The Book of Joby

The BOOK of JOBY

MARK J. FERRARI

TOR®

A TOM DOHERTY ASSOCIATES BOOK

NEW YORK

THE BOOK OF JOBY

Copyright © 2007 by Mark J. Ferrari

This book is printed on acid-free paper.

A Tor Book
Published by Tom Doherty Associates, LLC
175 Fifth Avenue
New York, NY 10010

www.tor.com

Edited by David G. Hartwell

Tor® is a registered trademark of Tom Doherty Associates, LLC.

ISBN-13: 978-0-7653-1753-7 (trade paperback)
ISBN-10: 0-7653-1753-2 (trade paperback)
ISBN-13: 978-0-7653-1686-8 (hardcover)
ISBN-10: 0-7653-1686-2 (hardcover)

First Edition: August 2007

Printed in the United States of America

0 9 8 7 6 5 4 3 2 1

To Josh Morsell,
who rekindled my desire to write,
Debbie Notkin,
who taught me how,
and the children of Taubolt
to whom I owe more than I can ever pay

ACKNOWLEDGMENTS

I've been improbably fortunate in both the number and quality of people who helped make this book a reality. Among the many, many who have helped and encouraged me, I am particularly grateful to:

Steve Ettinger and Kyala Shea, for wading through very, *very* early drafts which were *not* the polished work of genius presented here; Will Stenberg, Kenyon Zimmer, Pam Wilson, Patrick Curl, and other members of the occasional Weekly Writers Group, who suffered through eons of revision because they wouldn't stop providing such valuable feedback; my good friend, Brendan McGuigan, without whom this book would be of far poorer quality if it had ever been finished at all; Bill Jones and Marcia Muggleberg for their invaluable input, encouragement; and beyond-the-call promotional support; Debbie Notkin, whose editorial assistance, professional advice, and tenacious friendship have literally made this book, and no small part of my preceding illustration career, possible; John Dalmas, Dean Wesley Smith, Jane Fancher, and Jon Gustafson (if you're watching up there), who all kept my faith alive with their generous interest and counsel; and Patricia Briggs, who provided not only encouragement and counsel, but steered me toward an agent too!

My particular thanks to Tom Doherty, David Hartwell, Denis Wong, and everyone else at Tor for daring to publish such an—er—unusual first novel, and prodding me to make it even better; and to my agent, Linn Prentis, for her good advice and patient, persistent support through fair weather and foul.

Love and thanks to my parents, Andrew and Jackie, and my brothers, Matt and John for their faith in my ability to do this crazy thing.

Finally, my lasting gratitude to Jenny Rose Gealey whose inspiring life *and* death spurred and informed much of the story I've tried to tell here, and to her wise, warm and generous family for allowing me to incorporate some of her extraordinary poems in this work.

I can think of no remotely sufficient way to reward these people except to say that I am inexpressibly grateful, and otherwise unable to pay, so don't call us, we'll call you, et cetera, et cetera . . . (mischievous grin, fade to black).

The Book of Joby

PROLOGUE

(This same stuppid bet)

When he unlocked the verandah that morning, the young waiter found two men near his own age already sitting at a table, quietly watching the new sun drift from orange to gold above the sleepy Atlantic harbor beyond. He had no idea how they'd gotten in an hour before the restaurant opened, and headed out to make them leave, but found himself apologizing for the wait instead, and asking if they wanted menus. They already knew what they wanted, so he took their order and went vacantly back inside wondering why his head felt so cotton-stuffed this morning.

❋

"It's *magnificent,*" said the younger patron, gazing at the opalescent sky. His liquid brown eyes and beautiful copper features were framed in curly locks so black, one might have looked for stars among them. His feet were bare—a blatant violation of restaurant rules, though the waiter had not seemed to notice—and the soft white T-shirt untucked over his khaki shorts reflected more radiance than the sunrise alone should reasonably have lent it. "I could watch just this one thousands of times," he murmured. "Thank You for bringing me."

"The presence of a friend improves the view, Gabe," replied his host, the smile in His wide gray eyes spilling out across a face both older and younger in some elusive way than His companion's. He wore ragged tennis shoes, weathered blue jeans that precisely matched the changing sky above Him, and a short sleeve gray cotton shirt that seemed to shift between shades of warm shale and cool morning fog.

No sooner had they resumed their silent contemplation of the sunrise, than a dignified gentleman appeared, wearing an impeccably tailored suit of charcoal tweed. His pale, handsome features were set in stony determination, at odds with the pleasant morning, as he tugged natty pant cuffs away from elegant dress shoes, tossed an early paper onto the table, and sat down across from the two younger men, largely eclipsing their view of the bay.

"Lovely view," he offered without looking back to see. "Bit chilly for summer, but nice enough, I suppose. Imagine my excitement when I heard You were in the neighborhood!" he added with overtly false enthusiasm, then gestured at the newspaper lying between them. "Seen the latest on that massacre of villagers in Abudaweh? It seems the international tribunal has found *no one* to blame at all." He smiled and shrugged. "Perhaps the tricky bastards slew themselves, just to stir up trouble. Can no one be trusted anymore?"

The waiter arrived with two lattes and a plate of pastry, taking the newcomer's unexpected appearance in stride as well. "Shall I bring a menu, Sir?" he asked.

"I'd like everything *they* have," the gentleman said severely.

"Certainly. Will that be whole, low fat, or nonfat?"

"What?"

"Your latte, Sir."

The man regarded the waiter sternly, as if deciding what to do to him, then laughed suddenly. "Men of my age can hardly be too vigilant, young man. Better make it nonfat." He sent the waiter away with an ingratiating smile that faded to deadpan contempt as soon as his back was turned. Looking back to his tablemates, the gentleman's icy blue eyes came to rest on the dark-haired youth. "So, what do you think, Gabe? Did the buggers do for themselves, or is the tribunal in bed with Abudaweh's military elite?"

"I'd say you've been as busy as ever, brother," Gabriel replied coldly.

"Let's stick with *proper* names, shall we?" replied the older man with even greater chilliness.

"Which one?" Gabriel shrugged. "You keep so many."

"Morgan, at the moment. *Mister* Morgan, to *you.*"

"Boys," their gray-eyed companion interjected mildly, "you know I hate it when you fight like this. It demeans you both, and it's ruining My all too brief vacation."

"Were I allowed to visit You at *home,* Sir," Morgan protested politely, "I would gladly do so. But, given the circumstances, I have little choice but to intrude upon Your . . . 'vacations,' especially when they're held right here in my humble little *cell.*"

"Gabe was just telling me how lovely he finds your *cell,*" mused the gray-eyed man, tearing off a morsel of the pastry none of them had touched, and tossing it to a gull who'd come to perch on the railing behind his adversary. "Said he could have watched that one sunrise a thousand times."

"I haven't my little brother's overweening ambition to be Teacher's pet," Morgan replied, turning to grimace at the bird as it gobbled down the offering. "Such filthy creatures," he complained. "Really, You demean Yourself by catering to their mindless, vulgar greed."

"Why have you come to darken such a splendid morning?" the gray-eyed man asked wearily, tossing the gull another scrap. "If I wanted this sort of thing, I'd have gone to work today, Lucifer. You don't mind, do you, if I use that name? On you, Morgan seems so *guttural*."

Lucifer turned away as if to appreciate the view, and asked, "How long must You disgrace us all by propping up this doomed and depressing enterprise?" When his Lord made no reply, Lucifer's expression soured. "Is it my fault this blighted orchard bears such bitter fruit? *I* did not invent their deceitful hearts. Yet *I* am punished for their disobedience. *Why?* You cannot really believe I ever wished to challenge Your supremacy. *Principle* has ever been my only motive. I am guilty of nothing but insisting that *Your* laws be obeyed, that *Your* perfection be *perfectly* reflected!" Trembling with the effort of reining in his own consuming frustration, Lucifer whirled back to face his Master, the illusion of his human form dissolving into brilliant auroras of such dazzling beauty that the morning behind him suddenly seemed little more than a dingy rag thrown up against the heavens. *"Look at me!"* he demanded in a voice that rolled like muted thunder from all directions. "Do *I* belong *here*, penned up in this failed experiment with a race of flawed apes who, by their very nature, mock your majesty?" Gabriel looked away, finding his fallen brother's awesome beauty too painful to endure. *"Why do You fear me so?"* Lucifer demanded, reluctantly surrendering to human form again. "What ambition do I entertain but to serve a God not degraded at every turn by His own creation? You're the *omniscient* One! You must know it's true! Why will You never *listen* to me?" He fixed his Creator with a gaze of fearful defiance and desperate longing for recognition as old and unresolved as their dispute. "Admit it, Sir. This race of churls You indulge is the flop I have always said it would be. By now, the rot in this insufferable contrivance of Yours has gone clear to the core."

The Creator grew very quiet, and his gray eyes closed in concentration. He cocked His head, as if listening for something very small or far away. "No," He insisted quietly. "The core is as sound as ever . . . better, I'd say." He opened his eyes and gazed gravely at Lucifer. "But I do have this awful feeling that I know what's coming next."

"Then, as You doubtless *know*," Lucifer said with a feral grin devoid of mirth, "my sources are fearful of a monstrous new civil war brewing in the Congo that will make anything they've seen before pale in comparison. . . . I know how You despise all that death and suffering; and this could easily spill across all of Africa before it's done. Then there's all the influence even hotter heads, *war*heads one might say, are stealthily cultivating in India's parliament these days. After so many delays, the nuclear fruit is nearly ripe, and I have an almost infallible inside tip that by century's end nothing will remain of poor Kashmir but a glowing, glassy crater. It could all get so much messier in such a hurry then. All the global shock, the *righteous rage.* So *many* great nations at fault," he said with almost bestial ecstasy. "So much *blame* to go around. Messy, messy, messy," he lamented, shaking his head in a hideous parody of regret. "I'm not sure even *I* will be able to restrain such an *angry* world. The whole thing could just blow up in my—"

"Your point?" the Creator asked with a placidity that immediately reduced the rabid inferno in Lucifer's eyes to mere embers of sullen resentment.

"My *point,*" Lucifer said, with a sudden bland smile, "is that I might be able to pull some strings and slow things down a bit . . . at least, long enough to resolve a small wager, if You—"

"I thought so," the Creator sighed. "This same stupid bet. How many times have we done this, Lucifer? Ten thousand? Twice that perhaps?" He leaned forward, bringing the full weight of His suddenly devastating gray gaze to bear. "And how many times have you won?"

For a moment there was silence. Then, *"Twice,"* Lucifer breathed, neither looking away nor, to his credit, losing his smile.

The Creator shrugged. "They are allowed to fail."

"Yes, yes," Lucifer sighed, the steam seeming to leave his pipes all at once. "*Free will.* . . . I heard You the *first* time. Of all Your reckless gestures, that's the one that really lost You my vote."

"If you *had* heard Him the first time," Gabriel taunted, "the night sky would be far brighter now, wouldn't it."

"In a more *perfect* world," Lucifer retorted, rounding acidly on his onetime sibling, "*servants* would know not to interrupt their *betters* during *adult* conversation!"

"I believe your conversation was with me, Lucifer," the Creator reminded him. "And I really don't see why you—"

"I will not be mocked!" Lucifer snapped, forgetting himself entirely. "Certainly not by simpering songbirds like this impudent youngster you insist on—"

"What were you just saying about interrupting one's betters, Lucifer?" The

Lord of all creation asked with a level quiet that brought the devil instantly to wise if sullen silence. "As I was saying, I don't see why you keep subjecting yourself to these punishing humiliations. Even your two so-called victories did little but improve things."

"My only mistake with that wide-eyed couple in the garden was aiming too low," Lucifer complained. "As for the second time, I still insist You cheated. Judas *failed solidly,* and we clearly agreed that if I won, Jesus—"

"We've been through this a million times," the Creator interrupted. "I never suggested that Jesus would *stay* dead. It's hardly My fault you didn't think to inquire about that ahead of time."

"Well, what was I supposed to think?" Lucifer protested. "You said, *dead!* And dead is—"

"Evidently not," His master cut him off again, then smiled and shook His head. "Really, Lucifer, if I'd been you, I'd have quit while I was still just way, way behind."

"Well, You'd best not count on my errors this time," Lucifer insisted, visibly leashing his temper. "I've a delicious feeling that it's finally Your turn to blow it."

"Aren't you gung ho!" the Creator observed. "I don't recall having agreed to any wager yet."

In a moment of atypical unself-consciousness, Lucifer's face scrunched comically around so much constipated ambition.

"What would you want *this* time, if My candidate failed?" the Creator asked, tossing still more pastry to the flock of gulls that had gathered densely around them.

"Everything," Lucifer said, unable to suppress his eagerness. "This whole declining ball of sepsis You've indulged for so long goes! Its people, these vulgar birds, *the whole planet!* We start again, and this time You *listen* to *my* advice. Oh, You'll still be God, of course. I do know my place, whatever You think. But this time we'll try it without any of that *free will.* We'll have an *orderly* universe. A *virtuous* creation! No debauched little freelancers running about blithely denigrating their Maker and, by inference, the rest of us who must *obey* Your will. You do not seem to appreciate, My Lord, how deeply wounded I am by Your failure to recognize the value I place on Your dignity! If you had—"

"Stop," the Creator said patiently. "I heard *you* the first time as well. . . . Let's make sure I understand this. You'll spare a few thousand lives in the Congo, and a few million more from whatever atomic debacle you're arranging after that, if I agree to wipe every last scrap of My creation utterly from existence, should My candidate lose, and start over heeding *your* instructions. Is that right?"

Lucifer spent a moment scrutinizing the Creator's wording more carefully than he had on certain other occasions, then said, "That seems accurate."

"And if My candidate wins?" the Creator mused.

"Negotiable."

"Beyond that, the usual terms?" the Creator asked.

"Of course," Lucifer answered, his hopes visibly inflamed. "Are You *agreeing?*"

Gabriel turned to the Creator in clear concern. "My Lord, You're not seriously—"

"What did our distinguished guest say about interrupting?" the Creator interrupted.

"Of course," Gabriel said, glancing nervously away. "I apologize."

Throwing the last of their pastry to the gulls, the Supreme Being turned back to Lucifer. "I'm game. I'll want a little extra time to find a candidate, of course. Such stakes demand a certain attention to detail, and I do have the whole world to sift through. Shall we say . . . tonight sometime? Gabriel will officiate. I'll send him to tell you where and when, so don't make yourself too hard to find."

"Of course not!" Lucifer exclaimed, nearly swallowing his long tongue in euphoric astonishment. "I will be at Your every beck and call, My Lord. . . . At least, for a short while longer."

Lucifer was so excited, he failed to notice that one of the freshly glutted gulls had just defecated on his shoulder, and another on his expensive shoe. In fact, he had so forgotten himself that he carelessly popped from sight right in front of the waiter just arriving with his latte and another plate of pastry. There was only so much even mortal minds could be made to ignore. The Creator sighed and shook His head as the young man and his tray of food hit the pavement in a dead faint.

"Leave a generous tip," He told Gabriel. "I've got a lot to do before tonight." He turned to go, then stopped to smile mischievously back at His beloved angel. "I'm sorry if I seemed harsh with You a moment ago, My friend; but you nearly blew the whole deal. What if you'd made that ass stop to think things through?" He gave the unconscious waiter another rueful glance. "In fact, see that *all* his tips today are generous."

Then he was gone, leaving Gabriel to contrive some damage control, and wonder anxiously what on earth His Master knew that he had overlooked. It seemed a terribly reckless bet to him. Did the Creator not care that Gabriel himself was part of the creation to be erased should their human champion fail? Still, doubt was not strong in Gabriel's nature, especially regarding his Lord's judgment, so he just shrugged uncomfortably and bent to care for the fallen waiter.

PART ONE

�֎

Innocence and Guile

I

(Only name the quest)

"*Run! . . . Run, you scaredy cat!* The king will always beat you, Zoltan! And all your dumb ugly creatures too! *Ha!* Just *one* of Arthur's knights is better than your *whole stupid army*! *Ha, ha ha haaaa*!" Joby laughed in unrestrained exultation, brandishing his wooden sword from the castle walls as the humiliated enemy fled yet another great battle in disarray.

"Joooooby! . . . Joby?"

Joby's shoulders slumped, but he ignored his mother's voice and waved his sword once more at the fleeing horde. "I've got better monsters than *you* out of my *cereal*!" he hollered in contempt.

"Joby. I know you can hear me," his mother called, from the side yard this time. "Did you leave all this stuff on the driveway again?"

It was the kind of question Joby had never figured out how, or why, he was supposed to answer.

"I don't *think* so," he called back lamely, turning reluctantly from the battlefield beyond their backyard fence.

His mother came around the corner of the house carrying a large disk of cardboard in one hand, painted yellow, a red dragon scrawled uncertainly at its center, a banged up book in the other hand, and a tattered red bedspread draped over her arm.

"It must have been some other knight then," she said with the grim half smile that meant she was annoyed, but not enough to cause him any real trouble.

Joby remembered having left these encumberments behind in the heat of battle, but, like any knight worth his salt, he knew when to keep his own counsel. Did she really think warriors could run around *cleaning up* in the middle of a *battle*? Girls could be so pathetic!

His mother set his book, cape, and shield on the lawn in front of him and said, "If you do find the knight who left these there, please point out that your father could have driven right over them when he comes home. Unless that *other* knight wants tire tracks added to his family crest, he should find someplace better to leave his things." Her grin widened. She seemed very pleased with herself for no reason Joby could see, but since this meant he was in even less trouble than he'd thought, he obliged her by grinning back. "You might also tell him," his mother added, "how tired I get of reminding Arthur's knights not to leave their things where someone will break a leg on them."

Her grin faded as she reached up to tuck a stray lock of mahogany hair behind her ear, and went back to whatever she'd been doing.

"Break a leg on them," Joby scoffed quietly, stooping to pick up his things. She *always* said that, as if people were out there snapping limbs off on every little thing they passed. His toys, his books, his trading cards, even his *underwear*? Heaving a long-suffering sigh, he went back to the fence, dragging his cape behind him. God help his mother if she ever got into a *real* battle. She'd find out in a hurry how much more damage a mace could do than any pair of underpants she'd ever seen.

After looking out hopefully over the battlements again, Joby sadly decided that the enemy had truly given up and gone away. He slumped down against the fence, and wondered what to do, almost glad school was starting again soon. He'd heard terrifying stories about what fifth and sixth graders did to fourth graders at recess—especially during the first few weeks; but he was practically dying to be an "upperclassman" at last. For one thing, he'd finally be allowed to play dodge ball! Sadly, all that was two weeks off yet. Practically forever. At the moment, it seemed practically forever just until lunch.

Almost unconsciously, he opened the book, his most sacred possession; the dog-eared, grime-smeared, finger-smudged, broken-spined, long loose-leafed tome around which his entire cosmology revolved: *A Child's Treasury of Arthurian Tales.* It had been a gift from his grampa, entrusted to his parents on the day he was born; and the very map and outline of his boyish soul had formed slowly around its contents. Even after nine years of punishing use, a marvelous smell still wafted from its pages whenever it was opened, like some pungent musty incense rising from within the cathedral of his most secret, joyful dreams.

It had long since ceased to matter what page he opened to. Just lifting the *Treasury's* battered cover transported Joby instantly to Arthur's vast shadowed throne room, dappled in misty rays of jeweled illumination streaming from stained-glass windows high above his head. He waited, as always, on one knee before the High King's dais, his eyes cast respectfully toward the black-and-white marble floor tiles at his feet, his heart filled with the kind of urgent devotion that perhaps only a child can countenance—though here he was no child. Sir Joby was a knight; handsome, brave, and loyal, awaiting, as always, some new adventure in service of the glorious Roundtable and its beloved lord.

At Arthur's command Sir Joby had battled countless tyrants and terrible beasts, withstood searing temptations, and defeated devious wizards, armed with nothing but unyielding faith and courage. In victory, Sir Joby felt his liege lord's approval like a shimmering song through his entire being. And on those rare occasions when the beasts proved too fierce, the wizards too crafty, or the temptations too great, Joby had only to call out for rescue, knowing that Arthur would instantly appear with whatever feats of skill or miraculous power were required to save the day. Joby's heroic liege lord, his finest friend, had never failed him, nor ever would.

"My King," Joby whispered, eyes closed in delicious expectation over the open book, quoting lines he'd long since memorized, "I would serve you with my life. Only name the quest."

❈

Michael sat alone on the bright summer headlands, gazing out to sea, as still and silent as another pale outcrop of weathered coastal stone. Out wandering the dun-colored cliffs two days before, he had suddenly been taken by the sparkle of afternoon sunlight on the restless Pacific surge beneath him, and sat down to watch awhile. He had neither slept, nor moved, nor blinked since that moment, but had given his entire attention to the theater of water, sky, and stone constantly transformed before him by starlight, moonlight, and sunlight in the dark breathless hours before dawn . . . and day and dusk and night and dawn again.

He had served his Master here for nearly two hundred years, and still the novelty of so much beauty so completely unmarred by the Dark One's touch had yet to wear thin for him—which is not to say that angels are easily entertained, only that they find more meaning in the least fragment of shell or surf-polished glass than the most appreciative mortal mind might draw from a Russian novel or a week at the Grand Canyon.

His eyes and the summer sea passed a single shade of blue between them, back and forth, back and forth; a private and familiar rhyme shared by friends too long and well acquainted to have need of words. Back and forth, back and forth: his long ruddy-gold hair matched the tall dry grass around him, step for gentle step, in a long soft dance called by the warm wind sighing past them, headed north. He eavesdropped as the ocean whispered sweet cool nothings to distract the land while slyly dragging smooth round stones, one upon another, off the beach into its deep and secret pockets. Back and forth, back and forth; the world around him swayed to rhythms with which he seemed to sway as well, despite his utter stillness.

This reverie was finally broken by a thin column of pale smoke rising from a distant beach hidden behind the cliffs. It was Michael's charge to know what passed in this favored place, down to the silent flutter of moth wings at any evening porch light in the village. But when he cast his quizzical awareness toward the beach, he sensed no one where logic told him someone ought to be. A moment later, above the spot where he'd been sitting, a white gull wheeled on updrafts and turned to glide swiftly toward the mystery.

Arriving there, Michael spread his wings and landed gracefully well down the strand from a grizzled old fisherman in heavy, salt-stained waders, standing at the ocean's edge, patiently watching the tip of his long pole. Higher up the beach, a small driftwood fire blazed cheerfully in its ring of smooth gray stones.

Maintaining his disguise, Michael aimed another mental probe. This time the man registered perfectly, his long life wound and stretched within him. A child's simple pleasures; laughing adolescent mischief; early loves; earnest youthful dreams and ambitions; a radiant woman's beaming face; a child held; flashes of joy, gratitude, and pride; moments of affection, fear, and wonder; griefs endured; losses survived; arrangements made; acceptance; in time contentment; and finally . . . the deep and lasting peace that comes to some fortunate few with age. A remarkably lovely life, but nothing unexpected within a very fortunate old man's memory. Yet Michael's concern remained.

The old man's presence should have been as easily detected before. There was nowhere he could have gone to or come from in the few moments it had taken Michael to fly from where he'd first seen smoke. He probed the old man's mind again. Such broad passion and earthy understanding gradually unfolded amidst the small triumphs and crises of a modest life well and wisely lived. It all seemed too perfectly complete. *Too* beautifully drawn. Whatever the old man was, Michael felt certain he was *not* what he seemed; and the presence in this protected refuge of anyone pretending so well to be what he was not could only spell very serious trouble.

The old man reeled in his heavily weighted line, then cast it out again, seeming to relish the labor. An angel's eyes are quick and keen, and Michael's concern suddenly dissolved. He laughed a gull's shrill staccato laugh, spread his wings, and flew to the fisherman's side, where he resumed his human form.

Seeming unstartled by the bird's sudden transformation, the old man merely grimaced in good-natured chagrin.

"Welcome, My Lord," Michael smiled. "I confess, You took me by surprise."

This seemed to please the ancient angler, deepening the leathery filigree of wrinkles around his wide gray eyes into a crinkled smile that barely brushed his lips.

"How'd you guess?" he grumbled.

"Your illusion was too perfect," Michael replied, "though perhaps a moment late in coming. Then You reeled Your line in, and I saw You had . . . ," he smiled, "no bait."

The old man shrugged. "So? Sneaky buggers tease the bait off all the time."

"Nor even any hook, My Lord," Michael chided. "I know few others so in love with fishing for its own sake that even the hook is dispensable."

"Wanna know the secret of long life?" the grizzled old man asked gruffly.

"Assuredly, Lord," Michael replied with as straight a face as he could manage.

"Don't sweat the small stuff." The Creator eyed Michael sagely for a moment, then barked an old man's raspy laugh. "Saw that on a bumper sticker comin' over here. Ain't that a good one? *Don't sweat the small stuff.*" He shook his scruffy head in bemusement. "Too bad the stress-case drivin' that car doesn't read his own liter'ture." He looked joyfully at Michael then. "My friend," he said with soft but fierce affection. "It's so *good* to see you after so much time." He reached up to grip Michael's wide shoulders firmly in his weathered hands. "You look happy."

"I am," Michael replied, quietly. "Any sadness I feel is reserved for the world beyond this place. To what do I owe this unexpected pleasure, Lord?"

"Let's talk over breakfast," the Creator said, nodding toward his little fire. "Had some coffee with Gabe a while ago, but I didn't get a lot to eat."

"With pleasure," Michael replied following him toward the fire ring. "But . . . what shall we breakfast *on?*"

"*Fish,* of course," the old man replied as if Michael hadn't the sense God gave him. "Fried up fresh with garlic salt and lemon!" He produced a large unblemished lemon and a pale blue saltshaker from one of His small pockets.

"But I see no fish, Lord?" Michael teased. "Did the 'sneaky buggers' refuse to hold Your empty line bravely in their teeth while You reeled it in?"

The old man's answer came suddenly, from the air, as a line of pelicans swept in above the beach, each dropping a fish at their feet as it passed. The fourth and last of these offerings, not a small fish, hit Michael squarely on the head before bouncing limply to the sand beside him.

"That," the old man said with ill-concealed mirth, "is for doubtin' My skill as a fisherman." He took a large frying pan from the same small pocket, and placed it on the fire.

"I'm sure I never doubted any such thing!" Michael laughed, raking silver scales from his hair, and handing the somehow already gutted and cleaned fish to God.

"You doubtin' My word again?" the Creator retorted, laying them in the somehow already greased pan, and seasoning them.

"I doubt You not at all." Michael smiled back, warming to the game.

"I know," the old man said, his manner suddenly devoid of play, though no less affectionate. "I trust you too, Michael. I'm countin' on that trust just now."

"How could I behold all this," Michael insisted, arms spread wide at the scene around him, "and not trust the One who made it?"

"You've got it pretty bad for this place, haven't you, Michael."

"It's surely the fairest place left on *this* continent," the angel answered. "I've come to love the villagers; especially the children. . . . What's wrong, My Lord? Do you need me elsewhere? I confess, I'll miss them terribly; but if You ask it, I will gladly—"

"No," the Creator assured him softly. "You'll be needed here worse than ever now." He turned a troubled countenance toward the horizon. "Michael . . . I mean to let our old enemy—yours and mine—in on the secret of this place, and . . . well, more or less let him do what he likes about it."

There was a moment of stunned silence. Even angels can be surprised.

"This?" Michael whispered at last in something close to disbelief. "You're giving it to *him*?" He searched the timeworn face his Master wore, barely, to accept, but not to understand. "Have we done something to displease You, Lord?"

"Heavens no!" the old man rasped.

"Then *why*?" Michael pled.

"This morning, I agreed to join that old lamprey in a certain wager. You'll know the one, I expect."

"And this place was forfeit? This morning... and he's already won? How—"

"Course not," God growled, patiently. "I haven't even named my candidate yet. This place is as unknown to him as it ever was. But that'll have to change before much longer." The old man's fog-colored eyes fell full on Michael. "Still trust Me, friend?"

Michael's consternation dissolved into contrition. "Of course, My Lord. As much as ever. It's just that . . ." He bowed his head, gazing first at the sand between his feet, then at the fire where their fish were burning. "You *have* taken me *badly* by surprise."

"I'm sorry, Michael . . . deeply sorry. There *are* reasons. You know Me at least that well. . . . You also know how damned little I can say about it. That slippery eel claims I've compromised the wager; I'll have to forfeit. None of us wants that—'specially this time. I only came to warn you and make sure that when the storm blows in you make no move to stop it, even though the poor lad's wake'll surely be full of sharks and worse. You've guarded this place well, My friend. You have My heartfelt thanks. But when he comes, you'll have to let the whole filthy cargo come ashore with him. That's about all I can say. You, better than most, know the usual rules of this engagement."

"Then . . . I may do nothing," the angel pleaded, "but stand and watch all we love here trampled by that pestilent boar?"

"There's times it doesn't serve our friends to fight their battles for 'em, Michael."

"But, who *here* knows the first thing about fighting?" Michael pressed in frustration. "Half of them are utter innocents! The rest are refugees! They'll be helpless as feathers in a gale! If I'm forbidden to interfere—"

"With the *candidate*, Michael. Don't go belly up on Me now. The folks here are still under your care. The wager don't change that. You've many years by *their* reckoning. Mustn't tell them of the wager itself, of course. That would be blatant grounds for defaulting to Old Sulfur Stacks. But there's no law sayin' you can't teach your little flock to read the weather, and rig a tarp or two against the smell of rain."

Michael's troubled heart grew calmer as understanding dawned. "That much I will surely do," he answered grimly.

"Good. . . . I don't mean to sound insensitive, Michael, but I haven't seen your wits this addled since that old blowfish made war on Heaven."

Then something else occurred to Michael. "Are they to lose the Cup then?"

"No," the Creator said. "It stays, if they can keep it." He sighed heavily, and looked up at the sky in consternation, or a damn good impression of it. "I've got pretty deep faith in the boats I build," he said. Then, more quietly, "May *they* have faith in *Me*."

"How am I to know when it is time to step aside?" Michael asked.

"You'll know him when the time comes," the Creator said sadly. "He'll be pretty banged up and full of leaks by then, I imagine. But you'll know him. 'Til then, keep guarding the borders, and teach the villagers . . . something of caution. Once it starts, everyone's on their own."

There was a long silence on the beach then. Even the surf seemed pensive.

"He'll need a friend, Michael. Awful bad, I expect. A whole fleet of friends, if he can find 'em. That'll likely be harder than it sounds, by then." The Creator looked out to sea, and Michael wondered if it were tears he saw in the fisherman's rough gray eyes, or just the watery seep of old age. "You should see him *now*," the old man sighed. "You'd love him, Michael. You'd love him *fiercely*."

They were tears all right. And Michael understood them all too well.

❊

Miriam turned to gaze back through Joby's bedroom doorway at her son's shadow-softened face. Locks of shiny raven hair covered one closed eye. His breath had already fallen into the soft, slow rhythms of sleep, and, under the worn red bedspread that served as Joby's cape by day, he still clutched his precious storybook. She smiled, wishing her father could see how much Joby had come to treasure the simple gift. Her father had always seemed to know precisely what was wanted, quietly providing no more, no less.

As joyful as her own childhood had been, Miriam was certain she'd never shone half so brightly as Joby did. Like a cascade of pennies, images flashed through her mind: Joby standing utterly still to watch a spider spin its iridescent orb; charging shirtless through the house in summer with all the frightening combustibility little boys so wantonly squander; Joby lost in his storybook, wide blue eyes like whirlpools sweeping streams of dream and glory into the insatiable sea of his imagination. He was an intelligent and thoughtful boy, the sort who might have been cruelly treated by other children, she thought, had he not been such a charismatic little athlete, gleefully pulling a train of other boys behind him half the time, all parroting the things he said and did, for good or ill. Her smile widened. This marvelous, incandescent little boy was all her joy . . . he and Frank.

Though Frank sometimes laughed at her "silly superstitions," Miriam had sensed a kind of ambient brightness around their son from the very day of his birth. Times had been far harder then. Frank's mother had been killed by a drunk driver two months after Miriam and Frank were married, and his father had died eight months later of "severe angina"—the medical name for a broken heart, Frank had insisted. Frank had been unable to find work both equal to his talent and sufficient to support a family, and as Miriam had grown larger with Joby, he had begun to grow more distant.

Then Joby had been born.

She could still see Frank's radiant expression as he'd held their son at her hospital bedside, a renewed confidence in his voice and gestures, and an affectionate delight in her that she had feared gone forever. He'd gone home that evening to find a message on the answering machine from an architectural firm he'd applied to three months earlier, offering him a good job more than lucrative enough to meet their needs. Ever since, life had been almost alarmingly kind to them.

Now Frank was a partner in the firm. Surrounded by wonderful friends, they had a lovely home in a pleasant California suburb, completely paid for thanks to the surprising sum left them when Miriam's father had died. With the exception of her father's sudden but peaceful death five years before, they had encountered not a single crisis or hardship since Joby's arrival.

While Frank seemed to take all their remarkable fortune appreciatively in stride, Miriam occasionally found herself wondering what price might be demanded of them later. Now, watching Joby sleep, she found herself chasing that ridiculous thought away again. *Sorry,* she apologized silently to the empty air. *I can't seem to help my silly superstitions. No one's perfect, I suppose.*

Frank topped the stairs just then, coming quietly up behind her to wrap his arms around her waist and kiss the back of her neck before looking in at their sleeping son.

"Dropped off pretty quick, huh?" he whispered.

"It's tiring work," she smiled, "saving the world again every day."

Over dinner, Joby had told them all about routing Zoltan and his horde of evil monsters before lunch, then of being sent by King Arthur to slay two bloodthirsty ogres under the backyard deck before coming in to wash up for dinner. It had been a pretty big day, even for a great knight like their son.

"Did you read to him?" Frank asked.

She nodded. "The last one again. He keeps wanting that one lately. I really don't know why. It's so depressing."

"Arthur's death?" Frank asked.

She nodded again. "I asked him what he liked about it, and he said it was the part about Arthur coming back when the world's in trouble again."

Frank chuckled under his breath. "That boy wants to be a knight so bad. . . . I think he'll take the news about Santa okay; but I dread the day we have to tell him Arthur's just a fairy tale too."

She turned and kissed him sweetly on the lips. "That would be a *father's* job."

"I would never presume to diminish a woman's potential like that," Frank murmured. "Besides, *I'm* the one who'll have to tell him about sex. What happened to fair distribution of labor?"

Her smile widened, and she put her arms around his neck. "The way things work these days, he'll be telling *you* about sex."

"Then we'd better make sure I'm savvy enough not to embarrass us, hadn't we?" He took her hand and led her smiling toward their own room at the end of the hall.

✳

"Can't help her silly superstitions," Lucifer drawled, watching them tease each other down the hall into their bedroom. "Did you hear that? Oh, the irony!"

Neither the Creator nor Gabriel replied.

"So this is Your candidate," Lucifer mused, gazing down at Joby as the three of them settled invisibly around his bed. "It's hardly surprising he's so well behaved. Look at the life You've given him! One long, golden stream of blessings! We'll see how long that cheery disposition lasts when his picnic gets rained on, won't we." He looked up at God expectantly. Still no response. "Dying to be a knight, is he? And you've decided to grant his wish. I never cease to be astonished at Your capacity for *kindness,* Sir. Your proclivity for subjecting innocent children to these rather gruesome trials is rather intriguing. Perhaps I've failed to appreciate the *complexity* of Your character."

The Creator only waited patiently without reply. That, Lucifer realized, was what irked him most about God: His smugly passive-aggressive tendencies. The Creator never allowed the anger He must surely be feeling to slip out where anyone might see it. Lucifer found such saccharine duplicity disgusting.

"Who proposes this wager?" Gabriel asked, launching the timeworn ritual without preamble.

"I, Lucifer, Angel of Light, Mirror of Dawn, propose this wager."

"Who joins in this wager?" Gabriel intoned again.

"I do," the Creator answered.

Between them, Joby sighed in his sleep, and turned to rest facing God.

"Who will witness our agreement," Lucifer asked in accordance with the ancient rite, "and truthfully attest to its conditions and outcome if so required?"

"I will," Gabriel answered. "Is this acceptable?"

"It is," answered the Creator and Lucifer in unison. And it was. Lucifer might despise his younger brother, but the dusky little do-gooder had never demonstrated the wit to lie, and Lucifer doubted him capable of it, even if he wanted to.

"Then speak your terms with care," Gabriel said, "for each word spoken here will henceforth be binding and immutable. What do you wager, Lucifer?"

"I wager," Lucifer smiled, "that this candidate, deemed faithful and steadfast to our Lord, will, when put to the test and left to choose of his own free will, unequivocally renounce the Creator, brazenly defy His will, and commit great wickedness instead."

Joby's hand moved toward his mouth, as if he might suck his thumb. But the habit had fallen beneath his dignity even in sleep many years before, and the gesture was arrested as suddenly as it had begun.

"What would you claim if this were proven?" Gabriel asked.

"That this creation be immediately and completely expunged from space and time," Lucifer breathed, overwhelmed by an almost erotic longing, "and another commenced by the Creator in its place, subject to whatever specifications *I* shall advise."

"Your terms?" Gabriel asked Lucifer.

"First, that the Creator forbid all immortal beings in His service from intervening unless directly asked to do so by the candidate, lest his fate be decided for him by others. Second, given the Creator's advantage as first cause, and His supremacy over even me, I propose that He promise not to intervene directly, or by command, or by any word or act that may be construed as expression of His will in this matter for the trial's duration."

Gabriel turned to the Creator, forbidden to call Him God or Lord within the ritual, and asked, "Are You content with these terms?"

"I Am."

There was a moment of astonished silence, during which Lucifer hoped his own surprise wasn't as transparent as Gabriel's. He had never expected such conditions to go unchallenged, and wondered uncomfortably what the Creator's complacency could mean.

"Have you terms to add?" Gabriel asked the Creator uncertainly.

"Only that Lucifer not deprive the candidate of life itself or the power to choose unless and until the boy's unequivocal failure has been confirmed before valid witness, and that Lucifer's victory, if any, be achieved before the candidate's fortieth year of life, lest even in triumph the child be deprived of any peace."

"Are you, Lucifer, content with these conditions?" Gabriel asked.

"Yes," he replied. The Creator's terms were frightfully routine. It was sometimes tempting to wonder if his Master had any imagination at all.

"What would You claim if victorious?" Gabriel asked the Creator.

"Restitution to the candidate according to My terms; that the candidate remain completely unmolested by Lucifer or any that serve him for the remainder of his natural life; and that any benefit coming to the candidate or the world at large from this contest remain unchallenged by Lucifer or his servants, so long as the candidate lives."

"Will you, Lucifer, concede to these conditions if proven wrong?" Gabriel asked.

"I will."

"One thing remains to seal the wager," Gabriel proclaimed, "that you make, each, your case to the candidate, himself. For from the first day it has been ordained that mortal men and women shall be free to choose."

"By right and tradition, the Creator is first," Lucifer replied, constrained by form to say so, though he preferred this anyway, since it gave him power of rebuttal.

Between them, Joby's eyes moved rapidly behind their soft, smooth lids, already deep in dream; for it was not to the conscious child that the Creator and His adversary would appeal, but to the deeper self that moved relentlessly like magma beneath the cool, slow crust of Joby's waking life.

⊗

"My King, I would serve you with my life. Only name the quest."

Sir Joby knelt again before Arthur's dais, eyes cast reverently toward the floor, eagerly awaiting his lord's will.

"Should friendship be hobbled by such formality, Sir Joby? Rise, and add the pleasure of your countenance to that of your courtesy."

"As Your Majesty wills," Sir Joby replied, unable to suppress the smile that fountained from deep within him as he rose and looked into the laughing gray eyes of his beloved lord, Arthur, King of Briton, and Master of the Round Table.

"We have much to discuss, Sir Joby, but I would be out in the light and air on such a splendid morning. Will you consent to ride with me a while?"

"I am yours to bid, Sire," Joby beamed, "but I would be well pleased with such a privilege."

"Then I extend it on one condition," Arthur said, "that we put aside the manners of majesty for now and speak instead as friends. A king may command what he likes, I am told, but I often wonder of late if I am yet allowed friends, or only subjects now."

"Does the king truly doubt my friendship?" Joby smiled.

"Nay, *the king* does not," Arthur answered dryly. "Nor do *I*. So pray, for this short while, let us have none of *the king* between us. I will call you Joby, and you shall call me Arthur."

"As you wish, my—Arthur. I am deeply honored."

"As am I," Arthur replied, descending to clasp Joby's hand.

A moment later, they were riding at a joyful speed through one of Camelot's lesser gates. Joby dimly remembered the royal stables, the grooming and mounting of horses; but the day was so bright and fair that all else was quickly forgotten. The companionship of his king, and the swiftness and vitality of their horses left Joby giddy with the love of life, as glossy ravens scattered before them, cawing complaints as they sought refuge among heavily laden apple trees nearby. It was all so perfect.

After a long and boisterous ride, they stopped to rest their horses within a lofty wood. Joby felt the glade's deep, cool silence like a large, soft hand upon his shoulder as he dismounted. Rough, ruddy trunks of immense girth soared from burled bowls half as wide as houses into a dense canopy that cast its own twilight, pierced only by occasional shafts of green and silver sunlight. Swept by breezes that did not reach the forest floor, the immense trees swayed together in a ceaseless, solemn dance that seemed to engender the stillness beneath their branches. A liquid trill of bird song from somewhere deeper in the wood spiraled upward into silence. A tree frog chanted quietly nearby. A squirrel rustled in the branches high above them. These and the wind's voice were the only sounds.

Arthur found a seat on one of the great, mossy tree bowls, and beckoned Joby to come sit beside him. "Joby," he said gravely, "you have served me faithfully on too many occasions to count, and the love you bear me brings me deep joy and gratitude."

"I have no greater satisfaction than knowing we are pleased with one another," Joby replied.

"Nor do I," Arthur said. "I have need of a champion, my friend."

"I would serve you with my life, Sire. Only name the——"

"Yes, yes, I know," Arthur said, waving him to silence with a sad smile. "But I would not have an answer before you've heard me out. This is not *remotely* like before."

"I beg pardon, My Lord. I did not mean to interrupt——"

"None of that, Joby. You promised." The king sighed, then smiled. "I am entangled in a contest, Joby, with my oldest and most formidable enemy. It is a desperate and deadly affair with more than mortal parameters."

"Magic?" Joby asked.

Arthur nodded grimly. "Of the darkest kind. And, as you know, where magic is involved there are strange and immutable conditions laid on all concerned, even kings."

Joby nodded.

"That is why," the king continued, "I can tell you so little; only that the fate of all Camelot is at stake. The enemy is vastly more subtle, powerful, and vicious than any I have ever sent you against; the quest will be long and terrible beyond your imagining, and—mark this well, Joby—I will be utterly unable to aid you in any way whatsoever while it lasts, which may well be half your lifetime. Your entire youth, my friend. Consider it well. Should you fail, we all fail. There will be no rescue this time, no second chances, no further hope at all. Do you understand me?"

After a moment, Joby nodded, daunted despite himself.... Half a lifetime ... without Arthur's help. "My Lord," Joby began from force of habit. Arthur frowned. "I mean, Arthur ... I am willing to try, but ... how can I hope to win such a contest without your aid? What am I that the fate of all should rest with me alone?"

"You are the friend I trust," Arthur said, "the champion I choose." He paused to consider Joby thoughtfully, then said, "Make no mistake, my friend. You owe me *not* this undertaking! I will take no less joy in you should you refuse. It were far better to do so now, than to agree in vain bravado. But, should you agree, know that though I, myself, can help you not at all, everything else of mine in Camelot, every loyal subject, every inch of my realm, will be at your disposal if you but *ask*.

"Most of all, hear this, Joby. I know beyond question that you will give everything to this pursuit, but should you fail despite that, the fault will be my own, not yours."

"This is meant for comfort?" Joby asked, smiling wanly. "That my shame would fall on *you*? Pray, encourage me some more, Arthur. Tell me I am to ride to battle on a giant snail, or minus an arm."

"It is good to hear you jest." Arthur grinned. "But nay, Joby, I think I have encouraged you enough. Think on what I've said, and answer in your own good time."

Joby felt no need to think. "I will do this thing for you, Arthur, whatever it is, or die trying."

"Do not be hasty, Joby. There is time to let it turn."

"That is my answer, Arthur," Joby insisted. "If need be, that will be my answer tomorrow, and tomorrow, and tomorrow after that, until this trial has passed us by."

For a moment both men were silent, gazes locked. Then Joby recognized the tears in Arthur's eyes, and looked away lest they be answered in his own.

"There is no other man in Camelot, I think," Arthur said quietly, "who would have answered so without at least first inquiring after his reward."

Joby snorted, still not trusting himself to face his king. "Arthur, what reward have you to tempt me with that approaches the honor of . . . of your faith in me?"

"Behold my choice," Arthur whispered to the empty air around them, "and tremble."

Joby looked up to see who Arthur spoke to, but saw no one else. A shiver ran down his spine, and he was about to ask if they were alone when Arthur said more loudly, "Come, Joby, we must return to Camelot before sunset. The trial is upon us soon enough."

With one last glance around the clearing, Joby followed Arthur to their horses, fierce pride, swelling affection, and twining dread at war within his breast. He still did not know what task he had agreed to. Longer and more terrible than he could imagine, Arthur had warned. Well, he had no small imagination.

The ride home passed in thoughtful silence. Not until they were just miles from Camelot, trotting through an open riverside stand of alder trees, did Joby speak again.

"How am I to know it, Arthur?"

The king looked at him blankly.

"The test," Joby said. "What is it? When does it begin? Surely I must know *something* of it beforehand, mustn't I?"

"I have told you all I may, Joby, lest I violate the trial's conditions and forfeit all to my opponent at the start."

"But . . . how shall I prepare then? How am I even to recognize the enemy?"

Arthur shrugged. "How is evil ever recognized, Joby? What does it look like? How does one oppose it?"

Joby reined his horse to a halt and stared, beginning to comprehend the true difficulty of his position.

"I told you the trial was long," Arthur said, and wheeled his horse around to go on. "Come, Joby. The sun slows not at all in deference to our troubles."

Shaking himself from disbelief, Joby spurred his horse and followed.

Neither of them spoke again until they had stopped on the brow of the last hill overlooking the coastal headlands of Camelot. They had beaten sunset by half an hour, and the scene before them was so beautiful that even Joby's solidifying distress could not prevent him from being moved.

Graceful stands of pine and cypress, weathered and sculpted by salt and storm, stood nearly black against the green-gold fields and the glittering sea beyond. Out past the cliff tops mammoth stacks of rock thrust out of the water, their heads bent back above the mist, as if gazing at the sky in prayer. The distant boom and sigh of surf was mixed with the musical bark of seals, the strident cry of seabirds, and, from somewhere, the measured tolling of a bell. Out over the water, long lines of pelicans skimmed the troughs between huge swells moving ponderously toward shore. A high whistling cry drew Joby's gaze up to find hunting osprey hanging nearly motionless above the river mouth, waiting for their dinner to swim past below. The air carried scents of iodine and sea salt, wood smoke and dry wayside herbs, cedar bark, and weathered stone. And rising at the center of it all, the walls and roofs and spires of Camelot.

"Look at it Joby!" Arthur exclaimed. "Is it not lovely?"

"In truth, it is worth . . . anything to defend, My Lord," Joby sighed mournfully.

Arthur frowned and turned to look at Joby. "It is always ill advised to fill a bright moment with some future darkness, friend. Your trials, whatever they may be, have not yet begun. Can you not be here now, with me?"

Joby took a deep breath, nodded, then surprised himself by laughing aloud. Arthur was right. Who knew how many more such moments he would be afforded?

"Care to place a wager, My Lord?"

Arthur looked startled.

"I will beat you to that lookout on the river's mouth by three lengths!" Joby shouted, spurring his horse so that he was well away before half the words were spoken.

"You cheat!" Arthur shouted, prodding his mount after Joby's. "That bodes well!"

Joby did beat him, and when the two men had finished laughing and impugning one another's character, they sat their horses quietly in the spreading shadow of a giant old cypress, gazing at the beach below. Well-formed waves stood up and filled with light, like walls of brilliant jade, then tumbled down in creamy gouts of pure white foam, rolling in to spread across the sand before hissing back into the bay.

"You neglected to say what was forfeit if I lost that race," Arthur observed.

"I neglected to think of anything," Joby replied.

"You are truly not much suited to the business of reward, my friend. It is wise to look after one's own interests, I think—at least a little. No one else is likely to."

"This is all I want. . . . All I'll ever want," Joby murmured at last, still gazing at the sun-blazed bay and the dark-cliffed, wood-crowned headlands beyond. "To breathe this air, and gaze at all that lies about us here. There is no fairer prize."

"Lovely, yes," Arthur replied. "But is it good?"

"Of course, My Lord," Joby said, wondering if the question were some trick. "How could this be anything but good?"

Just then, an osprey plunged like thunder into the river mouth, and rose again to flap heavily inland toward its nest, a silver fish hanging in its talons.

"Death just came to some hapless creature there," Arthur replied. "Life *and* death go on all around us here. The fragrant wood smoke we smell bespeaks the end of some fair tree even as it warms some cheerful hearth. Are you certain all you see is good?"

"As I am certain of anything, My Lord." Joby answered. Then understanding dawned. "And you think this evil that I am to confront will be as easily recognized?"

"Nay," Arthur conceded, "though one may learn to know it as certainly, if not as easily. Still, perhaps it was unkind to conjure such dark clouds just when you had let them clear. See? The sun leans down at last to kiss the water. Let us ride out farther, you and I, and watch their embrace."

Moments later they stood together upon the western-most cliff tops, gazing out at one small band of fog poised above the farthest horizon. As the
sun fell behind it, its edges burned like molten gold, and elusive rays of
peach and salmon, powder blue, and palest yellow stretched briefly up into
the lavender sky.

As stars began to bloom above twilight's fire red, green, and cobalt
bands, Arthur broke their long silence. "At the worst of times, friend Joby, I
look most keenly for whatever beauty may be near at hand, and drink as
deeply as I can. I cannot recommend such drafts highly enough for those
who would learn to recognize evil, and remain proof against it. Feed your
heart, Joby. I trust *your heart* more than I trust the wisest head in Camelot. . . .
Now come. At the castle they will think us drowned or kidnapped by now.
You will have a meal fit to your courage, and a night of peaceful sleep in our
finest chambers."

They had barely entered the castle when Arthur was scolded off to some
too long neglected urgency by a flock of long-suffering advisers, leaving
Joby to wander on his own until the service of dinner in Arthur's hall.

❈

"My congratulations, Sir, on such a *lovely* presentation," Lucifer fawned as
God looked up from Joby's bed. "*Stunning* use of landscape! But, lovely as
they are, spun glass castles are so easily fractured. Just a little tap is all it takes
at times. . . . Goodness!" he enthused, glancing theatrically at the Donald
Duck wall clock over Joby's bed. "Is it my turn? So soon?"

Knowing the old stick would never stoop to take the bait, Lucifer plunged
into Joby's dream without waiting for the Creator to reply.

❈

Joby found himself on a balcony overlooking a moonlit rose garden, distant
merriment still audible within the palace behind him. The banquet had been
grand . . . he thought . . . well, rather vague actually, but definitely grand . . .
he was fairly sure. A breath drawn in appreciation of fragrant yellow roses
that climbed the trellis from below became yet another sigh. Each sigh had
been longer than the last that night.

"That sounded rather laden with care," offered a grave voice behind him.

Joby whirled to find a tall figure standing in shadow at the balcony's far
end.

"I . . . I thought I was alone," Joby stammered, disconcerted. Then, "I beg
pardon. That is rude greeting, but I was—"

"Please!" insisted the other, stepping out into the moonlight. "It is *I* who must apologize, lurking in the shadows so. I was here when you came out, and did not know whether to disturb you or merely keep my peace until you'd gone. Stupid of me really."

The stranger's voluminous robes were rich with velvet and gems, his silver-templed mane swept back regally, his brows thick and wise above icy blue eyes so penetrating, even by moonlight, that the strong compulsion to stare into them was quickly at war with an equally uncomfortable urge to look swiftly away.

"I'm at a loss," Joby said. "You seem familiar, but I cannot summon your name."

"I am not easily summoned," the other said, smiling at some private joke with a look so shrewd that Joby knew suddenly who he must be.

"Would you be the king's adviser, Merlin?"

"Why . . . yes! That's exactly who I am," the man said, seeming first surprised, then pleased. "How perceptive of you to guess. Most don't, you know; by design actually. I am often more useful to the king *un*recognized." Merlin waved the matter away with an ingratiating smile. "Be at ease, Sir Joby. I well understand how preoccupied you must be given the perilous quest you have undertaken. And I must say, I am well pleased with the king's excellent choice of champions. I have long been an admirer of yours, myself."

Joby's eyes widened. "You know of my quest?"

Merlin offered a self-deprecating smile. "Who *would* know, if not the king's *highest* adviser?"

"Well, yes. Of course," Joby blushed. "I . . . I am deeply flattered by your esteem, though I would take even greater comfort in knowing what, precisely, I am such an excellent choice *for*."

"Perhaps I can assist you then," Merlin replied.

"I would be deeply in your debt," Joby sighed. "But the king has made it plain that I may be told nothing of my ordeal beforehand."

"Not by himself," Merlin said, smiling. "That *is* one of the conditions laid upon him in this matter. But not all are subject to such restrictions. Myself for instance."

"*You* can tell me what this concerns?" Joby blurted out. "It is allowed?"

"I can," Merlin smiled, "and it is. Ask what you will."

"Thank God we meet!" Joby crowed.

"Indeed." Merlin smiled again.

"Well, to begin, with whom must I contend?"

Merlin's smile vanished. He seemed almost to shrink in upon himself. "You demand the cruelest answer first. Are you steeled to hear it, Sir Joby?"

Joby nodded, though Merlin's expression sent shivers down his spine.

"Evil itself, Sir Joby," Merlin whispered, as if afraid to speak the words aloud. "God's own enemy."

Joby felt his mouth fall slowly open. "Surely . . . you cannot mean—"

"The devil," Merlin said more resolutely. "You are sent on your king's behalf to oppose the devil himself. May God and all his angels go with you."

"How . . . how can a mere man . . . defeat the *devil*?" Joby murmured in dismay.

"I cannot say," Merlin sympathized. "But it must be possible, or Arthur would not have sent you, would he? He loves you deeply . . . does he not?"

No longer trusting his legs, Joby turned to lean against the balustrade. "If I fail . . . ," he said miserably, "all is lost. . . . For Arthur. For Camelot. That is what he said. . . . But how can I hope to succeed?"

"Now, now, Sir Joby!" Merlin protested. "Despair at the very beginning can lead to nothing good! You must not fail, and so you shant'! Come, walk with me in the garden below, and I will arm you with what advice I may. What say you, *brave* Sir Joby? Will you not entertain some *little* portion of the hope both I and Arthur place in you?"

Abashed, Joby, gazed down at the flagstones. "You are right, Merlin. I . . . I am deeply ashamed to have wilted so before the first faint breath of battle. I *will* succeed, for my lord, Arthur, and now, for you as well!"

"That's better!" Merlin laughed. "I should be honored to have any part in the outcome of your trial! Come! Let us away to the garden!"

Merlin took Joby's arm like an old uncle, already advising as they stepped into the torch-lit corridor.

"Vigilance must be your cornerstone, Sir Joby. The enemy you face will exploit every weakness you expose, leverage any smallest flaw, so you must steel yourself to offer him none! This may seem impossible at first; but those who claim that perfection is unattainable are weak and lazy men who care only to justify their own poor quality. You *can* attain it, Sir Joby. But there must be *nothing* you are unprepared to sacrifice. Not even your own heart! *Especially* your own heart. God's own Son laid down His very life. You must be prepared to do no less."

Merlin turned to face Joby at the garden's entrance. "Sir Joby, believe me when I say that no one wants to see this fight won more earnestly than I do.

Nor has anyone greater confidence in you than I have. In you I find nothing but hope for victory."

"I thank heaven for your candor," Joby replied. "The truths you speak are grim, but I would rather face any doom fully illuminated, than concealed in shadows. You have greatly steadied my resolve, Merlin. If it is the end of my life that I am pledged to, then for Arthur's sake, so be it."

Merlin nodded sagely. "If you are steadfast, you will not fail to realize my brightest hopes for you. I *feel* it, sir! I *feel it*! Come now," he smiled, turning toward the garden door, "let us put such sad concerns aside, and revel in the scent of roses while we may."

✷

"Of course, the trick is knowing precisely where that tap must be administered," Lucifer chortled, looking up in turn from Joby's bed.

"Shall we finish?" Gabriel asked flatly.

"Has no one here any sense of *humor*?" Lucifer protested sadly.

"If our solemn ritual seems a laughing matter to you," Gabriel said, "it can yet be declared null and void."

"Heaven forbid," Lucifer drawled. "By all means, continue."

"The candidate's consent having been attained," said Gabriel unhappily, "will you, Lucifer, submit to this wager and all its conditions as stated in my presence, bound by every word thereof, win or lose?"

"I will."

"And will You," Gabriel asked the Creator, "submit to this wager and all its conditions as stated in my presence, bound by every word thereof, win or lose?"

"I will."

"The wager is sealed," Gabriel said dolefully, "which none, even God Almighty may unsay. The contest begins. . . . By right and custom, Lucifer is granted first blow."

"Done that," Lucifer sighed, examining his nails. "Why not leave our young hero to enjoy that peaceful night's rest you promised, Lord? God knows, he'll need it."

But when Lucifer looked up, both the Creator and Gabriel were gone already, leaving him feeling snubbed and vindictive. Thinking to take it out on the Creator's pathetic little champion, Lucifer attempted to rejoin his dream, only to find himself nursing a hellish headache after banging his being against the barriers the Creator had placed to guard Joby's sleep that night.

"Enjoy whatever pretty dream he's left you child." Lucifer sneered. "It'll be His *last* favor for a *very long time!*"

Then Lucifer was gone as well, leaving only the slightest stink of brimstone to dissipate over Joby's peaceful, softly smiling form.

✤

Sunlight was streaming through Joby's windows when he woke feeling deliciously rested and intensely excited. He'd really been there! He was sure of it! Everything had been so real! And the way he'd been able to talk! Just like someone from his book! Trying to remember how he'd done that, he found his memories of Camelot already vanishing in the sunlight.

Quick! Quick! Quick! he thought, scrambling from his bed. *Write it down!*

Yanking open drawers, and scattering piles, Joby found a few crinkled sheets of wide-ruled newsprint and the iridescent stub of a Disneyland pencil, then rushed to his desk. But the courtly words were already gone, and the very ideas were fading fast.

"I woud rather fite my enemy in the lite then in the shadoes," Joby scrawled, recalling the scent of roses.

He waited, pencil poised, face scrunched in fierce concentration, then lunged to write again.

"You must be brave and give up your hart. . . . You must be . . . *What?* . . . vijilint." *Yes, that was the word.* What did it mean? "You must be perfect Sir Joby or the enemy will win!"

But these were all Merlin's words. What Joby wanted most to capture were Arthur's. *Think, think, think! What had Arthur said?*

"What dose evil look like Sir Joby? . . ." *Yes!* "How do you fite it?" *Yes! Yes! What else?* Then he remembered, and his face went slack with worry.

"I cannot help you anymore, Sir Joby. If you fale we all do."

I have to fight the devil, Joby thought, *all by myself.* He stared at the sheet of paper before him. Was this all he had left? . . . No. The words had fled. Perhaps he'd only imagined talking like that. But he still remembered riding with Arthur through the fields and hills. He remembered the solemn grove, and the birdsong spiraling up into echoes, the swaying trees, and the laughter and love in Arthur's eyes. He remembered Camelot on the sea, the seal song and the bird cries, the waves of burning jade, and the sunset—especially the sunset. Arthur had placed the fate of all this in Joby's hands. The words were gone, but Joby knew the core. The rest he would figure out somehow. Hadn't Arthur said there would be clues?

One last fragment came to mind then.

"Drink alot of beutey Sir Joby. . . . Feed your hart."

When nothing more came, Joby stood up with his little bit of writing and went to find his mother. Merlin had said he must be perfect. He figured he'd better start with this.

He found her in the kitchen making cinnamon rolls.

"Mom, will you check if I spelled these right?"

"Good morning, Joby! . . . You sure slept late. Must have had good dreams, huh?"

Joby smiled. "It was the best dream ever! I went to Camelot. . . . But I was forgetting everything, so I wrote it down. Can you check what I wrote, please?"

He handed the paper to his mother, who smiled and began to read. Joby watched her purse her lips, raise her brows, smile, then concentrate and frown again.

"What's this word?" she asked, holding the paper down so he could see it.

"Vijilint," Joby told her. "That's what Merlin said."

"Vigilant!" she exclaimed. "My goodness, Joby! Where did you hear that?"

"I told you, from Merlin. . . . What does it mean?"

"Well, it means . . . paying very close attention, I guess, or being very careful."

"That's what I thought," Joby said. "How do you spell it?"

"How 'bout I finish reading this first." His mother smiled.

As she reached the bottom of the page, Joby saw her eyes go moist and pink.

"What's wrong?" he asked.

She looked up, seeming startled. "This is what you dreamed, dear?"

Joby nodded uneasily. "Is something in my dream bad?"

"No! No, Joby," she said, reaching down to wrap him in a hug. "It's just . . . I had no idea little boys had such big ideas. Drink beauty? Feed your heart? Did you really think of that all by yourself?"

"No," he admitted. "Arthur told me. . . . Do you know what it means?"

She shook her head. "No better than you do, I'm sure. But it's a beautiful idea, and I'm glad you wrote it down." She squeezed him again. "There's just no end to you, is there, sweetheart!"

"I want to get a book," Joby said, pulling away from her embrace, "like the one Amy Holten has, with no words in it, so I can write these down, and all the other clues too. But first I want to make sure it's all spelled right."

"Well, your spelling's good enough for government work," his mother said, setting the paper down to go back to her baking. "Why don't we get some breakfast in you first. I'll put these rolls in, then we'll get you some juice while—"

"No!" Joby protested. "You need to check my spelling! There can't be any mistakes! Merlin said I have to be perfect to win the contest!"

His mother looked startled.

"Joby . . . no one's perfect."

"I know it's hard," he frowned, "but I have to. . . . Merlin said I can."

"You'd really rather do *spelling* than have cinnamon rolls?" she asked.

Joby nodded gravely.

"Well . . . all right," she said softly. "I'd be the last one to stand between you and academic excellence. Let's go over here, where we won't get food on it."

2

(Dodge Ball)

"If I may, Sir," enthused the obsessively brushed and Brylcreemed young sycophant rushing a respectful two steps behind Lucifer, "I'd just like to say how honored I am to be of assistance on a project of this magnitude! It seems an eternity since I've gotten to work on anything that really mattered here. Not that my regular work doesn't matter!" he rushed to add. "But *this*! Well, *this* is the kind of creative challenge one can really sink one's—"

"Career on," Lucifer interjected without turning or slowing down. The sudden silence was gratifying. He could almost hear the damned brown-noser's pasty little feet sweating under those gleaming black dress shoes. Why, he wondered wearily, with so many souls at his disposal, did he seem to end up with nothing but mediocre losers like this Williamson fellow?

Relieved of Williamson's annoying chatter, Lucifer fell to inspecting the severely modern makeover his labyrinthine headquarters had recently undergone. After centuries of lavishly baroque decor designed to affirm his stature as the earthbound world's premier power, Lucifer had suffered a spasm of aesthetic discontent and remodeled. The heroic scale remained, but Lucifer's vast environment was empty now, for empty had become synonymous, in his mind, with clean, and Lucifer craved nothing more than *cleanliness*. Long straight lines, perfect right angles, orderly grids, practical materials in sober, undistracting colors, naked utility uncluttered by frivolous decoration. After centuries of baroque excess, these were the breath of sanitized air that Lucifer had contrived to ease his confinement here. Every floor was carpeted in soil-resistant gray. Even the walls were constructed of acoustically absorbent materials so that his immense nest should remain clean even of unwanted sound.

Concerned for the aesthetic nourishment of his staff and tenants, Lucifer had taken care that this new industrial monotony be tastefully punctuated with priceless examples of *appropriate* artwork. Bad Dadaist painting, Neo-brutalist sculpture, Pop art, Op art, and original animation cells from *Beavis and Butthead* were displayed, not as expressions of Lucifer's taste but as evidence of mankind's depravity. *That* was what Lucifer collected most avidly.

Entering the conference room, Lucifer settled unceremoniously into a large gray chair at the near end of a massive, gleaming graphite table. Williamson walked around a large obelisk of polished obsidian to join two more conservatively dressed project recruits already seated at the table's far end, the dour tension in their faces magnified by a sourceless, color-leaching light from overhead. There was no other kind of light in Hell. Lucifer regarded windows as nothing but inducements to reduced productivity.

He considered the three damned souls awaiting his will and sighed despondently. "Before we waste any time *brain*storming," he announced dryly, "you'll want to give your full attention to the following presentation."

The room fell dark as a large screen appeared from within the wall behind him. It flickered blue-green for a moment, as if illuminated by firelight through twenty feet of seawater. Then a young man in medieval garb appeared on bended knee, his pale face cast down reverently, half-hidden behind locks of shiny raven hair. "My King," he murmured, "I would serve you with my life. Only name the quest."

Lucifer's three servants watched in utter silence as Joby's entire dream of Arthur and Merlin was replayed. When the screen flickered to darkness, the overhead illumination resumed, and Lucifer turned back to face his functionaries.

"Lest I steal anyone's *thunder*," Lucifer drawled sardonically, "I'll hear *your* ideas before expressing my own modest thoughts."

The team sat like deer staring into the headlights of an oncoming truck.

"Lesterman," Lucifer sighed, "let's begin with you."

"Certainly, Sir." Lesterman pulled an attaché case from beneath the table. "Well, Sir," he said, proffering a thick sheaf of manila folders, "I've prepared these personnel rosters, materials requisitions, and logistical outlines for a variety of strike scenarios ranging from the immediate mutilation of his parents at the hands of a serial killer currently stationed in the area, to the destruction of his entire town by direct meteor impact in late March. Of course, I've researched a number of more prosaic options; the collapse of their home during an earthquake, financial catastrophe, public disgrace, the usual things, but I thought . . ." Lesterman stammered to a halt as Lucifer dropped his face into his hands, and began to shake his head. "Sir? . . . Is something wrong, Sir?"

"Are you deaf and blind, Lesterman," he asked without looking up, "or just out to break the Guinness World Record for lethal stupidity?" When he did look up, Lesterman flinched, and dropped half his files. "Were you paring your nails when that young zealot leapt up and volunteered to end his life for *Arthur*? Striking hard at such a fellow will only galvanize him into full-blown martyrdom! Our Enemy would love that, wouldn't He! I'd *lose*, Lesterman! I'd lose *right out of the gate!*"

"I . . . I . . . Of course," Lesterman stammered. "That is—I just—"

"I don't think you'll be needed after all," Lucifer observed wearily.

There was just time for pure animal terror to register on Lesterman's face before he and all his folders vanished without sound or fanfare.

Seeing the obvious distress this caused Lesterman's remaining teammates, Lucifer drawled, "Calm yourselves, gentlemen. I know we all abhor waste here, but Lesterman will still have ample opportunity to be of service." He smiled unpleasantly. "Even here, folks have to eat . . . don't they?"

His amusement soured as he noticed the chunky one called Lindwald salivating rather conspicuously at the idea of dining on Lesterman. *Oh, God,* Lucifer groaned mentally. To be free at last of these revolting maggots!

"On second thought," he told the two remaining functionaries, "I don't think I can endure any more of your genius just now. Someone must survive to do the footwork, after all, so, I'll just spell it out for you.

"You're fairly new here Williamson, but Lindwald's been around long enough to understand how rudely we've been surprised on previous occasions just when we were sure of victory. Though some of those reversals seemed utterly unexplainable, I've never been able to *prove* the Enemy's unlawful interference, which leaves us to assume that the devious Deity is able to anticipate our strategies impossibly far in advance—or has somehow booby-trapped virtually every aspect of creation itself. Any questions so far?"

The two damned souls shook their heads in perfect unison.

"Therefore, we must begin with meticulous observation," Lucifer continued, "followed by patient, careful execution. During this initial phase of our campaign, the candidate must perceive our presence no more than the hare perceives the circling hawk. We must test him, but do nothing major—*nothing,* you understand—until we have grown to know his fears and insecurities as well as what he *doesn't* fear; what he loves, and what he hates; his dreams and ambitions—especially his ambitions; his favorite and least favorite colors, foods, smells, sounds. Anything—*anything*—might tip the balance.

"That's why you're here, Williamson," Lucifer continued. "My attention is required in too many places to be watching the child eat and sleep and piss at all hours. That will be your job. Report *everything* to me. I want you to dust off every least skill acquired during that illustrious career in advertising, and research this boy like you never researched any market in your lamentably brief life. Got it?"

"Yes, Sir," Williamson replied. "When I'm finished, your biggest problem will be chosing which of the available buttons to push for the desired result, Sir."

"That may be *your* biggest problem," Lucifer replied. "*I* will have no problems at all. Is that understood?"

"Perfectly, Sir."

After an uncomfortable silence, the fat one, Lindwald, cleared his throat softly, and asked, "What about me, Sir?"

"I think that you, Lindwald, may finally be ready to enter the fourth grade."

❈

"Quick, Sir Benjamin! Up the castle wall!" Joby raced to scramble up the live oak tree that spread its old arms over a quarter of their backyard. "The dragon can't get us up there. We'll make a new plan!"

"How come it won't get us?" Benjamin asked, racing after Joby. "Can't it fly?"

"It broke its wing!" Joby shouted without slowing.

"How'd it break its wing?" Benjamin pressed, waiting impatiently for Joby to climb above the first branch so he could follow.

"It tripped on my underwear!" Joby answered in exasperation. "Don't ask questions, Sir Benjamin! Just *climb*! You wanna get us both eaten?"

From inside the house, Miriam watched the elaborate play of little muscles across the small bare backs of her son and his new friend as they scrambled up into the tree's higher branches and fell into earnest conversation. She was still astonished at how quickly they had fallen head over heels into friendship. An after-school fight over some trivial violation of boyish honor had brought them together. Benjamin had bloodied Joby's nose, Joby had blackened Benjamin's eye. Two days later, Joby had knighted Benjamin on King Arthur's behalf, and they'd been inseparable ever since. Boys, she thought with a smile. Go figure.

Besides the boundless energy native to most children, they shared a natural athleticism, vivid imaginations, and a predilection to laugh at anything with the least potential for humorous interpretation. But, while Joby was a born leader, Benjamin was content to follow, constantly asking questions for which Joby happily invented answers. While Joby talked, laughed, and decreed incessantly, Benjamin tended toward thoughtful silences. Even their appearance was day and night. Deeply tanned, with large brown eyes and nearly white-blond hair, Benjamin seemed a golden noon beside the lunar radiance of Joby's pale skin, blue eyes, and midnight locks. Miriam always enjoyed seeing them together. They seemed two halves of some marvelous whole.

"Hey you," Frank said softly, coming up to give her a squeeze.

"Have a good nap?" she smiled, still watching the boys.

"Best nap I ever had—since the last one." His eyes followed hers. "Those two spend half their lives up there. Think we should build 'em a tree fort?"

"Let's not encourage them," she said. "Half the time, they don't even hold on to anything."

"Boys are climbers," Frank smiled, "and not half as fragile as us old folks. We don't want to make a wimp out of him." He squeezed her again. "Worst thing could happen to a boy. Lot worse than fallin' out of a tree."

"I'm sure you're right, dear," Miriam said, turning with a flirtatious smile to slide her arms around his waist. "Maybe we should find him a sister, so I'd have another wimpy girl to keep me company."

"Mmmm," he purred, leaning in to kiss her. "Wanna twist my arm?"

❧

Going through Williamson's first report, Lucifer had to admit that a few of his observations might be useful, though he had no intention of saying so. One shred of acknowledgment was all it took to render such creatures utterly unmanageable.

He went to the transmission obelisk beside his office door, placed a hand on its glassy surface, closed his eyes, and focused on a name. *Kallaystra . . . Kallays—*

"Bright One?"

Lucifer opened his eyes to find Kallaystra standing serenely at his side, looking, as always, like the wholesome ingenue she wasn't. Along with its fiery fantasies of Hell, the mortal world seemed to forget that demons were nothing more or less than angels swept to earth with Lucifer after their failed campaign against the Creator. Driven by rage or despair at their devalued state, some had fallen into madness, making themselves animal and ugly, or wandered off to become solitary rogues. But many, like Kallaystra, had remained as lovely as ever—on the surface at least. Kallaystra was one of very few, however, who still came readily when Lucifer called, one of even fewer he still dared rely upon. That, and the fact that she was an immortal being like himself, not some damned flake of once—human dryer lint like Williamson or Lindwald, earned her a very different degree of courtesy.

"Thank you for coming so swiftly, Kallaystra. I hope my summons didn't interrupt anything of import."

"Only boredom, Bright One. They are dull to watch."

"The boredom you endure magnifies my gratitude. What do you make of them?"

"The boy is certainly bright, but hardly so remarkable as many of his predecessors. The parents seem utterly mundane. Had bitter experience not taught us otherwise, I'd think all this caution wildly excessive."

"As it would be," Lucifer conceded, "had our Oppressor less power to complicate even the simplest endeavors. Someday I will catch Him meddling, and make Him pay." The idea made him smile. "This would be the very wager to force by default!"

"Would it?" Kallaystra asked. "You still haven't told me what the stakes *are* this time." She gazed at him inquisitively.

Caught off guard, Lucifer hesitated. He could hardly tell her that if he won she and all of Hell's other inmates would be eliminated with the rest of Creation.

"I . . . don't want this widely known, Kallaystra, for I'm testing loyalties; but as your faith is well proven, I'll trust you with a secret, just between the two of us. Agreed?"

"Of course, Bright One," she replied, eyes agleam with the delight conspiracy always brought her.

"You'll remember that little war some time ago, in Heaven. . . . The one we lost."

"What of it?" she said flatly. It was considered poor manners to mention it.

"Perhaps you'll forgive me for bringing it up when I tell you that, should I win this wager, the outcome of that contest will be reversed."

"What?" she gasped. *"He agreed to this?"*

"He did," Lucifer grinned. "He seems to have grown cocky in His old age."

"I can't believe He consented! What can He be thinking?"

"That is precisely what we must discover," Lucifer cautioned. "He's surely got an ace hidden somewhere. We need to find it before committing ourselves to anything of consequence."

"How can I be of service?" she asked, her enthusiasm clearly trebled.

"First, my trusted accomplice, by remembering that *no one else* must know what I have told you," Lucifer insisted. "When I am elevated to my rightful place in Heaven, proven loyalties will be rewarded; and proven disloyalty as well. Let the others reveal themselves *without* knowing what is at stake. Understand?"

"Rest assured, Bright One, your confidence in me is not misplaced."

"Had I doubted you in the least, Kallaystra, I would have said nothing at all."

"I am yours to command." She fairly bubbled.

"Good. I thought we might start by cultivating a small conundrum for Joby to navigate—just to see what boils up at higher temperatures." He went to his desk, glanced at Williamson's report, then smiled at Kallaystra. "Reconnaissance suggests that the boy's mother possesses a latent tendency toward anxiety, and the father attaches rather a lot of importance to his little boy's budding masculinity. I thought we might employ your extraordinary skill with dreams to whip these small flaws into a proper froth."

"Sounds fun." Kallaystra grinned. "What do you have in mind?"

"Briefly, I want his mother driven to strangle the boy in apron strings, while his father worries that Joby isn't 'man enough.' No matter what the child does, someone disapproves. Think you can manage it?"

"With ease, Bright One. Is that all?"

"Well, if you're left with time on your hands, you might help me locate a fifth-grade teacher more resonant with our point of view than the one they've got at that school of his. Someone with a love of conformity and a severe allergy to imagination."

"That will not be difficult, Bright One."

"I won't keep you then. Go with my profound appreciation."

"To the triumph so long denied us." She smiled, then vanished.

"Well . . . to *my* triumph at any rate," Lucifer murmured.

He was sure, of course, that she'd leak their little "secret" all over the cosmos. All Hell would soon be scrambling to assist him as he could never have coerced them to do directly.

"Had I doubted you in the slightest, my dear," he said, chuckling softly.

✖

"*Ha!* Yer *out*, Benjamin!"

"I am not! It didn't come *near* me!"

"*Liar!*" snarled the big, sweaty boy who'd thrown the large, red dodge ball. "I hit you clean enough to eat on, *didn't* I, Stives! Now you get out!" he hollered without waiting for Stives to answer. "It's *my* turn t'go in!"

"You didn't hit him," Joby said. "We all saw."

"You *would* lie for yer *liar friend,*" Lindwald sneered. "Why should I believe *you,* you skinny prick!" Balling his meaty hands into fists, he looked menacingly around the dodge ball circle and asked, "Anybody else think I didn't see what I saw?"

No one answered. Lindwald had come to their school only a week and a half ago, and already everyone was scared stiff of him—even Tommy Stives, who had been the school's uncontested bully until Jamie Lindwald's family had moved here and enrolled their hulking, vicious, foul-mouthed, lying, smelly, sweaty kid in the fourth grade.

"Seeeee?" Lindwald jeered. "Nobody says I didn't hit yer wussy little friend but *his* wussy little friend. So both you wussies are lyin'. Get out, Benjamin."

"Lindwald," Benjamin persisted, "just 'cause nobody but Joby's got guts enough to say so, doesn't mean—"

"He's not worth it, Benjamin," Joby sighed. "He'll just use up the whole recess fighting about it. Let him go."

"But—"

"Benjamin!" Joby growled as meaningfully as he could. "Let him go *in!*"

"Yeah, *Benjy!*" Lindwald taunted. "Listen to yer chicken little *boyfriend*! Least *he's* got the sense t'be *scared.*"

Benjamin was staring at Joby in confusion, but Joby gave him a tiny nod, hoping Lindwald wouldn't see, and pointedly squeezed the oversize red rubber dodge ball, which he'd been holding since Lindwald had missed Benjamin with it. Seeming to get it at last, Benjamin shrugged back into the dodge ball ring as Lindwald sauntered smugly to its center for his turn at being "it."

"You think yer gonna tag me," he grinned at Joby, "but ya better not throw too hard." He smiled nastily. "Wouldn' wanna hurt a innocent bystander, would ya."

Lindwald began to dance back and forth opposite Joby, hands slightly out from his sides. He *was* a lot lighter on his feet than his lardy appearance suggested, but Joby had no intention of trying to hit him—yet. He only raised the ball above his head, and threw it up and over to Benjamin, calling, "Just throw it back!"

Ever faithful, Benjamin did as Joby asked.

In possession of the ball again, Joby looked cheerfully through Lindwald at his friend, and said, "Since he just lies, and everybody lets him, what's the point in playing, right? Why don't you and me just keep the ball 'til recess ends, eh Benjamin?"

Benjamin shrugged, deferring to Joby as always.

Joby tossed the ball up over Lindwald's head again, and Benjamin arced it easily back.

"What a pair a *tutu girls*!" Lindwald barked, ceasing his agile dodge dance and stepping toward Joby. "You can't just take *our* ball, and play with *each other*!"

Joby lobbed the ball back to Benjamin. Lindwald turned to rush him for it, but Benjamin threw it up and over to Joby who caught it just as Lindwald turned to charge back at him. That's when Joby swung his arms back and hurled the ball with all his pent-up fury straight at Lindwald—who dodged with unbelievable swiftness, so that Joby's killing shot passed him completely, and hit Laura Bayer right in the face. Her glasses flew away as she fell to the ground to lie stunned until the blood began to trickle from her nose. Then she clutched her face and began to cry, louder and louder.

"Nice work, *butthead*!" Lindwald jeered at Joby.

Pale and trembling, Joby stood immobilized between white-hot rage at Lindwald, and horrified guilt over what he'd done to poor Laura Bayer. His guilt won out, and he rushed to stand helplessly over the wailing little girl, and blurt out apologies.

"Laura! I'm *sorry*! It was a *accident*! Are you okay? Stop crying! *Please* stop crying! I didn't mean to hurt you!"

"Didn' I tell ya not to hurt the *innocent, Joby*?" Lindwald laughed. *Actually laughed*—while Laura Bayer lay there screaming and bleeding on the ground!

Like an angry cat, Joby whirled and leapt at Lindwald, sending a fist into his face hard and fast, but what happened was so incomprehensible that Joby simply froze, mouth agape in shock. As his punch had landed on Lindwald's nose, Joby had *felt* it in his own face: the terrible ringing impact, the crunch of dislocated cartilage, the warm gush of blood in Lindwald's sinuses. Yet, reaching up to touch his own nose, Joby found it undamaged.

Lindwald's nose was already swelling as the blood appeared on his upper lip; but he just grinned hideously, and asked so softly that perhaps only Joby heard, "What's a matter, *lady-killer*? Hurt yerself on my nose?"

Almost involuntarily, Joby's arm swung back to launch another punch, but this time he could feel the terrible violence of it against Lindwald's already broken nose even *before* the punch had landed, and his swing veered wide almost of its own volition, missing Lindwald entirely.

Only *then* did Lindwald strike back, knocking Joby onto his back next to

Laura Bayer and jumping down to slam him in the face, so that Joby's nose ran red as well now.

"Give up, *dickhead?*" Lindwald demanded from astride Joby's stomach.

"No!" Joby hollered.

Lindwald hit him in the face again. "Give up?"

"No," Joby said again, vaguely aware that his own pain seemed oddly dim and distant compared to the still resonant memory of Lindwald's.

Lindwald was pulling his fist back for another punch when someone yanked him away so fast that the huge boy seemed lifted by a sudden wind. Then Joby saw Benjamin on top of Lindwald, thrashing him with both fists, his arms swinging like the little wooden windmill duck in the garden next to Joby's house.

There was hardly time to feel grateful, though, before his teacher, Mrs. Nelson, and the sixth-grade teacher showed up and waded in to separate the boys. They were joined a moment later by the fifth-grade teacher, who brought wads of wet paper towel and said the principal was on his way. Everyone was picked up, dusted off, wiped clean, and dressed down by the time he arrived.

"I will see *you,* and *you,* and *you* in my office right *now!*" Mr. Leonard fired, pointing at Benjamin, Joby, and Jamie Lindwald.

As the three boys shuffled after him and toward their doom, someone ran up behind Joby and touched his hand. He looked back to find Laura Bayer peering at him contritely through her somehow unbroken blue plastic-framed glasses.

"I'm sorry, Joby," she whispered. "I know you didn't mean to hit me."

She turned before he could reply and ran back to where the others stood, watching them go as crowds have always watched condemned criminals being marched to the gallows. As they walked, Joby hung his head and imagined kneeling before King Arthur to explain what had happened, but it was *Merlin's* voice he imagined. *You must be* perfect, *Sir Joby,* the wizard admonished, *or the devil will win. and Arthur will lose, and Camelot . . . Camelot will* burn.

Joby wondered miserably if he would get a second chance to be perfect. *Arthur, help me!* he thought, then remembered that Arthur *couldn't* help him anymore. It was in the rules. Arthur had said so.

"Joby Peterson, stop straggling!" Mr. Leonard scolded over his shoulder. "If you're man enough to punch people, you should be man enough to face the consequences. Now hurry up."

"Yeah, Joby," Lindwald whispered without turning around. Joby didn't need to see his face to hear the wicked grin in his voice. "If yer *man enough.*"

Joby waited for Mr. Leonard to yell at Lindwald for talking; but the principal just walked before them as if he hadn't heard.

❄

Trying to avoid her son, the school bus fishtailed, tires screaming on the asphalt, then slid full around, swatting Joby's bike like a bug onto the pavement. Rigid with terror, Miriam watched, unable even to cry out as the huge yellow juggernaut screeched sidelong over her son's doubled-over body, crumpling it savagely into the twisted blue wreckage of his bike. Only as the huge machine swiped two parked cars, and shuddered to a halt did Miriam find her voice, and fill the sudden silence with her scream.

Her eyes snapped open with a jolt, and she sat up breathing hard. *Oh God! It had seemed so real!* She looked frantically at the clock. 4:00 P.M.! Joby should be home! *Dear God, where was Joby?*

Then she remembered the phone call from school—Joby's detention—and slumped in relief. The whole day had been difficult. An inexplicable depression had settled over her shortly after Frank and Joby had left the house that morning. The phone call from Joby's school had seemed the last straw. She'd gone to the couch for a nap, wondering if she were coming down with something.

What an awful dream, she thought, rubbing her eyes and getting up to start on dinner. But for all she tried, she could not set the image of her son's violent death aside.

She'd never have admitted it, even to Frank, but there had been a few times, a *very* few, when her dreams *had* seemed to come true. They'd all been about silly things: missing a bus, spilling a load of groceries, the trivial comment of some friend; things hardly worthy of premonition. But her father had always taken a surprising interest in dreams as well, both his own and hers, and had seemed to anticipate little things with uncanny accuracy at times. It had all combined to leave her with a nagging awareness of the *possibility* of . . . well . . . it was ridiculous. Dreams were nothing but dreams, thank God. Nothing but dreams.

❄

They waited in Mrs. Nelson's room while she corrected spelling tests, sitting well apart, hands folded, and silent. Jamie fidgeted impatiently. His nose was huge and purple by now, and the rigid plastic desk chairs were too small for his considerable bulk. Benjamin gazed toward the windows as if trying to flee through them with his eyes. Joby stared at his folded hands and relived Mr. Leonard's humiliating judgment:

I don't care what you think of Jamie's sportsmanship, young man. You threw that ball far too hard, apparently on purpose; and then you were the first to throw a punch. Fighting is not acceptable here for any reason, and YOU, Joby Peterson, clearly lit the fuse. That is why I am giving Ben and Jamie just one day of detention while YOU will stay after school every day this week.

Mrs. Nelson looked up at the wall clock behind them.

"All right boys. It's four thirty. You may go."

They erupted from their chairs like greyhounds through the starting gate.

"But, Joby, I'll see you here again tomorrow. Remind your mother to expect you home late this week."

"Yes, Mrs. Nelson."

Outside the room, Jamie turned back to grin at Joby. "Don't forget to tell your *mommy*," he jeered, then turned and charged through the hallway door to freedom.

"What a *loser* he is," Benjamin muttered. "Joby . . ." Benjamin hesitated, "Why'd you just lie there like that when he hit you?"

Joby felt his cheeks flame. What could he say? *I felt my own punch hit Lindwald's face?* That sounded stupid even to himself now. He still couldn't understand what had happened. Had he just imagined it? Was he chicken, like Lindwald said? What if it happened again every time he tried to fight someone?

"Joby?" Benjamin pressed.

Joby's mind raced to invent some answer that didn't sound crazy or chicken; but all he could think of was the truth. "Promise you won't laugh?"

"Cross my heart," Ben said.

Joby steeled himself. "Something so strange happened when I hit him, that . . . I don't know what it was. But—"

"I knew it!" Benjamin blurted out. "He did something to you, didn't he?"

Joby stared at Benjamin as his thoughts did a sort of flip-flop. He'd spent all afternoon trying to make sense of what had happened, but somehow it had never occurred to him that Lindwald might have *caused* it!

"You went all stiff right after you punched him," Benjamin said, "and I knew he did something to you—but I couldn't see what it was."

Joby was still too amazed by the idea forming in his head to speak.

"Come on, Joby! Trust me!" Ben insisted. "What'd he do?"

"Magic," Joby whispered in astonishment.

"What?" Benjamin asked.

"I know it sounds impossible," Joby said uncertainly, "but when I hit him,

I *felt* it, just like it was *my* face getting slammed. Everything—even the bleeding. And when I went to hit him again, I felt my own punch before it even reached him."

Joby braced himself for Benjamin's ridicule, but all his friend said was, "Whooooa! How'd he do *that?*"

"Benjamin, I got a secret I haven't even told my mom. I can only tell you if you promise you'll believe me no matter what. And that you won't tell anyone else, ever."

"Okay." Benjamin nodded excitedly.

"No matter what?" Joby pressed.

"Even if Lindwald punches me 'til I die," Benjamin assured him solemnly.

"Okay," Joby said, "but if I tell you, it's a sacred oath—like in my book. We're sword brothers then, forever."

"Cooool!" Benjamin exclaimed.

Joby spat on his hand. "We must shake on it, Sir Benjamin."

Benjamin spat in his hand too, and they shook on it. Then they wiped their hands on their pants, and Joby told Benjamin about his dream, and the secret mission for Arthur. Benjamin listened with growing amazement and admiration.

"You *really* went there?" Benjamin enthused when Joby had finished. "Did you have a sword?"

Joby looked thoughtful. "I don't think so. Just a horse."

"So, when do we start fighting, Joby?"

"Don't you get it, Benjamin? We already have! Lindwald works for the *devil*! That's how he made me feel that punch. *Black magic!* When I hit him, he just said, *What's a matter Joby, you hurt yourself on my nose?* He *knew*, Benjamin! *You* made me see it! If he knew, he must have made it happen! Right? And if Lindwald can do magic, he must be working for . . . for *him*," Joby said, suddenly nervous.

"Lindwald works for the *devil?*"

Joby waved Benjamin quiet. "Don't go shouting his name like that!"

"What? Lindwald's?"

"No, you freak! The other one! . . . The *enemy's*! The *real* enemy!"

"Oh," Benjamin said, looking abashed. "You mean the dev—"

"Don't!" Joby urged. "Don't even say it. We'll just call him the enemy. Okay?"

Benjamin's eyes widened, and he looked around nervously. "You think he's listening, Joby? The . . . enemy? Like, right *now?*"

"I don't know," Joby said. "But he could be. Come on. We gotta go home and make a plan, Sir Benjamin. We can't get caught by surprise again!"

⁂

"That idiot!"

Lucifer whirled in fury from the bowl of water on his office desk through which, alerted by the ever-vigilant Williamson, he'd watched the disastrous scene unfold.

"I'm plagued with an endless army of morons!" he shouted at his office ceiling, then strode to an obsidian obelisk like the one in the conference room, slammed his hand against it and shouted, *"LINDWALD!"*

Instantly, the terrified soul, still guised as a chunky little boy, materialized, cowering in a corner of the large office as far from his employer as possible.

"What's wrong, Sir?" he quavered.

"Watch!" Lucifer yelled, thrusting his hand toward the wall behind him, where a screen appeared, flickering bluish green at first, then resolving into images of Joby and Benjamin in the hallway at school. When their entire conversation had been replayed, Lucifer turned to flay Lindwald with his eyes.

"What a hoot, eh, Lindwald?"

"Sir, I—"

"Shut up!" Lucifer bellowed. *"There is nothing I want more right now than to eviscerate each and every droplet of the mist you're made of!* All it would take to shatter my restraint is one tiny excuse."

Trembling visibly, Lindwald seemed almost to merge with the wall behind him.

"I said, *test* him!" Lucifer snarled. "I said, *n-o-t-h-i-n-g m-a-j-o-r! I sure as hell* said *nothing* about the blatant use *of power* against him, *did I!"*

Lindwald had become virtually inert with terror.

"Well?" Lucifer demanded. *"Answer me!"*

"No, Sir. But it seemed like such a little thing to—"

" 'No, Sir' would have done nicely!" Lucifer raged. He began to breath deeply, like a giant bellows, gathering the shredded remnants of his patience. When he spoke again, it was at a fraction of his former volume, if no less angrily. "One stupid, self-indulgent bit of braggadocio, and *look* at what you've accomplished, Lindwald. Your cover is blown; he's fully marshaled around his dream of *Arthur* again—which he'd almost forgotten; he even has an ally now! An *ally!* You're a flaming *genius!"*

Lindwald seemed both surprised and alarmed by the whimper that escaped his own pouty little lips.

"Do you know why you're not already being filleted for table service, Lindwald?" Lucifer asked in suddenly mild tones infinitely more frightening than his earlier rage.

The shake of Lindwald's head was barely perceptible.

"Because, as personally satisfying as I might find your immediate destruction, your sudden disappearance now would only confirm their suspicions, and I don't want that. So I'm sending you back to convince them that you're nothing after all but a nasty little boy like any other juvenile sociopath they know. Try thinking *obedience* this time."

After several moments of agonized silence, Lindwald dared to squeak, "How?"

Lucifer merely smiled. "I am not a monster, Lindwald. I understand your limitations. We are not all born to brilliance, so to spare you any further gaffs, I'm sending you back without any special power at all. You needn't worry about tipping your hand again, because you really will be nothing but the helpless little bully we want them to believe you are. Of course, your ... *parents,*" he smiled cruelly, "will still have *their* abilities, and I'll see that they provide the kind of *disciplined* home life required to nurture your success."

Lindwald looked like he might puke on Lucifer's elegant gray pile carpet.

Lucifer turned to wander his office pensively. "You're strategy now is to get soundly *thrashed* by these boys. Do you understand? Take care to make it happen naturally and look convincing, but when you're done I want those two boys to look and feel like heroes ... while *you* look like the ass you are!" Lucifer turned to face him again. "I'd go now, if I were you. It's getting late there. We wouldn't want your *parents* to worry, *would we.*"

This last admonition held fearful implications, but Lindwald needed no prodding. He was gone before Lucifer's words had left the air.

3

(Religions)

"Frank? You coming?"

Lost in thought, Frank looked up to find Sidney Mason at his office door. "The Goldtree Mall meeting. Ten minutes, dude."

"Oh! Sure. Thanks, Sid. Be right there."

Sidney left him with a high sign.

Frank stood to gather what he'd need. His mind had been wandering all morning. His sleep the night before had been plagued by that same weird dream: racquetball at the health club. Unable to see the ball or move beyond a snail's pace, he'd endured the same humiliating defeat on court, then opened his locker to find Joby hiding there, dressed like a girl, lipstick, mascara, and all, sucking his thumb while the laughter of all Frank's acquaintances grew loud enough to wake him. That was how it always ended. He'd had the dream at least four times already, and wondered more and more anxiously why anyone would dream such sick things about his own son even once?

Juggling cost estimates, design documents, and blueprints, he shoved the whole matter from his mind once again and headed for the conference room. He had a shopping mall to plan, and important people to impress. There was no time to worry about dreams.

⌘

Lindwald sat alone, hunched and brooding at a corner of the playground. The pointed animosity of his schoolmates since the fight with Joby meant nothing to him; but the torments he'd been made to endure at "home" each night since that dreadful audience with his master had been all the more horrendous for knowing they'd grow steadily worse until he managed to get "thrashed." He'd been goading Joby and Benjamin relentlessly, but for some reason the contemptible pissants wouldn't fight back now.

Looking up, he caught Laura Bayer gazing adoringly at Joby as he played tetherball with Ben. *The guy practically takes her head off with a dodge ball,*

Lindwald thought, *and she goes soft for him!* He spat between his feet, and wondered what made abuse such an aphrodisiac. The day after he'd hurt her, Joby had brought Laura a tree frog in a mayonnaise jar tied 'round with a green ribbon, and she'd fawned over the gift as if it were *chocolates! Ye gods and little daisies!* It was *insulting* to be in so much trouble over such imbeciles! Nonetheless, if Lindwald didn't find some convincing way to make them thrash him soon, his so—called *parents* would put scars on the scars he already bore beneath his clothes, which were no less painful for the contrived nature of his boyish seeming flesh.

✼

When Joby slammed the winning shot high over Benjamin's head, Laura bounced to her toes, but just managed not to clap. She didn't want to hurt Benjamin's feelings. He was really very good, just not as good as Joby.

"Beating you's getting boring, Benjamin," Joby crowed, arresting the tetherball as it swung back around the pole.

"Then I'll beat *you* this time," Benjamin offered unperturbed. "Loser serves."

Joby swung the ball to him, but shook his head. "You'll have to beat Laura—if you *can*," he teased, turning to grin at her. "I gotta go write a idea down before I forget."

As she watched him run off to write in his secret book, Laura sighed. She'd always liked him, of course. Most everybody did. He was nice, and smart, and good at sports, and *very* handsome. But what had really won her heart was how deeply he had cared about what happened in the dodgeball game. She was glad he'd tried to hit Lindwald. She'd have done the same thing if she'd had the ball. But Joby had been so sorry, and so sweet to her ever since, that she'd have forgiven him no matter what. Joby had something none of the other boys did. He had a heart.

"So . . . wanna play me?" Benjamin asked shyly.

Turning from her thoughts of Joby, she smiled and nodded, stepping into the ring around the pole. Benjamin was very nice too, of course, and almost as handsome as Joby. When she and Joby got married, she hoped Benjamin would be their best man.

✼

Hunched down against the school building, Joby slipped his "clue book" from a coat pocket. Its royal-blue cover was decorated with silver stars around a golden sun. His mother had gotten it at the stationery store, but Joby pretended it was a magic book conjured up by elves. He never wrote on its blank pages with anything but pencil, so that he could go back later and fix his spelling, which had improved so much that both Mrs. Nelson and his mom had noticed. *A knight must practice,* Joby reminded himself whenever learning to be perfect began to seem too hard. Since the disastrous fight with Lindwald, Joby had been careful to make sure his temper didn't mislead him again. He was also careful now to be polite to adults, wash his hands before every meal, and keep his room clean . . . well, cleaner anyway. He did his schoolwork first thing after detention each day . . . or almost first thing . . . most of the time. But he was still determined to do better. No more mistakes. *A knight must practice.*

Planning their strategy against Lindwald, Joby and Benjamin had started looking through his *Treasury of Arthurian Tales* for ideas. Several stories had mentioned a magical cup called the *Grail,* which nothing evil could come near, so the boys had started paying close attention to any cups they encountered, in case one of them should be it. Many of these same stories mentioned people called priests or bishops, who seemed to know a lot about fighting the devil. When Joby had wished aloud that they could find one, Benjamin had assured Joby that they had *lots* of priests at the church he and his parents went to, though he'd never seen any bishops there.

Joby had never been to church. His parents had never even talked about it. And when Benjamin told him that priests wore long robes like the people in Joby's book, and that the church looked like a castle, Joby had nearly flipped. "Maybe they're from Camelot!" he'd exclaimed. "Maybe they can tell us how to get there and talk to Merlin!"

Emboldened, Benjamin had explained that the church was at a school where people learned how to be priests, and suggested they ride over on their bikes that weekend, and talk to someone named Father Crombie.

"Why do you call him that?" Joby had asked.

"'Cause that's his *name,* you dork! They get different last names, but their *first* name's always Father."

"But—"

"I don't *know* why!"

"Oh."

"He's pretty old, but he's real nice, and he knows all *kinds* of stuff. I bet he can tell us *everything* about fighting the devil."

So it had been agreed. They'd go on Saturday morning.

Their best idea, however, had been to start their own Roundtable. It still amazed Joby that they hadn't thought of it sooner. They weren't going to tell anyone about their secret quest, of course, but if they knighted a bunch of their friends and got them to swear to fight the wicked and defend the weak, they'd have more than enough might to keep Lindwald in his place.

The idea had received mixed reviews so far at school, but Johnny Mayhew and Peter Blackwell had already signed up enthusiastically, which meant Duane Westerlund was in as well, because he did everything Peter did. That was only five, but Joby was sure more would want in once they saw how cool it was. There was even a big, round table in the library, which was always open after school. They'd agreed to have their first meeting there on Monday afternoon when Joby's detention would finally be over.

When Laura had heard about it, she and Paula Guarachi had asked to join too. But the boys had all agreed that girls could not be knights. Joby felt kind of sorry for Laura, but she was pretty cool, especially for a girl, and he was sure she'd get over it.

In the mean time, Joby had been getting ready for their first meeting by writing ideas for the Roundtable in his book. He'd come up with six already:

1. The meetings should be secret!—which is hard in the library, but maybe we could just shut up if someone comes until they leave again.

2. The knights should vote on everybody's ideas.

3. The knights should be like secret helpers and do good things for people without getting caught like Santa Claws.

4. The knights should always stick up for each other and help anyone who is getting picked on more than they should.

5. There should be tests everybody has to pass to get in. Even me and Benjamin.

6. The knights should have contests on weekends in the woods to get better at sports and fighting.

Joby read over his list with satisfaction, taking special note of words whose spelling he'd had to correct. Then he wrote: "7. The knights should all have bycicles." He thought for a moment, chewing the end of his pencil, then added, "And maybe help any guy who passes the tests to get one if he doesn't have it all redy."

Just then, the school bell rang, commanding everyone back to class, but as Joby stood to go inside, he found Lindwald standing in his way.

"Whatcha got in the book?" Lindwald sneered. "Names of all yer *boyfriends?*"

A knight must practice, Joby reminded himself, and walked around him without even meeting his eyes.

⚜

Saturday morning, after forcing down two pancakes and a few forkfuls of scrambled egg to please his mother, Joby bounded from the table, ran outside, leapt on his bike, and lit out for Benjamin's house.

As Joby arrived, his friend peddled out to meet him so that they didn't even have to slow down. Then they rode and rode and rode, until houses gave way to fields of dead corn or bare, furrowed dirt already showing the first green fuzz of winter grass. This was so much farther than Joby had ever ridden, it seemed as if they might really be riding all the way to Camelot.

"You sure you know where we're going?" Joby called to Benjamin.

"See that?" Benjamin shouted, pointing at a distant oasis of wide lawns, trees, and dark buildings nestled beneath the round dry hills ahead of them. "That's it!"

Twenty minutes later, they rode between the seminary's massive wrought-iron gates onto park-like grounds lushly landscaped around huge brick buildings older than any Joby had ever seen. The roofs were shingled in slate, the eaves and gables trimmed in gothic masonry. The many-paned windows were glazed in wavy glass, elaborately leaded and framed; nothing at all like the aluminum-trimmed plateglass familiar to Joby. But the church itself was by far the best thing there.

Many stories tall, the building was fronted in giant stone columns and elaborate reliefs. A wide cascade of steps led up to large, richly carved triple doors of dark wood hung on heavy wrought-iron hinges. The windows were all of stained glass. One, huge and round, hung like a giant spiderweb above the doors. Intricate towers rose to either side of the building's facade, topped in pillared openings filled with bells. Joby stared up at the edifice, barely able to breathe. It was his book come to life—his dream come true!

"Come on," Benjamin said, climbing the stairs two at a time. "It's neater inside."

One of the three big doors stood open, and as they walked into the church's dark interior, Joby looked up and gaped. Nearly lost in shadow, the ceiling was a lacework of vaulted masonry impossibly high above their heads. The huge stone columns supporting it were shod and capped in marble carved to look like giant thistle leaves. Statues gazed down from domed alcoves like giants solemnly considering Joby's worthiness to interrupt their deliberations. The mysterious gloom was broken here and there by patches of soft varicolored light from the stained-glass windows. Joby had never encountered incense, but traces of its unfamiliar scent gave him shivers. This *was* Arthur's throne room. Peering through the shadows past rows and rows of polished benches, where he imagined the court must sit in their finery for coronations and knightings, Joby saw the royal throne itself beside a beautiful marble table. On the wall behind these, a whole other castle was carved in miniature relief around a large, richly ornamented golden box.

Joby's rapture was suddenly unsettled by an awful sight. Above the golden box hung the realistically painted sculpture of an almost naked man nailed by his hands and feet to what looked like a sawed-off telephone pole. A circle of long thorns made his forehead run with blood, and his face was clenched in pain and grief. Joby stared at this terrible thing, filled with a powerful sense of dread and wrong. Why would Arthur keep such a terrible statue? He was about to ask Benjamin when he saw, higher still, a far larger statue hovering half in silhouette between the stained-glass windows around it. The regal figure wore voluminous robes and a high, pointed crown, holding an orb in one hand and a staff in the other. It was obviously a king; and Joby was sure which one it must be.

"*Arthur,*" he whispered reverently.

"What are you doing?" Benjamin asked.

By reflex, Joby had gone down on one knee.

"It's Arthur," he said without rising or looking away from the statue.

Benjamin followed his gaze, and said, "No it's not. It's God."

"God's a king?" Joby asked.

"I guess," Benjamin said. "Joby, you're only s'posed to kneel by the benches when you sit down, or in front of the altar. And you're s'posed get right up again."

Joby got to his feet, realizing that Benjamin would not understand what it meant to kneel before Arthur. His friend hadn't known anything at all about Arthur before Joby had knighted him back in September.

"Where are the priests?" Joby asked.

"I don't know. Since the door was open, I thought there'd be somebody in here." Benjamin peered around uncertainly. "It's kind of spooky without the lights on. Maybe we should go try one of the school buildings."

They were turning to leave when the whisper of rustling cloth made them stop and peer back into the darkness. Something moved beside the big table at the front of the church; a column of deeper shadow seemed to pull away from the lesser gloom around it. Both boys froze, and Joby felt deadly certain they were in trouble. The tall shadow drifted toward them, its dark robes swirling as if borne on some silent, ghostly wind. Then it entered a patch of colored light, and was suddenly just a man. Joby saw Benjamin unclench and let out a gush of breath, then realized that this must be a priest.

"Can I help you, gentlemen?" The priest smiled pleasantly. His charcoal hair was shot with silver, and there was a regal grace and confidence about him that seemed familiar to Joby, though he didn't know why.

"We're looking for Father Crombie," Benjamin explained. "The door was open . . . I thought he might be in here."

The priest's expression became apologetic. "Unfortunately, Father Crombie is away at the diocesan office all day. Might anyone else do?"

"Oh," Benjamin said in obvious disappointment.

"Have you come a long way, then?" the priest asked sympathetically.

"We just . . . We had some questions." Benjamin shrugged. "I sort of know Father Crombie. . . . But . . . I guess it doesn't have to be him."

"I'm Father Morgan." The priest smiled, extending his hand to Benjamin. "I'm just visiting, but I'd be delighted to assist you if I can. Were these *personal* questions?"

Shaking Father Morgan's hand, Benjamin said, "This is my friend, Joby. They're really his questions."

"Joby! I'm delighted to make your acquaintance. How can I help?"

"Well, first," Joby confided, seeing no reason not to get straight to the point, "we were wondering if you know how to get to Camelot."

Father Morgan looked nonplussed, then smiled slightly. "Camelot," he said, seeming amused. Joby felt himself flush. "As in *King Arthur's* Camelot?"

"Yes! That's it!" Joby blurted out, his embarrassment swept away in excitement. Joby had known the priest would know! His clothes, this building! Where else could it all have come from? "Have you been there? Do you know King Arthur?"

"May I ask what inspires this unusual query?" Father Morgan asked wryly.

At a loss, Joby timidly admitted that he didn't know what a query was.

"Forgive me," Father Morgan smiled, "I've embarrassed you. All I meant was, why are you asking these . . . rather remarkable questions?"

"Well . . . because . . ." Joby looked to Benjamin for help. Their quest was a secret. Somehow it had not occurred to him that anyone might ask *why* he wanted to know about Camelot. Joby felt more foolish by the minute.

"No matter," the priest assured him. "I was merely curious. Regrettably I have never been to Camelot, nor do I know how to get there."

"But . . . I thought— Isn't this a castle?" Joby asked in dismay. He pointed up at the kingly statue high above the tortured man. "Isn't that Arthur?"

The priest followed Joby's gaze, then shook his head. "I'm sorry, Joby, but this is just a church, the product of an unconscionable number of collection plates; and *that* is just a statue."

"But . . . it's *of* Arthur, isn't it?"

The priest shook his head again. "It's just a bishop, Joby. A very dead bishop, at that." He offered Joby a sympathetic smile. "I wouldn't want to dampen your faith in Camelot, child, but I'd be lying to pretend you might find it here."

"Oh," Joby said, feeling terribly deflated.

"Was that your only question?" Father Morgan asked.

Joby looked at Benjamin, then shook his head, took a deep breath, and asked, "What's the best way to fight the devil?"

Father Morgan's brows arched high above his pale, almost icy blue eyes. "I must say, Joby, you are full of surprising questions."

But Joby hardly heard him. Those eyes! Those *pale blue eyes!* He knew them now! The silver-shot hair, the regal bearing! Of course!

"Merlin?" he whispered.

Father Morgan seemed surprised, then smiled shrewdly. "Do you mean me? Joby, what would a *wizard* be doing in a *church,* disguised as a *priest?"* Then he winked, and Joby knew that Father Morgan was Merlin, though why he should be disguised as a priest, he could not imagine.

"But if you want advice about fighting the devil," Father Morgan continued, "perhaps a priest is of more help than a wizard anyway. God's own Son once fought the devil, Joby. Did you know that?"

"God had a Son? . . . Like *me?"* Joby asked, incredulously.

Father Morgan nodded.

"A *kid* whose dad was *God?"* Joby pressed, finding the idea almost absurd.

"Yes," Father Morgan said, unsmiling.

Joby shook his head, trying to imagine his own dad being God.

"His name was Jesus, Joby; and one time He was all alone in the desert for forty days without anything to eat. Forty days! Imagine how hungry He must have been! So the devil offered Him some bread. Just one harmless piece of bread. What could be wrong with that, eh, Joby?"

Joby shrugged. He couldn't see anything wrong with taking a piece of bread from someone, especially if you were starving.

"But Jesus wouldn't take it, Joby." Father Morgan smiled, driving into him with those strange blue eyes, compelling him to listen, to hear something *be-tween* the words, *behind* his disguise. "As hungry as He was, He denied Himself even a simple piece of bread, lest the devil use that little weakness somehow to gain power over Him." Father Morgan smiled down on Joby. "Think on that, child. To be faithful at all, you must be absolutely faithful. Nothing less will do. If you truly want to beat the devil, you must be prepared to deny any hunger he might use to breach your defenses." He ruffled Joby's hair, which seemed such an un-Merlinish gesture, that Joby almost pulled away. "Are you that brave, Joby?"

Joby nodded gravely, and Father Morgan laughed. "Ah, Joby. I'm rather glad Father Crombie wasn't here. I'd hate to have missed this chance to talk with you. I am sure you'll give the devil quite a run for his money. Just remember to be very, very good."

"I will," Joby promised, bothered by a sense that, despite his smiles, Merlin was angry with him for not trying hard enough to be perfect.

"Good lad. Was that all? Or are there still other marvelous questions weighing on that noble mind of yours?"

"What is that?" Joby asked, pointing to the statue of the suffering man.

Father Morgan turned toward it, though his eyes remained cast down, and his smile fled before a frightening expression that made Joby think he should not have asked.

"That," said Father Morgan very sternly, "is the price of failure. Remember that as well, Joby, if you intend to fight the devil."

⁂

"Damn," Lucifer cursed, the clerical robes dissolving around him like smoke as he returned to his office. That had been far too dicey. Who'd have thought the boy would recognize him? The boy's memory of that dream should have been virtually gone after so much time—had it not been for that useless wag *Lindwald.* But Lucifer had to congratulate himself on turning that surprise neatly to his own advantage. Allowing the boy to suspect "Father Morgan" of being Merlin had doubtless ensured that his poisonous advice would be taken all the more to heart. Lucifer smiled. God played a nimble game, but this time Lucifer would be nimbler.

Williamson's surveillance was proving more valuable than Lucifer had expected. Heaven forbid they had actually gotten to that priest, Crombie. *He* was precisely the kind of interference Lucifer did *not* need. Still, Lucifer did *not* want to be pressed into playing foot soldier again. Even such fleeting personal exposure to the degrading squalor of mortal creation left him feeling unclean for weeks. That's what chaff like Williamson and Lindwald were there to spare him. It seemed Kallaystra would have to find him a suitable priest as well as the new fifth-grade teacher, and swiftly. Things were not going at all as he'd anticipated, not that he would tell *her* that. Lucifer did not take kindly to being caught off guard, and even less liked to having others know of it.

※

Frank could hardly believe his ears! "Was this Ben's idea, Joby?" he asked, trying to hide his irritation.

"No," Joby replied hesitantly. "I just want to go to church with him. That's all."

"Did Ben's parents suggest this?" Frank persisted.

"No," Joby said again. "Are you mad at me? . . . Benjamin said you'd be *happy*."

"We're not mad, Joby," his mother intervened. "I think it's *nice* you want to go."

"Miriam," Frank began, but she gave him no opening.

"We're just surprised, dear. It's not something boys your age usually want to do, and . . . well, we're kind of curious what you hope to find there."

Joby shrugged uncomfortably. "*I* don't know. It just sounds interesting, and . . . and Benjamin's my best friend, and *he* goes. . . . So . . . I just thought I'd like to go with him tomorrow. . . . Can I?"

"Yes, of course, if you want to," Miriam said before Frank could open his mouth.

He nearly groaned. Could she be falling back into this madness too?

"Miriam," he said, "I think we should talk about this."

"Me too," she answered crisply. "Joby, may I have a moment alone with your dad, please?"

Joby nodded, and left the room looking like a boy in trouble, no matter what they'd told him.

Frank spoke up even as the door latched behind their son.

"Miriam, I—"

"You're scaring him to death," she cut him off, "and making him feel ashamed, which, as I recall, is why we decided to keep him away from churches to begin with."

"I didn't mean to scare him. You know that. It's just—"

"I know what it's *just*," she interrupted again. "You must have explained it to me a hundred times before we were married. And . . . okay, I bought into it. But—"

"But *what?*" Frank cut in. "You think I was wrong now? Is that why you're mad at me? Come on, Miriam. They'll turn him into a neurotic little basket case who spends all his time apologizing to God just for existing; or switches his conscience off altogether just to get *them* out of his head. Is that what you want? Wait 'til he hits adolescence and they start trying to unman him with all that crap about—"

"Is that what you're worried about?" she snapped. "Afraid they'll *unman* your little *stud?* He's nine, Frank! *Nine!* Not nineteen. And he's the most rambunctious, *manly* little *war chief* in the neighborhood, in case you haven't noticed. Besides," she said more quietly, "the church isn't always like it was for you. My father's faith was at the heart of everything I loved about him; and . . . yes . . . sometimes I miss it too."

"Why'd you stop going, then?" he asked flatly, torn between growing resentment, and a sudden twinge of guilt.

"I guess . . . I guess it just didn't matter to me as much as you did."

"And now?" he asked, struggling with a host of confusing emotions.

"Is it still a choice?" she asked, looking up at him. "Was it ever, really?" She looked at him, smiled fondly, then shook her head and laughed, "Frank, if we're smart enough not to turn religion into Joby's forbidden fruit, you know what will happen as well as I do. He'll go once or twice, find out it's boring, and forget all about it."

Knowing she was right, Frank reached out to embrace his wife, wondering, not for the first time, if she weren't the more sensible one after all.

When they had hugged and kissed their differences away, Frank called Joby's name, and he came so quickly that Frank suspected he'd been listening at the door.

"Joby," he said dryly, "your old man's a reactionary iconoclast."

Joby stared up at him, clearly unsure whether it was all right to ask what that was. So Frank reached down, lifted his son into the air and whirled him around before pulling the now giggling boy into a fidgety embrace.

"That means sometimes I'm a *weirdo,*" Frank explained playfully. "But I get better after your mother works on me, so we've decided you should go to church with Benjamin tomorrow, and the week after that if you want to. And when you get home, I hope you'll tell us all about it, 'cause we don't know much about church either. Okay?"

"Okay, Dad. I'll do a oral report."

"My son the genius!" Frank replied, setting Joby down with a groan. "Your brain's getting too heavy for me to lift like that anymore. You know that?"

"Not just my brain!" Joby bragged, pulling his sleeve back with a fierce expression, and bending his arm up to make a muscle.

"*Oh* my gosh!" Frank laughed. "Did I just hoist all *that* up in the air? No wonder my back hurts!"

"No *wonder!*" Joby proudly agreed.

"Tell you what, sport," Frank informed him. "From now on, you lift me. Okay?"

"Okay, *sport!*" Joby replied.

❧

"I don't know," Joby whispered, "but they sure didn't *act* happy." The boys had lost Benjamin's parents in the milling throng headed out of Mass, and were taking advantage of their first chance all morning to talk privately.

"That's so *weird,*" Benjamin whispered back. "I never heard of *anybody's* parents not wantin' 'em to go to church before . . . At least they let you come." He shrugged.

Joby could hardly wait to talk with Father Crombie. He had liked the old priest the minute he'd seen him at Mass. His kindly expression and cheerful smile had reminded Joby of Santa Claus, and he made funny jokes in the middle of his speeches. Joby hadn't always understood them, but people had laughed so hard that he hadn't been able to keep himself from laughing too. When Father Crombie had talked about people being lights in the dark, Joby had imagined himself surrounded by glowing candles—as if standing in a giant Christmas tree. It was such a neat idea that it had made him fidgety.

Of course, he'd been a little disappointed to see the polished benches filled with normal people instead of lords and ladies, but the Mass had still been wonderfully strange. There'd been a great deal of kneeling and standing, and sitting, and standing, and kneeling again, just when you started to get comfortable and weren't expecting it. Joby suspected this was all meant to spy out people like himself who didn't belong there, though Benjamin insisted they only did it so that people wouldn't fall asleep. Joby couldn't imagine anyone going to sleep in the middle of something so interesting. His admiration for Benjamin had grown in leaps and bounds as he'd watched his friend stand and kneel, and mouth the long, intricate prayers with the casual ease of an expert.

Not everything about the Mass had been pleasant, though.

Joby still hadn't gotten over the idea that God had a kid. He figured Geezez must have been more like a superhero than a normal kid, since no normal kid could go forty days without eating. But the more Joby had thought about it, the more Geezez seemed like a dumb name for a superhero—or for anyone at all. It sounded like "Cheesz-Its," or "Geezez Krised!"—which he'd heard people say when they were surprised or upset. It was like being named Dang it or Holy Moley. But not until halfway through the Mass, as he'd sat listening carefully to the prayers being read and chanted around him, had Joby slowly come to realize that God's superhero son, Geezez, and the frightening man nailed to the boards above the table for failing to beat the devil, were the same guy!

If Geezez, who wouldn't even take a piece of bread when He was starving, had lost to the devil anyway, and ended up like *that,* what was going to happen to Joby? Joby didn't know how long he could go without eating, but it wasn't anything like forty days! He'd spent the rest of the service reminding himself that Arthur wouldn't have asked him to try if there was *no* way he could win. He just wouldn't have!

Before church, Benjamin had asked his folks if he and Joby could go talk with Father Crombie afterward. So now the boys were waiting for the crowd of old ladies around the old priest to dissipate. When the last chatty old woman finally let him be, Benjamin walked boldly up with Joby in tow.

"Hello, Benjamin." Father Crombie smiled mischievously. "I saw you over there. Why didn't you come over sooner and rescue me from Mrs. O'Hearn?" He turned his kindly smile on Joby who suddenly felt shy. "Who is your quiet friend?"

Benjamin laughed. "He's not quiet! That's Joby, Father Crombie. He's not Catholic, but he's my best friend."

"Benjamin said I could come," Joby said. "Is it all right?"

"Of course!" Father Crombie gasped, looking scandalized. "Our Lord welcomed every child he ever met! I don't think He even asked if they were Catholic!"

"We've got some questions," Benjamin said. "Have you got time to talk to us?"

"There's nothing I'd rather do." He smiled. "Ask away!"

"They're . . . kind of private," Joby said. "Could we go . . . somewhere?"

"Oh. Certainly," Father Crombie replied. "Would the sacristy do, while I put away these vestments?"

When Benjamin nodded, Joby did too.

The sacristy turned out to be a small room to one side of the altar. As they entered, Joby saw closets filled with royal-looking robes, and shelves cluttered with mysterious boxes, bottles, books, and candlesticks of gold and silver. It was like a treasure trove! On one shelf there were two large golden cups, one with rubies set in its stem. As Father Crombie turned to hang the long embroidered scarf he'd worn over his robe in a closet filled with other such scarves, Joby caught Benjamin's eye and pointed urgently up at the golden cups, mouthing the word "Grail." Benjamin shook his head no, just as the old priest turned around and sat down in a chair by the scarf closet.

"Well, boys," he said pleasantly, "what shall we talk about?"

Benjamin looked to Joby, who turned to Father Crombie, shy once more, and unsure of how to begin.

"If it's a secret," the priest assured them, "I promise you that nothing said here will ever leave this room. That is a sacred oath, Joby."

After his embarrassing interview with Father Morgan, Joby had given considerable thought to making his questions sound less foolish.

"I have this book about Camelot and King Arthur," Joby began apprehensively, "and I wanted to ask if you think Camelot is a real place anybody could get to."

Looking neither surprised nor amused, Father Crombie thought for a moment, then said, "I do believe in Camelot, Joby. But I suspect it can only be reached these days through the dreams and intentions of good men and women like yourself."

Though not what he'd hoped for, the answer fit Joby's own experience.

"So, it's not real anymore?"

The priest looked startled. "Of course it is!"

"But you just said . . . What do you mean?" Joby asked.

Father Crombie put a hand to his chin in thought, then grinned. "Is money real?"

Both boys nodded, looking slightly confused.

"See?" Father Crombie beamed. "You both say yes. Yet money doesn't exist any more than Camelot does."

"What?" Benjamin said. "*Everybody's* got money."

"Do they?" Father Crombie asked with twinkling eyes.

Benjamin reached into his pocket and pulled out a crumbled dollar bill. "Look!"

"Is *that* money?" Father Crombie asked, as if he knew a joke they hadn't got yet. He rose to snatch a sheet of paper from the nearby counter top, and held it up for them to see. ST. ALBEE'S PRIORY CHURCH BULLETIN was printed in large green letters across the top. The rest was columns of black type. "What about this, Benjamin? Is *this* money?"

"No, Father," Benjamin said, beginning to look worried.

"Why not?" the priest insisted. "It's paper just like yours. It's even got green and black ink on it. It's bigger, but that should only make it worth more, shouldn't it?"

"But . . . you know it's just a church bulletin, Father Crombie!" Benjamin protested.

"Yes, I do," he smiled, "but the only thing that makes *your* little sheet of paper *money,* and mine worthless, is that everyone *believes* they're different *here* and *here.*" He pointed first at his head, then at his chest. "Money is the biggest fairytale you ever heard! Yet, just because we all *believe* in it, money is, sadly, more real to many people these days than you or I are."

Joby sort of got what he meant, but he couldn't see what it had to do with Camelot, and said so.

"Yes, well . . . what I mean to say, Joby, is that, just because a place like Camelot exists only in our minds and hearts at present, doesn't mean it isn't real, or that it can't be as solid as this church someday. If everyone believed in it as you do, Joby, it would soon be at least as real as money." He smiled. "Wouldn't that be wonderful!"

"You mean, Camelot could come back?" Joby asked excitedly. "Like King Arthur's s'posed to?"

"Oh, I'm sure it could," Father Crombie sighed, "if only people dreamed more wisely."

Joby fell silent, eyes wide but hardly seeing. As if a door had opened inside him, the whole quest suddenly made sense! Maybe Arthur had sent him to bring Camelot back—and the devil didn't want that! That would explain why Arthur couldn't help him 'til he won and why Camelot was doomed if he failed. Revelation surged through Joby like a heady explosion!

"Are you well, child?" Father Crombie asked, leaning forward in concern.

"Yes," Joby said. "I just . . . What if the devil didn't want Camelot to come back?"

"I'm sure he wouldn't," Father Crombie said, still looking oddly at Joby. "It's an interesting question, though. What makes you ask it?"

Filled with his own fierce purpose now, Joby ignored Father Crombie's question, and asked his own instead. "Father Morgan already told us that to fight the devil I had to make sure I never took anything from him, even a piece of bread, no matter how hungry I was. Do you know anything else about fighting the devil?"

Father Crombie sat down, gazing all the while at Joby. "Who is Father Morgan?"

"We rode out here yesterday," Benjamin said. "But you were at the . . . somewhere else all day, so we talked to Father Morgan instead."

"Here?" Father Crombie asked in surprise. "There is no Father Morgan here. . . . And I went nowhere yesterday."

"He said he was just visiting," Joby added, sure now that it *had* been Merlin. *Just visiting.* It was funny if you knew the secret.

"Perhaps," Father Crombie mused. His gaze became probing. "I'd be interested to hear what else he told you, Joby—if you wish to say, of course."

Joby recounted what he could recall, omitting his convictions about who Father Morgan really was, of course.

" 'The price of failure'?" Father Crombie asked when Joby had finished. "Those were his exact words?"

Joby nodded.

"And that's all he had to say about it?"

Joby nodded again.

For a time Father Crombie sat in silence, looking at Joby with bemused concern. Then he said, "Do I gather that you plan to fight the devil for the return of Camelot?"

Joby couldn't hide his alarm. He hadn't meant to tell Father Crombie *that.* He should have asked his questions more carefully. He looked to Benjamin, who looked just as worried and confused as himself.

"Don't worry, Joby," Father Crombie reassured him. "I meant what I said about not betraying your secret, which I think a very fine one, by the way."

"So . . . can you help us?" Joby said, not happy about the addition of a third party to their secret, but seeing no help for it now.

"I'd be happy to try," Father Crombie replied.

Seeing no reason anymore not to ask, Joby pointed at the golden cup he'd noticed earlier, and asked, "Is that the Grail?"

Benjamin rolled his eyes and looked embarrassed.

Father Crombie looked at the cup, then blinked at Joby. "Do you know what the Grail was, Joby?"

"Arthur had a magic cup that could do things and cure people," Joby answered. "Nothing bad could get near it." He gathered up his courage and added, "If that's it, I thought . . . maybe . . . Could we use it to fight the devil?"

Father Crombie's kindly smile widened, but he looked almost sad as well.

"Joby, there are so many, many things we should discuss, but Benjamin's parents must be waiting, and there are places I must be soon as well. Would you two consider coming back to see me later this week perhaps, when we all have more time?"

"We could come next Saturday," Benjamin suggested. "Couldn't we, Joby?" Joby nodded.

"For now then," the priest said, "may I just add a little advice of my own to what this Father Morgan gave you?"

"Sure," Joby said.

"Thank you. . . . First of all, I'm not certain it's helpful to be as careful as Father Morgan seems to have suggested. To thwart the devil we must be good, certainly, Joby, but not *too* good." He smiled. "The best way I know to fight the devil is to love God with all your heart, and love life as deeply as you can, for *life* is what *God* loves." He smiled affectionately. "I can tell that you are already very good at loving life, but that may become much more difficult if you give yourself no permission to fail at all, Joby. We must all fail a little now and then. If Father Morgan did not make that clear, I'm sure he meant to.

"Secondly, I would recommend laughing at the devil whenever possible," Crombie added. "It is said the devil cannot stand to be laughed at."

"But what if he sends people to fight you?" Benjamin asked. "You can't just laugh then, can you?"

"Defeat your enemies with kindness," Father Crombie replied. "Hate *feeds* hate; only love slays it. That is why God wants us to be great lovers, not great punishers. It is punishment enough to be a servant of the devil, justice enough to be the *delightful* people we are." He grinned.

Struggling to choose between Merlin's advice and Father Crombie's, Joby asked, "Did Geezez fight the devil the way you're saying?"

"Yes, He did," Father Crombie replied.

"But didn't He lose?" Joby asked.

Father Crombie looked confused, then sighed, "Oh yes: the *price of failure.* . . . Come boys. Let's go see that crucifix before you leave."

They followed him out to the altar and turned to gaze up at the terrible sculpture.

"In a way, what Father Morgan said was true," Father Crombie explained. "That *is* the price of failure, I suppose; but not *His,* Joby. *Ours.* We would hardly hang a statue of God's failure right here in His own house, would we?" Father Crombie smiled. "So why do you suppose this awful image is here?"

"I don't know," Joby said, glad that someone was finally going to tell him.

"Have you ever heard how God brought His Son back to life after He'd been dead for three days?" Father Crombie asked.

Joby gaped, and shook his head. "Is it true?"

"*I* believe it," Father Crombie nodded. He pointed to the kingly statue high above the crucifix. "That one up there is of God's Son after He had risen from death."

"That's *Geezez* up there too?" Joby asked in surprise.

"I told you," Benjamin muttered.

"But . . . Father Morgan said it was just a dead bishop!" Joby exclaimed.

"*Did* he!" Father Crombie said in obvious amazement.

Joby was more confused than ever. Surely Merlin would not have lied. Had Father Morgan not been Merlin? Why had he winked then, when he said he was just a priest?

"But . . . if Geezez didn't stay dead, why don't you get rid of that one then?" Joby asked, pointing to the crucifix. "Why not just keep the good statue?"

"We keep them both, Joby, because neither has any meaning without the other. You probably don't understand what it's like to be hopeless. I hope you never do. But there are people who lose everything they ever wanted, even the power to hope for it. They long for another chance, but they think it's just too late. Well, can you think of any time when it's more too late than after someone's dead?"

Joby shook his head.

"Yet *that* is precisely when God helped His Son," Father Crombie said. "You see? God waited until anyone could see it was far too late to help His Son at all. Then God helped Him anyway. *That* is hope, even for the hopeless." Father Crombie nodded at the crucifix. "That's why we keep this horrible statue hanging there, Joby. God's Son *lived* for everyone, but He *died* so the hopeless would know it's *never* too late for God to help them. You may be glad to know that yourself someday."

Joby could barely manage his swirling thoughts. Only moments before, his mission had finally seemed clear. Now everything was mixed up again.

"So you see, Joby, the devil lost that fight—not Jesus."

"Hey, Mom! Dad!" Benjamin called, seeing his parents in one of the big doorways at the back of the church. "We're almost done!"

Benjamin's parents waved to Father Crombie, who smiled and waved back before turning to Joby again. "The important thing is this, Joby: what God *and* His enemy both want is your *heart*. It's your heart that's most important, not the rules, whatever Father Morgan might have said."

Sitting quietly beside Benjamin as they drove home, Joby could not get

Father Crombie's last words out of his mind: *It's your* heart *that's most important.* Father Crombie's advice seemed the same as Arthur's, but Father Morgan's seemed a lot like Merlin's. How could Merlin and Arthur disagree? All
the way home, Joby's head hurt from trying to untangle it, and strangely,
so did his heart.

❈

"It *was* a bishop, you know-it-all little prig!" Lucifer shouted, dashing the
bowl of water from his desk. "*You're* the one who doesn't know what he's
talking about!"

In fact, the bishop in question had been a particular favorite of Lucifer's,
with whom—or *on* whom, more precisely—he still dined occasionally.
"God's risen Son, indeed!" Lucifer muttered in disgust. That moribund lump
of funerary sculpture was to the Creator's risen Son what the pretentious
bishop who'd posed for it was to God! But *wise* Father Crombie knew so
much better!

Sadly, anything Lucifer could have done to prevent the meeting might
have tipped his hand too badly; and he was wise enough to know that the
entire war mustn't be jeopardized even for such an important battle. He'd
been stunned when Joby's father had allowed the boy to go. He had thought
that variable sown up securely, but no; *love* had intervened! God seemed to
have built an endless series of these absurd gags into the universe, and right
now Lucifer was less amused than ever!

Someone in Joby's family, or Benjamin's, could have died, of course. That
certainly would have forestalled their little expedition to see Father Crombie.
But Lucifer didn't have the boy's measure well enough yet to know which
way such a jolt would launch him. Father Crombie, on the other hand, could
have had a heart attack without much impact on Joby at all, but that was too
much to ask of the cosmos on its own, and irksomely, the decrepit old med-
dler was too well protected for Lucifer to have arranged it himself. More
angels hovered day and night around that old nuisance than Dante himself
could have invented names for. There were back doors, however, even
through defenses like Crombie's, and a whole week was *plenty* of time.

"We'll see how you *love life* in some God-forsaken little outpost far, far
away from your beloved seminary," Lucifer snarled. "Laugh at the devil then,
Crombie!"

4

(The Roundtable)

"Ugh!" Laura exclaimed softly, lifting her bare knee from the poor crushed snail very carefully, lest the dead leaves crackle and give her away. Fourth-grade boys kept secrets about as neatly as they kept their rooms, and no one had thought to look behind them for spies as they'd raced out to this wide clearing among the trees for their *top secret trials.* Once she found out what it was that *boys* could do so much better than girls, she meant to prove *she* could do it better than any of them.

Sweeping the long auburn hair out of her eyes, Laura crouched forward to see more clearly through the clump of foliage in which she was hidden. The boys had stopped roughhousing to listen as Joby gave some kind of speech she couldn't quite hear. Then they all threw their arms up with a loud whoop and holler. Laura's face scrunched in consternation. She couldn't tell what was happening. She'd have to get closer.

Before Laura could even look around for some better hiding place, she was alarmed to see Joby running across the meadow directly toward her. Had they seen her? She crouched down even farther as Joby trotted right up to her hiding place, but instead of calling her out and making her leave, he just draped a red bandanna across the thin screen of branches between them, and sprinted back to rejoin the others across the field. There was hardly time to sort relief from confusion before all the boys were charging toward the scarf! Making herself as small as she could, she watched in growing panic as the hollering pack raced toward her, Joby and Benjamin in front with Bobby Lehan just ahead of Duane at the rear. At the last minute, Benjamin pulled ahead of Joby and crashed into the thicket, making Laura cower and scrunch her eyes shut, but Ben still didn't notice her. He just grabbed the scarf amidst much hooting and groaning from the other boys, as Joby slapped him cheerfully on the back. Then they hung the scarf on the bush once more, and everyone trotted away to do it again.

Running? Laura thought, indignant with relief. *That's* all it took to be a knight? *She* could run! A *lot* faster than *Duane Westerlund*! Scooting quickly back behind a safer bush as they prepared to launch their second race, she watched in less and less impressed silence as Joby won the next race, and Kyle Evans the third.

When they'd finished racing, they all went back to the field's far end where Joby handed his watch to Peter Blackwell, pushed the red bandanna into his back pocket, and lit out for a large pine tree at the edge of the clearing. After waving his arms at Peter, he jumped to grab the lowest branch and dangled for a moment, struggling to kick his legs up around the thick arm of the tree. Then he was aloft, shimmying higher, hoisting himself from branch to branch, up and up until it made Laura nervous to watch. Even the boys had grown quiet by the time he reached the very top, which swayed frighteningly as he tied the bandanna to a small branch there. Then he came down, seeming almost to free-fall from one handhold to the next before jumping easily to the ground.

Peter called out something that brought noisy shouts of approval from the other boys, but, to her mounting frustration, Laura still couldn't tell what he'd said. The shouting increased as Benjamin walked to the tree and climbed quickly up to touch the bandanna before descending almost as recklessly as Joby had. Another unintelligible announcement from Peter Blackwell brought a second round of excited shouts.

As other boys took their largely more timid turns at climbing to touch the bandanna, Laura realized how she could get closer. Very near them, a large oak tree hung well out over the clearing. From up inside it she'd be able to see and hear everything. The problem was how to get there without being noticed. This difficulty was soon resolved, however, when Joby tied the red bandanna to his arm, and ran from the field while the others just stood listening to Peter count quite loudly. Laura still wasn't sure what they were doing when, with a wild shout, everyone charged into the trees after Joby.

Since they'd left their shirts in a pile right beneath her oak tree, Laura was sure they'd come back, and when they did, she'd be hidden practically straight above them. Climbing trees wasn't something she'd ever done really, but it hadn't looked too hard.

After listening to make sure they were really gone, she crawled from hiding, ran to the oak tree, and grabbed an easily reachable branch. A moment later, having skinned one knee a little on the tree's rough bark, she was up.

"I'd make just as good a knight as *Duane Westerlund*," she muttered contemptuously.

One more hoist up, a short crawl, and she was at the base of the long branch that hung out over the clearing.

It hadn't looked this high from below. For the first time, she hesitated. How on earth, she wondered, had they climbed clear to the top of that pine tree without having heart attacks? *Well,* she thought crossly, *if* they *can,* I *can!* She clung to the branch and began to wriggle on her belly away from the tree trunk. Halfway out it began to bounce and sway unpleasantly. She stopped to fend off a wave of panic before inching forward again. When she'd gone as far as she dared, she lay still for a moment, then sat up very carefully to straddle the branch. She looked down. Her position was good. Her confidence was not.

That's when she noticed the ants. A thick dark trail of the little crawlers moved along the branch like miniature rush hour traffic, passing right beneath her! Or they had until she'd blocked their path with her body. Now they scattered everywhere in agitation; down her legs, up her arms. *Yuck!* No improvement in view or acoustics was worth this! Conceding defeat, she started turning around.

Suddenly, there was shouting from the woods nearby. Before she could react, Joby burst into the clearing, leaves tangled in his hair, his shirt torn in back, followed close behind by Benjamin and Kyle, then all the others. Joby ran straight to the trunk of her tree, slammed his hands against it, and shouted, *"Safe!"* He started laughing between gasps for breath. "You guys are the lousiest bunch of boar hunters I ever saw!"

"We *had* you!" Benjamin exclaimed. "Grabbin' your shirt should count!"

"I said, I'd make it to the creek and back," Joby insisted happily, beginning to catch his breath. "And that's what I did."

"You were *lucky!*" Kyle insisted.

"It's not against the rules to be *lucky.*" Joby smiled.

Laura didn't know what to do! There were ants all over her, she was half-turned around in the most awkward position imaginable, and she didn't dare move. Some mean trick of perception made the ground seem terribly far away, while the boys seemed close enough to reach up and touch her. If she did *anything* now, they'd notice.

Soon the whole pack of them had gathered below her, teasing and congratulating each other for moves they'd made or failed to pull off during their hunt, in which Joby had evidently been the prey. To Laura's relief, it seemed they were going to go have another hunt, which would give her the chance to get out of this tree. This time the red bandanna was tied around

Benjamin's arm, but just as he was going to leave, several of the boys said they needed to rest first, and the whole group collapsed agreeably onto the ground beneath her. That's when she was bitten. The ant's tiny jaws were a searing needle in her armpit.

"Oh!" she gasped.

The word was out of her mouth before she could catch it. Everyone looked up. A few of them stood.

"Laura Bayer!" shouted Johnny Mayhew in disbelief.

"Laura?" said Joby. "What are you doing up there?"

"She's *spyin'* on us! *That's* what she's *doin'!*" shouted Duane Westerlund. He picked up a pebble and hucked it at her as if chasing a squirrel or a blue jay away from their picnic.

Flinching back from Duane's little missile, Laura lost her balance. Clutching at the empty air, she felt more surprise than fear. No one made a sound, and there was no time to think before she hit the ground with a sickening jolt, as if from some great distance. She knew something was wrong, but her brain seemed stuck and far away. Her glasses were gone. She wondered if she'd broken them and if she'd get in trouble for it. Had she told her mother she'd be home late? Did she have homework to do? All these thoughts passed ridiculously through her mind in an instant.

"Laura!" Joby cried. Suddenly unfrozen, he and several others ran to look down at her in horror. "Laura, don't move!"

She tried to sit up, and her left arm and shoulder were instantly lanced with a horrible fire. Hearing herself scream, she imagined white-hot sword blades slicing up her arm and racing for her head. She fell back onto the ground as if someone had pulled her plug. The boys above her looked sick. Some of them turned and ran away. Her vision shrank in, as if she were falling down a long dark tunnel away from Joby's stricken face. There was just time to hear someone moan, "She's turning *gray!*" and Peter Blackwell yell, *"Duane,* you *butt!* You've *killed her!"* Then the tunnel closed.

❧

Joby walked slowly down the long shiny hallway with a bouquet of flowers in each hand. He was nicely dressed, his hair carefully combed. They said Laura was healing well, but even after two days, he was scared to see her arm again.

His parents had offered to come up with him, but he had left them in the lobby. After hearing what had happened, his mother had tried to forbid Joby from ever climbing trees again. His father had told her that it wasn't fair to make Joby stifle himself every time someone got hurt, which had only made his mother even more upset, and Joby just didn't want them seeing Laura, and starting it up all over again.

It still made Joby shudder to remember how Laura had turned all pasty and passed out after the fall. He had thought she might really be dead. They'd been a long way from the nearest building, and her arm had looked so terrible bent back beside her like she had a second elbow. Bones and blood had erupted through her skin from when she'd tried to sit up. Some of the guys had thrown up. After telling Benjamin and Kyle to run for help, he'd stayed beside her, petting her hair, afraid to touch anything else, telling her and himself that it would be okay. It had seemed to take forever for the emergency people to come in their big truck with Ben and Kyle in the front seat.

She had regained consciousness then, and Joby still couldn't believe how brave she'd been. When one of the emergency guys had mentioned "giving her a hand," she'd actually joked about needing a new one. She'd only screamed once, when they put a big plastic splint on her arm. Joby couldn't imagine making jokes if it had been him. He figured he'd have screamed pretty much the whole time.

They said she was going to have to stay at the hospital until Monday, because there'd been dirt deep in her arm, and they were worried about infection. Joby was the first person to see her besides her folks, and he wondered what to expect as he found her room, and knocked softly on the door.

"Come in."

She didn't *sound* dead.

He pushed the door open to find her propped up in bed, watching a TV hung from the ceiling. There was a tube stuck in her left hand and another embedded in her cast, but other than that, she looked okay. When she saw who it was, her hazel eyes went wide behind the blue-framed glasses that had miraculously survived her fall, and she smiled brightly. Relief washed through Joby. He had wondered if she might be mad at him.

"Joby!"

"Hi, Laura." He walked to her bedside, and handed her the small bunch of iris and freesia his mother had picked out. "These are from me." Then he set the large bouquet of roses and carnations on the covers beside her. "And these are from Duane. . . . He's real sorry, Laura."

She looked uncertainly from Joby's bouquet to Duane's and asked, "Why doesn't he come say so himself?"

Joby shrugged. "He's scared. He knows you prob'ly hate him now."

She snorted, and set the roses on her bedside table, then stuck her nose in Joby's flowers, took a deep breath, and smiled again. "I don't hate Duane," she sighed. Then she grinned. "I heard Peter call him a butt."

Both of them laughed.

"A lot of people think he's kind of a jerk right now," Joby said.

"That's too bad," she said, sounding like she meant it. "Tell him to come see me, Joby. Will you? He probably won't believe I don't hate him 'til I tell him so myself, and he probably won't come see me unless you tell him to."

Joby stared at her. She sounded . . . older. And something about her request made him feel proud, though he wasn't sure why.

"I'll tell him," he said. "But I don't think he'll come."

"He will if you tell him to."

The pride in him swelled some more. He looked at her cast.

"Does it hurt a lot?"

"Yeah. Sometimes. But not too bad."

"What were you *doing* up there, Laura?"

She looked embarrassed and glanced away. "Like Duane said. Spying."

"Why?" Joby asked.

"'Cause I wanted to see what I had to do to be a knight," she answered, still not looking at him.

Joby's shoulders slumped. If girls could be knights, no boy would want to be one. He knew that. . . . but . . . she'd practically *died* trying to get in.

"I'll try," he said. The words just came out on their own. But as soon as he heard them he knew he couldn't take them back.

"Try what?" Laura asked.

"To make them let you in," he said, sure he was announcing the Roundtable's death sentence.

First she smiled, then she looked down unhappily. "I can't climb that pine tree, Joby. . . . I won't pass the tests."

"I couldn't make jokes if my arm was broke," he replied. "Far as I can see, that'll work as good as climbin' any tree. . . . I don't think they'll listen . . . but I'll try."

She beamed at him. "They'll listen to *you*, Joby."

Joby looked down, not wanting her to see that he wasn't so sure.

"And if they don't, it's okay," she added. "I don't want to be in unless they want me. It's just nice of you to try . . . and . . . and your flowers are much nicer than Duane's."

That clinched it. Joby would *have* to try.

※

As they rode back to St. Albee's the next morning, Joby tried his idea out on Benjamin. After visiting Laura, he'd gone home and scoured his book on Arthur for anything that might help him make his case to the other knights. The solution, when he'd seen it, was so obvious it had made him laugh.

"So that's my idea," he concluded. "Whadaya think?"

"I think it's awesome." Benjamin grinned. "After what happened, they'd be jerks to say no. It's *perfect!*"

"Good," Joby said. "That's what I thought too. I just hope it's okay with Laura."

"Hey, she'll be in," Benjamin said. "She'll get to come to the meetings."

The weekend had dawned threatening rain, and Joby wasn't as excited about going to St. Albee's as he had been before. The Roundtable had come to occupy nearly all the space inside him that churches and grails had claimed the week before. Still, they had promised Father Crombie.

At the seminary, they asked a man leaving the grounds where Father Crombie's office was. He gave them a strange look, then said, "Go into that building, and ask for Father Richter. He can tell you."

When they got to Father Richter's office, they found a new priest behind a desk, who turned out *not* to be Father Richter, but called Father Richter on his desk phone. A moment later the office's other door was opened by a middle-aged priest with thick glasses and thinning gray hair, who smiled, and said, "I'm Father Richter. You must be Benjamin and Joby! Please, come in." Joby followed Benjamin toward the inner office, wondering why the younger priest had called Richter on the phone when he could have just opened the door and talked to him.

"Where's Father Crombie?" Benjamin asked when they were inside.

"The bishop has assigned Father Crombie to another post," Father Richter told them. "I will be replacing him here."

"But . . . he told us to come see him today," Joby said.

"Yes," said Father Richter. "He felt very badly about having to miss this appointment. In fact, he left a letter for you." He went to pull an envelope from the top drawer of an expansive mahogany desk before a very large window, then came back and handed it to Joby, who tore it open to find a typewritten letter.

Benjamin came to read over his shoulder.

> *Dear boys,*
>
> *I've had to leave on important business, and will not be returning to the seminary. I am sure Father Richter will be delighted to offer you any assistance he can. I urge you to heed whatever advice he may offer. He is an invaluable mentor with whom you will not go wrong.*
> *Sincerely,*
> *Father John Crombie, O.F.M.*

"What's a 'mentor'?" Benjamin asked.

"A rather special teacher, I suppose," Father Richter replied, looking pleased.

"He's not coming back—*ever*?" Joby asked.

"It seems not," Father Richter said. "Father Crombie did not have time to tell me of your business with him. Is there anything I can do?"

Joby wasn't sure about letting Father Richter in on their secret, so he just shook his head, thanked the priest, and said they had to get back home.

"If I may be of any help in the future," Father Richter smiled, "I hope you will not hesitate to ask. I look forward to the pleasure of your company again."

They thanked him politely, and left feeling glum.

They reached the main door downstairs and yanked it open. It was raining.

"*Oh great,*" Benjamin moaned. "You'd think Crombie could've called, at least, and told us not to come all the way out here."

Joby thought so too. Father Crombie had seemed so nice.

⊗

Behind the gothic window high above them, Father Richter was already on his knees in earnest prayer. The boys had come, and the letter had been there in the top desk drawer, just as the angel had foretold in his dream. Father Richter could always tell true dreams from false ones by the angel's voice, so musical and pure. So virginal.

Father Richter had never seen her, though he imagined that she must be lovely beyond endurance. He supposed she hid herself lest he be tempted to impure thoughts. Even self-discipline like Father Richter's might crumble before the beauty of an angel. He often wondered if she wore clothing—but no matter. Until he was in Heaven, safe at last from fleshly temptations, he would be content with her lovely voice, and the tasks she brought him on God's behalf.

Nothing meant more to Father Richter than knowing himself one of the very blessed few whom God had chosen to be of *special* service. Well aware that smaller men were quick to regard gifts they themselves had failed to attain as mere insanity, Father Richter had never spoken of his angel to anyone. They would *all* know in heaven, when they saw Father Richter's glory at last revealed and were ashamed.

But, like any of God's gifts, Father Richter's prophetic dreams were a cross to bear as well. When the moment foretold had come and gone, he was always left to agonize over whether he'd tried hard enough or done his part correctly. He never dared assume success, for losing God's special favor to pride or any other least sin frightened Father Richter far more than any threat of Hell.

"Lord!" he moaned now, eyes screwed shut, hands clenched in painful petition. "I *tried,* but I do not know if I have accomplished your purpose. Please . . . *please!* Give me some sign, that I may have peace!"

"They will return . . ."

He looked up in astonishment and stared around the room. There was no one present, but he knew what he'd heard. She'd never come to him outside of dreams before! Despite himself, he'd sometimes wondered—feared that . . . But now he knew, beyond any doubt! The angel was real!

"Thank you!" he cried, not caring who might hear. "Thank you, my angel! I shall be worthy! When they come to me, I will lead them in the way that they should go!"

❧

Kallaystra chortled in quiet delight as she took leave of her lovesick admirer. When Lucifer had requested her help in finding a useful priest, she had known right where to look. She'd been entertaining herself with this one for decades. Some of these mortal creatures just seemed to cry out for special attention, and *this one* had needed to be special *so badly.* He was even more willing than the child's silly mother to believe that the Creator would waste time sending them dreams about every little thing. Such *simple* creatures.

❧

Laura mentally rehearsed her lines as Joby and Benjamin escorted her like an honor guard toward the library. She had accepted Joby's proposal instantly, not bothering to explain that what he obviously saw as a solution, she viewed as a fine first step. In another flash of surprising statecraft, Joby had decided that any knight who wanted to veto the plan should have to say so to her face. No doubt about it, Joby was the smartest boy she knew.

She'd spent the morning reading a book of stories about Camelot from the library, which had been more interesting than she'd expected. She'd felt tremendous empathy for Guinevere. She'd also composed an impressive little speech full of phrases borrowed from the book, in case Joby needed help getting those pigheaded boys to say yes.

When Laura walked into the Roundtable meeting, flanked by Joby and Benjamin, there was a moment of surprised silence, during which she pointedly adjusted her pretty blue sling and heavy cast. But, as Benjamin had predicted, none of them dared object outright to her presence. Some even frowned at Duane.

"Hi, Laura," Duane said lamely.

Everyone waited, clearly expecting her to cut him dead. She suspected that Duane had not told anyone of his visit to apologize, and decided to keep his secret safe for now.

"Hi, Duane." She smiled. "Thanks again for the flowers. That was nice of you."

Duane looked relieved, and the others began offering shy greetings of their own.

"Well, let's start," Joby said. "I call the Roundtable to order."

Some of the boys looked uncertainly at Laura, but Joby pulled out the chair next to his, and waved her into it. The other boys looked around at each other as if their feet were glued in place. Not until Benjamin sat down to Joby's left, did the rest join them.

Reaching into his knapsack, Joby pulled out his book of Arthurian Tales, opened it to the place he'd marked, then stood and read:

"'This,' said Arthur to all his knights, 'is the *new* code of honor you will uphold in all my kingdom!'" He read *very* well. Laura could tell he must have practiced even harder than she had. "'Wherever the strong oppress the weak, you will fight the strong until the weak live in peace; not for wealth or fame, but for the glory that comes with honor! It is for you to slay whatever vile beast should plague the land—whether dragon or griffin—and to rescue *damsels in distress.*'"

He closed the book, looked boldly at his knights, and said, "We did our best to rescue Laura." Laura noticed he was careful not to look at Duane.

"Benjamin and Kyle did a good job of getting help, and we stuck by her 'til they came, and she's all right now. So I say, a cheer for Laura—and for us!"

He raised his fist in the air and shouted, *"The Roundtable!"*

All the boys punched the air and shouted with him. *"The Roundtable!"*

Mrs. Escobedo, the school librarian, came rushing out of her office. *"Boys!* This is a *library*! Any more yelling like that and you'll all have to leave!"

They quieted immediately, and Mrs. Escobedo went back to her office, scowling and wagging her head.

"Laura was pretty brave too," Joby said, more quietly. "You all heard her joke with that man about her hand." They nodded, and some laughed. "Any of you think you could have laid there and not screamed your head off the whole time? I couldn't," he said before anyone could answer, though their faces all agreed with him. "You all know Laura's wanted to be in the Round-table since the day she heard about it." A tense silence fell again. "Well, you just heard with your own ears that being a knight partly means rescuing damsels in distress, which I think we did as good as we knew how last week. And I don't know about you, but I felt good to help Laura out." There were a few tentative murmurs of assent around the table. "So here's my idea," Joby continued. "She's brave as any of us, and she's a pretty good sport, I think, considering we sort of knocked her out of that tree to start with." Now he did look at Duane, as did most of the others. "And maybe she can't be a knight, but there's no reason she can't join up as our official damsel in distress, is there?"

There were confused looks all around, and Laura's confidence wavered.

"Think about it," Joby urged. "Damsels in distress don't just show up whenever you need 'em! What if we need one, and we ain't got it?" Laura had noticed long ago that boys always turned to bad grammar or foul language when they were nervous around other boys, and wondered if the others knew it too, but Joby pushed ahead. "This way we always got one handy, no matter what."

When no one spoke, she decided she'd better say her speech. She stood, trying to look at them all as boldly as Joby had. "Good knights, and gentle," she began. She didn't know gentle *what* exactly, but Guinevere had said it in the book, and it sounded nice. "I would not intrude upon your noble coun-cil, except to offer some small service in thanks for your brave service." The rest of what she'd memorized suddenly left her, so she went on in her own words, making them as fancy as she could.

"I have heard you are looking for good deeds to do in secret." Some of the

boys looked accusingly at Joby, as if *they* hadn't told everyone themselves after last week's meeting. "I can find out things which you might not hear
about yourselves for you to do. No one even has to know I'm in, but you,
good knights." A few of them clearly liked the idea of a spy—as long as it
wasn't *them* being spied on, she supposed. "Of course, if this idea sounds *un-
seemly*," she was proud of fitting that word in, "I would not wish to uglify this
noble brotherhood with my presence." She adjusted her sling again, then finished her speech with one last flourish gleaned from the book. "I thank you,
brave and noble sirs, for hearing my petition with such courtesy." She performed a grave bow, practiced exhaustively before her mirror at home, and
sat down. Joby was staring as if he'd never seen her before. It had been easier than she'd feared. The fancy parts had seemed almost familiar in some
weird way. In fact, she could hardly wait to talk like that some more.

To everyone's astonishment, Duane jumped up across from her, brought
his hand down flat on the table, and shouted, "I vote *yes!*"

Everyone looked back at Mrs. Escobedo's office window, where, sure
enough, the librarian was half out of her seat, scowling at them again. Duane
made an apologetic gesture, and sat down. Happily, Mrs. Escobedo shook
her head, and did the same.

"We ain't votin' on it yet, Duane," Peter griped.

"Let's vote then," Joby said. "I vote yes too. If anyone says no, raise your
hand."

Laura adjusted her sling a third time. Johnny Mayhew looked pretty unhappy, but no hands were raised.

"Lady," Benjamin said, surprising everyone, since he wasn't usually quick
to speak, "the knights are proud to have such a brave damsel in distress," he
looked defiantly around the table, "*aren't* we, guys."

"Heck, yes!" said Duane, with a "told you so" look to Peter.

"No ones s'posed to know you're in. Right?" demanded Johnny Mayhew.

"*I* won't tell anyone, if *you guys* can keep your mouths shut," Laura replied.

"Well, all right then," he grumbled. "guess I'm glad you're in too."

She was in! She wasn't a knight yet, but she'd gotten her foot in the door.

❋

Joby burst into the house filled with good humor. He was still amazed at
Laura's speech. She could have been right out of his book! Even Benjamin
had said it felt more like the real Roundtable now that she was in. Everything
was going great!

"Joby?" his mother called from the kitchen. "Is that you, dear?"

"Yup!" he answered.

"You got a letter, honey. It's on the table by the door."

He went to pick it up and saw that there was no return address, but his name and address were very neatly written—definitely not from a kid. Who then? Joby didn't get letters very often. He opened it and pulled out a two-page handwritten note on fancy beige paper bordered in green with the letters "J. C." at the top.

Dear Joby,

    I took the liberty of contacting Ben's parents for your address. By now I imagine our second appointment has come and gone, and I must apologize with all my heart. I was called away quite suddenly, and in all the rush, I am sorry to say, I forgot all about it. I hope you will forgive me. I cannot begin to tell you how much I enjoyed meeting you, and I hope someday to hear how your efforts turn out. Sadly, I have been sent rather far away and doubt that we will meet again any time soon. Father Richter will be replacing me at the seminary. I know very little about him, but I hope he can be of help to you.

    Being the old kibitzer I am, I have one last bit of advice to add to our last, very enjoyable, conversation. If you're hoping to outsmart the devil, put as much effort as possible into pursuing the best things you can think of, and as little as possible into struggling against the bad. I am sure you will understand what I mean when and if you need to. I have great faith in you, Joby. Good-bye for now. God bless!

    Remember! Love life!

    John Crombie

Joby stared at the letter in confusion. Father Crombie couldn't have forgotten about their appointment if he'd given that first letter to Father Richter, could he?

Just then the phone rang. Joby picked it up.

"Hello?"

"Joby! I got a letter from Father Crombie!" Ben's voice exclaimed.

Joby frowned. "Me too."

"You did?"

"Yeah. . . . Don't you think it's weird when he already wrote us?"

"Yeah," Benjamin said. "Joby? You s'pose there's something wrong with him?"

"Like what?"

"Well . . . before my grampa died, he got real confused. You know? You'd talk to him and then five minutes later, he didn't remember you'd been there at all."

"You think Father Crombie's gonna die?" Joby asked.

"I don't know," Benjamin answered quietly. "But maybe that's why he had to go away. Remember all that weird stuff he said about there bein' no money?"

"Yeah, but . . . he didn't seem like he was gonna die to me."

"Me neither, but I got a feeling there's *something* wrong."

❈

Williamson weathered this indignity as he had countless others: eyes glazed, countenance mute, stance straight but unchallenging. He'd known since long before his untimely death that swallowing all manner of crap with a smile and "thank you, sir" was just one of numerous unpleasant prerequisites to promotion.

"First Lindwald, then you! Can I rely on *no one*?" Lucifer raged. "That damn letter sat on that damn table all day! And what did we do about it? *Nothing!* Why? Because we didn't *know* about it until it was in the candidate's hands! I thought I sent you to *watch*, Williamson! It's lucky for you they just think the old fart is demented and dying," Lucifer growled. "So much the better. But I swear, if the more relevant discrepancies between our letter and his are ever noticed—by either of them—I promise to put an unbelievable crimp in your style. Do you understand me?"

"Yes, Sir."

"And while we're discussing *style,* Williamson, I had expected a great deal more from one of the most brilliant marketing strategists of your generation than these clumsy demographic travelogues you've been foisting on me. I'm not at all interested in your little ideas about wearing him down or beating him up. I want the Enemy's *hidden ace!* To win this wager, he must turn *willingly* from the Creator to *us!* And I can hardly know how to arrange that until I've found the one utterly unexpected, completely *impossible* thing that makes *this* boy unique among all that other human vermin. Got it?"

"Yes, Sir."

Lucifer gazed at him with disdain.

"Get out of here, you spineless toad, and try keeping your eyes *open* this time! I want the *ace,* Williamson! Not the king. Not the queen, or the jack. The *ace!*"

"Yes, Sir."

"Out!"

Williamson went, struggling to bridle his resentment. Once, the world's most powerful men had paid Williamson fortunes for the kind of analysis he'd been providing! *Just bend over and play the game,* he told himself. *Find that ace, and he'll* have *to acknowledge you.*

5

(Aces)

Benjamin stared at the pew back in front of him, searching for imaginary faces in the wood grain. As he'd feared, church was no fun at all anymore without Father Crombie. This morning's interminable sermon was about humility, which, as far as Ben could tell, meant you were supposed to be ashamed anytime you did something good—and to be *more* ashamed the better you did! How stupid was that? Joby's company was all that made coming to church tolerable now.

Around Joby, the world just seemed to get wider and better all the time. Benjamin would never have thought of something like the Roundtable in a million years! He liked the secret missions even better than the stories Joby told them about King Arthur and his knights, or the games they all played at their tournament field.

Three weeks ago, Denis Wong had brought his model stegosaurus skeleton to school for show and tell. He'd put it together himself—*every bone*—and was very proud of it. But Lisa Herman's sleeve had caught it just before lunch, and pulled it off his desk to smash in pieces on the floor. Denis had thrown it all in the garbage, and spent lunch in a bathroom stall, crying. But after school that day, Sir Bobby had gotten the pieces out of the wastebasket, then spent the evening with some of the other knights gluing it all back together. They'd snuck the model back onto Denis's desk before class the next morning along with the Roundtable's secret sign, a quarter-size disk of cardboard painted yellow with a red dragon drawn on it. That was how people knew the knights had done something, though no one would ever admit—outside their secret meetings, of course—exactly which knights had done it. Benjamin was sure nobody but Joby could ever have thought up such a cool idea.

Deanna Tepper's lost jacket had reappeared mysteriously on Monday after Sir Kyle found it out behind the playground fence, where someone had probably thrown it. On Thursday, after Lindy Jacomella fell off the jungle gym and put a tooth halfway through her bottom lip, a whole stack of chocolate bars had shown up on her desk wrapped in red ribbon, attached to another little red and yellow disk. Lots of new boys wanted to join the knights now, and even the teachers had begun to talk about it. The tests to get in had gotten harder, and a boy had to do one secret good deed on his own before he could be knighted, but new members still kept coming.

Lady Laura had told them how badly Tony Esquivel wanted to be a knight, but that he wouldn't say so because he knew the knights all had bicycles, and he was too poor to get one. Everyone liked Tony, and Sir Duane had gotten a new bike for his birthday, so he offered to donate his old one. They'd left the bike on Tony's porch one morning before anyone was awake, and four days later he'd passed the tests and been knighted by Joby out at the tournament field amid the cheers of his new sword-brothers.

Laura was the first girl Benjamin had ever really been friends with. He'd known she was different the minute she stuck up for Joby after the dodge ball accident. She didn't do dumb *girl* things like playing *horsies* at lunch. She liked real adventures, and she sure got hurt as often as any boy, which he respected a lot. The supposed "secret" of her strange semi-membership in the Roundtable hadn't lasted even days, but as she had predicted, it was the guys themselves who'd let it slip. Now, of course, other girls wanted to be damsels in distress too, but the knights had told them all that they had to break an arm or leg to qualify, and that had kept them away pretty good so far.

Noticing the sudden quiet, Ben realized that Father Richter's sermon was over at last, and, offering a silent prayer of thanks, stood with all the others to mouth the creed.

After church he and Joby raced to the car well ahead of Benjamin's parents, then stood panting for breath.

"Do you think what Father Richter said is right, Benjamin?" Joby asked.

"What!" Benjamin rolled his eyes. "You mean *humility*? Nobody feels bad for doing something good, Joby. That's crazy! Are you *ashamed* about the Roundtable?"

"No, but . . . what if the enemy wins 'cause I get too proud?" Joby looked away anxiously. "I'm not sure it's good that we got everybody making fun of Lindwald."

"Why not?" Benjamin protested. "He's a *jerk*! We s'posed to thank him? Father Crombie said to laugh at the devil, right? Well, that's what we're doin'!"

"Yeah, but Father Crombie also said to fight our enemies with kindness. Maybe Lindwald doesn't even want to work for the devil. Maybe he's like a slave or something."

"He *wants* to all right! I never seen anybody who likes bein' mean so much."

"But Father Richter said—"

"I think you're on drugs, Joby!" Ben cut him off. The very idea that Joby might take any of Richter's nonsense about "humility" to heart made Benjamin furious. "And you know what? I think Father Richter's talks are dumb, and he's *boring*! I *like* the Roundtable! I *like* that Lindwald's getting what he deserves, Joby, and I'm *not* gonna listen to anyone who says I'm s'posed to feel bad about *any* of it!"

"That's not very respectful," Joby murmured, looking down uncomfortably. "Father Crombie said Father Richter was a mentor, and . . . and I'm not sure we oughtta be makin' fun of a priest when we're fighting . . . you know—the enemy. He uses our mistakes, remember? Even little ones. Merlin said so."

Hearing Joby sound so timid and girly made Benjamin's anger so fierce that he wasn't even sure anymore whether it was Richter or Joby himself he was angry at, and that scared him somehow.

"I'm your friend," Benjamin growled, as if saying it might protect him from the things he was feeling. "I'm your *friend*. That's all I'm gonna say."

"You boys ready to go?" Benjamin's parents had arrived at last.

Benjamin blew out a big breath of frustration, wishing they'd come sooner.

⚒

At recess the next morning, Lindwald sent Joby sprawling to the ground, and got sent to the principal's office for his trouble, while Joby was congratulated by Mrs. Nelson in front of the whole class for not letting Lindwald "get his goat," whatever that meant.

But at their meeting that afternoon, several knights complained that if Joby didn't put Lindwald in his place pretty soon, people would be laughing at the knights instead of at Lindwald. Laura insisted that Joby's refusal to fight was very grown-up, and a good example for the rest of them, which had done nothing to improve Joby's position. Having promised to take care of it, Joby had left the meeting wondering how.

"Just fight him, Joby," Benjamin said as they rode home together on their bikes. "That's the only way to make him stop for good."

"Don't you remember what happened last time I fought him? That's just what he wants. There must be some other way to get to him. What would stop you, Benjamin?"

"I don't know. . . . My mom and dad, I guess. *They* can make me do anything."

"That's it! Benjamin, you're a genius!"

"What?"

"His *folks'll* make him stop! I should have thought of that weeks ago!"

"You're gonna *tattle* to his *folks?*" Benjamin asked in dismay.

"I'm gonna beat him without falling for his trap," Joby said. "That's all. We gotta find out where he lives."

"Tony knows," Benjamin volunteered despondently. "I heard him tell Duane that Jamie lives one street over from him. . . . I still wish you'd just beat the crap out of him."

❈

After school the next day, they got on their bikes and headed for the address Tony had given them. It was not a pretty neighborhood. The few trees on Jamie's street were small and sickly looking. Front yards were hemmed in by chain-link fence, and waist high in weeds, or carpeted in dead grass cropped so short that bare dirt showed through like bald spots on worn carpet. Driveways were cluttered with rusty, half-assembled hulks, as if some forgetful mechanic had wandered off years before in the middle of a major rebuild. The paint was dingy and peeling on all but a few of the houses, and there were bars over most of the windows.

Jamie's house was covered in ruined paint the color of old urine, and a woman sat on the porch, watching them come as if she'd been waiting. She was terribly thin, with stringy brown hair so greasy it looked wet. Her shapeless knee-length dress had been pink once, before someone had wiped a floor with it. She held a cigarette in front of her face, and smoke curled out of her half-open mouth, unstirred by any sign of breath. No one spoke. Her dark eyes were hard and flat, her closed face angry and sleepy all at once.

"Whadaya want?" she said at last, as if they were selling something distasteful.

"We're . . ." Joby stumbled. "My name's Joby. This is Benjamin."

She looked away and took a long drag on her cigarette.

"You're those little brats givin' my Jamie such a hard time at school, ain'tcha." She exhaled, then turned back to stare them down as if they were the worst kind of trash.

"Mrs. Lindwald—" Benjamin began.

"Spater!" she snapped. *"Not Lindwald!"* Then, more calmly, "I ain't the little bastard's mother. Just his stepmom."

"Mrs. Spater," Joby said. "If Jamie told you we're giving him a hard time, he's—"

"You callin' Jamie a liar?" she demanded, then leaned back and took another lungful of smoke, as if they'd gone away.

"Yes," Benjamin said, his fists clenched. "He's been callin' all of us names, and pushin' us around, doin' everything he can to make us fight. And Joby hasn't touched him the whole time."

"That what you call a broken nose?" the woman said without looking at them, or raising her voice. "I call that touchin' 'im pretty good."

"He *made* Joby do that!" Benjamin protested.

Her sneering smile revealed a line of crooked gray teeth. "Took your fist, and shoved it up his own nose, did he? *You boys* sound like the liars to me. You better get outta here," she drawled, "'fore I call the law, and tell 'em to *make* you go."

"It's a public sidewalk!" Benjamin objected.

"Benjamin," Joby said quietly. "Forget it. This isn't going to work." He stood on his pedals, preparing to ride.

"But—"

The woman laughed to herself, and murmured, "You're every bit the little wimps he said you were."

There was a shuffling racket from inside the darkened doorway behind her. The patched screen lurched open, and Jamie stepped out looking startled and angry to see Joby and Benjamin. His stepmom looked at him with even less sympathy than she'd shown the other boys. "You'd best go back inside, Jamie."

"What're they—"

"Make yourself scarce, boy," she hissed.

Jamie grew visibly pale and vanished back into the darkness, the screen banging shut behind him.

The woman rose lazily, took one last pull on her cigarette before tossing it casually onto the porch. "I'm goin' inside to call the police. You'd better be outta here before I finish dialin', or I swear, you'll be callin' your folks up from downtown."

She didn't wait for a reply, and when Benjamin had pried his angry stare from her retreating back, the boys didn't wait to find out if she meant it.

"She was *bluffin'*!" Benjamin insisted as they pedaled away down the dismal street. "She can't get someone arrested just for standing on the sidewalk, can she?"

"I don't know," Joby said. "But you know what? I think Jamie's whole family works for the devil."

"*I'll* tell *you* what!" Benjamin replied. "I think his stepmom *is* the devil!"

☒

Lindwald came to school the next morning as close to elated as he had ever felt. Joby had finally handed him precisely what he needed! Knowing that his master wouldn't want Joby getting in trouble again, however, Lindwald had been forced to wait until school got out before cashing in.

"Hey, Joby!" he hollered, charging angrily across the playground as everyone headed toward the bus stop or their parents' cars in the parking lot. *"Who the fuck didja you think you were—comin' to my house, an' tellin' my folks a bunch a lies!"*

The crowd of kids between them parted like milk before a chopping maul, and before Joby could react, Lindwald rammed him into the air and sent him flying for the second time in three days.

"Stop it! . . . Stop it this minute, you PIG!"

To everyone's amazement, Laura Bayer had leapt into Lindwald's path, planting herself firmly in front of Joby.

"I'm *sick* of this!" she yelled. "Who do you think you are!"

"Laura," Joby began as he stood up, clutching a skinned arm, "don't—"

"No!" she insisted. "If he wants to fight so bad, he should have to fight us *all!*" She tilted her head back, and peered belligerently up at Lindwald. "You that brave, mister jerk, bully, fat face?"

She stood there, a slight little girl in thick-rimmed glasses, wearing her cast like a shield of invulnerability, and Lindwald realized that she really didn't think he'd hit her. It was all he could do not to laugh. These little specks of dung dust were so *clueless!* He drew one arm back and hit her hard in the stomach. Joby would *have* to fight him now.

There was a horrified gasp from all around as Laura folded and fell, her mouth open, but no voice to fill it. Then every boy there lunged at Lindwald.

"Back!" Joby barked. Something in his voice froze all those angry arms and knees as if time itself had stopped, and Lindwald had just enough time to remind himself to make it convincing before Joby was on him like a crashing plane.

"Convincing" turned out to be no problem. Trapped in the illusion of flesh, stripped of any special power, Lindwald could do nothing to deflect the blows or mute the pain, and the unrestrained fury of Joby's assault was somehow far more frightening than the coldly calculated torments inflicted by his "parents" each night. His sudden panic was as genuine as it was unexpected.

"Stop it! I give up!" Lindwald wailed, falling to the ground, his head cradled under his arms. *"You're killing me! . . . HELP!"* he screeched.

Lindwald vaguely registered the confusion around them, some voices calling for Joby to stop, Laura's among them—others cheering Joby on. But Joby seemed too lost in rage to heed anything but his one horribly singular purpose.

Suddenly, Lindwald found himself in a room he had not so much as thought of in three hundred years, trying to press himself through a stone wall as his mortal father hammered relentlessly at his back and limbs with an iron hearth tool on the night that Jamie, himself, had died. It wasn't *fair*! He was already *dead*! They *couldn't* make him go through this *again*! The numb strength of pure transcendent terror possessed him then. Leaping up, Lindwald dimly felt Joby's weight tumble from his back like a load of wet leaves. Then he ran.

In seconds he was through the playground gate and into the field behind the school, but he heard Joby and Benjamin shouting right behind him. They were *never* going to let him go!

❈

Alerted by Williamson, Lucifer hovered over the viewing bowl in his office, watching Lindwald's long awaited rout with almost sensual relish. "I could almost forgive your bungling for the pleasure this affords me, you little bastard." The grin he wore threatened to overflow his face, and wrap around his head. *"Run Jamie! Run!"* he cackled in quiet falsetto. Then, even more softly, "Joby, my *angry* little friend, I never guessed you had such marvelous *potential*! Get him, boy! *Sic him!*" Lucifer howled with mirth, watching them corner Jamie in a small, dense copse of dusty trees.

"What's a matter, Lindwald?" Joby taunted as he and Benjamin dodged one way, then the other, to keep Jamie from bolting. "Don'cha wanna fight me anymore?"

"Let me go!" Lindwald wailed. "You win! I *told* you! *You win!*"

"Laura's arm is *broken*, you asshole!" Joby shouted. "What the hell made you think it was okay to—"

"I'M SORRY!" Jamie screamed. *"Don't hit me anymore!"*

"He's nothing but a yellow little stink ball," Benjamin jeered. "That the best a *demon* can do?"

"What're you talkin' about?" Jamie whimpered. "I ain't no demon."

"We know what you are, Lindwald," Joby sneered, "*and* who you work for."

"I don't work for anyone!" Jamie moaned. "You're *crazy*." He tried to rush past them again, but Joby reached out and grabbed his shirt, which ripped down one side, exposing his back as Benjamin threw him to the ground where he lay, shaking and rippling with sobs.

"*What* . . . is *that?*" Benjamin gasped, jumping back from him in revulsion. Joby just stared.

Lindwald's back was covered with livid welts like long, fat caterpillars made of raw hamburger.

Jamie's crying grew softer, and he rolled slowly over to face his tormentors.

"What're you starin' at?" he whined.

"What's that all over your back?" Joby demanded in disgust.

For a moment, Lindwald looked blank. Then he pouted, and said, "That's what they do to me." The calculating look that crossed his face was so brief that Lucifer doubted anyone but himself had seen it. "That's what *you* made my folks do to me," Lindwald pressed, looking as pathetic as possible.

"*Us?*" Joby demanded. "We had nothing to do with—"

"*You* made 'em *mad* at me!" Jamie whimpered miserably.

"Your *parents,*" Benjamin said in hushed disbelief, "did *that?*"

"*No way,*" Joby whispered in shock. "*Nobody's* folks, could . . . I mean . . ."

Jamie played his serendipitous lever for all it was worth.

"No one's s'posed to know," he said, his lower lip trembling. "If they find out you saw, I . . . I don't know what they'll do to me. Please! Please don't tell anyone!"

"Lindwald!" Lucifer murmured, impressed despite himself. "What happened to that stupid lump I've put up with all these centuries?"

Lindwald broke down utterly then, and it was all Lucifer could do not to applaud the performance. To think that such theatrical genius had lain dormant under that clumsy shell for so many centuries, waiting for sufficient fear to bring it forth! Lucifer was chagrined by a sudden suspicion that he'd grown too lax over the eons.

"*Oh no,*" Joby whispered. "*Benjamin* . . . He . . . What if he's not . . . Benjamin, I've done something terrible." He stepped closer to Jamie, and said, "We had no idea what you were going through. Why didn't you *tell* somebody? A teacher, or—"

"My folks'd *kill* me!" Jamie blurted. "I ain't kiddin'! Promise me you won't say nothin' to *no one*! *Please!*"

"We won't tell," Joby assured him. "We promise. Don't we, Benjamin?"

"Yeah," Benjamin said, beginning to look genuinely ashamed. "I promise."

"Jamie, if we'd known what was going on . . . ," Joby began. "I mean—"

"Oh *yesss!*" Lucifer breathed, bending closer to the bowl. "Do the *noble* thing, my little paragon! *Reach out* to the *darkness.*"

"I mean . . . ," Joby hesitated. "We don't have to be enemies. If you want . . . we could be friends, I guess."

"YES!" Lucifer shouted. He looked up and spread his arms in exultation, allowing the angelic radiance he so seldom revealed to blaze around him as if a hundred suns had suddenly risen in his office! What luck!

"I know how bad I'd feel," Lucifer heard Joby say, "if my parents—"

"Well they *don't,* do they!" he heard Lindwald growl, oozing scorn and wounded pride now that he had Joby where he wanted him.

Lucifer's radiance vanished instantly as he bent in alarm over the viewing bowl again and realized in horror that the unmitigated ass didn't begin to comprehend the strategic value of what he'd accomplished! In a roil of panicked fury, Lucifer literally flew to the gleaming obelisk beside his office door, slammed his hand against it, and shouted, *"Accept his offer, you worthless sack of excrement!"*

He raced back to the viewing bowl to see Lindwald look appalled, then confused, then turn to Joby with an expression of abashed contrition, and ask, "You mean it?"

"Course I do," Joby assured him.

Lucifer released a huge sigh of relief.

"Nobody ever . . . Who'd wanna be friends with *me?*"

"Stop pushin' everyone around," Joby told him, "and you could have all kinds of friends—couldn't he Benjamin?"

"Well," Benjamin conceded, "I guess . . . if he'd start actin' like he *wants* friends."

"I *do* want friends," Jamie mumbled. "You ain't gonna tell no one. About my folks. Right?"

"We promise," Joby said, sticking out his hand. "Shake on it?"

Lindwald took his hand with a timid smile, then turned and held his hand out to Benjamin, who, after a moment's hesitation, shook it too.

Lucifer stared thoughtfully at the bowl as they left together, Lindwald wearing Benjamin's coat to cover his back. Joby's marvelous capacity for rage could be just the handle he'd been looking for, once he knew how to leverage it without tripping the wrong wires. And Lindwald! What an act! Perhaps he'd try turning up the heat on Williamson now too. Who knew what marvelous potential lurked just below the surface there as well? In fact, perhaps he'd been too kind to everyone in Hell.

✠

Frank was in the locker room after a particularly satisfying round of racquetball. Karl wandered in a moment later, wearing a conspiratorial grin. The two of them had pretty well slaughtered Mike and Phillip.

Then Jack Stives came around the corner, and Frank's good mood went straight to hell. Stives was a tall, muscular man with the ego and manners of a rutting ram. His son, Tommy, was in Joby's class at school, and, like his father, always spoiling for a fight. Years before, after a few of their boys' early quarrels, Jack and Frank had run afoul of each other. That had been before Joby had learned to handle himself, of course. Tommy left Joby alone now.

"Hey! Frank!" Stives exclaimed as he headed for his locker. "Funny I should run into you! I was just hearin' about your boy from my Tommy not half an hour ago!"

"No kidding." Frank grinned back, carefully casual.

"Seems he's become quite an item at school these days!" Jack said. "I hear his little club's gettin' rave reviews. What's it called?" He grimaced, trying to remember.

"The Roundtable." Frank smiled. "Yeah, Joby talks about it all the time."

"That's right." Jack grinned, pulling the sopping shirt off of his broad back. "The Roundtable. I knew it was *something* magical, but I thought it was fairies or something."

Here we go, Frank thought wearily. He shoved the last of his things into the locker, and reached for his coat. "Good seeing you, Jack. See you later, Karl."

"Yup. Tommy tells me your boy put up quite a fight today," Jack said.

Frank stopped, and turned back to face him. "Did he? I haven't been home yet."

"Well, I'm only tellin' you what I heard from Tommy, of course. But he says this kid, Lindfield, threw your boy halfway 'cross the playground this afternoon. Not the first time either, I guess." Jack shook his head. "Awesome patience your boy's got. My Tommy'd been all over that clown weeks ago. Anyhow, when your boy still wouldn't fight him, that little girl, Laura Bayer, the one broke her arm a while back, she steps right in to fight for Joby, and this asshole decks her right in front of everybody! Cast and all! That's some popular boy you got there, Frank. Little girls throwin' themselves across the tracks to protect him." He winked. "Quite the little lady-killer, sounds like to me."

Karl barked one quick laugh, then looked apologetically at Frank, while Stives looked startled, then beamed, as if just getting his own joke. *"Whoa!"* he exclaimed. "I didn't even do that on purpose! *Lady-killer!*" He guffawed. "Get it, Frank?"

"Yeah, I got it," Frank said levelly. He gave Karl a reproachful look, and headed for the door, hoping he didn't look as humiliated as he felt. It was like goddamn Jack "crap-for-brains" Stives had been watching Frank's damn, sick dreams or something! Protected by little girls, for godsake! Something had to be done, but he knew he'd better cool down first. A drink or two at the Filling Station might do the trick. Then he'd talk to Joby and find out what this was all about.

❋

Trying harder than ever to be more perfect, Joby had finished his science report on sea life the moment he'd come home, then cleaned his room. Dinner was not for half an hour at least, but he'd already washed his hands twice. Now he sat on his bed, clutching his Arthurian tome, and trying to sort things out. The enemy had clearly tricked him into punishing an innocent person. Hadn't Joby told Benjamin on Sunday that persecuting Jamie was a mistake?

Now Joby couldn't stop wondering what it would be like to have parents who burned lines on his skin when they got mad, or called him a "*bastard*" in front of strangers. Joby had never thought much before about what *other* people might be going through. What was it like for Tony to be poor? How did Duane feel, getting picked on so often? How many of his other friends were going through terrible things in secret? In that moment, Joby suddenly discovered his heart's desire, though not quite how to express it. RHecalling Father Crombie's sermon that first time he'd gone to church with Benjamin, Joby wanted terribly to fix all the sadness and harm that weighed on people like Jamie. Lights in the darkness, Father Crombie had said. The image of candles bloomed in his mind. A circle of tiny lights in the darkness, growing in number, spreading like a wave, farther and farther in all directions from where he stood willing the darkness away.

There was a knock on Joby's bedroom door.

"Come in."

Joby's dad stuck his head in. "How ya doin' sport?"

"Okay, Dad. . . . How come you're home so late?"

"I just had things to take care of after work. Can I come in?"

"Sure," Joby said. Hadn't he just said "come in"?

When his dad sat down beside him, there was a funny sweet smell on his breath.

"How'd your day go, Joby?"

"Okay. I wrote a report on sea life."

"You did, huh." His father smiled.

"Yeah. For science, we're studying things that live in the ocean. You should see, Dad! Crabs, and seashells, and sea enemies that shoot little poison darts into anything that touches them! Only they can't hurt people, 'cause we're too big—only little fish. And starfish walk on little tubes with suction cups on the end, and when they clamp down almost nothing can move 'em. And you know what, Dad? Up close, they're like *monsters*! Last year, Mrs. Baker said monsters are just make believe, but she's wrong! They're just real small!"

His father's smile widened, and he ran a hand through Joby's hair, raven black, like his own. "You really like science, huh?"

"Yeah," Joby said. "I didn't like plants much. But sea animals are cool."

"I saw Tommy Stives's dad at the health club after work today. He said you've been having trouble with that boy you fought with back in September. Is that true?"

Coming right out of the blue like that, the question left Joby feeling caught out and ashamed somehow, though his dad didn't seem mad. He looked down and nodded. "We had a fight after school today . . . but—"

"Jack said Laura Bayer got hit," his father said before Joby could tell him everything had come out all right.

"Yeah," Joby said, "but she didn't get hurt. Well, not too bad. She's okay now."

"Why was she involved, Joby?"

"She stood up to Jamie when he tried to fight me."

"Why didn't you stand up for yourself, son?"

"What? . . . Dad, I—"

"Has someone been telling you it's wrong to fight?" His father was still smiling, but the smile seemed strained now. "Do they tell you that at church?"

"No," Joby said, feeling worried. Something was wrong, but he couldn't tell what it was. "Well, sometimes. But that's not—"

"They're *wrong*, Joby." His father's smile had vanished completely. He was definitely angry, and as he leaned closer to Joby, the sweet smell on his breath got stronger. "It's never okay to be a bully, son, but sometimes a man needs to stand up for himself, and then it's not just okay to fight. It's *right*. It's *good*. Next time this bastard picks on you, you just flatten him. Understand? No son of mine needs little girls taking his falls."

Joby wanted to tell his dad that Jamie and him were friends now; that Laura was proud of him; that Jamie wasn't a *bastard*. But he didn't dare speak. His father was mad at him, and he didn't know what it was safe to say.

"I'm not mad at you, Joby," his father said, sounding sad. He reached out to stroke Joby's hair again. "I just want you to be proud of yourself."

⁂

"I must say, Kallaystra, your versatility never ceases to amaze me."

"You flatter me, Bright One, but I rather enjoy bartending, really. The Filling Station has such a wonderfully *distressed* clientele, and I'm such a good listener, you know." She smiled thoughtfully. "The boy's father is rather charming really, by *their* standards, and *very* good looking." She giggled seductively, and Lucifer laughed as well. "The friction between him and the child's mother should ignite very nicely any time now. The boy's sudden interest in religion works greatly to our advantage in this as well."

"Indeed," Lucifer replied. "Williamson tells me your priest has Joby struggling with *pride* already. Imagine! Only *nine*!" he chortled. "What a precocious boy."

"I knew you'd be pleased."

"Oh yes. In fact, I'm especially happy about Richter's admirable concern for . . . physical purity." He chuckled softly. "Given our progress with Joby's father, Richter's paranoia provides some delicious opportunities to up the volume of Joby's little conundrum, wouldn't you say? Damned at home if he doesn't want a woman, damned at church if he does. That's always been one of my favorite recipes."

"Bright One, the boy is only nine," Kallaystra said. "Isn't that a bit early to be thinking about sex?"

"The most fruitful seeds are planted well before the thaw, Kallaystra. How far ahead do you suppose the Enemy has planned?"

Her skepticism vanished in a grim nod. "Too true, Bright One. I'll begin tilling the soil immediately."

They were interrupted by a soft chime.

"That will be Williamson." Lucifer frowned. "He's overdue for one of his dreary reports."

When he'd placed his hand against the dark obelisk beside the door, however, his startled expression told Kallaystra that the message must be anything but dreary.

"Forgive me, Kallaystra," he blurted out. "I think he may have found it!"

Lucifer vanished before she could ask who "he", or what "it" was.

          ✖

Laura had wisely left the meeting so that the knights could talk freely, and Bobby Lehan was now vehemently expressing his objections to Benjamin's proposal.

"I never saw *you* stand up to Lindwald, Bobby," Benjamin rebutted. "She's been brave as any of us a whole bunch of times, and I say it's *stupid* she can't be a knight."

"He's right," said Tony Esquivel. "Look how much she gets hurt all the time. She's plenty tough to be a knight."

"You're just on her side 'cause she got you in, Tony!" Johnny Mayhew sneered.

"Tony's in same as you," Joby objected. "'cause he passed the tests, and we all wanted him."

"Yeah, Johnny!" Duane said. "Don't be a jerk to Tony just 'cause you're—"

"Shut up, Duane!" Johnny pouted. "You been kissin' up to her ever since you knocked her outta that tree. If it weren't for you, none of this'd be happening!"

"What's your problem, Mayhew?" Joby asked. "Laura done something to you?"

"She's . . . *This is not a club for girls!*" Johnny spluttered. *"Girls can't be knights!"*

"Yes they *can!*" Benjamin beamed. "I got *proof*!" He lifted a volume of the encyclopedia from the table in front of him. "I asked Mrs. Escobedo, and she—"

"Mrs. Escobedo!" Johnny scoffed. "What does *she* know about being a knight?"

"Johnny, shut up and listen!" Joby insisted.

"Mrs. Escobedo showed me *this*," Benjamin said, glaring at Johnny Mayhew. He opened to a marked page, and, to Johnny's clear consternation, began reading the entry on Joan of Arc.

          ✖

High up near the ceiling, two moths lay flat against the wall, watching the Roundtable's proceedings in mothy silence. The larger insect was white with huge gray eyes, the smaller one, dark brown with bright black ones.

"Is he not a joy to behold, My Lord?" The stream of thought passing between Gabriel and his Lord was filled with affection for Joby. "Look at how proud he is of Benjamin."

"And of the girl," the white moth agreed. "The three of them have become quite the little trio, haven't they."

"In truth," Gabriel replied, "they often remind me of the very ones they imitate. She is much like Guinevere, and Arthur would certainly have taken a shine to Joby. Benjamin is so like Lancelot that, were his coloring darker, I'd—"

Gabe saw his master's wings quiver slightly, and sensed the soft puff of pheromones that passed for a smile among moths. Suddenly, the pieces fell together, causing his dark wings to flutter involuntarily.

"*Surely* . . ." the dusky moth broadcast in the mental equivalent of a gasp, "you *can't mean*— They're not *really*—"

"I did promise them a second chance," the white moth replied. "Remember?"

"But . . . *now*? I do not mean to question You, Lord, of course, but isn't this contest challenging enough without throwing that knot into it as well?"

"I promised them," the Creator insisted. "And if Lucifer should win, I'll never have another chance to keep that promise."

For a moment, Gabriel was struck speechless—even for a moth. "My Lord," his mind whispered at last, "surely You do not *anticipate defeat!*"

"Perhaps He does," came a sardonic mental voice from just behind them.

Both moths fluttered up and turned to land again facing the large, shiny black spider that had snuck up on them from above.

"Two moths out alone should be more careful," the spider admonished. "What if I'd been hungry and failed to realize who you were in time?"

"You'd have found yourself in the arms of a six-inch praying mantis," Gabriel blurted out, "getting your head chewed off!"

"Gabe," the Creator sighed, folding his wings calmly behind him. "Your goat."

Gabe was too busy wondering how on earth the Creator had let Lucifer surprise them to puzzle out what goats had to do with anything.

The spider turned its many glassy eyes toward the escalating debate below. "So *that's* Your *hidden ace*," it said dryly. Its palps did that little dance that passed for laughter among spiders. "Was this the best You could do? Dust off a proven failure, and trot him back out for the most crucial wager in human history?"

"Arthur was hardly a failure, Lucifer," the Creator replied. "If memory serves Me, you lost that wager, not I."

"On a technicality," the spider sneered. "And, if he didn't fail, *technically,* he certainly didn't succeed. In *my* book, that's virtually the same thing. Two adulterous traitors, and an incestuous infanticide," he said, dripping with disdain. "To *these* you give 'second chances'—but not to *me*."

"*They were sorry,* Lucifer," the white moth replied.

"*Sorry?*" Lucifer murmured. "When I'm in charge, *sorry* won't be nearly good enough." He turned his back on them then, and siddled up a strand of web toward the crack he'd come from. "I'd love to stay and gloat," he broadcast back with a mental grin, "but now that I've glimpsed the rather pathetic card up Your sleeve, I have *adjustments* to make."

In the room below, Laura was being escorted back into the library by her grinning champion, Sir Benjamin. Everyone was clapping, except for Johnny Mayhew, who had left the room. But Joby didn't seem to care about that. He just smiled at his two best friends with obvious pride and affection, clapping louder than anyone as they took their seats beside him at the table.

6

(Taubolt)

Joby reveled in the warm spring air that caressed his arms and played through his hair as he biked home from that confining compound for the last time until the unimaginably distant month of September. School was finally over, which meant not only three months of freedom, but the final countdown to his birthday too! In three days he would be ten years old! Double digits at last! And as if all that weren't enough, Mrs. Nelson had given him a letter for his parents, which, from her smile, he knew must say something good. Joby hadn't felt this happy since Christmas, when he'd gone into the living room to find his brand new bike beside the tree, flake red, with twenty-one gears!

His old bike had gone to Jamie Lindwald when they'd let him into the Roundtable in March. Jamie had never talked again about what his parents had done to him, and Joby had known better than to ask. But he'd gone without a shirt out at the tournament field recently, and no trace remained of the ugly scars Joby and Benjamin had seen.

By now the Roundtable was completely famous. There were *sixth-graders* who wanted to be knights! Even teachers came quietly to Joby, Ben, or Laura with suggestions about who could use a lift or a helping hand. Johnny Mayhew had come back to the Roundtable eventually, despite Laura's knighthood, and become fast friends with Jamie. All in all, it had been an amazing year. Joby pumped his bike pedals fiercely, howling like a wolf, and laughing at the sun, unable to contain the giddy joy that powered through his body. He was free! Free at last!

⁘

"Hit me," said the Creator.

"Again?" Gabe exclaimed. "You *must* be over by now."

"We're gambling," the Creator chided. "Pressing My luck's the whole point."

Gabriel dealt his Master a sixth card, and the Creator laid His hand down, revealing a ten, a two, a four, a three, and *two* aces, "Twenty-one," he grinned, "again."

Gabe shook his head in amazement. "I must confess, Lord; it's reassuring to see Your luck run so strong."

"You don't, you know."

"Don't what?"

"Have to confess."

Gabriel looked confused.

"Never mind," the Creator said.

"Lucifer's done *nothing* for *months!*" Gabriel murmured. "It's making me rather nervous. What can he be up to?"

"Little Joby could teach *you* a thing or two about keeping your goat, Gabe."

"My what, Lord?"

"Your goat, Gabe. You seem so anxious lately."

"Master," Gabriel dared at last to ask, "did we not betray Your *'hidden ace'* to Lucifer?"

"Is *that* what's been eating you?" The Creator smiled. "Well, you needn't have worried. There is no silver bullet concealed anywhere in Joby. There never was. So we can hardly have betrayed it to Lucifer, can we."

"*No ace?* . . . I thought—I mean, *Lucifer* clearly thought . . ."

"If I were hiding aces, Gabe, I wouldn't hide them in Joby anyway." He picked up the cards and began to shuffle them. "First place that old boar would look, isn't it?"

"Then . . . forgive me, Lord, but, the child does seem terribly vulnerable. If there's nothing more waiting in reserve, how can You be certain Lucifer won't win?"

"Of course he might win, Gabe. The fellow's an ass, but he's not an idiot. In fact," the Creator sighed, "I'd say he's already got the game he's been playing with poor Joby pretty well sewn up."

Gabriel could not hide his shock. "You think he's *won,* Lord?"

"Lucifer often wins the games he plays." the Creator mused, soberly. "You know that, Gabe. Thank heaven he so rarely plays the right ones."

✼

Gabriel had not been the only one puzzling over the Creator's game since that afternoon in the library. Realizing later that sneaking up on his "omniscient" foe had been far too easy, Lucifer's gloating had quickly turned to apprehension. The Creator must have *wanted* to be overheard, which could mean only one thing: there must be a trap hidden somewhere in this discovery, waiting to snap shut on Lucifer's overconfident fingers, just as it had so many times before. Well, he wasn't falling for it this time.

That these children, though unaware of it themselves, *were* Camelot's tragic trio returned to the wheel was undoubtedly true. Tricky as He might be, the Creator did not lie outright. Not ever. But Lucifer's oppressor had never had any qualms about *withholding* the truth. So what *hadn't* He let slip? Lucifer had no intention of rushing blindly ahead until he knew. Beyond Williamson's surveillance, and Lindwald's carefully monitored infiltration, Lucifer had called all activity to an immediate halt.

Kallaystra had complained rather stridently about lost momentum, but Lucifer had just insisted that allowing the boy and his family this brief hiatus would ultimately work even more to Hell's advantage. What was more demoralizing, after all, than lost hope resurrected—then dashed—again? Kallaystra had received these reassurances with cool skepticism, as had most of the others. To Lucifer's satisfaction, she had clearly not failed to betray their "little secret" to nearly everyone in Hell. Flocks of his usually uncooperative demonic siblings had been paying him deferential visits for months now, just to see if there were anything he might need. Each time, Lucifer had mentioned the wager as if reluctant to burden them, but they'd invariably insisted on helping.

Now, of course, all those recruits were whining about having to cool their heels, but Lucifer would endure such complaint five times over before being rushed into some disastrous blunder. His second shot at Camelot's charming little trio would wait until all the trip wires had been discerned. This time they'd find no refuge in *technicalities.*

❦

Humming softly as she rinsed lettuce and red bell peppers, Miriam glanced up through the kitchen window at a world awash in sunlit greens and blues. There was fruit already swelling on those tiny peach trees Frank had planted two summers before. Once again, she reveled in summer's arrival.

Her nightmares had finally ceased just before Christmas, though it had taken her months to trust their absence. Frank seemed less anxious too these days. With the drier weather, construction had begun on the shopping mall, and kudos on Frank's design were pouring in from both his partners and the client, which made her husband charmingly impossible to live with. Joby's grades had been better that spring than ever before, and she could not remember the last time she'd had to ask him to pick up his things or do his chores. Thinking back, it was hard to understand now what she'd been so upset about all winter.

As she laid the salad things out to dry, and went to finish dressing the chicken, she heard Joby burst through the front door.

"Mom?"

"I'm in here, honey!"

He came running across the dining room, and into the kitchen. "I got a letter from Mrs. Nelson!" He bounded over and thrust an envelope at her. "It's for you and Dad."

She opened it and scanned the page.

"Out loud!" Joby protested. "Please," he quickly amended.

"'Dear Mr. and Mrs. Peterson,'" she read, "'I just want to say that your son's unflagging desire to learn and improve this year has been an example to all of his classmates. His wonderful imagination and delight in life have enlivened our class again and again. His Roundtable club has instilled a sense of excitement about helping others throughout the entire school. My only regret is having to relinquish the privilege of being his teacher next year to Miss Meyer. I have never seen Joby's like, and I am convinced that Joby will grow up to do great things. You must be very proud. Sincerely, Alice Nelson.'

"Oh, Joby!" Miriam said, bending down to fold him in her arms. "I *am* proud of you! Your father will walk on air when he reads this." She pulled back for a better look at her marvelous child. "I think you're just *perfect!*" she said. This seemed to please Joby so much that she said it again, playfully pulling his giggling face around by the ears. "You're my *perfect little boy,* Joby!" She kissed his forehead, and let him go.

"Yahooo!" Joby cheered, running from the kitchen with his book bag. "I'm gonna go wash my hands for dinner! . . . It's *summer!*" he shouted. *"Ya-hooooooo!"*

❈

As Miriam's fine chicken dinner drew to an end, Frank leaned back and asked with studied nonchalance, "So, Joby, given any thought to your birthday plans this year?"

His son looked up blankly. "Gee. I forgot all about it." Then he grinned slyly, and Frank couldn't help laughing.

"Like hell you did," Frank chuckled. "Let's hear it. What are we doing this year?"

Joby's smile became gleeful. "I wanna go see the little *monsters!*"

Frank was nonplussed, and saw that Miriam looked just as confounded.

"Tide pools!" Joby said. "Mrs. Nelson says all those animals we studied live right at the beach in tide pools. I wanna go see 'em!"

Ah! Frank remembered hearing Joby talk about sea creatures before. In fact, he had seen library books about marine life lying around the house all year. His brows climbed slightly. His son, the marine biologist? That's when he noticed Miriam's strange smile. "Miriam? What's that look about?" he asked.

"Oh . . . I was just remembering some tide pools I saw once when I was not much older than Joby. I found a *huge* starfish there—at least twenty legs."

"That's a *sun star!*" Joby exclaimed. "Did you see the little tubes it crawls on?"

"I don't think so." Her expression softened further. "But there were lots of beautiful shells and it was so sunny and warm. You'd have loved it there, Joby."

"Where was it?" Joby enthused. "Let's go *there!*"

"It was at little town called Taubolt," she said. "But it's much too far away. I'm sure there are lots of closer tide pools."

Of course, Frank thought. Where her father had grown up. He'd never been there, but Miriam had mentioned it from time to time. He could see she'd like to go there . . . and it had been a long winter, and he knew he hadn't been easy to get along with. Watching her bemused expression, Frank felt its echo spreading across his own face.

"Want to go see the beach where your grandpa grew up, Joby?" he said, smiling at Miriam.

"Yeah!" Joby exclaimed. "That'd be *cool!*"

"Oh, Frank," Miriam said. "We'd just end up *driving* all day!"

"I wanna go," Joby pressed. "Did you live there, Mom?"

"No, dear. Your grandpa left Taubolt a long time before he met your grandma. We only went that once, on vacation, and I don't even remember how to get there."

"Well, it's on the coast, so it can't be that hard to find," Frank said, rising to get a map. "Gotta be on the coast highway somewhere. Let's see how far."

A moment later he was back, spreading a California road map on the dinner table. He traced the wavy red line of Highway 1 north from San Francisco, reading the names of each town along the way, but his finger reached the Oregon border without ever finding Taubolt. "I guess it's too small to list," he conceded.

"It wasn't much of a town," Miriam said, turning to clear the dishes with nearly concealed disappointment. "Out in the middle of nowhere. It might not even be there anymore."

"A whole town can't just go away!" Joby protested. "We should look for it!"

"It's *Joby's* birthday, Miriam," Frank said, following her into the kitchen with his own load of dishes. "If that's what he wants, let's just drive up the coast and find it. Whadaya think?"

"I think Joby won't want to spend his whole birthday in the car."

"We'll make a weekend of it then. I can take Friday off. Nobody's going to say I haven't been working hard enough." He turned to Joby, who had followed them in with the salad bowl. "Mind if we celebrate your birthday all weekend, sport?"

"Heck no!" He beamed.

"Well," Miriam laughed, kissing her husband lightly. "As long as you both remember it wasn't *my* fault if this turns out to be a wild-goose chase."

"All right!" Joby cheered. "Can I bring Benjamin, Dad?"

"Whatever you want, son. It's *your* birthday, so *you're* the king."

"I'm the king!" Joby shouted, thrusting his fists in the air.

❈

"You asked to see me, Williamson," Lucifer said without looking up from the huge open book on his desk. "Be quick about it. I've a lot on my plate."

Williamson schooled his resentment once again. In the months since he'd found Lucifer's damned *ace,* the bastard had never said so much as "thanks." Damned if you didn't, and damned if you did. That's how it seemed to work around here.

"Sir, I've been doing the research you requested . . . on the boy's background, and while there's nothing remarkable about any of his other relations, it does seem that the child's maternal grandfather came out of nowhere."

"What?"

Finally something more than bland disregard.

"The man has no verifiable past before marrying the boy's grandmother, Sir. No apparent lineage, and his birth certificate, high school diploma, credit records, are all fake. They list his place of origin as Taubolt, California, but no such place exists. I've checked every map and atlas—every reference of any kind. I've had your own angels employ supernatural means of finding it, Sir, and there simply *isn't* any such place."

"So?" Lucifer shrugged scornfully. "He used forged documents to hide his past. An encouraging discovery, certainly, but not very useful until we know why. Is that all you've got to show for so much time?"

"Sir, I—"

"Just find out *where* the fakes were *made,* Williamson. Need I guide you through every task you're given? Where there's a forgery, there's a forger—and that person would undoubtedly be one of *ours,* wouldn't he!"

"With all due respect, Sir, I *have* made every effort to trace the forgeries, and can say with complete confidence, that they have no more past than he did."

"Then where *did* they come from? They can hardly have burst fully notarized from the head of Zeus! You've just been lazy!"

"I shall scour our lists more carefully, Sir," as if he hadn't done so five times already. But he knew that any other reply would have seen him spitted and basting 'til dinnertime—*every* dinnertime for eternity.

"Do," Lucifer said shortly. "And let me know when you've discovered something *useful*. Until then, get out."

❈

They left just after lunch on Friday. Ben and Joby provided running commentary on every sight from the backseat of the Petersons' Land Cruiser as they left familiar dry grassy hills for East Bay cities, the bridge, and San Francisco's rolling skyline. When the ocean itself came into view, the boys threw themselves at the west window, yelling their heads off. But after three more hours of winding coastal highway, the novelty had worn off, and they were both reduced to sleepy silence.

Near five o'clock, they stopped for dinner at a fish place that sold seashells and carved redwood curios. Having all but lost hope, they asked the waitress if she'd ever heard of Taubolt, and cheered loudly when she said she had. She wasn't sure, but thought it might be just a few more hours up the coast.

"A few more *hours!*" Benjamin and Joby groaned in unison, sliding together off of the leatherette seats and under the table like gunslingers who'd been shot.

For an hour and a half after leaving the diner they saw virtually no sign of humanity along the two-lane rural highway. The road grew extremely windy, and once, as they passed an immense outcrop of pale stone wrapped in dark glossy shrubs, Joby suddenly felt dizzy, and asked his father to pull over. After a moment on his feet, however, Joby suddenly felt better than he could ever remember feeling—as if some greasy syrup had been taken from his bloodstream, or a sack of stones lifted from his shoulders. When he mentioned it, his dad told him it was the effect of clean sea air.

Near sunset, they finally saw a weathered, hand-painted sign that read

TAUBOLT—2 MILES. They all cheered again, and the boys leaned forward, searching for some glimpse of their long awaited goal. Beside the road, sheep grazed in fields high with mustard flowers and wild grass already going gold. Long windbreaks of immense cypress trees marched across the landscape like bent old men leaning away from the sea. A worn but charming Victorian farmhouse went by on their right, its large yard lush with vegetable and flower gardens. They came over a low rise, past a ruined barn covered in blackberries and climbing rose, and there it was, spread atop a long headland in the distance.

Joby gasped.

Graceful stands of pine and cypress, weathered and sculpted by salt and storm, stood nearly black against the green-gold fields and the glittering sea beyond. In the bay between themselves and Taubolt, mammoth stacks of rock thrust up out of the water, their heads bent back above the mist, as if gazing at the sky in prayer. Seals basked in the last light of day on dark rock shelves, and long lines of pelicans skimmed the troughs between huge swells moving ponderously toward shore. A subtle movement in the sky drew Joby's gaze up to find some large hawk hanging nearly motionless above the river mouth, waiting for its dinner to swim by below. Rising at the center of all this, was a rambling collage of old Victorian facades, steeples, water towers, and gabled roofs.

"Oh!" Miriam softly exclaimed. "It's just the way I remember!"

Joby almost blurted out, *me too.* He had never forgotten the view before him. It was all just as it had been in his dream, except that, where the walls and roofs and spires of Camelot should have been, stood only the rustic silhouette of Taubolt. He stared and stared, hardly able to breathe, not knowing what to think.

As the highway crossed a river running into the bay, Joby saw the broad gray beach he remembered. Well-formed waves stood up and filled with light, like walls of brilliant jade, then tumbled down in creamy gouts of pure white foam, rolling in to spread across the sand before hissing back into the bay. High atop dark cliffs over the beach, a giant old cypress spread its shadowed arms out into the air. He and Arthur had watched this very beach astride their horses from beneath that very tree.

"Hey sport," his father said, glancing at him in the rearview mirror. "You're pretty quiet back there. Not sick again, are you?"

"Dad," Joby began, not sure what to say, "could we go out *there* first?" He pointed at the headlands' western edge. "I . . . I wanna see the sunset."

"The sunset!" his dad replied. "That's a great idea, Joby, but how 'bout tomorrow? We've got to find somewhere to stay right now."

"No! Dad, *please!* It won't be the same tomorrow. I . . . I know it won't."

"My goodness, Miriam," his father teased uncertainly. "Our son has developed quite the aesthetic streak, hasn't he? Do you remember if there's any place to stay here?"

"We stayed at an inn when my father brought us. . . . Oh! Frank, I think this is where we turn."

They left the highway, and wound toward town, passing a quaint red barn with white trim and an old-fashioned windmill pump, then found themselves headed west past a row of beautifully preserved gingerbread cottages. Lovely English gardens bloomed behind white picket fences as houses gave way to shop fronts, and they saw the inn, brightly lit and obviously open. Feeling assured of a place to stay, they acquiesced to Joby's wish, and continued west toward the headlands' far end. The street ended well before the land did, so they parked and wandered out across the grassy headland on foot.

The distant boom and sigh of surf was mixed with the musical bark of seals, the strident cry of seabirds, and, from somewhere, the measured tolling of a bell. A warm evening breeze carried scents of iodine and sea salt, wood smoke and dry wayside herbs, cedar bark and weathered stone—all just as it had been in Joby's dream.

Moments later, as they stood together on the cliff tops, gazing out to sea, Joby was barely surprised to see one small band of fog poised above the farthest horizon, its edges burning like molten gold, while elusive rays of peach and salmon, powder blue and palest yellow stretched briefly up into the lavender sky.

"Isn't it *beautiful!*" Miriam sighed, and Arthur's words came back to Joby's mind as suddenly and clearly as if he had just spoken them.

. . . I look most keenly for whatever beauty may be near at hand, and drink as deeply as I can. . . . Feed your heart, Joby. . . . Trust your heart.

✠

"It had better be urgent," Lucifer warned, one hand to the obelisk in his office. Glyster, or Gizzard, or whatever his name, was suddenly silent.

"Speak up, man!" Lucifer snapped. "I've got things to attend to, and *your* attention should be on the *boy.*" He had recruited this oaf to watch Joby whenever Williamson's new research took him from that task. Now Lucifer was having second thoughts about his choice of stand-ins.

"I . . . I've, um. Well," the damned soul stammered. "I seem to have lost him, Sir."

"Come again?" Lucifer was suddenly very still. "Lost *who?*"

"The . . . the boy, Sir." His excuses tumbled out in a desperate rush. "I was right on top of him, Sir! Right on his back! One moment he was there—or, I mean, *I* was there, and then, I was somewhere else, and he was gone! Just vanished right into nowhere! All of them! Even the car! Honest, Sir!"

"You're not telling me you've lost track of the boy you were sent to watch?"

Silence.

"Come to my office immediately, Glister."

"It's Glazer, Sir."

"NOW!"

Vanished, indeed! Lucifer thought, suppressing an urge to vaporize this pustule on arrival. The idiot hadn't even guts enough to admit he'd fallen asleep at his post!

The jaundiced fool popped up, clearly braced for a blow. Lucifer took another deep breath. Mustn't scare him senseless until all the important facts were harvested.

"Where did this alleged vanishing act occur, Glazer? You mentioned a car."

"Yes, Sir. They were driving up the coast on *vacation.* Then they all vanished, Sir. Just vanished!" He gave an annoying little shrug. "In a flash, you might say."

"You might, huh?" Lucifer mused through clenched teeth. "Where were they going on this vacation, Glazer?"

"To the *beach,* Sir." Despite his obvious fear, Glazer seemed to find the concept amusing somehow. "Going to see *crabs,* Sir, and *gather shells.*" He performed that infuriating shrug again and added, "Someplace I never heard of. Towbolt, I think."

For a moment Lucifer simply gaped. Then, *"Taubolt!* They were going to *Taubolt,* and it just never *occurred* to you to inform me until *now?*"

"Going to the beach to pick up seashells, Sir? Why would I bother you with something like—"

"Bye now," Lucifer said, almost merrily, and Glazer was gone—*in a flash, you might say.* With fragile calm, Lucifer laid his hand back upon the obelisk, and said, "Williamson. Come."

The fellow was there instantly.

"Sir?"

"I've got a riddle for you, Williamson. If a damned soul screams forever in a void where there's no one to hear him, does he make a sound?"

Completely terrified, Williamson stammered, "I . . . I imagine so, Sir."

"Yes," Lucifer nodded. "I hope so too." He turned and walked away. "Here's another one. If a supposedly competent researcher, with all the resources of Hell at his disposal, is unable to find a beach town in California called Taubolt, how can a mere mortal family, with *no resources* to speak of, trot blithely off to *vacation* there?"

"Sir? . . . I . . . I don't under—"

"I just terminated your stand-in, Williamson, because he managed to lose track of Joby Peterson and his entire family on their way to vacation in—get this, Williamson—*Taubolt.* . . . Now, stop me if I'm wrong, but it seems to me that if *they* can find Taubolt," he rounded on Williamson again and shouted, *"we should be able to!"* He took a deep breath, regathered his self-control, and said, "Am I missing something?"

"Sir," Williamson replied, sweating artillery shells, "I truly cannot think of any natural explanation for this."

No natural explanation. It was all Lucifer could do not to slap his own forehead. Had they actually *vanished*? *Literally*? Lucifer had assumed Grizzled was lying, or at least exaggerating, but . . . if it were *true*! He rather regretted incinerating the fellow before checking more carefully.

"Exactly, Williamson. No natural explanation—once again, you've confirmed my own suspicions precisely." He walked to his desk, and whipped out a pen and sheet of paper. "I have an errand for you." He scribbled a few lines on the stationery, paused to think, then scribbled a few more, signed it, sealed it with wax from the candle on his desk, and held the note out to his trembling researcher. "I want you to deliver this letter to a certain member of the enemy camp."

"To whom, Sir?" Williamson asked nervously, coming to take the letter.

"Gabriel."

"Gabriel?" Williamson choked. *"The Arch—"*

"Yes, you little coward, the Creator's right-hand *boy,*" Lucifer sneered. "He's not going to bite your head off while you're about *my* business. Wait for an answer, and bring it to me immediately. Is that clear?"

"Yes, but, Sir. . . . I can hardly just waltz into Heaven. Where am I supposed to—"

"Just run to any trendy coffee house on this abysmal planet and yell his name!" Lucifer snapped irritably. "Better yet, yell, '*cheat*,'" He grinned. "that may bring him even faster." Lucifer turned away and said, "Why aren't you gone yet? Just because I've *got* forever, doesn't mean I can spend it all waiting for *you*."

When Williamson vanished, Lucifer closed his eyes and fortified himself for an *unpleasant* necessity. He had to be absolutely certain that Joby had truly vanished from the earth, and, sadly, the task was too important to delegate.

He gathered his awareness, then let it spread from the flawless order of his own domain out into the Creator's squalid slum of a planet, searching for Joby. The more deeply he was forced to delve, the more his angelic mind recoiled in rage and loathing from all the filth and imperfection it encountered. When he finally yanked his awareness back to safety, Lucifer stood gasping, as if burst from some putrid pool just shy of drowning. *Nothing* filled him with more rage than knowing Heaven blamed *him* for all of *that*!

Nonetheless, Joby was truly not to be found.

"Got you at last, *Master*!" Lucifer breathed. "Explain Your way out of *this*."

❈

Benjamin woke in the blue-gray hour just before sunrise, and turned to find Joby sitting by their window, staring out over Taubolt's roofs, just as he'd been doing the night before. When his parents had left them, Joby had sworn to Benjamin that *this* was where Arthur had taken him in his dream! Benjamin trusted Joby more than anyone except his own parents, but he still didn't know what to make of such a strange claim.

"It's not even morning yet," Benjamin yawned. "Why are you up?"

"I'm trying to figure it out. . . . In the dream, Camelot was right here, so . . . do you think this is where Camelot *used* to be, or where it's *going* to be?"

"What?"

"Remember when I asked Father Crombie if Camelot could ever be real again?"

"No. . . . Well, yeah, maybe."

"He said it could come back if people believed in it like they believe in money. Remember? Well, maybe Arthur showed me Taubolt in the dream so I would know this is where he's coming back to." Joby turned back to face the window again. "You know what I dreamed last night, Benjamin?"

Benjamin waited, wondering if Arthur had talked to Joby again.

"I dreamed I was in the dark with candles burning all around me. . . . Hundreds of them, as far as you could see. Like Father Crombie's talk.

Remember? About being lights in the dark?" Joby looked back out the window. "I have that dream a lot."

Benjamin just stared at Joby, thinking he'd never seen him farther off in that world of his than he was now.

✦

The inn clerk had told them they were in luck; spring tides were exposing even more of the sea floor than usual. They'd had to rise just after dawn to catch the ocean's lowest ebb, but for Miriam it had been worth it just to watch the tiny smile come and go on her husband's face all morning as he'd watched their son and his best friend crouch side by side among the weed-draped rocks, pointing, exclaiming, and occasionally thrusting a hand into the water after some darting creature or bit of shell.

Earlier, they'd been able to walk out to the closest rock stacks in what locals called Smuggler's Bay. Miriam had forgotten how much color the ocean hoarded. Pink, lavender, yellow, orange, brilliant red, violet, and blue flashed everywhere from beneath heavy shrouds of iridescent brown algae or bright green mermaid's hair. Glinting shards of abalone shell were wedged into every crevice. They'd found several of the sun stars Miriam remembered from her childhood visit. Kelp and porcelain crabs, like armored alien tanks; slithering brittle stars; bright red sea bats; sculpin like tiny water dragons; bright purple urchins as thick as carpet in the larger pools; huge fluorescent green anemones, and beds of smaller lavender ones. Joby seemed to know all their names, and had made it clear that seeing his library books come to life was the best birthday gift they could have given him.

Hours earlier pale spring sunlight had gilt the town, then crested the surrounding cliff tops to cast a brilliant glamour over the glimmering liquid landscape at their feet. Breathing the salt air, listening to the swish of surf and the cry of gulls wheeling in the clear sky above her, Miriam was overwhelmed by Taubolt's loveliness and wondered why her father had ever left it.

She supposed he'd fled the isolation. Taubolt seemed even farther from the real world than mere distance accounted for. The inn didn't even accept credit cards! Fortunately, they'd brought checks. Their rooms were furnished with large, four-posted feather beds, glossy mahogany wardrobes, and end tables that looked like real antiques, making Miriam feel as if she'd stepped back in time to her own grandmother's house in Salem, Oregon. There'd been lace curtains and fresh-cut flowers in every room. Yet the prices were so reasonable. She wondered if the proprietor was aware of how much such lodging went for in the larger world these days.

The night before, after the boys had been settled into their own room, Frank had taken her for a candlelit nightcap in the richly appointed bar beneath the inn's grand old staircase. There they'd met a few of the other guests and been amazed to discover that none of them had come to Taubolt intentionally. They'd all been drawn aside by whimsy or curiosity on their way to someplace farther up or down the coast. Later, in the privacy of their room, she and Frank had shared a good laugh over the bartender's almost frightened expression when they'd told him they'd actually come looking for Taubolt. "Like he'd seen a ghost!" Frank had laughed, suggesting it might be time to get a more effective chamber of commerce.

※

"He didn't even have the nerve to deliver it himself," Gabe reported indignantly. "There's some terrified little functionary outside, trembling so badly that I'm tempted to take his hand and help him find his mommy."

"Stress management, Gabe. Remember?" the Creator said, still perusing Lucifer's letter. "So . . . My wayward angel thinks he's caught Me violating the terms of our wager. I guess we'd better go dash his hopes before he gets too attached to them. I've no intention of letting him win *that* easily."

"Or *at all*, I should think," Gabe said pointedly.

To the angel's discomfort, the Creator only said, "Go tell Lucifer's messenger that we'll come resolve his master's *misunderstanding*. Suggest that park in San Francisco. I haven't been there in ages. It should be lovely this time of year."

※

"*. . . Happy birthday dear Jooooooby! Happy birthday to yoooooooou!*"

Everyone around them clapped and cheered as the singing ended. The waitress had brought out a chocolate cake festooned in candles, and Joby was determined to eat half of it himself, despite being stuffed already. The White Tern was the most amazing restaurant he'd ever eaten at. White beets, hearts of palm, quail stuffed with saffron and chanterelle mushrooms; Joby had never heard of half the things they served here! When he'd found boar meat listed on the menu, he'd nearly flipped. Taking his first bite, thick, savory, and as tender as custard, he'd felt just like a knight of old.

"You gonna blow those candles out?" his father chided. "Or you tryin' to seal that cake in melted wax for later?"

Joby laughed as he puckered up to blow and had to take another breath.

"Don't forget to wish!" his mom warned. "And don't tell, or it won't come true."

Joby stopped to think. *When I grow up, I want to live here,* he thought. Then he blew as hard as he could, knowing every candle must go out if he were to get his wish.

"Just the candles on *this* table!" his father teased, leaning back as if against a gale.

It had been Joby's best birthday ever. They'd picnicked on the headlands by a thicket of wild lilies and bramble rose, then gone hiking beside a shallow brook through a canyon full of redwood trees. It had taken Joby a while to realized that these were the same trees he'd seen in Arthur's solemn grove, though the ones here were smaller. He'd even heard the same strange birdsong, though he'd still never seen the bird that made it.

They'd run into more animals that day than he'd seen in his entire life: deer, and herons, wood ducks, otters, a fox, and too many hawks to count. And that was just the *big* ones! There'd been a gazillion smaller, even more exotic creatures flitting and wriggling through the water and the undergrowth! To Joby, Taubolt seemed as good as Africa!

In the end, his father had the waitress wrap the remaining cake, not even *offering* her his credit card. By now it had become puzzlingly clear that no one took them here.

There really was something strange about Taubolt, and Joby didn't think credit cards were the half of it. The locals all seemed very warm and helpful, but he'd seen the knowing smiles and cryptic remarks that passed between them when they thought no one was looking. At first Joby had figured it was just because they all knew each other. But he'd been to lots of places in the city where he'd known no one but his parents, and still never felt so much like an outsider as he did here, as if there were some kind of invisible barrier—nothing unpleasant, just . . . always there.

The shops were strange too—full of shells and glass fishing floats, telescopes and teakwood chests, large colorful candles, sticks of incense and dried apple dolls. Not one thing you'd see in department stores back home. The old buildings themselves seemed magical somehow, with high, beamed ceilings, creaking staircases, dark, spiderwebbed corners, and half-open doors into shadowed rooms that customers were clearly not meant to ask about. Joby thought Taubolt would be an awesome place to Christmas shop.

During their after-dinner walk through town the streets were eerily quiet. From within the other restaurants, Joby heard the laughter of diners through amber-lit windows, the clink of glasses, silverware on china. But outside, they encountered no one at all until they neared the west edge of town, where they passed a young man sitting on a split-log bench outside a closed quilt gallery. Joby could tell he was local. He wore weathered jeans and a red plaid flannel shirt. His flaxen hair tumbled from beneath a gray baseball cap that shaded eyes bluer than the sea. A fine gold stubble glittered in the late light on his chin and upper lip. He smiled as they walked past, following them with his blue, blue eyes. Joby wanted to turn and ask him for an answer to the riddle he felt so strongly all around him, but that barrier was there— outsiderness—and Joby couldn't bring himself to cross it.

❊

Michael watched them pass, saw Joby turn, then give up and go on in silence. The angel looked away in sadness. If only the child had asked.

The word had come that fall, on the sighing wind, in the sprouting grass, the rustle of leaves, and the splash of raindrops, to every spirit or creature that still recognized the Creator's voice. The lords of Heaven and Hell had made a wager, its fulcrum a little boy whom any serving Heaven should assist if he should ask it of them directly, but whom none serving Heaven might assist if he did not. Nothing further had been offered.

Then, just yesterday, Michael had scooped the hellish wraith from a boy's slight shoulders at Taubolt's southern border, as was his charge, being Taubolt's guardian, then followed Joby, curious to learn why such a delightful child should have borne such a loathsome burden. The gold-brown gull following high above them as they'd entered Taubolt had never drawn their notice. Nor had the tawny field mouse peering at Joby and his friend from underneath the wardrobe in their room last night, and again as they whispered together at dawn.

Only after hearing the boys' whispered confidences that morning had Michael realized who Joby must be, and been plunged into confusion.

His Lord had said the time was many years away, and that Michael would know the candidate when he came. Yet not one full year had passed, and Michael had *not* recognized Joby in time to let his filthy cargo enter with him as his Master had instructed. Had Michael misunderstood? . . . Had he failed?

Time after time that day he had cast these questions toward Heaven, and still there was but one answer in the rustling breeze and the whispering sea: *"All things happen as they must."*

Anxious and confused, Michael had remained cautious until now. The seal watching from out in the swell that morning, the hawk circling high above their picnic on the headlands, the squirrel following their progress through

the woods that afternoon; in all these forms, Michael had meant to elude
Joby's attention. But this time . . . this *last* time, Michael had hoped the boy
would notice, would ask the question Michael had seen burning within him
throughout the day. For, in this at least, his Master's will was clear. If the boy
should *ask,* assistance could be offered. . . . If only he had *asked.*

❈

Joby eased the door carefully shut behind him, then tiptoed past his parents'
room toward the stairs. He knew they'd have forbidden him to go out alone,
but once they were up, there'd be no time for anything but breakfast and
packing. If he wanted to see the beach again, it would have to be now. He
had awakened before sunrise again, filled with an urgent need to go out and
say good-bye to Taubolt. He'd thought of bringing Benjamin, but his friend
had still been dead to the world, so he had let him sleep.

At the lobby, Joby abandoned any pretense of stealth, bounding through
the inn's leaded-glass doors out onto the sidewalk. The air was chill for
spring. Taubolt's buildings huddled in blue silhouette against the pale dawn
behind them, and a single fraying shoal of fog climbed in wispy tendrils
over the wooded hills flanking the river mouth. The sea smell was strong in
Taubolt's empty streets, the silence thick and secretive, as if there were no
one left in all the village but Joby.

He trotted past blank-eyed shop fronts, through a gate in the fence across
the street, and out onto the grassy headlands still heavy with dew. Halfway
to the cliff tops, Joby turned to look back at the sleeping town.

"Good-bye," he whispered.

Then he turned and ran toward the cliff-side trail that wound down to the
beach. The tide was not as low as it had been before, but he ran out as far as
he could without getting his shoes too wet, and gazed into the tide pools all
around him, sensing the myriad creatures crawling, darting, swaying at his
feet, though he could not see them.

"I'll be back someday," he said fervently. "Don't forget me."

He loped across a flat expanse of mussel bed to the edge of a deep fissure
washed by foaming surf and stood peering down into its green, semi-
opaque depths. Long dark strands of kelp writhed and curled in the current.
As the wave receded, the water fizzed like soda, then began to clear. He bent
closer, hoping to glimpse some secret treasure trove of shells, or perhaps . . .

But something large was moving there—zooming right toward him!

Joby leapt back in alarm as it burst the surface, and found himself staring
down at a brown-haired boy near his own age, whose startled expression

mirrored his own! For a moment they both froze, openmouthed and speech-less. Then, as another wave rushed through the trench, the swimmer plunged back beneath the surface and disappeared. When the fizzing water cleared, Joby saw no sign at all of the astonishing boy. In stunned disbelief, he began to scan the bay around him. There was nothing.

Where could he have gone—or *come from*? What was he *doing* there? The water was *freezing,* and he'd been wearing almost nothing! *Had he drowned?* Twining strands of panic tightened around his gut. Joby was about to run for help when something splashed to the surface hundreds of feet away near a small cave mouth at the base of one of the bay's towering rock stacks. It was the boy! He bobbed on the surface, staring at Joby with a worried ex-pression visible across the distance. Then he dove again and vanished . . . like a *seal,* Joby thought in utter wonder. How could *anyone* have swum that far so fast, without even coming up to breathe?

For a long time Joby simply stood and stared out at the bay, wondering if the boy would reappear. But he did not, and Joby realized that the sun had risen, and his parents might wake at any moment. A boy who could swim like that was not in any danger of drowning. He turned and raced for the cliff-side trail, hoping his absence had not been noticed—even by Benjamin. He couldn't imagine how he'd explain what he'd seen to anyone—not even his best friend—and he didn't want to have to try.

✼

Gabriel and the Creator sat on a bench near the band shell in Golden Gate Park; two ragged transients feeding an aggressive crowd of sparrows and pigeons from a greasy dollar bag of stale popcorn. Lucifer was late.

When he finally arrived, dressed to the nines as always, he walked up, intentionally scattering the birds.

"With all due respect," he drawled, "may I ask that You dispense with the bird feed, Sir? I have no wish to be shat upon at the end of *this* conversation."

"Lucifer," the Creator replied amiably, "it's lovely to see *you* again too." He tossed the remaining popcorn onto an overfull trash can behind the bench, where the birds set upon it instantly. "We were only trying to amuse ourselves while we *waited.*"

"Traffic," Lucifer said blandly as he joined them. "I hope you two didn't get all dressed up on *my* account. Is that what passes for *holy raiment* these days?"

"Your invitation took us by surprise," the Creator apologized. "All our good clothes were in the wash. But you can't have called us here just to critique our sartorial image."

"No, I did not," Lucifer replied, looking away with disdain. "It seems that our boy, Joby, has vanished on his way to someplace that doesn't exist. In fact, his entire family and a little playmate seem to be gone as well. I mean, really *quite, quite gone.*" He looked frostily at the Creator. "A rather remarkable achievement for mere mortals, wouldn't You say?"

"If you've an accusation to make, Lucifer, please make it," the Creator answered.

"You cannot just *remove* him from the game whenever it looks like he's *losing*!" Lucifer snapped.

"Careful. You'll scare the birds," the Creator said, glancing back at the trash can. "Besides, it didn't look to Me like he was losing. I'd say he's been doing better than ever. Wouldn't you, Gabe?"

Gabriel nodded.

"Our agreement states quite clearly that *You* will not intervene in any way," Lucifer rasped, "and that Your servants be commanded to refrain from intervention too!"

"*Unless* he *requests* their assistance." The Creator turned to Gabriel. "Isn't that right, our official witness?"

"It is," Gabriel confirmed.

Facing Lucifer, the Creator asked, "Are you *certain* Joby made no such request?"

Lucifer glared at his Lord with naked ire. "*Did* he?"

"No." God smiled.

"Then *how* do You explain—"

"I assure you, it was completely coincidental. Joby and his family happened to cross a barrier that has nothing whatsoever to do with our wager."

"Coincidence!" Lucifer shouted. *"You expect me to believe that?"*

The birds scattered nervously before hesitantly returning to finish their feast.

"Do you suggest I lie?" the Creator asked quietly.

With obvious effort, Lucifer reined in his temper.

"If you *are* suggesting such a thing," the Creator continued dangerously, "I would be happy to convene a full celestial court, and try the matter. . . . If you're proven wrong, of course . . . Well, you know the consequence as well as I do, and it wouldn't be very sporting of Me to win our wager *that* way, would it."

"What *coincidental barrier* is this?" Lucifer demanded more moderately.

"It's none of your business," the Creator smiled.

"If it's *on this earth* it's *my* business!" Lucifer spat. "You *gave* this planet to *me*!"

"Lucifer, really," the Creator scoffed good-naturedly. "Do I seem easily confused? I gave *you* to this planet, if anything, and told you to do as you like. That hardly constitutes *giving* you—"

"What the hell is Taubolt?" Lucifer shrieked, literally purple in the face by now. Startled by his outburst, the entire flock of sparrows and pigeons around the trash can burst into flight above them. "If the *candidate* has gone there, then I'm *entitled* to know what's going on!"

"It's just a little place I set aside several centuries ago," the Creator replied sternly, "so that a few lucky people could live and die without having to endure your handiwork. I certainly didn't *send* Joby there. Nor did anyone I command. He just happened to go. Life's funny that way. Our agreement does not even *suggest* that I must suspend all My operations elsewhere. I admit that Taubolt's guardian did yank your sorry bugging device off poor Joby's back on their way in; but *not* at My command, nor, as far as I know, with any knowledge of who Joby even is. Keeping you and yours from Taubolt has been his job for centuries. If you don't like that, you can take it up with him. He's a very reasonable fellow. Name's *Michael*."

Lucifer grew pale, though whether from fury or fear was anyone's guess.

"Oh! But you've met him, haven't you," the Creator said without smiling. "Well, as I said, you're welcome to fight it out with him, but I'm staying out of it, just as I'm *supposed* to." He turned to Gabriel. "Isn't that right, our official witness?"

"It is," said Gabriel.

"It . . . is not *fair* to place Michael between me and the boy," Lucifer quavered, "no matter *where* he is, or *why*."

"Not *fair?*" the Creator observed, sounding incredulous.

"You *promised* the boy would be free to choose for himself," Lucifer insisted tremulously. "How can he choose, if you hide him where no choice exists but You?"

"Ah," God said quietly, "you've got a point." He paused reflectively. "But the issue is moot now in any case. Mortal vVacations are brief things, and I'm confident that Joby will be well within your reach again by this very evening. If he ever returns to Taubolt, Michael will not stop your servants from following. Until that day, however, *if it ever comes*, you've no more entrance there than you ever did. Our wager has nothing to do with Taubolt unless Joby is there, so don't even try to find it. Is that clear?"

"I still insist that this entire affair is outrageously inappropriate to the spirit of our agreement."

"Have your lawyers talk to My lawyers," the Creator drawled.

Gathering the remains of his dignity, Lucifer leaned forward to tug his pant cuffs up and saw the bird droppings spattering his knee and shoe.

"Pity," the Creator said soberly. "That fit of shouting a while back; seems you scared the crap out of them." He shook his head sympathetically. "Such nice clothes too."

7

(Lessons in Shame)

Malcephalon was the first of Lucifer's council to arrive. A dark mist seeped across the threshold, flowing like sump water down the length of the room before swirling sluggishly up into a chair at the opposite end of the table. Black vapor poured across the glossy tabletop, resolving into sinuous gray arms, then crept in viscous cascades up the chair back, thickening into dark robes and, finally, the long gray face that Malcephalon had donned and never abandoned after their fall from grace. The demon's stony black orbs focused down the table's length to fasten upon his ostensible superior.

"Here already, Bright One?" he murmured balefully. "Well . . . I share your eagerness after such . . . *lengthy* preparation."

To Lucifer's knowledge, Malcephalon had *never* smiled since their defeat in Heaven. Kallaystra claimed to admire the demon's subtle mind, but it still surprised Lucifer that such a lovely, vivacious creature should befriend this sack of ashes.

"Greetings, Bright One!" Kallaystra trilled, materializing in the chair next to Malcephalon. "So, the hunt is to be unleashed at last!"

"Yes, Kallaystra. I'll not spoil your *momentum* any longer."

Before she could reply, a rude gasp issued from the empty air halfway down the table, followed by an even ruder curse.

"You're crushing me, you cow!" snarled a disembodied baritone voice.

"You'd be easier to avoid if you weren't sitting in my chair!" retorted a shrilly feminine one.

"I was clearly here first!" grunted the male voice in outrage.

"I'm sick to death of your eternal bickering!" rasped a third voice. *"There are five other chairs at this table. Why don't you both just take one of those?"*

The Devil's Triangle, as they were known, appeared then, all piled into the same chair. A skinny, wan, and pockmarked fellow struggled beneath an obese and shrew-faced maiden with dirt-smudged clothes and wild, fiery hair, while an emaciated crone, little more than a jumble of sticks in a long shroud of rotten lace, rode the struggling heap.

"You only sat in this one because you knew I wanted it, Tique!" shrilled the maiden squirming between them. *"And you only want it,"* she screeched at the crone on her back, *"'cause I'm already sitting here, Trephila!"*

"Age before beauty, you impudent sack of flab!" replied the crone, her voice a thin fugue of rusty hinges and wrenching nails.

It was all an act, of course, in which they never ceased to find amusement.

"Stop disgracing yourselves," Lucifer commanded wearily. "Or has the Enemy Himself sent you here to ensure our failure?"

"Now see how you've both embarrassed us," Eurodia whined.

"Us?!" her companions protested in unison.

Without transition, the uncouth trio were transformed into three neat, attractive individuals seated side by side in amiable silence. Tique was now a trim and handsome youth in clean white samite; Eurodia a slender Celtic beauty in dark velvets and bright satin ribbons; and Trephila an image of regal splendor, robed in sparkling lace, her shining silver hair elegantly coifed.

"Better?" Trephila asked with arch dignity.

"Much." Lucifer rose and went to place his hand against the room's large obelisk. "Williamson," he said. "Lindwald. Join us."

At the appearance of Lucifer's once-human operatives, Eurodia said, "What is *this lot* doing here? I thought this was to be a *serious* council."

"Even lowly functionaries must remain on the same page as the rest of us," Lucifer retorted. "Have we not seen the littlest bugs derail the largest endeavors?"

Trephila sniffed contemptuously as everyone frowned or looked away in distain.

Lucifer leaned back imperiously in his chair. "Have we any *other* concerns to air before getting started?"

"Bright One," Malcephalon ventured morosely. "I trust I will not offend by asking why the child's Roundtable escapade has been allowed to go on so long. Has this not left him somewhat *strengthened*?"

"Ah yes. . . . My *lengthy preparations*." Lucifer smiled coldly. "Had I not taken time to observe our quarry unhindered in his own element, would we have discovered his true spiritual lineage, or that of his friends? Had I bowed even then to calls for hastier action, we would certainly have missed the subtler snares laid for us in *Taubolt*." He swept the gathering with a challenging look. "While I appreciate the exemplary patience you've all demonstrated, I believe the time to act has finally arrived."

"Well, I second *that!*" huffed Trephila.

"My own exhaustive observation and analysis," Lucifer continued, pointedly ignoring her, "has revealed a few particular useful insights regarding our target. During his furious assault on Lindwald, Joby demonstrated an unexpected and deeply encouraging aptitude for rage, which may turn out to be key. In addition, while some sympathetic resonance with their former lives seems, happily, to have them already heading down the same tragic path they followed last time, Joby's severe integrity and intense desire to be an agent of *good,* as our Oppressor defines it, opens him beautifully to the self-blame, perfectionism, and blind trust that helped undo him last time."

"That Arthur!" Tique laughed. "Always leaping into the fire for any pea-brained pauper with a sob story." He slapped the tabletop, grinning like an idiot. "I'm glad he's back! This is gonna be a *riot!*"

Fortifying his patience, Lucifer indulged the small spate of laughter that followed.

"Unfortunately," Lucifer continued when he had their attention again, "there are some worrisome pitfalls to be aware of. Despite the pervasive shallowness and cynicism we've cultivated in the world of late, the child still exhibits an astonishing capacity for imagination and faith. As Lindwald so stupidly proved, he cannot be counted upon to deny his own experience and explain away our careless slips, as most will these days, so we must still proceed with utmost caution and stealth."

"If he's so alert to the truth about us," Tique interrupted, "why not just torment him openly? It's not like anyone else would believe him if he sought help." He rolled his eyes. "All this *careful* skulking about is such a *bore!*"

"What you suggest might work, were this not *Arthur returned,*" Lucifer said with barely suppressed irritation. "A soul like his is not broken by handing it the very adventure on which it thrives. On the contrary, the most devastating assault against a child who feels the call to greatness in his very blood is a life of relentless mediocrity. To our great good fortune, no other time or place in history better lends itself to that purpose than this one. We need do little, in fact, but smooth the boy's way of meaningful challenges until his life offers no hope at all of any least meaning or achievement."

"Smooth his way!" Eurodia protested. "We're just to spend the next twenty-five years making him *comfortable?*"

"This is going to be *no fun at all!*" Tique groaned.

"Bloody ashes!" Lucifer yelled. "I said *nothing* about making him *comfortable!* Could I have made that any *clearer?*"

"Well, if we're to *smooth his way,*" Trephila demanded, "how are we to—"

"Of *meaningful challenges,* Trephila . . . not of *meaningless miseries.* That he must *never* be allowed anything truly interesting or important to do doesn't mean we shouldn't bury him in empty busywork and pointless obligations. While we avert any major crises in his *own* life, those *around him* ought to suffer terribly in ways he is utterly powerless to alter. Whenever he trusts, I want that trust betrayed, but only in ways too petty to pursue. His brightest achievements must never be opposed, only dismissed with empty applause followed by suffocating indifference.

"When he is reduced to ghostly impotence, defeated by no enemy he can point to but himself, left with no shred of faith in anything whatsoever or any meaningful contribution to make, despising his own existence even as he berates himself for ingratitude in the face of so many blessings, then, and only then, will I be able to *remake* him in *our* image. This is the one course our Enemy is unlikely to have anticipated. Now, does everyone understand?"

"I am *so* relieved!" Eurodia laughed. "You had me quite worried, Bright One."

"Beyond all this, I trust it is *obvious,*" Lucifer continued, barely suppressing his impatience with all of them, "that having discovered our opponent's invasive coastal sanctuary, Joby must be allowed nowhere near the coast again at any time for any reason. We need waste no valuable time parsing the Creator's convoluted strategies there, if they are just allowed to rust unvisited. Is that clear?"

"Do you take us for simpletons?" Tique asked.

Resisting the temptation to answer, Lucifer merely turned to Kallaystra and said, "I want you to start fanning his parents' troubles back into flame, of course. Nap time's over. Get that teacher into position, and make sure our long-suffering priest doesn't despair of Joby's eventual return to the fold. Richter still has a part to play.

"Malcephalon," he said without waiting for her reply, "I want you whispering that wise counsel you're so renowned for into Joby's ear night and day. Teach him everything there is to know about shame, self-loathing, and despair. And by all means, let's do unravel his Roundtable now that it serves no further purpose. Lindwald may be of some use to you there.

"Tique, Eurodia, Trephila. A flood of petty misfortune and frustration will be very useful now. I imagine you'll enjoy that. But remember; *nothing meaningful* enough to get his teeth into.

"Lindwald, your good fortune in winning Joby's confidence saved you once, but speak *one syllable* to him which Malcephalon or I have not dictated, and you'll grace Hell's dinner table faster than you can say, Pop-Tart. Is that clear?"

"Yes, Sir."

"Williamson," Lucifer said, as if in afterthought, "you may continue as our security camera."

Williamson, whose face had long ago gone purple, said nothing.

"Are we finished?" Trephila asked, impatiently.

"For now."

"Good!" she cackled, suddenly the hag again.

Eurodia and Tique resumed their ruder forms as well.

"I get first shot at his bicycle!" Tique exclaimed.

"You only claimed that because *I* want his bicycle!" Eurodia whined.

Their voices were the last part of them to vanish.

&

Williamson left the meeting consumed in a fury like few he'd ever known. "Lowly functionaries!" *Little bugs!* That might apply to nitwits like Lindwald, but Lucifer's damn campaign would have crashed and burned *months ago* if not for *himself*! Hadn't *Williamson* been the one to inform Lucifer of Lindwald's screwups in time to remedy them? Hadn't *he* alerted Lucifer to Joby's hidden lineage? Hadn't *Williamson* been the one to connect Taubolt with the Creator's dream of "Camelot"?

His "own exhaustive observation and analysis"? Williamson thought in outrage. *How dare he?! Their security camera indeed!* This was the *last straw*! It was time Hell's whole useless ruling class learned a lesson about those *little bugs* they relied on to keep the dirt from under their own celestial nails. If it took him years, he'd find some way to win Lucifer's precious wager *all by himself*. Let them call him a bug *then*!

&

California's Indian summer had been canceled this year. August's dry heat had surrendered overnight to September's crisp chill, as if summer were just too tired to fight about it. That was pretty much how Joby felt too, as he rode toward school for his first day of fifth grade. There'd been trouble at his dad's construction site almost the moment they'd returned from Taubolt. The people who'd hired his father's company weren't happy anymore, and his dad was being held responsible. His father had been grumpier than ever, always telling Joby he should "stand on his own two feet, and be a man," as if Joby were standing on his *hands* or something. His parents were angry at each other half the time now too, and Joby didn't understand that either, though more and more often it seemed to be his fault somehow.

A week after their trip to Taubolt, his dad had backed over Joby's bike while leaving for work one morning, smashing it completely. His parents had been furious, and threatened not to replace it. No one had believed him when he'd sworn to having no idea how it got there. Joby had loved that bike! It had still been practically new! Why would he have dumped it right under the wheels of his father's truck where any idiot could've seen it would get run over? He'd even asked Benjamin if he'd borrowed it without asking, but Benjamin had sworn he'd never touched it. Eventually, his dad had broken down and gotten him another one, mostly because they were tired of driving him around, but the new bike was only a crummy three-speed, and an ugly yellow color at that.

Since then, Joby had tried harder than ever to be good, but he couldn't seem to make it through ten minutes without tripping on something, or tearing his clothing, or bumping his head. At first, his mother had just smiled and called it "growing pains." But after he'd smashed a few juice pitchers and dinner plates, she had stopped smiling, and begun to act as if he were doing it on purpose. So much for her "perfect little boy." In fact, his mother had become so nervous and irritable that by now Joby automatically tiptoed whenever she was around. She didn't seem even to want Joby going out of the house anymore. Just this morning she'd tried to insist on driving him to school, then told him, "You be careful on that bike!" at least twenty times.

No doubt about it; Joby was glad to have someplace to go again besides his house. Now that everyone was back at school he'd get the Roundtable going like it had been, and that would fix everything else. He wasn't sure how, but he felt sure it would.

Approaching an intersection two blocks from school, he pulled his back brake handle to slow down, but nothing happened. He instinctively pulled the front brake handle, and that did nothing either. He looked back in surprise to see what was wrong with his brake shoes, momentarily forgetting the intersection.

A loud screech brought his gaze back around in time to see a beaten old town car on the cross street *accelerating* straight toward him! Joby turned his bike so sharply that he nearly flipped over, but the huge car clipped him anyway as it roared by without slowing down. Against a vague, astonished fear, and a barely conscious struggle to reclaim control of his body as it flew toward the sidewalk, Joby had only one clear thought: His parents would *never* get him another bike.

❦

Frank paced up and down the shiny pastel hallway like a shooting-gallery duck, careful to avoid Miriam's bee-stung eyes. They'd been examining Joby since before Frank's arrival half an hour ago. Was it supposed to take that long?

Along with everything else, Frank hated how perfectly this validated Miriam's damn dreams. Her nightmares had returned in mid-July. He'd done everything he could to be understanding, but she seemed to expect him to help her tie Joby to a chair until her sleep improved! She hadn't wanted Frank to replace Joby's bike. Now Joby had virtually handed her the final word, and she was acting as if that made the accident all *Frank's* fault somehow. Half of him wanted to let Joby *walk* until high school if that's how long it took him to learn a little caution. The other half didn't want to let Miriam win. She'd been having these damned nightmares for *months* after all. So one of them finally comes true? What did that prove? Law of averages, right?

To be fair, Cally, down at the Filling Station, had helped him put some of it in perspective. At first he'd been reticent to mention anything so personal as troubles at work and home to a bartender, however attractive, but Cally always seemed so happy to listen, and so good at seeing right to the heart of things. She'd put her finger on the source of Miriam's trouble right away, explaining that Frank's difficulties at work threatened Miriam's sense of security, and so, afraid to confront her husband about it directly, Miriam was trying to retrieve control of her life through Joby. When Frank had tried to talk with Miriam about it, however, she'd simply flown off the handle, and accused him of being every kind of pompous, manipulative ass. He shook his head, and tried to remember their last truly happy moment together.

Sooner or later, it all came back to those damned Goldtree bastards. He'd gone over every detail of that mall design with them a hundred times before construction began, and they'd applauded like trained seals. Not until the damned showplace had started going up had they begun squawking about the "pricey materials," and "architectural extravagances." Those damned *extravagances* had been their favorite selling points back when there'd still been time to drop them! And his *faithful* partners! They deserved medals for dodging bullets under fire, every one. He shook his head again. God! What was he doing thinking about *work* when his kid was lying in a *hospital bed*?

"Mr. and Mrs. Peterson?"

Frank strode quickly to where Joby's doctor waited outside the examination room. Miriam was right behind him. Without thinking, Frank reached back for her hand, but she wouldn't take it. God, she was angry . . . Then again, so was he.

"We've looked Joby over pretty carefully," the doctor smiled, "and except for a couple of nasty abrasions and a bump on the head, he seems fine. He's a very lucky boy."

Oddly, Miriam turned away then, looking angrier than ever. Not for the first time, Frank wondered if his wife was . . . *okay*. The thought sent chills down his back.

"We can take him home then?" Frank asked.

"I'd prefer to keep him overnight, just for observation," the doctor said.

"Is that necessary?" Miriam asked before Frank could reply.

"No," the doctor shrugged. "But he did have quite a fall."

"He'll stay," Frank said before Miriam could get started. "May we see him?"

"Of course," the doctor said, turning to lead them into the room. "I certainly hope they catch the guy that hit him."

"Amen to *that*," Frank replied, wishing fervently for someone he could hit without guilt or reservations.

⊠

After his night at the hospital, Joby had spent another very unhappy day at home before going back to school. His father had driven him there. The bike hadn't been that badly damaged, but they'd taken it away, and wouldn't say for how long. When Joby had explained about the brakes, his father had gotten the bike and shown him that they were working just fine, so, once again, he'd been deemed a liar.

At school, however, Joby discovered that being run down by a car was just about the neatest thing anyone he knew could think of, and was rather enjoying his sudden celebrity by the time the bell rang and his crowd of fans escorted him to their new classroom. There, instead of Miss Meyer, he discovered a young, primly attractive woman he had never seen before. She had short, dark, shiny hair, and wore a gray dress suit that made Joby think of bank commercials.

"Hi, Joby. I'm Miss Stackly, as your classmates *already know*," she said, as if he'd missed an assignment or something. "Miss Meyer broke her hip in a fall last month, and won't be able to teach this year, so I'll be your fifth-grade teacher." She leaned forward to shake his hand. "I'm *very* glad you're finally here!" She looked up and smiled at the class. "There must be easier ways to get out of school than throwing yourself in front of a car, mustn't there, children?"

Everyone laughed, and Joby knew it was a joke, but something in her voice had made it sound as if she really thought he'd just done it trying to get away with something.

Smiling down at him again, she said, "I'm afraid you've already got some catching up to do, Joby, so why don't we sit down at lunch and go over what you've missed." It was not a request. There went his lunch hour.

※

They were silent as they walked into Joby's school for their parent-teacher conference with Miss Stackly. Such silences had become so usual that Miriam hardly noticed anymore.

She had opened Joby's last report card expecting further evidence of the student Mrs. Nelson had praised the previous spring. Instead, she'd found a long string of C minuses above a handwritten list of concerns filling the "Comments" box. The teacher's words still seemed etched on her retinas:

> *Joby seems to like working at his own pace, and in his own way. This appears to be deliberate disobedience rather than mere immaturity or ignorance of school policy. He is not working to potential, or making wise use of his time, and he holds his pencil the wrong way when writing. I have spoken to him about this many times since school began, but he is still doing it!!! It has been a pleasure to have him in class.*

Miriam had found Miss Stackly's final blandishment as offensive as it was incomprehensible. Confronted with the report when he came home, Joby had simply burst into tears and run to his room. Later he had mournfully sworn to working harder than ever, claiming that Miss Stackly hated him, and that nothing he did was ever good enough. Miriam had come this evening braced to meet the Wicked Witch of the West, but the woman who greeted them was attractive, pleasant, and apparently very sincere.

"Thank you so much for coming." Miss Stackly smiled, waving them all toward seats. "I know Joby's very disappointed about his report card, and it must have come as a surprise to you too. That's why I'm really so glad we're getting this chance to talk."

"Us too," Frank replied evenly. "Joby's always done reasonably well in school before. My wife and I are rather concerned about the sudden change."

"I appreciate and *applaud* that concern, Mr. Peterson." She smiled earnestly. "And I'd like to start by reminding everyone that a grade of C indicates perfectly *acceptable* work. Joby is certainly not failing in any way, and he's been making a much better effort lately, so we're definitely *not* in any kind of crisis. I see this more as a valuable opportunity to steer him toward higher achievement."

"I don't want to sound defensive," Miriam said somewhat coolly, "but it's always seemed to me that Joby was already something of an *over* achiever."

Miss Stackly gave her a wrenchingly sympathetic smile. "I'm sure I don't have to tell either of you what an amazingly gifted child you have, but it's crucial that such children be challenged. After being allowed to glide by on his extraordinary talents for so long, being asked to truly stretch himself for the first time undoubtedly feels like persecution, but I assure you, nothing could be further from my intention."

Miriam wasn't going to let her off that easily. "On his report card," she pressed, "you expressed concern about the way he holds his pencil, but his writing seems very neat to me, and his spelling has improved tremendously during the past year. He's worked very hard at that. Shouldn't we be more concerned with these things, than how he holds his pencil?"

Miss Stackly didn't seem the least bit defensive. She merely nodded, as if carefully weighing Miriam's point. "You know, those comment boxes are much too small." She smiled apologetically. "I so often wish there were room to address more than the problems there.

"Joby is a wonderful child," she went on to assure them, "but his very rich imagination sometimes draws him into a kind of *fantasy world,* which is fine for smaller children, but Joby is reaching the age where, if we're not careful, he could start to become socially isolated, and functionally impaired in all sorts of ways. I'd really like to see him reading a little less fiction, and concentrating more on core academics. Some organized team sports might help his sense of discipline."

"My son has always been *plenty* athletic, Miss Stackly," Frank replied with barely suppressed rancor. "If I know *anything* about Joby, it's *that*. And I'm not sure what *social isolation* you're referring to, but he's about the most popular boy I've ever seen." His tone became more heated. "You're new here, of course, so you may not have—"

"*Frank,*" Miriam interrupted, blushing.

"Mr. Peterson, I could not agree more," Miss Stackly insisted. "And *really,* I am *so moved* and *encouraged* every time I meet people who love their children like the two of you so clearly do. But I want to help keep him in step with his peers, so that he'll still be that same wonderful boy when he graduates from high school." She offered them her most ingratiating smile yet. "I've enjoyed meeting you both so much that, well, I can hardly wait for our next conference!"

Miriam left not knowing what to think. She had often heard that even the best children went through difficult phases. Perhaps she had only herself to blame for being naive enough to think that *her* child would be different.

❧

Benjamin sat with Joby and Jamie outside the auditorium, still flushed and glazed in sweat. When they'd all decided to try out for Mr. Bingham's fifth and sixth grade after-school basketball team, Benjamin had thought a tub like Jamie's chances pretty poor. It had never even occurred to him that *Joby* might not make it!

Having once again proven faster and more agile than seemed possible from the look of him, Jamie had made the final cut. But Joby's weird new klutziness had been in full force; and, to everyone's astonishment, Mr. Bingham had suggested afterward that he sit the season out. *Joby Peterson! King of the Roundtable!* Ben could still hardly believe it. Mr. Bingham had assured Joby, where others would hear, that boys often went through an *awkward phase* when their growth started, and that Joby's troubles only meant he was on his way to being tall and powerful sooner than most of his friends. But that hadn't helped much, and now Joby sat between Benjamin and Jamie, head hung in shame.

Benjamin punched Joby's shoulder companionably, and said, "Mr. Bingham was right, Joby. You're gonna be wipin' us *all* off the court *next* year—lookin' right down at the tops of our heads—even Lindwald's."

"Course you will," Jamie agreed. "Who said everybody's gotta be a hotshot athlete like Ben here anyway? You got lots of other good points. Your brain, for one, no matter what Miss Stackly says. And meantime, you need any protectin' 'til your growth kicks in, I'm yer man! I ain't forgot what you did for me last year."

Joby stood abruptly, and walked away without speaking or looking back.

"*What!?*" Jamie called after him. "I just meant—"

"Give it up, Lindwald!" Benjamin growled. Really, it was hard not to hit him. If Benjamin hadn't known better, he'd have sworn Jamie was humiliating Joby on purpose.

❦

Laura endured this latest meeting of the so-called *Roundtable* daring everyone to notice the pointed scowl on her face. No one had. Their club was back in fashion, but fashion seemed to be exactly the problem. Who was cool, who was not, whose tennis shoes were coolest; that's all anyone wanted to talk about now. Should the knights get special T-shirts made? Should they all get identical haircuts? To Laura's irritation, Lindwald was among the worst practitioners of the Roundtable's new conceits. He'd somehow gone from being merely accepted last spring, to being the Chief of Status Police this fall, with Johnny Mayhew backing up his every decree.

They'd hardly done any secret missions yet this year. The two proposed that afternoon had been nothing but personal payback schemes against kids who had ticked off some so-called *knight*. With Benjamin's support, Joby had managed to get them both voted down, but it made Laura sick! Nobody but Joby and Benjamin even seemed to remember what secret missions had been invented for, and since Joby's failure to make the basketball team, no one paid him half as much attention.

Her thoughts returned to the meeting only when Joby stood up to speak, looking, Laura had to admit, far less confident than he once had.

"As most of you prob'ly heard already," Joby began, "Lucy Beeker's folks split up last week, and you prob'ly seen how much Lucy's been cryin' since then, so we all know she could use some cheerin' up."

The room's sudden silence was more embarrassed than attentive. Lucy was the school's number-one social outcast. Heavier than Lindwald, and shorter to boot, she talked like a baby, and wore thrift-store clothes. Her brittle blond hair was a fuzzy rat's nest. She'd already been out of school twice that year for head lice, and they said her dandruff rained down on people from clear across the classroom. Laura knew what Joby was going to say as well as anyone, but, unlike the others, she was proud of him.

"I think we should do a secret mission for her," Joby said. The silence became suffocating. Laura was bursting to get up and second the idea, but she had learned by now that support from the Roundtable's only girl usually hurt Joby more than it helped.

Peter Blackwell stood and said, "Lucy's . . . pretty weird, Joby. People'd think we're dweebs."

Laura was halfway to her feet, not caring what it might cost Joby or any-one else, when, to her astonishment, Jamie Lindwald stood, staring hard at Peter, and said, with a frighteningly quiet voice, *"So what, butthead?"*

"Jamie?" Peter said, looking frightened and surprised.

"Only popular kids need help? 'S'at whatcha mean, ya little prick?" Jamie asked, balling his fists.

"No," Peter quavered. "It's . . . I just—"

Jamie turned to Joby. "I'm in."

Looking chagrined, Benjamin stood up as well. "Me too."

"I think it's a great idea!" Laura announced, shooting to her feet.

For a minute, no one else moved or spoke, and Laura wondered if "the girl" should have waited longer to jinx it with her endorsement.

"I'll do it," said Duane Westerlund, looking far from thrilled as everyone turned to stare at him.

"Good," Joby said, looking at no one in particular. "That should be enough. Any ideas on what we should do for her?"

"Next Friday's her birthday," Lindwald said.

The silence that followed this announcement was purely astonished. *Jamie Lindwald knew when Lucy Beeker's birthday was?*

"We should get some stuff together," Jamie went on, "balloons 'n stuff, and fix up her desk maybe, so she's surprised when she comes to school."

"But when are we gonna do it?" Duane protested. "Her mom always drops her off way before class, and Lucy waits around to get picked up again 'til five o'clock sometimes—right on the front steps! Miss Stackly's room is in the front hallway. It's not like Lucy's not gonna see us."

"I can take care of that," Lindwald replied, but would say nothing of how.

✖

They'd all been pretty startled when Jamie finally told them his *simple plan* for evading Lucy's attention. While Laura, Benjamin, and Duane had agreed to help get the signs and decorations together, they had sheepishly declined to break into the school with him later that night to put them up, despite Jamie's assurances that he knew how to get in without damaging anything. Joby had wanted to back out too, but the mission had been his idea, and he wasn't going to let Jamie go it all alone after the way Jamie had backed him at the meeting. So, after telling his folks he was going to study at Benjamin's, he'd come here to school with the sack of balloons and crepe paper to join Lindwald under cover of darkness behind a row of hedges that grew against the building, sneaking toward Miss Stackly's classroom windows.

When they got there, Lindwald grinned back at Joby, then reached up to grab a short length of wire hanging from one of the metal sills. When he tugged it, the window tilted open, freeing a small slip of paper Jamie had left to keep the latch from catching. Joby almost laughed in relief. He'd been afraid Jamie might break the glass or something. Jamie pulled himself up through the window, then helped Joby in. Navigating by the glow of street-lights, they went straight to Lucy's desk and got started.

They had all the balloons inflated and taped to the desk, and were just starting on the signs and crepe paper when Jamie suddenly gasped and lunged for the floor. Joby looked up and saw the red *flash, flash, flash,* reflecting palely off the far wall.

"Get down!" Jamie rasped. *"Someone called the cops!"*

Joby dove for the floor, and hissed, *"Who? Why?"*

"'Cause we broke in, stupid!"

"But how did they know?" Joby insisted. "Are there alarms?"

"I don't know," Jamie growled, "but we gotta get outta here! Don't stand up. They'll see you. Crawl to the door, and run for the back of the school."

"But the hall doors are locked," Joby whispered, feeling drops of sweat trickle down under his shirt as he crawled after Jamie toward the classroom door. "How will we get out?"

"The doors only lock from outside," Jamie replied. "'Cause of fires. From inside, you just push 'em open."

Scrambling out into the corridor, they got up and ran toward the front hallway intersection, then turned down a second hallway toward the school's back exit, but slid to a halt when they got there, staring at the heavy chain wrapped and padlocked around the inside handles.

"What now?" Joby groaned.

"Another window," Jamie said without hesitation. "Come on."

He turned and bolted toward Mr. Bingham's room, but as they entered the room, a flashlight beam swept the glass from outside. Lindwald threw himself against the wall beside the windows, put a finger to his lips, and waved Joby frantically toward a narrow closet to his left. Joby dashed to the closet, and stepped inside. Feeling surprisingly messy piles of stuff around him totter and shift as he brushed against them, Joby held absolutely still, trying not even to breathe, for fear that his treacherous clumsiness might cause an avalanche and give them away, but it was not *his* body that betrayed them.

From out in the classroom came a horrendous crash of breaking glass.

Without thinking, Joby stuck his head out of the closet to see what had happened, and had only an instant to see Jamie standing sullenly amidst the tangle of Mr. Bingham's huge American flag, its heavy toppled pole jammed through the broken pane, before a flashlight beam hit Joby square in the face.

"Stay right there, son!" came an angry, authoritative voice from just behind the beam. "Don't move a *muscle*."

☒

Waiting mutely beside his parents, Joby stared at the Thanksgiving decorations plastered around the school office. The upcoming holiday seemed utterly absurd as he sat, still trying to map the full dimensions of his disaster.

The night before, while Lindwald and one officer had waited out in the patrol car, the other officer had stood in Joby's living room asking his stunned parents if they *wanted* their son "detained." After all the other trouble he'd been in that fall, Joby had been afraid they might say yes, but after assurances from his parents that Joby would be severely punished, the policeman had left him in their "custody," warning that the school might wish to pursue "criminal prosecution" of Joby's "offense."

When the officer had gone, Joby had tried to explain about the secret mission to cheer up Lucy Beeker, but his parents had just stared at him as if he were some creature left by aliens in place of their real child. And why not? He had lied about going to Benjamin's house. Why should they believe anything he said ever again? When they'd sent him to his room, he'd left the door ajar and listened to them argue about things Miss Stackly had said about him, and, to his deep dismay, whether or not to take away his book about Arthur!

"She's right, Miriam," his father had insisted, coming up the stairs toward Joby's room. "The whole thing has gone too far!" Joby had just managed to hide his beloved book behind the bed headboard before his father barged into the room, demanding that he hand it over. When Joby burst into tears instead, his father had insisted that Arthur was not, had *never been,* real, and that Joby needed to start learning to live in the real world. This had only made Joby cry harder. "Blubbering's not going to fix anything, Joby!" his father had scolded. "Sooner or later, a boy's got to stand up and learn to be a man!" He had stormed out after that without remembering the book, and Joby had gone to bed feeling more miserable than he'd ever known a person could feel.

Everyone at school this morning seemed to have heard about Joby's arrest. Benjamin and Laura had seemed afraid even to look at him. Lucy's birthday decorations had been cleared away before anyone even saw them. Some of the guys thought it was cool that Joby had gotten arrested, but others said it only proved Joby wasn't fit to be leader of the Roundtable, not that it mattered anymore, because the principal, Mr. Leonard, had declared the Roundtable over and done for good. Mr. Bingham's supply closet had been vandalized, everything tossed about in piles. Joby, Jamie, and by extension, the Roundtable in general were being blamed. Though Joby had sworn to having no idea how Mr. Bingham's closet had gotten trashed, no one had believed him. By then, Joby had been sure things could get no worse, but they had.

At recess Jamie had abjectly apologized to Joby for getting them caught, and when Joby had reached up to put an understanding hand on his large friend's shoulder, Jamie had flinched away as if Joby's touch had burned right through his jacket. It had taken only an instant for Joby to understand and grow sick with shame. Wrapped up in his own misery, he had failed to consider what Jamie's parents would do. With one stupid act, Joby had ruined everything!

Now, sitting with his parents in plain sight of half the school, waiting to be humiliated yet again by Mr. Leonard, Joby stared into the darkness behind his eyes feeling nothing much at all. Miss Stackly had pulled him aside before class and told him that the school wasn't going to press charges. They weren't even going to expel him, but he was going to be suspended and they were going to suggest to his parents that he see someone called a therapist. Miss Stackly had relayed all this in hushed, sympathetic tones, assuring him that she wanted to relieve his fears about the coming meeting between his folks and Mr. Leonard. But Joby had seen the gleam of satisfaction in her eyes, heard the gloating in her voice, and suspected that, behind his back, she was having the time of her life saying, "I told you so," to everyone at school.

Joby and his parents stood as Mr. Leonard arrived at last.

"We've all got better places to be," he said, waving them toward his office door. "Let's get this over with."

As he marched in shame behind his silent parents, staring at the floor, Joby thought again of Merlin's advice about offering the enemy no imperfections. Despite the wizard's warnings, it seemed pretty clear that he'd managed to defeat *himself* before the devil had even shown up to fight.

8

(A Dork Among Deities)

School had been out for twenty minutes, but biology was Joby's favorite subject, and Mr. Estes always let him stay after and care for the classroom's little zoo. When he'd fed the geckoes their grubs, the tarantulas their crickets, and finished cleaning the aquariums, Joby spent a while in silent communion with all the little captives, then gathered his books and headed out into the hallway.

Turning to make sure the door had latched, he managed to spill the contents of his binder, then smack his head on the door handle as he stooped to pick them up. He spent a moment rubbing the sore spot, but took it otherwise in stride. After three years, his "awkward phase" had still not passed. Nor had he seen any of that growth it was supposed to have foretold. He still looked more like a fifth-grader than the almost fourteen-year-old eighth-grader he was.

Outside, the afternoon was bright and warm with premonitions of spring, though March swas still a week away. Hearing the crack of a bat and a swell of approving shouts from the athletic field, Joby remembered that tryouts for the baseball team were today, and wistfully decided to go watch for a minute before walking to his therapy appointment.

Entering the stands, he caught his sleeve on the chain-link gate, ripping it just below the elbow. His mother would not be pleased—or surprised. With a resigned sigh, he sat on the first-row bleacher and spotted Benjamin waiting for his turn at bat between Paul Boser and Jamie Lindwald.

Jamie had grown even huger since grammar school, making him the eighth grade's uncontested giant, but it was Benjamin's lean and chiseled grace that Joby envied. Benjamin's lengthening frame had embraced its growth spurt with no awkward phase at all. Joby's friend had just grown taller, faster, stronger, and better looking on an almost daily basis since sixth grade, until now, watching him hurl a football, swing a bat, or trot with unself-conscious assurance around the diamond, often left Joby aching with an envy bordering on grief.

After a lame infield pop-up, Boser stepped back and surrendered the bat to Benjamin, who came to the plate, swayed fluidly up into his stance, and eyed the pitcher with hawkish concentration. The pitcher gave him a conspiratorial grin. He and Benjamin were future teammates, not opponents, and Ben was the kind of hero people wanted to be liked by, not the kind they tried to overthrow. That everyone knew Benjamin's *best* friend was still Joby Peterson was nine-tenths of Joby's social salvation now.

The pitcher stretched back and hurled the ball. Benjamin's swing was as sure and smooth as flowing water, the connection so hard and clean that no one in the field even raised a glove, but only turned to watch in admiration as it sailed up and over the fence. Benjamin watched as well, his satisfaction neither overblown, nor falsely disguised. With a grim smile, he stepped back and handed the bat to Jamie.

Golden, Joby thought. *Benjamin is golden.*

"Hi, Joby!"

Joby turned to find Laura walking through the chain-link gate to join him. Her hair was short and styled these days, and she'd taken to wearing dresses a lot more often than she had in grammar school, but she still carried herself more like a guy than any other girl he knew. Scanning the lineup, she plopped down beside him, and slapped her books onto the bench.

"You trying out?" she asked without turning from the field to look at him.

"What do *you* think?" Joby scoffed. She and Benjamin were the only two people in the world who still didn't seem to get that he had lost it—whatever "it" had been.

"*I* think you psych yourself out," she replied, turning to him with a challenging smile. "But I couldn't care less if you play baseball or not."

"Thanks," Joby said flatly. "You come to watch Benjamin?"

She whirled to look at him as if he'd thrown a slug at her. "I *came* to say hi to *you,* you *spaz!*"

"Oh," he said, "sorry." He was a geek. He'd been a geek for years now. So why did it still surprise him every time he proved it again? Desperate to move the conversation along, he asked, "What did you get on Carlisle's test?"

Laura rolled her eyes, and huffed, "B minus." She tossed her short hair back in irritation. "What'd you get?"

Strike two, Joby thought, not daring to answer, though she saw through his silence instantly. To his relief, she only laughed. "An A, of course. How *stupid* of me not to guess! Why didn't they just skip you into high school?"

"Too immature," he replied without cracking a smile.

"Joby!" she snorted in disgust. "Can't you ever just— Oh, never mind. Who are you taking to the dance?"

"What dance?"

"The *spring* dance. . . . *Next week?* Is there some *other* dance coming up?"

Joby adopted a comically exaggerated scowl. "Laura, think for a minute about *me* out on a crowded dance floor! People would get *hurt*—maybe *lots* of people. I'd feel responsible." She frowned. *"I really would!"* he insisted, still hoping for a laugh.

"See?" Laura demanded. "That's what I mean. You've made up this total jinx thing for yourself, and you *never* give it a rest! How can anyone as smart as you have so much trouble learning to say something *nice* about himself?"

Strike three. Joby looked glumly away, and said, "I bet Benjamin would give his right arm to take you. He can dance."

With a furious growl, Laura grabbed her books and sprang from the bench. *"Joby Peterson!"* she screeched. "Sometimes you just make me want to *scream myself hoarse!"* She whirled angrily away and started toward the gate.

"What?!" Joby demanded. "What did I do *now?"*

✖

For the fifth time, Miriam went out to peer through the living room windows, then turned to stare at the phone. Joby should have been home from school an hour ago. She had called the school office twice already, and gotten nothing but a recording. She paced beside the fireplace for a moment, then headed back into the kitchen where a meat loaf was taking shape much too slowly.

It wasn't just the nightmares anymore. She was ambushed even in daylight now by overwhelming premonitions of impending disaster as vivid as any TV news flash. She'd even started hearing voices: most often a woman's derisive laughter, though never for more than an instant—just enough to make her start and turn, unsure whether she'd really heard anything at all.

She wiped her hands on her apron, and pressed them to her temples in distress. Was she going crazy? Frank hadn't come right out and said so yet, but he'd implied it often enough. Miriam was sure it was that woman *Cally* putting such ideas in his head. He'd stopped mentioning her, but he spent half his time down at that damn Filling Station now, and Miriam knew what was going on. She also knew that if she brought it up, Frank would only call it more evidence of her lunacy! She hadn't any proof, and without that, she was helpless.

Dear God! Where is Joby?!

She started for the phone to call the police, then stopped, imagining the derision on Frank's face when he found out. Instead, she went back and began fiercely kneading the meat loaf again. If Frank's love affair with that bar weren't hard enough on *her,* look at what it had done to Joby's self-esteem! A boy shouldn't have to wait for his father to come home from the *bar* every afternoon. She wondered how Frank could pay Joby's damn therapy bills every month, and not see—

She froze, then closed her eyes and put a hand to her forehead, heedless of the grease. How could she have been so stupid? Joby was at his therapy appointment. She shook her head in helpless self-loathing. Thank God she hadn't called the police. She stared blankly at the meat loaf for a moment, then she sagged onto a stool by the counter, and began to cry.

Somehow, somewhere, everything had gone so wrong. If only there were someone to help her, someone to . . . to show her how to fix it all. *Oh, God,* she thought. *Oh, God, please, please, help us!*

It had been so many years since she had prayed that at first she didn't realize what she was doing; but the minute she did, it was as if someone had spoken straight to her heart, and told her exactly what her mistake had been. She had been a fool to think she didn't need God's help. Maybe, she thought, if she returned to Him, He would return to them. She got up and nearly ran to the phone book. If she was lucky, morning Mass would be late enough somewhere that she could go after Frank and Joby were gone.

❧

"No, Cally. It's my fault," Frank sighed. "Mason and Meyer would still be Mason, Meyer, and Peterson if I'd just kept my resentment to myself. The whole damn Goldtree fiasco would be nothing but a bad memory by now if it weren't for my *goddamn pride!*"

Cally gazed at Frank as if he were a pouty child. "I still say you're way too hard on yourself, Frank. You had every right to be angry."

Frank traced lines in the frost on his beer glass, and shook his head pensively. "Not for what it's cost my family. I should have bit my tongue and ridden it out." He took a long pull on his beer, then stared at the glass as if it held the ashes of his favorite dog. "The whole thing's driven Miriam right to the edge, Cally . . . and it's *destroying* Joby." Frank drained his glass, then looked up at Cally as if hoping she'd give in and berate him.

"Want another?" she asked.

"No. I should be going."

He made no move to leave, however, only sat staring morosely at his empty glass. "He used to be such . . . such an incredible little kid. Now, I can hardly look at him without dying of shame."

"Kids go through rough phases," Cally said, turning away to wipe down her back counter, "but they don't lose themselves forever."

"All I ever wanted," Frank murmured, "was to be a good husband, and a good father, Cally. Even in high school, I dreamed of having a family. Now I do, and I'm just . . . letting them down." There was a pressure in his chest that made him want to smash all the glasses behind the bar, or shoot out the mirror, or crash through the plateglass window, but he couldn't seem to move. He could hardly even breathe. *"What's wrong with me?"* he whispered harshly.

"You know, Frank," Cally said, turning back to face him, "I'm not going to feed this little pity party you've got going." She tossed her hair back, and offered him a reproachful grin. "There's simply nothing wrong with you!" She leaned forward to look him in the eye. "Miriam and Joby are two *lucky, lucky* people. If you'd just get that through your pretty head," she ran her fingers playfully through his hair, "the rest of this would sort itself out in no time at all." She leaned away again, continuing to wipe down her countertops.

She was so pretty. . . . And so kind. Almost . . . almost he told her about the depraved nightmare that still plagued him after all these years. A hundred times, he'd wanted to, sure that she'd understand, that she might even know how to make it stop. But just thinking of it now made him loathe himself; Joby hiding in that locker, his thumb jammed between lips smeared with lipstick, clutching at his little dress. . . .

No, if Cally ever saw how sick Frank really was inside, he'd never be able to look her in the face again. . . . As if she'd ever want him to.

※

When Benjamin went to Joby's house on Saturday morning and found him already out, he didn't needed to ask where he was. A short time later, he found Joby at their old tournament field bent down in the new spring grass, peering at something beneath the oak tree Laura Bayer had fallen out of back when they were kids.

"Whatcha lookin' at, Joby?" Benjamin called, as he started across the clearing.

"Damselflies," Joby replied without standing or turning.

Benjamin stopped carefully beside him, and saw two tiny turquoise dragonflies balanced atop a stalk of wild oat. One of the creatures was perched on the other's back, its long tail arched to clasp its companion.

"What are they doing?" Benjamin asked. "Fighting?"

"They're mating," Joby said with scientific dispassion.

Mating. The word evoked a slew of exciting, if somewhat embarrassing, associations in Benjamin's mind. It had been almost a year since he had begun to notice how good it felt to lie in bed at night wearing nothing but his skin, and a mere six months since he had discovered that certain even more awesome sensations could be conjured without waiting for sleep or dreams.

"Joby?" he said uncertainly. "Have you . . . do you ever think about—" As the word "sex" balanced on his tongue, Joby turned to face him with the same clinical regard he had trained on the damselflies. Feeling his cheeks flame, Benjamin aborted the question.

"About what?" Joby pressed.

"Nothing. . . . It . . . nothing." Suddenly, he knew that Joby wouldn't . . . that he surely hadn't . . . that he would think Benjamin a freak.

"Come on," Joby insisted. "What were you going to say?"

Benjamin scrambled for some plausible substitution. "Do you ever think about the Roundtable?"

Joby looked back down at the damselflies, his clinical expression replaced by sullen embarrassment. "Course not," he said. "I'm no kid anymore."

Benjamin was surprised at Joby's tone and at the depth of his own disappointment. Whole landscapes of memory stirred in Benjamin's mind, awakening thoughts that had been dormant for years. "Do you still believe in that quest?" he asked. "You know . . . against the enemy?"

"What do *you* think?" Joby mumbled scornfully.

"I don't *know!*" Benjamin said. "That's why I'm askin'!"

"Whadaya want me to say? That I still sit around figuring out how to visit *Camelot,* and help *King Arthur* fight the devil?" Joby swiped angrily at his suddenly reddening eyes. "I don't need *you* making fun of me too, Benjamin. There's enough people doing that."

"I'm not making fun of you!" Benjamin protested. "I . . . I just always wondered what happened to," he threw his hands up, "all that. . . . I miss it."

Joby sighed, seeming to fall in on himself. "I'm sorry, Ben. It's just that . . . I wish I could still believe it. You have no idea how much." He turned to stare off into the thickets that had been their boar-hunting forest in better times. "You remember that dream I used to have? . . . The one with all the candles?"

Benjamin, nodded.

"I still have it," Joby said. "All the time. . . . And I wake up feeling like somebody punched my soul right out of my stomach, and I have no idea where they put it."

Benjamin reached out and punched his shoulder, deciding it was time to change the subject. "You takin' Laura to the dance?" he asked.

"She asked me . . . but I can't dance. I told her that, but she got so mad I don't think she'd go anywhere with me now." Joby looked tentatively at Benjamin. "You should ask her."

"*Me?* Joby, you are such a *dork!* She doesn't wanna go with *me!*"

"Why not?"

"'Cause she's got a crush *this big* on Joby Peterson!" he laughed, stretching out his arms. "You must be blind, Joby! Just go with her, and stand around if you want to. Trust me. She's not gonna care if you dance."

"Why would she want to go *stand around* with the class spaz?" Joby frowned.

"Joby, if you don't take Laura to the dance, I'm gonna tell every guy at school you wear purple underwear, and suck your thumb at night."

"*No you won't.*" Joby grimaced. "That's *disgusting,* Benjamin."

"Yes, I will, Joby." He was careful not to smile. "I'm *dead serious.* Nothin's gonna happen at that dance half as embarrassing as what I'll do to you if you chicken out, so get your butt in gear and ask her. It's time you got a clue, Peterson."

"Who are *you* taking, *Vierra?*"

"I," Benjamin said, hoping to cover his embarrassment with a casual tone, "am going with Duane and Jamie, and Johnny Mayhew."

"*Oh!* So *I* have to ask a *girl,* but *you're* going with the *baseball team?*"

"I'm just keeping myself free to dance with *lots* of girls!" Benjamin bragged, hoping Joby would buy it. "Believe me, though. If I had someone like Laura drooling over me, I'd take her!"

"Okay," Joby moped, "I'll ask her, but if she says no, you can't get me for that."

"She won't." Benjamin grinned. "Shall we shake on it, Sir Joby?"

⚬

The big night arrived. Joby's mom had gotten him a new set of slacks and a button-down shirt for the occasion, and Joby had purchased a small cluster of freesia and iris at the supermarket florist, remembering how Laura had liked them so long ago in the hospital. He'd even spent half an hour in the bathroom before dinner, combing his hair. Feeling nervous and excited, he opened the refrigerator and looked in to make sure the flowers hadn't wilted, then sat down with his parents to eat dinner.

The hiccups started halfway through his meal. They got so bad, so quickly, that he had to stop eating and lie down in the living room. But they only got worse, becoming surprisingly painful, until it was hard for him to breathe. His mother made him lean forward and swallow cups of water, eat spoonfuls of granulated sugar, and breathe into a paper bag, but nothing helped. Finally, half an hour before he and his dad were supposed to go pick up Laura, Joby went to his room, as much to escape his father's disapproving scowls as his mother's increasingly frantic ministrations. He had never heard of such hiccups. They were bearable as long as he remained lying down, but the minute he stood, they became huge gasping spasms that hurt his throat, and threatened to burst his lungs.

Ten minutes before they were supposed to leave, Joby's father came into his room, trying to look amused.

"Hiccups, eh?" he said wryly, sitting down on Joby's bedside. "I got a rash before my first date. I ever tell you that, son?"

Joby shook his head, fearing that speaking might make his hiccups worse.

His father patted his arm, and looked away. "It's always scary to do things we've never done," he said. "But that doesn't mean we shouldn't try. Remember how scary it was learning to ride your bike? But you weren't sorry you tried, were you?"

Since they'd never given his bike back to him, Joby didn't think the example a very good one, but he shook his head anyway.

Seeming to realize his mistake as well, Joby's dad grinned crookedly, and said, "You know, it's probably long past time you got that bike back. I'll talk with your mother about it while you're at the dance."

Unable to believe this sudden burst of luck, Joby started to sit up, only to be wracked by another loud and painful spasm, forcing him to lie back down again.

"I can't go," he groaned. "I can't even stand up."

A flash of irritation crossed his father's face. Joby hoped that didn't mean he'd changed his mind about the bike.

"You told Laura you'd take her to the dance, son. I'm sure she's gone to lots of trouble to get ready, just like you have." He gave Joby another reassuring smile. "Tell you what, sport. I'll call Laura's house and let them know we're going to be a little late. You just relax for a while. Let those darn hiccups settle down, and then we'll go. Okay?"

"Dad, I'm not doing this to get out of the dance," Joby said, suddenly re-alizing that's what his father was mad about. "I *like* Laura. It's just—" He was cut short by another loud, hard hiccup, and realized he didn't want to talk about this.

"It's just *what*, son? Eighth grade seems a little late to still be doing the *cooties thing*, doesn't it?"

"It's not that," Joby said. "I just don't think I like her like . . . you know . . . as a girlfriend. I—" He gulped in another hiccup. "I just like her more with"—another hiccup, "—with my mind, I guess."

His father stood up, clearly more than irritated. "Son," he said, "you're not a little boy anymore, so, let's just lay it on the table. You like a girl with *this*," he pointed at his chest, "or *this*," he pointed at his crotch. "*Not* with *this*!" He pointed at his forehead. "Is that clear?"

Joby hiccupped.

At that moment, Joby's mother came into the room, but his dad told her that they were having a "man-to-man chat" and that she wasn't needed.

"What on earth are you so angry about, Frank?" she demanded. "Are you trying to make his hiccups worse?" She turned a worried gaze toward Joby. "Look at him! He's scared to death!"

"Course he's scared!" his father snapped. "He's even scared of girls now, 'cause *you've* turned him into one!"

"Well, if you don't like how *I'm* raising him, maybe you should come home from that *bar* occasionally, and try *your* hand at it!" she snapped back.

To his horror, Joby hiccupped again.

His father turned toward him like a huge wave about to break, and said, very quietly, "Maybe your mother's right, Joby. Maybe we should be doing more things together. Next weekend," he paused, in angry contemplation, "we'll go hunting."

"*What?*" Joby's mother shrieked. "That's *stupid*! People get *shot*! Just last—"

"*Listen to you!*" his father shouted. "Is there *anything* he's not supposed to be afraid of?"

"*I forbid it!*" she yelled.

"Dad," Joby quavered, terrified to hear himself speaking, unable somehow to stop, "I . . . I don't want to kill *anything*."

His father went oddly rigid. For an instant, Joby was afraid his dad might hit him, but his father turned to his mother instead with a face full of pain that scared Joby even more. "*Look* what you've done to him!" his father rasped. Then he stepped past her, and headed for the door.

"Where are you *going*?" Joby's mother said.

"Out," his father replied without turning.

"Out *where*?" she demanded.

"Just out."

"To that *bar*?" his mother shrilled.

His father didn't even pause.

"Come back here!" she snapped. *"Don't you dare walk out on me that way!"*

Joby's dad turned in the doorway, and Joby suddenly knew with dreadful certainty that this time he would not be coming back. "I am going," his father said with terrible calm, "to tell Laura's parents that my invalid son will be unable to escort her to the dance tonight. Then I am going to have a drink, yes."

✸

"Kallaystra!" Lucifer crowed as she materialized beside the obelisk in his office. "Congratulations! What a *triumph,* my dear!"

"It did turn out rather well, didn't it," she said, beaming. "I wish you could have seen his face when I—"

"But I did!" Lucifer enthused. "I watched the entire affair from here! It's *you,* I fear, who missed out on the *wonderful* scene at their home." He gestured toward the wall behind him and a flickering blue screen appeared. "Behold the marvelous harvest of all you've sown, my dear!"

They spent the next few minutes enjoying a surround-sound replay of the scene in Joby's bedroom. In this screening, Trephila could be quite clearly seen orchestrating Joby's hiccups, while Tique goaded Joby's father into a rage, and Eurodia shepherded Miriam in precisely on cue.

"Hiccups," Lucifer mused sardonically. "How like them."

They watched almost fondly as Frank raged into the Filling Station, ranting and moaning about having betrayed his family and destroyed all their lives. Kallaystra, in her well-worn role as Cally the wonder-barmaid, calmed him down and made him tell her the whole sordid story, heedless of the barely concealed attention afforded him by numerous scandalized patrons.

"Wait a minute," they watched "Cally" say incredulously at the end of his confession. "You accused your son of being *queer*? Frank! Are you out of your *mind*?"

Frank's mortified silence was just too rich. "No!" he stammered. "I never said that! I—I just—"

"Well, it sure sounds like that's what you *meant*!" Cally cut him off, shaking her head as if unable to fathom how such a smart man could be so horrendously foolish. "Frank, he's—*what? Thirteen? All* boys his age are afraid of girls. *You* know that!"

"Oh my!" Kallaystra laughed, fairly glowing with pride. "It's better than *being* there! Look at him! He'll *never* be able to go home *now.*"

"Yes," Lucifer breathed. The replay zoomed in and froze on Frank's devastated expression. "Look at that!" Lucifer exclaimed, enraptured. He turned to her gleefully. "I can hardly express my appreciation. Just think, my dear! When we win, this small pleasure will be multiplied *billions* of times!"

"Will it?" she cooed, seductively. "You must have such *grand* designs laid out in that relentless mind of yours." When he failed to take the bait, she asked, "What should our next move be?"

"Now that the child's father is securely out of the way, we must be sure to anchor the mother in place," he replied. "First, let's relieve her of those troubling nightmares. You might even arrange a few really *nice* dreams, just to hammer the point home."

"But, Bright One," Kallaystra objected, "she's this far from real madness! A few more well placed frights, and—"

"I understand your disappointment," Lucifer soothed. "But we don't want Joby taken away from her. No one can hurt a boy as badly as his own mother can, after all."

"Oh," Kallaystra pouted. "I suppose you're right."

"Besides, she's been sneaking off to morning Mass recently. I'm thinking that with 'damned if you don't' nailed down nicely, it's time to work on 'damned if you do.'"

"Ahhhh," Kallaystra replied, with a begrudging smile.

"I believe Father Richter's tireless prayers for *importance* are finally about to be answered." He grinned, but his smile vanished as quickly as it had arrived. "We need to stop retarding his growth, however. I've never been very happy about that, actually. I instructed the triangle to make him physically inept. I said nothing about turning him into a dwarf."

"I will speak to them, if you wish, Bright One," Kallaystra said, always looking for opportunities to ingratiate, "but I don't think it's any of their doing. I asked them about it once, and they assured me his failure to bloom was just a happy accident."

"An accident!" Lucifer said skeptically. "The boy still has baby teeth, for heaven's sake! At fourteen? That seems a rather remarkable accident. If we're not doing it, who is?"

"He's a late bloomer." She shrugged. "It does happen, and you know better than I how usefully such conditions can be leveraged. Why should it concern you so?"

"Because having yanked him one way, I can hardly yank him the other now if he's not equipped to go there," Lucifer said irritably. "More than that, it makes me nervous to see something so oddly amiss in his life that we didn't instigate. Think about who we're up against here, Kallaystra, and ask yourself what He might be trying to accomplish by stunting the boy's maturity this way?"

"A point," she conceded. "So what do you suggest?"

"If we're not the one's who've been preserving all that baby fat, then let's make it leave," Lucifer said crossly. "Must I spell everything out—even to you, Kallaystra? Have your esteemed colleague, Malcephalon, continue to nurture shame and guilt within him, but on the outside, I want him growing. Within a year, I want him to be as attractive to his lusty adolescent peers as he is unprepared to deal with what they're after. And by all means, let's get him back to church before he strays beyond your pet priest's reach."

9
(Sex)

Joby had ridden to St. Albee's that morning and hiked up through a wooded ravine behind the priory to celebrate his sixteenth birthday in blessed solitude. He'd grown quite accustom to his parents' separation by now. Once the sound of muffled weeping had finally stopped leaking from his mother's room at nights, Joby's sense of guilt had faded some, and all their lives had settled into manageable, if somewhat lackluster, routines. Though often rather boring, his life was far from restful. An endless landslide of homework, after-school tutoring, student government, therapy appointments, and church youth group meetings left Joby always feeling as if swarms of urgent tasks were being shamefully neglected. With all of that finally on pause until September, there had been no birthday present Joby wanted more than to sit alone watching herds of cotton clouds graze lazily from horizon to horizon as the day passed in quiet, unrushed communion with nature.

His father had called before breakfast to say happy birthday, and confirm their celebration plans on Friday night. Joby's birthday had fallen on a Monday this year, and his father was buried in work. He'd started a small architectural firm of his own, which made Joby happy because it made his father happy, though the venture had rendered his father poorer and less available than ever. They got along much better now, though Joby felt no more "manly" these days than he ever had.

For all Father Richter's recurring warnings against the snare of vanity, Joby could not help wishing he looked, or even felt, more like all the other guys. By now, Ben was every inch the proverbial bronze god, but, while Joby had finally begun to grow again a few years back, he was headed for his junior year still looking fifteen at best. His mother kept assuring him that everyone would be jealous when he looked twenty-nine at forty, but that seemed cold comfort. To cap his woes, botched dental surgery to get rid of his persistent baby teeth had made it necessary to put braces on him just as everyone else was getting theirs off. Sometimes, it felt like he was growing backward.

A large, glossy raven flew over Joby's head, audibly slicing the air with its powerful wings, then stalled, banking on the breeze, and returned to perch on a nearby branch, where it stared at Joby, then croaked and rattled some kind of greeting. Over the years, Joby had come to feel an almost urgent kinship with animals, envying their lives out here beyond the paved confines of his own world. Animals suffered no one's expectations but their own. They did not belittle or shame. They did not make promises—or betray them. Doing his best to match the bird's percussive sounds, Joby cawed and clacked an answer to the raven's address. The bird cocked its head, stared at him with one dark marble eye, then took wing and glided away swiftly down the hillside, leaving Joby to wonder what rude or ridiculous things he'd said to the dignified bird.

A glance at his watch told him he had better leave if he were going to get back in time for the birthday dinner his mother was preparing. He stood reluctantly, brushed off his pants, and made his way down the grassy slope toward the ravine, then hiked through the cool oak woods to where he'd left his bike stashed behind the priory.

During the past few years, Joby had become a kind of honorary member of the priory community. In the company of St. Albee's priests, he had finally found something to trust and care about as he'd once cared about his Roundtable club. Only this was something real—something lasting. Under Father Richter's tutelage, Joby had come to see that the Arthur he had once searched for in fairy tales might be found, after all, in God. Joby had been baptized on Easter Sunday, the year before last, and often found himself talking to God these days as he had once talked to Arthur. God did not talk back, of course, as he'd once imagined Arthur did, but it was enough just to know that someone *real* was listening now.

Father Richter had taken a remarkable interest in Joby from the day his mother had reintroduced them, teaching him far more about scripture and theology than Ben seemed to have learned in his entire lifetime as a Catholic. The old priest had even shyly confessed to regarding Joby as the son he would never have—though Joby had never found, in Father Richter, the father he had lost. God had filled that gap. It was *God's* knight Joby aspired to be now, for in God alone had Joby found a mentor who seemed to harbor any greater ambition for him than that he be as little trouble as possible.

The bike ride back was long and peaceful until, several blocks from home, Joby glanced down Ben's street, and saw his oldest friend standing by the car his parents had just helped him buy, kissing Rebecca Medina. Joby pedaled quickly past, not wanting to be caught looking, but three blocks later his mind still clutched at that one brief glimpse into an alien life furnished with cars and girls and confidence.

Laura was going out with super-jock Kevin Branscom now, a senior with a build like Ben's, and a shiny red Camero. Joby didn't even have a permit. His mother had refused to allow it, despite his A in driver's ed. Joby tried to imagine himself pedaling over to pick up Laura on his bike. *That* would sure have Kevin running scared.

At home, he parked his bike in the side yard and went in the back door, careful to wipe his shoes clean on the mat. The scents of cooking drew him toward the kitchen.

"Smell's awesome, Mom!"

"Hi, honey!" She turned to give him a hug. "Have a nice day?"

"Great." He smiled. "You?"

"Wonderful," she said. "Why don't you go wash up. This is just about ready."

Walking through the dining room, Joby saw that his mother had hung crepe paper and balloons everywhere, and set the table as if for two visiting dignitaries, but despite the festive decorations, the house seemed full of gloom. Joby told himself it came of staying so long out in the bright sunlight, and went to wash his hands.

❊

"Well, Karen, *Kevin* may be dating his car, but *I'm not.*" Laura looked at her watch. "Oh my God! If I don't hang up, my parents will call the phone police."

"They can't," Karen laughed. "You're on the *phone.* So, are you telling me you're dumping Kevin?"

"No," Laura sighed. "I'm just saying . . . he's wearing a little thin, that's all."

"You *poor thing,*" Karen scoffed. "Kevin Branscom's hands all over *everything.* I'm sure there's not a girl at school who doesn't thank God every night she's not you."

"Shut up, Karen. At least your boyfriend's idea of intelligent conversation isn't debating the weight-gain benefits of burgers versus Mexican food. That's the only thing Kevin seems to think about, besides his car . . . and getting . . . you know."

"Yes, I *do,*" Karen vamped. "And, FYI, Brian's interests aren't nearly as *broad* as you seem to think, which suits me fine."

"What!" Laura demanded. "You're not doing *that* with Brian!"

There was a somehow smirky silence on Karen's end.

"*I don't believe it!*" Laura gasped.

"Laura, grow up!" Karen scoffed. "We're not little kids anymore. Brian's *graduating* next year! Besides, he *knows* perfectly well we don't even get *started* until I *see* his little stash of Trojans. I can't *believe* you and Kevin really never—"

"With *Kevin*?!!" Laura blurted out. "*Where?* On the hood of his *Camero*—in between mouthfuls of *burger*? Don't make me *retch*!"

"Well, then with someone else," Karen said impatiently. "We're not gonna be beautiful forever, you know. Better get it while we're hot, I say."

"Oh, *please! Too late!*" Laura scoffed. "We're seventeen!"

"It's your call," Karen said, "but I'm not just going to wait around for *Mr. Perfect.*"

Laura shook her head, and turned to look out her bedroom window. "I wish Joby had a clue."

"*Joby Peterson?*" Karen said incredulously. "He's got pretty eyes, and nice hair—for a *twelve*-year-old. . . . Brian says he's gay."

"*Joby's not gay!*" Laura snapped. "Where does Brian get off spreading such bullshit?!" She heard Karen laugh quietly. "Look, Karen. He's into church, okay? He has a whole set of values. If you don't know what those are, you can look it up under, *'make the world a better place.'* That prob'ly seems *gay* to Brian the stud-wonder, but I—"

"You don't need to get *nasty*, Laura," Karen said frostily.

"You don't call what you said about Joby nasty?" Laura asked.

"*Okay! I'm sorry!* I had no idea you were in *love* with this guy."

Laura slammed the phone down without caring what Karen would think. "You can be such a bitch," she muttered, then went to her bedroom window to watch shadows stretch across her lawn in the last clear light of day, and wonder what had ever happened to the Joby she still remembered from so long ago.

✸

Disguised as a mourning cloak butterfly, Gabriel perched tenuously atop a wreath of chrysanthemums someone had left at the feet of a marble angel, then fluttered into the air again in Miriam's wake as she moved slowly through the Mt. Madonna Cemetery toward her parents' grave site. Her head was bowed, her hands thrust into the pockets of her coat, and her shoulders hunched as if against a cold wind, despite the pleasant summer morning. At the grave site, she pulled a handkerchief from her purse, and bent down to clean the black granite headstone's polished face. When she had finished, she remained hunched over and motionless, gazing at the simple inscription:

IN LOVING MEMORY:
ABIGAIL MARY EMERSON
1893–1956
EMERY MERRILL EMERSON
1880–1979

It seemed especially cruel to Gabriel that she should suffer such deception, even in this. The angel wondered, yet again, why the old man had chosen to perpetrate such a seemingly senseless fraud on his own daughter. How much better might both Miriam and her son have come through all of this, Gabe thought, had her father simply been there to turn to. The old wizard's untimely pretense made so little sense. Then again, when had the motives of wizards ever made sense, even to angels?

"How did you ever raise me without Mom there?" Miriam whispered before turning to sit down against the headstone. She folded her arms as if against a chill and, haltingly, started speaking to her father about how terribly she longed to repair her marriage and how unequal she felt to raising her son alone.

Perched on a small bouquet of daisies not fifteen feet away, Gabriel listened, slowly opening and closing his wings in the sunlight, and wishing with all his heart that he could do something. He had never understood why the Creator had agreed to such a one-sided set of rules for this wager. Especially *this* wager!

Filled with frustration, Gabriel realized that, strictly speaking, his Lord had only forbade him to help *Joby* uninvited, *not* those around him. Surely one fleeting bit of comfort for Miriam wouldn't constitute any real breach of the Creator's command.

He fluttered up to land unnoticed on Miriam's shoulder, and sent his faith in the Creator, and his own care for Miriam into both her mind and body, then watched her careworn face relax, her eyes close, her hand reach back to stroke the polished surface of the headstone. As Gabriel fluttered away across the cemetery lawn, her face softened in a smile, as rare these days as it was lovely.

❋

While Rebecca was still off in the bathroom with her girlfriends, doing God knew what, Ben began his second circuit around the pool deck, sipping at his drink, nodding at the occasional familiar face, bobbing his head to the music, and trying to look something other than bored. Pete Blackwell's Summer Kick-Off party was Hawaiian-themed, but the thought of donning some loud flowered shirt had made Ben feel like a corny lounge singer, so he'd opted for plain beach casual, and a simple onyx stud in his left ear. A year ago, he'd have given not a single thought to what he wore, but within days of their first date, it had become clear that if *he* didn't fuss over his appearance, Rebecca *would,* and while Ben liked some parts of her attention quite a lot, *that* kind wasn't one of them.

A burst of catcalls and laughter from behind him made Ben turn in time to see Kevin Branscom holding Laura's upper arms from behind, amusing his buddies by pretending he was going to push her into the pool, only to pull her back from the edge as she tried to wriggle free of his grasp.

"Saved yer life!" Kevin grinned, turning her around to face him. "You owe me now, girl. Come on. You know what I want," he burbled, as if addressing a toddler while he puckered up and leaned in for a kiss.

To Kevin's obvious displeasure, Laura twisted away before his visibly greasy lips found any purchase. "Try asking again," she said with an almost unforced laugh, "when you've wiped that big string of cheese off your chin, Kevin." Kevin's friends clearly found her gambit even more entertaining than his, which didn't pleased Kevin. Letting go of her to reach up and wipe his face, he found the long string of cheese left there from nachos he'd been wolfing down a moment earlier. Looking first at it, then at her, as if the disgusting artifact were entirely her fault somehow, he huffed, "Whatever," and waved her away as if she'd just blown the opportunity of a lifetime.

Ben tried pretty hard not to judge people, but for all Kevin's ability on the field and reputation as a hunk, no matter how Ben sliced it, Kevin Branscom was just an inexcusable jerk. Ben never understood what someone as sharp as Laura was doing in his clutches to begin with, much less why she'd stayed this long. For all his own reputation around school as a ladies' man, girls were as mystifying to Ben now as they'd been when he was ten.

As Laura seized the opportunity to escape Kevin's presence for a more secluded corner of the yard, Ben followed, and sat down beside her on a bench beyond the light of Pete's tiki torches.

"How ya doin'?" he asked, casually.

"I'm tired," she said, and sounded it.

"Good," Ben said, looking back toward the crowd of partyers around the pool. "Does that mean you're finally dumping meathead? Like, *tonight, I* hope?"

"I've been meaning to for months," she conceded without objection, or even attitude. "I don't know why I haven't."

"Me neither," Ben said, still not looking at her for fear of seeming too interested and shutting her down. "You could have anyone at school you wanted, Laura. He's not even close to worthy of you."

"You offering?" she asked, almost defiantly.

Ben turned to her in surprise. "I'm with Rebecca," he said, before he could check himself.

"Who's about as worthy of you as Kevin is of me," Laura said, still sounding as if this were some kind of dare.

"Yeah, okay. You got me," Ben said, looking down into his glass of cola, and wondering how much she'd seen before he'd recovered his composure.

"It's probably not my place to say it, Ben—especially right now—but you really ought to hear the way she talks about you when you're not around. She's probably off with her little fan club right now, parading every detail of your sexual exploits together."

"Our *what?*" Ben said, whirling to face her.

Laura studied him for a moment in the dim light, then nodded. "I didn't think so," she said, managing to sound both satisfied and apologetic at the same time.

"Well," Ben said, grinning in embarrassment, hoping the light was too dim for her to see him blush, "I guess she's got appearances to think about." He shrugged ruefully, still grinning. "Probably hasn't done my rep any harm either. Maybe I should get her some kind of little thank-you gift."

"I'm sorry, Ben," Laura said, laying a hand gently on his arm. "I knew she was lying. Really."

"Yeah," Ben sighed, "well, I guess while we're bein' all honest like this, I should admit that it's not like I haven't come plenty close a few times—like, every other day." He shook his head. "The thing is, I just can't ever figure out what I'm gonna say to her afterward. 'I love you? No wait, that's a lie?' What we have is fun enough, Laura, but I just can't see going any further until I have *some* plan I can at least pretend to believe in about the 'ever after' part." He looked up at Laura's shadowed face, realizing how much he trusted her, and, in contrast, how little he had ever trusted Rebecca. So little, in fact, that he really wasn't that disappointed, or even surprised, by what Laura had told him. "I'd never risk saying this to anyone but you, Laura, but I think I'm going to wait until I've found someone I really love, or at least really think I love."

"So," she said, almost timidly, after a lengthy pause. "That brings us back to my question. If not Kevin and Rebecca, who?"

Ben looked away, aching to keep on being as honest as they'd suddenly become for just one more moment. But, as with Rebecca, he couldn't quite kid himself into dismissing what he knew was true—even in pursuit of what he wanted.

"I'd leave Rebecca for you in a heartbeat, Laura," he said soberly, "if I really thought your heart wasn't already spoken for." He turned to look her in the eye again. "Just tell me you're all done waiting for Joby, and I'll go put Rebecca's hand in Kevin's right this minute." He looked back into the crowd around the pool. "Hell. She'd probably go for it without a thought. Kevin's car's more tricked than mine. And Kevin's the *senior* varsity quarterback. Rebecca won't mind tradin' up." He looked back at Laura. "So, are *you* offerin' Ms. Bayer? . . . Cross your heart and swear on Arthur's sacred sword?"

To his horror, Ben realized that Laura was crying.

"Oh my God," he whispered, pulling her into his arms without thinking. "What is it? What's wrong? Did I do this? I didn't mean to."

She shook her head against his shoulder. "What if Joby never gets it?" she whispered back, her voice trembling as she cried. "Am I just supposed to wait forever? It's like you could hit him with a shovel, and he wouldn't even notice."

Ignoring the pang of disappointment he felt at hearing what he'd always known confirmed, Ben just said, "Have you tried?"

"What!" she said, hiccupping a laugh, and disentangling herself from his embrace with a quick glance around them to see who might be looking. "You mean really hit him with a shovel?" She laughed again, wiping at her eyes. "Well, no. I'm not sure that would really work so well."

"Sometimes, that's exactly what guys like Joby need," Ben said. "As usual, you're way ahead of us all, Laura. I haven't got a clue who my real match is, and Joby hasn't got a clue about, well, much of anything. But you've known what your heart wants for years. He's a dense son of a bitch, but he's like a brother to me, and, pitiful as it is to say, I think you'd better stop waiting for him to step up to bat, and just make the things you want happen. If that takes a shovel, it'd give me more satisfaction than you know to lend you ours from home. It's pretty big," he added with a lopsided grin. "Oughtta hurt enough to make even Joby notice."

✶

Mentally rehearsing her lines, Laura rang the bell and waited. Taking Ben's advice, she had decided to throw pride to the wind, and take the direct approach. She heard footsteps on the hardwood inside, and braced herself as Joby opened the door.

"Laura! . . . What are you doing here?"

"Was I supposed to make an *appointment*?" So much for her lines.

"No!" Joby apologized. "I didn't . . . I just meant, well, you know. School's out and all, so I just didn't expect . . ."

It was all she could do not to roll her eyes. She decided she'd better just get on with it before things got worse.

"Diane Kelty invited me to her pool party next Saturday. I was wondering if you would go with me."

Joby looked startled. "What about Kevin?"

"Kevin and I aren't together anymore."

"Why not?" Joby asked, looking concerned.

"Oh for *Pete's sake,* Joby. Will you go with me or not?" This wasn't going at all like she'd hoped.

"Well . . . sure," he said, sounding dazed. "I mean, I should ask my mom, I guess. You wanna come in for a minute?"

She nodded, and stepped inside as Joby jogged off to get his mother. Something smelled wonderful. She looked around the entranceway, wondering why Joby needed permission to attend a *daytime* party.

"Hello Laura!" Mrs. Peterson smiled as she came from the kitchen. "It's been such a long time! Can you come in for a minute? I've just finished a batch of cookies. I'd love to catch up on what you've been doing!"

"Thanks," Laura said. "I'd be crazy to turn down anything that smells *that* good."

Mrs. Peterson looked pleased as she led Laura and her son toward the living room, where a plate of M&M oatmeal cookies was already laid out on the coffee table.

"Have a seat," Mrs. Peterson offered, settling onto the couch.

Laura sat down beside her, while Joby sat across the room in a rocking chair by the fireplace.

"Joby says you've invited him to a party," Mrs. Peterson said, handing her a cookie. "That's very nice of you. Where's it going to be?"

"It's a pool party at Diane Kelty's house. She lives up on Viewline Drive."

"Oh! That's a very nice neighborhood, isn't it," Mrs. Peterson said brightly. "I'll bet they have a *lovely* home! What time will it be over?"

"It's an afternoon barbecue," Laura said. "It'll be over before dinner."

"So, it won't go after dark?" Mrs. Peterson pressed.

Laura shook her head. No wonder Joby still looked so young. His mother had probably forbidden him to age. "I have other plans that evening, so I won't be staying even if it does. I'll have Joby back by five thirty at the latest."

"Oh! You're *driving* now?" Mrs. Peterson said, sounding astonished.

"No. But I will be by the time school starts. My parents are really tired of having to drive me around all the time." Laura said, thinking, *Hint, hint.* "My mom can take us to the party though, and bring us back."

"Well," Mrs. Peterson smiled. "It sounds like lots of fun, Laura." She turned to Joby. "It's fine with me, dear."

Joby smiled with what seemed relief. "When should I be ready?" he asked Laura.

"We'll pick you up at noon," she answered, suddenly afraid of saying something stupid and blowing the whole deal. "I hate to eat and run, Mrs. Peterson. The cookies are great, but I have to get my hair cut, and I'm walking, so I'd better go."

"Oh, that's all right," Mrs. Peterson said warmly.

Laura stood and looked at Joby. "I'll see you on Saturday."

"Okay. Should I bring some food or anything?"

"Just a beach towel," Laura flashed him a flirtatious smile, "and plenty of suntan lotion."

Joby looked surprised, then a little flushed, and Laura turned to go, reassured to see that maybe he was not completely dense.

✖

"Well, why not?" Lucifer demanded. "It's been over two years, and he still looks like a choirboy!"

"We've tampered about as much as we can without killing him," Kallaystra protested. "He just doesn't age any faster. What are we supposed to do; put him on the rack and stretch him that way?"

"Don't be obstinate with me," Lucifer warned humorlessly.

"My heartfelt apologies, Bright One," she said in flawless imitation of contrition. "It is just that I share your frustration. I begin to wonder, as you did from the start, whether his condition indicates some new threat to our campaign."

"Oh, mark my words," Lucifer said with unconcealed rancor, "the Enemy is behind this in some way. This boy was not chosen for being unremarkable. The question we seem still to have failed at answering is, 'Remarkable in just how many ways?'"

For a moment, Lucifer simply paced his office, massaging his temples. Then said, "For now, we'll do the best we can with what little you've achieved. Tell the Triangle to dispense with all his physical handicaps. Perhaps if he discovers sports again he will at least put on some muscle tone."

"Might that not revive his self-esteem as well?" Kallaystra dared hazard.

For the first time during their meeting, Lucifer chuckled. "Not if our esteemed counselor has done his job. If, after all these years of conditioning, Joby retains any capacity to see beauty in his own form, I'll have your friend Malcephalon's hide for it. Feel free to tell him I said so, should you feel inclined."

⚏

"I think that's it then," Father Richter said. "Thank you for your help, Joby."

"No problem," Joby replied, looking around, hoping they'd overlooked something. He'd stayed to help clean up after the youth group meeting because there was something he needed to discuss with the priest, but he still hadn't quite worked up the courage to begin. "Can I help you carry those back to the priory?" Joby asked, reaching for the small stack of songbooks tucked between Father Richter's folded arms.

"I'm not *that* old yet," Father Richter said. His smile became concerned. "Is something the matter, Joby?"

Joby looked up and opened his mouth, but no words were in it.

"I've plenty of time, if there's something on your mind," the priest insisted. "Why don't we walk back to the priory?"

Joby and Laura had been "together" for over a month. He could still hardly believe that she was dating *him* instead of *Kevin Branscom,* or that Kevin hadn't beaten him to a pulp over it, though he'd heard that Kevin was already dating a cheerleader named Cherryl Bassetti. Nonetheless, Joby's inexplicable good fortune had not arrived without its catches.

Whatever his classmates thought, Joby's body had awakened long ago to the possibilities of sex just like everyone else's. The dreams, the sensations, the private experiments; Joby had greeted them all with enthusiastic if carefully concealed curiosity at first. Then, lying in bed one morning two summers back, enjoying the afterglow of one of those still very novel "test runs," the memory of Father Morgan's words during Joby's first trip to St. Albee's Church years before had suddenly returned to him from nowhere.

He denied himself even a simple piece of bread, lest the devil use even that little weakness to gain power over him.

Joby had gone still as stone, then weak as water as the rest of Father Morgan's words had come rushing back as if whispered in his ear.

To be faithful at all, you must be absolutely *faithful. Nothing less will do. If you truly want to beat the devil, you must be prepared to deny any hunger he might use to breach your defenses.*

The trap had closed around him with an almost electric shock. Unable to wash his guilt away in the shower, Joby's dread had grown worse and worse until, mastering his shame, he'd gone to ask Father Richter if what he'd been doing was wrong.

Despite Father Richter's obvious effort to be gentle, he had made it clear that Joby must bridle such "impure thoughts and actions" at any cost. Joby had not needed to ask what that really meant. God might leave him, just as Arthur had . . . as his father had. Though Father Richter had assured him that the sacrament of confession would cleanse him of any sin, even this one, Joby hadn't been about to risk God's friendship on cheap rationalizations. From that moment forward, he had promised God that he would utterly renounce, until marriage, the impure thoughts and deeds that had almost cost him his heart's deepest desire—the chance to be God's knight. That goal had proven excruciatingly difficult, but in time, he had learned to keep both impure desires and acts utterly at bay—even in dreams—until now.

Laura had a way of looking at Joby when they were together, of leaning too near, or brushing against him in passing, that had quickly reawakened everything Joby had worked so hard to put to sleep. He had begun to dream of her; wonderful, terrible dreams that he could no longer control, often culminating in the very pleasures he had fought so hard for so long to refuse. He was glad to have a girlfriend at last, *very* glad that it was Laura, and, frankly, deeply relieved to have an answer, finally, to the humiliating rumors he'd always known were traded about him behind his back. But he could not risk losing the battle he had waged so fiercely for so long, not even for Laura.

"Well, Joby," Father Richter said when they were settled alone in the priory's sun porch, "what's got my favorite pupil in such a turmoil?"

"Father," Joby said, "I'm having trouble with . . . with impure thoughts."

"Ah," the priest said. "Is *that* all. You had me worried for a moment. I trust you are repelling them?"

"Father? Is it a sin if . . . if it happens in dreams?"

"Of course not, Joby. God holds none of us accountable for what we cannot control." He smiled. "But our dreams *are* less likely to move in such directions if we are careful to keep our minds pure during the day. Are you doing that?"

Joby haltingly explained his budding romance with Laura, and his anxiety about having a girlfriend without being tempted to impure thoughts and actions.

"Joby," Father Richter said when his confession had exhausted itself, "you are a good boy. I know how your heart burns for God, so I will not trouble you with unnecessary admonitions. God does not hate the gift of sexuality. He made it after all, and wants us to enjoy it fully in marriage. It is the devil who hates God's gifts, and wants to see *us* destroy them through misuse. As I see it, the problem is one of ownership. Anything *we* own can be used against us by the devil, because he's so much more powerful and clever than we are. But the devil can use nothing that *God* owns, because *God* is more powerful than *he is.* We all desperately want to own our bodies, Joby, but if we let *God* own them instead, then the devil can *never* use them against us again. Do you see?"

"I guess," Joby said. "But how do I let God own my body?"

"Every time you are tempted, Joby, just remember that God wants you to sacrifice your sexuality to Him, so that He can give it back to you later, in marriage, immeasurably improved. Every time you put your own desires to death, you can take comfort and courage in the expectation of some even greater pleasure after marriage, when God returns what you have given Him, multiplied many times over."

"Does that mean . . . Should I give up dating Laura then?" Joby asked apprehensively. "Sacrifice it, like you said?"

"Absolutely *not,*" Father Richter replied sternly. "She must be a very special girl to have won the affections of such a fine young man." He smiled. "The thing to do, Joby, is devote yourself to learning how to *love* her, instead of *lusting* after her. That way, if you are ever married, the difficult part will all be done, and the easy part will merely complete your joy together."

Joby was filled with relief. Laura had always mattered to him, always made him feel proud—of her and of himself. Perhaps . . . perhaps they really would be married someday. The thought set everything within him singing.

"Thank you, Father." Joby beamed. "I feel much better now."

Father Richter grinned. "Your purity and devotion to the faith are an example to everyone." He leaned forward to pat Joby's shoulder. "I'm *proud* of you, Joby."

Never one to cut corners, especially with God, Joby still resolved, as he left the church, that he would learn to wake up if he had any more of those dreams. He still wanted God to know that there was nothing for which he would ever renounce Him, not the smallest piece of bread or the greatest pleasure.

❈

Williamson hovered like a chill at Joby's back as the boy finished overdressing for Lindwald's party. Getting Joby to attend at all had proven harder than prying hallelujahs from Hell. They'd already had to postpone the event twice. Lindwald had always taken pains to arrange things so that Laura couldn't come, of course, but Joby hadn't wanted to go without her. Ironically, that snag had finally been resolved by Laura's own well-meaning insistence that Joby start developing a more independent social life. Even then, weeks of persistent pressure from both Lindwald and Mayhew had been required to convince Joby he'd have any fun with a bunch of people he didn't know. And getting past Joby's mother had taken a performance by Lindwald's young henchman, John Mayhew, worthy of Eddie Haskell at his smarmy worst.

Williamson had to concede that this evening might actually be *amusing*. Only half the guests would be human. Joby would finally come face to face with the very demons who'd been tormenting him for years—though he'd not know it, of course. Malcephalon would be there disguised as a young Goth pseudo-poet; Tique, Triphila, and Eurodia as a rudely attired skate punk, a teenage wannabe gypsy, and a slutty cheerleader. Kallaystra was scheduled to show up later as the femme fatale. Even Lindwald's so-called parents, supposedly out of town for this party, would actually be attending as a wiry skinhead and a preppy teenage lush.

After all these years, Williamson thought with the ghost of a smile, finally something fun.

❈

Forbidden to enter any teen-driven car, Joby was forced to ride his bike to Jamie's party. He'd forgotten how bad the neighborhood was. After chaining up his bike, he headed toward the front door and knocked, but the music was so loud that no one heard him, so he pushed the door open for himself.

Throbbing heavy metal and dense, acrid smoke drifted past him through the opening, as if desperate, themselves, to flee toward fresher air. The shades were drawn, and all the normal lightbulbs replaced with red, blue, or green ones, turning complexions lurid, and filling the room with shadows, though it would be light outside for hours yet. Joby's first impulse was to leave, but Lindwald suddenly appeared wearing a wide, slightly bleary grin.

"Hey Joby! *All right!*" He threw an arm across Joby's back, and ushered him deeper into the house. "I was afraid you weren't gonna show! Wanna beer? A cigarette?"

Joby stared at him incredulously. This was not at all what he or Mayhew had led him to expect. "Jamie . . . I . . . I can only stay a little while. I—"

Jamie hooked his arm around Joby's neck, pulling their heads close enough to talk more quietly. "Look, Joby. Don't freak out, okay? I know you're new at this, but that's why I worked so hard to get you here. You'd be a lot more popular if you weren't so uptight." He gave Joby a conspiratorial grin and a good-natured thump on the back. "Just loosen up a little and hang out. That's all I'm sayin'."

Before Joby could answer, Johnny Mayhew popped up with a slutty-looking brunette under one arm, and a beer in his hand. "Joby!" He smiled. "Glad yer finally steppin' up to the plate, dude! The drinks are in there." He pointed at the red-lit kitchen doorway. "Grab yourself some brew!"

"Is there anything nonalcoholic?" Joby asked.

"What?" Jamie smiled, cupping his ears to hear over the music.

"I said, is there anything besides beer?" Joby yelled, just as the song ended, so that everyone turned to look.

"Oh. . . . Sure," Jamie said, glancing self-consciously around them. "There's vodka, rum, schnapps, whatever you want, bud. Come on." Jamie pulled him toward the kitchen as the music started up again: gangster rap this time, which was quieter at least. In the kitchen, Jamie pulled Joby aside, and said, "Look. Joby. Just be cool. You embarrass yourself here, you embarrass me, okay?"

"Jamie, I appreciate what you're trying to do, but, I don't think—"

"Just take a soda," Lindwald said, grabbing a 7UP off the counter and thrusting it into Joby's hand, "and I'll introduce you around. Give it a try, Joby. They're people too, ya know. Just be friendly, and you'll have a great time."

Soda in hand, Joby followed Jamie back into the crowded living room, where they were enthusiastically assaulted by a skater and his gypsyish girlfriend.

"Gonna be a *rager,* bra!" shouted the skater, slamming Jamie an exuberant high-five while his girlfriend threw herself around their host in a wild embrace.

"Damn straight, Skat!" Jamie shouted back. "Hey you guys, this is Joby."

Joby was shifting his soda around to shake Skat's hand, when Skat launched another of his mad high-fives, knocking the can out of his grip to gush its contents over Joby as it fell, leaving a dark stain down one leg of his khaki slacks.

"*Whoa!* Sorry, bra." Skat grinned. "You better clean that up. Look's like you pissed yerself." His girlfriend laughed uproariously. "Hey, Jamie! Where's the juice?"

Jamie nodded toward the kitchen, then surveyed Joby's new look with a grimace. "Come on. The bathroom's upstairs."

As Jamie led him toward the staircase, Joby realized for the first time how horribly wrong his clothes were, soaked in 7UP or not. He'd dressed for a party while everyone else there was dressed for Halloween or heavy yard work. *What a geek I am,* he thought just as Johnny and his girl popped up again.

"Nice look, Joby," Mayhew scoffed. "Can't even hold yer soda, huh?"

"Back off, Mayhew," Jamie growled.

Mayhew shrugged, and vanished back into the swirl of partyers.

The upstairs landing was blocked by an entourage of dark-clad girls surrounding a teenage boy with thin hungry features, dark eyes, and black hennaed hair. His long coat, heavy sweater, and ragged jeans were all black as well, right down to his battered steel-toed boots. He sat in a cloud of pot smoke, a joint hanging loosely from one hand.

"Out of the way," Jamie jibbed. "Wounded comin' through."

The vampiric crowd scrunched aside enough to let them by.

"*That's* who you should meet," Jamie said, when they'd gotten to the bathroom. "Seth's got a brain, unlike Skat 'n' Anna down there. I bet you guys would totally relate. When yer cleaned up, just introduce yourself and hang out up here for a while."

Joby nodded, relieved at any excuse not to go back into the full melee downstairs.

Unable to do much with the towel Jamie had given him but spread the dampness around, Joby finally gave up and left the bathroom. Back out on the landing, he found Seth reading poetry from a crumpled piece of binder paper. Not wanting to interrupt, Joby waited politely to squeeze past them.

". . . And since these things are bound to die," Seth intoned.

> *"Why drag their corpses after you?*
> *Surrender them.*
> *The looming shadow we call death*
> *is only freedom after all,*
> *back lit by the sun."*

Seth folded up the crumpled sheet, and stuffed it into a coat pocket.

"That was sooo cool," sighed one of his female entourage.

"Yeah," cooed another. "I loved the part about the night eating the moon." She looked at Joby, and asked, "Wasn't it beautiful?"

"I—um—I only heard the last bit," he said, "but it was pretty interesting." He thrust his hand out to Seth. "My name's Joby."

"Seth," the poet answered, ignoring his hand, but waving him to sit and join them. "I've never seen *you* at Jamie's parties."

"No," Joby conceded, sitting down. "I . . . Jamie just invited me this time. I'm . . . I'm kind of out of my league here, I think."

"Honesty!" Seth mused. "How refreshing! Jamie's taste in friends must be improving." He offered his joint to Joby, but Joby shyly refused.

"You're cute," said one of the girls, smiling, her lips blackened, her eyes heavily lined in mascara. "Your girlfriend here too?"

"She couldn't come," Joby said, unnerved by the calculating smile this elicited.

"Ah, so you're lonely," Seth commiserated. "Loneliness can make you wise, you know. Wiser than those morons downstairs."

"Yeah," one of the girls concurred mournfully.

"Wise and free," Seth said. The others all nodded gravely, as he took another hit off his joint. "It's the things we love that destroy us in the end," he grunted, holding in the smoke.

"That is soooo true," gushed one of the girls.

Joby's head felt strange. He suspected it was the smoke, and decided to brave the downstairs crowd again after all. "I'm kind of thirsty," he said, standing up. He looked sheepishly at his slacks. "I didn't get much of that first drink. I guess I'll go try again." He stepped across the bunch of them, and started down the stairs.

The music had gotten loud and fast again, and everyone was hurling about in some kind of mad slamming dance. Joby was trying to find Jamie in the crowd when someone ran into him from behind and sent him flying onto an end table beside the couch. The lamp sitting on it crashed to the floor in a burst of broken glass and laughter from all around him. Joby sat up to find the tall skinhead who'd run into him still gyrating to the music and leering at his half-drunken partner as if nothing had happened. Feeling honor bound to apologize for the lamp before he left, Joby got carefully to his feet to continue his search for Jamie. That's when he saw her.

Her sequined, knee-length dress seemed to catch all the light in the room, as if she were a bright silver fish darting through a fetid pool. She glanced at him suddenly, as if aware of his attention despite the chaotic crowd between them.

Forgetting to look where he was walking, he ran straight into someone large, and found himself belly to belly with Bobby Boggs, a senior lineman on the football team.

"What'er you, a *faggot?!*" the beefy giant bellowed. Then he recognized Joby, and laughed. "*Joby Peterson!* At a *party?* Didja wander in here lookin' fer, a gay bar, ya little squid?"

The music stopped abruptly as Bobby shoved Joby roughly away and opened his mouth to humiliate him some more. But, suddenly, the angel in silver sequins was standing between them, frowning up at Boggs.

"We haven't met," she coyly told Bobby, "but I thought someone ought to tell you that you smell."

Bobby leered down at her, beginning to smile. "Maybe I should take a shower then. You wanna help?"

"I don't think a shower will do it," the girl said, wrinkling her nose. "What is that, rotten hamburger?"

Suddenly, Joby smelled it too. From the gasps and rude exclamations around them, it seemed that everyone had noticed. Even Bobby's face crinkled in distaste, then he looked surprised and, without seeming to think, raised an arm and sniffed his own armpit.

"What the fuck?" he said, looking up in shocked mortification.

"You know," cooed the sparkling girl, "I'd stay on ice if that's how you smell when you heat up." To Joby's amazement, she turned briefly and flashed him a conspiratorial smile, then looked back up at Bobby and said with sexy ease, "By the way, Joby and I go *way* back, and I can *assure* you that he's *no* faggot."

Though stunned, Joby had the sense to keep quiet.

For one strange, long moment, the silver girl just stared up into Bobby's eyes as his expression shifted from anger, to bewilderment, to plainly visible fear. Then he shoved his way through the crowd and out the front door as if he'd seen a ghost. Except for a few quiet objections to the smell of Bobby's passing, the room remained eerily silent until the girl smiled again, and said, "Come on, Joby. Why don't you get me a drink?" She tucked her arm under one of his and led him off, still speechless, while the music came back on and the dancing resumed.

When they got to the kitchen, Joby turned and said, "Who are you, and— and why did you—"

"I gather from our departed friend, *the jerk,*" she cut him off, "that you're Joby Peterson." She flashed him another of her devastating smiles and reached out to shake his hand. "I'm Allaystra Bennit."

Joby was overwhelmed by her sheer beauty. Her large, liquid eyes were the color of perodite. Her thick, silky brown hair fell like a feathered veil around her face and throat. Her skin was flawless and pale, her lips full and dark, the shape of her under that dress was like a smooth ride over rolling country in a fine car. As he took her hand, he had trouble speaking. "Thank you," he managed. "I . . . I owe you."

Her smile widened, and Joby realized two things at once. The first was that he felt strange all over. His skin seemed to burn, and there was a pleasant, tingling pressure building underneath his nearly dry soda stains. The second was that he would die of humiliation if she noticed.

"Well, thanks," he said again, "Really! I'm sure you've got people to see though, so I'll . . . I'll just go now, but I sure do appreciate—"

"Wait a minute." She frowned. "Don't I even get to meet the guy I just rescued?"

"Well . . . well, sure," Joby stammered, "I didn't mean . . . I'll get you something to drink first, okay?" He turned away quickly, hoping to get himself under control down there before she noticed. That's when he saw Lindwald already at the beverage counter, and wondered how long he'd been there. "What would you like?" Joby asked Allaystra as he moved toward the liquor supply.

"Just soda," she said. "I'm not much of a drinker."

Relieved, Joby moved in next to Jamie to grab another 7UP.

"Way to go, Joby," Jamie whispered. "Yer ship's finally comin' in, eh?"

"What are you talking about?" Joby whispered back.

"Come on." Jamie grinned and said under his breath, "She *wants* you, dude! And I saw you puttin' up that little pup tent." He nodded unobtrusively at Joby's crotch. "It's nice to see they're wrong!"

"What? Who?"

"All those dickheads who say you're queer." Jamie grinned. "This'll shut 'em up." He nudged Joby's shoulder. "Go for it, stud." He left with a drink in each hand before Joby could close his mouth. Happily, Joby's other difficulty seemed to have settled down, so he went back to Allaystra with her drink.

"Thanks," she said, lifting the cup to her lips without taking her eyes from Joby's. "There must be somewhere in this house where we can hear ourselves think. Why don't we go talk, okay?" She smiled down at her sleek silver dress. "I'm not really dressed for slam dancing anyway."

Under control or not, Joby still felt terribly self-conscious, but she had saved his butt, and he wasn't about to be rude. "Okay," he said. "Wanna go outside?"

"Not so much," she said, wrinkling her pretty nose. "It's hard to make intelligent conversation with people puking in the bushes all around you. I'm sure it'll be quieter upstairs."

Joby had no argument to counter that, so he followed her through the crowd of dancers, who parted very courteously this time, and up the stairs past Seth and his poetry circle, in the midst of a decidedly more erotic poem, and finally found themselves in a nondescript bedroom where Allaystra closed the door behind them—against the noise, she said.

She sat on the bed and waved Joby down beside her. Joby tried to sit at the other end of the mattress, but Allaystra simply scooted up to join him. His palms were sweating, his skin was tingling, and he didn't know what he'd do if . . . if things started getting out of control again, but to his relief, Allaystra simply began to talk. She asked where Joby lived, how he knew Jamie, what his interests were. She asked about his views, and expressed her own on an amazing variety of subjects, and Joby soon realized that this girl wasn't just beautiful, she was really smart! He became so absorbed in their conversation, that he didn't notice how close she'd come until she put her hand on his chest as he was telling her about his secret desire to talk with animals.

"Joby Peterson," she crooned, "I've never met anyone so intelligent and, well, *deep*, I guess, at one of Jamie's parties." She leaned in even closer, and Joby noticed her perfume, too subtle to be detected from more than a few inches away. It was so lovely that his first instinct was to lean in farther just to get a fuller breath of it. "In fact," she sighed, "I don't think I've met any-one like you *ever.*" Her finger's slipped between his shirt buttons to touch his bare skin.

He was as astonished by the swiftness of his body's response as by its intensity. Hard in an instant, the desire to press himself against her went through him like a shout. One corner of his mind screamed back that this was *sin,* but as she began to undo the buttons on his shirt, the fear of betray-ing all he most believed in strained in stalemate with his body's agonizing desire to capitulate. Then, something turned within him, and he stood, not caring what she saw, only desperate to leave before he lost all control.

"Joby?" she breathed, reaching for his hand.

He could not remember leaving the room, nor fleeing down the stairs past Seth, as he must have done. He vaguely noticed laughter as he bolted through the front door, fumbled in the near dark with the lock on his bike, and ran with it out into the street. Only after a car screeched around him, blaring its horn in protest, did Joby come fully to his senses. He mounted his bike and rode away as fast as he could, his body still burning with the need for release, resigned to the certainty that he had narrowly escaped one sin only to embrace another when he got home. He could only hope that God would understand.

❈

"Bless me, Father, for I have sinned," the boy's voice came mournfully from beyond the screen. "It's been three weeks since my last confession."

Though a pretense of anonymity was germane to the sacrament, Father Richter could hardly fail to recognize Joby's voice, any more than Joby would fail to know his.

Hearing the boy's account of the previous evening's excesses, the inten-sity of his desire to sin, and the remedy to that desire he had been unable to avoid later, the priest's alarm steadily increased. The angel had emphatically warned him that sexual impurity posed the greatest threat to Joby's spiritual destiny, and thus to Father Richter's own ambitions as well. He had worked too hard and brought Joby too far toward holiness to see it all undone now by mundane adolescent urges.

"My son," Father Richter said, steeling himself for greater severity than he had ever shown Joby before, "I must be clear. The wages of sin is *death.* Our Lord taught that it would be better to sacrifice any part of our bodies and enter Heaven crippled, than to be cast whole into the fires of Hell. Is any passing pleasure really worth the loss of your soul? God called Abraham to sacrifice his own son. Next to that, how difficult is the small sacrifice of flesh that God asks of you?"

Of course, God had *spared* Abraham that sacrifice at the last moment, but Father Richter had no intention of weakening the boy's resolve by including that point. Given the raging storm of hormones any boy of Joby's age endured, it was unlikely enough that Joby's virginity would last much longer. Why give the devil any extra help?

"You say this young temptress was a *stranger*?" Richter asked.

"Yes," Joby whispered.

The anguish in that whisper nearly broke Richter's heart, but he knew there was no room for sentiment here and asked God for strength. "Have you a girlfriend?" he asked, knowing the answer, of course. "Someone you *truly* care about?"

"Yes," Joby murmured forlornly.

"Do you realize," Father Richter pressed, "that it was not merely God you wished to betray last night, but this girl you love, as well?"

There was an even longer silence. "Yes," Joby said at last, sounding on the edge of tears.

"It is good that you do," Father Richter said, suddenly feeling terribly weary. "Have you other sins to confess?"

"No, Father," Joby murmured.

"Then I absolve you from your sins, in the name of the Father and the Son and the Holy Spirit," Father Richter said. "For your penance, I want you to prove your worthiness of God's love by devoting yourself to loving the girlfriend you speak of without any lust whatsoever, and valuing *her* spiritual welfare as well as your own at all times, lest you subject *her* to an ordeal like that which you, yourself, have suffered. Do you understand me, my son?"

"Yes, Father," Joby said with audible resolve. "I will never be unworthy of God or her again. . . . I promise."

"Then go with God's forgiveness, and sin no more," Father Richter said, and slid the panel shut between them.

10

(*Too Late*)

As they walked, hand in hand, toward her front door, Laura smiled at Joby and leaned up to kiss his cheek, eliciting a smile twin to her own. The evening had been everything she'd hoped her senior prom might be. She'd been the envy of every girl there, dancing in the arms of their class valedictorian, so tall and handsome in his black satin tux. During their senior year Joby had finally becoming taller and better looking than Laura thought Kevin Branscom had any hope of being. Seeing even her lascivious friend, Karen Tyler, cast covetous glances at Joby that evening, Laura had barely restrained herself from drifting over to murmur, "Not bad—for a *twelve-year-old*—is he, *dahling!*"

As it happened, Laura's parents were gone for the entire week. By some miracle, they'd won a cruise trip in some contest they couldn't even recall entering. With the house all to herself, Laura had decided earlier that evening that the time had come to do Joby, and herself, one last, huge favor before graduation forced them to part.

For two years now, Joby had been sweeter and more sensitive than any boy she'd ever known, even Benjamin. He'd carved tremendous amounts of time from his frenetic schedule to spend with her. He had always listened when she wanted to talk, seeming both to care and understand. He was always surprising her with small insights, little gifts, and kind gestures. He had become a *very* good dancer, once she'd convinced him to try. And yet, there was still a part of him Laura had never gotten within shouting distance of.

From the very beginning, Joby had kept everything between them so terribly chaste. He kissed her often, but only as storybook princes kissed; lips warm and soft but barely open; embracing her with grace but never real passion. As he'd grown taller and more beautiful, she had hoped this would change, but it never had, though the passion missing in his kisses was more than evident in his eyes and voice. In the fall, Laura would leave for Brown in Rhode Island, while Joby went to Berkeley. But Laura had grown more determined than ever to have him completely, if briefly, at least once before she to let him go.

At the door, she turned, and Joby kissed her as sweetly, and as ever, inaccessibly.

"It was *wonderful*, Joby," she said when he leaned away. "I wish it wouldn't end." She smiled plaintively, taking his hands in her own. "I'm not *ready* for it to end yet. Come in and keep me company for a while. . . . *Please?*"

❦

Kallaystra stood gazing down on the pretty couple, sleeping peacefully in each others arms, naked but for the girl's covers wound about them. In one way at least, the unfortunate girl was not deluded: Joby really had become a very beautiful young man. Looking at him now, Kallaystra even felt some small regret at having failed to seduce him herself at that party two years earlier.

Steering the *girl* through this seduction had been child's play. It was never difficult to compel such creatures toward what they so deeply wanted to begin with, though the child might recall some of her tactics this evening with great discomfort in the morning. Winning past the *boy's* defenses, however, had required a subtle skill and surgical precision that left Kallaystra once again in awe of Malcephalon's abilities.

Her part in this finished, Kallaystra took one last appreciative look at Joby, and murmured, "I hope you enjoyed your meal, pretty lad." She glanced at Malcephalon, looming in the shadows beyond their bed, and quipped, "Here comes your waiter with the check."

❦

Joby woke in darkness without opening his eyes, still clinging to the most deliciously sinful dream he'd ever had. Thankful that God didn't hold him accountable for dreams, he opened his eyes and began to stretch. As the muzzy confusion of sleep suddenly receded, however, two things became apparent. He was in a room he did not recognize, and he was naked, though he *never* slept naked.

With a jolt, he sat up and turned to find Laura lying beside him, as naked as he.

Oh God! he thought, immobilized by shock. *What have I—How could we—*

His mind raced backward, scrambling for explanations, but everything was fuzzy and disjointed. For an instant, he even wondered if Laura had slipped him something somehow, then shoved the idea furiously away. Slowly, it all started coming back. There had been . . . an argument, about why he wouldn't ever touch her, why he wouldn't even look at her as she . . . as she had let her *dress slide to the floor.*

He shook his head in denial.

"You think I'm ugly, don't you," she had wept. "You must despise me!"

She *couldn't* have done that. She would *never* have . . .

He half-remembered his own urgent denials, his attempts to explain, his need to stop her tears, to comfort her, to hold her, the warmth of her through his clothing, the dampness of her tears on his face and neck as she clung to him. The elusive sense of manhood he had always longed for and never found within himself; the chance to be everything he'd ever seen in Benjamin; an answer to his father's shame; an end to the terrible gaping hole that had haunted his wounded, empty heart for so many years; every physical pleasure Joby had ever denied himself and hungered for; all this had suddenly been his—to seize or lose forever.

Despite the darkness, Joby covered his eyes, desperate to avert the memories even as he felt himself stiffening with new desire. Shame and dread leapt up inside him with explosive intensity. He had *used* Laura *terribly,* betrayed her love *completely,* broken *every vow* he'd ever made to God, ignored *every warning* Father Richter had ever given him! Yet, on the very heels of such horrendous treason, he *ached* to wake Laura and do it all again!

As stealthily as panic allowed, Joby slipped from bed and began to pull his clothes on. Laura drew a sudden breath and turned beneath the covers. Grabbing the rest of his things, Joby ran from the room before she could awaken and confront him. Fumbling for his car keys, he dashed from her house in his pants and shirt, tossing the rest of his clothes into his mother's car, then jumping behind the wheel to start the engine. As he lurched from the curb he glanced at the rearview mirror and saw Laura's pale form, robed now, sway onto the porch, illuminated in the green glow of street lamps. There was just time to see the dismay on her face before he gunned the engine and sped away.

By the time he got home, the first gray smudge of dawn had cut distant hills from the sky like paper silhouettes. There was no way to change what he had done, nor any way to live with it, so he had just retreated altogether into numb denial. He dragged his shoes, socks, tie, and coat from the backseat, shuffled up the walk, and opened the front door to find his mother standing there in her nightgown.

"Where have you been?" she asked, sounding torn between fear and fury.

"Out," Joby said, his gaze falling to the hardwood floor in shame at his half-dressed state, a virtual confession.

"Out *where?*" she demanded.

"Just out," Joby said without looking up. Then memory of his father's departure hit him like a pile driver; his parents' fight, their final words:

Out.

Out where?

Unable to endure it, he pushed past her and walked woodenly toward his room.

"Come back here!" she snapped. *"Don't you dare walk out on me that way!"*

Oh God, the very words!

Some barrier inside him shattered, and he ran for his room, gasping animal cries of misery. Behind him, his mother's silence suddenly seemed more filled with fear than anger.

⚬

Joby flushed the toilet and finished tucking in his shirt just as the second bell rang. One more class, he thought dully, and he could flee all these people. He didn't know where he would go. Not home certainly. He had spent the weekend locked in his room, despite his mother's pleas that he come out and tell her what was happening. Maybe he would just wander all night. If he was lucky, he thought, he would simply lose his mind soon, and forget himself entirely.

He pushed the stall door open, and found Jamie Lindwald standing in his way.

"Joby, what's up?" Jamie demanded.

"I'm late for class." He tried to walk past, but Jamie stepped into his path again.

"I been watchin' you all day, Joby. What the hell is wrong?"

"Nothing, Jamie," Joby mumbled. "Please get out of my way."

"Not 'til you tell me what's goin' on," Jamie insisted. "You look awful."

Joby began to feel angry. Since that party two years before, their friendship had been tenuous at best. So why the hell should Jamie suddenly be so concerned *now?*

"Jamie, I don't wanna talk right now—to anyone, okay? Just let me go to class."

"You know your problem?" Jamie said. "You always gotta be the hero—always givin', never takin'. You were the first person in my whole life who ever tried to be my friend, Joby, but I don't get to be *yours* now, do I. I just get to feel *grateful.* 'S that it?"

"Jamie!" Joby snarled. *"My whole life is fucked!* You can't *begin* to *imagine*

what a *fuckup* I am! So take your *hero* shit, and ram it up your nose, 'cause you never came *close* to fuckin' up like me!"

"Whadaya think?" Jamie pressed. "*I'm* gonna look down on *you?* Come on, Joby. Gimme a chance. Whatever you did, I done worse, or . . . or I owe you fifty bucks."

The offer's absurdity almost made Joby smile, but he remembered what he'd done, and his capacity to smile fled again. Suddenly, it seemed right though, to have to say it aloud, to let Jamie see what he truly was, like the beginning of some kind of penance. He looked Jamie squarely in the eye, determined to spare himself nothing, and said, "I slept with Laura Friday night after the prom."

Jamie looked incredulous, then blurted out, "*That's* what all this is about? I wondered why you been running off like that everytime you saw her comin'. *Joby!* You should be the happiest guy on campus!"

"I knew you wouldn't understand," Joby sighed, realizing that he'd just dragged Laura's reputation through the mud as well. "If you meant what you said about being my friend," he said, "*please,* don't tell *anyone* about this. For Laura's sake, if not for mine." He hung his head and turned to go. "I should never have said anything."

"No, Joby! Wait a minute!" Jamie moved to plant himself in Joby's path again. "I'm sorry. I know how much bein' good matters to you. I *like* that about you. But, there's stuff *you* don't get either!" He began steering Joby toward the door. "Give me ten minutes, okay? Then, you can go jump off a bridge if you want."

What the hell, Joby thought. It was too late to go to class now anyway.

Moments later they were sitting on a patch of half-dead grass out behind the wood shop trailer. Lindwald had talked all the way there with such unexpected frankness and sensitivity that Joby had begun to feel a little better despite himself.

"You try too hard to be *perfect!*" Lindwald insisted. "Who ever said you couldn't make any mistakes? *No one's* perfect!" He sat up and grinned at Joby. "Ben's slept with Rebecca, you know. You think God's gonna send *him* to Hell?"

"No he didn't!" Joby gaped.

"Yes he did," Lindwald insisted. "Cross my heart and hope to go to Hell."

"He'd have told me!" Joby said.

"You think he'd tell *Mr. Perfect* a thing like *that?*" Lindwald scoffed. "That's what I mean, Joby. Even your best friend's afraid to tell you stuff, but if you're ready to start carin' about somethin' besides bein' the school's top *egghead,* maybe you can finally *belong!* See?" He shook his head good-naturedly.

Joby was so wrung out, he didn't know what to think. *Benjamin* had done this with *Rebecca?* Joby couldn't imagine God throwing Ben in Hell. Moreover, it suddenly dawned on him that Jamie's revelation hadn't lowered his own opinion of Ben either.

"Tell you what, bro!" Jamie announced. "Now that you finally got a life, we should go celebrate! I know someone who can get us a couple six-packs. We'll go out to my personal spot, have a few laughs, loosen up, howl at the moon a little! Hell, Joby! Now you finally been *born,* you gotta come out an' get *baptized!*"

Joby shook his head. "I'm in enough trouble already, Jamie. I don't think breaking the law is—"

"Joby, what does it take to get through your thick skull? Your 'perfect' days are over, and I bet even *God's* relieved! You finally got *laid, bro!*" he crowed. "You're a *man* now! So you're gonna worry about one or two little sips of *beer?*"

"It's—not—*legal,* Jamie."

Jamie looked at him askance. "For chrissake, Joby. We're *seniors!* You think *anybody* at that college you're goin' to won't be drinkin'? The cops ain't gonna arrest the whole freshman class at Berkeley, are they?" He shook his head. "Just one little time 'fore we're outta high school, let's go celebrate *life,* huh? *Your* life!"

Joby stared at his friend as if seeing him for the first time.

"Tell you what," Jamie announced. "I'll only have one beer. That way, you can leave your mom's car at home, and I'll be your *designated driver.* Isn't that *responsible?*"

✿

Joby had never guessed how really *enjoyable* Lindwald's company could be! Amazing, outrageously . . . really *bitchin'* company!

In fact, it seemed that six or seven beers with Jamie had done more for Joby than many years of counseling. There was something *tremendously* therapeutic about needing such utter concentration just to . . . to walk . . . upright. He had no attention left to spare for any of the other things he was so glad not to be able to think about while he was . . . walking . . . but . . . he didn't care, because the other good thing about being drunk was that all he felt was one big, warm, drowsy buzz, much too large to leave room for any other feelings, like the ones he was so happy not to be feeling now, while . . . while Jamie was laughing . . . at *him,* Joby realized, and laughed too, then went sprawling to the ground, scattering his armload of empty beer cans in all directions, and laughing even harder. It felt *so good* to laugh!

"Good-bye, Mr. Perfect," Joby burbled as Jamie helped him to his feet, and stuck a few of the fallen beer cans back into his arms. Jamie's "personal spot" had been a small clearing in the woods outside of town; and, drunk or not, Joby had seen no point in leaving piles of trash to spoil such a pretty place. Jamie, who had consumed much more than one beer after all, had found the idea of cleaning the place up hilarious, and enthusiastically gathered not just their own empty cans, but many of the moldering beer cartons left by "previous campers."

The hike out seemed far longer than the hike in had been, and Joby's ability to walk had improved a lot by the time they got to Jamie's truck. So had his ability to think.

"Come on," Jamie ginned as they dumped their empty cans and cartons into the bed of his truck. "We can drive around a while before I drop you at Ben's. That way, you won't show up there lookin' as wasted as you do now."

"You don't look so good yourself." Joby frowned. "I don't think we should drive anywhere yet. Why don't we just hang out here for a while, 'til this stuff wears off?"

"Don't talk dumb, Joby. Beer ain't new to me like it is to you. I'm nowhere *near* too heated to drive! Get in." He yanked the driver's door open, jumped up behind the wheel, and reached across to unlock the passenger door.

"Jamie, I'm just gonna walk," Joby said.

"I ain't spendin' no two hours walkin' around," Jamie complained, "and I ain't waitin' around for you to come back here when you figure out what a dumb-ass you are neither. So what's it gonna be?"

"I'm walkin', Jamie," Joby said irritably. "And *you* shouldn't be drivin'."

"Suit yourself," Jamie growled. "You sure still got a lot to learn about loosenin' up." Without further ceremony, he started the engine and left Joby in a spray of gravel.

Joby watched him go, pissed that Jamie could be such a pal one minute and such a bastard the next. When his eyes recovered from the glare of Jamie's headlights, he discovered there was enough light from the nearby town to see the road by, and began the long walk to Ben's house.

After half an hour of walking, his pleasant buzz had given way to sore feet and growing fatigue, but the evening had left him clear about *one* thing: He loved Laura. He had always loved Laura, just as he knew she had always loved him, and what they had done on Friday night had been purely wonderful. He wondered how it had taken him so long to see what had been right there in front of his face.

He was going to marry her. He knew that now with every molecule in his body. The decision was no frivolous by-product of his fading inebriation. It was the most quietly sober, absolutely *right* decision he had ever made in his life. If he could find some way to fix things after the way he'd acted, he'd ask her to marry him right away. They could go to Berkeley together, or he'd apply to Brown with her; it didn't matter. Father Richter had told him to learn to love her without lust. Well, he'd spent two years doing just that. Wasn't that long enough? Wasn't it time for "the easy part" now?

With that decided, he walked on through the lamp-lit town feeling lighter than he could remember feeling ever before. His feet hardly seemed to touch the pavement now. His head was clear. The night seemed beautiful. He even felt ready to face his mother, now that he knew what to tell her. She loved Laura too, after all.

❈

Lucifer hovered over the viewing bowl in his office, watching Lindwald climb into his truck to leave Joby behind in the dark.

"Lindwald, my dear friend," he murmured, as if the damned soul's watery image could hear him, "you've played your small part beyond my wildest expectations, every line, parroted to perfection. It's time for that reward I promised you." Lucifer chuckled in delicious anticipation. "It's a little joke, actually, just between the three of us. Alas, poor Joby will not likely get it," he grimaced in mock regret, "and only *I'll* have time to laugh."

As he watched, the Triangle joined Lindwald in the scene; one to hold Jamie in his seat, lest he leap out of the truck and spoil it all; one to steer his truck toward the embankment; and one to light the spark in his gas tank. Lucifer shook his head and *tsk*ed. Given the incredibly thorough illusion of flesh in which Lindwald was trapped, this was probably going to hurt . . . a lot.

As anticipated, Lindwald had no time to laugh, but he did have time to scream.

❈

Ever since Joby had awakened to his first taste of debauchery's secondary rewards, Ben had wavered between sympathy founded in certain stark recollections of his own wilder nights, and an urge to smirk. Joby was the *last* person he had ever expected to see hungover, but when he'd shown up last night, Ben had refrained from pressing him for explanations. That morning as they'd gotten ready for school, Joby had finally told him all about his drinking spree with Lindwald, but refused to tell him why this sudden surrender to indulgence after so many years of respectable sobriety.

As they neared school, however, Ben's curiosity finally got the best of him. "So, how long do I have to wait to hear the rest of it, Joby?" When Joby didn't answer, Ben shrugged and let it go again, but then he saw a weird little smile on Joby's face, and really had to know. "Come on, dude. What drove you to drink?"

"This may seem a little sudden," Joby said, "but I was wondering if you'd consider being best man at my wedding."

Ben took his eyes off the road to glance at Joby. *"What?"*

"I'm gonna ask Laura to marry me," Joby said, straight-faced. "Today, I think."

Ben's mouth fell open. "Is that a joke?"

"Hey! It's red!" said Joby, pointing through the windshield.

Ben slammed on his brakes, and, when the light had changed, turned the corner and parked the truck.

"It's not a joke," Joby said, then smiled like Ben had not seen him smile since they'd been boys. That's when Ben knew he was for real.

To Ben's surprise, his own first reaction was a sudden stab of loss. He'd never realized until that moment, or acknowledged anyway, how much he'd hoped that somehow, maybe, someday, he and Laura . . . But then he took a second look at his friend's radiant face and realized that Joby was *finally, in love!* A frantic burst of excitement and delight instantly eclipsed any other feelings.

"You son of a bitch!" Ben shouted gleefully, reaching across to grab Joby up in a bear hug. "Who ever thought you'd beat me to the altar!" He let go of Joby, and leaned back so they could beam at each other until Joby laughed out loud. Then they both were laughing themselves sick. "When you gonna ask her?" Ben said.

"Well, I've got some patching up to do first, I think," said Joby. "We had a little . . . *thing* . . . after prom, but that's what made me see how much I love her, Ben. I just hope she'll have me now."

"Ha!" Ben laughed. "She's been trollin' Joby bait for six years, and you think she'll say no?"

To Ben's consternation, Joby's easy exuberance vanished as quickly as it had appeared. "It was a pretty serious *thing,*" he said. "I blew it real bad, but I'm gonna get her out of homeroom this morning, and try to work it out." He smiled a bit more wanly. "The valedictorian can pull some strings and get her a pass, I guess."

"Finally! He gets it!" Ben exclaimed. "Let's go get her, Joby."

He pulled back into traffic, and minutes later they were walking toward the school's main entrance. Crossing the lawn, Ben's attention was drawn to a group of girls clustered mournfully around one of their number who was crying. Ben was curious, but felt too buoyant to linger on it. As he pulled one of the school's big glass doors open for Joby, however, they saw another group of grieving kids at the end of the hall, and recognized Johnny Mayhew standing sullenly at the group's fringe.

"Lotta girls must've got dumped after prom," Ben said, oddly afraid to dignify his own joke with a smile.

"Hey, Johnny," Joby called quietly. "What's wrong?"

Mayhew turned and stared at him, then turned angrily and walked away.

"What's *his* problem?" Ben griped.

Joby looked around, and spotted Pete Blackwell. "Hey Pete, what's with all the crying around here?"

Pete looked glumly past them at the group down the hall. "Nothing like *dying* to get friends you never had popping up all over, is there?" he mumbled.

"Who died?" Ben asked with a chill of alarm.

"Jamie Lindwald," Pete said. "Crashed and burned his truck last night, outside of town. They say there were empty beer cans all over. Fresh ones."

Ben turned to find Joby's face painted in stark horror.

Pete looked abashed. "Sorry, Joby. I guess you were friends, huh? I should have—"

Before he could finish, Joby whirled, and slammed back through the big glass doors, half-running toward the lawn. Ben dropped his books and ran after him.

"Joby!" Ben yelled, "Wait, damn it!"

Joby ran even faster, right toward the street.

Ben poured on all the speed he had, and managed to throw him to the grass just before he reached the sidewalk. Joby writhed beneath him, but Ben kept him pinned to the lawn. As students gathered at a distance to point and gawk, Joby began to sob.

"It's got nothing to do with you!" Ben exclaimed. "You told him not to drive! You told me so last night. It was *his* choice! *His,* damn it!"

"I should have stopped him!" Joby wailed. *"He was out there 'cause of me!"*

"Goddamn it, Joby! *You* were out there 'cause of *him*! What the hell were you s'posed to *do*? Stand in front of the fuckin' truck?"

Joby stopped struggling and lay facedown, crying into the grass. Ben loosened his hold, but didn't let him up. After a moment, Joby's crying tapered off, and he mumbled something Ben didn't catch.

"What?" Ben asked.

Joby rolled over and stared up at him like a man already hanged. "The wages of sin is death," he said without inflection.

Ben could make no sense of it at first. Then he understood, and his anger flared white hot. *"That's fuckin' bullshit!"* he yelled. *"Fuck Father Richter, Joby!* I wish I'd never *mentioned* church to you! I wish I'd never gone *myself*!"

"No!" Joby moaned. "He was *right,* and I *ignored* him! He *told me* what would happen if I—"

"*I've* been drunk *lots* of times!" Ben shouted him down. "I got drunk in *junior high* sometimes! Nobody died! *Everybody* does it, Joby, and *nobody dies*!" He grabbed Joby's arms again, as if he might somehow force him to listen.

"Someone did die," Joby whispered. His eyes glazed even further. "It's different for you, Ben. . . . It always has been."

Ben was relieved to see Mr. Thompson, one of the school counselors, hurrying across the lawn, but when he got there, Joby wouldn't speak, so Ben explained as best he could.

"Joby," Mr. Thompson said calmly, "Ben is right. This wasn't your fault. In fact, your good sense in refusing to ride with him has saved us all from twice the grief. I can't tell you how grateful I am—how grateful we *all* are."

Joby remained silent, looking at the sky as if none of them were there. Ben felt his own eyes burning, wondering whether it would be good or bad for Joby to see him cry.

"Joby, let's go somewhere and talk, okay?" Mr. Thompson said.

Joby looked at him for the first time, then nodded slightly, as if movement itself were painful for him.

"Ben, thank you," Mr. Thompson said. "You can let him up now."

Ben got up, and reached down to give Joby a hand.

But as Joby reached his feet, he tore from Ben's grasp and bolted down the sidewalk away from school. Ben and Mr. Thompson were after him instantly, but Joby's speed seemed almost supernatural. Thompson soon fell away and ran back toward school. After three blocks, Ben started losing ground. Half a block later he gave up and turned back toward school himself. He'd get Laura, and they'd go find Joby together. He had a few ideas where Joby might go, and Joby wouldn't run from Laura . . . he hoped.

❈

"Absolutely *not,*" Lucifer barked. "I don't care how you do it, just get him *down* from there. I win *nothing* if he dies now."

Lucifer had canceled all appointments to stand over the viewing bowl and direct his team via the office obelisk. The moment Joby had stopped to loiter on the overpass, he'd gone to the obsidian pillar and contacted Malcephalon.

"No! Suicide will not *begin* to satisfy the wager's terms. . . .

"Yes, that's fine. . . .

"No. Eventually, he's got to be working for us, and he might be of no use whatsoever mad. I want him down, *and* sane, and I want it *now*! Must I be clearer? . . .

"Good. Now take care of it."

❈

Joby didn't know how long he'd watched the freeway traffic rush below him. For some time, only one thought had occupied his mind: *The wages of sin is death.*

But why Lindwald's? he thought at last. *Joby* was the sinner. Fornication, drunkenness, murder, all in one weekend. Why should Jamie have been the one to pay?

He remembered Lindwald flinching from his touch after Lucy Beeker's birthday mission . . . recalled the scars exposed on Lindwald's back after he and Ben had beaten him for being a "demon." Lindwald had paid over and over for Joby's mistakes. "Let's go celebrate *life,*" he heard Jamie laugh again. "*Your* life!"

"My life," Joby whispered dolefully. Just a quick climb over the railing, a single mindless jump. . . . People might grieve, but they'd get over it and go on with their lives.

Only . . . even now, in the middle of this desolation, he knew they wouldn't.

Every time he'd set his hand to the railing, his mind had filled with vivid, awful images of what his death would do to everyone he had cared for: Laura, Ben, his mom and dad. Though he'd lost any of fear of hurting himself, he could find no way to live *or* die with hurting all those others so terribly . . . so permanently. There seemed no way to make anything better, but it seemed he would be forced to live anyway, just to keep from making things worse.

Drained of feeling altogether, he wandered off the overpass at last, and, like a wounded animal driven by instinct toward its den, finally found himself at home, relieved to find his mother's car gone. He unlocked the door, and went inside fearing he had little time before she returned.

In his room, he pulled some clothes into a bag, then, hardly able to think, scrabbled through his shelves and desk drawers for anything else he might need, until, buried in the very back of his bottom drawer, he came across a thin book bound in royal blue, its cover decorated with a golden sunburst in a field of stars. Beneath that was his *Treasury of Arthurian Tales,* both stored there, out of sight and out of mind, since childhood. He sat numbly on his bed, and began to flip vacantly backward through the small blue book.

It was filled with large, childish writing, smudged in pencil. "Taubolt." "Taubolt." "Taubolt." The name appeared again and again across the last few pages. Then, "A knight must practice." He felt blood rush to his face, and flipped quickly to the front of the book. "Drink a lot of beauty, Sir Joby. Feed your—" He flipped that page so hard, it tore, wanting to close it altogether, but he couldn't seem to stop flipping through its pages, as if the answer to all this might still be hidden somewhere between all the things he was trying not to read . . . until his eyes caught a single heading, and his fingers froze.

"Ideas for beating Lindwald."

He was on his feet, running from the house, madly down the street without a plan, oblivious of the books still clutched in his straining hands. He ran and ran, trying to outdistance the torrent of memory: childhood dreams of Arthur; candles in the darkness; reconciliation of enemies, comfort to the suffering, help for the weak; candles burning by the hundreds, off into the night. . . . The knight. . . . *The knight of God! "Ha!"* he shouted, hardly able to bear his own scorn. What an ass! If he ran forever, he *might* not make it all any *worse!* . . . *That* was the brightest dream left him.

He ended up in a field, doubled over in the grass, vomiting a single plea, over and over, until his raw sobs mocked the raven's voice: *"Forgive me! Forgive me!"*

There was no answer in the silence, and in time, he ceased to speak at all, but merely sat and stared as sunset came and he realized, with dull surprise, where he was.

The tournament field.

He got up still clutching his two small talismans of childhood, went slowly to the clearing's edge, swung his arm back, and threw them as hard as he could into the trees.

❈

Across the field, concealed in knee-high grass and weeds, a glossy tortoise-shell cat stood stock-still, watching, with strange dark eyes, as Joby shuffled miserably away. When the boy was gone, the cat turned to mew mournfully at a cricket perched atop a long tendril of vetch beside him.

"He begs forgiveness he does not need," the cat mewed in frustration. "Why does he not think to beg for *help*, My Lord?"

"Lucifer's creature spoke truly before he was destroyed," the Cricket chirruped softly. "Joby has been well trained to think only of his debt to others. And in any case, he can hardly have guessed that you were here to offer *directly* help, Gabe."

"But he has many years of religious instruction now, Master. Why should it not occur to him to call upon one of us?"

"Oh, he'll call upon Me," the Creator sighed. "But Lucifer's terms forbid Me from answering. As for you and all My other servants, Gabe. I sadly suspect that for Joby you are precisely that, and nothing more: 'religious instruction.' He may have been taught all your names, but it will not occur to him that any of you are actually there watching, except, perhaps, to judge and condemn."

"Then how can he ask any of us for help at all?" Gabe asked, greatly distressed. "He cannot. It is not fair!"

"Nonetheless, it is the deal I agreed to," the Creator chirruped gravely.

"He will want those books back someday," Gabriel mewed in agitation. "They contain a portion of his heart. . . . Surely it would not violate the wager's terms if I retrieved them so that they can be returned, should he think to ask it someday?"

"That's for you to say, Gabe."

"Me!" the cat complained. "Since when is it my place to define Your will, Lord?"

"You know I am not allowed to speak on any matter touching the wager. *You* are the wager's official witness and arbiter, are you not? Who should know better?"

Gabe batted the grass with his tail in agitation. He had *never* had to *guess* his Master's will. A moment later, where the cat had been, a young man stood, with dark eyes and lovely copper features framed in curly locks as black as night. He walked resolutely toward the thicket of trees where Joby's books had vanished, but came back moments later empty-handed.

"They are gone!" Gabe said quietly to the cricket. "I searched quite carefully! Where can they have gone?"

"The world is full of mystery, Gabe," the cricket chirruped back. "Dryer lint, for instance."

"What?" Gabe, asked.

"Does anyone ever see it on the clothes when they go in?" the cricket mused. "Do the clothes seem much smaller when you take them out? . . . Of course," the cricket chirruped pensively, "clothes do shrink sometimes, but that hardly seems to account for all the sheets of it left over in the end."

"My Lord, forgive me, but . . . I haven't the slightest idea what You're talking about. What happened to Joby's books?"

"There's another mystery, Gabe. Shall we head back? I've a sudden hankering for cards. Care to join Me in a game of poker?"

"*Cards*, My Lord? . . . *Now?*"

"If not now, *when*?" the cricket chirped.

❈

Their fruitless search ended where it had begun: at the school parking lot. Ben stared wearily through the windshield, his hands still on the wheel, trying to think of someplace they might have missed, while Laura sat in like silence beside him. They had combed the grid of streets around campus first, then gone to the tournament field and half a dozen less and less likely places after that. They'd even gone out to St. Albee's, where Ben had derived some small, cold pleasure from the look on Richter's face as he learned of the disastrous fruit all his guilt-mongering had produced.

They'd found Mrs. Peterson a tearful wreck at Joby's home. After Mr. Thompson's call that morning, she'd spent a few panicked hours waiting there, then gone to church to pray for Joby's safety, only to come back and discover he'd been home while she was out. Ben and Laura had stayed with her until Joby's dad had arrived.

As Ben tried in vain to think of some stone unturned, Laura began to cry again.

"Hey," he crooned, sliding an arm across her shoulder. "Joby's okay. He's just gone somewhere to sort things out."

"I've made such a mess of everything," she moaned, swiping at her running nose. "I've driven him completely away just when he needs me most."

"No, you didn't," Ben insisted.

Laura just cried even harder, burying her face in his shoulder, soaking his sleeve with her tears.

While they'd been searching for Joby, she had told Ben all about seducing Joby after prom, and how horrified she'd been afterward at what she'd done. He'd been tempted several times to tell her of the marriage plans Joby had confided in him that morning, but he knew those were not his to tell, and certainly not under these circumstances. What unbelievably sucky timing.

"I wanted him to love me, Ben," she wept. "I wanted us to stay together. But I . . ." for a moment she simply shook with sobs. "I didn't want to *trick him* into anything!"

"Shhhh," Ben said, hugging her even tighter. "He loves you, Laura. He told me so. When we got to school this morning, he said he was going to . . . to go find you and talk." His hand came up to wipe Laura's tears away. He kissed her cheek where they had been, then kissed the top of her head. She looked up at him, so near, so hurt, so desperate for comfort . . . and somehow, it was her lips that his brushed next. She looked startled, but did not protest or pull away. Instead, she seemed to hold her breath, gazing at him uncertainly when he leaned back at last. Ben knew what he had done was wrong, but Joby had left Laura here with no one to turn to except . . . except . . . Laura leaned up and kissed him again, as if testing some confusing, utterly unexpected hypothesis.

"Well, screw me blind! *Looky here!*"

Laura jumped convulsively in Ben's arms, as he whirled around, slamming his arm painfully on the steering wheel Johnny Mayhew's face was practically pressed against the driver's window.

"King Joby's girl, frenchin' his best friend. That's *sweet!*" Mayhew crowed.

Ben was so horrified—both at what he'd done and at Mayhew's sudden appearance—that, for a moment, he couldn't even move.

"Looks like Joby's havin' a pretty rough day," Mayhew sneered. "Not as bad as Lindwald's, though. Yer just the kinda friends that murdering son of a bitch deserves."

Suddenly blind with rage, Ben was out of the car in a tangle fists and flailing, but Mayhew had already fled, stopping only once halfway across the lawn, and turning to jeer, "I'm gonna tell 'im, Ben! I'm gonna show 'im there's karma out there after all!"

⊠

Joby sat vacantly adjusting the sleeves of his robe, the tilt of his cap, waiting for them to call him to the podium to make his little speech. He just wished the ceremony done with. His pointless years of high school, his childhood in this town, his life with these people; he wanted it to end.

Having suffered terrible nightmares where Jamie's horrible parents shouted accusations at him over his friend's open grave, Joby hadn't found the courage to attend the funeral. When Johnny Mayhew had come later to accuse him of being a fake friend to Lindwald and gloat about Ben and Laura's betrayal, Joby had only taken Johnny's news as bitter confirmation of his own failure. To think that only hours after he'd told Ben he meant to marry her . . . But what did that matter now? Joby wasn't worthy of her. They must both have seen that. He wasn't even safe for her. He wasn't safe for anyone.

Even now, two months later, neither he nor she had talked with him about it—any of it. Two weeks earlier, as Joby had entered the hallway to the music room after school. He was getting some books he'd left, and he'd overheard them around the corner; Laura in tears—groaning about how if Joby knew it would destroy him and how she'd never dreamed this could happen to her and Ben agreeing that telling Joby would only make things worse. Joby hadn't had to guess what it was they didn't want him to know. He had just snuck quietly away again, wanting to spare them all yet another painful scene. As the weeks had passed, he and they had treated each other more and more like cordial strangers.

He could still see Ben's closed face earlier this evening, as they'd lined up for their graduation procession.

"You'll stay in touch, right?" Ben had asked, as if Joby were a distant relative, or a business associate.

"Sure," he had smiled as politely, "I'm just going to Berkeley, not the moon. I hear they've put up phone lines to Colorado now."

That had been it. Laura hadn't spoken to him at all that night, just smiled from her place near the front of their line. Joby hadn't been able to keep himself from thinking of the three of them together as kids, out at the tournament field, at his house or Ben's . . . at Roundtable meetings in the grammar school library. . . .

"And now," the principal announced, "I invite our class valedictorian, Joby Peterson, to the podium to share his thoughts on behalf of the graduating class."

Joby stood to polite applause and went up to mouth the words his adviser had helped him craft. He saw his parents sitting side by side, clapping with embarrassing enthusiasm. His brief tantrum after Jamie's death seemed to have brought them a little closer. The only good anyone had to show for that ordeal.

Placing the text of his speech on the podium, Joby fought an impulse to run off the stage completely. He had never been shy about talking before an audience. But this . . . it seemed too sickening . . . too lonely, somehow, to end his life here with one last big lie. But, what choice did he have? . . . What choice had he ever had?

"Parents, faculty, and fellow graduates," he began at last. "As we go out tonight into a wider world, I am compelled to ask one question: What it is that we hope to achieve? Just the next in a long series of rote steps toward acceptable membership in society? Just a job? A house? More income than the Joneses'?"

He swept the audience with his eyes as he'd been coached to do, seeing nothing.

"I hope, rather, that each of us goes out into the world tonight searching for some way to leave this planet a better place than it was when we arrived."

Or at least not damage it more than we already have, scoffed some ugly voice at the back of his mind.

"Tonight," Joby hurried on, "I hope we might resolve to forego some measure of wealth in pursuit of human wholeness and well-being. We must be ready to struggle harder for resolution of our conflicts than for victory over our opponents. We must be prepared to—"

Fake our way through an entire lifetime! cackled his tormenting mental auditor. Joby grabbed the glass of water left for him on the podium, and he took several long swallows to cover his dismay.

"We must be prepared to find *solutions* to our problems, rather than just people to punish for them."

He seemed to hear actual laughter in his own head then. Angry, accusing laughter.

"Tonight, I hold one wish above all others for my fellow classmates; that in twenty years the world will judge each of us successful, not by our wealth or personal importance, but by our capacity to dream a better world and to realize those dreams. As for myself, I would rather be the least happy man in a happy world, than the happiest man in a sad one."

Done at last, he fairly raced from the podium, hardly aware of the thunderous standing ovation he was receiving. Only when he was safely seated did he see his parents standing side by side, pounding their hands raw with approval, his mother's face awash in *happy* tears for once.

Too late, he thought bleakly as the applause rang on. *I've already failed . . . at all of it.*

PART TWO

※

Taubolt

(Downward Mobility)

Most of the others didn't seem to give a shit how people looked at them, but even after three years on the street, Gypsy still hated begging coins from folks who pretended not to see him even as they dropped change into his hand. It was hard to say which humiliated him most; the vacant stares, the guilty glances, or the outright sneers—not that Gypsy ever let it show, of course. He'd learned that lesson the hard way within days of leaving home. Let it show, and the cash cows walked right past you, while your fellow panhandlers turned on exposed fear like sharks come to blood in the water.

He had imagined none of this on the day he'd fled his parents' house to find "a more meaningful life," but there was no going back now. He'd never been able to keep a job for long. Too much bullshit, too little patience. So, much as he hated sitting against this building, sticking out his hand as strangers looked away, the need to eat and feed his dog had taught him to smile at every one of them like they were long lost lovers, offering cheerful little compliments to those who gave, and to those who didn't—long as they didn't swear at him, or spit, or kick.

Then again, there were a few on any street who'd never learned to look away at all. Easy marks. You could spot 'em blocks away, and Berkeley seemed to have more of them than any city Gypsy'd lingered in so far. He watched one of them get off a bus down on the corner. Young guy, about his own age, arms around a box of something. Normally that would have knocked him right off Gypsy's radar. Hands full was the best excuse around to pass you by, but everything about this guy said, "easy money." Gypsy'd never seen a face so vulnerable of vulnerability, or body language that screamed, *Please don't ask. I'll have to help you,* more loudly. No charming smile for this one, though. This guy was a bleeder. Suffering was what made him tilt. Gypsy could tell. Christ! This guy wore so much on his face, he might as well be naked!

When the guy was close enough, Gypsy looked up wearily, and said, "Hey, bud. Any chance you'd help my dog 'n' me get a bite to eat?"

The guy turned uncomfortably toward him, not quite meeting Gypsy's eyes, then, sure enough, set down his box, pulled a surprising wad of change out of his pocket, and dropped it all into Gypsy's hand. *Bonanza!* Gypsy thought gleefully. Had to be five dollars there, maybe more! To his surprise, the guy checked his other pocket too, and gave Gypsy what was there as well.

"Good-lookin' dog," the guy said, suddenly meeting Gypsy's eyes, and actually smiling, if a little wanly.

"Hey, thanks!" Gypsy said, forgetting not to smile as he stashed the loot inside his jacket. There'd be meal tickets and dog food for a couple days in this chunk of change. "His name's Shadow."

"Suits him," said the guy, turning his attention back to Gypsy's black lab.

"He's friendly," Gypsy said. "You can pet him if you want."

The guy reached out and ruffled Shadow's head.

"I'm Gypsy," Gypsy said, reaching out to shake hands before realizing how grimy his had gotten from hours of sitting on the sidewalk.

"Joby," said the other guy, grabbing Gypsy's hand without hesitation. "Well, you guys hang in there," he offered, picking up his box of stuff, and turning to go.

"You too," said Gypsy. "Hey, thanks again, man. God bless you, man. I mean it."

Joby looked back long enough to nod and smile, then turned again to go his way, but a portly man scowling at him from the entrance of a convenience store said, "It's stupid to encourage them, you know."

"Pardon me?" Gypsy heard Joby say, turning to face the man.

"Thanks to people like you," the man complained, "more of those bums clutter the sidewalk outside my shop here every day. I don't much appreciate it."

"You wouldn't. You're not hungry," Joby replied, and made to walk on.

"You think he'll spend that money on food?" the shopkeeper sneered. "You just bought that bum a beer, or a joint, more likely. Don't you get it?"

Instantly pissed, Gypsy stood up intending to go set this asshole straight, but before he'd taken three steps, Joby said angrily, "I'm not here to manage everybody else's life. What he does with that change is his responsibility. My responsibility is not to join the obscene surplus of mean-spirited tightwads ruining this whole planet!"

Whoa! Gypsy thought, coming to a halt. This was different.

"I'm not the one who's ruining things!" the shopkeeper snapped. "My taxes pay for the sidewalk these bums sit around on all day. *I'm* productive! *I* have a *job.*"

"Lucky you," Joby growled and turned again to leave.

"How do you know they're even really poor?" the shopkeeper sneered at his retreating back. "Half of them just dress up in rags and bum fortunes in spare change here every day. You must be new to Berkeley, young man, or you'd know that. Everyone else does." He turned away and muttered scornfully, "You're so gullible," then disappeared into the recesses of his shop.

"Least *I* don't believe the homeless are all *rich*," Joby grumbled as he left.

After three years on the street, Gypsy hadn't thought anything could still surprise him. Calling Shadow to his side, he started after Joby. "Hey, man!" he called. "Wait up!"

Joby turned around, looking tired and a little impatient.

"Man, that was awesome!" Gypsy grinned as he caught up to Joby. "Thanks, dude! *Nobody* ever sticks up for us like that. *Nobody.*"

"That would be me," Joby shrugged. "Nobody."

Thinking maybe this guy wasn't as easily read as he'd thought, Gypsy asked, "Why'd you do it, anyway? You don't even know me."

"You mean, tell that dickhead off?" Joby shrugged. "Wasn't hard. Hell, I've been getting mad at dickheads all my life. One of the few things I do really well, it seems."

"Why are you so down on yourself?" Gypsy asked.

"I've got a ways to walk still, and this is getting kind of heavy," Joby said, nodding at the box he carried. "I should get going." He turned and started up the street.

"Hey, I'm sorry," Gypsy said. "I didn' mean to dis you, man. Here, I'll carry that for you." He caught up to Joby again and reached to take the box.

"That's okay," Joby said. "I can manage."

"You gave me some decent change back there," Gypsy pressed. "Whatever that ass-wipe thinks, I got no problem workin' for my daily bread."

Joby stopped again, and turned to Gypsy with a bleak expression.

"My big nose gets me into all kinds of trouble," Gypsy pled before Joby could speak. "But I'll be honest, you got me pretty curious. I just wanna know why you been so cool to me when mostly people just wish I was gone."

This had the surprising effect of making Joby look . . . not guilty, exactly, but something close to it.

"You gonna let me carry that?" Gypsy pressed.

"Sure. Why not?" Joby sighed, handing him the box. "Thanks."

"No problem," Gypsy said. The box had no top, so he figured it was okay to look. There were some pens, a coffee cup, a half-empty bottle of mouthwash, a soft pack of CDs, a few bottles of lemon iced tea and several pieces of fruit, three fantasy novels, and a mechanical monkey on a tricycle. "What is all this anyway?" he asked. "You movin' or somethin'?"

Joby sighed again as they began to walk, and said, "It's stuff from work. I just lost my third job in six months."

"No way!" Gypsy said.

"Way," Joby replied humorlessly. "At this rate, I'll be sitting outside that asshole's shop myself within a month."

Gypsy stopped walking, utterly at a loss.

"Why the hell'd you give me all that change then?" Gypsy asked. "Ain't you gonna need it?"

Joby shrugged. "I'll go broke an hour sooner now. Doesn't matter much to me. Matter to you?"

"A lot," Gypsy said, realizing that after all these pointless years, he'd finally stumbled into someone he might actually want to know.

❧

Joby's studio apartment was four flights up in a converted Victorian hotel with cracked Tiffany windows, scarred parquet floors, and beamed ceilings enameled in garish yellow. It shared a wall with the moldering Art Deco movie theater next door, so that late at night, if he pressed his ear to the plaster, he could hear snatches of sweaty passion or melancholy dialogue in foreign languages. He'd already paid this month's rent. There might be just enough in his bank account to cover next month's too, if he didn't eat. He'd called this charming little dump home for nine long years. The only tenants who'd lived in the building longer were its cockroaches, but Joby harbored no illusion that his long tenure would win any lenience from the landlord.

After dropping his box of stuff on the threadbare couch, he went to the window and stared down at Shattuck Avenue's busy traffic, wondering what to do with his untimely freedom. It was too late for a matinee and too early for anything else. Perhaps, he thought sardonically, he should have invited Gypsy to come up and chat some more. By the time they'd gotten here, the young vagrant had begun to grow on him a little, in an *Oliver Twist* sort of way. Learning of Joby's dilemma, Gypsy had been full of useful tips about where to eat on twenty-five cents a day, and how to sleep warmly outside in winter.

With a heavy sigh, Joby turned from the window and wandered toward the alcove pantry that doubled as his bedroom. Sitting down there on his narrow cot—or, more precisely, on the pile of dirty laundry covering it—he tried to come up with yet another plan, though he doubted it would matter what he tried. Since getting himself kicked out of school nine years earlier, Joby's life had seemed to decompose as inexorably as all those soggy newspapers heaped up in the apartment building's leaky basement. Each tedious, menial job he'd lost had led to some even more meaningless job, until now it seemed he wasn't even equipped to enter columns of pointless numerals into a database all day at InfoStream. He had certainly done his best—at all the jobs he'd lost—but any expectation of cause and effect between effort and results had abandoned him long ago. He hadn't so much as one good reference to show for all those years of futility.

Turning to his parents for help was out of the question. Joby had concluded long ago that it was best for them, and for himself, that they know as little as possible about what his life had become. He called them several times a year to let them know he was alive, and assure them, however fraudulently, that all was well. Probably sensing that the truth would be unpleasant, they seemed content to let things go at that.

Trying to find some more comfortable perch on the pile of clothes beneath him, Joby conceded that he might as well bundle this mess up and walk it to the Laundromat. The apartment's gloom made him feel claustrophobic anyway.

Moments later, he walked back through the dingy lobby of his building and stepped into the frenetic stream of pedestrians outside. Squinting against the bright September afternoon, he hoisted his trash bag of clothing over one shoulder and started toward the corner, where yet another specimen of ravaged humanity was hunkered down against the wall. Sitting in her long, ragged skirts, weaving strands of yarn around a tiny cross of sticks, the weathered old woman looked like an apple doll someone had left out all winter in the rain. As he passed, she offered him a merry, half-toothless smile.

"Sorry," he grunted, looking away. "Gave it all to the last guy."

❈

Sometimes every moment in Hell seemed an eternity to Williamson. Halfway through Malcephalon's interminable presentation, he had begun counting silently backward from 666,666 just to combat the boredom. Now, he was starting to wonder if some larger number might not be called for.

Lucifer's conference room had been enlarged several times during the past ten years to accommodate the swelling legions of Hell's most renowned glitterati sitting around it now. Williamson was still accorded no loftier role than "security camera," of course, though Lucifer continued to demand his analysis in private, only to credit himself later for all the best ideas.

"Malcephalon!" blurted out an enormous pile of demonic flab named Basquel. "While we all stand in awe of your inexhaustible expertise, eternity *is* ticking by. Is the boy ready yet, or isn't he?"

Malcephalon fell silent, glowering at his detractor.

"Don't be petulant, darling," teased a stunning succubus wrapped in glimmering silks, "Basquel's just admitting that brilliant insights like yours are wasted on minds like his own." Basquel shot her a threatening frown. "But surely you can understand our eagerness to know. Is he soup yet, or not?"

"Not," Malcephalon intoned. "Yet," he added to stifle the rustle of discontent rippling through the assembly.

"We're twenty-four years into this campaign," Lucifer growled impatiently, "which, by the wager's terms, leaves us only *seven more* to bring *some* plan to fruition. How long can it take to break one pathetic boy's spirit?"

"You insist on cautious subterfuge," droned the dour demon. "Give him no meaningful crises, you say, nothing to battle but himself, yes? Such strategies require time. The boy's will is strong, his character sadly well intentioned. By now he is very angry, of course, but directs that anger largely at himself, just as you commanded—which causes him to rot, much as a pear does, from the core outward. The skin will be last to go. I fear we can expect little visible satisfaction until all he's stored inside these many years exceeds capacity. Then, I assure you, the whole structure will collapse at once, and we will have a victory as swift and devastating as its construction was . . . meticulous."

"Which should occur *when,* exactly?" Lucifer pressed in overt exasperation.

"You ask me to read tea leaves, Bright One," Malcephalon complained, "but, if we continue to be *very* careful . . . I think, perhaps . . . within the year."

At the resulting clamor, Williamson sank farther into his chair, demoralized. If he didn't find some way to grab the ball soon, he might never get the chance.

⚜

Autumn had blown fiercely into winter. Rain gusted through Berkeley's streets now, slicking asphalt and concrete to a gloomy sheen. Heavy fabrics in dark colors were back in fashion for those who could afford to care. Joby could not. His job interviews always seemed to go well, then—*nothing*—as if all his applications had simply vanished behind him. In October, he'd finally taken young Gypsy's advice and started dining here, at the Berkley Public Meal Project, to conserve his dwindling funds. Dinner could be had each night for twenty-five cents in the basement of this Unitarian Church.

Standing in a cold drizzle amidst the smoky, milling throng waiting for the dining hall to open, he looked around for Gypsy. Joby's initial forays into Berkeley's street culture had been awkward at best. Having no idea how to behave around people he did not remotely understand, he had behaved badly at first. Had it not been for Gypsy's almost eager willingness to mediate between Joby and the others, he might never have been accepted here. As Gypsy had helped him discard his distorted preconceptions, however, Joby had come to enjoy the companionship of his new peers. Now dinner was the highlight of his day, and Gypsy was one of the best friends he'd made in years.

To Joby's disappointment, the boy was nowhere to be seen tonight. Across the parking lot, however, by a cluster of rumpled men drinking from paper bags beside the Dumpster, he saw "the little old yarn weaver," as he'd once thought of her. Joby smiled and raised a hand in greeting. She waved back with one hand, waving off a proffered bottle with the other. Their friendship had been born gracelessly as well.

As Joby had wandered the city that fall looking for employment, she had come to seem almost omnipresent in her mass of fraying skirts, weaving her little ornaments of brightly colored yarn. She'd never said a word to him, much less asked for money, but had often smiled when he passed, as if they were old friends. This strange attention had come to cause him such discomfort that he'd started turning corners at the sight of her. Not until Gypsy had finally introduced them at the Project, one clear October evening, had Joby learned her name. Mary, it turned out, was regarded by nearly everyone here as the unofficial queen of Berkeley's streets.

No one seemed quite sure where she had come from, or how long she'd been around, but all agreed it had been longer than most among this transient crowd. Nor could anyone say where she went at night. But there was no one easier to find by day, as Joby had already discovered, and once he'd quit avoiding her, he'd quickly come to appreciate her marvelous sense of humor and great trove of earthy wisdom.

"What are you doing here?" rasped a voice at Joby's shoulder.

Joby whirled to find a gaunt man of sickly gray complexion whose short pewter hair seemed more bitten off than cut, and stumbled back, as much from the reek of urine, sweat, and stale smoke as from surprise.

"I know what you're doing up there!" the man insisted in a rapid-fire staccato. "I hear you through the floor! I hear everything!" He wrung a knot of greasy rags nervously between his hands. "I know all about Nixon's daughter."

"You've got the wrong guy," Joby stammered, struggling to conceal his alarm.

"Don't fuck with me!" the lunatic shouted. *"I know where you've got me buried! I know where all of us are buried! I hear everything you do up there!"*

"Silverjack! Down boy!"

Joby turned to find Sundog, the Project's self-appointed peacekeeper, coming toward them across the parking lot, his beefy hands held up in placation. Mary followed close behind, looking somber. Passing Joby by, the burly red-haired vet placed a hand gently on the maniac's shoulder and said, "Joby's okay. He's a friend of Mary's. See?" He turned to Joby, one hand still on Silverjack's shoulder. "Joby, this is Silverjack. He gets a little freaked around strangers."

"You know Mary?" Silverjack asked Joby suspiciously.

Joby nodded.

Silverjack looked past him at Mary. "You know him?"

"We're good friends, dearie," she assured him with one of her toothless smiles.

"He's okay?" Silverjack pressed.

"Would I be eatin' with 'im if he wasn't?" she asked, coming to stand beside Joby.

Silverjack gave Joby a decisive nod and said, "You're okay then," as if it were Joby who'd been uncertain, then thrust out a filthy hand, which Joby shook once, trying not to grimace.

"There you go!" Sundog roared happily, slapping Joby on the shoulder with one arm, and rocking Silverjack in a half hug with the other. Then, with Mary in tow, he yanked Joby brusquely off toward the basement door where those with tickets were finally being admitted.

"Thanks for bailing me out," Joby said turning first to Sundog, then to Mary.

"No problem," Sundog rumbled. "Everybody gets along. That's what matters."

❧

Wishing another of his "neighbors" good night, Drusaffa left their porch with his stack of pamphlets, and stopped to watch the last few stragglers shuffle out of the church basement down the street. The one they called Silverjack was still pacing and muttering erratically to himself back by the Dumpsters. Drrusaffa grinned, focused his mind, and hurled a barb in the man's direction.

Sure enough, the vagrant turned, peering fearfully into the streetlighted dark-ness around him until he met Drrusaffa's gaze across the distance. The demon's hideous grin widened unnaturally as Silverjack's frightened eyes went round as moons. Drrusaffa chuckled as the ruined man ran screaming from the lot, nearly bowling over two terrified old women walking home.

Drrusaffa's "neighbors" knew him as Bob Mackley, that nice young man who'd moved into the neighborhood several months ago, or had it been longer? Such a civic-minded young man, active in so many good causes, like . . . like, well, people had trouble remembering just what exactly, thought they'd been told all about it . . . by someone.

It had been rather dreary, really, drifting around for three months in an empty apartment, doing practically nothing when he wasn't out ingratiating himself to the neighborhood, or vandalizing their cars, or burglarizing their homes.

He mounted another flight of steps and rang the doorbell. A middle-aged man answered, looking vaguely irritated until he saw who it was.

"Why, hello Bob." He smiled. "What's got you out after dark?"

"Hello, Mr. Kerry." Drrusaffa smiled back.

"Who is it, dear?" asked a woman's voice from down the hall, where Drrusaffa noted the bluish flicker and mumbly voices of a TV. *Wonderful things, TVs,* he thought.

"It's Bob Mackley, honey."

"Ohhh!" exclaimed Mrs. Kerry, coming swiftly from the living room to stand beaming at her husband's side. "Won't you come in, Bob?"

"Thanks, but I can't stay. I just came by to let you know about a meeting I'm hosting next week."

"A meeting?" Mrs. Kerry asked, as if the word were foreign.

"Well, I've just been hearing so much concern about what's happening around the neighborhood," Drrusaffa said. "Seems like everybody I talk to—"

"Happening?" Mr. Kerry interrupted. "What's happening? I haven't heard."

"Oh. Sorry," Drrusaffa said. "I assumed you knew about the burglaries, at least."

"Burglaries?" Mrs. Kerry gasped. "Around here?"

Drrusaffa nodded gravely. "The Fowlers' house a month ago, and Mrs. Bennet's place just last week."

"Oh! That poor old woman!" Mrs. Kerry said, a hand flying to her mouth. "Mike! That's just up the street!"

"And all the vandalism, of course," Drrusaffa added.

"What vandalism?" Mr. Kerry asked unhappily.

"Gardens torn up in the middle of the night, houses spray-painted." Drrusaffa gave them his most guileless expression. "It just seemed like a good idea to get the neighborhood together and see if there's anything we might be able to do." He frowned uncomfortably. "I'm the last person who'd want to sound uncharitable, Mike, but . . . well, some people are starting to worry about the Meal Project's impact on our neighborhood."

"Why, yes!" Mrs. Kerry exclaimed. "Those people are crazy! I don't walk past there in the evenings anymore."

Drrusaffa held up his hands as if to forestall her conclusion. "Personally, I think what they're doing over there is important. People have a right to eat, and hunger certainly doesn't make vagrants any friendlier or safer."

"Well, then what are you proposing we do, Bob?" Mr. Kerry asked.

"Oh, I'm not *proposing* anything," Drrusaffa protested pleasantly. "I'm just providing a place for people to get together and talk about what *they* want to do."

❈

"I'm not kidding!" Gypsy insisted. "This guy told us pigeon-kicking was some big sport in Canada, and when we told him he was full of shit, he went to show us how they do it. Walked right over to these pigeons by the fountain, and launches this big kick at one. By the time he figures out the dumb bird's just gonna stand there lookin' at him, it was too late to stop his foot." Joby's hands flew up to catch the fruit punch jetting painfully out his nose as laughter erupted around the table. "You should have seen his face, man!" Gypsy laughed. "The bird goes flyin' 'cross Sproul Plaza and flops down right in this bunch of girls eatin' lunch. Dead as a doornail. Oh God!" Gypsy gasped, barely able to speak through his own laughter now. "You shoulda heard 'em scream! The guy's so horrified, he just . . . he just ran away like . . .'" Gypsy couldn't go on, clutching at his sides as he gasped for breath.

"You're so full of crap!" Sundog roared when he could speak again. "Don't your ass ever get hoarse from spoutin' such bullshit?"

"Got a whole barnyard into that one!" Mary cackled. "All but the chickens!"

"I'm totally serious!" Gypsy protested. "Tell 'em, Sarina! You were there. I ain't smart enough to make up shit like this."

"You are too!" she protested, slapping Gypsy's shoulder. "It's true though. Just like Gypsy said. I felt sorry for the bird though."

"Well," said Mary, "the man'll know better now what's meant by 'bird brains.'"

"Yeah," Sundog said, smirking. "Prob'ly still wipin' 'em off his shoe."

"You guys are terrible!" Sarina said, smiling reproachfully at everyone as she stood up, straightening her tie-dyed skirts. "I'd better get back there. I'm supposed to help clean up tonight." She leaned down to brush Gypsy's cheek with her lips, hiding his face inside the curtain of her ropy braids for an instant before squeezing his shoulder, and heading off to the dining hall's kitchen.

Gypsy watched her go with what a truly goofy smile.

"Someone's in love," Sundog crooned, lampooning tenderness.

"Jealous?" Gypsy asked, turning back to grin at Sundog. "You should be."

"Play nice, boys," Mary smiled. "Love's no laughin' matter."

"Not for Sundog," Gypsy scoffed. "For him, it's just a cryin' shame."

"I'm hit!" Sundog grimaced, clutching at his barrel chest. "God, that smarts." He pushed his chair back and got up with a smile. "Sarina's right. You're too smart to tangle with, monkey boy. Think I'll go drown my sorrows for a while. Care to join me, Mary?"

"Not if it's that diet horse piss you're offerin' me," she said daintily.

"What is this?" the big vet whined melodramatically. "Sundog piñata night? If my whiskey's not good enough for you, I'll take back the invitation, then."

"Whiskey, did you say?" Mary's eyes lit up as she gathered her skirts and climbed from her chair. "You might have mentioned it was whiskey, dear, 'fore lettin' me insult you that way. I was just thinkin' what a lovely night it was to share with friends." She batted her eyes comically at Sundog. "And I've no better friend than you, darlin'."

Sundog laughed, and took her arm as they headed out into the evening.

Alone at their table, Joby and Gypsy shared a meditative silence.

"She's a great girl," Joby said at last.

"Sarina? Yeah." Gypsy smiled. "She's so awesome." He fell silent again, then said more quietly, "My life always felt so pointless. You know. Endin' up like this, on the street? But now it all seems different, you know? 'Cause now I know it all led up to her. If I'd never run away . . ." He trailed off and shrugged. His smile faded before some more unhappy thought.

"Why the frown?" Joby said.

Gypsy shrugged again. "What am I gonna do, though, Joby? I mean, she ain't gonna marry some homeless street punk."

"You want to *marry* her?" Joby asked, somewhat surprised. Gypsy and Sarina had only been together for a couple months as far as he knew.

"Hell *yes*," Gypsy answered with sudden vehemence. "Joby, I left home to find somethin'. Somethin' to do, or be, that mattered. *Someone,* even. Someone I could believe in and, and, I don't know, follow, I guess, you know?" He shook his head. "Course, I was a clueless little twad. Don't think I haven't kicked my own ass almost every day for that. I let all that go years ago. Then Sarina came . . ." The light bloomed again in Gypsy's eyes. "She's all the meaning I could ever need, man." He looked back at Joby in excitement. "You know what I mean?"

To his dismay, Joby found that he did. Without warning, Gypsy's words plunged Joby into sudden, painful memory of another evening, impossibly long ago.

"I just . . . I gotta find some way to keep her though. Some way to be worthy of her," Gypsy said, his voice suddenly filled with angst. "I'm so afraid I'll lose her. That's what I do, man. I'm a loser! How do you change that, Joby? I gotta change that, now, before she goes. I *have to*! But I don't know how."

"I don't know either," he said, struggling to swallow a lump in his throat as he relived that long walk back to Ben's house on the night he had decided he would marry Laura. The last happy night of his life. "No. Wait. I do know how you change that," he said, feeling as if someone else had commandeered his voice. "You walk right through the door marked NO ADMITTANCE." He looked desperately at Gypsy, willing the boy to understand what he himself had not seen in time. "The things you're sure will kill you: do them, right away, even if it feels like dying on purpose. Defy everything you know about what won't work, what isn't allowed. If you want to marry her, ask her. Ask her now! And if she'll have you, do it right away." Joby couldn't stop the tears that splashed his cheeks. "You can lose her, Gypsy. I lost mine."

"Hey, I'm sorry!" Gypsy said, looking at Joby in distress. "I didn't mean to—"

"You didn't!" Joby snapped. "If you mean what you just said, don't sit there apologizing, go find her, right now, and tell her what you just told me. Do it now! I know what I'm talking about!"

Gypsy stared at Joby as if he were the Ghost of Christmas Future, then bolted from his chair and headed for the kitchen doorway.

❈

On his hands and knees in the darkness, Silverjack peered around nervously through clouds of his own steaming breath, then went back to scrabbling in the dirt. He'd uprooted half a dozen plants already, and pocked the lawn with shallow craters, but still no beacon!

The warning had come to him right after that alien thing had smiled and pointed at him two weeks earlier. They were all aliens! All these smug, so-called normal people in their normal little houses. The voices had explained it all. Not the old, fake voices. Real voices! He knew they were real because the meds didn't affect them.

The voices had told him of the alien beacon buried in one of these gardens, pulsing its traitorous signal to the invading armada groping through space toward his unsuspecting planet. No one knew but himself, and the alien vanguard of course, but *they* weren't going to warn anybody! There was no one to save the world now but poor Silverjack, laughed at and abused all his life just because his brain was tuned to alien frequencies. Well, they wouldn't laugh so hard after he saved them all, would they! But the thing was damn well hidden! This was the third garden he'd tried this week!

Suddenly, a window filled with light and slammed open on the second floor.

"What in God's name are you doing?" screeched an angry man silhouetted in the open window. *"Sweet Jesus! Look at my garden! Merideth, call the police!"*

Silverjack was already running. He could hardly save the world if he was in jail. Near the corner, he looked back, and nearly fell over his own feet. Well up the street stood the very alien who'd leered at him before! Silverjack stumbled to a halt, immobilized by fear, as the creature's terrible lips parted in hideous parody of a grin, wider and wider, as if some invisible knife were slowly gashing its face open! Then its laughter erupted inside Silverjack's own head, mixed with ragged screaming, which he realized a moment later, was his own.

The wail of approaching sirens finally broke the spell of terror that had kept him rooted to the pavement. Silverjack bolted into the darkness and vaulted a fence behind the Meal Project basement, sprinted through a darkened yard, and fled into the night.

❊

The dining hall doors were just being opened, and the jostling crowd starting to move, when Joby saw them coming, hand in hand, across the parking lot.

"Hey!" he called happily. "It's the happy couple!"

"We were just about to sell your seats!" Sundog teased.

Gypsy smiled shyly as Sarina beamed beside him, and Joby suspected they were late because they'd been off necking somewhere. Everyone had heard the news by now, and because Gypsy couldn't seem to tell anyone about their engagement without crediting Joby for "scaring him into proposing," Joby had been getting almost as many kudos as the couple had. Mary, in particular, had drawn Joby aside one evening to say what a fine thing he'd done, though a minute or two of crying over spilled milk didn't seem all that heroic to him. In fact, he tried not to think about that part of it.

"My *fiancé* has some awesome news!" Sarina said, as they joined Joby, Sundog and Mary in the now moving dinner line.

"She's pregnant?" Sundog blurted out merrily. There was an awkward silence. "Sorry." Sundog shrugged. "I was just joking."

"I got a job," said Gypsy with quiet pride. "Right here at the church. It's just janitorial and maintenance work, but it comes with an apartment, right here behind the Meal Project kitchen!" An ecstatic grin transformed his face. "We got a place to live!" he shouted. *"Is that fuckin' awesome, or what?"* He looked suddenly abashed, and said, "Guess now that I'm workin' for the church, I better watch my language, huh?"

"That might be advisable," Joby said, trying not to laugh and bursting with affection for Gypsy, who'd become something like a little brother to him now. "Man, when you make up your mind to go, you go, don't you," Joby said, trying not to think about the fact that he'd most likely lose his own apartment in the next few weeks.

"I've got reasons now," said Gypsy, turning to smile at Sarina. "Turns out that was all I needed."

Sarina leaned in to give him a lengthy kiss as they reached the dinning hall doors, where a woman on that evening's volunteer staff was handing out some sort of flyer.

"What kind of shit is this?" someone bellowed angrily ahead of them in line. Joby saw the man waving the flyer over his head and realized that there was a lot of angry buzz inside the dining hall.

Sundog, who was first to reach the pamphleteer, began to scan one of her flyers, then barked, "Awww, Christ!"

"What's wrong?" Joby asked, reaching for a flyer.

"Fucking self-righteous bastards!" growled the normally sanguine giant. "Look what those assholes do with all their fuckin' free time!"

"We're asking you all to go to this meeting down at city hall," said the volunteer at the door. "The city's got to hear from all of us too, or this could really happen."

"This is so fucked!" said Gypsy, as he and Joby scanned the flyer.

"Relocate?" Joby asked the pamphleteer. "Where would they relocate it to?"

" 'Relocate,' my rosy fuckin' ass," Sundog snarled before she could answer. "They'll just close us down and promise to find another place someday when we've all starved to death. That's what they always do. All those *'residents'* pay taxes. We don't. End of story."

"No!" Joby said indignantly. *"No! They can't keep doing this!"* The after-school tutoring program for which he'd once volunteered had lost its funding two months later; the Refugee Assistance Network had been shut down on legal grounds weeks after he'd signed up to help, and Joby's "little brother" had been busted for selling a palmful of pot to two of his friends. Watching the once gentle boy harden over the six months in juvenile custody while his permanent placement was arranged had filled Joby with despair. He was fed up with having his life shut down every time he found a bench to sit on. In fact, he was enraged! Sweeping his companions with an angry glare, he said, "We're going to that meeting, and showing that commission we're as scary as any little clutch of housewives and accountants."

"Hell, yes!" Gypsy said, looking at Joby with a brand-new kind of light in his eyes.

12

(Runaway)

Gypsy leaned forward, amazed by Joby's performance. The neighborhood's "legitimate" residents had been given so much time to vent that Gypsy hadn't been sure anyone from the Project's side would get to talk at all. When the planning commission's chairman had finally given Meal Project proponents there chance, a few dumb protests had been followed by an embarrassed silence as their side realized how outclassed they were at fancy speech-making; until Joby had gotten up and begun to speak, that was.

"I still haven't heard a shred of hard evidence it was us," Joby continued politely.

"A man of clearly vagrant appearance *was* seen vandalizing several neighborhood gardens," said the commissioner chairing the meeting, "and a Meal Project ticket was found inside one of the burglarized homes. That constitutes as a 'shred of evidence.'"

"If residents said they'd seen someone of 'clearly *teacherish* appearance' digging up their gardens," Joby asked, "would you be shutting down the nearest school?"

"We've told you repeatedly, Mr. Peterson, no one's proposing that anything be shut down, only a brief suspension of services during relocation."

"Then I'll rephrase my question. Would you *relocate* the nearest school to some as yet *undetermined* location?"

He's not even scared! Gypsy thought, in awe of Joby's composure.

"You're wasting our time with nonsense," said a second commissioner with wiry black hair severely pulled back from a pinched, unpleasant face. "There's no such thing as *teacherish* appearance, and schools are a basic service relied upon by the entire community."

"Not a *frivolous* service like feeding people their only daily meal," Joby replied, just short of scornfully.

Yeah! thought Gypsy. *Joby scores!*

The chairman looked bleak.

"All right," Joby shrugged. "Even if your suspect does eat at the Meal Project, this relocation proposal punishes an entire community of people for no crime but dressing vaguely like the offender. Has anyone dressed like you been arrested in this city lately? Should we relocate all men wearing ties?"

"Mr. Peterson, these residents have been subjected to real and intolerable offenses which—"

"Who hasn't?" Joby interrupted, gesturing toward his downtrodden compatriots in the audience. "I agree that the guilty party should be arrested and tried, but what's that got to do with exiling everyone who offends the aesthetic sensibilities of—"

"May I remind you," another commissioner angrily interjected, "that these residents are legitimate property owners, Mr. Peterson, while you and your constituency are merely *guests* in *their* neighborhood!"

"There it is!" roared Sundog, leaping to his feet. "I told you, Joby! Own a chunk, got rights! No chunk, no rights! There's the constitution *they* all follow!"

As Joby tried to wave him down, a short, wild-haired woman in tie-dye stood up and shouted, "The rich don't need no Meal Project! They just eat *us!*"

"The rich eat their own young!" bawled a man who looked like Santa Claus moonlighting as a chimney sweep.

Neighborhood residents in the audience began shouting and jeering insults of their own then, as the chairman banged his gavel. By the time order was restored, all five commissioners were clearly out of patience.

"Mr. Peterson, you have more than exhausted your turn to speak," the chairman said frostily, "and this meeting has run well over schedule. I call for a vote on the proposal to suspend operation of the Berkeley Public Meal Project at Castor Avenue Unitarian Church while an appropriate site for relocation is determined."

"I second," said the wire-haired woman to his left.

"In favor?" asked the chairman.

Five hands were raised.

"The motion is passed unanimously," said the chairman.

His last words were nearly drowned out by angry protests from the homeless audience, but Joby whirled around to wave them silent with such angry intensity that, to everyone's surprise, they obeyed him almost instantly. Then he turned to face the commission again, his tone no longer mild.

"For fifteen years, we who have our daily bread at the Meal Project have bothered no one," Joby said, his face a mask of contempt, "but—"

"This meeting is adjourned," the commissioner said, rising, to leave, along with the other commissioners.

"But these mean-spirited property owners," Joby continued unfazed, "may have a lot more noise to deal with now. You can turn your backs on justice, but *don't think we'll go quietly!*"

There was loud cheering from the homeless contingent, as neighborhood residents in the audience fled the chamber in unconcealed apprehension. The commissioners continued to file through their side door without acknowledging the upheaval at all.

As Joby stood with stormy dignity watching them go, Gypsy stared at him in open-mouthed admiration. Here, at last, was just the someone he'd left home so many years ago to find. Someone he could follow clear to Hell and back, if that's where this fight took them.

⍟

Hell NO! We won't GO! Hell NO! We won't GO!

For all its unoriginality, everyone had conceded that the phrase would likely serve their interests better than, "Eat ME!", which Sundog had suggested to much laughter. As he carried his BREAD, NOT BUNKERS! picket sign that morning, Gypsy thought that it had never felt so good to be alive! After nearly two weeks of their marching in rain and drizzle, the sun had come out at last, and they'd been on television too! The mobile news trucks were becoming a daily source of embarrassment to the "neighbors" and their commissioners. Public opinion seemed to be swinging their way. Lots of people passing by were offering their support these days. Normal people! Some of them had even joined the marching! Though it made him feel guilty to admit it, Gypsy half-hoped it didn't all end too soon. After a pointless life of suburban obscurity followed by an even more disgraceful life on the street, Gypsy was feeling proud of himself for the first time in many years. He'd even written his parents a letter telling them how well everything was going for him now.

Gypsy's happy reverie was shattered by a burst of shouting from behind him, and he turned to see other protesters pointing down Hearst at two police cars that had turned across traffic to block the street. An instant later, someone else was shouting and pointing down Castor, where a column of officers in riot gear was coming slowly toward the church.

Jesus! Gypsy thought. *Where are the fucking news trucks when you need them?*

"I knew it!" Sundog bellowed. "I knew the bastards'd fuck us over!"

"But we're not doing anything illegal!" protested one of the newer marchers, a woman who might have been anybody's mother.

"You're with us, lady," said someone else. "That's wrong enough."

A few of the latest recruits dropped their signs and ran up Castor away from the advancing police force.

"She's right!" Joby yelled, climbing onto the bumper of a car to be seen over the crowd. "We haven't broken any laws! We've just embarrassed city hall, so they're trying to scare us off! But we don't have to let them do it!"

"Yeah!" Sundog called. "Just stay peaceful! They want you to give 'em an excuse, so don't be stupid. We stay peaceful, those tin soldiers'll just have to go right back to their little toy box!"

"Look! There's more!" someone shouted.

Everyone turned to see a second force of riot police coming slowly up Hearst from behind the patrol car barricade.

Most of the crowd was clearly on the edge of fleeing.

"This is what we've been marching for!" Joby shouted. "To make them pay attention! Well, now they are, so let's show them what we're about! Do just what Sundog said! Stay peaceful! If they arrest you, let them arrest you, but do nothing to make it seem right! If this city wants to shame itself, let's not give them any cover!"

It was true, Gypsy realized with excitement. This, right now, was their moment! His heart swelled with pride in all of them who were standing up for what was right.

Joby continued calming and encouraging the crowd, and those who hadn't already run began to grow quiet and grim, raising their signs and planting their feet against the coming confrontation. This, Gypsy thought, was how it felt to truly matter in the world! He had never felt so complete.

In eerie silence, the two columns of police came closer and closer, converging at last, and massing to a halt in lines across the intersection opposite the church. An officer raised his bullhorn, and said, "This assembly has been declared disorderly, and is ordered to disperse immediately."

No one moved. To Gypsy's relief, no one even heckled the force. He suspected that, like himself, they were probably too scared to make a sound.

The tense silence continued as the two groups faced each other in frozen tableau, until the officer raised his bullhorn again. "Anyone refusing to disband now will be arrested. This is your last warning."

"We're on private property," Joby said, his voice even, though pale beside the amplified commands of the bullhorn. "The owners haven't asked us to go. We've a legal right to free speech and peaceful assembly."

"You are disobeying a direct order from a duly appointed officer of the law," the policeman bullhorned back. "That is an illegal act. If you do not disperse now, you will be arrested."

"Bullshit!" Sundog roared, but Joby immediately waved him silent, and looked again at the crowd around him. "If we go, we're finished," he said just loudly enough to be heard. "I believe we're in the right here, and if we have to prove it in court, I say, so be it. I'm willing to be arrested. But I respect anyone who feels different. If any of you wants to leave, I'll understand completely. Go with our thanks for the support you've already given." His face was guileless as his eyes swept the crowd.

For a moment, no one moved. Then the woman who'd spoken earlier said, "I'm so sorry, but my family needs me at home. I'm . . . I'm sorry." She put her sign down and walked rapidly up Castor opposite the direction from which the officers had come. A few other protesters followed suit as the police force watched in disciplined silence. But most of the crowd stayed, and Gypsy felt his pride in Joby swell. His friend had never seemed more rock solid and heroic.

"Anyone else?" Joby asked.

Silence.

Turning back to the line of officers, Joby called, "We believe we have a right to be here, and we're willing to test that right in court. I'm afraid you'll have to arrest us."

The officer in charge shook his head wearily, and turned to speak to someone behind him. When he turned back, Gypsy thought he heard the man heave a tired sigh.

Silverjack had been so quiet, Gypsy had forgotten he was there, so for an instant he was stunned motionless with everyone else when the madman screamed, *"Fucking alien shit!"* and raced from the crowd to charge the line of officers.

"Jack, you ass!" Sundog screamed. "Get back here!"

Damn crazy bastard! Gypsy thought.

Shields were instantly raised, and nightsticks drawn, as Silverjack crashed into the barrier of officers. Then he was on the ground, being beaten by at least four men.

They'll kill him! Gypsy thought, barely aware that he'd started running forward. "Stop!" he yelled. "He's harmless! Stop hitting him!" He heard several voices, including Joby's, call him back, but couldn't seem to stop. There was blood on the pavement under Silverjack's head. Nearly close enough now to yank the crazy fool away from them, he only vaguely registered the order to halt that came from somewhere in the mass of officers. When he saw the gun drawn, he thought, with an electric jolt, that they were actually going to shoot Silverjack!

"Noooo!" he shouted, doubling his speed, and hadn't even time to be surprised when the gun was raised on him instead. There was a shot.

Something hit his shoulder like a car at freeway speed. There was a second shot, and Gypsy fell back onto the pavement as if he'd hit an invisible wall. For a moment there was neither sound nor pain. Then he heard Sarina scream, and his chest seemed to explode in flames. He tried to call for help, but his throat was full of something that made him choke and the pain became unbearable. The street around him erupted into roaring voices, officers raising shields and rushing forward, closing ranks on people he knew, people who were now swinging signs like bludgeons. His vision began to gray, but to his relief, the pain receded some as well.

Then there was a man smiling down at him as if oblivious to the chaos all around them. He seemed about Gypsy's age, with night-black hair, and beautiful dark eyes. In fact, he was the most beautiful person Gypsy had ever seen. In that smile, Gypsy found everything he'd ever wished for in a friend, a brother, a parent, even a lover. It was the strangest, most wonderful feeling.

"Hello, Matthew," said the man.

"How . . . how . . ." Gypsy wanted to ask how the man knew his real name. But he still couldn't talk without choking, which made the pain leap up again.

"I'm Gabe," the man said, reaching down to touch Gypsy's chest.

Suddenly, there was no pain at all. In fact, Gypsy felt incredible!

"What did you do?" Gypsy asked. "Who are you?"

"Come on, Matt," Gabe said, looking up for the first time at the angry tumult around them. "This is no place to linger."

"Where are we going?" Gypsy asked.

Gabriel smiled again, and Gypsy felt a kind of happiness he didn't think he'd ever be able to explain to Sarina. "First, to the absolute best birthday party you've *ever* had. After that, it's up to you." The man shrugged and grinned. "Sky's the limit."

Gypsy's heart swelled with excitement as his mind filled with so many, many possibilities he'd never even thought of before. Getting to his feet, he saw that the police lines had fallen back, drawing the struggle away from the church by half a block. Silverjack had dragged himself to the curb, where he lay holding his bloodied head, whimpering but alive. Someone else nearby was crying much harder though. Wailing in fact. Gypsy turned to find Sarina rocking his own body against her breast, sobbing hysterically. Joby was beside her, holding them both in a crushing embrace, tears streaming down his face. The chest of Gypsy's shirt was soaked nearly black with blood. Only Gypsy wasn't in it anymore. It was the strangest thing.

"Can Sarina come?" he asked Gabe, hopeful.

"Not yet, Matt." The angel turned to smile at him again. "We'd really better go."

❧

After guiding Matthew home, Gabe had spent the night and morning helplessly at Joby's side as he lay in his cell alternately sobbing and staring vacantly into the darkness. Having decided that pressing charges against the demonstrators might not be politic given current public sentiment, they were letting Joby go now. Clearly he had no intention of going quietly.

"Not pressing charges?" Joby snapped at the officer handling his release from behind a wire-reinforced glass window. "An innocent boy is dead, a dozen more of us are in the hospital, and *you're* not pressing charges? God, am I impressed! Maybe *we're* pressing charges! That cross your mind?"

"Your acquaintance ran at officers under attack, Mr. Peterson," the officer intoned from behind his thick portal, "and disobeyed a clear order to halt."

"So you *killed him*!" Joby yelled, his voice trembling again, as it did whenever the moment of Gypsy's death came too clearly to memory. "He was twenty years old!" Joby rasped. "He was engaged to be married!" As his fury collapsed again into hopeless grief, Joby grabbed himself in a kind of spastic hug, and began to cry. "He worked for the goddamn church. He was just trying to save . . . We just wanted a place to eat. Why did . . ." Joby slumped onto a bench and shook with sobs.

"How do you suppose the officer who shot that man feels, Mr. Peterson?" the policeman asked coldly. "People like you should think about what their do-gooding might cost before they get everyone stirred up. It's not all just heroic poses, is it?"

Joby's sobbing ceased abruptly, and the unrestrained rage in his eyes when he looked up eclipsed any hope left in Gabriel's heart.

"There are laws in this state," the officer pressed. "Holding the instigator of a lethal situation responsible for resulting deaths. You could still be charged with murder, Mr. Peterson. If I were you, I'd be grateful to get off with nothing but a painful lesson about stirring up trouble you can't control. Before someone loses patience and presses charges after all, I'd suggest you go now and behave yourself."

Joby shot to his feet and stormed down the hall toward the doorway. But as he reached to pull it open, he turned and shouted, *"I hate you! I hate what you stand for! And if there's any justice in this whole goddamn world, this fucking city will pay for every last minute of the life you stole!"*

Then he threw the door open hard enough to shake its frame, then stalked through the precinct lobby. Outside, Gabriel watched him storm down the street, kicking at garbage cans and slapping at parking meters as he passed.

The angel looked up at the crisp winter sky, dotted with small clouds. He watched the remnants of last summer's leaves skitter across the street on a chilly breeze. He watched people walking toward him, away from him, oblivious to his presence, each one unique, worlds unto themselves. He took in the brilliant flashes of sunlit color reflected from passing cars, the twinkle of tinsel and Christmas lights on all the lampposts, the sounds of traffic and laughter, birdsong, and music from a boom box at the corner.

He laid his invisible hand against the cold granite facing of the precinct building. Every layer of wonder and sensation lead to yet another, on and on, a million deep, even here, in this most unremarkable corner of the world. He let it all fill him, as he contemplated the end of everything. After what he'd seen so clearly in Joby's eyes, heard so unmistakably in his voice, there seemed little doubt that Lucifer's victory now could be long in coming.

❈

"Definitely soup," Malcephalon told the expectant assembly, managing to gloat somehow, despite his eternally drawn expression. "When his rage has given birth to action, he will lose any claim to conscience. After that, our victory is assured."

"Let's not sink all the life boats just yet," Lucifer drawled, barely able to rein in his own giddy anticipation, given the week's achievements. "Our plan does seem to have unfolded perfectly for once, but let's not get careless with self-congratulation." He stared pointedly at Malcephalon. "To win, we must prove 'brazen defiance' and 'great wickedness,' remember, not just some half-baked little lapse in judgment. I want no risk of losing another one of these things on some tawdry technicality. Our Enemy's very big on that sort of thing, remember. So let's keep whispering in his ear until his rage has come to full fruition, and please, let's make sure that he's not caught or, God forbid, killed somehow before he's done all that is required of him."

❈

The Christmas decorations and choral music hailing Joby from every storefront seemed a vicious mockery, as he strode down street after street lacking any destination. Two days ago he'd ripped out his answering machine to stop the frantic messages left by his parents, who'd apparently seen his picture on the evening news. He ignored the uncertain greetings received from acquaintances he passed on his manic walkabout. He did not want to see them, or be seen, by anyone ever again. He wouldn't have left his apartment at all had he not been driven by a desperate need to move—move and think.

By night he dreamed of grief and guilt. By day he dreamed only of rage and revenge. The papers were full of Gypsy's death, and the city's defensive explanations. Public outrage had stirred demands for outside investigation and immediate the reopening of the Meal Project, but Joby didn't care. That officer had been right. All Joby's moronic candles in the darkness were a useless, wicked fraud! Nothing anyone now did could bring Gypsy back. When the city's detractors had squeezed sufficient political capital from the scandal of Gypsy's murder, it would be quickly forgotten. It would go unavenged. Any real justice was up to Joby. In this one last thing, he did not intend to fail his martyred friend.

He had no care for consequences now. He hated his life, had always hated it, and would happily see it end, so long as justice was served first. How did one learn to build a bomb? he wondered. How many would it take to level city hall? Who most deserved to die? Could he get enough of them with just a gun before being stopped?

"Ouch!" Joby gasped, nearly sprawling to his face. "Goddamn it!" he spat, looking back to find Mary stretched halfway into the busy sidewalk, looking crossly up at him as she rubbed the foot he'd stumbled over. "Damn it, Mary! Can't you stay out of my way?" he raged at her, heedless of the stares from passers-by. *"What's your problem?"*

"Have *I* the problem?" she asked severely. "I'd say it's *your* manners have slipped a bit." She gave him one last scowl, and went back to reading the book in her lap.

Joby turned angrily to go, then realized what she was reading, and spun back, sure his mind had gone at last. Yet there it was: *A Child's Treasury of Arthurian Tales!*

"Where did you get that?" he demanded, his fury momentarily displaced by astonishment.

She looked up from her reading, seeming irritated to find him still there. "Thrift store," she said, curtly. "The throwaway bin. Seemed too pretty t'toss out without one more readin', not as I can see it's any of your business."

"I . . . I had a book like that once," Joby said. "It was a gift from . . . Can I see it?"

She held it up for him to take, still looking cross.

The book was as worn as his had been, in virtually the same places. He held it to his face, and breathed in the very scent he remembered. Knowing there was no way it could be his own, he lifted its faded cover anyway, turned to the first blank page, and froze, open mouthed.

> *To my beloved grandson on his first day of life,*
> *May you grow to be a knight Arthur would be proud of. Do great*
> *things with a large heart, beautiful child. I am proud of you already.*
> *With much love, your Grampa Emery*

For a moment, he could hardly breathe. Then his eyes began to well, his breath to come in gasps, as his exhausted mind and ravaged heart collided, the first propelled by shocked disbelief, the second by grief and shame.

"How did you get this?" he demanded, trembling.

"I told you," Mary said.

"No!" Joby shouted. *"I threw this away! How did you get it?"*

"Haven't we a temper today!" Mary replied sternly. "Thrown-out things is what thrift stores sell, lad. Stompin' on my feet, yellin' like a drunkard. Now yer callin' me a liar. Your company's gone sour. Think I'll go find better." She started to get stiffly to her feet. "Keep the silly book since you seem to own it. Cost me little enough."

"No, wait! I'm sorry," Joby said. "It's just that . . ." The last frayed lines of defense inside him collapsed like the ruins of Jericho. "I can't . . . ," he pleaded. "Not now! Not now!" Clutching the impossible book to his chest, he doubled to his knees in unchecked misery, oblivious of those who gaped or turned away on the street around him, only half-aware of Mary's arms folding him toward her breast. *"I tried,"* he sobbed as Mary pulled him closer, kissing his head, and rocking him in her arms. *"I ruin everything I do, everyone I care about!"* he wailed into her lap. *"I just come near them and they die!"*

"There, there, child," she cooed sadly. "I know. It's been an awful thing. . . . Just cry now, 'til it's done. . . . I ain't goin' nowhere, my dearie."

Twice, as Joby sobbed into her lap, he felt her stiffen convulsively, and wondered fearfully if she were going to have a heart attack and die now too. He wanted to run away, and couldn't stop crying, and didn't want her to let go of him, all at the same time.

When his sobbing finally ended, he lay empty and exhausted in her embrace, ignoring the respectable people who hurried by averting their eyes, or shaking their heads, until Mary broke their silence.

"You should leave here, dearie. This town's got nothin' but pain for you now. Go someplace far off where there's no past to haunt you."

"I tried that," Joby murmured without raising his head. "When I came to Berkeley. . . . Start again. Someplace new. . . . There is no such place." He sat up, wiping ineffectually at his eyes.

"There must be," Mary pressed. "Ain't nowhere ever made you happy?"

"Well . . . there was one place," he said, surprised to think of it so suddenly after so many years. "There was this town called Taubolt. But I don't know anyone there, or have anywhere to stay. Not on the twenty or thirty bucks I've got left."

Mary nodded soberly, and said, "That's it, then. If I was you, I'd go there right this minute, and not look back."

"What? But . . . I just told you. Where would I stay? What would I do for food?"

"Homeless is homeless, one place or another." She shrugged. "And if all you've left is thirty dollars, that's what you'll be soon either way. Small towns ain't no meaner to such folk than big ones are. There's all manner of things t'eat in the sea, child, and who's to say there ain't a job waitin' for you there?"

"Oh sure," Joby scoffed, wearily. "I can't get work for love or money here in the metropolis, but up in 'two-store Taubolt,' I'll be first in line, right?"

"You're doin' it again, dearie," she said, absently pulling one of her yarn ornaments from somewhere in her skirts. "Always rollin' out that dark carpet in front of you. Them two stores will also have fewer folks to choose from, I imagine." She began to wind and weave the trailing yarn around its small frame. The little diamond shape looked nearly finished. "Have you really anything t'lose by tryin'?"

Joby saw her wince and flinch again.

"Are you all right?" he asked, anxiously.

"Indigestion," she huffed. "An old woman's stomach is no pretty sight, child. Are you goin' or not?"

"Mary, I don't even have a car. How am I supposed to get there?"

"You'll find a way once you decide," she said. "Decidin's the hard part, ain't it, dearie." She yanked the last strand of yarn tight, and tied it off.

"What are these things you're always making?" Joby asked.

"Just little charms." She smiled. "For friends I meet here and there. . . . Brings 'em good luck. Keeps the dark away some." She held out the one she'd just finished. "This one's for you, dearie. Been makin' it special."

"Thank you," Joby said, abashed. "You've been so nice to me, after the way I—"

Her face spasmed, and her arm jerked, as she held the ornament out to him.

"Mary, what's wrong?"

"I told you, dearie, bad chowder," she said shortly. "Take it now."

After shoving her gift into Joby's hand, she began climbing to her feet.

"Where are you going?" Joby asked.

"I got places to be some time ago," she said a bit breathlessly, and turned to leave. "As do you, my dearie, if you've the brains God gave you."

"Mary, wait!" Joby said, leaping to his feet.

"What is it?" she asked brusquely, looking back over her shoulder.

"I just . . . Thank you," he said, embarrassed. "For these." He held out her woven gift and his long-lost book. "I've never said it, but . . . I really . . . you're one of the kindest, wisest"—he struggled for some way to express what he was feeling—"most patient people I ever met. . . . I just wanted to say that."

Her eyes grew shinier and more pink-rimmed than usual. "Whatever fool things you must think about yourself, child, I've always been proud of you. Now, for God's sake, get out of here. Wherever your life's waitin' now, it ain't nowhere 'round here." She turned again, and walked off toward the corner without a backward glance.

"Good-bye," Joby said quietly, amazed to realize that the consuming rage that had driven him for days had simply vanished, like a spent fever, though, like a fever, it had left him feeling weak and insubstantial. Willing himself to look away from Mary's retreating back, he turned and headed home down Telegraph, his book in one hand, her yarn charm in the other, wondering if she could be right about going to Taubolt.

※

Merlin's skirts were bunched in white-knuckled hands as he left his grandson behind, straining to hold the demon's onslaught at bay until he could be sure the boy was out of sight. The jig was clearly up for this disguise. A pity really. With a saint for a mother and a demon for a father, it wasn't easy to invent personas effectively beneath the interest of both Heaven *and* Hell. Still, "Mary" had served her purpose, he hoped.

"Who are you, woman?" The demon demanded, appearing directly in front of him, steps short of the damned corner. "*What* are you?"

Knowing that no normal mortal would see the apparition, Merlin vainly pretended not to, hoping to confuse his tormentor just long enough to achieve his escape. Though twelve years spent waiting unobtrusively to act had seemed hardly any time at all to a man of Merlin's age, reaching that corner ahead of him seemed to be taking forever.

"I know you see me, hag!" the demon snarled. "Your concealments are a marvel, I confess, but no merely mortal thing sloughs off *my* attacks one after another. You weaken though. I feel it. Tell me what you are, and where you got that book, and I may let you live. Resist me further, and I will simply tear the answers from you."

Merlin just kept walking.

"Fool!" the demon snarled. "Where do you think to hide from me now?"

Fool, Merlin thought back through gritted teeth. *Around that corner will do nicely.*

"Do you think your noxious little knot of spells can save the boy?" the demon pressed. He raised a hand and redoubled the barrage of strokes and heart attacks he'd been hurling at Merlin, sufficient some time ago to drop any normal mortal woman where she stood. Throwing all his remaining strength into the shields that wreathed him, Merlin walked straight through the shadowed ghost, to its clear amazement.

"What *are* you?" it snarled, in angry dismay.

"If you don't know by now, dearie, it's too late t'care," Merlin cackled, turning the blessed corner at last. No one at all came around the other side.

⚗

"He was there then, wasn't he?" Gabriel asked. "With us in the glade when Joby threw his books away. That's how they disappeared."

"It would seem so," mused the Creator. "He hides quite well, you know, even from angels."

"But not from You, My Lord," the angel pressed. "Why did You not just tell me?"

The Creator shrugged. "I just assumed that if he'd wanted you to know what he had done, he'd have told you himself."

Disguised as a pigeon, Gabriel had watched the confrontation between Merlin and Malcephalon from atop a nearby record store, but, unlike Malcephalon, Gabe had quickly guessed who the old woman must really be. The sudden cessation of Merlin's anguished pleas to Heaven on his grandson's behalf, the angel now realized, had coincided too perfectly with "Mary's" appearance. The book's unexpected reappearance had removed any remaining doubt—regarding Merlin's involvement, at least.

"But . . . does all this not suggest he's been planning to disobey You from the start?" Gabriel asked anxiously. "He serves Heaven and received the same command all others did, not to interfere unasked, yet he disobeys. What are we to do, My Lord?"

"You know I'm not allowed to answer such questions, Gabe," the Creator chided. "Keep this up, I could get confused and say something I'm not allowed to. Then Lucifer would win. That what you want?"

"No, My Lord. Of course not."

But can that be what You want, Lord? Gabriel thought, unable to expunge the shameful thought.

As worded, Lucifer's condition forbidding the Creator's servants from helping Joby uninvited had applied only to immortal beings, but Merlin, though uniquely long-lived, was certainly not immortal. It had been the perfect loophole! The one remaining mortal able to hide from angels and contest with demons would have been free to help Joby, had the Creator not gratuitously upped the ante by addressing His command against unsolicited aid to "all serving Heaven." *Why had He done that?* The Creator *never* used words carelessly!

No one knew better than Gabe that the Creator's decisions were infinitely above any angel's right, or ability, to question. And yet, for the first time in all the angel's eons of experience, there it was . . . doubt. Gabriel didn't want it, didn't know what to do with it. But now it *was* and could not be unmade. Could the Creator *want* Joby to fail? Had He given up on creation? . . . Or was there something else between the lines? Gabe was failing to perceive here that.

"You won't punish him then?" Gabe dared to ask.

"I can hardly imagine doing so would not constitute an expression of My will in this matter," the Creator replied patiently.

Gabe looked down uncomfortably, wondering how much of his own newly-minted doubt the Creator had already divined. "Lord," he said, as dry of mouth as an angel is capable of being, "these conditions You have agreed to are so impossibly unfair. It might seem to some . . ." He shook his head. "No. It is *I* who wonder. Have You intentionally set this contest against Joby for some reason?"

"Why would I do that?" the Creator asked casually.

"I cannot imagine, Lord. But . . . it seems to me that Joby would certainly have failed had Merlin *not* disobeyed Your command."

The Creator shrugged. "He may still fail. What is it you really want to know?"

"Is that what You intend, Lord?" Gabe pleaded in sudden desperation. "That he fail?"

"I can't tell you what I *intend,* Gabe. You know that. I'm quite out of the loop until this wager is ended, though I may have much to say then, if anyone is left to hear it. How about a hand of cards, Gabe? Would that cheer you up?"

Gabriel could hardly believe his ears. *Cards?* The Creator sounded almost cheerful! Didn't He care at all?

"My Lord," he said palely. "I fear I have no appetite for cards. May I decline?"

"Why, of course, Gabe." the Creator sounded nonplussed. "Would I *make* you play? How much fun would that be?"

❦

Williamson hovered anxiously amidst the cloud of demons wreathing Joby's bed. Despite Malcephalon's efforts to dissuade him, Joby had hung the old woman's charm around his neck on a strip of ribbon, where, to everyone's livid consternation, it had blunted their influence ever since. The boy had even considered going into a *church* to *pray for guidance!* It had taken the combined strength of six different demons just to make Joby tired enough to come here and sleep instead. Adding insult to injury, the thing cast off a prickly energy difficult for Williamson, or even his superiors, to endure.

"Impossible!" Malcephalon kept hissing. "This cannot be happening!"

The Triangle, who might ordinarily have made quite a joke of Malcephalon's disgrace, were too dismayed to do more than grumble agreement.

To Williamson's concealed satisfaction, Malcephalon was in dire trouble for having failed to recognize the old woman's purpose and power in time. In fact, the once-dominant demon hadn't a friend in Hell now.

It seemed the old sorceress had left the world without a trace. Since she'd tried to send the boy to Taubolt, most thought it likely that's where she'd gone as well. Lucifer had ordered that Joby be allowed nowhere near the coast on pain of punishment far worse than death. Ironically, it was that very command that had caused Williamson to realize that his long awaited chance to grab the ball had finally come. It was common knowledge by now that not even Lucifer had been able to find the place, or Joby in it. Thus, if Joby were to get back there now, and Williamson were with him when he did, Lucifer, for once, would be powerless to prevent Williamson from calling the shots alone and engineering Hell's victory all by himself. Not even Lucifer would be able to deny him credit then! The one remaining problem was how to get sufficient time alone with Joby.

"Watching him snore is a bore!" Tique whined. "If you can't that thing off his neck, Malcephalon, then——"

"He can't wear it forever!" Malcephalon cut in angrily. "The moment it comes off, he will pay dearly for that old hag's cheek."

"Well, he's not likely to wear it into his morning shower," Eurodia said. "Why can't we just come back then?"

"What!" Malcephalon snarled. "Leave him here unguarded all night so the Creator's cheat can come steal him away for good? Are you mad?"

"Who suggested leaving him unguarded?" Eurodia sniffed. She waved contemptuously at Williamson. "If anything happens, our security camera here just squeals and we're back in a snap, right? So why hang around and watch the child sleep?"

It was too perfect! Trying to sound offended, Williamson, whined, "You guys can't just leave me here alone with this thing he's wearing. It's not *my* fault we're in this mess, and what if——"

As expected, Malcephalon whirled to face him in a rage. "*You dare assign blame here, worm?* If we tell you to watch, watch you will 'til Hell freezes, or you'll grace our dinner table for as long! Is that clear?"

"Yes, Sir," Williamson whimpered, silently congratulating himself.

"See ya in the mornin', *bug.*" Tique smirked and vanished.

"Watch well, fool," Malcephalon warned. "Hell's master is as close to fury as I have seen him in an age." Then Malcephalon vanished with the others.

Williamson glanced at the digital clock glowing beside Joby's bed. Seven hours 'til dawn. There might just be time if he could force the boy's hand quickly. With a smirk, he began humming at the walls, extending his modest little lure down into the building's filthy bowels.

※

Joby was grudgingly tickled from sleep by a feather-light touch on his bare shoulder. Reaching up to brush it away, his hand found something brittle that wriggled frantically under his fingers. With a jolt he was awake, swatting in revulsion at his shoulder as he threw the covers off and leapt up to slap the light switch. In the sudden glare, he saw the cockroach scuttle through a crack beneath the floorboard.

Joby sat down heavily on the bed, nursing a hellish head rush, and looked at the clock. Nearly midnight. Vowing to seek employment as an exterminator himself in the morning if his sleep was not quickly retrieved, Joby reached up, turned off the light, and settled hopefully under his covers again.

Only then, lying in the darkness, did he notice the soft, sporadic tapping sound. At first, he thought it might be rain on the windows, but it seemed to come from too nearby. He got up again, went to the doorless jamb that separated his sleeping quarters from the kitchen, and reached through to flip the light switch just inside. As illumination flooded the room, he jerked his hand back with a gasp, and stumbled back in horror.

Roaches rained from the ceiling, swarmed across the countertops, and scuttled across the kitchen floor in frenzied retreat from the light. Joby leapt back farther, looking down in alarm at his bare feet, then around the pantry space in which he stood. For some reason the incomprehensible invasion seemed confined to the kitchen despite the absence of any door to hold it there. He had no intention, however, of waiting around to find out how long this fortunate condition would persist. As he'd struggled that evening with Mary's advice about Taubolt, Joby had kept wishing for some kind of sign to guide him. Well, if this wasn't one, he didn't know what was. Holding her yarn charm against his chest with both hands, he knew Mary had been right. He had to get out of here! Now!

After yanking his clothes back on, Joby grabbed the duffel bag he used as a suitcase from the pantry cupboard he used as a closet, cramming as many of his warmest clothes inside it as would fit, glancing periodically at the kitchen doorjamb. After one last look around the pantry, he grabbed his newly-recovered storybook, and shoved that in his bag just as a roach scuttled down the pantry cupboard door, and free-fell to the floor. Joby whirled to find several more insects scuttling from their kitchen stronghold. As he'd feared the tide was starting to advance.

He dashed into the living room and looked around. His rent was due in less than a week, and he had nothing to pay it with. In truth, there was nothing here he really wanted that much anyway. Jogging into the bathroom, he shoved his toothbrush and a few other things in with his clothes, then fled his apartment without looking back. *Let the roaches have it all,* he thought. It felt almost good to be so free.

Half an hour later he was standing at a sodium-lit freeway on-ramp with his thumb out. Despite the hour, or maybe because of it, it was hardly any time before a small blue compact pulled over and waited while he ran toward it with his bag. Joby pulled open the passenger door to find a young man with dark, curly hair, and coffee-colored eyes grinning at him from behind the wheel. "Where you headed?" he asked.

"Up the coast," said Joby. "But I'd be happy just to get across the bay for now."

"Well, it's your lucky day. That's where I'm goin'."

"Across the bay?"

"Up the coast."

"You're kidding!"

"I don't kid 'til after eight A.M.," the guy said. "Where to on the coast?"

"No place you've heard of," Joby answered. "A place called Taubolt."

"No shit!" the driver laughed. "That's exactly where I'm headed!"

"No way!" Joby said. "No friggin' way!" He laughed, throwing his bag in the backseat, and climbing in. "God! I ask for one little sign, and now I'm livin' in the tabloids!"

13

(Home Free)

The sky had paled to a slate gray, and still this rural no-man's-land they'd been driving through for hours showed no sign of ending. Any minute now, his superiors would return to Joby's apartment and find them gone, Williamson thought anxiously, watching Joby's head loll against the passenger window. The boy had fallen soundly asleep even before they'd left the main route for this winding country road that called itself a highway. Their driver, on the other hand, seemed surprisingly alert for a man who'd driven all night.

"Joseph," as he called himself, had told Joby he was going up to spend Christmas with friends in Taubolt, but Williamson didn't buy it for a minute. At midnight? Just when they'd needed a ride? Then again, if this was Heaven's cheater in some new disguise, why hadn't he done something about the wraith in his backseat?

Suddenly, the air was charged with a frightening new presence—something powerful surging toward them at terrible speed. Williamson cringed in terror, sure his superiors had found him, but then the presence seemed to hesitate and veer away. An instant later, something stood in the road ahead. It seemed to be a man, though Williamson knew an angel when he felt one! Of course Taubolt's borders must be guarded! How could he have failed to anticipate this? What was he going to do? The angel would sense him in an instant!

Joby didn't stir as Joseph stopped their car and rolled his window down.

"What am I to make of *this*?" the tall, denim and flannel-clad "man" outside asked with obvious displeasure.

In a mindless panic, Williamson tried to flee the car.

"Stay, fiend," the angel growled. "You are in no danger. I am commanded to let you pass. Welcome to Taubolt, wretched soul," he added sullenly.

"We're . . . in Taubolt?" Williamson murmured weakly.

"We are at the border," said the driver.

"And you're not going to stop me?" Williamson squeaked in astonishment.

"I am forbidden to deny your kind entry now that the boy has returned," the angel said unhappily.

"Then we have to get inside!" Williamson blurted art. "It's almost dawn! I have to be inside before—"

"Is it not sufficient that you survive?" protested the angel. "Keep silent now. Gabriel and I have much to discuss."

Gabriel?! He'd ridden for five hours with an *archangel?!*

"In truth, Michael, I wish you'd let him go," Gabriel said. "There is much I would rather not discuss in his presence."

Michael?!! Two archangels?!!! Williamson burst from the car in panic, and fled down the road without thought of anything beyond escape, somehow, into Taubolt.

✿

"Gone where? What are you talking about? . . .

"What? I ordered no roaches!"

Lucifer's face became an increasingly exaggerated mask of incredulity as he stood at his office obelisk, listening to Eurodia's unthinkable report.

"Where were all of you when—

"No one but Williamson?" he yelled. *"All night?* I'll have your worthless hides for *shoe leather!* Why haven't you summoned him and found out where they—

"What? . . ." Lucifer asked quietly. "That's not possible. . . .

"Well find him, you idiots! Find them both, or flee for your worthless lives!"

He removed his hand from the obelisk just long enough to slam it down again, and shout, "Williamson! Answer me! *Now!*"

As the silence stretched, a thrill of rare dismay coursed down the devil's spine.

✿

"The presence of Lucifer's creature is not surprising," Michael said after casting an even deeper sleep over the boy. "But what are *you* doing here, brother?"

"The boy wished to come here," Gabe said. "He prayed for a sign."

"To you? Directly?" Michael said skeptically. "*I* pray my ears mislead me, Gabe! Our Lord clearly commanded—"

"A command already broken," Gabriel said defiantly, "by the boy's grandfather. Driven by *love*, Michael. Think on that! Since when has love been called sin in Heaven?"

"Love and obedience are close kin, brother," Michael said dangerously. "Mortal kind is weak and easily confused. Their errors may be excused. But we are always in His presence. Of us all, I never thought to hear *you* rationalize."

"When I discovered Merlin's disobedience," Gabe said, "I tried to ask—"

"Merlin?" Michael interrupted, his brows arched in surprise. "*The* Merlin—is this boy's grandfather?"

"Yes. And when I asked the Creator what was to be done about his defiance, Our Master just invited me to play a hand of *cards*! When I declined, He said that He would never *make* me play."

Michael looked askance at his sibling. "I fail to see what—"

"You have not been there to watch as I have, Michael," Gabriel pleaded, "but I fear Our Master's plan has gone awry! He is in danger of losing all He loves but forbidden even the least expression of concern by the terms of this wager. So He tells me that He would never *make* me play cards. Now do you see?"

"I see only that you've assumed far more than you've any business doing," Michael answered. "Do you suggest that the Creator didn't know what He was about when He agreed to these conditions?"

"If I am in error, brother," Gabe replied sadly, "then I can only think Our Lord has turned His back on everything He loves, including us, and I *cannot* believe *that*?"

"*Us?*" Michael scoffed. What have we to do with—"

"If this boy fails," Gabe interrupted softly, "all creation is to be erased, and made anew according to Lucifer's precise instructions."

Stunned to incredulous silence, Michael stared first at Gabe, then at the sky, as if some explanation or assurance might await him there.

"I will hide nothing I have done from Him," said Gabe. "Do you doubt He knows already? But I love Him, Michael. And I will endure even damnation to help Him."

"I only pray that help is what you've brought Him, brother," Michael said quietly, "for I love Him also and have never known disobedience to serve Him best. I love you as well, and I dearly hope you have not sold yourself in vain."

❧

"Hey, pal. Time to rise. We're here."

The voice seemed more dream than real as it drew Joby from the well of slumber. Then a hand was laid gently on his shoulder, and Joby opened his eyes to find his face against a window, beyond which narrow green paths wound off through tall dry grass toward cliff tops and the sea. Far offshore the rising sun shone brightly on a slow procession of billowing white thunderheads migrating north against the blue, blue sky. A double arc of rainbow glowed luminous beneath them as sunlight hit the cliffs. The fields glowed golden, and a dazzling regatta of white gulls wheeled gracefully above the bay.

"My God," Joby whispered, wondering if he might still be dreaming.

"Sure is pretty, isn't it?" said his companion.

Sitting up, Joby drew a long shuddering breath, and smelled sea salt, wood smoke, cedar bark, and weathered stone. Somewhere to the south, sea lions trumpeted greetings to the day above the muted boom of surf. Then he turned to find Joseph smiling against a backdrop of Victorian cottages, gnarled cypress trees, and gardens full of flowers even now, in late December. Farther up the street, he saw shops, water towers, and the old hotel looking just as he remembered them. "Twenty years," he murmured, "and nothing's changed at all."

"Hope it never does," his companion smiled. "Don't mean to rush you off, but I'm expected up the coast a ways for breakfast. This okay?"

"This is great," Joby said, opening the door, and reaching for his duffel bag. "I feel like I should give you some gas money or something, but I haven't got—"

"Don't worry, pal. Just do some other guy a favor, and the world won't miss your gas money. Merry Christmas!"

"Yeah," said Joby, remembering that it was Christmas Eve. "Merry Christmas. And thank you so much!"

Joby stepped out, shut the door behind him, and raised a hand in farewell as the car pulled away, then he turned and looked around him, memories of his boyhood visit welling up at every sight. It hardly seemed possible that he was really back . . . after so much time . . . so much water under so many bridges.

Hoisting his duffel bag, he strode across the field to go look at the bay, marveling at how much it felt like coming home, though he'd only been here once so very long ago. At the cliff tops, he sat and gazed down at the water.

"I'm back," he whispered to all the teeming creatures he knew were there beneath the surface. "Remember me?"

He was hungry, but it was much too early for anything to be open, and he had so little cash. He had no idea where he'd stay that night. Finding any kind of job would clearly have to be his whole focus once things opened. Someone here must need some yard work done, he imagined. While waiting for the town to stir, he decided to walk around and reacquaint himself with Taubolt until he could get a bite to eat. Then he'd find a public rest room to wash up in before going to charm Taubolt's throng of eager employers.

He was heading back across the headland toward town, still marveling at the beauty of everything around him, when he heard hushed voices from inside a dense stand of bishop pines a short ways off the path. Without thinking, he stopped to listen.

"They're so sad," said a girl's voice. "The whole grove. Can't you feel it?" There was a pause. "I think we'll need to dance."

"Oh good," said a second girl's voice. "Sunday? After breakfast. I'll tell Otter and Jessie. You get Ethan and Sophie."

"And Hawk for seven. . . . Don't you think he's cute?"

"I'm telling him you're in love," laughed the second girl.

"No, you're not," said the first with comical severity. "'Cause, I'll tell Ander what you said to Molly at Sky's birthday party."

"No!" shrieked the second girl. "You take everything so seriously."

"You shouldn't tease then," said the first.

There was another pause. Joby imagined them sticking their tongues out at each other, knowing he shouldn't be eavesdropping. But it was such a strange conversation. Sky? Otter? Ander? Hawk? It sounded like some kind of Indian tribe.

"What about Mrs. Farley's garden?" asked the second voice at length.

"If she doesn't stop fussing at those flowers," said the first, "they'll uproot themselves and run away. Mr. Farley's been dead for years. It's time she found a new husband. That would give her something better to work on."

"Mr. Templer's single," giggled the second girl.

"Bellindi! He's got nose hair!"

"I know," the second girl laughed. "But—"

"Shhh!"

A sudden silence fell, punctuated by scuffling noises, then thrashing about on the thicket's far side. Before Joby realized what was happening, the girls were peering wide-eyed at him around the thicket's edge. They seemed in their early teens. One had startling blue eyes in a pale, freckled face framed by long, wavy strawberry hair. The other had dark eyes in a heart-shaped face, and straight dark hair tied back with ribbons. They wore jeans and

T-shirts, and had chains of pansy flowers woven through their tresses. In startled disbelief, they stepped out from behind the trees to stare at Joby.

"I'm sorry," he said, feeling deeply embarrassed. "I didn't mean to . . ."

They turned to look at one another, then burst out laughing and ran off, hand in hand, into the field, their flower chains scattering on the breeze behind them.

❈

"Of course you can follow him," the Creator said pleasantly. "Didn't I say so last time?"

Gabriel watched a series of confused expressions struggle across Lucifer's face as the confrontation he'd clearly been expecting didn't occur.

"Well . . . how am I to find it, then?" Lucifer sputtered.

"I'll draw you a map," the Creator smiled, producing, as he spoke, a sheet of paper with several simple features already drawn upon it, and handing this to Lucifer.

"This is all?" Lucifer asked, perusing the map suspiciously. "Just follow this little highway? That seems awfully simple."

"The best hiding places are," said the Creator, "or *were.*"

"You're so smug." Lucifer frowned. "But we both know it was some creature of Yours who pulled Joby from the fire just as I had won."

"If you had won, we wouldn't be here debating the outcome, would we?"

"I *had* won, and you know it!" Lucifer snapped.

"Gabe," the Creator asked, "under oath as the wager's official witness, have I broken any least term of our agreement?"

"No, Lord," Gabriel answered, trying not to look ashamed. "Under oath as witness, *You* have not."

"There you have it, Lucifer. My servant does not lie any more than I do. If you've some proof to the contrary, present it. Otherwise, I've things to attend to."

❈

Day's end found Joby back on Main Street, wandering wearily past shops decked in gold and silver, scarlet and evergreen. Cheerful conversation and occasional carols wafted from every doorway. Everyone had been very friendly, but none had been hiring. Next time, Joby chided himself glumly, he'd have to run away earlier in the season.

Outside a candy shop, he was arrested by the scents of peppermint, cinnamon, and chocolate, but the smell was all he could afford. Sunset was not far off, and the clear evening was quickly growing chill. He'd still found nowhere to stay that night. It was Christmas Eve. Shouldn't there at least be room for him in a barn somewhere?

At the thought, he realized what any more-veteran bum would have known from the start, and turned back to head up Shea Street toward Taubolt's only church. Like everything else here, it was just a short walk away, on a hilltop at the north end of town, next to the cemetery. Where better to seek food and shelter on Christmas Eve?

The sign out front read, ST. LUKE'S. Joby found the door unlocked, and walked inside to find candles burning unattended on the altar.

"Hello?" he called.

Silence.

A huge mural of waves out on the luminous night sea covered the entire wall behind the altar. In front of this hung a crucifix. On a stand below that rested a modest gold tabernacle. *Catholic then,* Joby thought. The other walls were paneled in darkly gleaming redwood, the high ceiling supported by heavy crossbeams. The air smelled of wood polish, candle wax, and age. Stained-glass windows lined either side of the building: abstract designs radiant with the last fiery light of day. Evergreen garlands and wide velvet ribbon in crimson and white festooned the walls. Small white lights twinkled on Christmas trees to either side of the altar. Joby had not been inside a church since before Lindwald's death. It felt both comfortingly familiar and vaguely incriminating, as he walked forward and stepped into a pew.

It was impossible to gaze at anything but the mural, and to gaze at that without coming again and again to the crucifix at its center. Across the many years, fragments of his conversation with the old priest, Father Crombie, returned.

They long for another chance. . . . It was far too late to help his Son . . . he helped him anyway. . . . Hope, even for the hopeless. . . . You may be glad . . . someday.

With welling eyes, Joby dropped his head onto his hands atop the pew back. "God." The whisper left his constricted throat almost of its own volition. "If you're ever going to help me . . ."

The only answer he received was the sound of his own breathing in the gathering gloom. Then a soft shuffling sound brought his eyes up to find an ancient man in black clerical suit and collar tottering with obvious difficulty through a door to one side of the altar. With an oversize prayer book gripped in both hands, he went slowly onto one knee, rose even more slowly to place the book upon the altar, then stepped back and looked around the apse, as if to check the decorations.

The longer Joby looked, the more familiar the old man seemed. Knowing it could only be wishful thinking, Joby murmured, "Father Crombie?"

Clearly startled, the old priest turned and peered into the unlit church. "Who is that?" he asked in a kindly, still strong voice that Joby remembered with shocking clarity, even after so much time.

❈

The wretched traitor's trail wasn't hard to follow. Most of a day later, the wraith's fear still hung on everything he'd passed, like a long sulfuric fart through the countryside.

"Let's hope the boy is with him still," Kallaystra said, wrinkling her pretty nose.

"Security camera," Malcephalon growled. "I'll make him wish to die over and over again before I'm finished."

It rankled him that Kallaystra spared not even a glance in response. Clearly, Lucifer had only sent her along to humiliate him further. Someone "trustworthy" he'd said, to guard against "further incompetence." Who was Lucifer to talk of incompetence? Malcephalon suspected that, if their glorious leader had ever risked doing anything himself, he'd long ago have proven the most incompetent wretch in Hell. Why couldn't Kallaystra see that? It was well past time for a change of leadership. If Lucifer lost this wager, his position would certainly be weakened; not an unsatisfying thought.

"This place is noxious," Kallaystra said crossly. "It's beginning to distract me."

Wrapped in his own resentment, Malcephalon hadn't noticed. But she was right. Some offensive quality was growing stronger all around them as they moved farther into the Creator's newly-revealed preserve.

"Yes. I've felt it for some time," Malcephalon lied, not wanting to seem less observant than his chaperone. "Hardly surprising given the nature of this place."

"Let's find that little worm, and get out of here," Kallaystra complained.

As they pressed farther into Taubolt, the sun fell beneath the treetops, and the unpleasant sensation grew steadily stronger until it threatened to eclipse Williamson's trail altogether. Malcephalon thought the smell of it familiar. It tugged almost savagely at his memory. But of what?

"This is unendurable!" Kallaystra fumed. "If it gets any worse—"

"There he is!" Malcephalon snarled, pointing at a smudge of vapor hanging motionless against a thorny clump of foliage ahead of them.

What was left of Williamson simply stared with dull resignation as they approached. His form was pale and ragged, as if the torture he so richly deserved was already well along without them.

"The air," Williamson slurred as they arrived. "Burns . . . burns . . . I was tricked. . . . Cheating. . . . Angels cheating."

"Fucking flake of dung! You've betrayed us all!" Malcephalon shouted, raising both hands to strike.

Williamson shrieked as Malcephalon's blazing stream of blue fire hit him, but Kallaystra swiftly deflected the killing blow.

"Fool!" she snapped at Malcephalon. "You would destroy him before learning what he knows of the boy? Lucifer was right. You have lost your mind."

Malcephalon barely kept himself from launching another stream of fire at her. The impudent whore! When she had proven the little rat knew nothing worth saving, not Lucifer himself would prevent his revenge.

"Where is the boy?" Kallaystra demanded of Williamson.

"Took him . . . ," he panted, "to . . . to Taubolt."

"Who took him?" Kallaystra pressed. "Why didn't you alert us?"

"Tricked," Williamson gasped. "I know things . . . things Lucifer must hear. . . . They tricked . . . tricked us all."

"Who tricked you?" Kallaystra demanded.

"Only Lucifer's ears," Williamson moaned. "No one can be trusted."

"He's lying!" Malcephalon sneered. "Can't you see he's just trying to buy time?"

"Spit it out," Kallaystra snapped at Williamson, "or I'll let this fool do what he likes with you. *I* can be trusted with anything your master needs to know."

"He . . . ," Williamson breathed, raising a limp hand toward Malcephalon, with the tattered shreds of pure contempt in his eyes. "He . . . cannot . . . be trusted."

"You worthless, lying piece of—" Malcephalon's hands flew up to hurl fire again.

"Stop!" Kallaystra shouted, whirling to confront Malcephalon, her own hands raised to strike. "Why are you so eager to destroy him? . . . Why *was* he left alone all night to guard the boy? I am beginning to wonder. *Was* it just stupidity?"

"He thinks to spare himself by implicating me!" Malcephalon yelled. "Isn't it obvious what he's—"

"Stop!" Kallaystra shouted, whirling to where Williamson had been.

Only then did Malcephalon realize that Williamson had slipped off while they were arguing. The pathetic wraith was already several hundred feet away, struggling farther into Taubolt as if against some fierce, invisible current.

Kallaystra surged after him, but stopped with an obscene exclamation as Williamson screamed in torment, and began to stretch into attenuated fragments, his face drawn taught in silent agony. Then even the fragments of his substance blew apart like smoke on a puff of wind.

Malcephalon hovered in stunned astonishment. He had not seen this for many, many centuries, but he knew now what it was that filled the very fabric of this place, becoming more and more intolerable with each step farther into Taubolt. Being full demons, he and Kallaystra might have gotten much closer and survived, but a frail wisp like Williamson had been too vulnerable.

"The fucking Cup!" Kallaystra hissed. "That's what this place stinks of!"

"We are indeed betrayed," Malcephalon murmured palely. "If the boy is in its presence, we will never reach him."

"Come!" Kallaystra snapped. "There is nothing more we can do here. Lucifer must know of this immediately."

❊

"Father Crombie?" Joby asked in astonishment.

"Yes?" the priest said, taking the one small step down off of the altar with difficulty. "I'm afraid you have me at a disadvantage. It's so dark, and I cannot place the voice. Let me come a little closer." He shuffled forward, pulling a pair of wire-framed glasses from his shirt pocket, and setting them carefully in place. "I'm sorry," Father Crombie smiled, as he came abreast of Joby's pew, peering down through thick lenses, "but I still can't place your face. Are you a visitor to Taubolt?"

"I'm Joby Peterson," he said, struggling not to laugh aloud at the sheer impossibility of what was happening. Suddenly the world seemed full of unlikely coincidences. "You wouldn't remember me. We only met once, a very long time ago, when you were still at St. Albee's."

"St. Albee's?" Father Crombie exclaimed softly. "My! That *was* a long time ago!"

"Ben Vierra introduced us."

"I certainly remember Ben! A delightful boy. What's your name again?"

"Joby." He held his hand out, and Father Crombie shook it with a strength that belied his frail gate. "We came to see you one day after church about . . . well, silly kid things, really," he said, abashed.

Crombie's grip tightened convulsively, as he leaned forward to stare intently at Joby's face. "Joby Peterson?" he asked, astonished in his turn. "The boy who wished to fight the devil?"

Immediately, Joby was filled with shame. *No,* he thought. *The bum who's looking for a handout on Christmas Eve.*

"Have I got it wrong then?" Crombie asked, mistaking his silence.

"No," Joby sighed. "That was me."

"Well I'm astonished!" said the priest. "And delighted! I've never forgotten our meeting, you know. You made such an impression on me! How is Ben? He's not here with you in Taubolt, is he?"

"No," Joby said. "We haven't really seen each other . . . for a long time."

"Ah. Well, of course," Father Crombie said, sounding disappointed. "People grow and drift apart." He smiled again. "You're not boys anymore, are you. Probably have families now, and lives of your own, eh?"

Before this could become even more humiliating, Joby said, "I'm kind of stranded here, Father Crombie. I have nowhere to stay tonight, and I was hoping I might get something to eat." His face felt like stone. He imagined it crumbling off in shards as Father Crombie's smile gave way to a sad, half-stricken look.

"You've clearly a story to tell," Father Crombie said, "and I'd like to hear it, if you'll do me that honor. Would you consider coming back to the rectory and having dinner with me tonight?"

"That's very kind," Joby said, startled by the priest's generosity, though he dreaded such a conversation with this kind old man who'd thought so highly of him.

A cheerful blaze already crackled in the rectory hearth as they entered. A modest meal was laid out on the table. The old priest went to fetch a second set of dishes, insisting that Joby sit and warm himself. Moments later they were at the table, heads bowed, while Father Crombie thanked God for reuniting them.

It was just a hearty soup, a warm and fragrant loaf of bread, a simple salad, and a bottle of white wine, but it seemed tastier than any meal Joby could recall. Hoping to deflect Crombie's impending questions, Joby quickly asked the priest where he'd gone off to so suddenly all those years ago.

"Oh, that was a sad affair," the priest replied. "Seems the bishop had been finding some of my *liberal views* a bit offensive." He took a spoonful of soup.

"I was sent off to a poor urban parish in Chicago where I spent more time burying parishioners than preaching to them." He shook his head sadly, and spooned more soup. "Those were hard days. I did the best I could, though, as did they."

Joby shook his head in empathy. "I've gotten fired that way. Not a clue you're in trouble, then, bam! You're out the door."

"Really?" Father Crombie said. "When was that?"

"It's a boring story," Joby said, regretting his carelessness. "How'd you get here?"

"Oh, that's a long and boring a story too." Crombie smiled. "It seems I had detractors in Chicago as well. The superior who sent me to Taubolt had, happily, never been here and clearly imagined it nothing but the furthest outpost of un-civilization. Said he *feared* the damp air and rough rural life might be hard on my arthritic hips, which perhaps they have been, but the joke has been on him, Joby. I regard this place and its marvelous people as my life's reward." His bemused gaze wandered toward the fire.

"But enough of me," Crombie said at last. "I am eager to hear of your life. I sense it may not be an easy tale, but I think you'll find me a sympathetic listener."

By now Joby saw that Father Crombie might know more about disappointment and disgrace than he'd expected. Still, he felt unprepared to answer.

"Tell me about Ben," Crombie said, as if sensing his difficulty. "I was very fond of him, you know. You said it's been a long time, but you'd still know more than I."

"Ben liked you too," Joby said. "I don't think he cared for church much after you left."

"Ah. That's unfortunate."

"I haven't seen him since my freshman year at Berkeley." Even now, the memory hurt. "He came out from school in Colorado to visit during spring break, but things weren't going too well for me then." Joby found himself drawn up short by the irony of this statement, given his current circumstances. "I was pretty lousy company, I guess." In truth, he'd been *worse* than lousy company from the moment Ben had told him about Laura leaving school to marry some guy she'd supposedly met at an off-campus bar.

"What did you study there?" Father Crombie asked when the silence stretched.

Joby shrugged, and took a long pull of wine. He was going to have to do this. Why put a polish on it? "I studied expulsion, Father," he said without meeting the old priest's eyes. "I went through some bad depression my first year and flunked out of school. Ben came right in the middle of that, and wasn't up for any second helpings, I guess. We wrote a few times afterward, and then just . . ." He fluttered his hands stupidly.

"And after your departure from Berkeley?" Crombie asked, unfazed.

What would it take to make him get it? Joby wondered. *And then, Father,* he imagined saying, *I became an unemployed bum who's accomplished nothing but getting a few good people killed—before coming here to beg for charity, that is.*

"I got a degree in English at Hayward State," he said instead.

Crombie watched him for a moment with the same kindly expression Joby remembered from their other conversation twenty years before. "And then things grew even harder, I take it," he said at last.

Biting down hard on a sudden swarm of cynical responses, Joby nodded without looking up, trying to seem engrossed in his food.

"What brought you to Taubolt?" Crombie asked, refilling Joby's wineglass.

"I ran away," he said quietly, startled at his own candor. Then he set down his fork and looked Father Crombie in the eyes for the first time since he'd started talking. "A friend of mine was killed in Berkeley last week, Father, by policemen. . . . It was my fault." He looked away, suddenly feeling only empty and exhausted. "I was so angry, if I'd stayed in Berkeley, I think I'd have done something terrible. . . . I meant to . . . do something terrible."

He braced himself for a barrage of well meaning questions, but all Father Crombie said was, "Taubolt seems a rather unusual place to run away to. Most people haven't heard of it."

"I came here with my family once as a kid," Joby said, surprised and grateful to be released without interrogation. "My grandfather grew up here."

Crombie, who had hardly blinked all evening, even at Joby's reference to Gypsy's death, suddenly looked startled. "Your grandfather is from Taubolt? What's his name?"

"His name was Emery Emerson," Joby said. "He died when I was five."

Crombie shook his head, looking pensive. "I've never heard of him."

"You wouldn't have. He left a very long time ago. Just after high school, I think."

"Ah," Crombie said, as if Joby's answer explained nothing at all. "Well, I admire him for having the good sense to be born here, and for his part in bringing you to us, Joby." He paused thoughtfully, then added, "Though you seem to think otherwise, I have a strong sense that your arrival here had nothing at all to do with failure. This place has a strange way of attracting those it wants. If you'd like me to, I'm sure I can find you a place to stay until you find some work. I've someone in mind whom I'm sure would be delighted with your company. I'll call her after dinner. She may need some odd jobs done until you find better employment."

"That's . . . Thank you, Father," Joby said, startled by the sudden scope of Father Crombie's hospitality. "That's much more than I ever expected. . . . But, I hope you won't pressure her. I went looking for work today, and I think it's going to take a while. I don't want anyone feeling stuck with me."

"Where did you look? The stores?" Crombie smiled. "On the day before Christmas?" He shook his head and chuckled. "That's not the place. No, I'm sure we'll have no trouble finding something for a bright, good-hearted boy like you to do around here. Just let me ask around a bit."

To be called good-hearted by a man like Crombie filled Joby with an utterly unlooked for warmth. Would the old priest have thought so, he wondered, if he knew that Joby had been planning bombings and shooting sprees a day before? Probably not, but Joby couldn't seem to fill the objection with any real conviction. The old man's kindness was too large to fight, and Joby suddenly allowed himself to feel gratitude. He'd needed help, and here it was, like a miracle. When had that last happened? Feeling Mary's charm under his shirt, soft against his chest, he sent a grateful thought her way as well, for the wise and patient shove she'd given him. How the world could change, in just a day!

❧

Lucifer had done nothing but pace his office in frightening silence since Kallaystra had informed him that Taubolt harbored the Cup. She was beginning to wonder if he might actually have forgotten Malcephalon and she were present when Lucifer stopped without turning to face them and said, "So, my esteemed colleague, you've wasted twenty-four years of precious opportunity, only to lose the whole game in one spectacular lapse of judgment." He did turn then, to gaze at Malcephalon with a look that made Kallaystra wince. "And now, it seems, you've denied me even the consolation of punishing Williamson. Have you yet some other brilliant plan to salvage this catastrophic cavalcade of blunders?"

"I would not presume to eclipse your own brilliance, Bright One," Malcephalon intoned savagely. "Pray, reveal your own vastly superior plan."

Kallaystra barely concealed her shock. What in Hell was Malcephalon thinking?

"You *dare?*" rasped Lucifer.

"*You* dare?" Malcephalon replied. "You, who do virtually nothing but *observe* as others labor on your behalf? *I* did all the work, *Bright One,* while—"

"Slowly, stupidly, and unsuccessfully!" Lucifer snarled.

"It is child's play for those who risk nothing to criticize those who act!" Malcephalon snarled back.

With a startled curse, Kallaystra fled to the margins of the room as Lucifer's hands shot up to attack.

"Risk this, you traitorous imbecile!" Lucifer screamed, launching a wall of green and amber gas hotter than a star at the coal black demon.

Malcephalon was as fast. The gaseous cloud met an ethereal barrier of crackling blue and white with a detonation heard throughout Lucifer's domain. The walls of this and every other room in Hell shuddered and dissolved as Lucifer's carefully sustained illusions of space and material substance became momentarily tenuous. Struggling to place herself further from harm's way, Kallaystra turned back to watch the conflict in dismay. They would tear all Hell apart!

With a celestial roar of rage, Lucifer abandoned the illusion of human form, his skin seeming to rupture before an explosion of inner white light. Where Malcephalon had stood, darkness deeper than that between the stars strove to swallow and quench Lucifer's deadly radiance. Vast arcs of raw power slithered and snapped across the indefinable spaces that were Hell's real fabric, catching multitudes of mortal damned in the inexpressible torment of that crossfire.

Struggling with everyone else to avoid the onslaught's deadly backwash, Kallaystra suddenly found herself with an open shot at Malcephalon's metaphorical "back." Realizing that she might be next in line for Lucifer's wrath, merely by virtue of her onetime friendship with the moronic demon, she wasted no time in clarifying her position. Summoning every shred of force at her command, she launched it all at Malcephalon's unprotected flank.

There was a barely audible gasp of astonishment as Lucifer's unimaginable brightness flared around Malcephalon's position. Then, unearthly silence.

A moment later, Hell's vast labyrinth of corridors, chambers, and severe furnishings shivered back into being, and Kallaystra found herself half-embedded in one of Lucifer's office walls. Disengaging herself, she stepped forward as confidently as she could to stand before the victor.

"God, that felt good," Lucifer murmured dryly, shrugging back into his illusory form. He turned to stare humorlessly at Kallaystra. "Very astute decision, my dear."

There was no sign of Malcephalon. Angels left no bodies when they died.

"Though bitter experience leaves me less than hopeful," Lucifer muttered, "I suppose I must pursue the one tiny shred of potential salvage from this catastrophe: angels cheating. You're certain that's what Williamson said before he was destroyed?"

Kallaystra merely nodded.

"Did the ass elaborate at all?"

"No, sir," she replied, knowing every word was dangerous at present.

"Then I'll have to go abase myself again, I suppose," he sighed, "as fruitlessly as ever, I am sure." Without sparing her another glance, Lucifer walked past Kallaystra to lay a hand on his office obelisk. "Tique, Eurodia, Trephila, a word please."

The Triangle appeared, looking as pale and shaken as angels can.

"There have been some changes," he told them calmly. "Malcephalon is no longer in charge of this campaign."

"There were . . . rumors," Tique joked nervously, then looked quickly at the floor.

"I've not forgotten who else decided to leave the boy alone that night," Lucifer said flatly. "Let Malcephalon's fate serve as an object lesson. . . . There will be no further fooling around. Is that clear?"

Kallaystra found herself nodding with the others.

"Sir," said Trephila, always the boldest of the three, "I'm told the Enemy promised us access to Taubolt should the boy return. Does not the . . . *situation* there constitute a breach of that promise? Could we not—"

"Sadly, no," Lucifer cut her off. "He said we could follow. He did not say we'd enjoy it. We must do what we've done before," he replied. "Send mortals in to neutralize the Cup, and its . . . *company*," he sneered, "before going in ourselves to finish the job."

"But . . ." Eurodia looked caught out, and fell silent.

"But?" Lucifer insisted.

"I . . . I only meant," she stammered quietly. "Is there still time for that?"

"An excellent question," he mused grimly. "If we do run short of time now," he looked pointedly at each of them, "so do you."

"What are we to do?" Trephila asked with admirable dignity.

"Though we cannot go there yet in person," Lucifer said, "I don't see why we shouldn't send Taubolt a neighborly little greeting of some sort. I think a bit of meddling with the natural order might be in line. You three are fairly fond of that, aren't you?"

The Triangle nodded again. Tique even managed to smile.

"I'm putting Kallaystra in charge now." He turned his uncomfortable gaze on her. "We'll need a moment or two to strategize." He turned back to the Triangle. "Then she'll tell you what to do."

How wonderful, Kallaystra thought as the Triangle vanished, *to be rewarded for loyalty with command of a full-blown disaster.*

※

Joby clutched the table edge, while Father Crombie clung to the kitchen door frame as the small house gradually ceased to groan and sway around them. After the moment of breathless silence that always seems to follow earthquakes, the tension broke, and they both began to laugh.

"Wow! That was a pretty good jolt!" Joby said, as the adrenaline hit him.

"My goodness, yes." Father Crombie smiled. Somewhere nearby, a dog began to bark, then another farther off. "Let's hope that was centered nearby, or some other town may be having a very unhappy Christmas indeed."

"Well," Joby said, looking around. "Looks like you came through it okay."

"Yes. Nothing seems to have fallen." Crombie smiled again. "Should make for a lot of talk tomorrow, though . . . which," he said, looking at his watch, "it will be in just a few hours. As I was saying when all the excitement started, here are directions to Mrs. Lindsay's inn." He held out a small scrap of paper. "She'll want help with the wood and things, and after that quake, she may even have some cleaning up to do tonight."

"It'll be my pleasure, Father," Joby said, rising to take the directions. "This is so kind of you both. I don't know how to thank you."

"When you've gotten settled, come back and keep an old man company. That will be more than sufficient thanks. Any chance I'll see you at Mass tomorrow?"

Joby hadn't been to church in years, but could deny this man nothing after all he'd done. "Absolutely," he said. "This is already the best Christmas I ever had."

"Which makes mine the same," said Crombie. "Merry Christmas, Joby."

"Merry Christmas, Father," Joby replied, and stepped out into the night.

The sound of surf seemed magnified by the darkness as Joby stood, letting his eyes adjust. The air was redolent of sea smells and wood smoke. He looked up and drew a sharp breath. So many stars! Below him, the quaint town twinkled in holiday lights, seeming to mirror the sky.

"I'm living in a Christmas card," he murmured happily.

West of town, the sea was gilt in ghostly silver, the horizon washed in mist aglow with starlight, and . . . there was someone standing motionless atop an isolated knoll out on the headlands. Despite the darkness and the distance, Joby suddenly felt certain he was being watched in return. As he stepped forward, straining to see the figure better, something dark rushed by in eerie silence just above his head. He whirled to see an owl's silhouette against the starry sky, gliding over the cemetery toward the woods east of town. Laughing at the scare it had given him, he turned back to find his watcher on the headlands gone. Had he just imagined it? Shaking his head, he hefted his duffel bag, and started down the hill. Out of the kindness of her heart, Gladys Lindsay was waiting up for a stranger on Christmas Eve.

Brightly trimmed in small white Christmas lights, the Primrose Picket Inn was impossible to miss. The two-story white Victorian slumbered under the expansive arms of two ancient cypress trees. The glow of all those lights revealed well-tended gardens, as inexplicably full of flowers in December as every other garden in the town.

Up on its porch, Joby let the inn's large bronze knocker fall twice before wondering if he'd wake Mrs. Lindsay's guests, then lowered it with care, hoping he hadn't already offended his new benefactress.

His worry vanished when the door was opened by a smiling, white-haired woman not much more than five feet tall.

"You'd be Joby, I assume!" she enthused. "Come in! You must be freezing!" She hugged herself and shivered as Joby came in with his duffel bag.

"Thank you so much for putting me up like this," Joby said.

"Oh, it's no trouble. Winter's slow here, lots of empty rooms just gathering dust. Father told you I needed help with a few chores, didn't he?"

"Absolutely. I'm happy to help out any way I can."

"Well then," she chirped, "I'm getting the best of this bargain." She gave him a quick look up and down. "Father didn't tell me you were so handsome!"

"Well . . . thank you." Joby smiled uncertainly. "Looks like you made it through the quake all right."

"Oh yes! Wasn't that something though? I just now got the last of my guests back to bed. Up jabbering like excited children. You'd think they'd never felt a little shake before. Father Crombie said you're tired from your trip, so I won't talk your ear off." She turned spryly away. "I've made up your room on the second floor."

She led him past a small rosewood table in the entryway. It was graced with fresh-cut flowers on a white lace doily. An old postman's clock ticked quietly on the wall above it. The short hallway opened on one side into a large sitting room papered in Victorian floral patterns and comfortably furnished in dark, well-polished antiques. Joby paused to get a better look. Etched glass lampshades fringed in dangling crystal pendants glowed softly on the walls. The embers of a generous fire smoldered behind an old wrought-iron grate under a large carved mantel. Large windows were curtained in ruffled white lace. A colorfully lit Christmas tree stood in the corner, draped in silver rain and old blown-glass ornaments. Its resinous scent filled the room.

T'was the night before Christmas, Joby thought. It was the kind of house one found in fairy tales, not in real life. "This is beautiful," he said aloud.

"Thank you," Mrs. Lindsay smiled, her wizened face radiant with pride. "This room is full of wonderful memories for me, especially at this time of year. You picked a good time to come."

She turned and started up a banistered flight of hardwood stairs. Joby followed her to the second floor landing where she opened the last door they came to, reached in to flip the light on, and waved him in ahead of her.

Just inside, Joby halted in surprise. This was no tastefully generic guest room, nor Spartan servants' quarters. Bookshelves above a pine desk were crowded with sporting paraphernalia, model airplanes, an insect collection, a harmonica, a corncob pipe, and what looked like prom pictures of a lovely red-haired girl in turquoise satin on the arm of a jet-haired boy with movie-star good looks. *Huck Finn, Little Big, Once and Future King, and A Separate Peace* shared the higher shelves with old high school math and science texts. In one corner sat a small wood-burning stove, its pipe chimney rising to pierce the ceiling. The large, high bed was covered in a thick quilt sewn in fan designs of russet brown and hunter green.

"I hope you'll be comfortable here," Mrs. Lindsay said. "It was my son's room before he went off to college." She paused, seeming awkward for the first time since Joby's arrival. "If all this stuff bothers you, there are other rooms of course."

"No, this is great," Joby said, "if your son doesn't mind. He's not coming home for Christmas?"

"No," she said. "He's been far away with a family of his own for many years."

"Oh. Sure," Joby said, realizing the Mrs. Lindsay was hardly young enough to have children still in college. But it all looked so much as if the boy had just left.

"You should sleep then," she said warmly. "Bathroom's at the end of the hall. When would you like breakfast in the morning?"

"You don't have to do that," Joby said.

"You'll be no help to me starving." She smiled.

"I . . . Whenever you're having breakfast, I guess," he said sheepishly.

"That's awful early. Seven o'clock. The guests don't eat 'til nine."

"I'm an early riser," Joby assured her.

"Great then," she beamed, "I'd love the company. I'll cook something special. It's Christmas after all. Forecast says it will be lovely tomorrow. You'll have dinner with us, won't you? It's the finest feast in town, if I do say so, and Father Crombie will be there."

"I'd love to," he half-laughed, wondering if she thought his social calendar might be full, or something. "Is everyone here so generous? Or did I just happen to run into the two nicest people in town first?"

"Welcome to Taubolt," she smiled, "and sweet dreams, dear." She closed the door behind her.

Joby looked around the room again with a surreal feeling that he'd actually come home to some former life he'd just forgotten until now. He dropped his duffel bag, and went to the window for one last glance at the starry night outside, then turned out the light, pulled back the covers, and dropped onto what felt like a real feather bed. Moments later, he fell asleep trying to recall when he had last felt so content.

❈

Michael sat perched atop the dead fall on which he'd come to rest after Joby caught him watching. That had been careless, but Taubolt's guardian had hardly been himself since his disturbing discussion with Gabriel. Michael's younger sibling had always been a bit high strung, but reckless disobedience? Michael didn't know what to think, except that disaster was woven all through the news.

And then there was Joby himself. The delightful child Michael remembered was gone, his once radiant heart a cauldron of conflicting emotions of which Joby himself seemed hardly aware.

He wondered what the world's scientists would make of a seismic event felt over half the globe with no identifiable epicenter, and might have smiled at Hell's apparent tantrum over Joby's escape, were it not for what he saw approaching Taubolt now.

Out on the horizon, farther than any normal owl could possibly have seen, a vast boiling shadow gathered and grew, eating the stars as it came. *Already, it starts,* he thought bleakly, *and I may do nothing but watch.*

Below him, a twinkling village of innocent souls slept peacefully, dreaming Christmas dreams with no inkling of how their long peace was about to crumble.

14

(Christmas in Taubolt)

Fierce with joy, Joby ran through dark woods trailing spreading waves of light, candles lighting candles lighting candles in his wake. An exuberant wind roared through the canopy above him, filling the charged air with swirling leaves. The gale grew louder around him until a blinding flash lit the wood as bright as day.

Joby started awake to find the wind's roar undiminished, mixed with what sounded like a shower of nails on the roof above him. Another stuttering flash lit the room, followed by a volley of crackling thunder as Joby sat up in bed.

He went to the window, and swept aside the curtains just in time to see a long arc of violet lightning hurled across the roiling sky like some attenuated tree, followed by a more muted rumble.

"Wow!" he murmured, filled with boyish delight at the display.

Just outside, tree limbs thumped against each other and the walls, sounding like a delegation of clubfoot drunkards stumbling down a flight of wooden stairs.

Another clap of thunder ratcheted through the air, and the roar of wind began to build, as if some immense train were rushing headlong toward the house. Across the yard trees whipped suddenly low to the ground, and Joby stepped backward from the window in alarm.

Churning with hail, leaves and twigs, the mammoth gust struck like a tidal wave, causing the house to groan and shift around him. Joby stumbled farther back as the windowpane bulged inward and the stovepipe began to shake and screech against the gale with a sound like some tormented tractor engine. The great cypress trees that had seemed shelter to the house before, beat upon it now like savage giants. Joby glanced apprehensively at the ceiling, wondering if the top floor was such a safe place to be.

Hearing another powerful gust surge across the headlands, he pressed himself against the wall, and waited, mesmerized, as trees across the street thrashed low again. The sash rattled violently as something large slammed

256 ⬧ MARK J. FERRARI

against the west side of the house with a battering boom. A string of Christmas lights torn from the inn's eves swung past the window. Across the street, power lines arced and flared, launching sparks into the wind like silver dandelion seeds. Then everything went inky black as Taubolt's power failed. The solid darkness around him magnified the roar of driving hail and raging wind until the storm seemed more a malevolent animal trying to break into the house than a mindless tantrum of air and water.

Outside his room, Joby heard muffled voices, a thud, a curse, quiet laughter. He groped along the wall until he felt the doorjamb and opened the door to find several narrow beams of light playing across the hallway. Dressed in nothing but his briefs, he closed his door to a crack before one of those flashlights found him.

"Everyone, please stay put 'til I can get some lamps lit." Mrs. Lindsay's voice floated from behind one of the flashlight beams. "Joby? Is that you, dear?"

"Yes, Mrs. Lindsay."

"Can you come help me, please?"

"Sure," he said. "I'll get some clothes on."

By what little light spilled through his narrowly open door Joby found and donned his jeans and T-shirt, while the house continued to creak and boom around him. Then he was out passing other guests with hasty greetings as he rushed, barefoot, to catch up with Mrs. Lindsay, who was already headed for the stairs.

"This is wild," he whispered when he caught up. No longer alone in the dark, his fear was giving way to excitement again. "I've never seen a storm like this."

"It's a pretty bad one," she said almost cheerfully as they descended the stairs. "But we've seen worse, I think. Hard to tell 'til morning. Sorry to press you into service so soon, dear, but I need you to bring some lamps back up to the guests' rooms while I light a few more downstairs."

"My pleasure, but, well, is it safe to stay up there? I mean, with the trees and all?"

"Those trees are half made of such weather, young man. They've stood through storms like this for a hundred years, and I'll be truly surprised if they surrender even a limb to anything this one has to offer. So when you bring the lamps up, please don't go scaring my guests with such ideas. All right, dear?"

"I'm sorry. I didn't mean—"

"I know." He saw her smile in the wan glow of her flashlight. "But a word in time saves nine, to mangle the proverb. We must remember that some of those city folk may not take the same delight in such little adventures as people like you and I do."

Joby had to smile. *Those city folk?* Who did she think he was? Then the rest of her remark registered: *people like you and I.* Suddenly, he ached with wanting to belong—really belong—here in Taubolt. *Like you and I. . . . Yeah,* he thought. *Thanks, Mrs. Lindsay. That's the best Christmas present I ever got.* "I thought you said Christmas was going to be lovely," he teased as they headed for the kitchen.

"Well, here's more proof that weather's a famously imprecise science, dear," she laughed. "Welcome to the wild frontier, Joby."

❈

In all his existence, Gabriel had never endured anything so shameful as knowing that he alone was to blame for the euphoric astonishment dawning on Lucifer's face.

"Do my ears deceive me, little brother," Lucifer gasped in unbridled delight, "or did they just hear you *admit* to having blatantly cheated?"

"Joby prayed for a sign," Gabe said palely, "and sought—"

"I've finally got You!" Lucifer crowed, turning with glee to face the Lord of all Creation. "The wager is forfeit to me!" He actually chortled. "I don't think I'm going to make You wipe it all away just yet though. I want a little time to enjoy *his* humiliation first!" He pointed vengefully at Gabriel. "Well, little brother? Have you nothing to say? Aren't you going to stammer explanations? Apologize perhaps? Grovel? Anything?"

The Creator gazed sadly at Gabriel, who looked abashed, and said, "I did nothing to influence his choice. I only answered his prayer for a ride."

"His prayer to you personally?" Lucifer demanded.

"No," Gabe said without hesitation.

"His prayer to angels in general? To God even?"

Again, Gabe shook his head.

"Just his *wish,* then," Lucifer scoffed. "It was no prayer at all." He turned insolently to God. "I tire of all this stalling. The victory is mine. I claim my prize. It is time to unmake this miserable travesty."

"Of course," the Creator said. "As soon as you explain which of the wager's terms has been violated."

Lucifer looked incredulous. "Our terms clearly stipulate that no immortal servant of Heaven may intervene without explicit invitation to do so by the candidate! My overzealous sibling here is certainly an immortal being, and he has, by any *honest* definition, intervened on his own initiative," his expression became sly, "unless You put him up to it, of course. . . . You didn't, I suppose."

The Creator's silent stare grew chilly.

"Just asking." Lucifer shrugged. "Pays to be thorough, You know."

"I have yet to see Your point," the Creator said, unamused.

"What's not to understand?" Lucifer snapped. "He interfered! The terms say—"

"That I was to *command* him not to," the Creator interrupted coldly, "which I did. There is no term requiring his obedience."

While Lucifer gaped, Gabriel struggled not to stagger from sheer relief.

"You . . . you cannot be serious!" Lucifer choked at last. "The assumption of obedience is obviously inherent in any mention of Your command!"

"You'd be proof of that, I suppose," the Creator observed dryly.

"Then . . . then I demand that he be punished," Lucifer spat. "The penalty for angelic disobedience is damnation, if I am not mistaken."

"That I cannot say," the Creator replied.

"You *cannot say?*" Lucifer shrilled. "You had no trouble finding your voice when it was *my* turn!"

"Your terms," the Creator calmly reminded him, "forbid Me from anything that might constitute expression of My will in regard to any issue touching on this matter prior to the wager's resolution. Thus, I cannot say."

Gabriel and his Master waited in silence, until, after much ranting, pacing and heavy breathing, Lucifer was able to go on.

"A touch. I confess it, Sir," Lucifer said, still struggling toward calm. "You are . . . stunningly resourceful. But as Your *angel* has proven himself a liar and a sneak, I must at *very* least insist he be deposed as Our wager's official witness."

"I'm sorry, Lucifer, but, once again, your logic escapes Me. He has answered every question put to him freely and without distortion. How does this constitute lying?"

"Ridiculous! What of timely disclosure?" Lucifer insisted. "If concealing the truth all this time doesn't qualify him as a liar, it certainly still makes him a sneak."

"But he concealed nothing." The Creator shrugged. "He confessed everything to Me as soon as he returned from conveying Joby to Taubolt."

Lucifer's eyes grew wide with fury. "And you said nothing to me at that park, when I specifically challenged you about—"

"You asked if *I* had broken the terms of our wager, and were told that *I* had not," the Creator cut him off. "I must also remind you that, as there was no other witness to our agreement, we would have to null the entire affair if Gabriel were removed. Can't conclude the rite without a witness, can we?"

Lucifer lost his briefly regained control. *"You . . . I . . . I insist . . . He can't . . ."*

"Complete sentences, please. Do you wish to dismiss him, and put this whole affair behind us, or not?" the Creator asked politely.

"Of course not!" Lucifer yelled.

"Please watch your tone," Heaven's Master said amiably. "My patience may be infinite, but it does not extend much past that. Now, unless you possess some further pressing revelation, I presume our business is concluded?"

"You're so *clever,*" Lucifer hissed, trembling with rage. "But who in Heaven or earth do you suppose will trust You when this affair is finished, knowing how You allowed this blatantly biased and disobedient conniver to remain at Your side through the remainder of these proceedings?"

"I fear he may be right, My Lord," Gabe said, bowing his head in shame.

Lucifer turned to look at him in surprise, the Creator in sad acceptance.

"Though I do not know what Your judgment regarding my disobedience will be, Lord," Gabe said quietly, "I have no desire to cast suspicion upon You through my continued presence. Therefore, I ask leave to remove myself from Your presence until the wager is concluded and You are free to make Your opinion of me known."

"You must do as you see fit, Gabriel," the Creator said quietly. "For the very reasons already mentioned, I may provide no guidance."

"Then I would go now, My Lord," Gabe said, fighting not to weep in their sight.

"As you wish," the Creator said quietly. Then he turned back to Lucifer with frightening sternness. "As for you, *Bright One,* I grow weary of these rude displays. I assure you, by the power of My Name, that when and if I lose this wager, you will not need to seek Me out like some recalcitrant schoolboy. I will come to you! Until that day, however, think very carefully before wasting more of My time."

❈

Joby woke the next morning in near darkness to quiet clinking and scraping sounds coming from the kitchen. Apparently Mrs. Lindsay was already cleaning up. When they'd gone in for lamps and candles, they'd found a length of picket fence shoved partway through the shattered kitchen window. As the storm had grown worse, they had helped the guests bring their bedding down to the main floor after all. They'd all camped out together in the parlor and the dining room, as far from the windows as possible, listening to the world moan and crash outside until exhaustion had finally dragged them once more into restless slumber.

Joby turned and stretched, then rose quietly from his tangle of quilts, and went to help Mrs. Lindsay, whom he found with a dustpan beside a wastebasket full of shattered glass. A wet mop stood in its bucket near the broken window. The floor and counters were already clean and nearly dry.

"Oh, Joby," she whispered as he entered. "Am I waking everyone?"

He shook his head. "I'm a light sleeper. Looks like I'm too late to help, though. How long have you been up?"

"Just a while. I wanted things ready to go in here. After making them sleep on my parlor floor, I'm hoping an impressive breakfast might appease them some."

"I don't think they'll blame *you* for last night. How will you cook without power?"

"It's gas, dear," she said, waving at the oversize stove. "I went out to have a look." She grimaced. "It's quite a mess out there, but the tank and lines look fine, so it should be safe. Afraid I'll need all the help you can give me today."

"Happy to be of service, ma'am," he said in a silly cowboy twang, grinning.

"Good. There are a few things I need from the grocery and the hardware right away. I've made a list." She took a slip of paper from the countertop. "Would you mind heading over now to pick them up?"

"Sure," Joby said, "but won't they be closed still?"

"Given the state of things, Franklin's probably had the hardware open all night." She smiled grimly. "The grocery's his too, so if it's still closed, you just tell him it's for me. He'll let you in. You know where they are?"

"Yup." Joby smiled. "Noticed 'em yesterday. I'll get my shoes on, and go."

"Thank you so much, Joby. You're a godsend!"

"All in a day's work, ma'am," he twanged again, not sure where the cowboy persona had come from, but liking the feel of it.

A moment later, as he stepped out into the pewter morning, Joby stopped and looked around in awe. Most of the inn's westward picket fence was now up against the house in chunks, along with the ruins of a small shed blown from God knew where. Mrs. Lindsay's cypress trees still stood, but two large limbs lay across her flowerbeds, while a third leaned up against the house, having torn away a good length of gingerbread molding in its fall. Shingles from who knew how many roofs lay scattered across the yard like oversize leaves. Ragged shreds of cloud crept sluggishly across the drizzly sky, as if even the air hung in tatters now.

One of Mrs. Lindsay's neighbors had been far less fortunate. A tall bishop pine leaned well through the second-story wall of a house across the street. There was no one to be seen outside the building.

As Joby walked farther into town, the true dimensions of Taubolt's disaster became increasingly apparent. A fallen cypress had crushed the corner of the health food store on Alland Street. The roots of another had torn up a large chunk of Shea Street as it fell, turning a length of old plank sidewalk into a length of old plank fence between an art gallery and the music store. Up toward the graveyard, a pickup truck lay crushed beneath a third downed tree. Two teenage boys and a girl stood staring forlornly at the wreckage, the girl in tears. Dead power lines drooped into the street. Christmas lights hung in sad, limp strands from every storefront. Bits of holiday merchandise snatched from broken display windows had come to rest in odd places. A large plastic punching clown, awol from the toy store, leered down from its new perch between *Father Time and the Maiden,* a sculpture atop the bank building. Joby shook his head again in wonder at the mess Mother Nature had made of last night's perfect Christmas card.

He found the grocery full of people, though none seemed to be customers.

"Holy cow," he gasped, staring up at the gaping hole left when a large span of roof had been torn from the back half of the store over the meat counter and the produce.

"Least it didn't come off over the dry goods," quipped a blue-aproned clerk wheeling her full mop bucket past him. "Produce don't mind the water so much."

Joby offered a sympathetic smile. "I hate to even ask this right now, but Mrs. Lindsay sent me over from the Primrose Picket for some things."

The clerk smiled wryly. "Gladys pressin' her guests into service now? How'd you all come through it over there last night?"

"Better than you, I guess." Joby grinned ruefully. "I'm not exactly a guest, though. I'm sort of her new hired hand. My name's Joby."

"Oh?" said the clerk. "Well I'm Dahlia. Never seen you around before."

"I just got here yesterday, actually." Joby shrugged awkwardly. "I'm a friend of Father Crombie's. He sort of fixed up the deal with Mrs. Lindsay."

"Oh!" the clerk said. "Where'd you know Crombie from?"

"He used to be at St. Albee's Seminary where I went to church."

"Well!" the clerk laughed. "Ain't you had a fine introduction to Taubolt, then! Really rolled out the old red carpet, didn't we? First that quake, then this!"

"Made quite an impression." He grinned. "I suppose I should go tell Mrs. Lindsay when you'll be open."

"Oh, help yourself to whatever she needs." The clerk smiled, waving at the store. "Just keep the list. Gladys can settle with Franklin when the war's over."

"Thanks," Joby said, rather startled at her ready trust. He glanced at his list and asked, "Um . . . where should I look for . . . maraschino cherries and walnut halves?"

The clerk's eyes widened. Then she laughed, "Real emergency supplies, is it?"

"I think she's trying to appease her guests with a special breakfast," he offered.

"Well I hope they appreciate it," the clerk chuckled. "Those are over on the first aisle by the cake mixes. Pickled eggs are by the champagne over there," she joked, "in case Gladys can't make it through the mornin' without them either."

By the time Joby left the adjacent hardware store with plastic sheeting, duct tape, and carpet tacks, it was all he could do to carry his purchases. Stopping to consolidate his load, he glanced down Shea Street toward the bay just as a mountainous comber surged through, its top blown back like thick white smoke. As he stared, the entire bay heaved upright with a grating rumble, as if the ponderous wave were tearing everything off the bottom as it came. Then it hit the cliffs like cannon fire, and shot into the air like Niagara Falls in reverse before plunging down onto the rocks and seething back into the bay.

"Oh my God!" Joby exclaimed. He'd heard of storm surf, but never imagined anything so huge!

Heading down for a closer look, Joby was so absorbed in the spectacle that he missed the curb and found himself performing feats of juggling and contortion to make any circus proud. Barely managing to retrieve his footing and the bags of food, he wasn't fast enough to catch the rest. The plastic box of carpet tacks burst open on the sidewalk as the rolls of duct tape fled in three directions and the plastic sheeting started to unwind. Had he been watching someone else dash after so many fugitives at once, he'd have found it very funny.

Chasing a roll of duct tape that had just vanished around the street corner, Joby nearly collided with a distinguished older man coming from the building's other side, who held out the runaway, and said, "I am guessing this is yours?"

"Thanks," said Joby, sheepishly accepting the roll. "I dropped some things."

"So I see," the man chuckled, looking past him toward the field of scattered carpet tacks. "Let me help you gather these," he said, already heading toward the task.

"Thanks, but I can do it," Joby said, jogging to retrieve the other rolls of tape.

But the man was already bent down, sweeping the spill into a pile with his hands. "I've no pressing engagements," he said cheerfully. "My pleasure. Really."

"Everyone's so *kind* here," Joby said, somewhat embarrassed as he came to help pick up the more far-flung tacks and return them to the still serviceable box. "I was watching those waves down in the bay instead of where I was going."

"Quite a sight this morning isn't it!" the man agreed.

"Sure is," Joby said. "Is it always like that after storms here?"

"Not usually this impressive," said the man. "Then, neither are our storms, fortunately." He turned, extending his hand. "My name's Solomon, by the way."

"Oh. Sorry. Joby," Joby said, shaking his hand. "You're from here, I take it?"

"Yes . . . and no," Solomon replied. "Just returning after a long absence, actually."

"No way!" said Joby. "I just came back here after a long absence too, sort of. Got here yesterday. You live here in town?"

"I'm not quite settled yet," the man said evasively. "You?"

"I'm helping out at the Primrose Picket Inn. I've got a room there."

"Ah," Solomon smiled. "I've many fond memories of that place."

"Oh! You know Mrs. Lindsay then?"

"No, no," Solomon said. "It was all well before her arrival, though it's clear she's done a fine job with the place."

"Yeah, she's great." Joby smiled, gathering up his packages again. "And I'd better get back there with all this, or she'll think I jumped ship. Thanks again for your help, and, uh, welcome back to Taubolt, I guess."

"Same to you, Joby," Solomon said amiably. "Merry Christmas."

"Hey, yeah! You too," Joby said, resuming his progress toward the inn. He looked back a moment later, intending to invite the man over for a visit, but Solomon had vanished, back around the corner, he presumed.

✼

Mrs. Lindsay's breakfast was magnificent: fresh-squeezed orange juice and champagne; chanterelle omelets with Edam cheese; home-canned peaches; fried potatoes with rosemary; and a pastry wreath dripping in a brown sugar cinnamon glaze with walnuts and cherries baked into the crusty top of every fluffy bite.

Despite their rough night, her guests were surprisingly jovial.

"That was something!" said a grinning young man at the table's far end. He turned to his pretty wife and joked, "Just think! We nearly missed it, honey!"

His wife smiled ruefully at everyone. "We had reservations at some motel down the coast. But we stopped here for gas, and it was just so charming, we figured, why drive all that way for some other place we'd never seen?" She shook her head. "I can't believe you put all this food together without any power or water, Mrs. Lindsay! I'd have just huddled in my sleeping bag 'til the National Guard came."

"We're used to making do here in the country," Mrs. Lindsay said modestly.

"You know," remarked a fashionable-looking woman at the other end of the table, "I'm here by accident as well. Isn't that strange? Three days ago, I drove up the coast intending nothing but a day at the beach somewhere. When I found this place, I had to buy everything from toiletries to extra clothing here in town." She smiled at Mrs. Lindsay. "Can't say I'm sorry though. Been the best three days I've had since my husband died, and I'll certainly have better holiday stories now than any of my friends."

The older couple seated next to Mrs. Lindsay exchanged a look and laughed. "We were going to spend the holidays visiting friends up in Ferndale," the man said gleefully, "but they both came down with the flu."

"It was disappointing," his wife added, "but they'd made us reservations at a B&B up there, and it seemed a little late to invite ourselves for Christmas with our daughter so we drove up anyway."

"Took the scenic route," her husband said, "and just stopped here for lunch."

"But like they all said, it's just so charming!" his wife laughed. "So here we are, someplace we never heard of, for the storm of the century."

"Well, I, for one," said the young husband who'd begun the conversation, "would be happy to help out with repairs this morning, Mrs. Lindsay."

"Me too," said the widowed woman. "I'm pretty good with a rake."

They all jumped on the bandwagon, and Mrs. Lindsay happily offered a free night's lodging to everyone on what she called her "chain gang." After breakfast, Joby marveled to watch these well-heeled vacationers cheerfully attack the ruined yard and house with rakes, saws, and hammers. With so many hands, they'd gotten breakfast cleaned up, all the broken windows covered in plastic, the ruined fence and shed mostly cleared away and the fallen tree limbs half sawed up by eleven thirty, when Mrs. Lindsay announced that everyone should take a break while she and Joby went to church.

※

They were nearly late to Mass and had to stand in back with a crowd that overflowed onto the steps outside by the time everyone stood up to sing "Away in a Manger," as Father Crombie made his slow way toward the altar, nodding cheerfully to people along the aisle.

After Lindwald's death, attending church had seemed too hypocritical to face. Later, simple despair had displaced painful concepts like hope or trust—in himself *or* God. Now, all at once, here he was. After more than a decade away from church, Joby didn't remember enough to do much more than follow along until the scripture readings were finished, and Father Crombie stood to deliver his sermon.

"I am told," Father Crombie began, "that Tom and Margie Faulkand found themselves lying in the manger quite literally this morning." He turned to grin at a stout, balding man and a plump, rosy woman near the front of the church, who blushed and smiled at those around them. A ripple of quiet laughter spread as those who knew the story started passing it to those who didn't. "Seems the roof of Joe Lima's barn, a good deal of hay, and a chicken, if I've been correctly informed, blew across the road and right through Tom and Margie's bedroom wall," Crombie continued.

"Oh dear!" Mrs. Lindsay gasped, craning her neck to inspect the couple more carefully. "Was anyone hurt?" she asked the man next to her, as if expecting he'd know.

"Not a scratch on either one is what I heard," smiled the man, "though I did hear somethin' 'bout a chicken dinner at the Faulkands' tonight, so I can't vouch for the bird."

"Happily, however," Father Crombie said when the laughter had died down, "despite the real losses many are coping with this morning, I've not heard of a single person seriously injured or, God forbid, killed last night. Has anyone heard otherwise?"

There was a silence filled with shaking heads and pensive smiles.

"Then I trust it will not seem too out of touch," he smiled, "to say, Merry Christmas, my friends!"

"Merry Christmas, Father!" the congregation roared back.

"Our Savior must have experienced dismay very like the Faulkands'," Crombie smiled, "when He woke on that first Christmas to find Himself, not in Heaven where He'd gone to bed, but in the feeding trough of a drafty barn, with a long hard haul ahead of Him. On this Christmas morning, we are blessed with an opportunity to have *compassion* for that little child, as He had *compassion* for us." He swept the congregation with a gentle smile. "True compassion does not just reach down to help the suffering, but joins them in whatever they endure—*and* in whatever they celebrate. This, my wonderful neighbors, is what *you* have taught *me* in the years since God brought me to this marvelous town. You who do suffer trials this morning know you will not suffer them alone. We will join with you. And what I most wish to say to you all this Christmas morning is simply *thank you*, . . . each of you, for being who and what you are, every day. You are all God's greatest gifts to me. As you celebrate today, may God bless you all, and, through you, everyone you meet. Amen."

He returned slowly to his chair beside the altar and sat in quite contemplation before continuing the Mass.

It was, without a doubt, the shortest sermon Joby had ever heard; also the most genuine, and, to Joby's dismay, the most distressing. The obvious affection between Crombie and his parish spoke straight to the heart of everything Joby had once believed in and aspired to, which left him feeling now as if all his deepest wounds had been torn open, every desire he'd ever put painfully to sleep, awakened against its will. The temptation to hope that all those lost dreams might be redeemed at last here in Taubolt was as painful as it seemed suddenly impossible to suppress. Afraid he might be going to cry, Joby held himself very still and shoved down hard on everything he felt, praying only for control. In the still moment of reflective silence that Crombie allowed to linger, Joby's prayer was answered. The turmoil within him solidified into a hard, aching lump somewhere between his Adam's apple and his heart; painful, but blessedly contained.

This respite was short-lived, however. Mere moments later, as Father Crombie raised the ceramic Eucharistic chalice, Joby's attention was drawn by a chance trick of light on its plain exterior. There were sudden rainbows in the glaze; subtle but astonishingly beautiful colors. As Joby stared, something in the sheen itself returned him entirely to an instant in his boyhood. He could feel the sunlight on his back, see his old storybook open on the ground before him, smell the pages and the scent of cut grass, hear the clack of grasshoppers in the field beyond his parents' fence, the trill of a mocking bird. . . . *My king, I would serve you with my life, only name the—*

Joby covered his eyes, and bowed his head, as if in prayer, to hide a sudden surge of inexplicable grief and the tears streaming down his face, indifferent to his efforts to prevent them. *Stop this!* he demanded silently, whether of himself or some ethereal persecutor he wasn't sure.

He spent the entire Eucharistic prayer hidden behind his hands. When he finally dared look up again, the cup was just a cup once more, but he no longer quite trusted it, or himself. When communion was distributed, the profound reverence on Mrs. Lindsay's face as she started forward made Joby feel like an unworthy pretender, and he could not follow her. As the communion line dwindled, he caught Father Crombie looking at him with an expression of unnerving sadness.

When the Mass was ended, it was all Joby could manage not to rush from the church as Mrs. Lindsay lingered to chat with virtually every person there. When they started walking home at last, Joby glanced out toward the headlands west of town, and was greeted with yet another puzzling site. At the edge of an isolated grove of gnarled old cypress trees, seven adolescent children stood with hands joined in a ring around one partially blackened trunk leaning away from its fellows, and, as Joby watched, began to make a careful stepping dance counterclockwise around it. That's when Joby recognized the two girls he'd startled out of hiding on the headlands only yesterday.

Hadn't they spoken of some grove? *Sunday . . . And Hawk for seven.* Now, here they were, it seemed. Joby wondered idly which one of them was Hawk.

❧

Mrs. Lindsay's Christmas dinner was clearly going to be a banquet of legendary dimensions. To everyone's delight, power had been restored to Taubolt at around three, and her guests had gone upstairs to enjoy long forestalled showers now that water could be pumped again from the inn's well. Apparently, it was Mrs. Lindsay's tradition to have a few friends join her guests for Christmas dinner, and the invitation list had expanded after church to include Tom and Clara Connolly, and their daughter Rose, whose house had been so badly damaged across the street.

At five o'clock, just as Joby finished helping Mrs. Lindsay get the quail in the oven, a man's voice called from somewhere near the parlor, "Anybody home?"

Mrs. Lindsay straightened with a smile. "You know perfectly well where I am, Jake," she called back. "And I've got plenty of help already, so it's safe to come in."

A tall, blond, thirty-something man with remarkably blue eyes walked into Mrs. Lindsay's kitchen with one large, callused hand wrapped around the necks of two bottles of white wine, and a raffish grin on his face. He seemed instantly familiar to Joby, though he couldn't think why.

"Just didn't wanna disturb an artist at work," the fellow teased.

"You get smoother every year, Jake." Drying her hands on her apron, she walked over and stretched up to give him a hug, for which he had to stoop almost comically. "Merry Christmas, dear."

"You too." He smiled, offering her the wine.

"Oh, thank you," she said. "These are much nicer than what I've got!"

"Liar," he grinned, "but I couldn't think what else to bring, with you already serving up half of Taubolt's winter food supply."

"All I needed was your charming company, dear." She turned to Joby, and said, "This is Jake: one of Taubolt's local heroes. When he's not out cutting everybody's firewood, he's in charge of Taubolt's volunteer fire department and emergency response team, which means he probably hasn't slept since yesterday."

"Got a nap this afternoon." Jake shrugged. "I'm good to go."

She smiled skeptically, and said, "Jake, this is—"

"Joby Peterson, I'll bet," Jake said, reaching out to shake Joby's hand.

"How'd you know?" Joby asked, wondering if perhaps they had met.

"Oh, everybody's heard about you." Jake grinned. "We're all wonderin' how Mrs. Lindsay knew to hire on extra help just in time for all this storm repair."

"He's been worth his weight in gold, I have to say." Mrs. Lindsay beamed.

"I'm the lucky one." Joby smiled. "You look familiar, Jake. Have we met?"

"Don't think so. You just got into town yesterday, didn't you?"

"Yeah," Joby said, still certain that he knew this face.

"Well then," Jake said, grinning, "you're probably just mistaking me for some other good lookin' woodcutter you knew down in the city." He turned back to Mrs. Lindsay, and asked, "Maybe I could help you with the table?"

"That would be lovely, dear. You know where things are."

Joby watched him go, feeling certain he was missing something.

Half an hour later, the table was clothed in white linen and lace, bone china and sterling settings, cut-crystal tumblers, and graceful long-stemmed wineglasses. The fish was on, the fowl and venison were almost done, the salads and side dishes were on the table, and a lovely version of the *Nutcracker Suite* wafted from the parlor stereo.

Bridget and Drew O'Reilly were first to arrive. Mrs. Lindsay introduced Drew as a local apple farmer, and Bridget as "head teacher" at the town's high school. Thirty-five at most, Bridget had sparkling gray eyes and short, dark blond hair agleam with sunny highlights. Her smile was wide and frequent. Joby could picture her as a ski instructor, or a triathlete, but not a head teacher. Then again, her husband looked younger than he'd ever imagined any farmer looking. They had just begun to talk when another knock at the door turned out to be the Connollys.

"Hello, Clara! Hi, Tom," Bridget said brightly. She smiled warmly at their daughter. "How ya doing, Rose? A little too exciting at your house last night, huh?"

When Joby saw Rose's pale, heart-shaped face and long dark tresses, he felt a flush of embarrassment. Rose stared back at him with the same startled expression that he realized he was wearing. Their mouths snapped shut in unison.

"Joby," Mrs. Lindsay said, seeming unaware of their mutual discomfort, "these are my wonderful neighbors, Tom and Clara Connolly, and their daughter, Rose. And this," she said to the Connollys, "is my new righthand man, Joby Peterson. He got here yesterday, just in time for the storm."

"Your daughter was pretty much the first person I met here," Joby said self-consciously, shaking Mr. Connolly's hand. "She caught me sort of eavesdropping on her while I was out walking on the headlands."

He turned awkwardly to Rose. "That's really not like me at all. I just heard voices in the trees, and turned to listen without thinking. It's, um, nice to meet you more . . . formally, I guess."

"No big deal," Rose said, recovering her smile. "It was just . . . we'd never seen you before. . . . That's all."

"Saw your house," Joby said, trying to flee the subject he had broached.

"It's a little crunched," Rose said, smiling ruefully. "Our bedrooms are all in back, though. So that was good."

"I wish my office had been in back," Tom said, trying to sound cheerful.

"One of Tom's many hats here is real-estate agent," Mrs. Lindsay explained. "He works out of his home."

"*Really* out of my home now!" Tom laughed. "For a while, at least."

"Well, you know Bridget and I will be by to help tomorrow," Drew assured him.

"Thanks," Tom said. "We've gotten offers all day, and I can't tell you how much it means to us. I just hope the weather cooperates long enough to get it done quickly."

"So, what brought you to Taubolt, Joby?" Mrs. Connolly asked.

"Father Crombie and I are friends," Joby replied, having figured out by now that this was the simplest answer to that question. "He set me up here with Mrs. Lindsay."

Joby had just started to tell them about St. Albee's when Father Crombie himself arrived bearing two small but handsomely wrapped packages.

"Hello, everyone!" he said cheerfully. "Hope I haven't kept you all waiting,"

"You're right on time," said Mrs. Lindsay. "Joby was just talking about you."

"Well, I hope he hasn't spilled too many of my secrets." He gave Joby a conspiratorial wink, then handed one of his packages to Mrs. Lindsay. "Merry Christmas, Gladys." To Joby's surprise, he handed the other package to him. "And this is for you."

"Thank you," Joby said as Father Crombie shrugged out of his coat. "I . . . didn't expect this. . . . I—"

"Should open it and refrain from silly protests." Father Crombie grinned, handing his coat to Mrs. Lindsay who smiled and took it up the stairs with her present. "It's a sneak attack, Joby. You're only responsibility is to be surprised and delighted."

Joby removed the wrapping to find a richly bound anthology of American poetry.

"You mentioned a degree in English at dinner last night." Father Crombie smiled. "I hoped you might enjoy that. I own a well-read copy myself."

"Well, thank you so much," Joby said again, then surprised himself by leaning forward to hug the old priest, who returned the gesture warmly.

Mrs. Lindsay reappeared and ushered everyone toward the dining room, where the large, elegant table waited, alight with candles.

Even having helped to prepare it, Joby was astonished at how good the meal was. The candlelight made everyone look youthful and merry. Mrs. Lindsay's paying guests chastised her for spoiling them so badly, insisting they'd never be able to enjoy normal food again, while Rose began to quiz Joby about his tastes in music and what city girls were wearing these days. Soon they were talking and laughing as if there'd never been an awkward moment between them.

"Father said you have a degree in English, Joby?" Bridgett asked as soon as Rose gave her an opening.

"Just a BA," he replied. Hoping to avoid talk about his past, he turned quickly back to Rose, and asked, "Wasn't that you down on the headlands this morning, around that tree with a bunch of other kids?"

Suddenly uncomfortable again, Rose gave Joby a weighing look, then said, "We were praying for the tree that got hit by lightning last night."

"Praying for a tree?" Joby said. That seemed . . . a little weird.

"That particular grove of trees is pretty special to us all," Mrs. Lindsay said. "We have weddings down there, and memorial services, and all kinds of things. I can't begin to guess how many marriage proposals have been made under those branches."

Joby saw Tom and Clara Connolly smile knowingly without looking up from their meals, and suspected their initials might be down there somewhere.

"We pray a lot around here," Jake said to Joby with an oddly pointed grin. "We're too far from everywhere to get help any other way."

❧

When everyone had gone, and Joby had finished helping Mrs. Lindsay with the cleanup, she had surprised him with another wrapped box pulled from far under her Christmas tree. It had contained an old-fashioned writing kit: stationery, quill pen, inkwell, even sealing wax and a stamp engraved to emboss the letter "J" in the blob of wax. "For writing home," she'd told him, saying that the kit had been her son's before he went away. When she saw Joby glance again at the monogram stamp, she said, "His name is Justin."

Now, up in his room, Joby sat flipping through the poetry anthology Father Crombie had given him, thinking about how generous everyone had been to him, and how strange it felt after . . . so much time.

He still hadn't called his parents. The memory of their frightened messages on his machine back in Berkeley stung his conscience. He should have called, especially on Christmas, but he still couldn't face . . . what? Their fear? Their anger? . . . Their shame? . . . His own perhaps? Still, he couldn't just leave them wondering if he was even alive. If they hadn't learned of his sudden disappearance yet, they would soon. He was sure their names and address were on the rental papers somewhere. His landlord would probably be after them to get rid of all the stuff he'd left behind. He'd left a lot of details untended in his flight from Berkeley.

Amidst these thoughts, he noticed a page corner that someone, Crombie, he supposed, had bent down. It marked a poem by Longfellow, and one stanza caught Joby's attention immediately:

I remember the gleams and glooms that dart
Across the school boy's brain;
The song and the silence in the heart,
That in part are prophecies and in part
Are longings wild and vain,
And the voice of that fitful song
Sings on, and is never still:
A boy's will is the wind's will,
And the thoughts of youth are long, long thoughts.

He stared at the page, then closed the book, thinking of the storybook Mary had returned to him, stuffed now in his duffel bag across the room. Taubolt already felt so much like the home he'd wanted for so long without knowing. He was already determined to belong here, whatever it took. But in part, he knew, it would take laying his past to rest somehow . . . or at least cleaning it up enough to move on. *For writing home,* Mrs. Lindsay had said. Could she know him that well already?

A moment later he was seated at her son's old pine desk, staring at a blank sheet of cream-colored stationery, dipping and redipping the old pen into the bottle of ink.

"Dear Mom and Dad," he wrote at last. "I'm sorry I never answered your messages last week. A lot has happened, but first let me say that I am very well." His pen hung thoughtfully over the paper for a moment. "In fact, I'm better than I have been in years. You'll never guess where I am living now. . . ."

15

(Migration Season)

"In the headlines this morning: five people were killed, and seventeen injured in the bombing of an outdoor market in Belfast. No one has claimed credit for the attack, but members of Parliament were adamant in demanding harsher measures against such extreme elements.

"Senate Republicans held a press conference outside the Capitol building in Washington this morning, calling again for tougher economic reforms, including a crackdown on abuse of the Federal Welfare system, and the elimination of capital gains taxes. Across the street, protesters branded Republicans, 'the party of punishment,' accusing them of trying to divert responsibility for the nation's current economic woes from America's wealthy elite by penalizing the country's poorest citizens instead.

"In Los Angeles this morning, two teenage boys were gunned down outside a Tastee Freez in Pico Rivera. Police say the killing seems to have been gang-related, and that suspects are currently in custody for questioning. This latest instance of youth-related violence has spurred new calls in the California's Senate for legislation permitting youthful offenders to be tried and incarcerated as adults.

"The Dow is up 257 points this morning, to 9435. The NASDAQ is up as well, 70 points to 2381. Analysts say there seems to be no end of good news in sight."

Agnes Hamilton got up from her breakfast to turn the radio off. Being reminded that the world was going to Hell on a bullet train did nothing good for her digestion.

Getting rich had done little for it either. Two years after winning the California lottery, her life offered little more satisfaction than it ever had.

She sat back down, wincing at the pain in her spine, and the wind in her stomach.

Now she had a beautiful mansion in the Oakland Hills. Surrounded by lavish gardens it was a true estate. But this had only left her coping *with* swarms of annoying housekeepers, gardeners, and administrative assistants whom she kept having to fire for betraying details of her private life to solicitors or the press.

The one thing she really had hoped for after her sudden rise to riches was influence. All her life she'd watched the world go to ruin around her while the nation's rich and powerful seemed to pursue no greater purpose than keeping themselves comfortably entertained. This outrage had fostered a cold fury within her breast for so many years that she could no longer remember being without it. Then her numbers had come up, one after another on that fabulous, impossible evening, and she'd thought that, finally, she'd have the power to halt the disintegration of at least some small portion of her world.

Since then, she'd sent sizable checks to an impressive array of politicos, attended countless fund-raising dinners and exclusive salons, even stooped to speaking up at public meetings. But all her ideas about restoring some semblance of decency to modern society were still ignored. Oh, for what she paid them any number of public officials were happy to sit there nodding for as long as she had breath to go on. But while her money, it seemed, interested them as much as anyone else's, her thoughts on law and order did not.

Memories of that disgraceful riot in Berkeley two months past resurfaced like putrid bubbles of marsh gas in her mind. To have put people through all that just days before Christmas! *Should have shot them all,* she thought crossly.

Feeling weary, she pushed her plate away unfinished and stared out the window at her garden, suddenly imagining a quiet little village full of charming cottages where life went on graciously from day to day, as it had done in better times. Someplace at the edge of the world, where the urban madness encroaching on her here was still just a dim, unpleasant rumor.

Vivid pictures bloomed in her mind: neatly trimmed lawns, a rose-covered arbor, a sunny table on a bluff top, tea laid out against a backdrop of blue summer sky and untroubled ocean bordered in clean white surf. *Yes,* she thought. *Out on the coast there must still be any number of quiet, isolated little towns.*

Suddenly afire with dreams of escape, she left the remains of her breakfast for what's-her-name, the latest housekeeper, and went upstairs to pack. It was a lovely day for January, and she'd still gone hardly anywhere in the sporty little car she'd bought that fall. A pleasant drive up the coast seemed made to order. Who knew? Perhaps she'd find her little Shangri-la, and leave this squalid city to collapse under the weight of its own depravity.

❀

"Thank you for making the time, Jake."

"My pleasure, Father Crombie." Jake stomped as much of the mud and sawdust off his boots as he could, then wiped them thoroughly on the rectory's broad straw mat before following the old man into his living room. "So what's the problem?"

"Well, it may not be a problem. It concerns Joby Peterson."

"Ah," Jake said, seeming unsurprised.

"What do you think of him?" Crombie asked.

"Nice enough. A little unsure of himself. Spends a lot of time fixin' things that aren't broken, but good at heart, I think." Jake paused, seeming to study Crombie before adding, "And maybe a Trojan horse?"

"Yes, I was certain you would notice," Crombie sighed.

"Well, there was that little quake, and then that little storm, within hours of his arrival," Jake drawled grimly. "You know something more specific, I take it?"

As Crombie related his first encounter with a nine-year-old boy seeking advice about fighting the devil and asking questions about the Grail, Jake listened with quiet intensity. Crombie went on to describe Joby's reference to a grandfather from Taubolt, and the other small fragments he'd gleaned of Joby's more recent past during their occasional chats since Christmas. "Do you recognize the name?" Crombie asked at last. "Emery Emerson?"

"I remember him," Jake said. "Left here as a boy. Haven't seen or heard of him since. So what are you suggesting, Father?"

"That Joby may, in fact, be involved in some conflict with Hell of which he has become unconscious through the years and, therefore, may both need our help and pose a threat to our well-being."

"Interesting theory." Jake smiled. "You've waited to tell me all this 'cause . . . ?"

"I'm not certain of these assertions," Crombie shrugged, "and thought others here should have a chance to know the boy better before judging him." He looked down and sighed. "I like him, Jake. I've liked him since the day we met, and I feared that, on the heels of that storm, he might not receive the fair hearing he deserved." Crombie looked up expecting to see disapproval on Jake's face but found there a broad smile instead.

"You've been smart to keep this to yourself," Jake said. "Spread such tales, he'd get wind of it soon enough, and if he really doesn't know such a thing about himself, there could be some damn good reasons he's not supposed to."

"Then, should the Council know?"

Jake shook his head. "I don't think so. Not yet at least. It's lucky you've got such a good line on the boy. Forewarned is forearmed and all. But you could be right about that fair hearin'. Folks are still pretty skittish after what went on here over Christmas. I say we just watch him like hawks until the evidence points to somethin' clearer. In fact, we should keep him where he'd be visible to more people more of the time."

Crombie allowed himself a smile at last. "I'm relieved that you feel this way, Jake. It so happens I have a notion about what we might draw him into, if you think it safe to put him in closer contact with the children."

"Nothin' more watched, or better guarded 'round here than the children," Jake said. "What'd you have in mind?"

✸

As he wheeled another load of newly split firewood toward the backyard, Joby couldn't help feeling proud of how good the inn was looking. Mrs. Lindsay had kept him working hard, chopping and stacking wood, repairing her fence and gardens, hauling away storm wrack, fixing the eaves. Taubolt had recovered from the storm with amazing speed. The whole town had worked together, until there was hardly a reminder to be seen of the "hundred-year storm" as people were calling it.

Joby was really getting into the whole country living thing. Jake had come around after Christmas with the load of wood that Joby now was splitting. He had what a "cord" was—and the distinction in utility between softwoods and hardwoods—without once making the boy feel foolish for not knowing. He'd even shown him how to swing a maul, "so they won't think you're new," he'd said with a wink.

By far the strangest bit of rural lore Joby had encountered so far had come when Mrs. Lindsay sent him to the hardware store for "a bottle of lion piss." Sure he must have heard wrong, he'd asked for clarification, and she'd explained that squirting it on her gardens kept the deer away. So Joby had headed for the hardware store apprehensive that this was some kind of joke played on newcomers. But Franklin Clark had handed him an eight-ounce squeeze bottle of mountain lion urine without cracking a smile, and Joby had chuckled all the way back, trying to imagine how they got mountain lions to piss into a bottle, and wondering if deer could really be dumb enough to think there were lions hiding in some little clump of geraniums.

All in all, not an evening had come since Joby's arrival that he did not climb into bed feeling dazed with gratitude for the way his life had been so suddenly transformed.

Nonetheless, he was aware of another, darker feeling that sometimes

lurked behind his gratitude. He'd done his best to forget the strange experi-
ences he'd had in church on Christmas morning, but in the rare, undistracted
moment late at night or when he hadn't anything to do, Joby still felt
hunted . . . by what, he didn't know. Nor, to be honest, did he want to. He
just did his best to focus on the future and hoped that time would erase
whatever strange discomfort was continuing to plagued him.

Shaking off these shadows yet again, he went back to the wheel barrow
just as Mrs. Lindsay leaned out an upper-story window and called down that
Bridget O'Reilly had just phoned to ask if Joby would mind coming up to
see her at the high school.

"Want me to finish up the wood first?" he asked.

"There's no hurry about that, dear. You'd best go see what she wants."

❊

Perched just below the church on a hillside above the headlands north of
town, Taubolt's high school was a single, surprisingly modern building:
square, with low white walls and high red-tiled roof, like a squat pyramid. A
circle of teenagers stood in the pale winter sunshine on the small front lawn,
deftly using their feet, knees, and foreheads to pass three small cloth balls
through the air between them. A second group sat clustered in animated conversation near the school's main doors; one wore a giant foam rubber top hat,
while a taller boy with large obsidian eyes and handsome, dusky features had
wrapped his brown shirt, turban-like around his head, like a young maharaja.

Jaunty greetings forming in Joby's head evaporated as the Hacky Sack
balls fell to earth with quiet slaps and everyone turned to watch his arrival in
silence.

"Hey." He smiled as he approached the group beside the doors.

"Hi," replied the turbaned boy. Two others tentatively raised their hands.

Careful to keep smiling as he pulled open the large plateglass door, Joby
felt their scrutiny like the sudden silence after a trapeze accident at the circus.
Then he stepped into a single large room, two stories high, reverberating
with the musical roar of forty or fifty more kids laughing, chasing, teasing,
tossing, ebbing, and flowing like a swirling flock of blackbirds. At first he
thought the whole building just a shell around this one huge chamber. Then
he saw doors and interior windows opening onto this central hall from what
he surmised were classrooms and offices. Ample light found its way in
through a crazy assortment of windows, skylights, and glass block walls.

Once again, however, as the kids began to notice Joby, a sudden silence
swept the room as everyone turned to look at him.

"Hi, Joby," said Rose, emerging from a group of girls across the room.

"Hi, Rose." He smiled, feeling a palpable shift in tension around the room, as if some corporate intake of breath had been released. But still, no one spoke. "Is Mrs. O'Reilly around?" Joby asked.

"I'm here, Joby," O'Reilly said brightly from a door behind him. "Thank you for coming so quickly and, please, call me Bridget."

A rustle of murmurs and whispered laughter quickly swelled back into the hubbub Joby had first encountered, as conversation and horseplay resumed around him.

"It's lunchtime," Bridget said more loudly, smiling and pretending to cover her ears. "Let's talk here in my office, where we won't have to yell."

"I hadn't realized Taubolt had so many kids," Joby said as Bridget closed her office door behind him. The room was small with only one long, horizontal window high in the wall, like an archery slit in some medieval fortification, though it allowed a surprising amount of light into the room. The walls were covered in bright posters, photographs of students, and artifacts of kid-made appearance.

"Taubolt's not as small as it seems," Bridget said. "Three times as many people live in the hills around us as here in the village." She waved him toward a well-stuffed chair across from her desk. "Make yourself comfortable."

"This building's a lot newer than anything else in town," Joby said.

"The old building burned a few years back," Bridget said wryly. "A newly arrived architect designed this to replace it. It's a bit industrial for some of us, but wonderfully functional. Want some tea?" She gestured toward a hotplate and kettle on her desk.

"No, thank you," Joby said. "I'm kind of curious about why you asked to see me."

"Father Crombie tells me you're looking for work," she said, pouring herself a cup of tea, and sitting on the edge of her desk. "Interested in teaching high school?"

"I'm not qualified," Joby said, startled.

"You have a degree in English, don't you?"

"Well, yes, but—"

"Can you diagram a sentence?"

"I suppose," Joby said, "It's been years since I—"

"Know what a 'predicate' is? How to punctuate a prepositional phrase? The difference between an essay and a novel?" she joked.

"Yes," he said, "but I have no experience."

"None at all?" she asked.

"I did a little tutoring with grade-school kids in college, but—"

"Ah!" She sounded triumphant. "Then you're the most qualified candidate I have at present. You seem to have strong language skills. Father Crombie says you like to write. From what I heard on Christmas, you're a born story-teller. Do you like children?"

"Yes," Joby said, "but . . . I hope Father Crombie hasn't pressured you into this as some sort of favor, because I—"

"Of course not!" Bridget laughed. "I really don't want to pressure you, Joby, but I'm sort of in a fix right now. Are you interested at all?"

"Well," Joby said, still trying to sort out his questions. "I might be, but . . . what about a credential and all that?"

"Here's my situation," Bridget said, getting up to refresh her tea. "Charlie Luff, our current English teacher, is ill." Her smile wavered and vanished. "It's come on suddenly, and he'll be out at least through summer. If I'd had more warning, or it were earlier in the year, I'd go looking for someone with all the right paper and more experience, but by the time I found anyone willing and able to come here now, the term would be over. So if you're at all interested, I'd like to have you come meet the kids at morning meeting tomorrow. If that goes well, we could try it for a week or two and see what happens." She gave him a sympathetic smile. "I know this is sudden, but what do you think? . . . Eighteen dollars an hour if you pass muster," she added, hopeful.

Joby could hardly believe his luck. "I don't know if I'll be any good," he smiled, "but I'll give it a try. When would you need me to start actually teaching?"

She looked apologetic. "Is Monday too soon?"

❈

"It's fabulous! And so affordable! I'll take it."

Tom Connolly could count on one hand the number of real-estate clients he'd had from outside of Taubolt during the past ten years, so he'd been caught somewhat off guard when Agnes Hamilton had shown up at his home, steered by someone in town, to ask about houses for sale in "this simply exquisite little village of yours!" He knew the drill of course. Occasionally, one of Taubolt's visitors got it into their heads to stay. If Taubolt really wanted them, no amount of discouragement could dissuade them. If not, almost none was more than enough.

There were only two houses available within the village proper—the same two that had been available for years. He'd shown Hamilton the more decrepit one first, and he quoted an outrageously high price, hoping to get this over with quickly. To his surprise, she had happily examined the leaking roof upstairs, the loose and blistering gingerbread trim, the cracked windowpanes and crumbling glazing, the sloping back porch covered in now barren wild rose vines, chattering all the while about the deplorable state of the urban world and its distressing disinterest in her solutions to its problems.

So, he'd moved to phase two: casual banter about how depressed real-estate values were at present in these parts.

"Glad to hear it," she'd replied. "I'd hate to see this place go suburban."

"No worry there," he'd jovially assured her, jumping to phase three. "Lots of people talk about moving here, but most find it's just too big an adjustment."

"What kind of adjustment?" she'd asked.

"Poor roads," he'd mused. "Hard on your car, and takes forever to get anywhere. Social isolation—our nightlife here is all on four legs. Having to chop wood and light a fire every morning. Electricity's twice as costly up here as everywhere else, and it goes out practically every week in winter, which means you've got no running water at all unless you've got a generator to run the pump. There's no water system, you realize. Got to maintain your own well, truck water in if it goes dry in summer. No, this life wears most people out in a hurry."

"Well, aren't you the salesman, Mr. Connolly," she'd scoffed, seeming more offended at his lack of showmanship than put off. "You needn't worry though. I'm a woman of exceptionally strong character, and quietude is precisely what I'm seeking."

So it seemed she was actually going to buy. Wouldn't Stan Weston be surprised!

"Well, that's great," Tom said, trying to sound enthusiastic. "Guess we should go back to my office and start on the paperwork."

"I'm so thrilled to have discovered all this!" Ms. Hamilton said. "You know, I had a sort of premonition at breakfast this morning and just drove right up here! It's all so beautiful! Taubolt must be California's best kept secret."

"Oh, that it is." Tom nodded.

"Well, I hope it stays that way," she said. "Though I suppose there might be one or two people I wouldn't mind importing once I'm settled. Particular friends of mine. But don't you worry, Mr. Connolly, they're all people who see things precisely as I do."

No, Tom decided, *this could not possibly be anyone Taubolt wanted.* She'd undoubtedly go home and reconsider, or just forget completely, like so many before her. He wasn't going to bother Stan about it yet, whatever papers she might sign today.

☀

"That's one launched," Kallaystra said, "and the fire's being lit under a number of other useful minds as we speak. What amazes me, now that we're looking, is how many little fragments of this place already litter the world. I've found photos, letters, newspaper clippings, even postcards! How could we possibly have overlooked all that before?" she asked breezily.

Lucifer didn't answer, suspecting her question of being a veiled barb. But he couldn't help contemplating the kind of power it had taken to keep them blind for so many years to an entire domain and all its myriad little traces, even one as small as Taubolt must be.

"How long before they're all placed?" he asked.

"It's hard to say for sure," Kallaystra answered. "By fall, I hope."

"I had expected greater efficiency from you, Kallaystra."

"Well, I can't push them much harder," she protested. "Most of them would be far less cooperative if they knew who was pulling their strings or that we existed at all."

"The instant you have them settled," Lucifer said wearily, "I want every detail you glean on my desk without delay." He allowed himself a small sigh of resignation. No doubt years of their best work with Joby were being washed away in Taubolt like so much monsoon mud.

☀

As Joby approached the school that morning, there was no one to be seen outside, nor any ruckus as he walked inside to find the students standing hand in hand in a large ring around the perimeter of the room. Their heads were bowed, their eyes closed, as if he'd walked in on the middle of a prayer. Joby stood by the entrance, pale sunlight streaming through the doors and glass-block wall behind him, and waited uncertainly.

Glinting moats of dust drifted through shafts of light descending on the silent circle of kids from various windows and skylights, lending the scene a radiant serenity both beautiful and surreal. Whatever Joby had expected, this wasn't it. Were these teenagers, or Tibetan monks? A moment later, at some cue Joby didn't discern, the students all looked up at once, smiling across the circle at one another, and chorused, "Good morning." Then their buoyant silence dissolved into the kind of conversational babble he'd expected.

"Hi, Joby!" Bridget said. "Come join us." The kids all sat down on the floor where they'd been standing, turning to watch as Joby came and sat beside her. "We take a minute every morning to get focused," Bridget told him, as if perceiving his unasked question. "Everyone, this is Joby Peterson. I've been talking with him about filling in for Charlie until he's better." She turned to Joby. "Want to tell us a little about yourself?"

Gathering his thoughts, Joby noticed that not all of the circle's attentive faces were young. A woman with sharp, bird-like features and long, dark hair streaked in silver wore layered, green silk skirts, knee-high boots, and a black lace shawl. A silver stud pierced one of her nostrils—which he found surprising, given her age. Directly across the ring sat a snow-haired man, his wide, toothy smile bright in a well-tanned, lined-leather face. He wore jeans, tennis shoes, and a woolen crew neck sweater. Surmising that these were his fellow teachers, Joby was glad he hadn't worn a coat and tie.

"Well, you know my name," Joby said, and launched into the well-rehearsed remarks he'd been practicing all morning. "I studied English in college . . . but my interest in language goes a lot further back than that. When I was a kid my grandfather gave me a book about King Arthur and the Roundtable: knights, dragons, magic, wizard, witches, all that stuff. I pretty much lived inside that book for years, but only later on did I began to realize how powerful language really is. We take words for granted; talking, writing reading, but we're the only animal on this whole planet who can do it. It's made everything we are, everything we make and do, possible. In ancient Europe, men called bards sometimes had even more power than kings. Their ability to use the language was considered magical."

A hand shot up across the circle, it's owner a lean boy with straight, shiny dark hair, liquid brown eyes, and a shy, quicksilver smile. Joby nodded at him.

"Do you still have that book?" the boy asked.

"Actually, I do."

"Charlie brings books for us to read out loud in class," said a small girl with wide doe eyes and a cloud of wavy brown hair. "Could we read yours?"

"I suppose so," he said, wondering at the way everyone kept referring to Mr. Luff as Charlie. Teachers had never been called by their first names when he'd been in school.

Joby was immediately barraged with more questions having nothing whatsoever to do with English. Where was he from? What had his high school been like? What were his favorite movies, music, sports? Was he married? Did he have a girlfriend? So much for his prepared statements. Some of their questions, like why he had come to Taubolt, required carefully incomplete answers, of course, but soon Joby began to relax and enjoy the banter of his soon-to-be students.

"What about you guys?" he said at last. He looked at the boy who'd first asked about his book. "What's your name?"

"Ander."

Ah, Joby thought. So this was Ander of the secret conversation he'd overheard on the headlands. "And what's your favorite subject, Ander?"

"Surfing." Ander grinned. "But I like writing stories and poetry a lot too."

"That makes two of us," Joby said. "Writing, I mean; I've never surfed." He turned to the doe-eyed girl who'd asked if they could read his book. "And you?"

"My name's Autumn. I like botany and music." She smiled shyly. "I play flute."

He remembered her name as well from the headlands tryst.

Joby recognized the strawberry-haired girl next to Autumn. "I think we met," he said bashfully.

"Rose told me how freaked you were," she smiled, "but it was no big deal. We get spied on by strange men all the time, don't we Rose." Judging by the giggles this elicited, the story had clearly circulated. "I'm Bellindi," she said, "if you don't remember."

"Hey, I really didn't hear a thing!" Joby fibbed. "I swear!" Turning quickly to a butter-haired boy beside Bellindi, Joby asked. "What about you?"

"I didn't hear a thing either," he said with exaggerated innocence. "Honest!"

Everybody laughed again, as Joby honored his quick wit with a wry smile.

"I'm Jupiter," said the boy. "My best subject's ornithology." A new round of giggling left Joby sure he'd missed some inside joke.

"You like birds then?" Joby pressed, hoping for a clue.

"Some of them are my best friends," the boy said brightly, drawing more suppressed mirth from the others.

"Uh-huh," said Joby deciding to cut his losses and move on. "And who are you?" he asked a short, fire-haired boy with devilish eyebrows next to Jupiter.

"Nacho," the boy answered with a taunting grin.

"Interesting nicknames, you guys have," Joby said. "Is anyone here just named Bob?" With surprised expressions, three boys sitting in a row across from him raised their hands in unison, eliciting the loudest burst of laughter yet. "Ooookay," said Joby we'll get to you guys in a minute, but back to Nacho, first. Got a real name, Nacho?"

"That's it!" Nacho protested. "What my mama gave me."

"Oh," Joby said, unconvinced. "Got a last name then, or is it just Nacho?"

"Mama," said the boy, clenching laughter behind his grin, "Nacho Mama."

The back of Nacho's head was immediately slapped by a tall, freckled scarecrow of a boy with tousled black hair sitting next to him.

"Hay! Watch it, Sky!" Nacho snapped, whirling to frown at the boy.

"You behave then, monkey boy." Sky grinned. "Can't you see we got company?"

Sky, Joby thought. Another name from the mysterious headlands conversation.

"Ignore junior here," Sky smiled lazily at Joby. "His last name's Carlson, not Mama, and he's our perpetual freshman. He's goin' for the school record in broken rules."

"Hey!" Nacho protested with exaggerated dignity. "I can test the limits of appropriateness without breaking the mold of propriety."

Wondering what the heck that was supposed to mean, Joby only realized their whole conflict had been a joke when the two boys performed some secret handshake and began to laugh.

As all this had been going on, Joby had noticed the trio of Bobs whispering and smirking at each other between furtive glances at himself. One of them was the swarthy kid who'd worn his shirt as a turban the day before. The second wore a backward baseball cap over wavy blond hair and the face of a mischievous cherub. The third had dark eyes, pale gnomish features, a thick lower lip, and short-cropped, curly black hair.

"How about you three?" he asked them. "Larry, Moe, and Curly, I presume?"

Seeming not to get the reference, the blond boy adopted a comically serious expression, and said, "I'm Cal Bob." He pointed to the gnomish boy on his right. "This here's Cob Bob," then to the Indian boy on his left, "And this's Swami Bob."

"Cal Bob, Cob Bob, and Swami Bob," Joby said dryly. "You're related then?"

Cal nodded soberly. "Brothers."

Joby nodded. "The family resemblance is remarkable. And what are you guys' into? School-wise, I mean."

They glanced at each other, then turned to him with uncannily identical deadpan expressions and said in perfect unison, "English."

"I'm doomed," Joby moaned theatrically.

"Hey, relax, man," said Cal. "We like you."

"How reassuring," Joby drawled.

"I hate to stop all this," Bridget said, "but I'm afraid we're out of time. Thank you so much for coming down this morning, Joby."

"My pleasure," Joby replied with a quick bob of his head. "It was fun."

"Don't forget to bring that book," said Ander as they all got up and started heading for class.

"Don't forget your lunch money," said Nacho with a leering grin.

"Don't listen to Nacho," said Sky. "There's no cafeteria."

"Richard!" Nacho retorted.

"Ognib." Sky grinned, chasing Nacho into another classroom.

"Why don't you come around at lunch," Bridget said, smiling. "I'll introduce you to Ariel and Pete, and we can talk about next week. The kids obviously like you, so unless they've managed to scare you off, you're in."

"Me? Scared?" Joby smiled. "What's to be scared of?" He grinned, hoping those weren't famous last words.

❊

"That's all he said?" Hawk asked, brushing locks of dark auburn hair up out of his fog-colored eyes. "Just heard you and stopped to listen?"

Rose nodded, along with several others, their attentive silence broken only by the swish and gurgle of surf outside the cave, and the tinkling spatter made by tiny rivulets dripping from the algae-covered ceiling onto wet, gray stones and gravel.

The kids had all kinds of hideouts around Taubolt; different places for different times and purposes. Today they'd gathered in one of the many sea caves that riddled the headlands around Taubolt to discuss the growing swarm of mysteries surrounding their new teacher, Joby Peterson.

"How did he hear anything outside a closed ring," Bellindi insisted. "Stopped and stared like we'd put out a sign or something! How accidental can that be?"

"So, he's of the blood and doesn't know it yet," said Sophie. "Hawk didn't know it either when he first came, remember? Lots of people don't."

"He knows what he did, all right," Nacho said. "Look how tweaked he got about it when he saw Rose on Christmas. I say he's a spy."

"A spy for who?" the honey-haired girl protested.

"I don't know, Ray," Nacho complained. "Whoever we're all hiding from."

"Maybe Bellindi or I just kicked one of the stones out of place without noticing," Rose said. "It's not like we were being super careful. It was hardly dawn. We never thought there would be someone out there."

"But there was, and neither of you noticed," said Cal. "How's that work?"

"And what about the earthquake, and that storm the night he got here?" Vesper asked, as if the matter hadn't been discussed a hundred times already.

"Doesn't prove nothin'." Sky shrugged. "We've been through all that."

"Everyone knows it weren't no natural storm, though," said Cal. "It's the bad thing comin', ain't it, Swami!"

"It might be," Swami replied, tossing pebbles toward the cave mouth without looking at any of them. "But I don't think it was him either. That's not what I got."

"Do we trust him then?" asked Jupiter. "You know what Jake says."

"Yeah," Otter agreed. "Pleeboles ain't to know a thing!"

"He's not a pleebole," huffed Rose. "He lives here now. He's probably not even an ognib. Mrs. Lindsay likes him, and so does Jake, I think."

"Seemed nice enough to me," Ray concurred, prodding large green anemones closed with a wand of iridescent brown kelp.

"He's hiding something," Nacho insisted. "I can tell a snarker when I see one."

"Snarkers see snarkers wherever they look," Jupiter teased.

Nacho wrinkled his face in offense.

"Why would Bridget hire him if he were dangerous?" asked Cob.

"I think he's gonna matter," Swami said, turning to look at them, "but . . ." He shook his head, and went back to throwing pebbles. "But not in any bad way."

"Well it wouldn't hurt to try an' flush 'im out a little, would it?" Nacho pressed. "We could lay some kinda trap, and see if he goes for it."

As he said this, three figures rose smoothly from the water at the cave's mouth and crept in toward the gathering. Hawk and the others facing the cavern mouth struggled not to smile as the central figure put a finger to its lips.

Flanked by his two best friends, Blue and Tholomey, Ander crept up behind his sister, raised the abalone shell he'd been carrying and tipped it out over her head, pouring a thin cascade of frigid salt water onto her hair and face.

"You foam-headed freak!" Sophie shrieked up at her brother, trying without much success to keep from laughing with the rest now that the fright had passed.

"Tide's comin' up, you know." Ander smiled. "You'd all better go soon, 'less you're gonna swim out of here with us."

The thought of swimming out with Ander's crew made Hawk's heart ache with envy. If only his father had run off earlier, he thought bitterly, maybe he'd have come to Taubolt sooner, and learned the kinds of tricks Ander and the others took for granted.

❅

The new Sykes-Mundi Building, twenty stories of odd angles in gray-mirrored glass just outside of downtown proper, was a critical success architecturally and a prestigious reflection on its corporate tenants. Floors eighteen and nineteen currently housed the Los Angeles offices of West Meridian Timber Products, the corporate alias of Robert Ferristaff, who sat gazing out the windows of his corner suite wondering how much better the twentieth-floor view might be, when his assistant, Larry Bruech, knocked perfunctorily at the half-open door and entered with a single black folder in hand.

"I think you'll want to see these," Bruech said, laying the folder on Ferristaff's expansive, gleaming, granite desk top.

Ferristaff swiveled around and opened the folder to find a small assortment of very old black-and-white photographs.

"They were found archived in the other building," Bruech informed him.

They were aerial shots: mile after mile of densely forested hills—virgin timber, or Ferristaff was a two-bit shoeshine boy. *Those were the days,* he thought, shaking his head. Didn't see wood like that anymore, except in a few damned national parks. "Gut-wrenching mementoes," he quipped sardonically. "What's your point?"

"Look at the ledgers in back." Bruech reached down to flip one of the photos over. "See? They're all referenced to a place called 'Taubolt.' There was no documentation, so I had Linea look the place up in our archives here. She found nothing, so I had her check a whole slew of outside sources, including the NGS, and still nothing. Then, yesterday—you'll never believe this—Linea's sister calls to tell her she's losing her position with that lottery winner in Oakland, because the old woman's moving to someplace called Taubolt."

"Well, you're right, Bruech. That's a humdinger," Ferristaff conceded dryly. "I assume there's a punch line somewhere?"

"Turns out Taubolt's just a few hours north of San Francisco. We've turned every stone looking for records of ownership or harvest, but there's nothing; no deed or claim; no harvest plan, or reference of any kind with state or federal land management; not even the interior department's ever heard of it." Bruech smiled and shrugged like Houdini out of chains a minute early. "*We* never harvested anything up there. I had Linea look into that weeks ago. I've checked on all the other major players as well—discreetly, of course. If any of them ever cut near anyplace called Taubolt, I'm a—"

"Don't, Bruech. You'll hate yourself in the morning." Ferristaff couldn't help smirking. "You trying to tell me there's some giant stand of virgin timber just sitting up there on the California coast—unnoticed for all these years?"

"I know how it sounds, Robert, but it's starting to look that way."

"That's the best one I've heard in—well, maybe *ever*, Bruech. If you found this stuff in our archives, then I'll bet you lunch for a month, and I don't mean Burger Barn, that we're the ones who cut it, probably back when my grandpa was too young to drive a truck. We just lost the paperwork, that's all."

"And every state and federal agency we file with lost it too?" Bruech protested. "I'm not kidding, Robert. I've checked, or I wouldn't be bothering you, would I?"

"Well, I'd go back and look a little harder before you bet the farm, Bruech." Ferristaff's smirk soured. "It's probably a goddamn national park."

"You think I didn't check that first?" Bruech insisted.

"All right," Ferristaff sighed. "Have them send someone up to check it out. But when they come back with photos of some suburban housing development, or Mr. Ranger checking in a bunch of happy campers, his travel expenses come out of your paycheck." Ferristaff's smirk returned. "I'd believe in fairies before I'd believe the timber in those photos is still standing unclaimed anywhere in this state—or this country, for that matter."

16

(Leaving the Path)

A playful breeze followed Joby up the forest path, sighing through the massive redwood trees, ruffling through the lush undergrowth. Tumbling water and birdsong echoed softly through the warm arboreal twilight. The weather was clear and unusually mild for February. Where sunlight reached the ground, a delicious green smell arose, evoking memories of childhood summers, despite the season. Joby could imagine no more pleasant way to spend a Saturday than wandering alone through such a paradise.

After just a few weeks of teaching, he felt he'd truly found his place in Taubolt. Bridget, Pete and Ariel had shown him the ropes without ever making him feel like the utter neophyte he was, and his students seemed the very incarnation of Longfellow's poem about the thoughts of youth, their luminescent natures brimming with laughter and imaginative mischief, creativity, and surprising flashes of wisdom.

He stopped to watch a pair of tiny flies hover and dart, like airborne diamonds, in a shaft of light among the fir boughs. All around him, misty rays pierced the forest's shadowed depths. Beyond the streambed, every dark needle and leaf was limned in silver. a lacework of brilliance and shadow, from which a boy, silent and still, suddenly appeared as if from thin air. Joby started and stared before realizing that he must have been there all along, backlit and invisible until Joby had looked right at him.

"Jupiter!" he said. "What are you doing over there?"

The butter-haired boy only turned and walked into the dark woods behind him.

Joby gazed after him for a moment, then shrugged and continued his hike. The kids at school had warmed to him considerably by now, but a vague skittishness remained at the edges of their friendliness, as if he were a new dog in the neighborhood, one of whom they were fond but not yet entirely trusting.

"Like to hike?" laughed a brazen voice directly above him.

Joby stumbled back in surprise, then looked up to find Jupiter perched high in the fir tree above him. "You scared the crap out of me!" Joby gasped.

Laughing even louder, Jupiter half-climbed, half-plunged toward the ground. Scorning the lowest branches, he leapt down and unbent his knees to stand grinning before Joby, who vaguely remembered climbing like that himself once, and wondered, now, how he'd ever lived to be fifteen. Looking back across the streambed to where the boy had just disappeared, he asked, "How'd you get all that way so quickly?"

"Climbed," Jupiter said, glancing at the canopy over their heads. "Trees're thick up here. You can go a long ways without comin' down."

"Aren't you afraid of falling?" Joby asked.

"Aren't *you* afraid of falling?" Jupiter parried.

"I'm on the ground," Joby said.

"So am I!" Jupiter grinned.

Joby narrowed his eyes reproachfully.

"My limbs work just as good up there." Jupiter shrugged. "Wanna go hiking?"

"If it's on the ground," Joby replied dryly.

"Come on." Jupiter grinned, striding briskly away up the trail while Joby hustled to catch up. The boy seemed well named. A patch of gold in the dusky shade, he exuded a jovial confidence that made him seem effortlessly capable of anything. Demonstrating precisely this quality, Jupiter stopped abruptly to point up a steep incline covered in densely tangled foliage and debris. "Let's go that way!"

The ascent, if not altogether impossible, looked like far too much work. "Don't forget to write," said Joby. "I'll stay on the path, I think."

Jupiter looked at him scornfully.

"Hiking off the path causes erosion, doesn't it?" Joby said lamely. "Have you ever even been up there?"

"No," Jupiter said, clearly wondering what that had to do with anything.

"Okay," Joby said wearily. "Just don't get us lost. We've got to be back in time for the potluck at school tonight, you know."

With a radiant grin, Jupiter began bounding up the hill like a startled deer, while Joby sighed and started picking his way slowly through a sea of obstacles.

"Not like that!" the boy laughed, turning to look back at him. "If you wanna be a Taubolt stud, you have to barge up here, not pizzel like a narning pleebole!"

"What's a Taubolt stud?" Joby asked, feeling heat in his face. "And what makes you think I want to be one?"

"A Taubolt stud is me!" Jupiter crowed. "*Of course* you want to be one!"

The boy's sheer conceit made Joby laugh and filled him with an urge to match such ridiculous audacity. As he leapt clumsily up and over the fallen tree in front of him, a wave of antic energy surged through him like a shout.

"YES!" Jupiter shouted as Joby came abreast of him and kept going. "Another Taubolt stud is born!"

"I was a stud years before you were an idea!" Joby shouted back in delight as the two of them continued charging up the hill together. When they finally reached the hilltop, Joby braced his hands against his knees, and gasped, "Okay. . . . I've got to stop."

"Good," Jupiter panted back. Joby looked up to find him red-faced, and breathing as hard as he. "You're not as wobbity as you act," the boy conceded.

Once recovered, they followed a streambed downhill through more dense underbrush before heading up again through drier woods of oak, fir, and laurel. Joby wasn't sure anymore where they were in relation to town.

"You're not gonna get us lost, right?" he asked Jupiter.

"Fold your feathers!" Jupiter scoffed. "All these streams lead back into the canyon. Do I look like a pleebole?"

Still struggling with the local lingo, Joby asked, "What's a 'pleebole' again?"

Jupiter hesitated, then said, "I'm just sayin' only tourists could get lost here."

"Okay," Joby said. "Just making sure."

After following a new path for some time, Jupiter suddenly shouted, "Yes!" and ran up the hillside ahead of them. *"Oh YES!"* he crowed again, thrusting his hand into a low bush covered with small, bright green leaves. When Joby caught up, Jupiter offered him a handful of tiny, round berries, almost black in color.

"What are these?" Joby asked.

Jupiter's eyes went round. "Don't you know *huckleberries?*"

"I've heard of them," Joby said nervously. "But . . . are you sure these are okay?"

"Only since I was three!" Jupiter scoffed, shoving a fistful into his mouth, and groaning in delight. "I've never seen so many! It's the lost huckleberry homeland!" he enthused, reaching out to rake another handful from the bottom of a clotted branch. "What are you waitin' for," he mumbled to Joby around the mouthful, "a fork?"

Joby tried a single berry, then threw the rest in, smiling as their surprisingly potent sweetness exploded on his tongue. After that, they ate, and laughed, and ate, and ate. Later, as Joby tried to lick the purple stains off his hands, Jupiter assured him they would be the envy of everyone who heard about it at school that night.

"What I can't understand," Joby said, "is what all these berries are doing here. It's February. These bushes must have bloomed in, what, December? That can't be right."

"Happens sometimes." Jupiter shrugged uncertainly. "Taubolt's got some kind of special climate, I think. Pete told us about it in science class. 'A microclimate,' he said. So things just sort of grow when they want to here."

"How weird," Joby mused. "Thanks for getting my butt up here, Jupiter. It's been a lot of fun. A lot more than I was expecting, really."

"Gotta leave the path sometimes," Jupiter said, smiling pointedly at Joby.

"Yes, yes. Point taken, professor," Joby drawled. "It's getting late, though, and I need to get cleaned up before the potluck. Maybe we should start heading back?"

"No problem," Jupiter said, giving his stomach one last pat. "Just follow me."

The hike back seemed much longer than the hike there, and none of it looked familiar. Finally, Jupiter stopped and turned to stare up the hill they had just come down. Then he grinned without meeting Joby's eyes, and said, "You know, we might be lost."

"Oh great!" Joby exclaimed, looking at his watch. "The potluck is in one hour, *stud,* and it's gonna look pretty flaky if I'm not there. Got a plan B?"

"Keep heading down this streambed, and hope it crosses the path somewhere, I guess," Jupiter offered sheepishly.

"Oh no," Joby said. "I don't know where the path we started on is, but I think I can get us back to Blueberry Hill, so I say we go there and start again more carefully."

"That sounds good too." Jupiter shrugged.

Fortunately, they found the site of their berry spree, and, after looking around, cut off the crest trail earlier as Joby began to recognize obstacles he'd worked harder to get past than Jupiter had. After a tense half hour of trailblazing, they stumbled, with deep relief, back onto the original canyon path about a mile east of Taubolt.

"We have fifteen minutes," Joby said, checking his watch again and beginning to trot toward town. "We might just make it if we run all the way."

"See?" Jupiter grinned. "No problem! Just like I said."

Joby gave him what he hoped was a dangerous smile, sure that more than a few parents would wonder why the new English teacher looked like he'd just crawled out of the forest on his knees.

※

I was a whisper
 conceived in the golden time.
Summer
  turning
   to
    Fall.
And mountains, the only ones
  silent enough,
   heard me mumbling songs
 in my first unborn moment.
But in this deep basin
  between Earth's rocky fingers
  I could not stay long.
  Fall
   to
    Winter
     to
     Spring

The next chapter begins
 in a hospital bed
touched by the ocean breath
  born in the emerald time.
   Spring turning
  to Summer.
Kelp castles and
  driftwood fortresses
heard my songs bounce off cliffs
  and ripple the ocean.

And Summer
  to
   Fall
  to

Spring
    to
       Summer again
7 times until I returned
       to the mountains.
In a blink
    I had grown my own
        eyes,
   my own
     voice,
and to rock peaks
   and cradles
I returned
  and returned
Summer to
    Fall to
      Winter,

Where an icy wind
  stole my songs,
made me afraid
  to raise my voice.

And now the power
  of that speck of child
against jutting peaks
  returns with the hail,
   rides the winds
    of midnight
saturates me with
   the rain.
Child of salt water
   and rock,
words now lost
   in thunder.

Hawk stood before the display of work from Joby Peterson's English classes. He read Rose's poem a second time, and a third. She'd read it to him herself on the day she finished it. She read him a lot of her poems before showing them to anyone else. Everything she wrote, or said, or did seemed perfect to Hawk. She was the most amazing girl he'd ever met. She was also the school's best student, while he was its worst. Her family was the cream of Taubolt society; his was a disgrace. They were friends. Hawk was too smart to wish for more than that, or too smart to let it show, at least.

Though he'd been cutting class for weeks, Hawk never missed a potluck or an open house. No wobbity-wah about tests or homework at a potluck, just the other kids and a full-surge smorgasbord. He hadn't mentioned the event to his mother, of course, doubting she'd have come even if he had. She didn't cry much anymore, thank God, but she didn't much like socializing either, since his dad had left. When she wasn't working, she just stayed home now, seeming to believe whatever Hawk told her about his own life.

Just then, Hawk saw Jupiter run in, followed by the very person Hawk had come to spy on: the mysterious new English teacher, Joby Peterson. To Hawk's surprise, their clothes were filthy, and they had bits of twig and leaf tangled in their hair.

"Sorry I look like a cat toy," he heard Joby say to Bridget. "Jupiter got us lost on a hike, and I figured, better on time and ragged than cleaned up and late. Hope I was right."

Hawk wasn't sure whether to laugh or sneer as Bridget reached up to brush the forest out of Joby's hair. As Joby move toward the food line, greeted by a steady stream of parents, to whom he apologized over and over for his unwashed condition, Hawk rolled his eyes, sure he'd never seen a more pathetic suck-up.

Then, just as Joby finally got a plate of food, the Bobs descended on him like a small tribe of gangster-rap Indians. Joby was clearly charmed to silliness with their little act, and Hawk had to admit they were funny but thought they hogged a lot of attention.

"You guys are total sitcom material," Hawk heard Joby laugh. "You thought about taking this to Hollywood?"

Cob looked offended. "You haven't seen our TV show? I'm hurt. You hurt, Cal?"

"I'm hurt bad." Cal frowned. "You hurt, Swami?"

"Yup," said Swami. "I'm pretty hurt."

Cal turned back to pout at Joby. "We're pretty hurt," he said.

"Hey! I'm sorry." Joby grinned. "Something I can do to make it up to you?"

"You could take us out to dinner somewhere," Cal said brightly.

Cob nodded happily. "That'd even us up."

"I'd love to," Joby said, and started dishing lasagna from his paper plate onto Cob's. "Everything's on me tonight. All you can eat."

"Hey!" Cob yelled, yanking his plate out of Joby's reach. "Get that off! How do I know where your food's been?"

"We didn't mean *tonight*," Cal griped. "You can just owe us later. Right?"

Wrong, thought Hawk. *Say wrong, or you're—*

"Sure," Joby said.

Screwed, Hawk thought with a grim grin. The last thing anybody with a clue would want was to owe the Bobs. God knew what they'd ask for.

"Whadaya think, Cob?" Cal asked. "The Heron's Bowl?"

"Naw!" Cob scoffed. "That slop house? Let's go someplace nice."

"Yeah," Joby concurred theatrically, "this is a special occasion! We don't just want some canned food crap at gourmet prices. Let's go someplace *good*."

What a full-surge idiot! Hawk thought, watching Cal and Swami struggle to keep straight faces as Cob's expression darkened ominously.

"Who told you that?" Cob growled.

"Told me what?" Joby asked uncertainly.

"About the Heron's Bowl," Cob frowned, his impish brows drawn down.

"Well . . . *you* just did," Joby said, sounding confused. "I was just—"

"That's my *mom's* restaurant," Cob frowned.

"Oh, God," Joby groaned, closing his eyes. "I was only— You said . . . I've never even been there! I just . . ." He looked around nervously, and asked, "Is your mom here?"

By now Cal and Swami were laughing so hard, Hawk thought Cal might throw up. Even Cob was smiling, though it was, Hawk thought, a pretty scary smile.

"She's over there," Cob said, pointing at a cluster of chatting women across the noisy room. Hawk saw Joby slump in relief, then Cob said, "I think she'll want to know about this, though. The restaurant's reputation is very imp—"

"Don't you dare, Cob!" Joby cut in. "You totally set me up, and you know it!"

"Well, I suppose I don't *have* to tell her," Cob mused, gazing petulantly at his twiddling fingers. "We'll need to talk about what my silence is worth to you though."

"I'm buying you dinner, aren't I?" Joby protested.

Cal shook his head. "That was a previous debt."

THE BOOK OF JOBY ✷ 297

"Why, you little thugs," Joby said. "My firstborn child then? A pound of flesh?"

"Gentlemen," Cal said officiously, "I don't think we should discuss this anymore without our lawyers present." He turned to his cohorts and said, "Conference." They stood in unison, leaving Joby to stare after them as they walked in theatrical silence across the room and out the main doors.

Hawk had no idea what everyone had been freaking out about. This guy was no scary spy. He was just a full-surge dufus. . . . Or was he? Might a spy not try to look foolish, just to throw folks off?

"Why are you avoiding everybody, Hawk?"

Hawk turned to find Rose at his shoulder. "I am not," he said.

"Yes, you are. You've been here half an hour and haven't even talked to anyone." "I'm just . . . in a quiet mood." Hawk shrugged, embarrassed to admit that he'd been stalking Joby Peterson.

Rose looked down self-consciously and asked, "Is something wrong?"

"What would be wrong?" he said, flustered.

"I don't know. I just . . . well, wasn't it around this time last year when your dad—"

"Oh please!" Hawk exclaimed. "Everyone knows that was the happiest day of my life!" He looked away, appalled at taking such an angry tone with Rose. "I'm sorry, Rose. I . . . It's just . . . I didn't mean to sound like that."

"It's okay," she said. "A bunch of us are going to the headlands. Want to come?"

"Sure! Gotta take a leak though. Will you wait?"

She rolled her eyes and nodded as Hawk raced off toward the bathrooms. When he arrived, however, the door swung open, and he came face-to-face with Joby Peterson.

"Sorry," Hawk said, looking down and stepping back to let Joby pass.

"No problem," Joby said, but instead of walking by, he added, "I don't think we've met. You a student here?"

Hawk knew it would be dumb to lie. They were bound to meet sooner or later. Besides, hadn't he decided the guy was harmless? "I'm Hawk," he said.

"Well!" Joby grinned, stretching out his hand. "At long last, the famous Hawk! You're supposed to be in one of my freshman classes. How come I haven't seen you?"

"I've been sick," Hawk lied. "Flu. Bad. . . . How come you know me?"

"I . . . I don't," Joby said, "I just—"

"You just said, 'the famous Hawk,'" Hawk insisted, suddenly tired of all the sneaking around. "How come I'm famous?"

Joby gave him an odd smile, then shrugged and said, "Well, my first day in Taubolt, I happened to hear Rose and Bellindi talking out on the headlands. They mentioned a bunch of pretty cool names, and yours was one of them." He shrugged.

But how'd you hear them through the ring? Hawk barely managed not to blurt it out.

Perhaps his frustration showed, because Joby grinned sympathetically and leaned in even closer. "Can you keep a secret?" he asked quietly.

Hawk's skin prickled. Was this guy going to tip his hand at last? Hawk nodded gravely, half-thrilled and half-afraid.

"Well," Joby took a quick glance around, and said, "don't *ever* say I told you this, 'cause I kind of fibbed a bit to Rose and Bellindi about it, but I did hear Rose tell Bellindi that she thinks you're cute."

Hawk couldn't keep the sudden smile from his face, no longer caring how Peterson had gotten through their ring, just very, *very* stoked that he had!

✺

Raphael stood, balanced in perfect stillness atop the minaret's topmost needle, gazing down at the still waking city of Damascus. As the first rays of dawn touched his perch, the angel assumed corporeal form just long enough to feel the sunlight burnish his gleaming ebony face with luminous highlights of violet and indigo darker and richer than the city's fleeing shadows. This was his favorite time of day, the moment of trembling, sunlit silence just before the muezzins began their hauntingly beautiful call to prayer throughout the city spread beneath him. He smiled gravely, imagining what someone looking up just then might think to see him balanced on the head of this great pin. It was doubtful anyone would lift their eyes so high. Nonetheless, he released his momentary body and faded from sight again.

"Raphael."

The voice, more felt than heard, would have broadened the smile on Raphael's vanished face. "Master?" he whispered in a bass voice softer than the morning breeze.

"Attend Me."

"Your command is joy to me, My Lord."

An instant later, the minaret's needle was as empty as it seemed.

Raphael found his Master sitting alone among the stars, looking pensive and improbably melancholy.

"What do You require, Master?" Raphael asked, eyes cast down, despite the joy his Lord's presence brought him.

"Company," the Creator replied.

"I am here, My Lord. But . . . where has my brother, Gabriel, gone?"

"Gabe is off on business of his own," the Creator sighed.

"Forgive me, Master," the angel asked in graceful astonishment, "but since when have angels business of their own?"

"An excellent question," the Creator mused. "Let's go for a walk, Rafe. I've a thirst for conversation."

They stepped together into the bright purity of Mt. Chomolungma in Tibet, and started out across the glittering slope, heedless of the shearing wind and drifting snow.

After a time, the Creator asked, "So, My friend, what shall we talk about?"

Raphael looked over in surprise. "Whatever You wished to discuss, My Lord."

"I was rather hoping you'd think of something," the Creator answered.

Puzzled, Raphael searched himself for some worthy subject, and finally said, "Where I am, there is little more than rumor of Your latest wager with Lucifer. How does it proceed?"

"Ah," the Creator said. "An interesting choice."

As the Creator filled him in, Raphael's inner smile grew increasingly grave. "It does seem to me at times, Lord," Raphael said deferentially, "that Lucifer could not manipulate mortal kind as he does if they were more obedient to You. May it not displease You, Master, but I have wondered why You allow humanity such free rein."

The Creator nodded, seeming to approve of the question, much to Raphael's relief, "Have I ever told you how I created the world, Rafe?"

Raphael had heard the story too many times to count, of course, and witnessed some of it himself. But he never tired of hearing it again, for his Master told it differently each time. So Raphael smiled, and said, "It would please me greatly to listen, Lord."

"Well, Rafe," the Creator began, "believe it or not, I wasn't always perfect."

Raphael looked doubtful.

"No. It's true," his Master said. "Not only was I lonely once, I didn't even know that's what it was. I thought I was just bored. It was just Me and My shadow then, you know, in this big empty void." He shrugged. "A shadow's pretty poor company, Rafe—especially in a void.

"Anyhow, thinking I just needed a hobby, I took up pretty much every craft there was back then, and put together this fairly sophisticated performance piece where I juggled a lot of clay spheres on long curvilinear continuums in front of this humungous astronomical mural I'd painted, but with no audience to impress, except my shadow, it was kind of like TV. You know? Just a lot of motion without any real meaning."

Raphael shrugged politely, as they stopped to watch a snow leopard wander the icy waste ahead of them.

"It wasn't just motion I wanted, Rafe. It was *conversation*: honest-to-God debate, witty repartee, juicy gossip! But with whom?" The Creator shrugged. "My shadow never had anything to say I hadn't already thought of on my own. I needed something more than just a better sock puppet. I needed real company! This had never been done before, of course. I had to start totally from scratch. My first breakthrough was single-celled organisms, but they were a total bust as company—like talking with your lava lamp." The Creator shook his head. "More television, really. And scale was a problem. Developed some serious eyestrain issues trying to see what I was doing for such long periods. That's why I made dinosaurs, really, so I could step back a little and still see the game."

The Creator's story was interrupted again as a great slab of ice and snow crashed down into the vast gorge ahead of them. Avalanches are majestic things, especially at a distance, and they were both silent in appreciation until the last drifts had settled.

"But you know, Rafe, it still wasn't scratching that itch. None of it." The Creator paused thoughtfully, then asked, "Ever been to Disneyland all by yourself, Rafe?"

"I must confess to having missed that pleasure," Raphael replied respectfully.

"Must you?" the Creator asked.

"Well . . . yes, My Lord," Raphael answered in surprise. "I've never done it. Would I lie to You? Why even try?"

"Yes," the Creator sighed wistfully. "Why even try?"

"My Lord?" Raphael asked, worried that he'd said something wrong.

"It's nothing, Rafe. Anyway, you haven't missed much. I've tried it, actually." Raphael looked up, startled.

"Oh. Not lying." The Creator smiled. "The Disneyland thing. Went in while it was closed one night and turned on all the rides, set off some fireworks, made Myself dinner at the best restaurant—you know, the one above New Orleans Square that only VIPs ever get to see? But the whole night was a crashing bore. 'Oooooh!' you say when the fireworks explode, and nobody says, *'Yeah! Look at that!'* 'Isn't this salad superb!' you say, and nobody says, 'God! It's delicious!' It's just not that much fun waving your arms around and screaming on a roller coaster all by yourself, Rafe."

Raphael was completely nonplussed, but one look at the forlorn expression on his Master's face kept him silent.

"It was like that with My creation too," the Creator said. "Every day I saw interesting courtship rituals, combat, storms, earthquakes, floods, volcanoes. Like summer at the movies. But when you say, *'Look at that volcanic sunset, will you?'* to an animal, the most you're likely to get is a brief look up from chewing cud or licking scales. Nothing was ever special or surprising to them because it never occurred to them—*couldn't* occur to them—that things might be any other way.

"I began to get seriously depressed, Rafe. Why be Supreme Being if I couldn't make anything that wasn't just more of *Me*? I started talking to my shadow again, each conversation darker than the last, until . . ." The Creator became pensive again, then asked, "Do you know why teenagers get roaring drunk, and zoom around wrecking cars, and bungee jump off bridges, Rafe?"

"I must confess to having wondered on occasion why they don't behave more wisely," Raphael replied politely.

"There it is again," the Creator said looking vexed. "Raphael, I wish you'd stop using that phrase."

"My Lord, I'm sorry. What phrase?"

" *'I must confess.'* . . . I'd rather not hear that again."

"Of course, My Lord," Raphael said without rancor. "I shall do as you ask."

"Yes. . . . I know," his Master answered wearily. "Well, I'll tell you why they do it, Rafe. It's because they're so terribly thirsty for some shred of proof that they matter—that they even really exist." The Creator looked away and shook his head. "I did My own share of roaring around wrecking things, I suppose. Just got wilder and wilder in My desperation to be 'real,' until, finally, I pulled that stunt with the comet." The Creator scowled at the memory. "Pouf!" He sighed. "No more dinosaurs. There wasn't even anyone to apologize to. You can't imagine what it felt like to be that lonely.

"In a fit of desperation, I took all the best things about myself; creativity, intelligence—though you'd never have known it from that comet stunt—beauty, immortality, consciousness, everything I could think of including free will, and I made you, Raphael, and all your brothers and sisters, including Lucifer. Then I stood back and said, 'Surprise Me! I dare you!'" Raphael's Master stopped walking, and gave him a sympathetic look. *"I must confess,* My friend, that Lucifer was the only one who did.

"Don't get Me wrong, Rafe. You make My heart swell with pride and affection every day. But you all did exactly what I wanted you to, all the time, except for Lucifer. He'd hardly opened his eyes before he started looking around and making *'suggestions.'* This tree was crooked. That sky was a jarring color. Those creatures were as ugly as sin, though I had no idea what *that* was then." The Creator smiled ruefully. "It bugged the hell out of Me, at first. But it was also fun to have someone I could finally really argue with." The Creator's smile faded. "I think it bothered him terribly that no one ever took his side. The rest of you were always thanking Me, and telling Me what a *wonderful* job I was doing. Maybe that's what finally drove him to try making company of his own."

Raphael hoped his Master didn't expect him to feel sympathy for Lucifer. He'd convinced plenty of angels to take his side in the end, and look what it had cost them all.

"He couldn't create things out of nothing of course," the Creator continued. "Even in My most reckless adolescent moments, I'd known enough to leave certain fail-safes in place. So he found a pair of foraging apes, happily minding their own business, and gave them half the things I'd given him, including his contrary nature. Not enough to make them his equals, of course, just enough to make them conscious of his own superiority, and articulate enough to tell him he was right."

This Raphael remembered all too well. What a storm there had been in Heaven when his Master had found out!

"Remember how miserable the poor creatures were?" the Creator said sadly. "Reason? Consciousness? What did they want with all that? Eve suddenly convinced she had a weight problem? Adam looking at the elephant's penis, and the boar's, then down at his own? What a mess.

"If Lucifer had just stepped up and owned his mistake, I suspect we'd have patched things up. But his pride would not allow it. To err is one thing, but to go down there and tell the poor creatures it was *their* fault! Well, you'll remember how I hit the fan then, I'm sure. The rest . . . is history, I suppose.

"You know how much time I spent down here trying to fix the massive neurosis Lucifer had inflicted on those sad innocents. But they were too convinced I was angry at them to trust Me. I tried reassuring them. I tried jokes. I even tried punishing them, hoping they'd feel expiated and leave it behind But nothing worked. . . . And that's when it hit Me, Rafe."

Raphael saw his Master's face grow radiant with excitement. The wind picked up speed, and he heard the mountain groan and rumble at its roots.

"I remember standing on a hill one day, watching them burn down each other's little villages, all trying to shove their own shame onto other's' shoulders, just as Lucifer had done to them, and suddenly thinking, 'Oh my God! They really are totally out of control! Even *Mine!*' Raphael, as awful as I felt about what they were *doing,* I could not have been happier about what they *were!* I swear, Rafe, if Lucifer could just have stopped trying to eradicate his shame by getting rid of them all, I might have invited him back with open arms and a hero's welcome!"

This assertion made Raphael quite uncomfortable, but his was not to question.

"Of course, this hardly excused Me from addressing all the damage My own angel had inflicted. So I hung around, trying to shove them back on course: forcing them to apologize when they'd maimed someone, thwarting their little wars, telling them over and over that they couldn't be God no matter how angry they were, scaring the crap out of them when it was necessary. Let's face it, Rafe, I was a world-class party pooper, and yet the most amazing thing happened! A few of the little buggers began to get what I was after, and, Rafe, they liked Me!"

Raphael's Master smiled a childlike, almost silly smile that, for a moment, tempted Raphael to jealousy of poor mortal humanity. The wind died suddenly away, as if the very mountain held its breath. The Creator's eyes were suddenly agleam with unshed tears. "Love. My greatest creation took Me completely by surprise."

"But . . . I do not mean to contradict You, Master," Raphael said, hesitant after his earlier "I must confess," gaff, "but, how could Your own creation take You by surprise?"

"Oh, I created the things that created love," his Lord replied. "But, while I was more than able to make them *obey* Me, nobody *made* them *like* Me, not even Me! This wasn't just an empty imitation. It was the real thing! Don't you see? They *chose,* Rafe!

"Well, I saw right off that the whole thing had to stay free, or none of it

would be real. You can't control the bad stuff and pretend the rest is spontaneous. So I backed off. I still do what I can of course. I'm not one to leave
the building before the fire's out, especially when I helped set it. But even
knowing too certainly that I exist would kill the whole thing. Like what you
said earlier, why would you lie to Me? Why would you try? You wouldn't,
even though you could. And I don't really want you lying to Me, Rafe. But,
in another way, you'll never love Me the way they do—the ones that do love
Me, at least."

He gave Raphael a reassuring smile, and being what he was, the angel
accepted the truth without discontent.

"So you see, Rafe, I could make that perfect world Lucifer imagines, where
everyone always does just what they're supposed to—a world where no one
had any option but to believe and obey." The Creator smiled sadly. "To do it,
I would only have to murder choice, and with that, any real being, and, with
it, love itself. But, I won't murder love, Rafe, just to conquer hate, however
tidy the corpse. Unlike my angry angel, I have known eternity in that lonely
void. If Lucifer's part in refining my creation is ever finished, I may give him
that perfect world he claims to crave, but he'll be its only truly living citizen,
and, trust Me, Rafe, he'll complain. Bitterly."

17

(Waking)

. . . and stare into the embers
searching for some mislaid compass,
until, grown warm and drowsy,
I surrender to the press of blankets
drawn and tucked around me
by deft and unseen servants
of the soft, suppressing night.

Joby stared at the poem he'd been crafting, as if some final stanza might magically appear to resolve the riddle tugging at his metaphorical shirt-sleeves. Ever since his hike with Jupiter, Joby had been haunted by thoughts of the boy's easy laughter, adventurous spirit, and utter lack of self-doubt, until, by now, the bright sap that seemed to flow through all his students here had him feeling such desperate need of some defining answer to a question he could hardly name that he'd started writing *poetry* again for the first time since college! Things were that bad—*here*—where everything was always good!

With a sigh and a crooked smile, Joby set his pencil down, pulled on his coat, and set off for one of his now frequent after-work wanders on the headlands. Was there enough of whatever fuel had once burned within him to ignite again? Could he still shine as brightly as his students did? Had he ever been as luminous in youth as they were, or did he only wish he had been now? The more he struggled to remember, the less certain he became.

Gotta leave the path. Jupiter had told him. At times, it seemed almost as if they were trying intentionally to teach him something. But they never told him precisely what. Leave what path? How? Joby hadn't asked, and wasn't going to, because he didn't want to see the boy's blank look, and face the fact that they weren't trying to teach him anything at all—that there was nothing to his vague new urgencies but vague imagination.

Lost in thought, Joby didn't see Hawk until he stumbled, almost literally, over the boy sitting cross-legged and silent in the tall, twilit grass.

"Whoa!" Joby exclaimed. "I almost stepped on you!"

Hawk shrugged without looking up. Joby was about to move on when he noticed Hawk's reddened nose and puffy, pink-blotched eyes.

"Everything all right?" he asked.

Hawk still said nothing.

"Sometimes," Joby pressed uncertainly, "it helps to talk when things are bad. I've had a few bad times myself, and once, when I really didn't want to talk at all, someone—"

"What would you know?" Hawk demanded, finally turning to look at Joby, his face an angry challenge.

"Only what you tell me," Joby answered, fearing he'd been wrong to push.

"Bet you got As in everything," Hawk scornfully accused. "Bet your folks were proud as could be of their little genius."

"You got that wrong," Joby replied. "My father left us when I was thirteen. My mother thought everything I did was going to destroy us all."

For an instant, Hawk looked confused. Then his angry mask returned.

"You're a teacher," he said, sneering, as if that proved Joby's every word a lie.

"By sheer dumb luck," Joby replied.

"Bullshit," Hawk said, turning away again. "Nobody gets hired to teach if they're stupid. I could tell if you were stupid."

"I could tell if you were too," Joby said, sitting down in the grass, not too close.

Hawk shot him an angry glare well suited to his name. Joby met his stare until the boy looked away again. After that, they sat.

. . . And sat.

Joby was about to give up when Hawk asked sullenly, "Why'd *your* dad leave?"

Ah, Joby thought, and his heart went out to Hawk with sudden ferocity. "I thought he went because he was ashamed of me, Hawk. He didn't think I was much of a man back then. It was a long time later before I realized it was mostly all about things between him and my mom." Hawk didn't move, but his posture softened some. "He's never been willing to talk about it," Joby said, "so I don't know what, exactly, those things were, but it hurt me for a long time . . . They've gotten back together since then, but I still have trouble even visiting them." When Hawk still said nothing, Joby took another risk. "Why'd *your* dad leave?"

Hawk turned toward him with an expression Joby couldn't decipher. Anger? Fear? Surprise? "Who told you that?" the boy demanded.

"Like you said," Joby answered gently, "I'm not stupid."

" 'Cause he's a fuckin', puck-eating, drunken dickhead," Hawk said quietly.

Joby hid his surprise. He couldn't recall hearing a single obscenity in Taubolt before, and had been lulled into assuming everyone here was innocent of the ugliness taken so for granted elsewhere.

"Do you miss him?" Joby asked.

Hawk's expression became incredulous, and Joby was sure he'd blown it.

"I don't *miss* him! . . . How could I miss him? He's still screwin' up every day of my life! He'll never quit!"

"How? What happened?"

"My mom won't stop bawling her eyes out! That's what happened. She's never gonna get over it, and I'm fucking tired of it!" He was trembling now, but Joby resisted an urge to reach out and embrace the boy. "If she wants to crawl into her hole and die, I wish she'd just do it and quit blaming everything on me!" He took an angry swipe at one of his eyes, clearly embarrassed by the tears gathered on his lashes.

"What's she blaming on you?"

"The fuckin' note!" Hawk spat, glaring at Joby. "Now she's all fucked-up again, 'cause of you guys and your Nazi little prison camp!"

"You've lost me," Joby said, laying Hawk's anger aside. "What note?"

"The notes you dickheads send to my house every three weeks," Hawk retorted. "I didn't find this one before she saw it, and now she's—"

"Notes about what?" Joby pressed.

" 'Hawk has been absent from school again this week,' " the boy said in an angry parody of adult authority. " 'Hawk is in danger of failing his courses. Hawk is a criminal disgrace who should be beaten with a pipe and executed for—' "

"Okay. I get the picture," Joby interrupted, resisting another urge to assert that Bridget had only Hawk's best interests at heart. "So, how does your father figure in here?"

"Your dad ever hit you?" Hawk demanded. "He throw beer cans at your mom, and slap her around, and fuck with you 'til you got angry, then hit you for mouthing off?"

"No," Joby said. "I was luckier than that."

"That's what I thought," Hawk said, turning away again as if Joby had fallen beneath his dignity to acknowledge. "You don't know shit."

Ignoring Hawk's taunt, Joby said, calmly, "I've been hurt, Hawk. I've lost family, dreams, friends. . . . I've done things that got people I cared about killed. And I've been arrested, if that helps any. So you can sit there and tell me off as if you knew anything about who I am, or you can give me a chance to listen and try to understand. But, whatever you think, I'm not remotely qualified to look down on you or anyone else."

Hawk gave him a skeptical glance. "What'd you get arrested for?"

"Starting a riot in the city I came from," Joby said, braced to finish what he'd started. "A good friend died that day. The police said it was my fault. In some ways they were right. . . . It's why I came here."

"They still after you?" Hawk asked, turning to look at Joby again, his anger turned suddenly to shy interest.

"No," Joby sighed. "My friend's death was even more their fault than mine, and they knew it. So they let me go." He saw Hawk's expression shift from interest to something terribly like admiration, and his stomach twisted. "There's nothing neat about it, Hawk." Joby's eyes began to burn, and his throat to tighten as he thought about Gypsy for the first time in months. "It was nothing to be proud of, and it hurts even to remember now. I just want you to know that I do understand what it's like to hurt."

The eagerness left Hawk's face. "I'm sorry," he mumbled, "for what I said."

"It's okay. You were angry, and it sounds like you've got plenty of cause to be."

Hawk looked down and began to pluck stalks of grass, thoughtfully twirling them between his fingers or bending them into simple shapes. "I got all Bs once, before we came here." His eyes stayed fastened on his busy hands. "Worked my butt off. But when my dad got the report card, he just said I had a knack for falling into a pile of shit and comin' up with a gold ring in my teeth, whatever that means. Told me not to expect him to get all impressed until I was really working *up to potential*." Hawk stopped fiddling with the grass, but wouldn't look at Joby. "My mom stood there the whole time and didn't say a thing." He shrugged, and sighed, "You had to be crazy to mess with my dad when he was in one of those moods. I know that. . . . Later she told me how good I did and how she was proud of me. But . . ." Hawk trailed off.

"Trying never did me much good either," Joby conceded, losing ground to the heat in his eyes and the lump growing in his throat, "Not 'til I came here, at least. Your dad was wrong about you, Hawk. Sounds like he was wrong about a lot of things." He struggled to find something wise and helpful to offer, but drew a total blank. "Is there . . . anything I can do, Hawk?"

No," he said. "I'm just a screwup."

"I don't think so."

"How would you know?" Hawk asked wearily.

"School is not the meaning of life," Joby insisted. "I forgot to mention that I also flunked out of college."

"Okay." Hawk shrugged. "So you're an even bigger screwup than me. You win."

"Winning's not the point."

"I want to try sometimes," Hawk said. "It'd make my mom happy. But I can't stand all the stuff they make you do. It's like everything's set up to point out what a dumb-ass I am." Hawk frowned. "It's always been that way."

"So what interests you, Hawk?" Joby said. "What do you really enjoy?"

Hawk looked up as if Joby had asked something dangerous.

"There is something then, isn't there?" Joby pressed.

Hawk shrugged. "Bein' outside." He studied Joby uncertainly, "Doin' things with the other kids."

"If you like hanging out with people, suppose you did your homework with someone who was there to make it a bit more fun."

"I tried that," Hawk said wearily. "Rose and Bellindi just kept tellin' me to shut up so they could do their homework."

"I didn't mean Rose and Bellindi." Joby grinned.

"Who then?" Hawk insisted.

"I used to tutor kids after school, and we did have some fun." He drew his hand across his chest. "Cross my heart. Real fun."

Hawk rolled his eyes.

"Just give me a chance, Hawk."

"Jupiter says you're cool to hike with," Hawk conceded. "I could show you something better than a bunch of huckleberries. You should hike with me."

"Sounds possible," Joby mused. "How long's the hike?"

"What's that matter?" Hawk protested.

"How long?" Joby insisted.

"Long," Hawk said defiantly.

"Equal swap then," Joby said. "I'll trade an hour of hiking for every hour of homework we do together after school."

"We could do my homework on the hike," Hawk said hopefully.

"I'm not stupid, remember?"

Hawk heaved a long sigh. "Okay. But we hike first."

Joby shook his head. "If the hike's that long, we can't go 'til Saturday, and that's three days off. I say we meet tomorrow after school, which, by the way, it might be good to try coming to for a while. Then we'll celebrate this weekend with that hike."

Hawk's face scrunched in world-weary disgust. "You know, you'd be a lot more fun if you lightened up some."

"All right. I'll tutor you in English, and you can tutor me in lightening up. Fair?"

"I guess."

"Shake on it," Joby said, sticking out his hand.

Hawk looked at the proffered extremity as if it were a rubber chicken, and said, "You're really weird, you know."

But he shook on it anyway.

✻

"Hello?" Tom took quick inventory of the young man at his front door, whose conservative business attire argued against "tourist."

"You're Tom Connolly?" the fellow asked a tad too cheerfully.

"I am," Tom cheerfully replied. "What can I do for you?"

"I'm told you're the man to see about real estate here." The gentleman smiled.

Tom managed not to roll his eyes. Undoubtedly another of Agnes Hamilton's disciples. Tom had already gotten two phone calls and one personal visit from "friends" she had lured here to get in on the ground floor of her *charming discovery.*

"That would be me." Tom smiled, all pleasant professionalism. "Is there some particular property you're interested in, Mr. . . . ?"

"Bruech. Larry Bruech" The man smiled and reached to shake Tom's hand. "No, I'm here on more of a fact-finding mission. Have you a few minutes, Mr. Connolly?"

"Certainly," Tom said, glancing overtly at his watch, in case this encounter wanted terminating. "I think I can squeeze you in before my next appointment. Please come in, Mr. Bruech."

"Thank you." He entered, peering curiously about. "What a lovely house. That paneling is redwood, isn't it? And those beams?"

Tom smiled and nodded.

"Been a long time since anyone's had wood like that to build with, hasn't it?"

"Taubolt's an old town, Mr. Bruech. Are you interested in finding a home here?"

"Not at the moment."

"Oh," Tom said, surprised. "Then . . . what—"

"I'm here on behalf of my employer, actually. Do you have an office somewhere, Mr. Connolly?"

"Sure. Upstairs. Follow me." Tom headed up the staircase, and asked, "You a friend of Agnes Hamilton?"

"Who?" Mr. Bruech replied.

"Sorry. I thought you might know her. Who did you say your employer was?"

"I didn't actually. He prefers to remain anonymous for now."

"*He's* looking for a house then?" Tom asked as they reached his office door. "Please, make yourself comfortable."

Bruech perused the well-furnished office with at least as much interest as he'd shown downstairs. "Very cozy," he said. "You must do a pretty brisk business here."

"Actually, Taubolt attracts a lot more lookers than buyers," Tom replied, poised to begin his preemptive routine. "Lovely to look at, but hard to love when it comes right down to it."

"Really," Bruech said, eyebrows arched. "Rather isolated, I suppose."

"Yes. That's certainly part of the problem," Tom said, surprised at Bruech's apparent unconcern. "Your employer doesn't mind isolation, I take it?"

"Oh no. In fact, he's rather counting on it." Bruech smiled oddly. "He's a very successful investor interested in purchasing a rather large amount of land somewhere in this area. Real quantities of unspoiled terrain are hard to come by now, as I'm sure you know, and a few inquiries leave the impression that much of this area is unowned, or at least, fairly unattended to. Would you say that impression is valid?"

It was all Tom could do not to gape. In his whole life here, he'd never encountered anything like this. He hadn't thought it possible. He sat down, scrambling for some response that would not give away too much while he decided what to do.

"Well, I might be better able to answer your question if I knew what your employer is hoping to do with this property. There are some serious impediments to development here, you understand. Water is a real problem in this—"

"Oh, he has no interest in development, Mr. Connolly. The world has more than enough suburbs, doesn't it? No, what he wants to invest in might best be called wilderness, the less disturbed the better."

"For what purpose?" Tom asked, more bewildered by the moment.

"My employer is a great admirer of the outdoors, Mr. Connolly; of open space, and untouched forest. As I said before, a rare commodity nowadays." He smiled again.

"To be honest, Mr. Bruech, I'm used to selling little but the occasional lot or parcel, I'm afraid. How much land are we talking about?"

"How much land is available, Mr. Connolly?" Seeming to perceive Tom's dismay, he added, "Money is not the primary issue. He's a practical man, but he'll pay a fair price. So, how much land might be available, say, in that range east of town?"

"I'm sorry, Mr. Bruech, but I have to admit you've caught me off guard," Tom said, trying to cover his increasing panic. "I can do some research and get back to you, but today, I'm afraid I'm just not prepared to be of much help. And while I certainly don't want to seem rude, I am due at that other appointment any minute. Perhaps if you could contact me again in a week or two?"

"I'd be happy to. I appreciate your time, Mr. Connolly." Bruech stood and reached to shake hands again. "I look forward to talking with you soon."

"Certainly," Tom said, reeling as much from relief at having bought some time as at the enormity of what had just occurred. "I'll show you out." Dared he hope this brush-off might offend the man enough to put him off for good? He doubted it, but hoped so nonetheless, having no better plan at hand.

❧

"'Lancelot put his shoulder to the massive wooden door and heaved. Its iron hinges groaned, but the door remained fast. The clash of swords beyond told him that Gawain still lived, but he did not care to guess for how much longer, alone against so many. Recalling the warnings his reckless companion had chosen to ignore, Lancelot charged the door again, his strength fortified by anger.'"

"Good. Stop. You read really well, Hawk. Better than most."

"Never said I couldn't read," Hawk growled.

"Okay, so let's go over this last part," Joby said. "Since you know all the basic subject, verb, object stuff, we'll get right to the tricky parts. First sentence, 'his.'"

Hawk puffed his cheeks out, then said, "Adjective?"

Joby shook his head. "An adjective describes a noun."

"So?" Hawk protested. "'Shoulder' is a noun, isn't it? And 'his' describes the shoulder. Can't I just read it? I wanna know what happens!"

"You like the story, huh?"

Hawk narrowed his eyes, and shrugged noncommittally.

Joby shrugged as well, drew the book off the table, and slid it back into his pack. "Let's find a more interesting book then. Maybe something on animals."

"Okay, I like it!" Hawk exclaimed. "Geez! I never heard of an English teacher who wouldn't let you read."

"My point," Joby said, putting his *child's Treasury of Arthurian Tales* back on the table, "is that there'd be nothing to read if the author hadn't known how to write it. If you like this book, then writing matters to you too, whether you knew it or not." He gave Hawk a pointed look. "Learn to write well enough, and thousands of people could be lapping up *your* stories someday."

"*Me* . . . write a book," Hawk said sarcastically.

"Why not?" Joby replied. "Do you think this writer was never a boy who rolled his eyes when his teacher pressed him about sentence construction?" He looked down, pretending to read the *Treasury's* cover, and said, "'The Adventures of Hawk! Thrilling Tales of Taubolt'!"

Hawk tried to cover his amusement by groaning, "You're such a narning dopletin!"

"At least *I* have made an effort to learn *your* language." Joby smiled. "A month ago, I wouldn't have understood a word of that insult."

Just then, Swami stuck his head in the classroom door. "You still takin' us out tonight?" he asked Joby.

Joby looked at his watch. "Wow! I didn't realize we'd gone on so long. You need to call your mom, Hawk?"

"She won't care. I'm staying in town at Reed's house tonight."

"Okay. What time are we meeting tomorrow?"

"Ten o'clock?" Hawk said. "Cal's gonna drive us to my place." He shook his head in mock disgust. "I still can't believe you don't have a car."

"Sorry, dude." Joby shrugged. "I didn't know you lived so far from town. Get your stuff. I gotta lock up and go pay my debt to society." He turned to grin at Swami.

⚹

"Damn it, Kallaystra, we need eyes!" Lucifer spat. "Anything at all could be happening in there! Can't you move them in faster? Three months, and all you've secured is one dull letter to his parents, and a handful of postcards from an old crone who babbles of nothing but gardening. What good is that? Has she even met the boy?"

"Actually, we have *three* operatives inside," Kallaystra insisted with imprudent brittleness, "and more under recruitment, but the place repels many of those we send, and it's difficult to push people who've no idea they're working for us to begin with."

"Then perhaps you should be cultivating a far greater flock of candidates," Lucifer pressed irritably. "A mere handful of blackbirds isn't likely to drive out that Cup."

"I've wondered, Bright One," Kallaystra dared ask, "why we don't just continue to assault the place with storms and whatever other woes can be launched from outside. Might the boy not just leave the place once it became unlivable?"

"What!" Lucifer growled. "Batter blindly at what we can't even see? What if he were to die under a falling tree, or drown in storm surf? I'd just loose the wager. And do you suppose our Enemy is likely to hand us such favorable terms again?" He paced the room, frowning at the walls, then turned an accusing glare on Kallaystra. "I would never have authorized even that first storm, had it not been necessary to appease the rage of our troops after Malcephalon's unconscionable botch-up."

Necessary to appease the troops, she thought in disgust. Everyone in Hell knew for who that meteorological tantrum had been thrown to appease. "Consider my efforts redoubled, Bright One," she said with chilly calm, then left without waiting for dismissal.

✠

Joby and Swami arrived at the Heron's Bowl to find Cal and Cob sitting on the sidewalk beside a broad bed of flowers like a couple of garden pests, caps on backward, chewing gum, and acting tough. A few rude comments were exchanged as a matter of form before Cob waved Joby toward the restaurant's bright red door, saying, "Our table is reserved!" But as Swami opened the door for Joby, Cob intentionally squeezed in beside them, momentarily jamming everyone in the door frame, so that they stumbled through together in a small explosion.

"Cob!" scolded a short, scandalized-looking woman, her wry face framed in a wild halo of frizzy black curls.

"Sorry, Mom," said Cob, sounding anything but contrite. "Joby, this is my mom, Muriel. Mom this is Joby," he gestured grandly toward Joby, "the guy who hates our food! Hope our table's ready. I sure don't want him thinkin' the service sucks here too."

Joby felt himself blanch.

"Pleased to meet you, Joby," said Cob's mother, "I'm glad you're giving us a second try."

"Good to meet you too," Joby replied, silently cursing her son. "Whatever Cob's told you, I really haven't eaten out much, well, at all, really, since I came here—to Taubolt, I mean, not your restaurant—I mean, I've never been to your restaurant, but Cob made this joke about—" He turned to Cob, who was the very picture of malicious glee, and pleaded, "Tell her!"

By then, everyone was laughing, including Muriel. "Cob told me what happened," she assured Joby, "and, anyway, I know all about my son's evil tricks." She grinned as if it made her proud. "For being such a good sport, though, your dinner is on us tonight."

Despite Joby's polite protests, she insisted, and they were quickly seated at a simply but elegantly appointed table near the center of the restaurant.

Their meal was remarkable, and the price tag made it even tastier for Joby, who'd come braced to invest a reckless portion of his first month's pay in dinner for four. Given the company, it was hardly surprising that their food was seasoned with considerable merriment as well until, as they were finishing their entrées and thinking about desert, Jenna, their waitress, arrived smiling uncomfortably.

"Sorry guys," she whispered, "but some customers over there have asked that you keep it down." She smiled apologetically, gave them a "what can I do?" shrug, and left.

Cal looked around in irritated disbelief. Swami gazed at his plate humorlessly, toying with a forkful of fish.

"Well, that's too damn bad," Cob protested in a stage whisper too loud for comfort. "This is my mom's restaurant, and I'll have fun here if I want to! Who are these whiny richards anyway?"

Jenna hadn't said. But Joby spotted two self-consciously dignified older women studiously ignoring them. One was dreadfully thin, voluminous coils of shinning black hair piled on her head and thrust through with red lacquered chop sticks. She wore ostentatiously stylish clothes, and carefully applied, if rather excessive, makeup. The other woman's hair was white, and bobbed off just below her ears. She was rather heavyset, with thick glasses and a fixed expression of unfocused discontent.

The boys noticed them too, and when Jenna returned for their dessert orders, Cob asked if they'd been the ones to complain. Jenna nodded sheepishly, then cut off Cob as he began to describe, in grizzly detail, what he intended to go say to them.

"Don't you dare, Cob! The thin one's local, and a regular customer. Your mother would kill you, and probably me as well for not doing something to stop you."

"Local!" growled Cob. "Since when? I never saw her before in my life!"

"Last month," Jenna whispered. "Bought that big house on Stevens Street."

Later, as they ate their desserts in gloomy silence, Joby couldn't help recalling all the other politely disapproving killjoys he'd run into during his life, from grade-school teachers to those "respectable neighbors" who'd helped engineer Gypsy's death. By the time he finished cobbler, Joby had conceived of a plan for one small sliver of revenge to which, he imagined, no one could object. Hoping that just being publicly acknowledged as the complainers would make them uncomfortable, he got up and walked toward their table, preparing a very thorough apology.

"Excuse me," he told them, brightly, "but I felt I should apologize for upsetting you earlier."

He'd been right. Neither of them even wanted to look at him.

"It was rude of us to laugh so much over dinner," Joby said, "and I'm glad you sent the waitress over. To be honest, it was kind of a relief to eat dessert in silence. Kids get so noisy when they're happy, don't they?"

"Oh yes!" said the dumpy one, clearly taking him seriously.

The dark-haired wraith gave her friend a disapproving look, then turned to Joby and said, "We're fine now." She went back to her food then, as if Joby had left. But Joby didn't feel their grievance had been anything like sufficiently aired. That was the game ladies like this played, wasn't it; flawlessly mannered malice?

"That's very kind of you," he said, "but I really should have done something to clamp down on all that fun, myself. In fact, worrying about it has completely ruined my meal. I'd feel much better if you'd let me make it up to you by paying for your dinners."

"Well, aren't you a nice boy!" the dumpier woman exclaimed in surprise.

The wraith gave her companion another tired look, the turned to Joby, and said, "If you're really so contrite, young man, I'd rather you taught your rude acquaintances something of silence in public places; and to dress appropriately for dinner." She looked disdainfully across the room at them. "They may get away with such behavior in this permissive backwater, but someday they'll find themselves out in the *real* world, and discover that civilized people are not so tolerant." She looked down her nose at Joby. "One wonders where their parents are."

Serving you dinner, Joby thought angrily.

"We didn't move up here," the dragon lady added, "to be bombarded with loud noise and rough language every time we step outside."

She returned to her meal, dismissing him with scornful finality. But Joby was too offended to contain himself.

"Rest assured Ms. . . ." He waited for a name.

"Agnes Hamilton," answered the woman's clueless companion. "And I'm Franny Tyndale." She smiled, seemingly oblivious to any nuance of the real conversation here.

"Rest assured Ms. Hamilton," Joby continued, coldly, "that everyone who *grew up here* will be informed of your arrival, and told to remain silent in your presence."

When Hamilton made no reply, he left them to their meals, wishing them every kind of indigestion and a bone-dry well that summer.

✠

When she'd gotten Jake his tea, Clara Connolly sat down and stirred some honey into her own, wishing their discussion were so easily sweetened.

Tom spread his hands in dismay. "I'm completely flummoxed, Jake. First that Hamilton woman, and now this! What's happening to the border?"

Jake shook his head. "World's been changin', Tom. More people out there every day, crowdin' up against us on every side. You know Taubolt's little charms are mostly sleight of hand. Such tricks don't work so good when folks get up too close."

Tom stared bleakly into his cup.

"Come on," Jake smiled. "Didja really think this was never gonna happen? People were only bound to overlook a big empty hole in their crowded little box for just so long, no matter what we did."

"So what do we do about Bruech?" Tom sighed. "A few questionable new residents is one thing, but it sounds like this mystery investor wants to buy the whole place, lock, stock, and barrel."

"Just tell him the owners don't want to sell." Jake shrugged.

"Sure," Tom said, "but what if Bruech goes looking for himself and finds a few willing ognibs, like Weston. They're not gonna see the bigger picture."

"Comin' to Taubolt ain't the same as stayin', Tom. You know that well as I do."

Tom shook his head, unsatisfied. "I've said it before, Jake. I think it's unwise to leave so many of Taubolt's own residents in the dark. Once it's clear they belong here, ognibs ought to be told the whole truth, not just tossed red herrings and innuendos. If the border's failing, it seems more crucial than ever that we all pull together. If I'd been able to talk openly with Stan Weston, Hamilton and Tyndale wouldn't be here now."

"I feel the same frustration all the time, Tom," Clara said, "but you know it wouldn't work."

"Why not?" Tom insisted. "They live here, for heaven's sake! They're good people! Look at Crombie. He's an ognib, but we made him a guardian! Gladys Lindsay's not of the blood, but the Council meets at her inn! If they know, why not the others?"

"'Cause a lot of 'em just don't want to," Jake said gently. "I admire your attitude, Tom, but a lot of people here just couldn't handle it. Look at our kids. They play their little games practically in plain sight, for all we warn 'em not to. You think the ognib kids don't see what goes on? But mention it to 'em, and most just go blank or explain it away somehow. It's not their world, Tom, and frankly, it's not their problem either."

"Besides, dear," Clara added, "you know that sooner or later someone would find it all too interesting to keep to themselves."

Tom threw his hands up. "Maybe you're right, but it would sure make a lot of things easier. Hiding from the world is one thing. Hiding from our neighbors is another. . . . So what about Bruech, Jake?"

"People throwin' big money around usually think they're doin' you a huge favor," Jake mused. "If you don't act grateful enough, they'll teach you a lesson by takin' their business elsewhere." He smiled. "Just keep rushin' him off like that. Wait a couple days to return his calls. Have a lot of trouble locatin' the owners. Act like you're only givin' it half your attention, and maybe he'll just get mad and walk."

"Okay," Tom said. "But if this invasion's going to continue, I think it's time the Council met and came up with some more focused approach."

Jake leaned back thoughtfully. "You're prob'ly right. I'll talk to the others and arrange it with Gladys."

Tom looked relieved, and Clara was too. Better the whole Council deal with this than leave her husband holding the bag. Still, she was surprised at how unconcerned Jake seemed and couldn't help wondering if the ancient knew something he wasn't telling.

⚘

With subdued farewells all around, Joby left the Bobs outside the Heron's Bowl, and went to walk off his lingering anger at that obnoxious woman on

Taubolt's now-deserted wooden sidewalks. Soon he had abandoned the darkened shop fronts of Main Street to wander out across the bright, moon lit fields and walk along the cliff tops, listening to the surf below, like the soft, regular breathing of some enormous sleeping child.

Before long, he'd grown calm enough to face the fact that his clever little plan to embarrass that woman had been anything but clever. He had only spread her stain even further over their evening by embarrassing himself. The Bobs' bad influence no doubt, he thought with a wry smile. He'd have to be more careful in the future to act his age, not theirs, however infectious their age did seem at times. He was supposed to be *their* role model, after all.

Feeling relaxed enough to sleep now, Joby turned to head back to the inn, but just then some new sound joined the ocean's rush and sigh beyond the cliffs. Someone down on the beach was singing—quite loudly.

Joby went back to peer over the cliff edge and soon spotted a somewhat portly man standing on an outcrop of rock jutting well into the water. His arms were spread theatrically as he sang at the top of his lungs—something by Gilbert and Sullivan, Joby thought, perhaps a bit off key. Then Joby noticed small bobbing shapes in the moonlit water at the singer's feet. As a wave came in, several of them submerged suddenly, only to resurface elsewhere seconds later. Who would be swimming this long after dark? Joby wondered. Then, one of the swimming audience began to bark almost as musically as the singer, and Joby realized that the man was singing to seals! And the seals were listening!

Joby turned to scan the headlands behind him, wanting a witness to confirm what he saw, but the fields behind him were empty all the way to town. Joby looked back down at the vocalist and his astonishing audience. Suddenly shy of disturbing them, he shook his head and turned for home, wondering whether Mrs. Lindsay would think him crazy or merely dishonest when he told her what he'd seen.

⚜

Something there is that doesn't love a wall,
That sends the frozen-ground-swell under it,
And spills the upper boulders in the sun;
And makes gaps even two can pass abreast.

Joby lay in bed, reading the anthology Father Crombie had given him for Christmas, as he did most nights now. He'd come across something familiar by Frost, and was going over it for a second time, struggling against encroaching sleep and distracting thoughts of what he'd seen out on the headlands that night.

Mrs. Lindsay had been amused by his astonishment. "That's just Dash Borden," she'd laughed. "He's out there at all hours singing to those seals." Then, more soberly, "I think it helps him with the loneliness since his wife died."

"But, they were listening!" Joby had insisted. "Right there at his feet!"

"Seals are a curious lot," she'd assured him. "They'll come 'round to check on almost anything that happens in or near the water."

Joby shook the idea from his head again, and went back to reading.

> *Before I built a wall I'd ask to know*
> *What I was walling in or out,*
> *And to whom I was like to give offense.*
> *Something there is that doesn't love a wall,*
> *That wants it down! I could say 'elves' to him,*
> *But it's not elves exactly, and I'd rather*
> *He said it for himself. . . .*

Unable to hold sleep any longer at bay, Joby set the book aside, reached up to douse the light, and closed his eyes. But even as drifted at the edge of sleep, the poem's last few lines still danced behind his eyelids like moonlight on the surge that night:

> *He moves in darkness, as it seems to me,*
> *Not of woods only and the shade of trees.*
> *He will not go behind his father's saying,*
> *And he likes having thought of it so well*
> *He says again, 'Good fences make good neighbors.'*

18

(Measure's Tale)

Joby was waiting, bag lunch in hand, when Cal's junker truck roared around the corner and rumbled to a halt in front of Mrs. Lindsay's inn. Joby didn't know too much about cars, but the truck's bulbous lines suggested a fifties or sixties vintage, and its once-green, flaking paint, elaborately detailed in rust, backed that estimate.

"This thing street legal?" Joby quipped, climbing in beside Hawk.

"You trashin' my truck?" Cal shot back.

"Seems a little late for that," Joby drawled.

"Better'n yours, ain't it?"

He had a point. "You coming on the hike with us?" Joby asked.

"Nope. It's a Bobber day."

"Which means?"

"Which means," Hawk grinned, "the Bobs'll be fryin' up a couple scrawny minnows and a whole lotta crow for dinner again."

"Last I heard," Cal mused, "you two wanted a ride somewhere. But now I'm thinkin' maybe I don't have time this morning."

"You're the best fisherman in Taubolt history," Hawk amended. "Okay?"

Mollified, Cal gunned the engine and lurched into the street with hardly a glance backward for traffic, not that there was ever much traffic to look for in Taubolt.

Hawk lived up Avalon Ridge, ten miles south of town. Beyond tumbling roadside fences half-buried in herbs and blackberry, wide fields of tall dry grass rippled in the wind, punctuated by isolated stands of redwood, old barns, and weathered homesteads. Ravens swooped and dove in the breeze. Grazing horses looked up as they drove by.

It took twenty-five minutes to reach Hawk's house; a piecemeal, wood-shingled structure halfway up the ridge, decked out in wind chimes, abalone shells, and odd little stained-glass windows. Cal dumped them out, honked farewell, and rumbled away.

The long flight of wood slat stairs up to Hawk's front door swayed so badly under their combined weight that Joby feared it might collapse. But he kept his mouth shut, cautious of offending Hawk. Once inside, Hawk called for his mother, but got no answer.

The entrance hall was dimly illuminated by a red and blue stained-glass window beside the door. A spindly vine covered in tiny leaves cascaded from its macramé harness over an end table cluttered with mail. An oval rag rug of green and gray covered much of the hardwood floor. The walls were dark, unfinished wood, and the still air smelled like a dusty copse of trees.

"Guess she's workin'," Hawk said, leading Joby into a kitchen and breakfast bar connected by a short, wide flight of stairs to a large, sunken living room. The furnishings were worn, but things were immaculately neat, clean, and well lit by several skylights and a wall of glass on the living room's far side. Joby's attention was immediately drawn to a large painting hung over the couch, a spectacular landscape rendered in what looked like oil pastels; rich orange afternoon light and dark blue shadows draped a desert landscape beneath a vibrant blue sky dramatically washed in clouds. Its beautiful composition conveyed a sweeping sense of airy space. Not a print apparently, it was, without a doubt, the finest object in the room.

"What does your mom do?" Joby asked.

"Different things," Hawk said, pulling sandwich makings from the refrigerator. "Helps people with their records and bills sometimes, or does cleaning and stuff."

"Sounds like she works pretty hard," Joby said.

"Yup," Hawk said, crinkling his sandwich into a brown paper bag. He grabbed two small bottles of drinking water for himself and Joby from a shelf above the countertop, and said, "Okay. Let's go."

As they left, Hawk stopped to leave a note for his mom. Joby read over Hawk's shoulder as he wrote that he was out hiking with his English teacher and would be home for dinner. He paused, then added a reminder that his teacher would need a ride home.

"You did tell her about that before now, didn't you?" Joby asked.

"Sure." Hawk shrugged without meeting his eyes.

Joby could only hope it was true.

Minutes later, they were headed farther up the steep ridge along a narrow, overgrown dirt road. It was almost one o'clock before they stopped to eat their lunches on a wide, grassy hilltop. The morning's gentle breeze had died away. The smell of warming straw and wayside plants was pungent. Songbird and raven-call joined the *clack, clack, clack* of grasshoppers, and the lowing of distant cattle.

After lunch, as they continued up what had become only the ghost of a trail, they surprised a wild boar and stood very still as it trotted away, tail stuck up like a flagpole. When it had run some distance, it stopped to look back over its shoulder, then crashed into the underbrush and disappeared.

"They can be real mean," Hawk warned. "Gotta be careful when you see one."

"I've never seen a real boar," Joby said reverently. "You're so lucky to grow up in a place like this."

"I didn't," Hawk replied, resuming his progress ahead of Joby. "We moved here two years ago from Phoenix." He fell silent for a while, batting at the grass with his hands as they passed, then added sadly, "Wish I *had* grown up here, though."

"What made your folks come here?" Joby asked.

"It was my mom's idea. She wouldn't stop buggin' my dad."

"How'd she hear about a place like Taubolt clear down there in Arizona?"

"Some friend of hers told her about it a long time ago. I think she thought my dad would get better if she got him out of Phoenix, but he's a prick no matter where he lives." He took a particularly vicious whack at some weeds leaning into their path. "Guess she knows that now."

They hiked uphill in silence after that, through a dense thicket of stunted conifers in which their path nearly vanished. Then, all at once, the trees opened into an abandoned apple orchard full of gnarled old trees. It was surprisingly warm out in the light. Something buzzed, cicada-like, from the shrubs around them.

Hawk stopped abruptly and motioned for Joby to be quiet, pointing to the field's far side. At first, Joby saw nothing but tall grass. Then several dun colored shapes resolved into the backs of browsing deer, heads down, foraging in the tall straw.

Oddly, Hawk began to hum very quietly. Joby could barely make out the pretty if repetitive melody until Hawk began to hum a little louder, and first the doe, then her fawns, raised their heads to stare at him. As Hawk added soft, flowing nonsense sounds to his tune, the deer twitched their tails, but made no move to flee. Still singing, Hawk reached slowly into his pocket and pulled something out inside his fist, then began to take slow, casual steps forward, one or two at a time, until he was halfway to the deer. There he sat down very slowly, singing all the while, and stretched his hand out, revealing two sugar cubes.

Joby watched in fascination as minutes passed. Neither Hawk's arm nor his tune wavered. Finally, the doe took a hesitant step forward, then several more while Hawk sang on. Within reach of his hand, the animal stretched its neck to sniff the sugar, then nibbled it quickly from Hawk's palm. Only then did Hawk's tune fall silent, and his hand drop slowly into his lap. When the doe had finished eating, she and Hawk gazed at each other while Joby held his breath in pure amazement. All at once, to Joby's even greater wonder, the deer sang back to Hawk. It was just a few atonal trumpeting sounds, but Joby had never known deer made any sounds at all. When her brief song was done, the doe turned to nuzzle her fawns toward the orchard's far side and through the thicket.

Hawk watched them go without moving, while Joby watched Hawk in envious wonder. "How did you do that?" he asked at last.

Hawk turned to grin proudly at him. "They're suckers for sugar." He shrugged, as if that explained everything.

"What were you singing?"

"Just made it up," Hawk said. "Doesn't really matter what you sing, long as it's quiet, and you don't stop. No animal sounds like that when it's attacking, and if *you* believe they're not afraid of you, they can tell, and they're not afraid either. That's all."

"But it talked to you!" Joby said, still unable to believe it was all so simple.

"Deer can talk." Hawk smiled. "They just don't want to most of the time."

As they talked, one thought had drown all others in Joby's mind: *How could any man have left a boy like this?* "Where on earth did you learn all this?" Joby asked.

"All the kids around here know this stuff. But that's not the best thing. Come on! I'll show you something really neat! It's why I brought you."

"Something can top what I just saw?" Joby asked skeptically.

"Back there," Hawk said, pointing toward the orchard's far boundary of brush and trees, "there's a haunted house! It's been empty so long, no one re-members who lived there. The windows are all smashed out, and half the floors have fallen into the rooms below them." His voice grew quieter as they crossed the orchard, as if he thought someone might hear him. "I even heard people say there's a body stuffed in the chimney, but I don't think it's true. You can tell it's haunted though. It feels like something's watching you, or about to talk in the next room, even in the daytime. Nobody goes there at night."

Hawk's excitement was palpable as they pushed stealthily through the thicket toward his house of horrors. But as they broke from cover, he stopped abruptly, crouching down to hide, and frantically motioning Joby to do the same.

"What's wrong?" Joby whispered.

"Someone's there!" Hawk moaned quietly. "They've ruined it!"

Joby crawled forward, coming shoulder to shoulder with Hawk, and looked out between the branches at an attractive, freshly-painted, two-story, wooden house. The lush green lawn around it was neatly mown, and wind chimes tinkled on a porch that wrapped around two sides of the structure.

"Looks like they even pulled that body out of the chimney," Joby said, glancing up at the smoke drifting cheerfully from the chimney. "Too bad. But don't worry, this hike's been plenty—" He fell silent as a man walked into view from behind the house, carrying a garden spade. A man he recognized. With a smile, Joby got up and began to press through the remaining bushes.

"What are you doing?" Hawk whispered in alarm.

"It's okay," Joby said. "I know this guy." Then he called out, "Solomon?"

"Joby!" Solomon said, clearly startled, then, more calmly, "What an unexpected pleasure." The old man set down his spade and came to meet him.

Hawk followed Joby out of hiding and stood staring from one man to the other.

"Hawk," Joby said, "this is Solomon. Solomon, this is my friend, Hawk."

"Pleased to meet you, Hawk." Solomon grinned.

"How come I never saw you before?" Hawk asked cautiously.

"Like Joby, I'm new to Taubolt, I and tend to guard my privacy rather closely."

"I hope we're not intruding," Joby said. "We were out for a hike, and Hawk thought this was an abandoned house."

"No bother at all," Solomon assured them. "I'm delighted to have your company. Care to come inside? I have some lemonade in the kitchen if either of you is thirsty. Gotten rather warm all of a sudden, hasn't it?"

Joby looked to Hawk, who shrugged uncertainly. "Sure," Joby said. "Thanks."

"It's amazing you could fix it up like this," Hawk said suspiciously as they headed for Solomon's back porch. "I thought it was way too ruined."

"It was work," Solomon conceded. "And expensive. Almost irretrievable when I found it. Such a fine house should never have been allowed to go to ruin like that."

"Did you have to clean out the chimney?" Hawk asked.

"Oh yes." Solomon grinned. "Completely blocked, when I came."

"By what?" Hawk asked with poorly concealed urgency.

"Leaves," Solomon said. "Sticks and birds' nests. Even a beehive! Everything that collects in chimneys over the ages. Such a moldy mess. To be honest, there might have been anything decaying in all that muck. . . . Anything at all." He winked at Hawk, then grinned at Joby.

Solomon's back door opened into a kitchen, neatly tricked out in white enameled furnishings, a red-checkered tablecloth, lace curtains, and blue willow-pattern china plates hanging up near the ceiling. An old cast-iron stove seemed all there was for cooking, and a hand pump over the sink was the only fixture. Solomon looked on, amused, as Hawk went over to give it a few skeptical pumps. When it gurgled and coughed up its first small stream of clear water, Hawk stepped back and said, "Cool!"

From there, Solomon led them into what he called, "the parlor," warmly furnished in comfortable old chairs and a thickly upholstered Victorian couch. There was a large wooden rocker facing the fire, but what seized Joby's attention was an aged spinning wheel in front of the lace-curtained window.

"My grandfather had one of these!" Joby said, walking over to place a hand lightly on the wheel, resisting the impulse to spin it as he had in childhood.

"Did he?" Solomon asked quietly.

"Yes. It belonged to my gramma. She died before I was born. But Grampa kept it in their living room." He shook his head. "He died when I was five. But I remember, whenever we went to his house I'd stand there spinning and spinning it 'til my mother made me stop."

"A lovely thing," Solomon said sadly, "from a time when there was still room for beauty as well as function." He turned and headed back toward the kitchen, saying a bit roughly, "I'll get that lemonade."

He was back a moment later, carrying a tray with three tall glasses of lemonade garnished with sprigs of fresh mint. "The real thing—not concentrate," he announced, any trace of melancholy banished.

Hawk thanked Solomon, took an eager gulp, and smiled.

"What do you do, Solomon?" Joby asked. "For a living, I mean."

"I'm a storyteller of sorts." He handed a glass to Joby. "Retired now, or nearly so. I've come here to settle my affairs, and move on to the next chapter of my life."

"How do you make a living telling stories?" Hawk asked.

Solomon's brows rose in surprise. "You've never read a book or seen a film?"

"Oh!" Hawk replied. "You're a writer? Why didn't you just say that?"

"You make it sound so pedestrian," Solomon said with a playful scowl. "But I've told my tales in many ways, as actor, poet, musician, soldier, merchant, politician. There are more ways to tell a story than you'll have guessed, young Hawk, and since the world is always hungry for another, there is never lack of work for one who tells them well. I've been rich and poor, famous and obscure, but never unemployed." Solomon smiled and winked at Hawk.

"Sounds like a cool job," Hawk said. "Could you tell us one now?"

"Hmm," Solomon mused. "Well . . . I don't see why not. Let me think."

Hawk and Joby waited expectantly.

"Once, long ago," Solomon began, gazing intently at Hawk, "there came a dark and bitter winter that would not give way to spring. At the height of summer's lawful reign, trees that should have been green and heavy with fruit, cracked under burdens of ice instead and toppled in the cold. Families huddled fearfully around their dwindling fires, their houses buried in snow, and still the days grew shorter, until it seemed even the memory of light might be extinguished. In that dark world haunted by dread and gnawed by need, greedy men of viscious cunning and brute, ugly force wriggled up into the failing light like maggots out of rotting meat, to oppress and devour a people grown all but ignorant of goodness, courage, or love."

Solomon spoke in dark, musical rhythms that struggled to rise, and fell again, making palpable the hopeless weight of that doomed world's slow collapse.

"Into this hopeless winter, a child named Measure was born, in whose heart the seeds of summer's resurrection were hidden, though no one near him knew it, least of all himself. Only the imperiled winter sensed the truth, for even the smallest flame cannot go long unnoticed by the darkness around it. Thus, the brightness hidden in Measure's heart drew torments from the darkness as a rubbed cat draws sparks, and Measure was no little god to lightly shrug off such assaults. He was just a very human child."

As Solomon went on to unravel the tale of Measure's desperate struggle, the villainous winter transcended mere season to become a person, malevolent and cold. Such was the old man's skill, that Joby saw, and felt, and was, somehow, whatever Solomon described. No book or movie he'd ever known had drawn Joby in with such immediacy. He both longed to know how it would end, and wished it would go on forever, but after what seemed far too short a time, the tale wound toward completion.

"And so, after all his many adventures," Solomon intoned at last, "it seemed that all was lost. But Measure's years of captivity in that black and empty cell had left him stronger than he knew. The darkness trembled at his touch now, though Measure did not see it, and the silence drew away in fear, though Measure did not hear it flee. Left to sit, and stare, and listen, unheeded, some part of him had, itself, become so dark and still, that he no longer feared those jailers, but now made ghosts of them who had so long made one of him, and they feared that soon he'd come to know it. Very soon perhaps."

Solomon fell silent.

Joby and Hawk waited.

Solomon leaned back, lifted his lemonade, and took a sip. Then he stretched and smiled and said, "Well, this has been a real pleasure. I'm very glad you all stopped by."

"What?" Hawk protested. "What happens to Measure?"

"That is not for me to say. But when you know, I hope you'll tell me." Adopting his grave storyteller's voice again, he added, "For countless are we who long to know how Measure's tale ends."

"No! You can't stop there!" Hawk exclaimed. "That's cheap!"

"You're not really going to leave us hanging like that!" Joby laughed in disbelief.

"What kind of mother," Solomon answered, "murders her newborn child just to satisfy her curiosity about how its life will end?"

"What's that got to do with anything?" Hawk demanded angrily.

"A *true* story is a very *living* thing," Solomon said, "and mine still has its life ahead of it. If I told you what you want to know, it would die right here without accomplishing its purpose. I am not that kind of mother."

"I bet you don't even know the ending," Hawk said sullenly.

"I know many endings to this tale," Solomon assured him gravely. "I'd be a very poor storyteller if I did not. I certainly know how I'd want it to end."

"Then tell us!" Hawk pled. "I have to know!"

"How badly?" Solomon asked.

"*Real* bad!" Hawk assured him.

"Good." He smiled. "Then you'll find the answer."

Hawk gaped in outrage.

"I am sorry," Solomon shrugged, "bards aren't all they're cracked up to be, but I promise, Hawk," he said earnestly, "that next time I tell you a story, I will finish it completely. This one simply wasn't meant to work that way. I hope you will forgive me."

Hawk frowned at him, fingering his empty lemonade glass.

Solomon looked at the clock above his mantel. "In the meantime, it's gotten rather late, and I recall you said something about a long hike home?"

Hawk looked at his watch, and gasped, *"Oh crap!"* He leapt from his chair. "Mom'll kill me if I'm not back before dark!"

"Right after she has me arrested for kidnapping," Joby said, getting up as well.

"I've enjoyed the company," Solomon said. "I hope you'll both visit again."

"And I hope you'll come have dinner with me at Mrs. Lindsay's inn some night," Joby said. "If you'll give me your phone number, I'll call to set it up."

"I have no phone," Solomon replied. "Part of my quest for peace and quiet. But perhaps I'll stop by the inn next time I'm in town, and we can arrange it then."

Joby said that would work, finding it hard to imagine doing without a phone, as Hawk rushed out the kitchen door ahead of them. A moment later, having hastily thanked Solomon for his hospitality, they trotted back across his lawn and headed for the path.

"Okay," Hawk said when they had reached the far side of the old orchard. "We're gonna have to run, but it's downhill all the way, so there's a fun way we can do it. You ever tried running like a deer?"

"I have trouble running like a slug," Joby joked.

"I heard how you almost beat Jupiter up that hill," Hawk scoffed. "So cut it out. This is serious. Deer don't just run. They bounce. Like this." He took a few quick strides downhill, bounded into the air, and glided nearly six feet before springing up to do it again. Then he stopped, turned back to Joby, and called, "Now you try!"

"Looks like a good way to break my leg," Joby said.

"My mom'll break more than that if we're late," he said. "Like you said, she *might* think *you* should have got me back earlier." Joby wondered if all of Taubolt's kids were such natural extortionists. "Come on!" Hawk urged. "It's fun. Your feet hardly ever touch the ground, so there's almost no chance to trip, and it doesn't tire you out like running either! That's why the deer do it!"

The kid seemed to know an awful lot about deer, Joby thought, as he jogged downhill, then took a timid leap, and bounced immediately up into another in imitation of Hawk. Surprisingly, the boy was right. His downhill momentum was so strong that he had plenty of time in the air to plan his landing and his next jump. In fact, there was almost time between landings to rest his legs. Minutes later, they were leaping and sailing down the hill at a speed that would have frightened Joby if he'd stopped to think about it. But he didn't. They were having too much fun, whooping and laughing as they barged between the evergreen branches that sometimes crowded the road.

❈

Merlin waited until Joby and Hawk were well out of sight, then growled, "Don't just hover there, old friend. Come in and visit for a while." He turned without waiting for an answer. *Gardening,* he thought with chagrin. All his defenses undone by a moment of careless absorption in mulching roses! Then again, he'd never expected anyone, least of all Joby, to come waltzing all the way up here unannounced. The world was strange with luck these days. Upon reaching his parlor, he was unsurprised to find Michael there ahead of him, seated in casual glory on the couch.

"You've done a marvelous job with this place," the angel said amiably. "But 'old friends' don't usually hide from one another, Merlin. Or is it Solomon now?"

"Have you no old friends in Taubolt then, Michael? Or should I call you Jake?" He smiled grimly as Michael conceded the point. "You followed Joby here, I take it?"

"Hawk actually," Michael replied. "You gave him quite a scare at first, and I pay special attention to Taubolt's children. Your skills have grown mighty indeed, Merlin. I'd not have believed even you could hide all this right under my nose for . . . how long now?"

"December, more or less."

"I thought so," Michael sighed. "What on earth are you thinking, Merlin? Did you really believe the Creator could be deceived just by covering my eyes?"

"Deceiving *Him* was not my concern," Merlin sighed. "It was only your own disposition toward my purpose here that concerned me." He shrugged and smiled. "I apologize, if that will help."

"To me?" Michael chided. "It is not *my* will you defy here."

"You won't hinder me then?"

Michael looked mildly surprised. "For all you've been set apart, you are still a mortal man, and like all mortal men, free to chose your own path, Merlin, for good or ill. You know that as well as I."

"I feared you might have been commanded to enforce His will in this matter."

"I have had no such command," the angel assured him, looking troubled for the first time in their conversation. "In fact, I have been left without any word from Him at all since this matter started. His decree against interference was the last instruction I was given." The angel's gaze hardened some. "The same decree you surely received."

"Yes," Merlin said sadly. "Which I find I cannot obey."

The angel shook his head. "Then the boy has not *asked* for your help."

"Me?" Merlin laughed bitterly. "How could he? He thinks his grandfather long dead, and, if I read his boyhood journal rightly, even my real identity has been usurped by the enemy."

"If you still call him enemy," Michael replied. "Why are you defying our Lord?"

"What do you expect of me, Michael?" Merlin demanded angrily. "Are *fifteen hundred years* of loyalty to Heaven not sufficient proof of my intentions?"

"Longevity was not thrust upon you unwillingly, as I recall," the angel replied. "You accepted your mandate as a gift, and of him to whom much is given, much will be required. I know it is hard, but—"

"Oh, spare me your platitudes, Michael!" Merlin snapped. "What do you know of perishable love?" Merlin looked away, unable to endure the angel's sympathetic gaze. "I am as loyal to the Creator as ever I was. What I would give much to know is why *He* has left *me and my family* in this abysmal circumstance with no right way to proceed."

"Surely you are too much wiser than other men to seek refuge in such confusion," Michael quietly insisted. "Obedience is the right way to proceed. What mortal man knows this better than yourself? Truly, you astonish me."

"Obedience to what?" Merlin demanded hotly. "To love? Has that not been the foremost law of Heaven since ever there were laws? The Creator knows I love Him well, but I love my grandson too, and my daughter!" He could not keep his voice from shaking, or tears from welling in his eyes. "How, in Heaven's name, am I to choose between love and love, Michael? How can the Author of love itself, demand that of me?"

Looking, perhaps, contrite, Michael said nothing.

"It still torments me to recall how I failed Arthur, who was, in all but fact, a son to me," Merlin said more quietly. "I will not fail this boy who is my grandson in truth. If our Lord should damn me for it, then I will be damned."

"You cannot know what that means," Michael said softly.

"No, I only know what it would mean to betray my grandson."

"You do not mean to tell him about the wager, do you?" Michael warned. "That would mean default."

"Do you think me *that* rash?" Merlin said wearily.

"Your artful little tale came perilously close," the angel pressed.

"But close only," Merlin insisted.

The angel sat in silence for a time, searching Merlin's face, then said, "There is one thing that deeply puzzles me. If you so love your daughter and her son, why pretend to die, and leave them?"

"You do have a talent, angel, for knowing just where to rub the salt."

"I do not seek to hurt you," Michael said. "You know that's not my nature."

"Nonetheless, you do," said Merlin sadly. "My gift for premonition is a chancy thing, being, as it is, the bequest of my demonic father, but bitter experience has taught me to ignore it to my peril. Having divined some imminent calamity aimed at my daughter and her family, I could secure no clue as to its nature or what might be required to protect them when it came. To my endless grief and disgust, I foolishly determined that I might help them more effectively unhobbled by the parameters of my disguise as a frail old man. There seemed only one way to free myself from that disguise, though severing a hand—both hands—would not have caused me so much pain. I told myself that I was doing it for them.

"Then the nameless crisis finally came and, with it, a command from no one less than Him we serve that I must not help the ones I loved at all!" Merlin looked back into the angel's eyes unsure whether to beseech or rage. "Do you begin to see what this ordeal has cost me, angel? How I am paid for all the centuries of faithful service I have rendered? Tell me again how obvious and simple such a choice as mine should be!"

Merlin's angry gaze wandered from the angel's face to Abigail's spinning wheel, and all his anger drained away like water into sand. Suddenly unspeakably weary, he simply bowed his head, half-glad that his beloved wife was not alive to see what had come of his one unguarded concession to love after so many ages alone.

"The Creator's blessings on you, friend," Michael said softly, rising to go. "Take care, and choose wisely. I wish this reunion had been a happier one. . . . And—" He fell abruptly silent, looking more troubled than Merlin had imagined one of his kind could.

"And what?" Merlin asked, wondering fearfully what could bring such distress to the face of an angel.

"Nothing," Michael murmured, turning away. "An unworthy thought." He looked back at Merlin, tried to smile, and failed, alarming Merlin more. Then he was gone.

⚬

It was twilight when they finally arrived at Hawk's house, winded but exuberant.

"Wow!" Joby gasped as they stood before Hawk's house recovering. "That's the funnest thing I've done since I was twelve, I think!"

"You did great," said Hawk. "This was a great day! You should have dinner with us before my mom drives you back."

"If that's okay with her," Joby said. "Just . . . let me catch my breath here first."

"Hey you two." Hawk's mother stood at the top of the stairs, silhouetted in the lighted doorway. "I was starting to wonder if you were coming back. Anybody hungry?"

To Joby's relief, she didn't sound upset. He couldn't make out much of her appearance in the growing gloom, but her voice seemed strangely familiar.

"Depends," Hawk called nonchalantly. "What ya got?" Joby caught the hint of a sly grin on his face in the low light.

"Lasagna, candied carrots, and shrimp salad," she said dryly. "That good enough, your majesty?"

"Got potential," Hawk teased. "Can my teacher stay too?"

"If you'd quit teasing me and get up here, Arthur. I still have to drive him home afterward, remember?"

"Arthur?" Joby said.

"It's my name," Hawk lamented, starting for the stairs. "Everybody calls me Hawk but her."

Mounting the jiggly flight of stairs in darkness was even scarier than it had been by daylight, and all Joby's attention went to keeping his footing until they'd arrived safely at the top. Then, he looked up, and saw Hawk's mother, who had stepped back into the lighted hallway to make room for them.

It took a second for the features to register, another to surmount his disbelief. Then, all Joby could do was stare.

"My God," she whispered.

"What?" Hawk said, looking from one of them to the other.

"Laura?" Joby said, still frozen where he stood.

"Joby?" Laura gasped. "How . . . What are you doing here?"

"You know each other?" Hawk asked.

"I live here, Laura," Joby said, hardly trusting his voice. "In Taubolt."

"You're Arthur's English teacher?" She sounded stunned, frightened, angry, many things at once, but happy was not among them.

"You're Hawk's mother," Joby said in tenacious disbelief.

"Yes," she said hotly. "I'm his mother."

"What's going on?" Hawk demanded. "Why are you guys acting like this?"

The question broke Joby's trance, and Laura's too, it seemed. She raised a hand to massage her forehead.

"Believe it or not, Hawk," Joby said, "your mom and I grew up together."

"What?" Hawk exclaimed. *"Where?"*

"Long, long ago, and far, far away," Laura said, letting her hand drop, and smiling wanly. "Why don't you come in, Joby, while some of the bugs are still outside."

"I'm sorry." He stepped in, and she closed the door. "I just can't believe it's you."

"Tell me about it," Laura laughed, starting to recover. Her hair was longer than he'd ever seen it, and there were lines in her face that hadn't been there before. It had been fourteen years, after all. But she was as lovely as he remembered. More so. "If I'd known you were coming, I'd have baked a cake," she quipped. "You do have time to stay for dinner, I hope?"

"Of course," Joby said, beginning to regain his balance. "My God! It's so great to see you!" he said, and thought, *What kind of asshole leaves a woman like Laura?*

"Wait a minute!" Hawk half-yelled. "You guys *grew up together?*"

"If you'd told me your English teacher was named Joby Peterson," Laura smiled archly at her son, "I'd have said so sooner."

"This is . . . *too weird!*" Hawk said.

"I'd like to eat dinner before it's all gone cold, Arthur," Laura said. "Go wash up, okay?" When he'd gone, staring back at them until he was out of sight, she turned to Joby, and said, "It is good to see you again, Joby, if a little amazing. But, since you're sort of the one who brought me here, I guess maybe I shouldn't be so surprised."

"I brought you?" Joby asked. "How?"

"You don't remember how stuck on this place you used to be?" She shook her head and smirked. "You almost never stopped talking about it when we were kids. Made it sound like the Garden of Eden, so I finally came to see for myself."

"You remember that?" Joby said, bemused.

"I remember everything." Joby's smile faltered. "You and Ben went off without me on your little birthday trip." Her grinned whimsically. "You never even noticed how ticked off I was, did you?" She turned to head for the kitchen, and huffed, *"Boys."*

❧

In truth, Merlin was relieved he'd been discovered. It had been a great nuisance, having to keep himself and his house shielded night and day from the angel's awareness. Knowing that Michael would not oppose him made everything easier.

He stepped onto the inn's porch, let the knocker fall several times, and waited until the door was answered.

"Mrs. Lindsay?"

"Yes?"

"My name is Solomon. Joby invited me to stop by sometime, and though I realize it's rather late, I happened to be passing and thought I'd see if he was here."

"I'm sorry. He's not," she said, looking startled. "But I've been expecting him. Won't you come in? He really should be back at any minute."

"That's very kind of you." Merlin stepped inside, and followed Mrs. Lindsay to her parlor. "Have you many guests at present?"

She shook her head. "It's the slowest time of year, Mr. . . . ?"

"Rand," Merlin said. "But I prefer just Solomon."

"Well, I'm very pleased to meet you, Solomon, and I hope you'll call me Gladys. Can I get you anything? A drink?"

"No, thank you. I'm quite content."

"You must be new to Taubolt?"

"Yes, actually. I arrived shortly before Christmas."

"Ah," Mrs. Lindsay said uncertainly. "I hadn't heard. Where are you living?"

"Quite a ways from town, actually. Up on Avalon Ridge. The place was in considerable disrepair. Restoring it has been a great deal of work; one reason I've been so scarce."

"I'm fairly familiar with the Ridge," Mrs. Lindsay frowned, "and I can't think what place you mean."

"It's quite isolated." He shrugged. "I doubt you'd know it. An abandoned fixer-upper near the top of the hill."

Mrs. Lindsay's eyes widened. "Not the old Emerson place!"

"Why . . . yes. I believe so." Solomon smiled to cover his surprise. "You have quite a knowledge of the past, I see."

"But that place is such a wreck!" she said. "I'd have thought it long past saving."

"So it seemed," he conceded. "But I assure you, it's quite lovely now."

Confusion warred with suspicion on Mrs. Lindsay's face, while Merlin quickly revised his strategy. He knew very well that Mrs. Lindsay was more aware of Taubolt's deeper secrets than most in town, and he decided that this turn of events might actually advance his plans some.

"Well, you're to be congratulated," she said skeptically. "That must have been a huge undertaking. I'm even more amazed that you could have accomplished such a project without everyone here knowing. Who did all that work for you?"

Merlin grinned sheepishly, allowing himself to look caught out. "Gladys, I am led to believe that you are acquainted with those in Taubolt who are 'of the blood.'"

Mrs. Lindsay grew very still.

"Please, don't be alarmed," Merlin urged. "I am one of these myself, returning to Taubolt after a very long absence. You are welcome to check my references with Jake." He suppressed a smile, imagining how Michael might answer that inquiry.

Visibly relieved, Mrs. Lindsay asked, "How long have you known Jake?"

"Oh, we go back a *very long* way, if you take my meaning."

"You're an ancient, then?" she said, eyes gone wide.

"Yes. I am. Now I'm sure you see how I was able to restore the house, and perhaps why I've been somewhat shy of company while learning how things have changed here since my departure."

"Well . . . this is marvelous!" Mrs. Lindsay said. "I've often wondered if Jake wasn't the only one left. Everyone will be so excited . . . that is, if it's all right to tell them," she added quickly.

"Oh, you're welcome to tell those who've any business knowing," he said. "Your discretion in these matters is well known to me, and Jake will doubtless have told many of them soon, in any case. Joby, however, must know nothing."

"Of course. I meant only the Council, really. Isn't he a wonderful boy, though?"

"As fine as any I've met," Merlin concurred. "You've been very kind to him."

"He's been a blessing to me," she said, then looked up at the mantel clock in concern. "I don't know where he is though. He should have been back hours ago."

"He came by my place with a young friend this afternoon," Solomon said. "They'd made a very long hike. Perhaps it took more time to get back than expected. Or perhaps they went somewhere afterward."

✳

"I can't believe you're as old as my mom," Hawk announced when they'd been eating for a while.

"He's a charmer." Joby grinned awkwardly at Laura.

"It's true, though," Laura said. "You've hardly changed."

"Neither have you," Joby answered, reaching for more carrots.

"So did you guys ever date each other?" Hawk asked.

Joby concentrated intently on acquiring another slice of lasagna.

"Yes, Arthur. We did," Laura said, a tight smile brushing her lips.

"I knew it!" Hawk enthused. "That's so cool! I wish you'd married *him*."

Joby felt his stomach tighten, as Laura's smile vanished. "But then you wouldn't be here, Hawk," he said levelly. "This is all really delicious, Laura."

"I might be," Hawk replied. "I'd just be someone else."

"I don't want someone else," Laura said, reaching out to brush Hawk's hair back with her hand.

Hawk leaned away to stop her, but smiled nonetheless.

When they'd all finished their ice cream, Laura sent Hawk off, under protest, to do his schoolwork. Then, over her objections, Joby insisted on helping her clean up.

"You're driving me to town," he said. "It's the least I can do."

"I owe you more than a drive to town, I think," she replied.

"For what?"

"Taking such an interest in Arthur. I hear he's even going to school lately." She gave Joby a frank smile.

"He doesn't think you know."

"Of course I knew." She shook her head. "Things have been rough around here. I've had to deal with one thing at a time, that's all. I'd have gotten to Arthur's trouble at school soon, but this is a much better way. I really do appreciate it."

"Well, it's no charitable sacrifice or anything," Joby said. "Hawk's a lot of fun."

"I know," she smiled, "but it's nice to know I'm not the only one who sees that."

"You're not," Joby assured her. "He's got lots of friends."

"I know that too, but he needs a man to talk to, someone he knows can see what he is, what he's becoming. . . . Children need witnesses to make them real, I think, and with boys, I guess it's got to be a man."

Joby remembered the look Hawk had given him after charming the deer, and knew that she was right. Laura was a wise woman. The thought that some idiot had left either her, or Hawk, roused his anger once again.

"What's that look?" Laura asked, setting down the cup she was drying. When Joby didn't answer, she said, "You can tell me. There isn't much around here that's not already broken." She gave him a smile that clearly had nothing to do with funny.

"I don't see how he could leave either of you," Joby said. "I don't know how I'd live with myself if I'd left a boy like Hawk." He was dismayed at the look of pain that swept her features. "It's none of my business, of course."

"No, it is," she said. "If you're going to be Arthur's friend. . . . I don't know how much he's told you."

"Only that his father was . . . not too supportive," Joby said. "Of either of you. . . . Hawk's pretty angry."

"He's got good reason," she said, dried her hands, and went into the living room to settle on the couch.

Joby took a chair across from her.

"I did love Sandy," she began without preamble, "He loved me too, in the beginning, just the way I was, with all my flaws." She paused reflectively. "I really needed that." She looked down at her hands, and shrugged softly. "I didn't think to wonder if he loved himself as well as he loved me." She stared out the window at the darkness. "I could see it some even then, the way he talked about himself, as if he weren't worthy of . . . of anything. But I was young and . . . I thought . . . I probably loved the idea of helping him; of being there to bandage his little wounds." She laughed, softly, derisively, at herself.

It had been impossible not to think of their past together, but Joby had managed, until now, to keep it all fairly out of focus. Now, there was no way not to wonder how different her life might have been if he'd had the courage to . . . to . . . "Are you sure you want—" he began. "I didn't mean to open old wounds."

"Too late," she said gently. "They were all wide open before you got here. It's nice to have someone who'll listen, really. Someone who . . . who knew me."

He saw the tears in her eyes and was silent for fear of what any sound or gesture might do to either of them.

She took a few deep breaths and went on. "By the time Arthur was eight, Sandy was miserable all the time. He wouldn't talk about it, but he couldn't just leave it there in plain sight unexplained, so he began to invent reasons. First it was the world in general; the government, the media, all the assholes at the top. Then it was his job. Then it was Phoenix; the smog, the traffic, the crowds, the house we lived in. Finally, Arthur and I became the cause of all his misery, every little thing we did or didn't do. He knew he was wrong, but he couldn't seem to help himself. He'd always liked to drink, but it hadn't been a problem before that. One night, he was very sloshed, and he got angry at Arthur for something—I don't even remember what—but he hit him, way too hard. I told him then to get help or we'd leave.

"For a while after that he tried. He really did. I wanted it to work, for all of us, Joby. I don't know if that just sounds stupid now, but I thought there had to be a way. When things started to slip again, I thought maybe, if we left everything behind, everything that kept reflecting who we'd been, and what had happened, maybe he'd be able to leave it all behind too. That's when I remembered the things you always said about this place. I thought it would be perfect, so I convinced Sandy to try it.

"It was so beautiful here. You were right about that, Joby. And for a while things really did seem better. But . . ." She looked away and gave her head a quick, frustrated shake. "You never leave yourself behind. I knew that." She shrugged it off. "He started drinking again. Just a little at first, then more. Pretty soon, he was taking it out on us again. Physically. I told him then that he could have his anger and his beer, or he could have us, but not both." She gave a helpless gesture. "You know what he chose."

"When did he leave?" Joby asked.

"A little over a year ago. . . . Took nothing but the car. Didn't even say good-bye."

"Have you heard from him?"

She shook her head. "I've finally decided he isn't coming back, but it's been hard not really knowing."

Joby sat and stared, struggling for some way to fill the silence without sounding utterly inane. Taking pity on him perhaps, Laura smiled and said, "You're a very good listener, Joby. You always were. And I know this wasn't easy listening. Thank you."

Joby's eyes were drawn again to the pastel landscape above her head.

She saw him looking and smiled. "Do you like it?"

"Very much," he said. "That's the original?"

She nodded, looking pleased.

"Must have cost a pretty penny."

She laughed and shook her head. "The artist gets a discount."

It took him a second to get it, then he gaped and said, "You did that?"

She nodded with the first truly happy smile since their conversation had started.

"It's spectacular!" Joby exclaimed. "You should be rich!"

"I used to show in a few galleries down south." She shrugged. "Did all right, but I haven't done much work since we left Arizona."

"Well, when you start again, put me on your mailing list. I'm sure I can't afford you, but I'd love to come gawk at your openings."

Hawk appeared in the doorway that led to the rest of the house then.

"Hey, Joby! I got this computer game called Smart Bomb. Awesome graphics! You wanna play?"

"Is your homework done?" Laura asked.

"Yeeees," he sighed with a pained expression.

Joby doubted it, but Laura didn't seem inclined to push.

"I'm not very good at computer games," Joby told him.

"You can watch *me* play," Hawk said.

"Okay." Joby gave Laura a knowing smile as Hawk went back toward his room.

As Joby started toward the doorway, Laura said, "I'm glad you're here, Joby. I . . . I've thought about you lots."

"I've thought about you too." Joby smiled. "Lots."

19

(The Emerald Time)

Not withstanding the hundred-year storm that Christmas, it had been a mild winter, even by Taubolt's standards, so no one was startled when spring came early, pouring into the air and earth like a sweet tonic of laughter and light. By mid-April, bare branches had vanished behind canopies of lime-colored leaves, and the emerald winter fields burst forth in brilliant flowers. Swallows returned to Taubolt's eves, quail chicks tumbled through the grass behind their parents like little fur balls, and deer wandered boldly through yards in broad daylight with their fawns. The relentless north breezes, that always accompanied spring there, blew flurries of white and pink petals through the blossoming apple orchards up on the ridge and back in the valleys.

For Hawk, however, spring's return was shadowed by a confusing tide of improved prospects and suppressed anxiety. There was his growing friendship with Joby, in which he was afraid to trust too deeply; his noticeable improvement at school, of which he was afraid to feel too proud; the increasingly frequent visits between Joby and his mother, in which he dared not place too much hope; and his deepening desire for Rose's affection, which still seemed too unrealistic to pursue. He was swimming in good fortune, but felt disappointment circling in the murky depths beneath his dangling legs.

Restlessness had sent him out hiking that morning, up into the hills with no particular destination in mind, at least none that he was conscious of until he stepped out into the abandoned apple orchard and realized he'd come to Solomon's house.

Hawk found himself sneaking through the orchard hedge, as if he might find the house reverted to the half-collapsed ruin it had been before. But, there it all was; the neat green lawn and border gardens, new paint, clean windows, wind chimes, and a cheerful stream of smoke rising from the chimney. If anything, it seemed eerily unchanged from his last visit.

He walked hesitantly to the back porch, and knocked softly on the screen door. When no one answered, he moved to go, then heard the inner door scrap open behind him, and turned back to find Solomon smiling in the doorway.

"Hello, Hawk! Sorry it took me so long. I was upstairs."

"Oh," Hawk said.

"Lovely day, isn't it? Out for another hike?"

Hawk nodded.

"Care to come in?"

"Okay." When they were inside and seated by the fire, Hawk said, "I heard you been comin' around town more."

Solomon nodded. "I'm more inclined to socialize now that my house is finally in order, and the weather's gotten so nice."

"Mrs. Lindsay sure likes you," Hawk said. "She's always tellin' Joby how charming you are."

"I'm happy to hear I've made a good impression." Solomon grinned. "She's quite a good cook. I would not wish to be unwelcome at her table."

Hawk ran out of small talk then and sat awkwardly, unable to find words for what he really wanted to say.

When the silence had begun to stretch, Solomon smiled and said, "Come up with any ideas yet about the end of Measure's story?"

Hawk shook his head. "I wish you'd just tell me."

"You'll never learn to be a storyteller that way," Solomon chided.

"You sound like Joby," Hawk huffed. "He's always sayin' I'll never write a book if I can't spell this, or learn that."

"Would you like to be a writer?" Solomon asked.

Hawk looked askance at Solomon. "You and Joby workin' together?"

"Believe it or not, Hawk, you made quite an impression on me the day we met. I watched you listening to my story and saw something in your eyes I know quite well."

"What?"

"A true love of stories. Not just the usual thirst for entertainment, but the kind of profound hunger that burns in the heart of a true storyteller." He leaned forward and said, "I'm asking very seriously. Would you like to learn to be a storyteller?"

"What? Like you?"

"Like me."

"I don't even know what you do, exactly."

"That's what I would teach you."

"Teach me?" Hawk asked. "To tell stories like yours?"

"Not just to tell them, Hawk—to *make* them."

"I . . . I don't know if I could."

Solomon leaned forward intently. "Do you wish to?"

Hawk felt strangely afraid of accepting Solomon's offer—and of letting it pass.

Solomon had been watching him keenly. Now he leaned back, looking thoughtful. "In fact, you impressed me so much the other day, I've written a story with you in mind."

"A story about me?" Hawk asked incredulously.

"Inspired by you," Solomon replied, "which may or may not amount to the same thing. You'd have to be the judge of that. Would you like to hear it?"

Hawk nodded, dying to know what kind of story it could be.

To his surprise, Solomon did not get up and go looking for the text, but simply leaned forward and began to recite from memory:

"Gold of feather!
Fierce of eye!
Defiance in its hunter's cry!
Clipped, its wings.
Baroque, its cage.
Deep, its grief and old, its rage.
Its master won it on a bet when it was just a fledgling chick. Thinking he'd acquired a pet, he clipped its wings and hung a stick for it to perch upon before his fawning friends and guests, and dream of aeries high and wild, swept clean of noisy pests.

Long it sat, and regal grew, and longed to soar but never flew. What kind of man acquires a hawk, to clip its wings so guests can gawk?

'Magnificent!,' the tired refrain of flatterers who stopped to gaze, but couldn't see the cold disdain with which the hawk returned their praise, nor notice how its talons clenched and gouged its polished perch, or feel their empty hearts laid bare by eyes God made to search.

But, oh, its master, he could tell. He saw the hawk's pain all too well. And soon he found he couldn't bear to meet the raptor's regal stare.

'Damn!' the angry man would cry, 'I wish to God I'd set it free! But now I dare not let it fly, for surely it would turn on me and have revenge for all the years I've kept it prisoner here. Why, I could never leave my house, and not look up in fear!

'There you sit, and there must stay. My mistake, but you must pay. I fear you've grown too fierce to free. But then, you'll live in luxury. I'll guarantee you that at least. Come now! What other bird of prey need only sit and preen and feast?'

The hawk's cold gaze said, 'Go away.'

And deep inside its master's gut, the grubs of conscience gnawed, and whispered that he'd ruined a creature made to fly by God.

In time the man would not go near the golden bird he'd once held dear. He didn't want it spoken of, this thing he owned but couldn't love. He bade his servants see that it got every kind of dainty fare in hopes it would accept its lot, and cease that cold accusing stare that fixed him now from in his mind, and haunted him in dreams, in which he fled in vain to hide from angry raptor screams.

But though he never saw the bird, it chaffed him raw to know that somewhere 'neath his roof, those eyes still glared their chill reproof, until, at last, a desperate man, knowing there would never be escape in any other plan, he told his servants, 'Set it free.' It had been a year and more since he had had it clipped, as no one would go near it now for fear of being ripped.

So, fearfully, they went to do the dreadful task, as ordered to, afraid that they themselves would be the ones it raked as it went free. But some while later back they came to say the cage was open wide, but that it seemed the bird was tame, for it just sat there, still inside. And none of them, for all they tried, could get the bird to leave. It didn't seem to comprehend the concept of 'reprieve.'

So! *he thought.* We set it free, but here *is where it* wants *to be. I've been driven mad with guilt while it's* enjoyed the nest I built!

And suddenly, where guilt had burned, leapt flames of angry fire, which quickly turned remorse and shame to proud and spiteful ire. And off he stormed to where the cage sat open near the sill, forgetting how he once had feared the bird he went to kill.

Through the door, in righteous rage, the 'master' burst, to find the cage open. And the hawk inside, with one shrill cry and wings spread wide, flew forth with talons raised to rake the man who now cringed down in fear, and saw too late his great mistake. The hawk had waited for him here.

But though he lay there now, defenseless, no attack occurred. Though it could have savaged him, the mighty hawk demurred.

And when at last the 'master' dared to look and see why he had fared so

well against the hawk's attack, he flinched to find it looking back from
where it perched upon the sill, eyeing him with such disdain, that just the
memory, even still, inflicts a wound of greater pain than any that its beak
or talons might have tried to tear—a wound from which the man still finds
no refuge anywhere.

Blazing, its eyes!

'Coward,' they said. 'An earthbound bug that's better dead.'

And then, with one defiant cry, the golden bird was in the sky.

'Watch me sail the endless blue!" screeched the soaring hawk on high. 'I
have sat the perch like you, but you will never learn to fly! I'd not stoop to
tear the flesh of one who clipped my wings for fear!'

'And then its 'master' wept for shame, and watched the proud hawk dis-
appear."

Solomon leaned back at last in silence.

Hawk sat amazed, still burning with the bird's longing for freedom, still
filled with its final, triumphant cry, wishing he too could fly free of every
cage, every captor. "Am I the hawk?" he asked timidly.

"I've heard it said that in dreams, all the characters are you," Solomon
replied. "Poems have much in common with dreams, I think."

"It all rhymed!" Hawk said, realizing that it had, in fact, been a poem.
"How did you . . . I wish . . ."

"What do you wish?" Solomon pressed softly.

"I wish I could make something like that."

Solomon smiled. "Then let me try to teach you." He got up and left the
room, but returned a moment later with a small roll of paper tied in ribbon,
which he handed to Hawk. "Here's a copy of your own. Take it home. Read
it, and think about what you'd like to do."

Hawk took the poem with a kind of reverence. "Can I show it to Joby?"

"By all means. I hope you will, in fact." Solomon's smile gave way to a
sober expression. "I know you've been disappointed all too often, Hawk, but
there comes a time to see the open cage and risk letting go of one's long
captivity. If I'm not mistaken, you'll know what I mean."

Hawk did know what he meant and so much wanted what Solomon
seemed to promise that he could hardly face the fear it caused him. And in
that moment, he saw that his fear of Joby, of success at school, of Rose, were
all the same fear. Somehow, as if by magic, Solomon had answered the question Hawk had not known how to ask!

✻

"So what do you think of him?" Mrs. Lindsay asked.

"Oh, Solomon's the real item all right," Tom replied. "It's odd Jake didn't mention him sooner, though, don't you think?"

"I think Solomon wanted some time to get his bearings." Mrs. Lindsay smiled. "And Jake doesn't say much unless there's reason to."

"Isn't that the truth. He's more tightlipped than ever lately. Have you noticed?"

She nodded. "It's a bit unnerving, with everything that's happening." She looked around as if to make sure they were unheard. "You know this spring I've had all kinds of guests who'd clearly planned to come here. It's as if the border has vanished altogether."

"I'd say it has." Tom frowned. "How else do you account for people like that Ferristaff fellow up on Turtle Pond? He's building a damn palace up there, and he's cut and milled almost every tree on that property to do it. Not exactly what I'd envisioned when his point man talked about *love of wilderness.*"

"I know. . . . I've heard the children are pretty angry."

"I can't blame them. There was a really ancient grove on Latham's back acreage, and that jackass cut it too." He shook his head and grimaced. "I told Jake this would happen. A few ognibs willing to sell, and now Ferristaff wants to buy the whole damn range. Fortunately, what he did to Latham's place and that crew of thugs he's brought in to do construction have made him pretty unpopular around here. I think he'll find a lot fewer sellers now."

✻

As they hiked farther into the woods, Hawk continued to talk enthusiastically about his "lessons" with Solomon. In the past few weeks, the boy had opened like a flower in the sun.

"So we made up this place called Ymril," Hawk went on, "where these people live called the Bannisklan. I got the idea from this other story Solomon told me about these people called the Sidhe in Ireland. Anyhow, the Bannisklan live in pools of—"

Hawk's narrative was cut short by the screeching tirade of a bluejay somewhere just off the path. Hawk stopped and looked toward the sound in surprise, just as Jupiter came crashing out of the foliage ahead of them.

"Some dogs got Nacho!" Jupiter gasped. "He's hurt bad! They got Rose and Tholomey cornered too! Come on!"

Jupiter ran back into the woods with Hawk and Joby close behind. Joby could hardly believe the speed and agility with which the boys surged through the forest ahead of him, dodging and leaping obstacles like a pair of hunting hounds. He had lost sight of Jupiter completely, and begun to worry he'd lose Hawk as well, when he heard savage barking ahead, and a girl's frightened scream. A wave of renewed alarm brought forth an extra burst of speed, so that Joby burst into the clearing just behind Hawk.

Jupiter was nowhere to be seen, but Joby had no time to wonder where he'd gone. Ahead of them, backed into a narrow cove between several high stacks of cut timber, Rose and Tholomey were pinned in place by two Dobermans growling and barking viciously as they strained at their long cable chains. An angry raven dove at the enraged dogs' heads and tails, causing them to spin and snap their teeth in fury. As Joby watched, a blue jay joined the raven's assault.

Not until Tholomey dodged to one side, did Joby see Nacho lying on the ground behind them, eyes closed, white as a sheet, dark blood stains drenching the denim around his torn pant leg and seeping through his ragged shirtsleeve near the wrist.

Hawk had begun to yell and throw rocks at the dogs to distract them. But the sight of Nacho's savaged limbs sent a shock wave of panic and anger through Joby's body, and in what he would later call a blind rage, he grabbed a large branch, and waded toward the dogs, swinging fiercely. Though close to five feet long, the branch seemed surprisingly light and immediately connected solidly with one of the dogs, causing it to keen as it flew several feet to land limply on its side. The other dog turned and sprung at Joby but the branch was there between them. The dog fell back and hunched to jump again, but Joby brought the branch down hard, grazing the dog enough to scare it off momentarily.

"Run!" Joby yelled to Rose and Tholomey.

Instead of fleeing, they dropped their sticks and grabbed Nacho's arms, assisted by Hawk, who rushed in to help them drag him toward the clearing's edge.

Meanwhile, the remaining dog charged back toward Joby at a gallop, ears back, teeth bared, silent with fury. Joby tried to ward it off again, but missed as the dog leapt and hit him in the chest with such force that he staggered back and fell. Joby flung his arms across his neck and face, expecting teeth to close somewhere on his upper body, but instead there was another whimpering cry, and the dog's weight simply vanished.

Joby opened his eyes to find Jake standing above him with a maul half-raised to strike again. But the dog lay unmoving a short ways off, bleeding from a wound on the side of its head. Its companion, whining pitifully, struggled to rise and flee on a hind leg broken by Joby's initial blow. On Jake's face, there was only sadness.

Joby began to shake, and fought an inexplicable urge to cry. Jake stooped to help him up, then went quickly back to tend to Nacho, who had regained consciousness, and was groaning in pain.

Joby looked at the dogs, one clearly dead, the other crippled and felt his stomach knot in empathy and disgust, despite what they had done to Nacho, and tried to do to him. He turned away, and watched Jake bind Nacho's wounds with strips torn from the boy's ruined shirt, while Tholomey and Hawk looked on in silence, and Rose stroked Nacho's hair, tears trickling down her face.

"Where's Jupiter?" Joby asked.

"I sent him for more help," Jake said without turning from his work. "He and Sky found me in the woods, but I'm afoot, and we'll need a truck to get Nacho out."

Joby looked around again. "You sure saved my bacon, Jake," he said soberly. "Thank you."

"Thanks for saving theirs," Jake replied, tightening one last bandage. Nacho seemed half awake now, but calm. Jake rose and looked back at the ruined dogs, then stepped over the dead animal toward the crippled one, which shied away, whimpering as he approached. Jake crouched down in front of it crooning soothing sounds, and after a moment, reached out to stroke its back, and then its head. The animal whined in high pleading tones, then licked Jake's hand. "I'd rather have taken that maul to this creature's owner," Jake said wearily. "It's a crime against nature to twist dogs like this."

The dog laid its head down between its paws then, and closed its eyes. As Jake gave it one more pat and stood, Joby realized it was no longer breathing.

"Is it dead?" he asked in dismay.

Jake nodded without looking back.

Joby felt a dreadful shame. Some dumb creature kept on a chain, bludgeoned to death for doing exactly what it had been trained to do.

As if reading his thoughts, Jake said, "We've just set them free, Joby." He shook his head, walked back to the others and gently asked, "What were you all doing here?"

"We—" Tholomey began, then seemed to think better of it and said, "He was cutting outside his property. We came up to . . . we . . ." The boy bowed his head in shame.

"You guys think something needs fixin'," Jake said quietly, "you come tell me, or Bridget, or some other adult. We'll take care of it."

"Will Nacho be all right? Rose asked.

"I think so," Jake said. "Looks like they missed his arteries. Don't think he really lost as much blood as it seems. It's just the shock that's got him. And the pain. But that'll all pass quick enough, once we get him down to Dr. Locke." For the first time, he grinned. "He'd be a lot worse off if you hadn't stood by him that way. That was pretty brave." He turned to smile at Joby. "There's likely to be some pretty grateful parents, Joby. You were quite the warrior there."

Joby shrugged, a blush of pride struggling with the sorrow he still felt for having killed the dog. "Wasn't any time to think, really," he said.

"It was like something in your book!" Hawk beamed. "You were like a knight!"

Tholomey agreed.

Embarrassed, Joby changed the subject. "You guys see those birds? That was pretty weird, huh?"

To his surprise, everyone looked embarrassed.

"Birds'll fight anything that threatens their nests." Jake shrugged. "Nothin' weird about that."

※

Tom shook his head in disbelief. "Really, Mr. Bruech, it was unconscionable to leave such dogs unattended without a fence. They could have killed my daughter. And to guard timber? Were you afraid someone might throw those logs over a shoulder and carry them off?" He shook his head again, and looked away. "Everyone here's grown rather sour on your Mr. Ferristaff by now, and they're just not interested in selling him any more of their property. Nothing I can do about that, even if I wanted to."

"The children *were* trespassing," Bruech insisted, "and we have agreed to pay Mr. Shandy for his timber. What else can be expected of us?"

"Oh, we expect very little of you, Mr. Bruech. And if those kids *were* trespassing, it wasn't on Mr. Ferristaff's property, was it?" Tom had lost all patience with this manipulative man. "Frankly, we don't consider a few kids tromping around in the woods that big a crime around here, especially where there are no fences. Unlike your employer, Mr. Bruech, Mr. Shandy really is a lover of wilderness, and none too happy about the gash you left in his woodland, payment or no. You're a fine one to talk of trespass."

"I have already explained; that was merely an error in our understanding of the boundary lines of Mr. Ferristaff's property. We—"

"I hope your lawyers are better equipped than your surveyors then, Mr. Bruech, because the way your client conducts himself, they'll need to be. I'm sorry, but I do have other business to attend to."

The polite expression Bruech had maintained throughout their meeting fell away before an imperious glower. "I must say, you are the most self-defeating real-estate agent I have ever come across, Mr. Connolly. I had hoped we might deal with each other on more amicable terms, but you leave me no alternative but to play hardball."

"Is that some kind of threat, Mr. Bruech?" Tom asked, no longer attempting to moderate his scorn.

"As you must guess, Mr. Connolly," Bruech continued calmly, "our research into Taubolt has been quite exhaustive, and it seems that this idyllic little outpost has been remarkably unforthcoming with county and state agencies about such things as, oh . . . its existence, for instance." He raised his brows a little. "What a lot of fees and taxes don't seem to have been paid over the many, many years your town has flourished here. So many licenses missing. I'm not impeaching anyone's integrity, of course. The whole thing is clearly some kind of gross bureaucratic oversight, which your lovely community can hardly be blamed for choosing to overlook, but a century of unpaid bills? Such a costly scandal might drive Taubolt right out of existence."

Tom sat very still, unable to believe what he was hearing. If there'd been any doubt about the demise of Taubolt's defenses, there could be none now.

"Don't worry, Mr. Connolly," Bruech smiled with nearly believable sympathy, "Mr. Ferristaff is a pragmatist, not a stickler for rules. If you and whoever you've been running interference for are willing to cooperate with him, he'll be only too happy to preserve your remarkable little secret, even, perhaps to bolster it."

"I am just a Realtor, Mr. Bruech," Tom said weakly. "I own none of the property you're interested in. There are others I will have to talk with."

"Of course," Bruech said, rising now to stretch and smile. "I never meant to accuse you of being more than a middleman. Talk with your clients. You have all the time you need. Weeks and weeks, if necessary." He turned to go, but turned back at the door to add, "It seems to me that Mr. Ferristaff is doing

Taubolt a favor. If you don't sell to us, what's to stop some truly ruthless tim-ber operation from moving in and clear-cutting these hills for as far as the eye can see?"

❧

As he labored painfully up the stairs behind the Primrose Picket Inn and toward the attic room where Council meetings were held, Father Crombie met Mrs. Lindsay carrying an empty tray back toward the kitchen.

"Hello, Father. They're all here, buzzing like a fallen wasp's nest."

"Who can blame them?" he sighed. "Have they started, then?"

"They're waiting for you, I think."

"Then I must redouble my pace," he joked, hoisting himself up another step.

A moment later, as he entered the high, peaked room with its pine rafters and dormer windows, conversation came to a halt as he was greeted courte-ously. "Sorry I'm late," he said, lowering himself into a chair beside Jake and near the head of the table. "Have you arrived at some solution without me, I hope?"

Alice Mayfield, who ran Taubolt's art gallery, harrumphed something that might have been a laugh, and replied, "We've all been counting on *your* plan, Father."

The Council consisted of five women, and five men, all but Crombie of the blood and longtime residents of Taubolt. At the end of the table opposite Jake sat the town's stellar new arrival, Solomon Rand, a nearly pure-blooded ancient like Jake, it was said, and thus invited to their Council meeting, though not yet an official member.

"I still do not understand what happened to the aversions we have always maintained," said Orrydia Honzel in her thick German accent, apparently re-suming the conversation interrupted by Crombie's arrival. "That people are finally beginning to notice our presence, I can understand, but why should one man have been able to pursue the facts of our existence with such focus for so long without being turned aside?"

"Our arts work fine on human minds, Orrydia, but not on machines," Jake said. "I suspect it's computers that're shortin' out our defenses. Ferristaff's lit-tle trap may not be quite as foolproof as he thinks, though, for the very same reason. Solomon and I have a plan, which I'll let him explain, since it's exe-cution will be largely his affair."

Solomon cleared his throat, and said, "First, let me say that I am honored by the reception you've shown me, appearing unannounced, as I have, in such troubled times."

"Any friend of Jake's is a friend of ours, Mr. Rand," said Bridget O'Reilly. "And the addition of a second ancient to our assembly right now is doubly welcome."

"Thank you." Solomon nodded. "As Jake indicated, my travels these many years have equipped me with considerable knowledge of the larger world's new technologies, and I believe they may be used to defuse Mr. Ferristaff's case against us. Unfortunately, I fear we will have to purchase the necessary time by giving Ferristaff at least a little of what he wants for now."

"You mean sell him all that land?" Tom Connolly objected.

"Not all the land he wants," Solomon answered. "Just enough to keep him interested and leave him cause to continue threatening us for a while. Given a year or two, I should be able to place sufficient 'lost' records in enough bureaucratic sinkholes to convince any thorough investigator that Taubolt has, in fact, been paying fees and applying for licenses all along and simply fallen victim to embezzlement and bungling."

"But, won't more land just make him harder to dislodge?" Bridget asked.

"It's pretty clear by now that Ferristaff plans to log whatever property he gets his hands on," Jake said. "Solomon's learned that he owns a huge national lumber company." There was a general gasp from around the table. "The mountains around Taubolt must look like the lost mother lode to him."

"This is intolerable!" snapped Alfred Cognolio, who ran what many affectionately called "the junk shop" on Main Street and was normally the quietest of them all. "I say we just pay the bastard an unfriendly visit tonight, and scare some virtue into him!"

"And when he tells everyone what he saw?" asked Florence Kellerman.

"They'll think he's mad, of course," Alfred shrugged.

"Can't risk it," said Jake. "To get his whole company out of here, we'd have to scare a lot of others too. 'Stead of thinkin' they're *all* mad, people might get interested in findin' out what's up 'round here. The last thing we need is more attention."

"What do you suggest then?" asked Franklin Holt.

"There's that old proverb about bein' careful what you wish for." Jake shrugged. "If half the trees he harvests turn out to be rotted useless with some new fungal disease, and enough of his equipment is trashed by rogue falls, landslides, salt-air damage, and such, we can make his operation cost him more than it's earnin'. His own stockholders might pull 'im out then." Jake smiled. "That'd also discourage other loggin' operations from comin' to take his place. Otherwise, as his Mr. Bruech pointed out, we might just get rid of one bastard to find ourselves dealing with another."

"All right," said Franklin. "The hardware store can play its part in slowing him down, certainly. But what about the Cup? If the border's gone, does it make sense to keep putting it so casually into public view on Sundays?"

Jake turned to Father Crombie.

"It would seem to me," said Father Crombie, "that in such times, the Cup's influence may be more important than ever. Most of Taubolt's own ognibs have never guessed the truth. I can't see that a few more strangers in town pose any immediate threat to its safety. In any case, Ms. Hamilton, Mr. Ferristaff, and all of their crowd has seemed disinclined to attend church."

"But if wickedness can enter Taubolt now, might not the Cup become aroused?" Orrydia asked. "Its nature might not be so subtle then. If the wrong eyes should see—"

"Evil, in Taubolt!" Daisy LeRonde exclaimed softly, as if this were too much to fathom. The room fell silent as her utterance struck home.

"Well, if it's evil we're up against," said Florence, "perhaps we should be moving the spring rites forward. There would be some added strength in—"

"If added strength is what's needed," Daisy interjected, "it makes no sense to weaken the rite by holding it out of time."

"Besides," Bridget said, "if we move it forward even a week we'd have to pull half our children from several days of school. How would we explain that to—"

"Hey, hey," Jake said, smiling reassuringly. "Let's not get ahead of ourselves. The border may be gone, but the Cup's as potent as ever, so it's not like anything monstrous is just gonna amble into town. I say we leave things be until we've got some better reason than vague fears of future trouble to change 'em."

"All right," said Alice. "But we'd still better be a lot more careful than we have been. Among other things," she gazed gravely at the Council's other members, "that means telling our kids to stop playing with power where anyone might see. That episode with Joby Peterson in the woods last week was downright reckless."

"That was hardly *playing*," Tom protested. "Jupiter and Sky were trying to save Nacho's life, not to mention Tholomey's and Rose's."

Many at the table nodded, but Alice stood firm. "I understand, and I'm grateful they succeeded, but, frankly, this was not the first time I've seen those kids act almost like they're daring Joby to get it. They've come to like him a bit too much, I'm afraid."

Father Crombie glanced toward Jake, and found the ancient gazing back. Given Taubolt's escalating troubles, it did seem time to stop hiding what they knew of Joby's past from the Council. People must know Joby well enough by now to give him a fair hearing and decide what should be done.

"That's because he's likeable," Bridget replied to Alice, then turned to Jake. "It's been months now, Jake, and I have yet to sense even a hint of threat in him. That storm may have had something to do with whatever's happening to our borders, but I've come to doubt that Joby's arrival was anything but coincidence. It does seem pretty likely that he's of the blood though, and I'm not entirely clear about why we're all still trying so hard to hide from him. Isn't it time he was helped to understand just, like all the others?"

Yes, Crombie thought, the time had come. To his surprise, however, Solomon spoke up before he had a chance to say so.

"Since coming here, I have had the pleasure of making this young man's acquaintance," the ancient said, "and have learned things about his earlier life which, in all sincerity, I do not feel entitled to relate, but which do leave me utterly assured that he has no secret designs of any kind on Taubolt, nor intends anyone here a shred of harm.

"That said, however, I am also persuaded that it might be best, at present, to leave him blissfully ignorant of whatever he has not yet guessed about this town, or about himself. Here in Taubolt, he has found the one thing he most desperately needs: *refuge,* both from the world that drove him here, and from himself. I fear deeply that the very things you would *help him understand,* might serve only to deprive him of that refuge once again. As I said, I am unable to elaborate without violating confidences I feel bound to honor. I am sorry to be so oblique, and will fully support whatever decision this gathering comes to, but I felt obliged to equip you with my counsel on the matter."

Crombie looked to Jake, as did all the others.

"I've got no cause to challenge anything he's said." Jake shrugged. "Joby seems a bright enough fellow, and such things are often best left to shake out in their own way and at their own pace. If he wants to know more about what's goin' on, he'll ask, I s'pose. 'Til then, let's just go about our business and leave him be."

20

(The Golden Season)

Joby was awakened from an afternoon nap by a tentative knock. It had been too soft for Hawk and too long for Mrs. Lindsay, who always tapped just twice. He shrugged off his bed and crossed the room to open the door.

"Laura!" he said, surprised.

"Mrs. Lindsay said I should just come up," she said. "I hope you don't mind."

"Of course not. Come in." He smiled and bowed her through the door, before remembering the rumpled clothes strewn across the foot of his bed, or the pile of assignments he'd left spread across his desk. "It's a little messy, I guess."

"Not by Arthur's standards." She smiled.

He pulled out the desk chair for her, then went back to sit on his bed. "To what do I owe this unexpected honor?"

"Arthur's report card came yesterday. His lowest grade was a C, and there were two Bs. I can't tell you how grateful I am, Joby."

"Well, it's his accomplishment, not mine." Joby smiled.

"I know that," she said, getting up to look out his window at the headlands already going gold with summer heat. "Someday you should really learn how to just say, 'thank you,' or 'you're welcome.'" She gave him a wry smile. "You're the best thing that's happened to Arthur since we came here. He talks about your hikes and your talks, and even your tutoring sessions, as if you were some kind of action hero."

Joby covered his bashfulness with a brief, sitting bow, and said, "I've done no more than chivalry and honor require, m'lady," then hastily added, "But your praise is rich reward. I thank you, and you're welcome."

She gave a light, uplifting laugh quite unlike the weary, cynical one he remembered from their first conversation. "I'd forgotten you could do that!" she said wistfully. "It's like being right back at one of our old Roundtable meetings."

"Well . . . I get a little silly, sometimes," he said, cringing at the memory of his childhood grandiosities.

"I wasn't teasing you," she said. "I just . . . it makes me happy, remembering how things were when we were kids."

"I know. I'm sorry," Joby said. "I'm being . . . It's great that Hawk's coming into his own." Laura got up and came toward him. "And I really appreciate your coming to—"

She bent down and kissed him on the cheek, trailing perfume as she drew away. Joby scrambled for something to say, but words deserted him.

"You've never known how to take a compliment," she teased, walking toward his door. She looked back before she left, and said, "If you have nothing else planned tomorrow night, why don't you get someone in town to drive you up to our place for dinner." She flashed him another smile. "I know Hawk would love to see you."

"Thanks. I'd love to," Joby said.

"We'll see you then," she said and left.

❈

"Thanks for the ride," Joby said, climbing into Cal's truck the next evening.

"When you gonna grow up an' get a car of your own?" Cal teased.

"On a teacher's salary, that might be a few years off yet," Joby replied self-consciously. "But I do appreciate your help, Cal."

"No problem." Cal grinned. "Course, you owe me now."

"What's it gonna be this time?" Joby groaned. "My lunch money for a month?"

"Think you're pretty fast, don't ya." Cal smiled. "School's out for summer, so there ain't no lunch money. No, I'll just think about it some and get back to you."

Joby laughed. "You Bobs have a bright future in the outside world, you know."

"Plan to be king," Cal grinned back, "soon as I graduate."

Spring had made the Ridge more beautiful than ever. Joby was so taken with the scenery that it seemed only moments before they arrived at Laura's. Cal parked the truck and Joby jumped out, then realized that Laura's car was nowhere to be seen.

"You sure they're here?" Cal asked.

"They invited me to dinner," Joby said. "I can't imagine she forgot."

"Well, better make sure before I dump you here," Cal said, getting out of his truck to mount the rickety stairs beside Joby. Joby knocked at the door, but got no answer. A second knock produced the same result.

Cal tried the door and found it open.

"That's weird," Joby said.

"Maybe we should go in and make sure everything's all right."

"I don't think we should go in when they're not home," Joby said.

"Aw, lighten up." Cal smiled, and pushed through the door into the entrance hall. "Hello? Anybody home?" There was no answer.

"I guess they forgot," Joby said, trying to shrug off his disappointment. "We should go."

Cal shook his head. "Hold on a minute. Somethin' don't feel right here."

He walked slowly down the hall toward the kitchen and living room as Joby followed.

Arriving first, Cal stopped, staring into the living room, mouth open in shock. "Joby, I think you better see this," he whispered, looking frightened.

Rushing to Cal's side in alarm, Joby stepped into the kitchen and—

"SURPRISE!"

All of Taubolt seemed to be there, laughing uproariously at Joby's frightened expression. Cal leaned against the kitchen counter behind him, half-crippled with mirth.

"What . . . the hell is this?" Joby asked.

"Happy birthday, Joby," said Laura, coming up to hug him.

Joby's mouth dropped open. "Oh my God! . . . I . . . It's June tenth?"

"You narner!" Hawk laughed. "Should've got you a *calendar* for your present!"

Joby turned and slugged Cal in the arm. "You had me thinking someone was dead in here." He scowled happily. Turning back to Laura, he said, "I can't believe you remembered."

"I can't believe you forgot," she teased.

"This is unbelievable! What if I hadn't come?"

"We had contingency plans," Mrs. Lindsay said.

"You were all in on this," Joby said in wonder. "Where'd you all park?"

"Way up the road!" Jupiter groaned. "Such a long hike back, I almost got lost again!"

Half the kids from school, most of their parents, and virtually everyone else he knew in Taubolt was there. Then Joby spotted Nacho's devilish grin at the back of the crowd, where he stood on crutches beside his parents. It was the first time Joby had seen him since he'd gone to the hospital in Santa

Rosa for reconstructive surgery. Joby went to greet him, returning a steady stream of cheerful greetings and good wishes along the way.

"Good to see you, Nacho." He smiled. "How's your leg?"

"Healing faster than medical science can explain." The boy grinned.

Nacho's father, a tall man with unruly currents of red sand-colored hair, nodded toward the window and said, "There's something out here we'd all like you to have a look at, Joby."

The room fell quiet as Joby walked to the window and looked down on the gravel drive that wrapped around Laura's house. Other than an old station wagon someone had parked there, he saw nothing but the usual scenery.

"It looks a little giddily," Nacho said, "but it runs pretty good. We've taken real great care of it."

"Well, Nacho's been a little hard on it actually," his mother said disapprovingly.

"Hey! I fixed up all the big stuff!" Nacho protested.

"He's quite a mechanic," Nacho's father conceded proudly. "It should last you a few years at least."

"What . . . are you talking about?" Joby asked, thinking they couldn't mean what it sounded like they meant.

"Everyone chipped in and bought it from us." Nacho grinned.

"It was time to get a new one anyway." His father smiled.

"But . . . Thank you, but this is too much. It's got to be worth—"

"A lot less than our son's life," Nacho's mother said.

"And we're all tired as hell of carting you around!" said Cal.

Everyone laughed, and Joby shook his head, trying not to get emotional. "Well, thank you all so much. I can't think of what to say except that, whether you know it or not, you've all saved my life too. . . . Taubolt's given me everything I ever wanted. I owe you all big time."

Someone started singing "Happy Birthday," and everyone joined in, while Joby stood grinning "like an eejit," Cal said later.

An avalanche of wonderful food began appearing then. By now, Joby had discovered that Taubolt was potluck paradise. Ian Kellerman had assembled a band of local musicians who played an odd but lively fusion of funk, blue-grass, and Celtic swing, better for dancing one's brains out than any music Joby had ever heard.

Finally Laura produced a blazing birthday cake, and Joby blew the candles out to much cheering, secretly wishing that Taubolt would never change.

A moment later, he saw Hawk and Rose heading outside together. Hawk's arm was around her waist, and she didn't seemed to mind.

Later, as he passed Hawk in the kitchen, Joby said quietly, "Way to go, bro."

"What?" Hawk replied.

"With Rose." Joby grinned. "I saw you puttin' the moves on a minute ago."

Hawk grinned back, and said, "Bet I know who *you're* in love with."

To hear it launched so boldly from the lips of Laura's own kid seemed somehow indecent, though Joby could not deny it. "And who would that be?" he asked lamely.

"I still wish she'd married you instead of Sandy," Hawk said shyly. "I'd rather have had you for a father."

"Well," Joby said, feeling touched. "Would being brothers do?"

"I guess," Hawk said.

"Brothers it is then." Joby grinned. "I'm honored as hell, Hawk. Best birthday present I ever got—even better than the car. I mean it."

"No problem." Hawk smiled, holding out his hand. "Wanna shake on it?"

"You're really weird, you know," Joby laughed. But he shook on it.

✵

"Who's got that avocado?" Jupiter asked, gingerly balancing a hot tortilla laden with beans and slices of pepper jack cheese.

"Blue ate it all," Ander said mischievously, his charcoal-smudged face aglow in the flickering firelight. Twilight deepened over the lake behind them.

"Hey! There was only this much left!" Blue protested, pinching his fingers together to show how little. "Ask *Tholomey* who ate most of it."

Blue's younger brother grinned sheepishly. "I thought there was another one."

"*Tholomey,*" Jupiter complained, "you packed in all the vegetables! How could you think there was another one?"

"He carried 'em, he should get a bigger share if he wants," Sky said, rolling his eyes, and tossing Jupiter a tomato. "Here, finish that, and you guys'll be even."

"Yeah, you narner," Tholomey taunted. "Don't get *precipitous.*"

There were chuckles from around the circle. Several weeks earlier, Agnes Hamilton had written a letter to the editor of Taubolt's weekly paper complaining about the "precipitous high jinks of Taubolt's loitering youth" on the streets that summer, and its "detrimental effect on tourism." Since then, Taubolt's kids had taken to abusing the word "precipitous" at every opportunity.

Joby's cheeks ached from smiling as he watched them negotiate the finer points of wilderness dining. Ms. Hamilton not withstanding, the summer had passed in delicious splendor. Perhaps because of the semi-celebrity conferred by his rescue of Nacho and the others that spring, or because he had a car now and was always happy to drive them around, or perhaps just because he truly liked them, Taubolt's youth had lured Joby into one marvelous escapade after another all summer, until, by now, he counted many of them closer friends than he'd had since he, Ben, and Laura had been children.

As the end of August had drawn near, a bunch of "the guys," as Joby now thought of them, had decided that a camping trip was in order before returning to their scholastic prison. Sky and Joby had offered to drive. From stashes of their own old equipment, the boys had outfitted Joby for backpacking up to a lake that Blue and Tholomey knew of high in the coastal range separating Taubolt from "the mainland." The seven of them; Ander, Sky, Jupiter, Hawk, Blue, Tholomey, and Joby, had driven inland for over two hours on half-ruined dirt roads, then spent a full day hiking ever upward beside a wide river that tumbled over huge stones between high rock ledges into clear, emerald pools filled with fish.

For Joby, who had never backpacked before, the hike up had been a vivid mix of stunning visual beauty, and slow physical torment. The day had been hot, the pack heavier and heavier, and the riverbed trail steep and boulder strewn. But first sight of the lake itself had been ample reward. Some ancient cataclysm had dumped great slabs of rock into the river, forming a wide, clear reservoir surrounded on three sides by low stony peaks, sheer rock ledges, and occasional evergreens. The gap through which the boys had come opened on a sweeping view of ridge after forested ridge, clear back to the coast.

Recalling their arrival still made Joby want to laugh. After the hot and arduous hike, the boys had all run whooping and hollering toward the lake, dropping their packs along the way, then, as quickly and carelessly, their clothes, before leaping joyfully into the water. Beyond the fact that Joby had always thought of skinny-dipping as a somewhat "shady" activity, he'd also been keenly aware of being the group's lone adult, not to mention their teacher. So when Hawk had loudly demanded to know what Joby was waiting for, he'd stripped off everything but his boxers, and hobbled uncertainly down to a stone ledge at the shoreline to dive in.

"What, yer gonna leave your shorts on?" Tholomey had teased. "Mama's boy!"

"Some of us are too modest to show off," Joby had parried, then dove in.

But the lake itself had overruled him, tugging his shorts off to drift somewhere behind him as he'd swept out of his dive in a long, swift arc beneath the surface. By the time Joby had come up for air, Hawk and Tholomey, who'd been close enough to see what happened, had been howling with laughter.

"Serves you right!" Hawk had laughed.

Tholomey had quickly disappeared underwater, then splashed up again to shout, "*That's* what you were worried about showing off? Don't make me laugh!"

After that, even Joby had been unable to keep a straight face. He'd gone under to retrieve his shorts, mooning Hawk and Tholomey in the process, and resurfaced to toss the sodden ball of cloth back onto shore before initiating a splashing war with his two gleeful detractors. Their war was quickly joined by all the others, and by the time they'd grown cold and tired enough to come out of the water, the issue of clothing had become as moot for Joby as it was for everyone else. They'd all lain about on the hot sunny shoreline to bake dry in the sun, and when it had come time to rise and go set up their campsite, Joby had donned his clothes again with dull regret.

For three days since, they had laughed and swum and hiked together through this pristine, sunny haven, high above the surrounding landscape. At night, they'd slept with nothing over their heads but the countless stars, watching the sun rise again at dawn without having to leave their sleeping bags.

This morning, Blue, Tholomey, and Ander had gone off early, coming back with enough fish to make breakfast for them all, though, when Joby had asked about their angling secrets, they'd just grinned at each other, and said, "If we told, we'd have to kill you." As Jupiter and Sky had fried up the catch on a patch of foil above the fire, shy, sunny Ander, and gentle, soft spoken Blue, had competed to describe the grizzly ceremonial techniques Joby's sacrificial slaughter would necessitate, gleefully inventing new and shockingly bloodthirsty details as they went.

Now, sadly, their adventure was finally at an end. Tomorrow they would hike back into the real world, and face the resumption of school. As if in denial of this melancholy fact, their rowdiness had climbed to new levels of intensity. They'd even concocted a bawdy song together, every verse ending with, "Wasn't that precipitous!" When they'd gone, earlier that evening, to rehang their extra food in a distant tree, Joby had joked that there was hardly any need, since their ruckus must already have scared everything with legs off the mountainside.

As Joby reflected on all this, a quiet finally fell across their camp. Some stared at the fire, others turned to watch bats flutter erratic zigzags over the dimming lake in search of summer's last mosquitoes.

"I can't believe I'll have homework on Monday," Tholomey lamented.

As a teacher, Joby felt he ought to cast the fact in some more positive light, but, in all honesty, he wasn't much happier about it than they were. He was grateful to be spending another year teaching, of course, though sorry that his good fortune should be founded on someone else's hardship. Charlie Luff's fight with cancer wasn't going well.

"I don't mind so much," Hawk said. "I'm kind of ready for a change."

"Yeah, right," Tholomey teased. "You just want an excuse to see Rose every day!"

Hawk smiled awkwardly.

"Hawk's in love," Ander whispered too loudly to Blue.

"You got any more of those Ymril stories, Hawk?" Joby said, trying to rescue him.

On the two previous evenings, Hawk had told them stories from the imaginary history of Ymril which he and Solomon had been inventing together all summer. They'd been surprisingly good tales, earning both rapt attention and outspoken praise from everyone. Tonight, however, Hawk just shook his head.

Ander looked at Joby, and said, "Tell us about that club you started."

Joby looked blank.

"The Roundtable." Ander smiled.

"How do you know about that?" asked Joby

"Hawk told us," Blue said.

Joby looked at Hawk, who shrugged and smiled. "Mom told me all about it."

"She did?" Joby asked uncomfortably. "What did she say?"

"She said it was cool." Hawk grinned. "Like being characters from your book, and you were like King Arthur."

Joby dismissed this with something like a snort. "I was more like a fourth-grader with pretensions," he said, then, surprised to find that it no longer shamed him to talk about it, he began telling them about games on the tournament field, and how Hawk's mother had gotten to be their official damsel in distress, and later a full-fledged knight. Warming to the subject, he went on to describe some of their more famous secret mission—and Laura's role in keeping the club appraised of who needed encouragement.

Jupiter turned to grin at Blue, and said "That'd be so damn fast, wouldn't it?"

"Yeah!" Tholomey replied.

"It was secret, right?" asked Ander. "No one else knew who did those missions?"

Joby nodded. "We left little yellow disks of cardboard with a red dragon on them to let someone know they'd been aided by the Roundtable, but no one outside the club was ever told who exactly had done the deed."

"Then shut up, you guys," Ander grinned at the others.

"How about this great weather," Jupiter mused, his face suddenly comical with feigned innocence.

Joby smiled, fairly sure the idea would be forgotten by morning.

❊

Joby woke to find the eastern sky aglow with approaching dawn, and himself filled with restlessness, as if he'd forgotten something urgent, or remembered something . . . almost. Knowing he was through with sleep, he slipped quietly from his dewy bag and left camp to relieve himself. After that, he went down to the water's edge and settled on a rock ledge above their swimming hole to watch the sun rise and bid the lake and all its pleasant memories farewell.

The water was glassy smooth, utterly silent. Not far off a trout leapt, then another. The spreading rings merged slowly as they move toward shore. Peaks around the lake turned rose then golden as the sun came up, until the rocks he sat on were gilded too, and the water at his feet changed from black to blue to emerald. In its glassy depths, hypnotic moirés of light moved slowly across the lake bottom. Two trout swam lazily by, utterly secure in their shimmering world. Giving in to the lake's allure, Joby stripped his clothes off, stretched his arms up, and dove far out over the water, seeing himself reflected in its still surface, as if in flight, before the stinging slap, the shock of cold, and the beautiful, gliding stream of motion through its liquid embrace.

After forty feet of freestyle to warm himself, he ducked beneath the surface, letting his breath go and plunging toward bottom. The water grew colder, but he loved the feel of it on his skin. Opening his eyes, he hung motionless in dancing, tranquil brilliance, lost in silence, utterly relaxed, completely alive. Only when his lungs lost patience with him did he push into the soft mud beneath his feet and shoot up and up, bursting back into the morning with a gasp.

Climbing back onto the ledge, he sat naked and dripping in the early sun, covered in undulating reflections of sunlight, and feeling suddenly as wild, as still, and as beautiful as everything around him. Lost in light and warmth, he gazed out across the dazzling water, and became aware of movement all around him in the silence.

Tiny flies danced on the lake's surface. Bees and dragonflies darted or hovered all along the shore. Ants searched the rocks and pebbles for morsels to bring back to their queen. Thistle seeds and iridescent strands of gossamer drifted through the open air, back lit with rainbow fire by the rising sun, until it seemed the entire world was one slow, swirling dance of glinting, golden illumination. It was the strangest feeling, yet familiar in some nameless way as well. A small wasp landed on Joby's arm, carrying the rainbow in its wings, but he felt no fear of being stung, only the tickling touch of kin. A bottle fly, also covered in rainbows, landed on his knee; one more intimate connection with the moving, luminous scheme of life that stretched away across the lake into the forest beyond, and on out of sight. With a surreal surge of wholeness and well-being, Joby wondered how he'd stumbled into this sudden fairyland, and what might happen if he tried reaching farther into—

"*Whaaaaaaawhoooo!*"

The shout and several pounding steps behind him were all the warning he received before Jupiter's body came hurtling past him to land like a depth charge in the lake, drenching Joby and his perch with spray, and shattering the spell. An instant of wrenching dismay at the loss of his fragile ecstasy was followed by a spontaneous explosion of pure wildness in Joby's breast, released in a banshee shout as he cannonballed into the water beside Jupiter. Within minutes, everyone had joined them, ending their retreat as they had begun it, in naval warfare.

❊

After breakfast, they packed their gear and reluctantly left the lake behind.

They'd been underway for several hours when they reached a particularly steep and rocky stretch of streambed. The trail switchbacked higher on the embankment, but some of the guys, impatient for speed, or just tired of eating one another's dust, hiked into the margins of the stream itself, and began to hop from boulder to boulder as if their packs weighed nothing.

"That doesn't look very safe guys," Joby called down to them. "Why don't you come back up on the trail?"

This earned him a withering look from Sky, who said, "We're not two-year-olds."

"Yeah, but who do you suppose your folks'll blame if something dumb happens out here?" Joby pressed. Ignoring him completely, Hawk jumped down from one boulder to another right behind Sky. "Come on, Hawk. Your mom'll skin me alive if I bring you back with a broken arm."

"Joby!" Hawk frowned. "Lighten up."

Seeing that he'd embarrassed Hawk, Joby shrugged and shut his mouth.

Sky hopped from one large boulder, onto a second smaller one at the lip of a pool, then down onto a third, as wide as he was tall, which rocked forward suddenly, and gave way underneath him.

"*Whoa!*" Hawk cried, as Joby whirled to see Sky flail in midair, then drop like a sack of sand, landing face down under his pack on the muddy bank as the huge rock tumbled over his legs and went crashing into the underbrush down stream.

There was a moment of shocked immobility before everyone hurried toward Sky, who lay facedown and motionless.

"Don't move him!" Joby shouted, rushing to the boy's side. When he got there, he knelt down, overtaken by an eerie calm, and said, levelly, "Sky?"

The boy did not respond.

"Sky, you hear me?" Joby said, trying to calculate how long it might take him to drop his pack and run back to their cars at the trail head. It would take hours to get help. Should he send someone else? The others stood around in helpless silence, pale with fear. Did any of them know enough first aid to cope until . . . what? A helicopter arrived? From where? No matter how they handled this, it was going to be a nightmare. Dully surprised at his own persisting calm, Joby wished with all his might for some kind of miracle, and said again, "Sky, if you're conscious, I just want you to move something. A hand or anything."

Slowly, Sky turned his head, revealing a pale, muddy face, and said quietly, "Just give me a minute."

Joby felt a wash of relief. At least he was conscious.

"How bad are your legs?" he asked, still embedded in emprobable calm.

To his amazement, Sky rolled over and said, shakily, "That was scary." Everyone seemed to breath again at once. Sky stretched out a hand to Blue, who'd been hovering over him all the while, and said, "Help me up."

"Whoa, whoa!" Joby said. "Don't put any weight on those legs! Aren't you hurt?"

Sky shook his head. "I don't think so. I'm just gonna sit up, okay?"

Joby could not believe that Sky was unhurt, but after Blue pulled him up into a sitting position, the boy bent his knees and said, "I'm fine. Really. I just wanted to be sure before I moved, that's all." He smiled wanly. "I guess I had that coming, huh?"

Weak with incredulous relief, Joby said nothing.

"You sure were calm, Joby," Tholomey said.

"Yeah," said Hawk. "I thought you were gonna freak for sure."

"Well," Joby said, suddenly wanting nothing so much as a long nap, "for future reference, when I get that calm, you can bet we're in deep, deep shit." He felt shaky now, and so, so sleepy. "Sky, are you sure you're not hurt? That rock rolled right across your legs. It must have weighed half a ton."

"It must've just looked that way from where you were standing," Sky said sheepishly. "'Cause I'm fine."

"But . . . Didn't the rest of you see it?" Joby insisted, turning to the others.

"Looked kind of like it bounced a little to me," Blue said nervously. "Maybe it just rocked over them, you know?" He didn't smile, seeming oblivious of his own pun.

"Mud's pretty soft here," Jupiter suggested uncomfortably. "Maybe that helped."

There were two deep indentations in the mud where Sky's knees had been, but Joby still couldn't trust such luck. "Don't stand up yet," he said, moving around to put his palms on the bottoms of Sky's feet. "Press your legs very lightly against my hands. If it hurts at all, stop." Sky did so. "Try a little harder, but just until it hurts." Joby pressed.

Sky pushed harder, and shrugged. "I'm sorry I scared everyone, but I'm really okay." He shook his head. "I really thought that rock was in there solid."

"Well, that's the damnedest luck I ever saw," Joby said. "Not that I'm complaining." He helped Sky up, still warning him to take it slow, but when the boy had gained his feet and started back for the trail, walking as easily as ever, Joby finally accepted that, for once, he'd gotten what he'd prayed for. "Okay, let's try to stay alive just a few hours longer," he said grimly. "No jumping off cliffs, swan diving over waterfalls, or handheld explosive devices 'til you're back at home, and it's your parents' problem. Got it?"

Everyone meekly reassured him, and trudged off looking at their feet, as if Sky had died. Joby followed them feeling so tired that he hoped they wouldn't have to carry *him* to the truck before they'd finished.

⚘

Dear Mom and Dad,

A letter from your son. Can you believe it?

I have no idea how to do this, so I'll just plunge in. I'm sure you've known I was hiding from you all these years, and I guess I've always known, deep down, how much it must be hurting you to let me do it. That's one of many reasons it's so hard to write this even now when I have only happy things to say for once. I suppose there were things I thought I should protect you from, or that I was just afraid to tell you, but I'm not going to fill this letter with excuses. I just hope that you're both well, and that, if you can forgive all these years of silence, you'll let me come out of hiding now, at last.

I am doing unbelievably well here. In Taubolt, I have finally found a place that feels more profoundly and wonderfully like home than I ever dreamed possible. I am teaching English in the high school here, and helping out at the Primrose Picket Inn, where I have a very cozy room. The innkeeper, Mrs. Lindsay, has been kind beyond all explanation. Everyone is kind here. It's like a completely different world. And I've become a completely different person. I end each day happy now, and grateful. I'm even in way better physical shape than I ever was before. I don't ever want to leave this place. I love everything about it, and everyone I know here—especially the kids—more than I know how to say. I love you guys too. And for the first time in far too many years, I'm not afraid to tell you so. I'm not sure why I ever was.

You should come visit me. Mrs. Lindsay says you can stay for free here at the inn. She's an amazing cook! I want you to meet my friends, and I want them to meet you. I have so many, many great stories to tell you, but I'd rather do it face to face over one of Mrs. Lindsay's delicious dinners. Do you think you could come? Pretty please?

> *Love,*
> *Your prodigal son, Joby*

P.S. You'll never guess who I found living here as well! Remember Laura Bayer? How's that for "small world"? She has an amazing son named Arthur, though everyone but her just calls him Hawk. Sadly, her husband left them just over a year ago. (I am trying hard not to seem too happy about that.)

Expecting a tantrum of historic proportions, even by Hell's standards, Kallaystra managed not to cringe as Lucifer finished reading, and let the boy's letter flutter down onto the conference table. Not a breath was drawn by any of the assembled throng as the unnerving silence stretched and stretched, while Hell's master stared down at the document outlining the un-raveling of all their efforts.

When the suspense became unbearable, Kallaystra took her life into her hands and murmured, "At least it was intercepted before reaching them."

Lucifer just went on staring, no longer at the letter, but at the empty air between himself and it.

"Love," he mused at last, "is a *many splendored* thing, is it not?"

Everyone stared in confusion, as unable as Kallaystra, it seemed, to imagine what this abstract utterance might portend.

Lucifer turned to Kallaystra with not half the ire she'd been braced for, and said, almost cheerfully, "See that it's delivered."

"The *letter?*" someone in the crowd blurted out stupidly.

"The boy's clearly put considerable effort into its composition," Lucifer answered mildly. "It seems rather peevish to waste all *his* work just because we can."

The gathering's confusion became as palpable as their dread had been.

"Bright One," Kallaystra said carefully. "It seems that you've conceived of some new plan the rest of us are failing to perceive."

"Ever the diplomat," Lucifer said with a predatory grin. "Surely I am not the only one who sees it." He looked around as if expecting some response.

"I fear you are," she said, well aware of how he savored such chances to make them all look stupid. "May we beg enlightenment?"

"But it's so obvious!" He smiled. "Everything the boy has ever desired is right there in Taubolt! Everything he *loves*! Everything that loves him! In one convenient location." Lucifer smiled craftily. "How desperate must our Master be to cheat so clumsily? Shortly after I blew the whistle on my lately exiled brother, the Creator condescended to assault me with a lecture on *love* and *compassion*. To be sure, a rather self-serving admonition from One so soon to be in need of both from me. But I found the ploy rather more instructive than He'd intended, for it, and this lovely letter, have provided precisely the key I've been waiting for. It seems we've been *pulling* on the rope when all the while we should have *pushed*."

Seeming to realize that he wasn't getting through, Lucifer exclaimed. "Don't you see? The Enemy's entire strategy is founded on the assumption that *love* will save the boy from himself! I'd have seen it far sooner if I'd been looking for anything so stupid. He's virtually handed us the whole enchi-lada!" He beamed around the table, clearly expecting some response, but Kallaystra was as lost as everyone else.

For the first time during their meeting, Lucifer seemed truly displeased.

"This," he growled to no one in particular, "is why *I'm* in charge here." He turned his back on all of them and began to pace. "At very least, we can hope his parents will answer that letter and initiate some regular correspondence." He directed a baleful gaze at Kallaystra. "The boy, himself, is doing more to keep us informed than you have so far. Your timid efforts to flood that town with mortal operatives had better be trebled."

"Bright One," she said, biting down on her frustration, "I've done everything I can without—"

"Then do everything you *can't*!" he snapped. "*Pay* them to relocate if necessary. I don't give a fig for subtlety anymore. We've only six years left! Bring more attention to the place. Bring attention to *us* if you have to!" A sly look crossed his face. "We'll fix that afterward. Right now, I want those idyllic streets drowned beneath a tide of vice and conflict fierce enough to drive that Cup clear off the continent!" He took a few deep breaths, and resumed his pacing. "If it takes a year or two to gather them in, perhaps that's not as much a problem as you thought. No harm in giving our boy time to fall even more deeply in *love* with all of it. I want the hook set irretrievably. Let's see that sentimental despot lecture me once He's been defeated by His own *greatest invention*."

PART THREE

�֍

The Final Measure

21

(Labor Day)

"Here they come," Joby announced, half-shouting to be heard over the crowd noise and the approaching blare of brassy instruments.

The last dry heat of summer shimmered off the pavement of Main Street, bearing scents of golden grass and ripening blackberries, tanning lotion, sweat, and popcorn into the bleached September sky. Taubolt's idea of a marching band led the festivities—a baker's dozen of musicians, no two wearing the same costumes, playing the same instruments or, perhaps, even the same tune; the noise of so many cheering or jeering onlookers made it difficult to tell. Taubolt's First Annual Labor Day Parade was one in a growing list of tourism incentives invented by the new Chamber of Commerce.

Despite the heat, Laura backed farther into Joby's embrace, pulling his arms more tightly around her waist for comfort. The crowd of strangers pressed to the curb around them felt more restive than festive, as if the parade were not something they'd come here to watch, but an unexpected obstacle on their way to other destinations.

"Where do they all come from?" Laura wondered aloud.

"What?" Joby asked, his chin bouncing against the top of her head.

"How do so many people even hear about a thing like this?" she asked more loudly, tilting her face up to help him hear.

She felt him shrug. "The Chamber's doing its job, evidently."

The Chamber, she thought again unhappily. A school board, the Historical Preservation Council, the Parks and Recreation Board, even a *local art's committee* for heaven's sake! Taubolt had gotten along marvelously without any of them for centuries, it seemed. Why did it need them now all of a sudden? Tourists and urban-flight refugees outnumbered Taubolt's original population three to one these days. Admittedly, she and Joby were fairly recent arrivals themselves, but they had come quietly to embrace Taubolt as it was, not to change it all into the very things they'd fled here to escape. Laura didn't even try to find a parking space within blocks of the post office anymore, much less the meditative solitude in Taubolt's streets that she had once so treasured. How had this many people found such an isolated place in just two years? In her opinion, whatever that Chamber of Commerce was doing should be outlawed.

"Hey, down there," Joby said leaning around from behind her to grin and give her a squeeze. "This isn't s'posed to be a funeral procession. Why the long face? You okay?"

"I'm sorry," she said, smiling apologetically. "I'm just missing the old Taubolt."

His grin twisted ruefully. "Yeah, I know," he said. "You wanna leave?"

"No. We're here." She shrugged. "I'll get into it. We've got to celebrate your last gasp of freedom after all. What better way than a parade?"

Joby nodded. "Hard to believe the school year's already here again, isn't it?"

"Hard to believe this will be Arthur's last one," she replied. "Seems only yesterday I wondered if he'd ever graduate at all." She turned in Joby's embrace to smile at him. "Then you came along, Sir Joby, and turned him into an honors student."

"Aw. T'weren't nothin' ma'am," he drawled, looking down, abashed, to scuff a shoe on the pavement. "Any ol' knight woulda done the same."

She leaned up to kiss him on the lips. The kiss he gave her in return was, as always, perfect. Perfect lingering length, perfect tenderness, followed by a perfect smile. Just like the kisses he had given her in high school.

Laura leaned away, covering her discomfort with a smile she hoped was as perfect as his own, then turned back to look at the parade as a float advertising Taubolt's upcoming Whale-Watching Festival passed by. Astride a huge, somewhat misshapened whale of papier-mâché, which there'd apparently been no time to paint, sat Karl Foster, the Chamber of Commerce's president, waving at the crowd, like Captain Ahab riding Moby Dick. A banner on the whale's side proclaimed, TAUBOLT: PARADISE BESIDE THE SEA!

⚈

"Look." Rose grinned. "There's your mom and Joby."

"Where?" Hawk said.

"Down there, across the street. See? They're kissing." Her eyes became as bright as her smile. "When's he going to marry her anyway?"

"I don't know," Hawk sighed. "When he finally gets off his butt and asks her, we should have another parade."

"Sometimes you sound like it's you he's supposed to marry," she scoffed.

"No way." Hawk grinned, leaning in to kiss her again. "Only one person I'll ever want to marry."

"I hope that's not a proposal," she smiled, dodging his lips to peck his cheek instead, "'cause you know what I'll say."

"Not until after college," he sighed, shrugging away from her to watch the parade again. "I know. You must have told me about two hundred times."

"It's hard to know when you're listening." She grinned mischievously. "If we both get into Brown—"

"*When* we both get into Brown," Hawk corrected with a smile.

"*When* we're at Brown," she smiled back, "we can take all our gen-ed classes together, and study together every night. It'll be almost the same thing."

"No it won't," he said, "but I can wait. Long as we're together. That's all I care."

"That's all I care too," she said, throwing her arms around his neck, and starting to rhapsodize again about going off to college and living in the wider world at last. Hawk couldn't suppress the silly grin that always crossed his face when she talked this way. He'd known that wider world all too well once, but never believed it could be lovable until she'd begun to show it to him through her eyes. Now, he couldn't wait to share it with her. Solomon had told him once that a true bard was only fully forged by pleasures and pains far greater than any Hawk had yet known. Listening to Rose now, Hawk felt sure that everything Solomon had meant awaited them at college. Just one more year.

"It's kind of strange," she said at last, watching the ladies of Taubolt's Historical Preservation Council pass in their old Model A Ford, decked out in antique frocks and wide, flowered hats. "Half our friends may never leave Taubolt at all. Don't they ever wonder about what's going on out there?" She gave him an earnest look. "I know some of it's awful, but there must be so much worth doing!" Her expression became dreamy. "Sometimes being cooped up here feels like," she smiled, "like sleeping through a parade."

"You think Taubolt's boring?" Hawk laughed. "Look at all these people! They'd have given anything for five minutes of what you took for granted growing up here!"

"I know," Rose sighed, pulling him back into the shop entryway where they could talk more privately, "I love Taubolt with all my heart, Hawk. You know I always will. But what are we doing with everything we have here? What's it for? Do we ever ask that? All these people seem so desperate for what we've been given, but we just hide it here, where it's nothing but a game—a game for children."

"It's not just *hidden* here," Hawk murmured gravely. "It's protected. Their world destroys what it *needs* as quickly as it destroys anything else, you know. Maybe Taubolt's *little game* is all that's kept what we have here alive."

"Maybe," Rose sighed. "But we must be keeping it alive for something more than just," she shook her head impatiently, "just keeping it alive." The excitement came back into her eyes. "Haven't you wondered why Taubolt's borders have suddenly failed after all these years? Maybe it's time to bring what we have *out* of hiding, Hawk! You know none of this is really ours, certainly not the—" Hawk started and looked around to remind her they were not alone. "Certainly not *it,*" Rose whispered, looking chastened.

"That's one thing I'm not looking forward to," Hawk said, taking her hand and leading her around the building into a small patch of garden away from the noisy street with its prying eyes and ears. "What's it going to be like," he asked softly when they got there, "living so far away from the Cup for so long? I can't even remember how that felt now, and I don't think I want to."

"We'll handle it," she assured him, "because we'll have each other, Hawk, and because we know there *is* something to believe in, and that there must be some way to share it. There must be a thousand ways! All we'll need to find is *one.*"

✼

Agnes Hamilton took a petite sip of iced tea, set her glass on the lawn table, and heaved a long-suffering sigh. A sudden blare of discordant horns from the parade route three blocks off was followed by a muffled swell of applause and laughter. "Listen to that racket, Franny! Did we move up here just to be assaulted by a bunch of yahoos trying to wake the dead?"

Franny shook her head obediently.

"Karl wanted me to ride with him on that ludicrous whale, if you can believe it," Agnes scoffed. "Imagine. Up on that monstrosity waving like some circus performer. I do wonder about the man sometimes."

"He's very proud of the new Chamber," Franny said with apologetic deference. "You did encourage him to form it."

"I encouraged him to organize this town's unruly flood of merchants into some more *manageable* body, not to make a *spectacle* of himself—or me! Parades! What next? *A kissing booth?*"

"Oh, I'm sure he would never ask you to do *that,*" Franny gasped.

Agnes gave her a sidelong glance, wondering, not for the first time, whether Franny's dim front were just disguised recalcitrance. "If he had to raise such a din," she growled, "he might at least have kept rabble like that *Greensong* woman out of it. It's disgraceful to legitimize such a harridan by letting her march down Main Street."

"What could he do?" Franny asked timidly. "It's against the law to stop her."

"Oh!" Agnes exclaimed sarcastically. "And *laws* are so important here, aren't they?" She was suddenly wracked with something close to despair at the overwhelming obstacles she faced. "No one seems to understand the price I've paid to help protect this town," she moaned. "The historical society was a useless gossip refinery before I took it under wing. *Preservation* hadn't even occurred to them! Can you imagine? Now we've got the teeth to keep people from painting their houses any old color they want, or plastering Main Street with neon signs, or . . . who knows; growing cactus in their yards! Just look at this influx of people, Franny! Taubolt's character would have been swept away completely by now if not for me. Just tell me I'm wrong."

Franny looked a bit unsure about whether to obey. "*I* know how hard you work, Agnes. So does Karl. . . . A lot of people do."

"Well, they don't work very hard to show it," Agnes pressed, speaking not so much to Franny anymore, as to some larger internal audience. "The school board still refuses to close that high school campus at lunchtime," she huffed. "You'd think they might remember who got them going in the first place. I mean, really, Franny! The school board, the Chamber of Commerce, the Botanical Council, even the committee to explore incorporation. *None* of these had even crossed this town's backward minds before I came." She exhaled as if some large animal had stepped on her chest. "Who knew it would be so much work to manage a little dolls' house like Taubolt?"

"It's a very nice little dolls' house though," Franny reassured her.

"Yes," Agnes conceded wearily, "but between the yahoos moving up here, and the native simpletons, one of me may not be enough to save the place." Somewhere down the street, a string of firecrackers exploded in rapid staccato. "Uhg!" Agnes exclaimed, sloshing her drink onto her blouse in alarm. "Oh! Those hoodlums!" she complained, brushing ineffectually at the wet spots on her breast. "If we had a standing police force here, these lawless children might develop some respect for the rights of decent citizens!"

Franny nodded solemnly, getting up to offer Agnes her napkin.

"It's disgraceful that we're reduced to importing officers all the way from Heeberville for events like this circus of Karl's! God knows what bedlam might erupt amidst such a mob!" Her tirade was cut short as a low flying helicopter thundered over her rooftop and across her yard on its way toward the parade route.

"God almighty!" she exclaimed, sucking breath like a landed fish. "Ferristaff! A man with his money has no excuse for such manners!"

⊗

"The earth is our mother!" Greensong shouted into the video camera trained on her cadre of protesters as they marched under signs and banners decrying Ferristaff's local logging operations. *"They're calling Taubolt paradise! Would men rape their mother in paradise? We want Ferristaff out of here NOW, with all his macho men stinking of money and steel!"*

"News crews in Taubolt," Franklin muttered, overlooking the angry spectacle from up on the Crow's Nest Bar and Grill's sundeck with Gladys Lindsay and the Connollys. "That I should have lived to see it."

"And policemen," Gladys lamented, gazing down at the two bored-looking officers escorting Greensong's company down the street.

"Came up here for a public interest story," Tom sighed. "Looks like they got it."

"Trouble in paradise," Gladys said grimly. "Far more titillating than the quaint parade they expected, I'm sure. She does put on quite a show. Look at her scream."

"Seems to me she might hate men a little more'n she loves trees," Franklin grunted. "Feelin's mutual from what I've heard. Not sure I like seein' so many of our kids out there beside her either. Couple of 'em came into the store last week to get stuff for those banners. Said she told 'em the planet's proper human population was zero."

"She opposes Ferristaff." Clara shrugged. "Of course the children back her. They're angry about what he's doing to our forests too. Aren't we all?"

"Not like that," Franklin said. "That anger's got nothin' to do with justice."

"For what it's worth, Rose agrees with you," Clara conceded.

"Smart girl, your Rose," said Franklin. He looked up and down the parade route with distaste. "Awful lotta bad seed gettin' spilled in our yard these days. Turns my stomach to watch 'em fight over Taubolt like we'd never even been here."

"There's a television executive from Los Angeles staying at my inn this weekend," Gladys said. "Some friend of Ferristaff's apparently. He tells me they're preparing to film a one-hour special here." She shook her head sadly. "I still can't understand how all this happened so quickly—or at all!"

"Ain't natural. I'll tell you that," Franklin grumbled. "Jake can say what he likes. This ain't just an overcrowded world stumblin' up against us. There's gotta be somethin' behind an invasion like this. Wish I knew what it was, much less how to stop it."

"Well, between the way Hamilton's buying up this town, and Ferristaff the woods," Tom said, "I don't know how much there'll be to save soon. I hate to say it, but maybe we should be looking for someplace else to go."

"Things here that're awful hard to move," Franklin said without looking away from the parade. "You know that well as I do, Tom."

"Yes, I do," Tom sighed. "But we may have to find some way to move even those, Franklin. Ferristaff's already started looking north."

"He won't find it," Franklin said. "Never get in on the ground, and we both know what he'll see from the air."

"Men like him destroy things they can't see all the time," Tom pressed.

"He tries," Franklin said quietly, "I'll do things to him personally that'll make any plans Ms. Greensong's got seem lovesick."

A rhythmic thrumming in the distance made them all look up, along with everyone on the street below, as a helicopter appeared above the roofs at Main Street's far end, and turned in their direction.

"Speakin' of the devil," Franklin spat.

✺

"There you go, Mr. Benzick," Ferristaff said, banking the copter to give his passenger a better view of Main Street. "Not exactly the Macy's parade."

"If it were, I wouldn't be here." Benzick smiled. "Wish we had cameras down there. This is exactly the kind of stuff we're going to want for the special."

"Oh, you'll have no shortage of quaint spectacle." Ferristaff grinned. "Not if the Chamber of Commerce has anything to say about it. Anyway, I heard something about a news crew up here today doing some kind of PR section for a Bay Area station. You'll probably be able to grab some of their footage." He searched the parade route. "There's the cameraman, in fact, ogling the latest little thorn in my side." He nudged the copter forward a few blocks until they were hovering right over Greensong's little band. "Hello, darlin'!" Ferristaff drawled under his breath as everyone below stared up at them. Greensong shook her fist at him, shouting in obvious rage. One more thing to like about helicopter travel, he realized; couldn't hear a damn thing from outside the cockpit. "We've probably ruffled enough feathers here." He grinned. "What next?"

"Well, I'd love a better look at the coastline," Benzick said. "North this time?"

"No problem." Ferristaff banked to head back across town.

"I appreciate your taking time to show me around like this," said Benzick.

"My pleasure," Ferristaff replied. "Shadwell and I go way back. If you all do this TV special, I hope he'll get up here himself, and visit me. You tell him I said so."

"I will." The young man smiled. "The show's already been green-lighted actually. I don't know if you're aware of it, Mr. Ferristaff, but this little town has become quite the hot ticket. You'd think it was Disneyland and Yellowstone rolled into one, the way people are panicking to vacation here now." He fell silent, gazing down at flocks of seabirds wheeling about the surf washed cliffs, amber fields of grass, and wooded knolls farther inland. In diplomatic deference to his host, he said nothing about the wide, muddy tracts of clear-cut scarring numerous slopes east and south of town. "It is beautiful," he mused. "I still can't imagine how all this went undiscovered for so long."

"Well, that might have something to do with Taubolt's stiff-necked natives," Ferristaff said dryly. "You say 'growth' to them, they think tomatoes and summer squash. Hell, this place has more potential per square acre than Laguna Beach. Every last one of them could be rich for life by now if they had the tiniest bit of business sense. But I'll tell you, Mr. Benzick, these are the sorriest tribe of backward yokels you will ever meet." He grinned humorlessly. "Though I can see that might be a source of some delight to your program director."

✻

"Why antagonize her like that?" Laura asked in disbelief as Ferristaff's craft veered from its brief pause up the street and headed away from town. "Isn't she causing him enough trouble without him poking at the wasps' nest?"

"You'd think," Joby said, as the distant ruckus subsided, and the parade began to move again. "Though she pokes plenty too. Can't expect the logging crowd to hug her for it." It seemed to Joby that there was altogether too much poking going on in Taubolt these days. Even the tourists had changed. Gone were the bemused, accidental visitors that had once wandered so cheerfully in and out of Taubolt's shops and restaurants. Now, the guests at Gladys's inn spent half their time complaining. Stressed and disgruntled couples in bright plastic sun hats and plaid Bermuda shorts moaned about the places they had come from, or irritably listed the ways that Taubolt wasn't living up to whatever they'd been told by magazines or travel agents, while their tetchy children cried or argued in the background. It all left Joby feeling not just glum, but vaguely anxious.

By any rational assessment, Joby's life here had gotten better with each passing year. He had a solid position now in the most idyllic place he could imagine. He was blessed with scores of remarkable friends, and, most wonderfully of all, he had Laura back; a gift he'd never hoped for in the dark years since he'd lost her. And yet, despite all this, there was still some small, hard, fearful knot at the center of him that Taubolt had never managed to reach; some elusive artifact of his unpleasant past. Unable to expunge it, he'd just done his best to ignore it altogether, but it seemed unwilling to ignore him.

To Joby's carefully concealed dismay, that dark lump had settled very quickly between himself and Laura. A creature filled with light and beauty, she gave him fistfuls of the treasure she contained whenever they were together. But each time he reached inside himself to reciprocate, he found that mute, intractable core of empty darkness where the laughter and delight he longed to give her in return should have been. The closer she came, the more frightened he felt that she would see what sat there inside him, and recoil. For more than a year now, he'd done all he could to keep her near, fearful of losing her again, but unable to let her in. Struggling all the while to find some way past the turmoil that stood between himself and all he most wanted, he feared Laura would not let him hide from her much longer.

"Uh-oh," Laura teased. "Better get out your can of crystal repellent."

Abandoning his ruminations, Joby looked up the street to find Molly Redstone, Taubolt's recently arrived New Age maven, and her circle of disciples, all in flowing gowns and ribbons, gliding toward them to recorded strains of ethereal music under a huge purple banner that read, HARMONY HOUSE HERALDS THE COMING DAWN.

Molly had appeared the previous year, insisting that Taubolt sat at the convergence of no less than five geological power vertices, and promptly opened Harmony House, a shop selling every accoutrement required by devotees of alternative health and spirituality. Her weekly meditation and discussion group was very popular among the newer brand of townie now, and her business thrived.

"God will not suffer a witch to live!" shouted a balding man in white shirt and black trousers standing nearby. Joby felt Laura tense in his arms as the man

leapt into the street, pointing, rod-armed, at Molly. *"A witch is an abomination before the Lord!"*

Joby groaned, unable to believe this was happening so soon after Ferristaff's disruptive appearance. A shocked silence rippled through the sea of bystanders in both directions as Molly and her followers sped their pace in stone-faced silence.

"Behold the whore of Babylon!" the man shouted. *"It's no dawn she heralds. It's the darkness!"* Rushing forward, he tried to grab one of the poles supporting her Harmony House banner, but the woman holding it managed to bang him in the head with it instead, sending him reeling back to the curb, clutching his forehead and looking around as if expecting someone to come to his defense.

"Your god is a bigot, and a murderer of women and children!" one of Molly's disciples spat scornfully at the man.

Molly stopped her with a glance, and said with a sad smile and a voice pitched to carry, "The enlightened are above such bitterness, Alicia." She looked theatrically at her wider audience, and added more loudly, "In becoming the enemy, only the enemy is served. Victory lies only in peace. Be peace." She turned serenely, and moved on, her contingent hurrying after.

"Concubine of the devil!" the man shouted after her, then fled the street, muttering something about the rejection of prophets in their own land as Joby saw the Heeberville police officers who'd been guarding Greensong and the crowd from each other come running in an attempt to intercept the lunatic.

"Laura, let's go," said Joby, as the knot of darkness he'd just been pondering seemed suddenly to squirm and kick inside him like a restless fetus. "This isn't the kind of celebration I was hoping for."

✼

The wind brought gusts of parade noise from the other side of town as Swami and Ander helped Father Crombie slowly up the chapel's back stairs. His hips and knees had grown much worse that winter. Even short walks were a painful labor now.

"Thank you for allowing this, Father," Swami said apologetically.

"We thought it might be safest while everyone is at the parade," said Ander.

"It's like a migraine," Swami groaned, "the constant press of all their greed and grief and . . . and anger. We wouldn't've bothered you, but we didn't know where else—"

"Boys," Crombie interrupted, "there is nothing to explain or apologize for. This is my sacred, and, frankly, most fulfilling task in life. I am well aware of how the particular gifts you two possess must chafe in such troubled times, and I am deeply gratified to help you bear these burdens in whatever way I can." After all these years, it still caused Crombie awe that such creatures should require anything from him at all, and pity, now, that they should reach manhood with so few tools, or even language, with which to cope with what had come at last to Taubolt's doorstep. Crombie took the key from his pocket, and turned it in the back door lock. "Ander, will you go make sure the chapel is empty, and lock the front doors, please?"

When Ander had gone in ahead of them, Crombie continued to lean on Swami's steadying arm as they approached the golden box against the wall behind the altar. Crombie fumbled beneath his shirt for the medallion Jake had given him.

None but the Council were allowed near the Cup now without Crombie's consent. Since the broken world had started pouring through Taubolt's borders, the unpredictable object had been given more and more frequently to spontaneous, sometimes spectacular displays of . . . who knew what? Anger? Fear? . . . Grief? It was impossible to know. But since its outbursts often involved strange plays of brilliant light and sudden flows of sound, soft and eerie or fierce and beautiful, which would be difficult to explain to those best ignorant of Taubolt's secrets, Jake had set wards around the Cup's housing now that none but Crombie and the other Council members could pass.

"Some say the Cup could leave us," Swami said anxiously. "Is it true, Father?"

"That it has a will of its own, and the power to come and go as it wishes is beyond dispute," Crombie replied. "What it will choose, or why, is as much a mystery to me as to anyone else," the priest concluded.

"What would we do if it were gone?" Swami asked even more fearfully. "I have had such terrible dreams."

From this particular boy, the remark was deeply disturbing, but Crombie kept concern from his voice as he replied. "I cannot presume to reassure *you* about the unreliability of dreams as I would most others, Swami. But it is God who protects us here, and the Cup serves God, just as we do. Even were it called away, our true protector would not abandon us. That much comfort I can offer with confidence."

As they reached the tabernacle, Crombie began to murmur the words only his voice could instill with power. At once there was the sound of choral song as if from very far away, innumerable vocal harmonies, lovely beyond any skill of human composition. As the tabernacle doors unsealed themselves, a warm radiance the color of sunlight through magnolia petals streamed from the widening seams. Father Crombie and his young companions were on their knees before the doors were fully open. What Crombie marveled over most at that moment was not the spectacle before them, but the utter absence of pain in his legs as they had knelt and the certain knowledge that he would have no trouble rising afterward. What the boys might be receiving, he could not guess, but their rapt expressions told him they had all they'd come for.

(Reunion)

"Well, I'd say you're a hit!" Joby enthused as he drove Laura home from her opening at Alice Mayfield's gallery. "Think you can paint fast enough to meet demand?"

"Praise is one thing," she temporized. "Sales are another. We'll see what we see."

"And you think *I'm* crummy at compliments!" Joby teased. "You sold three paintings just tonight! Isn't that a hint?"

"All to Hamilton," she said. "I'll need a larger customer base than that."

"I don't know," Joby mused, hunching his shoulders. "She's awfully rich. . . ."

"'Awfully' is right," Laura drawled. "I've never met anyone who made it so hard to smile when they're throwing money at you." She shook her head, staring out into the starry night. "She talked as if it were *me* she was buying."

"Well, I'm just very happy that you're painting again," Joby said. "I'm already saving up to expand your customer base by at least one, if that helps any."

"Aren't you sweet," Laura said, turning to smile at him in the moonlight. "But the day I let you pay for one of my paintings is the day—"

"What!" Joby cut her off playfully. "My money's not as good as Hamilton's?"

As they turned into the gravel drive, they were surprised to see another car already parked there.

"Who's that?" asked Joby.

"I have no idea," Laura said, sounding concerned.

As they pulled up beside it, Joby saw a tall broad-shouldered man sitting in the darkness on the steps to Laura's door, his face barely lit by the bounce of Joby's headlights off the house.

"Can I help you?" Joby asked, stepping from his car.

The man was silent for a moment, then said uncertainly, "I'm looking for Laura Bayer. Sorry, Laura Raulins, I guess. I was given directions to this house." He hesitated, then said, "Are you her husband?"

"No, he's not," Laura said, emerging from the other side of Joby's car. "And it's Laura Bayer again. Do I know you?"

"Laura?" the man said. The dim light glinted off teeth, and even in the strange half light, Joby could not have mistaken that smile. "Ben?" he said, incredulous.

"Oh my God!" Laura gasped. "Ben, is that you?"

"Joby?" Ben blurted out. "What are *you* doing here?" He laughed suddenly, and Joby rushed to embrace his old friend, a step ahead of Laura.

"I live here!" Joby said happily. "What the hell are *you* doing here?"

"You live *here*? With Laura?" Ben said, sounding even more surprised.

"Of course not," Laura laughed, hugging Ben in turn. "We're just coming back from an opening of my paintings in town. I wish you'd been there! Why didn't you tell me you were coming? And how did you find me anyway?"

"Your parents told me where you were. I thought I'd surprise you."

Joby's delight began to sour. What had Laura meant by "of course not"? And come to think of it . . .

"So what on earth brings you to Taubolt, Ben?" Joby asked a bit too cheerfully.

"I haven't seen Laura in years." He shrugged. "I thought I'd come visit. Her folks didn't tell me *you* were here though." He smiled that sunny smile Joby remembered so well. "Two for one! I feel like a lottery winner!"

I'll bet, Joby thought.

"Well, let's not stand out here in the dark," Laura said. "Come inside!"

"Whoa!" Ben said, as he followed them up the wobbly stairs. "You should fix these steps before they kill somebody."

"Sorry," she said self-consciously, "I've gotten used to it, I guess, and I'm not much of a handyman."

"Well, maybe I can shore it up a little for you tomorrow," Ben offered.

Joby silently berated himself for having failed to make the same offer long ago, but it had never wobbled this badly until Ben had thumped his bulk down on it. Their old friend had grown into quite the giant since college. Two hundred twenty, if he was an ounce. . . . All of it muscle, Joby didn't doubt.

They'd hardly gotten inside, when Laura realized she'd left her coat in the car, and asked Joby to go down and get it while she fixed them all some snacks.

Joby went, wondering why she hadn't sent Ben instead, as if that made any sense. Nor was his state of mind improved when he came back inside a moment later, rather quietly, and heard voices hushed in urgent conversation from the kitchen. He shut the door behind him as softly as he could, but the voices stopped.

"You want beer, Joby," Laura called cheerfully, "or soda?"

Ben came into the hallway holding a beer.

"Beer," said Joby.

Ben smiled and shook his head. "I can't believe we're all together again."

"Neither can I," Joby answered, forcing a smile in return.

"You're lookin' good, Joby. This place must agree with you."

"You look like a movie star, as usual," Joby said, unable to pretend it wasn't true.

Ben's smile became a bit uncertain. "That's some sky tonight," he said back through the kitchen door to Laura. "You guys have as many stars out here as I ever saw in the mountains. Think I'll go out and take another look. Want to join me, Joby?" he asked, as he passed, heading for the door.

"Sure." Joby shrugged.

They'd hardly gotten outside before Ben leaned up against the railing, and asked, "So, are you two together finally?"

Joby had to admire Ben's directness, and felt relieved that they wouldn't have to beat around the bush. "We're not married yet, if that's what you mean." He shrugged again. "But we've been dating for a year. You here for the reason I think you are?"

Ben looked away uncomfortably, grinning sheepishly. "Am I that obvious?"

Joby said nothing, caught between a series of conflicting emotions.

"Listen, Joby," Ben said, turning back to look him frankly in the eyes. "This isn't going to get complicated. Yes, I came here looking for Laura, and yes I was hoping she might be glad to see me. I've been a lot of places since we all parted company, and never met anyone who held a candle to her. But I had no idea you were here. I only phoned her parents once and said I was an old friend trying to track Laura down. They asked a few questions about me, but never mentioned you."

Wondering why they hadn't, Joby wondered even more uncomfortably whether Laura had ever told them she was seeing him, and if not, why not?

"I had no idea *what* I'd find here, Joby," Ben sighed. "I just figured I'd come see and play it by ear from there. Now I see you're here, my ear says butt out, loud and clear. I hated what happened to us all the first time. No way I'm going there again. It's really great to see you both, but if you'd like me to go, I'll understand completely."

"Well, no," Joby said, suddenly feeling catty and ashamed. "Of course I don't want you to go. I . . . I've missed you, Ben. It's great to see you too."

With a wry look, Ben said, "Then pray, accept my full surrender, your highness, and my renewed vow of fealty."

"Oh my God!" Joby chuckled. "You know, I teach at the high school here, and, you'll never believe this, but the kids have started up their own Round-table club. They even leave the same little tokens."

"You never could go anywhere without infecting people," Ben said. The fondness on his face was unsettling. "I've thought about you a lot, Joby. I can't tell you how happy it makes me to find you looking so much better than you did last time we met."

"A lot's changed since then," Joby said, quickly suppressing unpleasant memories of their last encounter, years ago in Berkeley. "Everything, really. I've finally found my place in the world." He couldn't help smiling. "I'm very happy now."

"I can tell." Ben grinned, setting his beer on the railing, and folding his arms. "I'd have tried to look you up before, I guess, but to be honest, it almost killed me to see you like that in Berkeley. I guess I just . . . hid from you after that. I'm sorry."

"I've done my share of hiding too," Joby said. "A lot more than you." There was an awkward pause, then he asked, "So how long can you stay?"

"No place I really have to be right now." Ben shrugged. "I've saved up enough money to drift for a while."

"I rent a room at the Primrose Picket Inn in town," Joby said. "The innkeeper is a very good friend. I'm pretty sure she'll give you a pretty sweet deal there."

"That'd be great." Ben smiled.

"Guess we'd better go in then," Joby said. "Laura will think we're out here jousting to the death or something."

"No," Ben smiled quietly, "she knows us both too well, and she knows *I* know who's always owned her heart."

Joby smiled gratefully and nodded toward the door, wondering how he could have felt so threatened by such a fine old friend. The finest friend he'd ever had, or likely ever would. With Laura back, and now Ben as well, he could think of nothing more to wish for. His happiness was complete.

✸

As much as Nacho resented the flood of strangers pouring into Taubolt, he had to admit they'd brought some pretty cool toys with them; like computers, which he'd taken to as a match takes to fire, and most of all, skateboards. From the moment he'd watched a child half his age "ollie" off a curb on Shea Street, Nacho had been hooked. Now there was nothing he enjoyed more than being out on a brisk morning like this one, pushing the envelope on his beloved skateboard, the *shraupmobile*. Nacho's board had become a virtual appendage, a second heart, a set of wings.

It was not entirely without malice, however, that he pivoted into a long, loud backside tailslide along the curb as he approached Karl Foster's chichi boutique. For Nacho, the man had come to represent all that was noxious about the invading hoard. Having purchased his little piece of the rock, Foster now treated people who'd been here for generations as if they were just so much trailer trash in his way. Sure enough, before Nacho had come within twenty feet of Karl's storefront, the man was racing out onto his deck like an angry dog.

Ignoring Karl's wild gesticulations and shouts of outrage, Nacho did a 180 nollie heel flip on the sidewalk right in front of him, then popped his board up into one hand and sat down on the curb with his back to the infuriated merchant.

"Didn't you hear me?" Karl demanded ridiculously from the deck behind him. "I asked you to leave! This is a place of business!"

"You didn't *ask*," Nacho said without turning to look at him. "You *ordered*. And this is a *public* sidewalk, so I've got every right to sit here and catch my breath." The man made no reply, but Nacho felt his angry silence like a furnace at his back. Turning to look at him, Nacho asked, "What's your problem, Foster?"

"My problem?" Karl barked incredulously. "You kids are out here every day, trampling my garden, damaging my stairs, leaning on my deck and fence with your dirty, baggy clothes and surly looks and foul language, like a gang of dope-smoking terrorists scaring off all my customers, and you ask what's *my problem?* . . . Don't you have parents? Didn't anyone teach you *anything* about being *human beings?*"

"Yeah," Nacho said. "They taught me for *twenty years* before dopeltons like you came here waving fistfuls of money and telling us all we had no right to be seen around *your* town anymore. This was our *home* before it was your *place of business,* Foster."

"Here you are," Foster drawled, "how many years out of high school? And what are you doing with your life?"

"As it happens, *richard,*" Nacho snapped, beginning to boil. "I do DHTML and JavaScript with back-end server perl/CGI scripts for high-profile e-commerce Web site architecture, as well as audio/video capture and digitized real-time media streaming. You ever thought about a Web site, Karl? You'd be amazed how it can boost business, even for a little trinket shop like yours. If you're interested, I could fit you in later this week sometime. How's Wednesday look?"

Karl just glared at him and curled his lip.

"Hey," Nacho said apologetically, "did I lose you with the technical stuff? Here, let's try it in simpler terms." He began talking very slowly. "A *Web site* is a—"

"You punks think you're so smart, don't you," Karl cut him off, "just because you sit around playing computer games while the rest of us are out here working for a living. But you'll sing a very different tune when we get a sheriff in this town. You try these tricks in front of my store then, I'll call the law down on you so hard it'll make your cocky little teeth rattle. What you do with that board constitutes a clear public nuisance, boy, and they'll confiscate it. Then you can *walk* here to make fun of me."

"Woof," Nacho said. "Woof, woof."

Karl clearly had no idea what to make of this response.

"What's it like, bein' Hamilton's little lapdog, Karl?" Nacho asked. "She feed her *pretty boy* yummy little doggy treats?"

"I don't have to take this." Foster sneered and turned to go back inside his store, but as he reached the entrance he turned back. "You know, there's a lot of support around here for making skateboarding illegal inside town limits, son. When they take your toys away, they may give you hoodlums tickets too. Hope your computer business pays well enough to cover the cost." Then he spun away into his shop.

Filled with disgust, Nacho jumped onto his deck, set his board down, and kick-flipped the steps back onto the sidewalk, leaving a splintered gouge in Karl's top stair.

Karl came racing out after him screaming like a banshee, but Nacho was already soaring down the street, too far away to hear, too free to care.

✖

"It's about commitment!" Greensong insisted. "You can't say, 'I stand for justice' and then do nothing!"

"Of course not," Rose said. "But there are ways to act without becoming just like what you're acting against."

"There's no resemblance between me and them!" Greensong shouted. "They trash whole ecosystems to enrich themselves! I'm saving whole ecosystems for free!"

"Saving lives by taking lives?" Bellindi asked quietly. "The kinds of things you suggested to those kids could have left men maimed or even killed. Do you think it'll be easier to save our forests when everyone thinks *we're* criminals and *they're* the victims?"

"Are a few dead men are worse than the extinction of every salmon on the West Coast?" Greensong screeched, waving toward the window of her rented cabin as if an entire school of them were swimming in the twilight just outside. "Everything that lives in these forests is in danger of extinction. *Men* aren't! I'm sorry, but you're a couple of very *nice* girls from a very *nice* place that knows *nothing* about the real world."

"If your 'real world' is about killing people to protest their lack of concern for the sacredness of life," Bellindi said darkly, "I don't think I want any of it here. And I doubt anyone else will either. If you think fighting Ferristaff all by yourself will be more effective, just keep spouting suggestions like the ones you've been making. You'll have your forces down to one in no time."

"If you're so sure of your position," Rose asked, "why did you propose these things to no one but a bunch of kids?"

"Because they can still hear me," Greensong spat. "They're not already brainwashed like the two of you."

"Or because they're so much easier for *you* to brainwash," Rose replied evenly. "We came up here because we want to see Ferristaff stopped worse than you do, and you're about to hand him the war. I'm not about to let that happen. Trust me, if there's one tree spiked, one *bomb* made around here," she rolled her eyes, unable to believe Greensong had even suggested such a thing, "we will know, and we will report you."

"You traitorous little bitches." Greensong sneered. "Are you sleeping with Ferristaff, or just running his errands?"

Rose looked at Bellindi, who was clearly struggling to keep her composure. "Hate us all you want," Rose shrugged, turning back to Greensong, "but if you come up with any more plans that stupid, at least have the courage to propose them to adults next time, not just Taubolt's kids."

She and Bellindi turned to leave, wanting to finish the long walk home from Greensong's isolated cabin before total darkness, but as they reached the door, something crashed through a window to their right, spraying glass onto the table there before skidding to a halt on the floor. As both girls froze, a second, closer window shattered. Greensong bit off a scream as a fist-size rock passed within inches of her shoulder and thudded off a low cabinet. Rose and Bellindi crouched down and scurried back toward Greensong who was cowering behind a kitchen chair—the only cover close at hand. The sound of laughter blossomed not far outside. Several men, from the sound of it.

"Hey, Greendyke!" bellowed one of the men outside. "Wanna get lucky?"

More laughter, loud and mean.

"We do!" shouted a second man. "Come out and dance, you tree-huggin' bitch!"

"Yeah!" laughed the first man, "I wanna spike *your* tree, darlin'!"

More hilarity, and the sound of boots crunching on gravel as the men approached.

"I've got a gun!" Greensong shouted desperately.

Perhaps it was the fear in her voice that gave her away, but the men outside just laughed. "So have I, lady!" jeered the second man's voice. "Hot, hard, and loaded."

"Know which end to shoot from, honey-cum?" called the first man.

Suddenly the back door just behind them shattered with a clamoring racket, causing all three women to scream and throw themselves against the farthest wall. A third man stumbled through its ruin, leering and obviously drunk. "Boo," he said, thinking this so funny that he could only lean against the ruined jamb and laugh at first.

"Oh, looky here!" exclaimed one of the men from out front, sticking his face in through a broken window. "Bonus points, Sandoval! One for each of us!"

"Three little tree huggers, lined up on a wall," chanted the man who'd broken in the door. "Tasty little rabbits, and I'm gonna eat 'em all." He bent double with drunken laughter as his two companions pushed the front door open and came inside as well.

✖

"What *kind* of animals?" Ferristaff growled in disbelief. "Didn't they have guns?"

"Of course," Bruech shrugged. "But it was dark, and they kept missing. Apparently this went on all night, and by morning they'd had enough. They packed up and high-tailed it out of there."

"Well, I didn't pay them to turn and run the minute they encountered a little wild life, you can tell 'em there's no check in the mail." Ferristaff ran a hand through his thatch of silvering hair, and went to stare unhappily out at the darkness through one of his expansive living room's picture windows. The house he'd built of local timber here in the hills outside of Taubolt had an impressive view of the coastline meandering north into the moonlit haze. "Frankly, I'm tired of all these ridiculous setbacks, Bruech. Why is it suddenly so hard to get a simple little survey done?"

"I'm as frustrated as you are, Robert, but I don't know what else to try," Bruech protested. "It's like sending men into the devil's triangle up there. I hire seasoned professionals—people we've used lots of times in much rougher terrain than this seems from the air—but they just end up wandering in circles, or losing their equipment. Now this. I don't know what to make of it."

"Well *someone* has to own that mysterious hole," Ferristaff grumbled. "Whoever that is could answer most of the important questions. Why haven't you found them yet?"

"Frankly, sir, I think they're hiding from us. Or being hidden. It's the same game these people have been playing since we got here."

Ferristaff said nothing to this. The memory of his embarrassment when he'd tried to leverage some cooperation from these yokels by reporting their tax evasion was not one he wanted stirred. Someone had beaten him to the punch there, and he wasn't going to try it again, even if he thought anyone would pay attention to his accusations a second time. "There must be something we can use to make them quit this shit," he muttered.

His thoughts were derailed by the sound of tires crunching across his gravel drive.

"Who would that be?" Ferristaff murmured, going to the door. Before he got halfway there, someone was banging on it to wake the dead. Angered, Ferristaff picked up speed, Bruech following behind, and yanked the door open to find Tom Connolly glaring at him on the porch.

"I want you out of here!" Connolly shouted so fiercely that Ferristaff balled

his fists, bracing to block a swing that didn't come. Connolly just stood there, shaking and livid, and continued to shout. *"Your whole goddamn company and these goddamn thugs you import had better be packed up and—"*

Ferristaff simply slammed the door shut again in his face, but Connolly resumed banging on it almost immediately.

"What the fuck is he about?" Ferristaff snapped at Bruech, who simply shrugged, looking startled. "If you can't calm down and talk to me like a civilized man, Mr. Connolly," Ferristaff shouted through the heavy redwood door, "then you'd better go because I'm about to call the police!"

"From *Heeberville?*" Connolly jeered back. "Now I'm sacred! As it happens, they're already on there way! I called them half an hour ago!"

"What?" Ferristaff asked, turning back to Bruech, who simply shrugged again and shook his head.

On the porch, Connolly had finally fallen silent.

"Mr. Connolly, I don't know what's happened, and I do want to," Ferristaff said more calmly. "If I open this door, will you tell me what's going on in some more reasonable manner, or do we have to wait until there are officers here to protect me?"

"Oh, that's *rich!*" Connolly snapped.

After another lengthy silence, Ferristaff, who had never had much trouble handling himself in a fight, shrugged at Bruech, and opened the door.

Connolly stood glaring as before, obviously struggling for control. "Three of your men," he rasped, "just tried to *rape my daughter.*"

Ferristaff's jaw swung down like the tailgate of a dump truck. *"My God!"* he breathed. This was trouble. Real trouble, if not managed carefully. Fortunately, his very real shock seemed to temper Connolly's rage, if only slightly. "Is she—" Ferristaff began.

"Jake happened to be nearby and got to them in time to stop it," Connolly grated. "But your presence here has got to end. By morning, you won't have a friend left in—"

"Mr. Connolly," Ferristaff cut in levelly, "are you suggesting that I had something to do with this appalling crime?"

"You came under false pretenses," Connolly accused, "and your *activities* here have been nothing but one big toxic spill ever since! We don't want any more of—"

"I am deeply, deeply sorry about what's been done to your daughter, Mr. Connolly," Ferristaff interjected again, "and I will spare no effort or expense to see that these man are found and—"

"They're already in custody," Connolly interrupted in turn. "The only thing you can do for us is leave. If you need help packing, please don't hesitate to ask."

"I own this land, Mr. Connolly," Ferristaff said, allowing just enough steel into his voice to cut through any illusions Connolly's distraught condition might have allowed him. "I *bought* every acre I'm harvesting up here fair and legal. I'm sure I'd feel just as you do, had it been my daughter, but I am not the guilty party here, nor in any way associated with what those jackasses did. Consider them fired, and I hope they hang, but I have no intention of going anywhere. I don't want you to leave here confused about that."

"It's your neck," Connolly said with pure contempt, and whirled toward his car.

A moment later, as Connolly sped off in a spray of gravel, Ferristaff turned to find Bruech looking rather gray. "Forget the north coast for now. First thing in the morning, I want everything there is to know about this whole sorry fuckup. We've got some serious damage control ahead of us. Stockholders hate this sort of thing."

※

"How's Hawk handling it?" Ben asked somberly.

"He's awfully torn up for Rose," Laura said, "and angrier than I've seen him since Sandy left. He'd like to see those men all killed, I think."

"I can't blame him," Ben replied, frowning more at the mention of her abusive ex-husband than of the would-be rapists. Over the years, it had become only harder to forgive himself for leaving her to such a fate.

They walked along the dry, grassy path in silence for a while, listening to the sigh and boom of surf from beyond the cliff tops. Laura had called him at the inn that morning to say she couldn't paint and didn't want to sit alone at home. Joby was at school, and Hawk was skipping classes to spend the day with Rose at her house. Ben had suggested lunch and a walk.

"That little flyer's not going to improve tempers either," Ben observed.

"What an ass," Laura sighed. "Pretending to sympathize, while virtually blaming her at the very same time. Who does Ferristaff think he's fooling?"

"Does seem like he'd have done better to say nothing at all," Ben agreed.

The half-sheet flyers were circulating all over town. With impressive speed, Ferristaff had arranged for someone to leave little piles of them everywhere. Laura had been shown one at lunch, by a friend at the restaurant, and been almost too angry to eat after reading it. While decrying the terrible act, and calling for the stiffest punishment allowed by law upon

Ferristaff's three now ex-employees, the flyer had also suggested that it might be safer for Taubolt's youth to avoid "associating with known provocateurs."

"She only went up there to talk that woman *out* of what she was planning!" Laura said heatedly. "He should be thanking her, not accusing her of asking for trouble!"

"In a town this size," Ben said, kicking himself for bringing it up again, "everyone will know that soon enough, and Ferristaff will only have slit his own throat further."

"I know," Laura said sullenly. "But any idiot should have seen how those flyers will infuriate all Rose's friends. If anything, he's just given them all one more reason to flock to Greensong's side. I hope whoever distributed those things had the sense not to leave any at the school."

"If they did, I'm sure Joby had the sense to get rid of them quickly," Ben said, eager for a change of subject. "I've gotta say, it's great to see him catch his stride again at last. It's even better to see you guys together finally," he added to be politic. "Took him long enough, but all's well that ends well." Receiving only striking silence in response, Ben looked curiously at Laura, and said, "Isn't it?"

For a moment, she just looked away uncomfortably as they continued to walk. Then she said, "Ben, I'm so glad you've come. There's been no one I could talk to here. Who knows Joby like you do, I mean."

"Hey," Ben said, touching her arm to draw her to a halt. "What's wrong?"

She turned back to look at him. "I'm not sure," she said. "Maybe nothing, but . . ."

"Is it Hawk?" Ben asked. "Do you think he suspects?"

"No," she said, looking suddenly older and more tired than he'd ever seen her do. "And he never will. It's way too late to change that decision now. But it's so hard deceiving him. And, for the rest of our lives, Ben? I wish we'd told him."

"I know," Ben said miserably. "I've always hated lying to him too, but I'm still not sure we had a choice. He was in such awful shape. One more blow, and who knew what he'd have done to himself? He was even worse when I saw him back in Berkeley. There's just never been any good time to tell him, and now . . . You two are together. That's the future. The past is past," he said, wondering how much richer and more joyful both their lives might have been if he'd just had the courage to stay with her and help her raise the boy himself. He hadn't felt remotely ready to be a father, or a husband then, but he'd have been better than Sandy, and now he'd have had everything his heart desired. Why, he wondered, did such clarity always seem to come so long after it was needed?

"But that's just it," she said unhappily. "I'm not sure the past is gone at all. Not for Joby. Sometimes, when we're together, I'd swear we're right back in high school."

"What do you mean?" Ben asked, both genuinely dismayed and uncomfortably curious to learn that all was not as well between them as he had assumed.

"We've been together for a year, Ben," she said, just above a whisper, "and we've still never slept together. We smile. We kiss. We cuddle. We talk. He says all the right things—*does* all the right things—until it's time to move ahead—*somewhere*—with what we have. Then ..." She raised her hands helplessly. "I've tried nudging him, but he's full of perfectly reasonable answers. 'Why rush? Let's enjoy all the seasons of our relationship! Lay solid foundations!' Ben, there's nothing there to argue with, but sometimes it feels so much like he's not there either!"

"Then nudge harder," Ben said, compelled to encourage her despite another wish he didn't want to acknowledge even to himself. "You've just got to tell him how you feel—what you want."

"And do what I did to him the last time?" she said.

"What?" Ben said. "I don't see how telling him—"

"That he's got to sleep with me or lose me?" she said, almost shrilly.

"No!" Ben said. "How do you ... That's not what I meant. Telling him that you want to move forward somehow, like you just said, doesn't have to be an ultimatum."

"What if he takes it that way?" she pressed. "What of he's acting like this because he still doesn't trust me, then I say this, and—"

"If he's even halfway worthy of you," Ben interjected firmly, "and I think he is, he won't. I think you know he won't too—or you wouldn't be with him to begin with." He gave her a skeptical look, and asked, "What's this really about, Laura? It's not just the sex. Not with you. What aren't you telling me?"

She was silent for a long time, again looking everywhere except at Ben. It was a moment before he realized that she was trying not to cry.

"Oh!" he said softly, and, without thinking, put his arms around her and drew her close. "What's up, Lady Bayer?" he crooned, as she wept into his shoulder.

"What if I don't want him anymore?" she barely breathed. "How could I do that to him?"

Ben felt ambushed, though he should have seen it coming. The conflict of emotions within him was immediate and titanic. "If you didn't want him anymore, I think you wouldn't be crying now," he said softly, holding everything else rigidly inside. "What makes you think—"

"It's not me he doesn't trust," she wept. "I know that. It's himself. *Still.*" She pulled away to wipe her eyes and face and try to gather her composure. "He keeps telling me there's never been anyone for him but me and never will be, and I can tell he means it. It's himself he doesn't love, Ben. No matter how recovered he may seem here. I know the signs all too well, because . . ." She began to lose it again, but pulled herself together with visible severity. "Because Sandy was exactly the same. Why do I keep choosing men who don't love themselves enough to love anybody else?"

"You don't," Ben said, adding both anger at Joby and grief for him, to the list of feelings at war within him. "You chose Joby way before he was ever such a man. We both did. It was Joby, King of the Roundtable we both loved, and—" Ben fought a lump growing in his own throat. "I can't believe he's not still inside there, somewhere." With that declaration, the war inside him seemed suddenly decided. "If you still love him, you've got to fight this out with him, Laura. He needs someone to do that for him."

"How?" she asked miserably, falling back into his arms, still leaking tears. "He's talked to me about all those years in Berkeley. All the awful things that happened. He says he's left it all behind. He lives as if he has, but . . ." She pulled away from him again, with a deep breath and an air of grim decisiveness. "You're right. I'm still in love with the Joby we knew as children, but that Joby has been pulverized for years. I don't know why, or whose fault it was, but it happened." She shook her head in frustration. "How do you fight a lifetime, Ben? How do you put a pulverized child back together, and fit it into the body and the life of a grown man? If you have any concrete ideas, I'm all ears."

Ben could think of no credible reply.

"I'm very certain of one thing," she said firmly. "I've been through Sandy once. I am *not* doing that, to myself or to Arthur, again. Not even for Joby. Not even for love."

"Then you have to tell him that," said Ben, "and convince him not to make you. Maybe Joby is the only one who can put that child back together, but at least you have to tell him what's at stake and help him try." Shoving the last inch of the blade into his own heart, Ben said, "I'll help you do that any way I can. Both of you."

23

(Conspiracy)

From the moment he'd come before the Cup three weeks earlier, Swami had understood that Joby was somehow key to whatever was unfolding around them and woefully unprepared for whatever part he was to play. There had been no vision or voices; only a visceral knowing like that which told him where his limbs were in the darkness, or what he wished to eat when he was hungry. Knowing was Swami's gift. The Council respected his talent, but not enough, he suspected, to approve what he intended now, so he had not asked their permission, or told anyone that he was bringing Joby here. Since that moment in the chapel, his sleep had roiled with vivid dreams, of Joby and of the Garden. If the Council condemned him for this later, so be it. Swami knew what he knew, and had learned to trust his gift.

Still, as he and Joby knelt by Swami's car, stuffing a few last items into their backpacks before hoisting them on and adjusting the straps, Swami was nervous.

"You ready?" he asked Joby.

Joby smiled and nodded. "You sure the car will be all right here, like this?"

"No one will come here," Swami assured him.

Joby glanced again at the car, pulled not quite out of the rutted dirt road onto a narrow, weedy shoulder against a high embankment, then grinned and said, "I suppose you're right. I didn't even realize this road was there until you turned onto it. How does anyone remember where that turn off is?"

"Anyone doesn't," Swami said, forcing a smile. "Let's go."

※

Coming to perch high atop a fir tree, Michael folded his hawk's wings, and watched Swami lead Joby down the trail toward what very few had any business seeing. Michael had no idea where the boy's reckless choice would lead, but the angel knew better than to interfere with anything in which Joby was involved. So he watched, contemplating the accelerating disintegration of Taubolt's carefully ordered existence.

As if yet another reason for concern were needed, something troubling had recently crossed into Taubolt. Michael was not sure how long ago, for it seemed able to hide from him—in itself, reason for apprehension—straying into his awareness only for fleeting instances since early September. It was nothing human, but too full of intelligence to be any mere animal either. The brief glimpses Michael had been allowed were fevered with despair, confusion, or anger. While the Cup's power still filled the land for such a distance, it could not be a demon, though that is what it felt most like, but whatever it was, Michael felt certain it should not be here.

As Swami and Joby disappeared around the bend, Michael's mind flew out again across the fields and ridge tops, deep into the forests, along the winding roads, searching for some further sign of . . . And there it was again! In the woods east of town! Much too close for comfort! Michael spread his wings and flew, but even as his mind reached out to pin the presence down, it flinched away from his awareness like a feral, frightened animal, and fled. What on earth could do that to an archangel? With Merlin accounted for, Michael could not imagine.

❀

All afternoon Swami had led him steeply upward over hillsides covered in the usual dry grass and dusty brambles. It had been a hard, hot climb under fully-loaded packs, making the few blessed stretches of shady woodland especially welcome. Not until early evening had they finally reached the ridge top, and stopped to gaze out over a breathtaking expanse of coastline stretching north, layer after paler layer, into the mountainous distance. Thickly forested hills of amazing height plunged down to meet the sea far below them, where mist churned up against the rocky shoreline spread into deep ravines giving the view a mythic atmosphere.

From there, Swami had led Joby down into woodland immediately different from any he'd ever seen. The trees here were wind-sculpted into graceful geometric shapes, as if decorations for a fairy tale, and the gargantuan ferns lining their path brushed at Joby's shoulders as they dropped farther into the gorge. Many of the tree trunks here were easily fifteen feet across, and an almost eerie stillness made the place seem even more primeval. When Swami had invited him to come backpacking for the weekend, one last time before the heat of Indian summer failed, Joby had expected nothing so remarkable.

"Where *are* we?" Joby breathed at last. It seemed no place they should have been able to walk to in a single afternoon. "How come I've never heard of this place?"

"We're on the Garden Coast," Swami answered, turning back to face him gravely. "This is one of Taubolt's most guarded secrets, Joby. You've must promise never to speak a word of it to anyone who hasn't spoken to you about it first."

Joby was unsure what to make of such a strange request.

"I'm serious," Swami pressed. "Please. Promise me you'll keep this to yourself."

"Sure." Joby shrugged. "Wouldn't want this crawling with tourists, would we?"

Seeming mollified, Swami turned and continued down the path.

It got darker as they hiked through stands of impossibly huge redwoods and other kinds of trees Joby didn't think he'd even seen before. No sound but their own footfalls disturbed the evening air. When it had grown almost too dark to see, they came to a small flat patch of grass beside the black glass pools of a gurgling brook, where Swami suggested they make camp for the night.

The place imposed its quiet on them as they prepared and ate a simple meal of tortillas and beans. After that, they sat watching sparks fountain up into the well of stars between the trees above their fire.

"This is real virgin forest, isn't it," Joby murmured at last.

"You can't begin to guess," Swami replied, his obsidian eyes and swarthy face grown suddenly fey and sad in the firelight. "I'm turning in. Long hike tomorrow."

"Yeah. Me too," said Joby and headed for his sleeping bag wondering what kinds of dreams a place like this might bring.

❦

As they packed up their camp after breakfast, a gem-bright bird of red and blue flashed down from the trees above them to snatch a crumb of oatmeal, and fly off again.

"What was that?" Joby exclaimed. "I've never seen a bird so beautiful!"

"It's called a ruby thrush," Swami replied, hoisting his pack onto one knee and over his shoulders with practiced ease.

"I've never even heard of it," Joby said in awe.

"There are some very rare things living here," Swami said. "This forest has never been disturbed."

Soon, they were on the trail again, and in the clear light of day, Joby began to notice all kinds of astonishing and completely unfamiliar plants. They passed beneath arboreal clusters of blue, thumb-size orchids, and crossed a glade of shiny crimson lilies. Joby stopped to finger a furry, silvery shrub trailing strings of what he assumed were berries, though they looked more like pearls. As the morning wore on, they hiked through glades with leaves that swiveled and shimmered in the breeze like a shower of gold-green coins, passed dwarf maples with leaves as wide as dinner plates, and waded through thickets of fan-shaped foliage the color of eggplant, which smelled of cinnamon and crushed celery.

Nor were just the plants remarkable. Snails with bright purple shells half as big as Joby's fist crawled up tree trunks. By a muddy streambed, swarms of large green butterflies fluttered into the air at their approach like an upward shower of windblown leaves. He saw two more ruby thrushes; a snow-white sparrow; a yellow frog; bright blue fish, whiskered like carp; a speckled, scarlet salamander the length of his forearm; an orb-weaving spider of pure metallic gold; and a sunning snake tiled in glassy, iridescent scales. Swami had names for all of them, none of which Joby had ever heard.

Joby's exclamations of surprise and wonder had soon given way to uncertain silence. Something odd was going on. He'd spent lots of time in Taubolt's woods by now, and never seen any of what they passed with such increasing frequency here.

Weird sounds issued from the hills around them: remarkable spirals of ascending birdsong, melodious strains of something like a high French horn, bursts of clucking chatter like musical monkeys. Even the air here was different somehow, or the light perhaps. Things seemed clearer, more sharp-edged and vivid. It all seemed impossibly strange, yet strangely familiar too. When he finally realized why, chills ran down his arms despite the morning's warmth.

"I had this dream last night," he said quietly to Swami, who was walking several feet ahead of him, "full of strange animals who were trying to make me sing a song I didn't know."

Swami stopped and turned to gaze at him intently. "What kind of song?"

"I can't remember," Joby said. "It was very beautiful. I wanted to sing it pretty badly, but it kept changing all the time. The point is, that red salamander we saw a while back was one of them. And I'm pretty sure that iridescent snake was too. In fact, I think a lot of this stuff we've seen was in that dream, but I've never seen any of it 'til today."

Swami smiled for the first time on their whole hike, Joby realized. "Maybe your mind is just inserting all of this into the memory." Swami shrugged. "Or maybe you were really meant to come here."

Wondering what he meant by that, Joby said, "You were in it too. Only you had huge eyes, like black glass, and the face of a ten-year-old child."

Swami's smile wilted. "What did I do, in your dream?"

"Tried to make me sing, like the rest," said Joby. "Swami, what is this place?"

"I told you," he said, turning to resume their hike, "a very old, and undisturbed forest. This is how the forests all were once. How they'd be now if it weren't for people."

"I used to study animals," Joby said to Swami's departing back. "How can I never have heard of any of these things?"

"Some of them live nowhere else," Swami said, without slowing ahead of him. "Many have not been discovered by anyone but us."

"Not *discovered*?" Joby exclaimed. "Swami, shouldn't someone—"

"NO!" Swami whirled to face him, angry or afraid; Joby wasn't certain which. "You promised you'd tell no one!"

"And I won't," Joby said, looking around in helpless frustration. "But this many rare species in one place—Swami, do you have any idea how important this is? It's got to be protected, or there will be nothing to stop someone like Ferristaff from—"

"There would be no protection!" Swami looked panic-stricken. "No matter what they promise, it would be . . . *disaster*. Joby, please listen to me. I wasn't even supposed to show you this. But—"

"Says who?" Joby interrupted. "Swami, what the hell is going on here? You make it sound like you're part of some conspiracy to—"

"I am," Swami cut him off, "part of some conspiracy."

"What?" Joby said, taken aback.

"There are . . . people here," Swami said, clearly struggling to navigate some very fine line, "who . . . protect this." He looked away, upset. "Please, Joby. I trusted you enough to bring you here. Trust me too. I . . . think we're going to need your help soon. I don't know how, but . . . for God's sake, keep your promise to me and say nothing about this place to anyone, or . . . or I've made a terrible mistake."

Joby didn't know what to say. He did not make or break promises lightly, but it seemed so wrong to know about this and tell no one. The *right* people, at least, should be aware that there was a veritable zoo of unknown species parked on the California coast. That might be enough to save all of Taubolt from guys like Ferristaff. After what had happened to Rose, Joby would have dearly loved to see the look on Ferristaff's face when the EPA told him to shut his whole claptrap down and go. And this conspiracy stuff? It gave him the creeps. "How can you and . . . whoever you're working with hope to defend this all alone against someone with Ferristaff's money and power?"

"No one like Ferristaff will ever find this place," Swami said with conviction. "Not unless he was shown. Taubolt was never hidden so well as this place is."

"Taubolt was *hidden*?" Joby asked. "Since when?"

Swami gave him an imploring look. "Please. For now, just *trust me*."

"All right," Joby said uncertainly. "I did promise. Consider me part of your conspiracy, I guess."

Swami smiled, somewhat anxiously. "Actually, you and I are sort of a conspiracy inside the conspiracy now."

"Uh-huh," Joby nodded skeptically, "and what exactly are *we* conspiring to do?"

"Protect all this," Swami said.

"From?"

"Something bad . . . that's coming. I don't know what yet. But when it comes, will you help us save this?" the boy asked urgently.

"If I can, of course," said Joby, more skeptical than ever. "Who wouldn't? But, what makes you think *I* can help? If you don't even know what this bad thing is—" He stopped in mid-remark, staring as a tiny stag stepped shyly into the ferny glade behind Swami. It was no larger than a small dog, and its horns were *silver*!

"What is *that*?" Joby whispered.

Swami turned, just as the first stag was joined by a second. The deer stared back at them, ears up, posture wary, but they made no move to flee.

"Pigmy silvertip," Swami said quietly. "They're not afraid of men here. Few men come, and none of those have ever hurt them."

"They have silver horns!" Joby whispered.

Swami shook his head. "It's just a fine, shiny fur. Only looks like silver." He turned back to grin at Joby. "They have a larger cousin who's pure white, with horns that look like gold. But those are even rarer."

Joby only shook his head and stared, quite certain that this animal had been in no nature book he'd ever read.

❧

From grammar school on, Joby's teachers had sternly assured him that "science" had mapped and paved every mystery of consequence on earth. There were no lost continents, no mythical creatures, nor had there ever been. The ocean floor harbored no sunken cities or sea monsters now, only tube worms.

The atom had been smashed into particles too tiny and technical to interest anyone but physicists. Even the vastness of space had been reduced, in the common mind at least, to little but a thin, lifeless gruel of gas, dust, and the occasional large rock. Since junior high, Joby's whole world had practically been summed up in the phrase, "there's no such thing." But three days on the Garden Coast had turned all that on its head. There *were* lost continents and mythical creatures, right here in Joby's own backyard.

Now, as Swami led them back into the normal world, Joby followed him up the last switchback in a daze, wondering how he was ever going to bear keeping such a secret. He was so lost in thought that he almost ran into Swami, who had stopped suddenly to stare up the trail ahead of them. Following his gaze up to the trail's next bend, Joby froze in fear. Gazing down at them in perfect stillness, with black, unblinking eyes, stood a mountain lion so dark in color that it might have been a panther.

"Sit down," Swami whispered in hushed shock. "Whatever happens, don't make a sound. Don't even move." He unbuckled his pack and let it slide from his shoulders to drop softly on the ground. Then he began to walk slowly toward the lion, looking back at Joby only once, very quickly, to say, "*Whatever* happens."

Through the sudden haze of fear, Joby vaguely recalled advice from somewhere that they ought to be making noise and throwing rocks. But Swami knew the ways of this place better than he could ever hope to, and the boy was already so far up the trail that Joby supposed there was nothing to do but obey his instructions. He sat down as slowly as he could, fearfully wondering how he would run if the lion charged, not that he was likely to outrun a lion either way.

Only feet from the animal, Swami sat down as well. Hardly daring to breath, Joby swept the trailside with his eyes, looking for a stick or a large stone to hurl if the beast leapt on his friend. That's when he realized that Swami was humming softly, just as Hawk had done one afternoon, years before, in the orchard below Solomon's house. Charming deer was one thing, Joby thought, but mountain lions? Absurdly, he found himself wondering if this were how they got lions to piss into those little bottles Mrs. Lindsay had sent him to the hardware store for.

As Swami's tune grew slowly louder, the lion took a tentative step toward him. Joby tensed in fear, sweat trickling from his temples and down the insides of his arms as the lion advanced again. Mere inches in front of Swami, the lion stopped, rumbling softly. It stared at Swami. Swami stared back, humming all the while. Joby waited, rigid as a stone Buddha, if nowhere near as calm. Then, to his astonishment, the lion bent its hind legs, and sat. Swami's humming ceased, but the staring match continued until time itself seemed to stretch and stop.

Suddenly, Swami gasped, and the lion raised its head and howled as if in pain. Joby tried to stand, but his legs were rubber, and his pack pulled him over so that he achieved nothing but a small lurch sideways. The lion surged to its feet, keening. Joby stared in terrified incomprehension as Swami wailed along in some shared agony, until, finally, the lion's cries abated, and Swami's wailing turned to quiet sobs.

Then, to Joby's horror, the lion thrust its head at Swami's face, opened its jaws, and . . . *licked Swami's forehead!* With a shuddering sob, Swami leaned forward and threw his arms around the lion's neck, as if it were the family dog, burying his face in its furry shoulder, while the beast continued licking him. Joby simply gaped, knowing that his deepest certainties about the world were lost forever now.

Just when Joby thought that things could get no stranger, both boy and lion turned in spooky unison to gaze at him. *"What?"* he wanted to say, but still could find no voice. For the first time in the entire encounter, Swami looked frightened, but not of the lion. Joby was gathering the nerve to ask what the hell was going on when the lion looked back at Swami and pawed gently at his chest, as if shoving him away, then turned and trotted off as tamely as an oversize house cat.

Swami watched it go, then looked down, letting more tears fall onto the dusty earth between his legs.

Joby's head swam with unanswered questions as he found his voice again. "What . . . was that?" he murmured at last. "What did you just do?"

Swami turned to regard him with a long, unblinking stare, but didn't answer, only got shakily to his feet and came back for his pack.

"Swami, I need to understand what I just saw," Joby insisted.

"There are things I *can't* explain," Swami said quietly, seeming somehow gun-shy of Joby now.

When he'd shrugged the pack back onto his shoulders, readjusted its straps, and refastened its buckles, Swami turned and continued up the trail. Joby followed mutely. Neither of them spoke again all afternoon as they made their slow way over and down the long ridge toward the world they'd come from three days and another lifetime ago. Only as they approached the car did Swami finally break their silence.

"Thank you, Joby," said the boy, uneasily, not quite meeting Joby's eyes.

"For what?" Joby asked.

"For accepting what you saw. . . . For trusting me. I . . . I need you to trust me."

"What happened back there?" Joby asked. "Why won't you tell me?"

Swami looked forlorn and helpless.

"Swami, did you *talk* with that lion?"

"If I said no, would you believe me?"

Joby thought for a moment, then slowly shook his head.

"And if I said yes?" Swami sighed.

Joby only stared, realizing that he could believe that even less.

"You see?" Swami smiled sadly. "There are times when answers just don't work." He turned to continue toward the car. "We should get moving. I need to get back, and . . . I have things to do. You will be welcome here now," he said quietly without turning. "But remember your promise."

✼

When he finally managed to find Jake, stacking firewood behind the Heron's Bowl, Swami almost fled without speaking. Before he could, however, the man he'd always thought he knew turned to gaze at him curiously, and asked, "What is it, son?"

Swami was still afraid to speak. For all his reputation as a seer, he had no idea what would happen when he did. With a glance around to make sure they were alone, he finally blurted out, *"You're an angel?"*

Swami saw it; Jake's surprise. It was very slight, but it was there. Could angels be surprised, or was he wrong? He hoped with all his might that he was wrong.

"Come with me," Jake said levelly, already heading around the corner of the restaurant toward the gardener's potting shed. When Swami hesitated, Jake looked back and said, "There's no need to fear me, Swami."

Finding no anger in Jake's voice or face, Swami released a pent-up breath he hadn't realized he was holding, and followed him.

As soon as they were in the shed, and Jake had closed the door, he turned, still not seeming angry, and said, "How do you know this, Swami?"

"You're an angel," Swami breathed, feeling weak. "Don't you already know?"

"Angels don't just violate the minds of mortals, child," Jake said gently. "We hear what is addressed to us. We see and understand much more than you can possibly imagine, but there are boundaries we respect, because our Lord has told us to."

"I've done something," Swami said, fearful despite Jake's assurances. "Maybe something bad."

"You took Joby to the Garden." Jake nodded. "I saw you." His voice held only reassurance. "Is that why you're afraid?"

Swami shook his head, faint with fear. If Jake were an angel, then the rest might be true as well. "Joby is the bad thing, isn't he," Swami said, feeling close to tears.

"No," Jake said, looking concerned for the first time. "The bad thing you've dreamed of follows him. But there is no more bad in Joby, himself, than there is in you."

This relieved the most painful of Swami's fears, but there were so many others.

"Swami, I need to know how you've learned all this. Was it one of your visions?"

"I . . . Your brother told me," Swami whispered, still dazed by the memory.

There was nothing slight about the surprise on Jake's face this time.

"He found us in the Garden," Swami said, the story tumbling from him in a sudden rush. "He was guarding it, I think, or guarding Joby, or the Garden from Joby. It was hard to tell. I'm not sure even he knew; his mind was such a jumble of pain and confusion. He was a lion. I thought it might be a demon until he touched my mind, but—"

"No!" Jake gasped, his gaze thrown at the ceiling in apparent grief. *"Oh, Master, No!"* he cried, covering his eyes with callused hands. *"Gabe, what have you done?"*

Swami stared in shock. In all his life, he'd never seen Jake even slightly ruffled, and feared to know what it could mean, wondering, still, if he might be at fault.

*

Merlin was at home, happily immersed in a gardening magazine when the room around him suddenly filled with radiance unlike any kind of sunlight. He whirled around, but couldn't find the source of it.

"Merlin! I have need of you!" Michael's voice boomed from all directions.

It had been centuries since Merlin had been summoned in this way by anyone at all, much less by an angel, and the distress in Michael's voice filled him instantly with apprehension.

"What has happened?" Merlin asked fearfully. "Where am I to find you?"

"Ride my voice!" the angel commanded roughly. *"There isn't time!"*

Clearly something dreadful was afoot. Without further questions, Merlin drew upon sufficient power to step into the ether where the angel's summons streamed away toward Taubolt like a ribbon of light. Willing himself along that ribbon, Merlin found himself standing in a potting shed beside the Heron's Bowl before a gaping, dark-eyed boy of East Indian complexion, and a frighteningly agitated archangel.

"What's wrong?" Merlin asked.

"The presence we've pursued since midsummer," Michael said, "is Gabriel."

"*What?*" Merlin exclaimed. "That can't be! Its mind is—"

"*Demonic!*" Michael groaned. "After bringing Joby here, my brother was exiled from the Creator's presence for the duration of the wager. He fears damnation, and it seems he has surrendered to despair."

Merlin was aghast. "And you never told me?" he asked, already guessing why.

"I thought to spare you the implications." Michael frowned, confirming Merlin's fears. "He allowed this boy to bond with him this morning in the Garden."

Merlin turned to look at the boy with greater interest. "Are you still bonded?"

"It was only for a moment. Then he left me," said the boy, still gaping at him. "You're *Merlin*?" he asked, lost in astonishment. "*The* Merlin?"

"For better and for worse," Merlin growled, "I am. And your name is?"

"Swami," said the lad.

"You were able to endure this bond then, Swami?"

"His mind is like a fire," Swami said. "But he meant me no harm. He broke the bond when he saw that it was hurting me."

Merlin turned to Michael. "Then he may not be past reaching."

"We must try to bring him back," said Michael. "While there is any hope at all, we must! Swami has agreed to help us."

"This mere lad?" Merlin exclaimed turning to the boy again. "How? Why?"

"For whatever reason, Gabe trusted him as he has trusted neither of us," Michael said, clearly pained by the admission. "They have a bond, however small. And I cannot be both channel and physician, Merlin. We both know how adversarial this will be."

"You intend to use this *child* as a channel?" Merlin said, appalled.

"His gifts and strength are greater than you credit, Merlin, or I would never have asked this of him. Particularly his capacity as an empath. Have you some secret store of that skill, which I am unaware of?"

It was a rhetorical question that Merlin didn't bother answering, but turned back to the boy. "Swami, have you any notion what this means? What it could cost you?"

"Michael has explained it very clearly," Swami said, demonstrating at least sufficient sense to look afraid. "I don't know if I'll have the strength to hold that much pain for very long, but I want to try. To save an angel," he added, still looking too wonderstruck for Merlin's comfort. Still, it had been bravely said, and it was doubtless true that Michael would not have asked the boy unless he really thought him able.

"We must go back there now," the angel pleaded, "before whatever remains of their bond fades." Michael turned to Swami. "Are you ready?" When Swami nodded, Michael smiled gratefully and took his hand. An instant later, the shed was empty.

❧

Swami rose toward consciousness as if through sodden velvet curtains, letting the rustle of breeze-born foliage, the smell of dewy earth, and the play of cool air across his skin draw him back into the waking world. When he finally opened his eyes, he was relieved to find them all still there. Merlin, the enchanter of ancient tales, sat propped against a stone, contemplating the morning sky. On a fallen tree beside him sat the two others, one dark and beautiful despite the weary sadness in his face, the other, golden-blond and familiar to everyone in Taubolt, yet truly known by none, it seemed.

Two archangels! It still dizzied him. Who was he to keep such company? And yet, *they* had needed *his* aid, and he had not failed them. That fact alone seemed sufficient to justify everything he'd been through, and a great deal more.

Though it seemed unlikely that he'd ever fully understand the bulk of what he'd been through, the ordeal had left Swami in possession, by default, of much of what the wounded angel knew. He understood now that Taubolt and all it protected were in far greater danger than anyone but these few around him guessed; that the things he had always taken for wonder were just the thinnest skin upon a world of marvels unimagined by himself or anyone he knew; and that Joby was the poor, unwitting fulcrum on which all their fates were balanced. Swami could only grimace now at the woeful ignorance in which he had risked bringing Joby here.

Despite all these revelations, what most occupied Swami's mind was the crucible he'd just been through. For two days and nights without ceasing, Swami had been the living link through which Merlin and Michael had waged war against the animal madness on which Gabriel had cast himself adrift. It had been inexpressibly painful, exhausting, fearful work, endured not in hours or even minutes, but instant by instant as the punishing current of their spiritual battle had passed through the fragile wire of his being. Much of what Swami could remember seemed just a fevered plunge through mental landscapes as incomprehensible to him now as they had been then, but, in the end, they had succeeded. Gabriel had returned fully to himself, relinquishing his lion's form, and Swami had been allowed, at last, to drop into exhausted sleep virtually where he stood.

Now, probing his own mind, Swami found the person he'd always been still there, intact, but stretched across a great deal more than he had never been, or at least never been aware of. It seemed that he would, and would not, ever be "himself" again.

He was about to sit up when the darker angel said softly to no one in particular, "My soul's become a foreign land. I feel such remorse. . . . What have I done to us all?"

"Gabriel," Merlin said gently, "you are hardly the first of your kind to flee the anguish of despair in that fashion. But you are one of very few to willingly return. I stand in awe of such great heart. Temper your remorse with that."

"I share the fault, brother," said the lighter angel Swami still couldn't help but think of as Jake, "I should have spoken less harshly when you brought Joby here. That you should think I would not let you stay . . ." He looked away. "You should never have been made to waste your strength in hiding from us all."

"Peace, Michael," Gabriel said. "I was hiding long before I came here." Swami saw his gaze grow distant. "With Joby gone, I had no purpose left to fill the time. No hope at all. Everywhere I went, Lucifer's minions taunted me with visions of my coming damnation. I was half-mad with their torment before I ever thought to seek the Cup's protection." He looked up at his brother, eyes glistening. "I remember, Michael . . . how you warned me." His face fell in shame. "You were right. I am a fool."

"I'll hear no more of this!" Merlin snapped with surprising vehemence. "There is only One with authority to assign your fate, and He has yet to speak. We have not all suffered these past two days just to have you sink back into despair and madness." He fell abruptly silent, then shrugged apologetically. "I'm sorry. Truly. We all have remorse to deal with, it seems, and I deal with such things less gracefully than angels." He offered Gabe a rueful smile. "No doubt my demon father's influence."

As Merlin spoke, Michael glanced at Swami and smiled to find him look-ing back. "Our hero is awake," he said.

"Good morning, lad," Merlin said gruffly. "Now I fear you've seen the mighty in yet another flattering light. Sorry for the rude awakening. I hope your sleep was good. God knows you earned it."

"I feel much better now," Swami said, sitting up stiffly, and rubbing at his eyes.

As Swami's fists fell away, he found Gabriel kneeling beside him. "I owe you more than I can pay," said the angel, leaning down to kiss his forehead. In awe, Swami watched him draw his perfect face away, as all the stiffness of his night on the ground suddenly departed. His body tingled with such en-ergy that he couldn't keep from standing; half-certain he'd be able to fly if he tried. "I am in your debt forever, little brother," Gabriel said, smiling un-certainly at Swami before returning to his place beside Michael and Merlin.

Little brother. He'd been called *little brother* by an *archangel!*

"I have lived a very long time," Merlin said, "and never seen a braver act than the service you performed here, young man."

"Thank you," Swami answered, not sure what to make of such praise from beings as far above himself as he was above an ant. "I'm not sure how I'll keep the rest of my life from seeming dull now."

Michael and Merlin laughed. Even Gabriel smiled.

"There will be some need of heroes around Taubolt for a while yet, I sus-pect," Merlin chuckled. "I doubt you'll lack employment."

"Believe me," Michael grinned, suddenly seeming more like "Jake" again, "it'll be good to have someone else who knows what's really going on around here. You have no idea how hard it's been havin' no one to talk with but this cantankerous old wizard."

"Michael?" Swami said uncertainly.

"Yeah?"

"Do you mind if I still call you Jake?"

Michael's smile softened. "You'll have to," he said. "More than ever, the folks in town have got to see me as a trusted peer, not some exotic icon from their mythic past. Besides, I *am* still Jake, Swami, much as I ever was. I'm just him and more. Can you see it that way?"

"I'll try," Swami said, uncertain. "I guess . . . I guess I'm that now too."

"You are," Merlin said gently, "as much yourself as ever, Swami. A passage like the one you've just been through cannot help but change you, but un-derneath every tree ring, the ring before remains. Rest assured, you've gained much, and lost nothing that would have been yours to keep in any case. Growth changes us all."

"As for that," Michael added seriously, "what you've touched inside my brother's mind still belongs to him and no one else. Hard as it may be, you must guard it all as someone else's treasure, for that is what it is. Do you understand?"

Swami nodded solemnly.

"Well then," Michael said, "glad you're awake. You should eat something while we all get our signals straight about how to handle things."

Merlin had already gone to their small fire, where he ladled oatmeal from a pot Swami knew they had not brought with them, into a bowl that had also come from who knew where. As he brought the bowl to Swami, Merlin glanced at Michael and said, "I assume that containment is still our primary aim?"

"If it's still possible," Michael nodded.

"In addition to providing some plausible explanation of what he's seen then, our story must discourage him from wanting to know more. Any ideas?"

Swami disagreed completely, but he held his tongue. Surely, such powers knew better than he what was best.

"Swami?" Merlin said. "You have something to say." It was not a question.

"Well," Swami hesitated, "if Joby's your grandson, then he's of the blood, more than lots of us are."

Merlin nodded.

"So, I don't see why we've all been hiding from him . . . or why you've hidden him from us."

"Swami," Michael said, "you were born in Taubolt, and embraced its secrets with a child's ease. Joby grew up in a different world, one that makes no allowance for even the possibility of such things. By the time he got here, Joby was a ruin of the man he might have been but for this trial he's caught in. He is so much better today only because the Cup and Taubolt's people have provided him sufficient protection to heal and find himself again—a task still far from finished."

"Yes, but how would telling him, or us, have changed that?" Swami asked. "We could have helped him even more if—"

"What Joby needed, and still needs, is *refuge*," Merlin insisted. "The truth would turn everything he rests assured of, the very bedrock of his daily reality, upside down. We dare add no such stone to the load he already bears. What if he fled Taubolt altogether?"

"There is another thing," Gabriel said softly. "Being of the blood, Joby has already used its power in many small unwitting ways since childhood. That things so often shift around him is not always merely Lucifer's doing. What he believes, be it hope or fear, has great effect. Were he to become conscious of his power, Lucifer would have a new and far more potent lever to manipulate him with."

"As for hiding him from Taubolt," Michael said, "you know how suspicious people were of him at first. How easily would Joby have found refuge here if others had known what you do? Even now, if they found out, he might suddenly be shunned by people whose welcome and friendship have been crucial medicine to him."

Their arguments made undeniable sense. Swami, himself, had been afraid of Joby after learning what the lion's mind had shown him. Still, he could not forget the look on Joby's face after watching his brief bond with Gabriel at the end of their hike, nor Joby's pleas for understanding afterward.

"You still are not convinced," Merlin said, looking at him curiously. "You know my grandson in ways different from our own. Tell us what you think."

"I think he loves Taubolt more than anything," Swami replied uncertainly, "and believes in us so deeply. What will it do to his refuge when he finds out we've never believed in *him* enough to come out of hiding . . . even now?"

All three gazed at him in silence, Merlin with obvious chagrin.

"It has the ring of truth," Michael conceded. "If trouble comes, we may have as much need of Joby's trust as he will have of ours. But it would still be very dangerous for all the reasons we've discussed, and, while I intend no offense to anyone here, we *must* be careful to avoid any further interference in Joby's trial."

At this, Gabriel looked forlorn, while Merlin looked offended.

"But isn't hiding from him interference too?" Swami dared to press. "Why is he here at all, if not to find us? It's his destiny to know. I feel it with everything inside me, and I don't think hiding from him's going to work for too much longer anyway. Not after . . . what he saw."

"From the mouths of babes," Merlin sighed, glancing at Michael, then back at Swami. "Having heard our concerns, what do you suggest we do?"

Swami felt far from easy about giving any more advice to his betters, or about bearing the responsibility if he turned out to be wrong, yet, it seemed so plain to him. "Stop deciding for him, either way," he said. "If Joby wants to hide from Taubolt, fine, but if he asks to know the truth, then . . . then warn him that the answers might be hard to hear, even frightening, and if he still wants to know, just answer whatever he asks."

Merlin drew a long, pensive breath.

Michael nodded. "Very well, but there are some things no one must be informed of. The wager is one. My true nature is another."

"And mine," Merlin added. "Not yet, at least."

"I think I have already had too much to do with all these matters," said Gabriel, breaking his long silence. "With your leave, Michael, I would stay here, in these forests, for whatever time is left to me, and care for all that lives here in solitude. May I remain?"

"Of course, brother. One has come to Taubolt who may pose a threat here if he cannot be dissuaded. Your help in guarding this place would be very welcome."

"I will go then," Gabriel said, rising to leave them. "Peace upon you all, with my unending gratitude." He turned to Swami and said, "Especially to you, my friend. If ever you need help, you have but to call and I will come." Then he took a step away from them, and vanished.

24

(Trick or Treat)

As October arrived, fall suddenly descended over Taubolt like a soft, smoky curtain, turning maples, oaks, and alders into bright splashes of fire among the evergreens. Mornings came chill and dewy for a week. Then the rain arrived, roaring on the roofs and hammering branches bare. Dry gullies became creeks again, while creeks became rivers, and rivers became raging torrents. Chocolate-colored cataracts spilled over cliff tops into the roiling bay whipped into rafts of marshmallow cream by storm surge thundering up the cliff sides to cast flurries of shredded foam and spindrift swirling across the headlands west of town. Not until the month was nearly over did the weather clear again, to everyone's relief.

Three nights before Halloween, as the sun set beneath a pale, cloudless sky, Taubolt's more enlightened ladies gathered in the back room of Molly Redstone's shop for their weekly New Age meeting. There was much to meditate upon. It had been a stormy month on *many* plains.

"He'll be crippled for life!" gasped Carolena. "That's what I heard. The poor man has a wife and two young children, and he's only twenty-seven! What an awful thing."

"It was obviously that Greensong woman," said Alicia. "I'm all in favor of saving the environment, of course, but she's taken things much too far. I can't stand her."

"Well, they did try to rape her," said Margery Baltore. "I might have gone out and driven a few spikes into those trees myself if someone had done that to me."

"But they already caught the men who did that!" Alicia objected. "They're being punished. What more did she want? Now she's ruined the life of a completely innocent man. How's that supposed to save the trees?"

"Oooooh," Carolena grimaced, her fists balled in anger. "People are so unenlightened! It just makes me want to go out and shake some sense into them!"

"Ladies," Molly interjected calmly. "Let's get recentered. Judgment can have no place in our endeavors. We are here for higher purposes."

"I'm sorry," Carolina said. "There's just so much stupid violence out there lately. It's hard to stay attuned."

"The secret," Molly said gently, "lies in staying focused on our goals, rather than our obstacles." She smiled in anticipation of what they were about to hear. "With that in mind, Cassey and I have been saving something special to end our meeting with tonight. Cassey, will you tell us all what you told me this afternoon?"

Cassey smiled, eyes gleaming with delight as everyone turned to face her. "I've seen the fairies!" she said in hushed wonder. "Just today, with my very own eyes!"

"What?" said Margery, sounding a tad skeptical.

"Ooooh, tell us!" squealed Lolly Berrit.

"I went out on the headlands to enjoy the nice weather," Cassey said gleefully, "and, from a distance, I saw several children go into that pretty ring of trees down below the church. I didn't think much of it at first, but when they didn't come out again, something made me wander up a little closer, just to see what they were doing. But when I got close, three birds flew out, and there was no one in the ring at all!"

"Couldn't they just have left while you weren't watching?" Alicia mused. "Or gone out the side you couldn't see?"

"To where?" Cassey protested. "That circle's got nothing but open fields around it in all directions. Three children, three birds. Isn't it obvious?"

"Wow! They turned into birds?" Carolena exclaimed. "Amazing!"

"A raven, a blue jay, and a seagull," Cassey said smugly. "What would three such different birds be doing in there all together anyway?"

"Goodness!" Lolly gushed. "This is it! The proof we've waited for, isn't Molly?"

"It has begun," Molly said quietly, looking meaningfully at each of them. "The devas have revealed to me that our purpose here is to reestablish contact with these spirit beings and help them usher in the coming dawn of enlightenment. The New Age is upon us at last, and Taubolt will be its portal to the world."

"How exciting!" Carolena squeaked, literally bouncing in her chair, while the other ladies in their circle received the news with varying degrees of satisfaction.

"Our enthusiasm must be tempered with great caution, though," Molly

warned. "As the sacred celebration of Samhain approaches, such spiritual activity is bound to increase, but we mustn't scare them off with tides of vulgar publicity. Be more attentive than ever to the signs, but I think it would
be best if our discoveries were discussed nowhere but here for now. Is this
acceptable?"

The women all nodded, and Carolena said, "That's very wise, Molly. We
all know what happened when those two English girls told."

"Oh, yes!" clucked Lolly. "The place was overrun, and all the fairies driven
out!"

"That's precisely what we must avoid." Molly nodded. "Our calling is to
guard the cradle of rebirth, not commodify it as so many others would."

"Like that Karl Foster," Sharine agreed. "Talk about unenlightened!"

"And Agnes Hamilton!" Margery added. "She wants to run this whole
town!"

"Ladies," Molly admonished. "Focus on the goals."

Everyone dutifully agreed.

"Well. This has been such an energizing meeting," Molly said with brisk
good cheer. "Thank you, Cassey, for bringing us such exciting news. What
momentous times! Shall we take a moment to reattune ourselves before
we go?"

The ladies all closed their eyes, embracing the meditative silence in which
all their meetings were concluded. Some did breathing exercises, while others simply tilted faces upward in gestures of blissful gratitude for the univer-
sal harmonies.

When they were gone, Molly went back to her apartment behind the store
to update her Harmony House Web site, hardly able to suppress her excitement, imagining the center of spiritual and healing arts that this small town
would someday be—and, of course, all the business this would bring through
her shop.

✷

"Hi, Laura."

"Ben!" she exclaimed. "What are you doing *here*?"

"Just thought I'd stop by to say hello." He shrugged, waving a moth
from between them in the porch light. "Is this a bad time? You seem kind
of startled."

"Of course not," she said, a trifle uncomfortably. "I just thought you'd be
Joby."

"He's not here?"

420 & MARK J. FERRARI

"No," she said. "There was some kind of Halloween thing at the school tonight. He said he'd come by afterward."

"Great! Then I'll keep you amused until he gets here." Ben grinned. When she still made no move to invite him in, he added, "If that's all right?"

"Yes!" she said, still sounding off balance. "I'm sorry. Come in." She stood aside to let him enter. "This is quite a bit out of your way, isn't it?"

"My way to where?" He grinned, brushing past her. "This was my destination."

"Oh," she said, leading him toward her living room. "That's nice of you."

"I haven't seen you in a while," he said, careful to sound casual.

"Been a busy time," she replied, her composure returning. "School starting up, Halloween and everything. The way the weather's been, I haven't gone to town much. Sorry about that. Have you been lonely down there?"

Now there's a fine question, Ben thought as they reached the living room. "Hawk here?" he asked, sitting on the couch as she took a chair beside the windows.

"No," she said. "He and Rose are at school too."

"Then we can talk," he said cheerfully, wanting not to waste whatever time they had before everyone got back. "Have you spoken with him yet?"

"I *knew* you were going to ask that," she said, sounding exasperated.

"I didn't think so." Ben smiled. "Is that why you're so glad to see me?"

"There's never been a right time," she pleaded. "He went on some camping trip just after we talked, and came home all upset. He won't tell me why. And I didn't want to stir up even more trauma while Hawk was dealing with what happened to Rose, and—"

"Hey!" Ben cut in. "You don't owe me any explanations. I was just curious, you know, after last time. I hope you haven't been avoiding me just because—"

"Don't be silly," she scoffed. "Like I said, there's just been a lot going on."

"Okay." He shrugged. "Just wanted to make certain."

"So how have you been?" she asked.

"Fine," he said wryly. "I've been working on my screenplay and designing that new atom bomb downstairs in my spare time. Then there's all the fan mail to answer."

"I guess Taubolt's pretty boring in the rain," she said apologetically. "Especially if you're new here. I should have made a bigger effort to get down and see you."

"Naw," he said, smiling like he meant it. "I see Joby every day at the inn, and I'm looking for a job. That'll fix me up."

"Money running short?" she asked, sounding concerned.

"Nope. Being a man of leisure's just not turning out to be as fun as I thought."

"There's a big Halloween bash at the Crow's Nest tomorrow night," Laura said sympathetically. "Joby and I are going. You should come."

"He already told me," Ben said. "I'll be there with bells on. Well, not bells, exactly, but something pretty flashy."

"What are you wearing?" she asked, smiling for the first time since he'd arrived.

"That would spoil the surprise." He grinned. "You?"

"If you're not telling, neither am I," she said with a smile he was sure she hadn't meant to seem so flirtatious, but it cut him nonetheless.

He'd come here planning to say all sorts of things he knew now he couldn't say, which, having barged his way into her home, left him with the awkward task of inventing some graceful exit. "Well, speaking of my costume, it still needs a little work," he said, getting up. "I should go back and get that taken care of. Just wanted to say hi."

"But you just got here," she said, getting up as well. "I'm sure Arthur would like to see you. They should be home any minute. Won't you stay?"

Suddenly, it seemed almost hard to breathe. "I really can't," he said, knowing that he must sound like a fool, but that there was no remedy for it now. He had to get away before he said or did who knew what stupid things. "Hawk sees me all the time in town. I'm sure he must be sick of me by now. Like you said, it's a long way back to town, and I've got interviews tomorrow, early." He forced another grin. "See you tomorrow night. Can't wait to see your costume."

"Okay," she said, looking at him strangely. "Can't wait to see yours too."

As he turned to go, she came and gave him a farewell peck on the cheek, which was all it took to send him bolting for the door. "See you two tomorrow!" he called back as he left the house, half-running for his car. He'd been a fool to come here; a bigger fool to stay in Taubolt once he'd found out Joby was already here; and a total moron to make so many stupid promises it was already killing him to keep. He'd be leaving Taubolt very soon, it seemed— for all their sakes.

❀

Six months after the Lord had led him to Taubolt, Reverend Samuel Cotter of the One True Gospel Church had yet to win a single convert. In part, he credited his failure to the foothold enjoyed by that papist outfit on the hill.

They had the only real church building here, and sinful folk always mistook such empty edifice for true spiritual authority. Sam's ministry, which did not enjoy the funding to support such vain facade, was housed in a small rental storefront at the farthest corner of town, and the few tourists who found him there at all invariably beat a hasty retreat upon discovering that he was no purveyor of filthy, overpriced mammon like the others.

Beyond these handicaps, Sam knew his poor showing was simply the inevitable result of having been sent, like Jonah, into such a heathen, unresponsive land. Taubolt reeked of pagan belief and practice. Halloween seemed bigger news than Christmas here!

This particular morning, however, Sam's ire had a far more urgent target. Hours of agonized prayer had revealed that his most urgent mission here must be to drive Molly Redstone from the streets of Taubolt once and for all. He'd felt constrained to lie low for a time after that ill-fated confrontation during the parade. God's grace had helped him to elude those misguided officers, but one did not ask the Lord to multiply such signs.

Wickedness like Redstone's could not be tolerated indefinitely, however. Thus, he had reluctantly decided to visit his only ostensible colleague here, papist or not, and see if they might join forces against the wicken whore of Shea Street and her nest of blasphemous followers. If nothing else, a life of itinerant preaching had taught Sam better than to scorn any tool, however offensive or demeaning, that the Lord might provide. The road to glory, he knew, was lined with thorns, and traveled on one's knees in humility, one painful step at a time.

So it was that Sam Cotter came knocking at the door of St. Luke's Parish rectory, that Halloween morning, prepared to extend the hand of ecumenism to his Catholic counterpart for as long as it took to get rid of Molly Redstone. When no one answered, he wondered if the old priest might be in his chapel, and walked around to the front of the church. The doors there were locked, but he knocked anyway. Receiving no answer here either, he turned to go in something of a huff. But as he reached the gate, he heard the door rattle behind him, and turned to see it swinging slowly open.

"Hello?" Father Crombie smiled.

"Hello, sir." Sam smiled back. "How are you this fine morning?"

"Well, but rather slow, I fear. My legs are not what they were. May I help you?"

"Actually, sir, I was hoping we might both help the Lord. My name is Samuel Cotter. I'm minister of the One True Gospel Church, here in town."

"Ah, yes," Father Crombie said uncertainly. "I believe I have heard your name."

"May I come in?" Sam asked.

"Why . . . yes, of course. This is God's house, not mine."

Sam was not surprised at Crombie's poorly concealed hesitation. It was only to be expected that a leader of the papist cult would feel some hesitation in the presence of a true man of God. He put on a pleasant face, and stepped inside, glancing suspiciously at all the papist gewgaws and idolatrous statuary as they moved toward the altar.

"Nice little building," Sam said. "You fill it up on Sundays, do you?"

"Attendance varies, of course," Crombie said amiably, "depending on how many of Taubolt's visitors happen to join us, but we've a goodly congregation."

When Crombie failed to inquire about the size of Sam's own congregation in return, he could not help feeling snubbed. As much as it would have embarrassed Sam to admit he had none, the old man's smug disinterest still offended him. *You shall know the tree by its fruit,* he thought with disgust, deciding it was time to get down to business.

"Sir, I'm here today because this lovely and deserving town is afflicted with a spiritual cancer that I expect distresses you as deeply as it does me. I am referring, of course, to that heretic, Molly Redstone, and her spiritual brothel down on Shea Street. The Lord knows I've labored to expose that woman for what she is, but one voice in the wilderness does not seem to have been sufficient. It was my thought that if you and I joined forces, we might have enough moral clout around here to drive her out, and return this community to the state of spiritual health I'm sure you also long to see restored."

Having said his piece with admirable brevity, Sam fell silent, assuming that not even a papist minister could fail to endorse such clear common sense. But Crombie just stared in apparent confusion, causing Sam to wonder if he might be a little senile, or just so out of touch that he'd not even heard about the witch in his own backyard.

"You are aware of Molly Redstone and her so-called Harmony House?" he asked.

"I have heard some about that, yes," Crombie murmured, "but, Mr. Cotter, though the woman clearly holds very different beliefs than my own, I am not sure it is my place to . . . 'drive her out,' as you put it."

Cotter was stunned, at the old man's bald admission, if nothing else. Hadn't he even the shame to *pretend* he was on God's side? "You're a Christian minister, sir, are you not?" Sam protested. "Are you aware of what this woman teaches, of how many people she has seduced into joining in her Satanic practices?"

"I've been led to believe," Crombie said, "that she sells bits of crystal, a little jewelry, some candles, tea, and vitamins there, and espouses a philosophy of vague goodness and optimism." He paused briefly, then added, "Some astrology as well, I suppose, but while I may not be as convinced as she that such things are efficacious, I would hesitate to call them Satanic."

For a moment, Cotter was reduced to drop-jawed, speechless astonishment. "You *back* this woman?" he blurted at last.

Crombie looked startled. "I said nothing of the kind, Mr. Cotter. You and I clearly disagree on several points, but that doesn't mean that I endorse—"

"Sir, I have spent my life reading and rereading the scriptures, and I can assure you, without hesitation, that *God* agrees with *me!*"

Crombie's expression became almost sympathetic, which galled Cotter more. "I propose, Mr. Cotter," the old man said gently, "that it might be wiser to agree with God."

"You, sir, are a danger to your congregation!" Sam snapped indignantly. "The immortal souls of your flock hang in the balance of what you teach them, and if that tripe is any sample, they are surely all bound straight for Hell in the same handbasket!"

"Mr. Cotter, I am afraid I must ask you to leave," Crombie said, no longer looking confused, or friendly.

"If this *was* God's house, I'd make *you* leave, old man!" Cotter spat. "But any fool can see it's not, so you bet I'll go, and shake the filth from my sandals as I do."

It was only as he turned to leave that Sam heard the sound of . . . music? It was quiet, and rather discordant, as if a large choir were warming up behind the door of some distant room. But this place was nowhere near large enough to hide any such choir. Cotter turned, looking for the source of the sound.

"What's that?" he demanded, but Crombie said nothing. In fact, the old priest suddenly looked almost frightened, which raised the hair a bit on Cotter's neck. "Where's that music coming from?"

"I...am an old man," Crombie demurred. "My ears have failed along with my legs, I fear. I cannot hear whatever you're referring to. Perhaps it's something outside."

But it wasn't outside. It was coming from somewhere just behind Crombie, and growing louder! It was coming from somewhere very near the altar!

"Liar!" Sam rasped fearfully. This was as unnatural as any sound he had ever imagined. "What kind of perversion are you hiding in this whitewashed tomb, old man?"

"Mr. Cotter, I really must ask you to go," Crombie insisted.

But Cotter's mission was to cleanse Taubolt of evil, and he knew now that he'd found its dark heart here, where no one would have thought to look; in a church! Ignoring Crombie's protests, Cotter pushed roughly past him, and marched toward the sanctuary.

"In the name of Jesus Christ!" he shrilled, *"I command the powers of—"*

That was all he managed to get out. Through the very seams of a golden box mounted in the wall behind the altar came a hideous light, which washed Cotter in such pure loathing and animal terror that he could only flee in panic toward the church's open doors. Some small part of his mind was salient enough to feel ashamed that he had met true black magic at last and fled before it without a struggle. But the rest of him was filled with gibbering pleas too backed up to do more than clot behind his mouth.

Only when he'd run several blocks down Shea Street did fear finally relinquish control of his legs, which clung now to his pants in a glaze of cooling urine. He stumbled to a halt, trembling and gasping, right in front of Redstone's wicked store. When the worst trembling had passed, he turned and screamed back up toward the unhallowed church, *"Thou art an abomination before God! Burn! Burn, thou consort of witches and demons! The fires of Hell consume you and your blasphemous temple!"*

❆

It was a perfect night for Halloween. Taubolt's antique skyline and hillside graveyard cut dark silhouettes against the clear, brittle wash of twilight. Jack-o'-lanterns glowed on nearly every porch and fence post, as Laura and Joby drove into town. The few pedestrians on Taubolt's quiet streets seemed to drift like phantoms, though this was likely due to viewing them through cheesecloth.

Joby had put together an elaborate "headless man" ensemble. His real head was concealed inside a tux jacket on a cheesecloth fronted shirt stretched over a wire frame. Its collar was stuffed with red crepe paper, as was the hideous pull-over mask he carried under one arm as his severed head. The costume left him less than ideal vision, of course, and very limited mobility, so Laura was driving.

She had dressed up as a renaissance maid in white petticoats under a long green velvet dress she'd made herself. Its low-cut bodice covered a puff-sleeved peasant blouse pulled down to bare her shoulders. A wreath of dried roses crowned her long auburn hair.

"Listen to this," Joby said, squinting through his cheese cloth portal at a copy of *The Lighthouse*, Taubolt's weekly paper, which he'd brought along to peruse during the long ride from Laura's house. "It's a letter to the editor. See if you can guess who from.

"'Dear Editor,'" he read. "'As we approach Halloween, I feel compelled to join numerous other concerned residents in imploring the parents of this quiet community to remind their children that prowling, vandalism, and other so-called Halloween traditions are not only dangerous, but illegal. Please, in the interest of safety, keep your children at home this year. If we all work together, we can enjoy this colorful holiday without fear of regrets the morning after.'"

"Oh my God," Laura groaned.

"'Sincerely, Agnes Hamilton,'" Joby smirked.

"Is she *nuts*?" Laura exclaimed.

"Might as well have painted a bull's-eye on her front porch," Joby concurred, "with a big neon sign: INSERT EGGS HERE."

"She'll act so victimized, too," Laura sighed, shaking her head as they pulled into a parking space just down from the Crow's Nest. "Oh, *look!*" Laura gasped, jamming the car into park, and killing the engine. "That's Ben!"

Joby turned his false torso until he could see Ben walking toward them, grinning rakishly in a costume to put any prince to shame. The stiff lace collar of his white linen shirt emerged from a black leather doublet with puffed sleeves slashed to reveal sapphire satin linings. A silver rapier sheathed in black leather hung at his hip. His black leather trousers were tucked into knee-high, cuffed black boots. A black velvet cape swept back over one shoulder, embroidered in silver and lined in more sapphire satin, was fastened by a silver broach engraved with Celtic knot work.

As Laura stepped from the car, Ben swept his cape back with one arm, in a formal bow. "Sir Benjamin, at your service, lovely lady. May I say, you are a vision tonight?"

"You are too kind, milord," she replied, dropping a quick curtsy. "I can't believe we match!" she said, straightening to give him an excited hug.

Joby's attention was so fastened on Ben's costume that he banged the top of his false torso on the doorjamb trying to get out of the car, and fell back into his seat. After a more careful exit, he joined them at the curb, and said from within his cheesecloth cage, "Let me guess, Ben. You were in a wedding once, and never get to wear it anymore."

"Close." Ben grinned. "I got it at a renaissance fair, years ago." He looked down at himself sheepishly. "Seemed like a good idea at the time."

"A little puerile," Joby joked, "next to the understated maturity of mine."

"You do look gruesome!" Ben said. "How you gonna eat and drink through that?"

Joby hadn't thought of this. "Through a straw, I guess."

"Party animal!" Ben grinned. "Can you dance in it?"

"Okay, so it's got a few design flaws," Joby said irritably. "We don't all have professional tailors, Ben."

"Hey, I didn't mean—"

"I know," Joby said, glad they couldn't see his beet-red face. "I just . . . lost my head for a minute." Laura groaned, but Ben was good enough to laugh.

Ben led the way upstairs through the old water tower that was the restaurant's entrance, while Laura hung back, helping Joby negotiate the rough wooden steps. "I knew I should have come as a cowboy," he murmured, wondering why on earth he'd chosen a costume that left him half-blind with no peripheral vision.

At the top, Ben pulled the door open and they were drowned in deafening music, laughter, and shouted conversation. Joby's lack of peripheral vision became an even greater challenge as they sought a table in the bar amidst the crowd of giant butterflies, ghosts, clowns, fairies, witches, ghouls, and superheroes. The place was a furnace, and Joby quickly discovered yet another of his costume's drawbacks. He was glad he'd worn nothing heavier than a black T-shirt underneath.

When the waitress came, Laura ordered coffee, Joby asked for grapefruit juice with a straw, ignoring the waitress's amused expression, and Ben ordered Glenlivet, up. At first, the party swirled indifferently around them, but soon, Joby and Laura's friends began to come around to *oooh* and *ah* their costumes Ben's, of course, got all the top awards, as he was introduced to anyone and everyone in Taubolt. When Bridget and her husband came by, she dressed in green balloons as a giant bunch of grapes, and Drew decked out as a "cereal killer," wearing a robe festooned in empty cornflake boxes decorated with bloody bullet holes or stabbed with rubber knives and cleavers, she became the fourth person to ask Joby if he weren't awfully hot in there.

"You know, you're right," Joby said, surrendering at last. "I'm hot, and blind, and claustrophobic in this dumb thing." He pulled his arms from the jacket sleeves, lifted the fake torso off his shoulders, and emerged feeling rumpled, sweaty and drably out of uniform in his sodden black T-shirt. "Decapitation isn't all it's cracked up to be," he growled comically, setting his empty shell on the floor. "Now I can order a burger."

"It was kind of neat though, talking to a stuffed shirt," Bridget pouted.

"Breathing's even neater." Joby shrugged. "Next year, I'm a cowboy for sure."

"Well, this isn't too well ventilated either," Drew said, turning to his wife and plucking at his robe. "How about we get some air out on the deck?"

They made their farewells and left, but, having taught school for three years, Joby knew half the families in Taubolt, and soon had a steady stream of visitors, to which Ben, and even Laura, mostly had to sit and listen. This receiving line went on and on, until, eventually, during a lengthy conversation about scholarships between Joby and Bellindi's parents, Ben and Laura finally excused themselves to go dance. Some time later, when Joby had finally run dry of visitors, he sat sipping his third grapefruit juice, and wondering when, if ever, Ben and Laura would return.

Finally, he got up and went to the restaurant's dining room, which had been cleared for dancing, where he leaned against the doorjamb, buffeted by the music, and watched Ben and Laura utterly lost in all the fun they were having. They made a lovely couple, and Ben's costume alone would have justified the attention they were getting from people all around the dance floor. Joby saw himself reflected in the darkened windows beyond them, looking plain, he thought, and rather thin in his black pants and T-shirt. His hair was sticking up ridiculously from having pulled his costume off. He reached up to rake it back into place, wondering why no one had said anything all this time, and he suddenly felt tired—and utterly out of sync with the celebration around him. With a last glance at Ben and Laura, he went back to get his ill-conceived costume in the bar, then headed for the door carrying his empty torso under one arm.

As he started down the stairs, however, Laura's voice called out behind him, "Joby, where are you going?"

Oh, he thought, *I've been noticed.* "I'm just a little tired," he said without turning. "I told Gladys I'd help her with some things around the inn tomorrow. I think I'd better get some sleep." He turned to smile at her. "It's just three blocks. I can walk."

Ben came through the door to stand beside her.

"You weren't even going to say good-bye?" Laura asked incredulously.

"You two were dancing, and . . . I didn't want to interrupt."

"For God's sake, Joby," Laura said wearily. "I can't believe this."

"Hey! It looked like you were having fun!" he sputtered, acutely embarrassed. "I just didn't want—"

"Save it!" she snapped. "I wouldn't dream of compromising your pity party." She whirled around and went angrily back inside, leaving Ben there in his elegant costume, staring down at Joby with a glum look that fanned Joby's shame into anger.

"Congrats, *Sir Benjamin,*" he sneered, "looks like clothes *do* make the man." He turned his back, and continued down the stairs.

"What's she supposed to do, Joby?" Ben demanded, starting down the stairs after him. "Throw herself at you? You want to dance, ask her to dance! For God's sake, she's wanted you for twenty years now! When are you gonna make your damn move?"

Joby could hardly see straight for the fury and shame he felt. He hurried down the stairs, just wanting to be anywhere away. At the bottom of the stairs, he crossed the street and stalked out onto the starlit headlands, tossing his ridiculous costume into the grass. When he realized Ben was still following him, he turned and yelled, "Go back and dance!" then stumbled in the dark over the uneven path.

"You're acting like a twelve-year-old!" Ben yelled back. "I didn't proposition her, I just danced with her!" He'd caught up to Joby now. "If you wanna know the truth, I'm sick of watching you sit around endlessly sorting through your ridiculous insecurities while Laura just hangs out to dry. If you want her, take her, or—"

"Or what, Ben? . . . *You'll* take her?"

Anger chased a startled look across Ben's face in the dim light. "Maybe I will," he said, trying unsuccessfully to sound as if the idea surprised him. "God knows you've had *your* fifty million chances."

"My best old friend," Joby heard himself growl, as something inside him uncoiled with a snarl, propelling him forward to shove Ben hard.

"What the— *Joby!*" Ben yelped, stumbling onto his back in the grass.

A second later, Joby was on top of him, his fist plunging toward Ben's face as some saner part of him wailed in dismay, helpless to contain the fury that possessed him. One punch was all he got before Ben threw him off, and rolled to his feet.

"Wanna fight, huh?" Ben rasped, reaching down to hoist Joby off the ground and hurl him into a patch of blackberry vines beside the path. As Joby struggled to his feet, hardly noticing the thorns that gouged his arms and hands, Ben unfastened the broach at his shoulder and let his entangling cape fall away. Then he waded in toward Joby, silhouetted against the stars like an angry bear. Joby leapt back onto the path, and backed away, but Ben lunged forward, throwing a punch to Joby's stomach. Joby bent back, softening the blow, but lost his balance and fell again. As Ben threw himself on top of him, Joby kicked out with one leg, catching Ben in the chest, so that he fell to one side, allowing Joby to roll away.

"Son of a bitch," Ben grunted, rubbing his chest. Then he scrambled after Joby and grabbed his arm. Joby tried to pull away, but couldn't and turned to throw another punch with his free hand, but missed. For a time, they writhed together on the gravel path. Then Ben wrenched Joby's arm around and rolled them over so that Joby was pinned beneath him, facedown in the grass. Yanking the one arm back and up as if to break it off, Ben brought his other hand down on the back of Joby's head, apparently intent on grinding his face into the ground.

Joby cried out in pain.

Suddenly, the pressure on his head was gone. Ben let go of his arm, but remained astride his back, breathing raggedly. "What the fuck is wrong with you, Joby?" To his astonishment, Joby realized that Ben was crying. "I wanted to be everything you were, once, you know that?" Ben said, clearly struggling to control his emotions. "Then . . . you just came apart. . . . What the hell happened, Joby? I tried to be there for you, but it was like you were buried in glass." He took a long shuddering breath, and was silent for a while, then stood up and stepped away. "What the hell are you hitting me for?"

Joby rolled over, cradling his aching arm, and lay on his back. "I don't know," he said at last. "I don't know what's wrong with me. I never have."

Ben said nothing, just sat roughly in the grass, staring up at the stars.

"Do you love her, Ben?"

"Maybe you can't figure out what's wrong with you because there *is* nothing wrong, under all that fear," Ben said, ignoring his question. "When you're good, you're great, Joby. The greatest person I ever met. Why can't you just relax and enjoy that?"

"Ben, do you love her?"

Ben turned to stare at him. "Yes."

It should have hurt him, should have rekindled his fury, but it wasn't even a surprise. Long before Ben had come back into their lives, Joby had known he was going to lose her, because, underneath the "whole new Joby" he'd plastered over himself since coming here, he could still find nothing bright enough to give her. Ben had always possessed brightness to spare. He and Laura were perfect for each other. They always had been. It was kismet. He was tired of fighting.

"Does she love you?" Joby asked.

"Not like she loves you." Ben watched him in the darkness for a time, then asked, "Do *you* love her, Joby?"

"Yes. . . . But—"

"Then *love* her," Ben cut him off. "Don't keep trying to spare her the risks. She's a big girl. She's been hurt plenty, and lived." He raised a hand to probe gently at his eye.

"I'm sorry I hit you," Joby said.

"Yeah, well . . ."

It took Joby a second to realize that Ben was laughing. "What are you laughing at?" he asked.

"I think you've given me a black eye," Ben answered, like it were the punch line to a really good joke.

"I'm sorry," Joby said, wincing as he put weight on his arm, but Ben kept laughing. "Why is that so funny?" Joby asked.

"You don't remember how we met?" Ben grinned, getting to his feet. "Things do come full circle, don't they, Sir Joby?"

"Oh, God," Joby groaned, remembering their fight in grammar school. "Does this mean I have to knight you now?"

"Done that," Ben said, reaching down to help Joby up. "We'll have to think of some new ritual." He clapped a hand to Joby's shoulder, and asked, "We all right?"

"Better, I think," Joby said. "Look, Ben. I just want her to be happy. If she'll be happier with you—"

"No," Ben cut in quietly. "No more of this stupid deal-making. Can't we just follow our hearts and let her decide?"

"You're right," Joby said. He stuck out his hand. "Best of luck, Sir Benjamin."

"And to you, Sir Joby." Benjamin grinned. They shook on it, and headed back to the Crow's Nest, grabbing Ben's cape and Joby's discarded costume on the way.

When they returned, however, both Laura and her car were gone.

"She done flown d'coop," said Ben as they stood confounded on the sidewalk below the restaurant. "After all this, she may choose neither of us."

"Guess we'd better drive up and apologize, huh?" Joby said.

Ben shook his head. "It's got to be almost midnight. If she's gone home, she'll probably be asleep by now, and I, for one, have been slapped around enough for one night. A breather between fights might be in order for all of us."

"Well, I'll see you tomorrow then?" Joby asked.

"You're going?" Ben protested. "I'm too wound up to go home yet. Let's hang out a while." He grinned in the lamplight. "I heard some kind of drumming down on the beach when we were walking back. Wanna go see what that's about?"

Joby was exhausted, but he was also happy that Ben still wanted his company, so they headed toward the cliff tops, dropping Joby's costume in Ben's car along the way. A moment later, they were staring down at the sandy rivermouth. It was ablaze with bonfires and crowds of rowdy revelers.

"Now *that* looks like a *real* party!" Ben exclaimed, already trotting down the path that wound toward the beach. "Come on!"

People of all ages mingled in raucous celebration around crackling fires. Shouts and laughter merged with the hiss and roar of surf as people danced wildly to the beat of many drummers. Bizarre costumes appeared and vanished at the edges of the firelight. The air was thick with wood smoke and the smell of beer. This, Joby thought, was really Halloween!

Turning to find Ben gone, Joby looked around and spotted him at a distant fire handing cash to someone, and heading back with several bottles dangling from one hand.

"Here," Ben said, shoving a bottle into Joby's hand. "You need a beer."

"Thanks, but I don't really—"

"You *need* a *beer!*" Ben insisted. "Pinch your nose and cope, bro!"

Ben already had the top off his, and raised it to his mouth. Joby shrugged and followed suit. He wasn't going to argue with anything Ben asked of him tonight.

Having been no drinker since Lindwald's death, the buzz was considerable and quick. The drumbeat began to feel like something coming from inside him. The blur of dancing, laughing partiers grew increasingly dreamlike, and Joby liked the feeling.

25

(The Morning After)

The cold came first, then the dampness. Joby opened his eyes and squinted into the too-bright fog around him. Where . . . ? What? . . . He sat up, groaning at the sudden throbbing in his head, and realized he'd been passed out on the beach all night. Ben's velvet cloak was thrown over him like a blanket, and Ben, himself, lay sprawled in his fancy costume not far away, asleep on the sand. *Like bums,* Joby thought in disgust. What if his students had seen him like this?

He scanned the mist-shrouded beach, relieved to find no one else in sight. The cliff tops were completely lost in fog, which, he hoped, meant no one up in town could see him down here. Counting his blessings, he got unsteadily to his feet, hugging his bare arms and thinly clad torso against the chill, then suffered a whole new host of unpleasant protests from his head and stomach. Every ten or fifteen years, he decided, one really *should* get roaring drunk, if only to remember why it was such a bad idea.

As the jarring gong between his ears subsided, fragmentary memories of the previous night began to break into focus, or as close to focus as ever seemed likely. To his distress, Joby vaguely recalled encountering several of his students at the margins of the firelight when he'd been very tanked. But the diaphanous, impossibly fantastic costumes he remembered them wearing led him to dismiss these memories as nothing but products of his ill-advised inebriation and an anxious conscience.

As unpleasant as the thought of further motion was, Joby hoped that a short walk in the brisk salt air might dispel his hangover, at least a little. Seeing no reason to inflict consciousness on Ben as well, Joby wrapped the cloak around himself for warmth and left his friend to sleep as he wandered toward the shoreline.

The fog grew even denser as Joby neared the water, reducing everything around him to ghostly suggestions in sopping shades of gray. Feeble tendrils of pale smoke drifted from wide mounds of blackened ash where last night's bonfires had burned down. Already deflating in nascent decay, jack-o'-lantern left lying in the sand stared blankly at the ocean from darkened, empty eyes. The surf was small and glassy now, flopping sluggishly up onto the beach. It felt almost as if Taubolt had died in its sleep while Joby lay unconscious.

A low stack of rock had been left behind by the receding tide, its feet collared in limp brown seaweed. Joby crossed the hard, wet sand, climbed its barnacled face and sat down on top of it to stare out at the bay and think about his new détente with Ben.

Last night, he'd been ready simply to surrender Laura's affections. Somewhere along the way, it seemed, that had become his default response to any hint of failure. Let go. Walk away. In fact, he'd felt almost relieved to see his worst fears finally realized and have it over with at last. But this morning, things looked different. Surrender wouldn't do. Ben had told him that, and he'd been right.

Joby and his best and oldest friend loved the same woman. That wasn't anybody's fault. Laura was the other best and oldest friend that either of them had. She'd been the most magnificent girl either of them knew ever since the day she'd fallen from that tree, while trying to be a knight. Even now, the memory brought a lump to Joby's throat and heat into his eyes. Who else should either of them love?

It had to be accepted. And sooner or later, one of them had to win her. Despite Ben's wry suggestion that she might choose neither of them after last night's foolishness, Joby knew it was the other way around. Laura loved them both—as much as they loved her. It must be killing her to have them both around again.

For all the "morning after" fog inside and outside of his head, Joby finally saw clearly that the only way such a mess could ever be cleanly resolved was for either himself or Ben to lose her, honestly and decisively, having truly done all he could to win her. Only then would nothing toxic be left dangling unresolved between them. As much as all the parts of him grown weary of defeat wished to lie down and flee the further pain, Joby was going to have to fight—for all their sakes.

Well out in the silvered bay, a seal was hunting. For some while, Joby had been watching idly as it thrust its head out of the water to look around, then disappeared beneath the surface for minutes at a time. Now, seeming to have finished its business, it surfaced and swam for shore, pushing little mounds of water before it as it zoomed just beneath the glassy surface toward a stretch of beach well down from where Joby huddled on his rock.

As it broke the surface, ten feet off shore, however, Joby gaped, surging to his feet in such a rush that he nearly toppled from the rock.

What had risen from the water was no seal, but his friend and former student, Ander, in a wetsuit. Joby's mind scrambled to explain as the boy began to wade toward shore, a large fish dangling from his hand, though Ander had no speargun, net, or knife.

The memory returned with shocking clarity. Joby had been ten years old, alone out on these very rocks at dawn, staring down at a half-naked boy in the frigid water who'd stared up at him in equal dismay before swimming off just like . . . It wasn't possible! No human being could swim like that! What he'd seen out there this morning had clearly been a seal, until . . .

Knee-deep in lapping water, Ander stopped to stretch like a man rising from bed, swinging his head around to whip the sodden hair out of his eyes. His face swung toward the rock where Joby stood. Their eyes met across the distance, and Ander froze in bald amazement. The fish fell from his fingers to float seaward, stunned or dead.

For a moment, they both stared. Then Ander donned his sunny, *guileless* smile and waved. Joby couldn't move. He might have laughed at the sheer audacity of such an attempt to play this off, but there was no laughter in him now.

Ander had already launched himself back into the water to swim, quite naturally this time, toward Joby's perch, as Joby waited, still motionless with shock. When he arrived, Ander stood, waist-deep, gazing up at Joby, and flashed another sunny smile.

"Hey, Joby. What's up?" Ander said, as if merely pleased to see him.

"You tell me."

Ander's smile vanished. "How long have you been up there?"

"Long enough," Joby said. "That *was* you fishing out there, wasn't it?"

Ander's shoulders slumped. He looked away from Joby.

"How's it done?" Joby asked, still hoping for some laughably obvious explanation he'd failed to think of. When Ander didn't answer, he said, more urgently, "Ander, please! I really need some answers. . . . Help me understand."

"I don't think you will," Ander said, looking trapped. "I'm not sure you can."

"Why won't anyone just tell me what's happening here?" Joby insisted, thinking immediately of Swami's trick out on the Garden Coast. "What harm could it do?"

"That's the question," Ander replied. "Ever since you came here."

"What?"

"Tell me what you are, Joby."

"What *I* am?" Joby gaped. "I'm not the one who's swimming around like a seal."

"No, you're the storm-bringer and boundary-breaker, the one who's always piercing our defenses like they weren't even there. Explain all that to me, and maybe I'll—"

"Ander," Joby exclaimed, "I don't know what you're talking about! I don't even know . . . what you are, but I thought we were friends! . . . Aren't we? . . . Weren't we ever?"

"Yes," Ander sighed, coming to slump miserably against the base of Joby's rock. "I've liked you from the day you came to school. We all did, mostly, but it's been scary too, and now . . . this totally blows."

"Okay, listen," Joby said, desperate for some answers. "I've clearly stumbled into something I'm not supposed to know about. But if it's any comfort, Swami kind of spilled the beans already, I think."

"Yeah," Ander shrugged, "I heard."

Trying to sound light, Joby pulled a smile from somewhere. "It's a little late to hope I'll just forget all this, isn't it? If that's what you wanted, you shouldn't have been zooming around like that out here in front of God and everybody."

"You weren't supposed to be here!" Ander protested. "I checked! There was no sign of—" His mouth snapped shut as a new wave of guilty chagrin swept his face.

"Checked what? How?" Joby pressed.

Ander shook his head. "I know you've got a million questions, Joby. But it's gonna take a lot more explaining than you think. If I start trying now, you'll just have even more questions, and it's not my place to answer most of them. Besides, I'm already late for work at the hotel." He began to wade around the rock toward shore.

"Late for *work*?" Joby exclaimed. "You can't just leave without explaining this! At least tell me how you swim like that."

"Joby, I'm sorry," Ander said. "It's gonna have to wait 'til—"

"Tell me!" Joby snapped in frustration. "Or I'll just start asking around until I find someone who will. I'm tired of all this 'secret' shit!"

"I wouldn't try that," Ander replied quietly. "Anyone who knows won't tell you. Not like that. And anyone who doesn't know will think you're crazy. Just . . . be patient."

"Patient 'til *when*?" Joby complained.

Ander looked pensively out to sea again. "The falls up Burl Creek Canyon; be there at sunset. Don't forget a flashlight. It'll be a dark walk back. Whatever answers I can give, I'll give you then." He looked up toward town and sighed, "The punch card calls." He splashed onto the beach and started heading toward the stairs.

"Ander!" Joby called.

"What?"

"What was the fish for?"

"Breakfast," Ander said over his shoulder and shrugged. "The hotel food's not so great."

He went on then, leaving Joby to wonder if he'd planned to cook it on the beach, or . . . whether he was into sushi.

☒

"*Look* at the *mess!*" Agnes shrieked. "*Look there!* They've *broken* my *window!* This is *exactly* what I *knew* would happen! I *begged* their parents to *prevent* this, but did anybody *listen? NO!*"

Karl certainly shared her outrage at this latest teenage crime spree, but her hysteria was beginning to grate a little. "I'm very glad you called me, Agnes, but—"

"I wanted you to *see* this, Karl! I wanted *somebody* who's not a complete *idiot* to *see* what they've *done* to my *house!* It'll take all *day* to clean this up! *All week!*"

"It's atrocious, Agnes," Karl commiserated. "Absolutely inexcusable. But they're only digging their own graves, you know. I'm coming back here with a camera, and we'll have pictures printed in the paper. Front page. That'll garner even more support for getting some police protection here in town. You may not want to hear it, Agnes, but they've done you quite a favor here."

"I don't just want *police* here now!" she wailed. "*I want a jail!* That's where these little *criminals belong!* I'm going to make sure you can't buy an egg in this *whole town* without *ID!*"

"Calm down, Agnes," Karl said. "We're going to make them pay for this, but you've got to take the high ground. Show 'em we still have our dignity. Revenge is best served cold, you know."

"Oooooh!" she blustered, struggling to master her frustration. "I'll have to get a bigger freezer then."

"That's the spirit," Karl said supportively. "Hit 'em with your sense of humor, Agnes. Show 'em they aren't getting to you."

☒

"*Ben!* Ben, wake up!"

"Joby? What—Oh shit." Ben clutched his head, and grimaced. "My mouth is full of sand. Where are we?"

"Ben, I just saw something. You're never going to believe me, but I swear—"

"Keep it down, will ya?" Ben complained. "God, I'm totaled. Why'd you let me drink so much?"

"*Me!*" Joby objected loudly, wincing at the gong this revived in his own brain.

"I'm joking," Ben growled. "Guess we overdid it, huh?"

"Ben, shut up and listen to me. I just saw Ander turn into a seal. I mean, the seal turned into Ander. And it's not just him. Swami talks to animals. He did it right in front of me. How do you explain that? No one will answer any of my questions, but something unbelievable is happening here! Everywhere!"

For a moment Ben just stared at Joby, then, though it really hurt his head, he couldn't keep from cracking up. "God, Joby! I knew you didn't drink much, but what a neophyte! You must have the mother of all hangovers in history!" He lay back down on the sand, struggling not to laugh himself sick, literally.

"Goddamn it! I'm serious, Ben! I'm telling you the truth!"

This just made Ben laugh harder—an increasingly risky activity, given the condition of his stomach. He had no desire to embarrass Joby, but he couldn't help it. The look on Joby's face was so hilariously tragic.

"Fine! Laugh!" Joby said, kicking sand at Ben, which helped him stop laughing as it got into his eyes and mouth again. "Keep right on laughing when I'm dead tomorrow!"

"Quit it with the sand!" Ben griped. "What's with all the being dead crap? If this is about Laura—"

"It's got nothing to do with that," Joby said exasperated. "There are other things happening in the world besides you and me and Laura!"

That got Ben's attention. "Since when?" he said, taking a second look at Joby's expression and feeling suddenly more sober.

"Since about ten minutes ago," Joby told him, looking as sober as a schoolteacher, which, of course, he was.

"Okay," Ben sighed. "So what happened again?"

"Look, Ben. I know how crazy this sounds, but if you won't trust me, who's going to? I really need you to believe what I'm telling you, okay?"

Ben took a deep breath, trying to suppress all the nasty sensations sloshing through his insides as he sat up again. "Tell it to me a little more coherently," he said.

"I was just sitting out there on the rocks, watching a seal hunt the swell for fish," Joby said gravely. "But when it swam to shore and came out of the water, it wasn't a seal anymore. It was this kid I know in town named Ander. He was still holding the fish."

Ben just stared at Joby, no longer laughing. Last night had been hard on both of them. Now Ben wondered if he'd grossly underestimated *how* hard it had been on Joby. "He was wearing a wetsuit, I assume?" Ben asked.

"Of course," Joby said. "He'd freeze out there without it."

"He got dark hair?" Ben asked.

"Yeah. You've met him?" Joby said, surprised.

"No," Ben said. "I'm just imagining the kind of guy who'd look like a seal until he came out of the water."

"You think I didn't think of that?" Joby asked crossly. "It was a seal's head I saw out there, Ben. There's no fur on Ander's face, and his nose is nowhere near that big. Besides, he stayed under water for five minutes at a time, and swam faster than a Jet Ski."

"The kid's spent all his life in the surf." Ben shrugged. "He's a great swimmer with impressive breath control."

"I mean *literally* faster than a Jet Ski, Ben. Under water." Joby rolled his eyes. "Listen, I'd be telling myself everything you're saying, because *I* know it's impossible as well as you do, except for one thing. When I confronted him about it, he told me to tell no one, then told to hike up to the Burl Creek falls at sunset tonight, where he's promised to give me some answers." Joby leaned back and spread his hands. "Explain that."

"Why not just tell you now?" Ben said, perplexed.

"Good question," Joby said pointedly.

"He said not to tell anyone? That's . . . pretty weird."

"He said they'd only think I was crazy." Joby said, folding his arms and looking accusingly at Ben. "I told you anyway, because I *trusted* you." Joby's smug expression faltered. "And because I have no idea why I'm supposed to go all the way up there at night to get the answers. I thought that someone I could trust should know where to go looking for my body if I don't come back."

"Hold on, pal!" Ben protested. "You don't really think you're goin' up there without me, do you?"

"So you believe me now?" Joby said, hopeful.

"I don't believe some guy really turned into a seal," Ben snorted. "But I do believe you've stumbled into some kind of very weird shit, and frankly, I think you're an idiot for going up there at all."

"I *need* some answers, Ben," Joby said earnestly. "If I don't go up there, I may never get them. Like I said, this isn't the first weird thing I've seen here, and . . ." He looked distressed again. "These people are my friends, Ben."

"You *think*," Ben interjected.

"These are my students and my neighbors," Joby insisted. "I've seen them every day for three years, and they've treated me better than anyone I've ever known except for you and Laura. I can't believe they'd hurt me, but I do have to know who, or what, they really are. I can't just go on here pretending not to care. Not now."

"Yeah, well, like I said," Ben pressed, "I think you're an idiot, but idiots like company, and if you think I'm gonna sit here on my hands tonight waiting for the news at eleven, you really *are* crazy. What good are answers if you're dead?" Ben grinned wickedly. "Or beamed up for a rectal probe on Pluto? This could be dangerous, dude!"

"But, if you come with me," Joby pressed, "how will anyone know what happened if neither of us comes back?"

"We'll leave a note, bright boy. That'll do at least as much good as I'd have done you here." He felt a winsome smile spreading on his face. "Just like old times, eh Joby? Two knights off to combat supernatural evil?" It made him almost giddy with delight. "Only this time, it's *real*! How cool is *that*?"

❊

When Ferristaff answered his front door to find Agnes Hamilton on the porch, he barely managed to suppress a groan. Had he not been subjected to enough harassment? Sadly, as she was the single largest owner of commercial properties in Taubolt, and its single biggest pain in the ass as well, he felt compelled to be courteous. The last thing he needed was to end up on *her* wrong side too.

"Hello, Robert," she said, offering him her signature grimace of a smile.

"Hello, Agnes," he replied. "To what do I owe this unexpected honor?"

"You're too kind," she said. "I just came by to offer my condolences."

"Regarding?" he asked, concerned that some new disaster had occurred of which he hadn't been informed yet.

"That poor young man who was crippled by the tree spike," Agnes said.

Thank God, he thought. *Old news.* "Well that's very kind of you," he said aloud.

"Actually, I'd like to donate some money to his family," she said. "Just to help them through until they get back on their legs."

What a tasteless choice of words, he thought, trying not to smile.

"I wasn't sure where to send it," she explained, "and thought it might be easiest just to give it to you personally. May I come in?"

The urge to smile left him, but he could hardly say, *I'll just take the check, good-bye.* "Yes! Please do," he said aloud.

"Thank you, Robert," she said, brushing past him. "My, what a lovely house you've built! I adore the look of finished wood."

"There is no substitute in my opinion," he concurred pleasantly, ushering her into the living room, where she took a seat. "Can I get you anything to drink?"

"No. I won't be staying long."

The urge to smile returned.

"Actually," she said, getting out her checkbook, "there was one other issue I was hoping to discuss."

The urge to smile vanished.

"I've penned a short letter to the county sheriff, asking that he give more careful consideration to our request for local law enforcement." Her pen paused above the check. "To whom do I make this out?" she asked.

"James Moss," Ferristaff said politely, wondering if she really thought writing a check to some employee of his was going to move him to her cause. "No, wait," he said. "Better make it out to Alice Moss. It may be a while before Jim can cash it very easily."

"Of course," she said, scribbling in the remaining details and reaching up to hand the check to him.

Covering his surprise at the five-figure amount, he said, "That's very generous."

"Contrary to popular opinion," she said, grimacing another smile, "I can be very generous, where generosity is deserved." She put away her pen and checkbook. "As I was saying, I suspect my letter might get more attention if it were clear that I'm not speaking solely on my own behalf, so I'm inviting a number of other influential members of the community to sign it. Quite a few of Taubolt's business people already have."

Of course they have, thought Ferristaff, *you're their landlord.* Though he didn't doubt that many of them had signed it willingly enough. He, himself, had managed, until now, to dodge this issue, having learned long ago that inviting law enforcement in the door could cut both ways. Not all of his own men were scrupulous law-abiders, as that damn circus in September had demonstrated.

"I thought, especially after what's been done to your poor Mr. Moss, that you might want to sign it too, Robert. I'm sure it must frustrate you terribly that the perpetrators of that heinous crime are still at large."

"There's only one perpetrator," Ferristaff said. "And I know damn well who she is, pardon my language."

"Not at all, Robert," she replied. "I assume you mean that Greensong woman."

"Of course I do," Ferristaff growled. "And to be honest, Agnes, I'm not sure why the expense and effort of importing an entire standing police force should be required to subdue one twiggy little ecoterrorist. There are investigators working on it, and when they find the evidence to prove what everyone already knows, they'll have no trouble coming out here to arrest her."

"That assumes, of course, that you are correct in assuming it was her," she said.

"Who else would it be?" he asked, careful to keep the scorn from his voice.

"As your flyer intimated," Agnes sighed, "the woman has attracted quite a few youthful disciples. Two of them were with her during that . . . unfortunate event last month, weren't they? Could none of them have been involved?"

"I have no reason to suspect that mere children—"

"I am not referring to *mere children*," she cut him off with startling sharpness. "There are some very nasty creatures roaming this pleasant little town in children's clothing, Robert, but they are in no way *mere children*. They've inflicted countless acts of truly hateful vandalism on many of our shop owners, and regularly terrorize their customers in broad daylight. Just last night they virtually demolished my own house."

Ah! Ferristaff thought dryly. He'd read her little letter to the editor, and he thought her more brainless than blameless there.

"I see no reason to assume that driving spikes into a handful of your trees would be beyond them. Not at all," she said, seeming sure she'd made her point. "Were there any real threat of consequences here, I think we might see a very significant decrease in the troubles that increasingly plague us all."

He was drawing breath to express polite condolences about her house, and demure her request, when a horrendous crash caused them both to spin and stare in shock at the scattered shards of glass that remained of one of his large picture windows, and the large rock resting at the center of the mess.

"Goddamn her!" Ferristaff raged, running to the shotgun he now kept by his front door, then racing outside in hopes of settling this escalating nonsense in the good old-fashion way. He found no one to aim at, of course. The woods around his property were as still and silent as ever. *"Greensong, you bitch!"* he shouted. *"I know it's you! Everybody knows! Your butt is bound for prison any day now!"* Unable to contain his rage, he fired both shells into the trees, hoping for a scream. But there was nothing. When he turned around, he found Hamilton standing on his porch, looking gallingly self-satisfied. "What the hell," he spat. "Put me on your roster. I'll sign the damn letter."

"I'm so sorry about your window, Robert," she commiserated. "But I do appreciate your help. I'll send the letter by tomorrow."

❉

"Gonna do some painting," Cotter explained with an uncomfortable grin, shoving two gallons of paint thinner onto the counter. "Time to spruce up the mission a little."

"Looks like you'll be sprucin' up things more'n a little." Franklin grinned, trying to be friendly, though Cotter had always given him the creeps.

"Gonna take a lot of painting, that old place," Cotter said defensively. "Inside and out, you know."

"Outside too!" Franklin said, trying to sound impressed. "Gotten that past Hamilton's Preservation Council, have you?" He gave Cotter a sympathetic smile to show he understood how trying that must have been.

But Cotter shook his head, and said, "That's next on my list to do."

"Oh," Franklin said, nonplussed, as Cotter paid him. *"After* the thinner?"

"Well . . . I can't get the paint 'til the Preservation Council tells me what color's okay, now can I?" Cotter sputtered irritably.

"Hey," Franklin apologized. "Didn't mean to pry, friend. Just makin' small talk."

"No harm done," Cotter said, leaving with his thinner, but forgetting his change.

26

(Revelation)

As twilight approached, Joby and Ben finally heard the falls ahead of them, having walked for half an hour in apprehensive silence.

"Maybe I should go up first and check things out," Ben suggested quietly.

"Yeah," Joby teased uneasily. "Then they can knock us off separately." He looked up into the woods overhanging the path; always so peaceful and picturesque before, they seemed full of lurking shadows now. "If they want to hurt me, they've had years to do it . . . I just hope Ander shows up at all when he sees you."

They crested one last rise and stood looking down on the ferny hollow into which Burl Creek plunged in lacy veils. A primitive wooden bridge spanned the pool beneath it, and, leaning heavily against the bridge's railing, stood the last person Joby had expected. Father Crombie looked up at them, and waved.

"What are *you* doing here?" Joby called.

"How'd you *get* here?" Ben added, before the old man could answer.

"Waiting for you, of course. And rather carefully," Crombie said amiably.

Unsure whether to feel relieved or dismayed that even Father Crombie was involved, Joby said, "I was expecting—"

"Ander," Crombie finished with a kindly smile. "I know. But it was decided I might be the better messenger, given our long acquaintance." As Joby and Ben descended toward the bridge, Crombie's smile faded. "You boys look as if I were a ghost."

"What about your hips?" Joby asked uncertainly. "I mean, I thought you were . . ."

"A cripple?" Crombie smiled. "I am, and had a great deal of help getting up here, of course. Now, please, relax—both of you."

"Are you going to tell me what's going on," Joby asked, wondering if anyone in Taubolt *hadn't* been deceiving him, "or just give me the runaround again?"

Father Crombie's expression grew sober. "I am prepared to tell you a great deal more than you may wish to hear," he said. "No one has ever wished to deceive you, Joby. But neither did we wish to trouble you with burdens that were not yours to bear. Even now, I must warn you that the answers you seek may leave you far more troubled than continued ignorance will. Are you really certain that you wish to know?"

Ben's laughter surprised them both. "Bull elephants couldn't drag me away without an answer now, Father. So, what's the story? You all Martians, or what?"

Father Crombie had the grace to smile. "Come, boys. This will likely be a rather lengthy conversation, and these old legs are no longer fit to stand through such endeavors. Let's find a place to sit while I abuse your credulity." He turned carefully, and began shuffling toward the far end of the bridge.

After exchanging a look, Joby and Ben followed him toward a jumble of fallen logs and mossy stumps. After helping Crombie to get seated, they found perches for themselves, facing him with their backs to the creek.

"I recall that you boys were fairly comfortable with miracles once," Crombie said after a reflective pause. "Do you remember asking me how to fight the devil?"

Joby felt his face grow warm. "We were little kids," he mumbled.

"And have you never found children wiser than their elders?" Crombie asked.

Joby shrugged uncomfortably.

"You asked that morning if the chalice in my sacristy was the Grail. Remember?"

Ben chuckled under his breath, intensifying Joby's embarrassment.

"What if I told you that the Grail is no myth, nor the devil, angels, or magic itself?" Crombie asked. "Could you still gather enough of that childish faith to trust me?"

"What are you saying?" Ben laughed. "That what Joby saw was *magic*?"

Crombie simply gazed at them with a kind of severity that made it seem he was saying exactly that and expected to be taken seriously.

"You don't mean *magic* magic," Joby insisted, ". . . do you?"

"I suppose I should begin by telling you a story that you'll likely find still harder to believe. I ask only that you listen until I'm through. Then you may write me off as mad and walk away, or . . . you can tell me how much more you wish to know. Agreed?"

Joby and Ben nodded together.

"Then, here is a bit of history I'm sure you've never been taught, though I've acquired ample reason to believe it true. I assume you boys have heard somewhere how the archangel Lucifer made war against God in Heaven when humanity was young."

Joby nodded. Ben shrugged.

"You may recall that Lucifer and the angels who sided with him were cast down to earth in defeat, like stars swept from the sky, to become the demons of Hell."

"What's that got to do with Taubolt?" Ben asked gruffly, clearly as uncomfortable with these old catechisms as Joby was.

"What's been forgotten," Crombie continued unperturbed, "is that a third group of angels sided at first with Lucifer, then, realizing their error, turned to fight at God's side against him. To this day, I am told, Lucifer blames his defeat on their defection."

"Told by *who*?" Joby blurted out. "I mean, who'd have been there to know?"

"Their descendants," Crombie said gravely, "whose very survival depends on passing down the memory of Lucifer's enmity even now, all these millennia later."

"Their *descendants*?" Ben scoffed.

"You agreed to listen," Crombie reminded him gently.

Joby saw the muscles in Ben's jaw clamp down around some further protest.

"Since they had sided with Lucifer, impartial justice demanded that this third angelic faction be cast to earth as well. But the change of heart that had led to their timely shift of allegiance also preserved them from becoming demons like Lucifer and his kind. Though barred from returning to Heaven, they still enjoyed the same rapport with their Creator that every other earthly creature does. They chose to make of their new home here, not a prison, but a garden reflecting what they recalled of Heaven, filling it with beauty and what we call magic, though to them it was no more magic than speech, thought, or breath are to us.

"So it was for ages afterward. The legends we know today of fairies, djinn, and spirit beings are not just empty tales as most suppose. They are our own distant memory of the time when these fallen angels, good and evil, still lived openly in our presence. At first, there was frequent conflict between the two factions, but as ages passed, they grew almost indifferent to each other. Finally, however, Lucifer saw how dearly God loved humanity and perceived his opportunity for revenge. When the fallen angels still serving Heaven sought to protect humanity from his attacks, his anger at them was rekindled.

"As more ages passed, the fallen angels still in grace longed ever more keenly for their lost celestial home, envying the mortal creatures around them who, dying in love with God, were returned to Him in Heaven. This made them beg their Creator for something no angel had ever suffered— mortality. They would gladly die, they told their Maker, if, in death, they could return to Heaven as well—no longer angels, just simple souls gathered back with all the rest into the intimate presence of their Lord.

"Moved to pity, God granted their request, offering the same to Lucifer and his demons. But Hell's proud and embittered faction refused the offer out of hand. Thus, only fallen angels loyal to Heaven became mortal, though their lives were still measured in centuries rather than in years. Made mortal, however, they became vulnerable flesh as well, and Lucifer's campaign to destroy them for what they had done to him in Heaven was renewed with vigor. The angels fallen in grace were still very powerful, but in time, more and more were overcome and slain defending themselves and those in their care.

"Grown more lonely as their companions died, some took mortal spouses and bore children with angelic blood running in their veins. These children grew to be powerful men and women with lives vastly longer than ordinary mortals. Some served the light heroically, others were legendary for their darkness, for Lucifer was especially keen to bring his angelic enemies to grief through their children, preferring to seduce rather than slay them when he could.

"As the Roman Empire waned, the last of the true angels fallen in grace died, but their descendants lived on, bearing new generations of children, each less potent in the blood than those before and thus more vulnerable to Lucifer and his horde. By the Renaissance, those of the blood were terribly diminished in power and lived always in hiding, hardly daring to reveal their heritage even to their own children. Many of these, left ignorant of their own nature, did not know to hide their strange gifts and abilities, so were easily found and destroyed by Lucifer's servants, who took particular delight in seeing these murders done in the name of God."

Father Crombie gazed sadly toward the falls. "The very church I have given my life to serve," he murmured, "has too often lifted in prayer hands spattered with such innocent blood . . . imagining that God was pleased." He shook his head and seemed to shudder. "How the devil must howl with laughter."

The old priest looked so forlorn that Joby was sure he believed what he was saying, but he felt Ben's rigid silence beside him like the charge before a thunderstorm.

"Father Crombie," Joby said. "I don't want to offend you, but if you're saying that Taubolt is full of . . . angelic half-breeds descended from demigods at the dawn of time, I, uh . . . I have some trouble with that." He glanced at Ben, who nodded once, sharply. "No one could still remember any of this, and any such bloodline would be spread atom thin through most of mankind by now. Besides, why Taubolt? Aren't there lots of more remote places to hide from . . . well, the devil, I guess, than a tourist town in California?"

Crombie gave him a weary, if unsurprised look. "They are here because there is something in Taubolt that protects them—something unique in all the world, Joby."

"And that is?" Ben asked in something close to a growl.

Crombie gave them each a measuring look, then said, "The Grail."

"Jesus, Mary, and Joseph!" Ben exclaimed, shooting to his feet in unbridled frustration to pace off toward the falls, where he turned back to snap, "What's next, Father? Merlin the Magician?"

"I know how odd all this must sound, Ben, but have you ever known me to lie?"

"Of course not." Ben scowled. "You're no liar, but—"

"A fool then?" Crombie cut him off.

"Father, you're the kindest, most honest, most . . . most *virtuous* man I ever met, but either people here are tangled up in some pretty delusional folklore or someone's been playing you for a sucker. And now they're using you to try playing us for the same."

"A fool then after all," Crombie said, unable to hide his disappointment.

"Have you actually seen this Grail, Father Crombie?" Joby asked.

"Almost daily," he said. "I have the unthinkable honor to be its principal guardian at present."

At this, Joby and Ben fell silent, staring first at Crombie, then at each other.

"You have seen it as well, Joby," Crombie said. "In church, your first Christmas morning here. I am not likely to forget the effect it seemed to have on you—as if the hounds of Hell were nipping at your heels. You nearly ran from church after Mass that morning." He smiled sadly. "Not the response I had hoped for, I'll admit."

Joby suddenly recalled his agony that morning, ignited by a single glimpse of— "The communion cup," he murmured in astonishment. The memory sent snowflakes down his spine. "That's . . . that's it? The *actual Grail?*"

"Joby," Ben said edgily, "Don't you go loopy too now."

"Ben, he's right," Joby said in a rush of wonder. "I remember seeing . . . colors, sort of, in the glaze, and . . . something happened. I don't remember what. But I freaked completely. I was afraid to go back into that church for, well, years."

"So you freaked out a little, Joby!" Ben protested. "After what Father Richter did for you, I'd have freaked out sitting in a church too. It doesn't take the Holy Grail to explain that! This is a full-on *myth* we're talking about! A Monty Python movie! Remember?"

Ignoring Ben's outburst, Crombie spoke solely to Joby. "Those of the blood have followed the Grail for centuries, because evil cannot come near it. The more evil the being, the more lethal the Grail's presence. But the Grail has a will of its own and may travel where it chooses without a moment's notice. About four hundred years ago, it chose to come here for reasons still a mystery today, and the remnants of what you and I might call 'fairy' found it and followed. Every year its presence draws more of those who possess any trace of the blood to this place, while keeping all others at bay—that is it did until you arrived. Since then, Taubolt's borders have failed somehow, and now it seems the world has found us."

"And you think that's because of me?" Joby asked in dismay.

"Hellooo!" Ben exclaimed in exasperation. "Can we step away from the edge, please?"

"I have no such conviction," Crombie said, still ignoring Ben. "I merely observe that the two events seemed to coincide."

"No wonder they've been hiding from me," Joby groaned. "Father Crombie, if the chalice made me freak . . . does that mean . . . am I somehow evil?"

"No No NO NO NO!" Ben suddenly roared, stamping his feet like a child in full tantrum. *"You're going to ruin him all over again!"* Swiveling to face Joby, he said with less volume but even more intensity, "This is totally, shit-for-crackers *crazy,* Joby! I am not letting you go back to being a self-doubting,

scared shitless, suicidal little wreck! You are *not* evil! You were *never* evil! And you're not *going* to be evil if I have to *beat* the sense back into you with my *bare hands!*" He seemed to run out of words then, breathing like a sprinter yards short of the finish line, while both Joby and Crombie stared at him in stunned silence. With a start, Joby realized that Ben might be going to cry. "Damn it, Joby," Ben pleaded, "you're finally happy. . . . We're all together again. Please, *please* don't go backward now!" He turned to Crombie. "For God's sake, Father, tell him!"

Nodding sadly, Crombie turned to Joby. "Ben is right, Joby; I was foolish not to see what my words might mean to you. If you were evil, the Grail would have driven you from Taubolt long ago, but you have been welcome and happy here where only the good are welcome and happy for long. So listen to your wise and faithful friend. You are, and have been as long as I have known you, as far from evil as the sun is from the sea floor."

"Then why did the Grail affect me that way?" Joby asked, unsatisfied. "And why did Taubolt's protection end when I arrived?"

"As for the first," Crombie shrugged, "the person you were may have found what he longed for as frightening and painful as what he feared—if not more so. As for the second, I cannot say, except that it can have nothing to do with your being evil, for you are manifestly not."

"This all means nothing anyway," Ben insisted, the tantrum seeming to have drained him, "unless that cup is really the Grail, and Taubolt's really a secret fairy refuge; which, I'm sorry to say, I still do not for one second believe, or understand why you do, Joby." He turned back to Father Crombie. "Or you either, frankly." His expression became contrite. "And . . . I'm really sorry I yelled like that."

"I am not," Crombie replied. "Your outburst was the roar of genuine love and loyalty." He tilted his head up to look Ben squarely in the eyes. "I believe these outlandish tales only because I have seen a steady stream of miracles performed, practically since the day I arrived here, by people more good-hearted and less deluded than any I have ever known. And, of course, I have held the Cup itself, in my hands, and been blessed to drink from it on too many occasions to be mistaken about its nature."

In the waning light, Ben looked uncertain for the first time that evening. "I don't know," he sighed. "It might be easier if I could see some of these miracles too."

"Have you not?" Crombie asked. "I thought that's what brought you here."

Ben shook his head. "Joby may have. I haven't. And . . ." he hesitated. " I'd just like to believe it way too much, I guess. . . . Maybe that's why I can't. It feels . . ."

"Like a potential disappointment?" Crombie asked.

"The truth is usually disappointing," Ben said. "That I understand. That I trust. But fairy tales come true? . . . That just scares the hell out of me."

"Think very carefully about what I am going to ask you," Father Crombie said, "both of you." He seemed to weigh his words before continuing. "Are you certain you could stand to live in the world I've been describing, if you were convinced of its truth?"

"Believe me, Father," Ben said, grinning sarcastically, "I'd like nothing better than to see a few bona fide miracles."

"Are you sure?" Crombie asked. "You'd gain a new set of marvels, to be sure, but a whole new set of fears as well. Are you ready to suffer a return to childhood so late in life?" He paused. "For all I care, we need never mention any of this again. Might it not be safer, even wiser, to simply go home now, have a laugh at one old man's wild imagination, and return to whatever you were doing before?"

"Are you saying you can show us some sort of proof right now?" Joby asked.

"Are you saying you want me to?" Crombie answered.

"It'd have to be something pretty damn impressive," Ben grunted. "A few really good card tricks aren't gonna cut it."

"There may be no going back once you've decided," Crombie insisted.

"There's already no going back," Joby said. "You know that."

"Yeah," Ben shrugged. "Show us. It's why we came here."

There was a quiet rustling in the foliage beyond the pool, and Joby turned to see a large raven burst into the open air, glide toward them, and land gracefully on the railing at the center of the bridge. It perched there for an instant, blinking at them; then, without transition, Sky stood balanced easily on the rail where the bird had vanished.

Joby almost forgot to breathe in the silence that gripped them all.

"It's a trick," Ben said, sounding torn between astonishment and anger. "Look how dark it's gotten. You could pull off anything in light like this."

"I can fix that," said another voice behind them.

Joby and Ben spun around to see Nacho walk out of the trees. Grinning mischievously at Ben, he reached up to touch a redwood bough hanging just above his head. Where his fingers made contact, a tiny green-gold glow was kindled—just a spark at first, but it grew brighter and began to spread from twig to twig, up one branch onto another and another. As Ben and Joby gaped, the entire tree began to glow, every bump and needle traced in pale golden fire. The luminescence quickly spread from tree to tree until the hollow in which they stood was bathed in more than ample light to read by.

Ben moved toward a glowing branch as if walking in his sleep, and reached up to finger a tuft of luminescing needles. *"Oh . . . God,"* he whispered.

There was a sloshing splash across the pool, and Joby turned again to watch several objects, large and dark, glide smoothly beneath the bridge, pushing the water's surface up before them. Joby backed away in dazed alarm as three seals reared up and began to splash ashore . . . miles up a creek too small for anything their size to navigate! One of them barked, as if in laughter, then, again without transition, Ander, Blue, and Tholomey stood grinning at Joby as if this were just another boyish prank.

"Man, I've waited years to show you that!" Blue grinned.

"How . . . How are you doing this?" Ben murmured, sounding on the edge of panic.

"We just do." Ander shrugged.

Joby had never seen Ben truly frightened before. Seeing it now sacred him worse than all the rest. Ben started backing toward the logs they'd been sitting on, looking dazed and short of breath. He stumbled into them and sat heavily, as if he might lose consciousness. Before Joby could react, Jake appeared from somewhere, leaning down to grab Ben's shoulders. Ben flinched and pulled away.

"Chill, dude!" Nacho said in obvious alarm. "We're not gonna hurt you."

Joby waved the others off. "Ben?" he said, uncertainly. The world he knew was doing flip-flops, just as Father Crombie had warned, but what he most wanted back was Ben—strong, sure, confident, Ben. "Freaking out's my job, remember?" he teased nervously. "You're kind of horning in on my territory here."

"Joby, look how they're . . . messing with us! They've slipped us something! We could be into anything here!" He looked around in fear. "What do you all want?"

"Ben, it's okay," Joby said. "I know these people."

"You don't know *jack*!" Ben blurted out. "People can't turn into . . . into things!"

"He's in shock," Jake sighed. "Just needs some time." He turned to Nacho. "The candle trick was a little much, don't you think?"

"Hey! He asked for more light!" Nacho protested throwing up his hands. "I was just trying to accommodate." But Joby saw contrition on his face.

"I guess we overdid it," Sky said, glancing at the others.

"Ben, it's completely okay," said yet another familiar voice, and Joby whirled to see Hawk walking toward them across the bridge. "No one's gonna do anything to you."

"Oh God," Ben groaned in what sounded like despair. *"Even you?* Is . . . *Laura—"*

"Mom's got nothing to do with any of it," Hawk assured him, stopping an arm's length away. "She doesn't even know. Not much blood in me either, I guess." He shrugged in obvious disappointment. "I can't do much compared to the others."

"Well, if you've got any at all," said Joby, "then Laura must too."

Hawk shook his head. "We'd have known by now. I guess it was my dad," he said, looking even more downcast.

"Hawk," Joby said. "What they're telling us . . . Is this all true?"

"Far as I know," Hawk said. "They believe it, and the things we do are real enough. I can do a few things."

Thinking of the deer, and half-afraid to know, Joby asked, "Can you turn into . . . something else?"

Hawk looked down sadly and shook his head. "Like I said, I'm too weak."

Ben was staring dully at Hawk, and to Joby's relief, his panic seemed to be subsiding. When he spoke again, his voice was filled with something more like resignation. "I was wrong," Ben said to Father Crombie. "About everything. I don't know if I can handle . . . any of this. I should have listened to you. I'm sorry. I just didn't—"

"I felt just as you do once," Crombie reassured him, "but I lived, as I suspect you will. My assumptions had been hardening for even longer than yours have, afterall."

"So . . . how many more of you are hiding in the bushes?" Ben asked, trying to smile.

"Only those Joby has known best have come," said Crombie. "We thought it would be easier that way. But there are many more in town."

"Come on out," Jake said to no one in particular, "but no more fancy stuff."

First Jupiter and Swami, then Tom Connolly and his daughter, Rose, appeared from between the trees a, bit too gracefully. Rose came to Hawk's side, smiling shyly at Joby. Then a sudden gust of wind blew up from nowhere, swirling leaves and trails of dust around Joby and Ben, and Cob was standing beside them, grinning like a lunatic.

"Asshole," Jupiter muttered.

"A little joke!" Cob protested, hunching his shoulders in classic Bob fashion. "I couldn't help it." His head bounced forward as if slapped from behind, and Cob yelped as Cal appeared from thin air at his shoulder.

"Couldn't help that either, fool," Cal growled at Cob. "Tryin' a give 'em both another heart attack?"

Cob gave Cal a shove, but Nacho snapped, "Cut it out, you clueless richards! Didn't you hear what Jake said?"

"Sorry," Cal said to Ben and Joby. "Cob don't know when to quit, sometimes."

Ben barked a quiet laugh, and the tension seemed suddenly to drain from all around the clearing. "Can't be *that* much angel in either one of you." He grinned wanly.

"It is hard sometimes to believe you guys are almost twenty," Joby agreed.

"Lot older than that," Cal bragged.

Cob ribbed him in the side.

"What!" Cal protested, rubbing at his ribs. "Don't matter *now!*"

"What does that mean?" Joby asked.

Cal looked guilty, but Sky said, "Hey, it's not exactly a secret anymore, is it?"

"Some of us don't age that fast." Cal shrugged.

"Ain't *that* the truth!" Nacho jeered, glaring at Cal and Cob.

"Look who's talking, *'perpetual freshman'!*" Cob jeered back.

Rose rolled her eyes and sighed.

"How old *are* you then?" Joby asked.

Cal shrugged. "'Bout thirty I guess. Ain't paid that much attention."

"No way," Ben said.

"So," Joby asked in renewed disbelief, "you were . . . *twenty-four* when you started high school?"

"We go more or less whenever we like," Cal said.

"More than once sometimes," Cob added.

"No one notices?" Ben insisted.

"Those who pay attention see as much as they wish to," said a familiar voice up on the rise above them. "Those who don't wish to know, don't pay attention." Joby and Ben looked up to see Solomon coming down the path toward the bridge. Joby was hardly surprised to find that Solomon was fey as well. The old man waved casually, and Joby found himself waving back, as if nothing were amiss.

Joby looked at Jake and asked, "So, how old are you?"

"I've been seeing to things around here for a pretty long time," Jake replied. As he spoke, the luminescence Nacho had cast around them glinted from the golden stubble on Jake's upper lip and chin, and Joby finally knew where he had seen that face before meeting Jake at Mrs. Lindsay's.

"It was you, wasn't it?" Joby said. "On that bench when I was here the first time."

Jake nodded with a small, wry smile.

Joby shook his head in dull amazement, then turned to Ander. "Was that you I ran into as a kid, swimming in the bay that morning?"

Ander shook his head. "That was Blue. He got all wadded up about being seen. We teased him pretty bad."

"Guess you won't be teasing anybody now," said Blue.

Ander looked abashed.

"So . . . are you *all* that old?" Ben asked looking from one to the next of them.

"I'm just twenty," said Rose, "pretty much like I seem. We all have different gifts. Some age slowly, some don't, but we're just human beings like you, really."

"Who turn into birds and seals," Ben replied. "What do you turn into, Rose?"

"Nothing," Rose said self-consciously. "I just talk to plants."

"Oh," Ben said, recovered enough to be sarcastic again. "Is *that* all."

"Lot's of us can't change," Swami said. "I can't. You've got to be pretty strong in the blood for that."

"And raised to it from the start," Solomon interjected. "Those born here are most apt to have the talent. The necessary faith is harder to learn the later one starts."

As they'd talked, the full wonder of it all had been dawning on Joby. There was magic, *real magic,* in the world! In some ways it was as scary as Crombie had warned, but in other ways . . . "What I wouldn't give to be like you guys," he sighed.

"You are." Ander shrugged. "How else to do you think you caught me this morning? Some of our tricks don't work so well on others of the blood."

Joby stared at Ander in utter disbelief.

"You were always stickin' your big nose where you shouldn't have been able," grinned Jupiter. "Like that day you saw me in the woods. Course, *some* of us were smart enough even then to figure out you must be of the blood too," he said, looking smugly at Nacho. "So I didn't mind too much. Just started training you to be a Taubolt stud."

Joby shook his head, knowing it could not be true.

"You did it the first day you got here." Rose smiled. "Me and Bellindi had set up a circle ward, but you heard us like it wasn't even there."

"Everyone thought you were some kind of spy," Hawk laughed.

"No!" Joby blurted out. "You can't be right! I've never done a magical thing in my—"

"Yes, you have," Ben cut him off.

Joby turned in disbelief to find Ben watching him with bald envy.

"Everything you did when we were kids was magic, Joby. Whatever you touched turned to gold." Ben looked down and sighed, "I should have known, you lucky bastard."

"Don't be an idiot," Joby growled. "If anyone was magic, it was you. All I ever wanted was to be what you were."

"Then you're a fool," Ben smiled sadly, "'cause you made things happen all the time I couldn't have thought up even if—"

"I'm sorry, but you're all just wrong!" Joby blurted out again, feeling confused and upset. "If I have a molecule of what you've all got, I'll be a monkey's uncle!"

"Ambitious," Nacho grinned, "but with practice you might pull it off."

"More fun to be a raven, though," Sky teased. "Don't you want to fly?"

"I'm serious!" Joby said.

"So are we," said Sky gravely. "You healed my legs, Joby. On that camping trip."

"Now *that's* ridiculous!" Joby scoffed. "Don't you think I'd know?"

"Not necessarily," Tom Connolly said quietly. "Intent by itself can be potent for our kind. How badly did you want him healed?"

"Well . . . of course I wanted him to be okay," Joby protested. "Who wouldn't?"

"My legs were broken bad," Sky said quietly. "When I came to, it was all I could do not to scream. Then, all of a sudden, they got real hot and I felt too weak to do anything but lie there, and then there was no pain at all. My legs worked fine again."

"Then obviously they weren't broken," Joby insisted, feeling flushed. "You were in shock. You got mixed up."

"They were broken," Tholomey said. "I've got some gifts for healing, and I could tell they were way worse than anything I had a prayer of handling."

"I thought it was Tholomey that fixed me up," Sky said, "or maybe the bunch of them together, but later they said none of them knew how it happened." He smiled at Joby. "That's when we really started wondering about you."

"Like I said," Ben leaned forward with an admiring smile, "you d'man, Joby."

"But . . . how could I not know?" Joby insisted.

"How could you know what you couldn't even believe?" Ander asked. "The Cup draws people of the blood to itself in lots of strange ways. You wouldn't be the first who didn't understand or even known about their gifts when they got here."

"Ha!" Ben laughed. "You're a goddamn wizard! That's perfect. All that Roundtable stuff; I should've known. It's in your blood, bro!"

Even Ben believed this? Joby was beginning to feel sick. First they'd turned the world upside down, and now they were insisting that he didn't even know *himself*?

"You know yourself better than we," Solomon said, as if reading his mind, "and it is altogether possible that we are wrong." He looked around severely at those who'd been intent on convincing Joby of his kinship, then turned back to Joby with a reassuring smile. "Don't worry, Joby. You are too vividly yourself to be erased so easily, I think."

"Nobody's trying to erase you!" Ander said in dismay.

"We like you fine the way you are," Rose said.

Hawk and several others nodded in vigorous agreement.

But Joby saw how Solomon was looking at them—as good as shouting, "back off." They'd only shut their mouths, not changed their minds. He didn't know what to think. It would be great if they were right. Heck! It would be unbelievable! But that's precisely what it was: unbelievable! They were only thrusting one more impossible expectation on him. He was just about to tell them so when a slow flare of light, pink and gold and pure, washed over the palely illuminated clearing as if dawn were coming early.

"*Jake!*" Rose gasped as everyone turned to behold a radiant cloud that hovered toward them across the water.

In an instant, everyone was on their knees except for Joby and Ben, who stared around them not knowing what to do or think.

"God . . . Joby!" Ben gasped, suddenly going to his knees as well. *"It's real!"*

Only then did Joby discern the brilliant form at the cloud's center—a chalice that seemed carved of sunlight. Joby knelt at last, hardly aware of what he did, as, from out of nowhere all around them, came the sound of voices lifted in inexpressible harmony at some unimaginable distance. Joby's mind emptied of words, even thoughts, but not of feelings. Those washed over him as if an ocean of warmth and reassurance had suddenly risen up and dragged him from some cold, rocky shore into its gentle depths. Joby wanted to speak—to sing—but nothing emerged within him but an unbearable longing just to touch the radiant vessel's gleaming rim with his half parted lips. As if in answer, the Cup within its blinding cloud began to move across the water toward himself and Ben.

"I . . . I can't," Joby heard Ben whisper.

But Joby knew to whom the Cup was coming, and distantly remembered that he had been frightened of it once, ought to be frightened of it still, perhaps. He hadn't been to church in years, but that didn't seem to matter now. Only the longing and the joy were real—possessing every inch of him. As it came to rest before his face, Joby's hands swam forward, as if through water, to grasp the Cup and pull it toward his lips. And then—

✼

He sat sheltered between his parents' backyard fence and the hedge that grew against it, a crimson cape draped across his child's shoulders. Between his small boy's hands, the book lay open, its delicious scent rising like the hot draft from a bakery, the cool, earthy damp of a primal forest, the incense of a great cathedral.

"My King, I would serve you with my life," he whispered with a reverent joy long forgotten. "Only name the quest."

And in that instant, every detail of his childhood mission, every joy and sorrow, victory and mistake he'd known in all the intervening years rushed up from those pages in a torrent of recall, not just known, but understood with impossible clarity. And amidst this nearly unendurable rush of more than memory, Gypsy's face appeared, looking up in surprise and unbridled delight.

"I'd have never even tried, except for you," Gypsy said.

"Gypsy!" Joby said, filled with joy at seeing him. "I thought they killed you!"

"You got somethin' real special, man," Gypsy said. "I mean it." Though his face still seemed as near, Gypsy's voice was growing pale and distant. "You got heart, man. Don't forget it, Joby. . . . Heart."

"Wait!" Joby called. "Don't go yet!" Then grief hit him like a slap of cold water.

✼

Joby gasped and dropped the Cup. It didn't fall, but hovered on the air before him as he struggled to understand all he'd just experienced. To his profound dismay, he was already losing nearly all of what he had momentarily grasped so clearly. He reached out for the Cup again, but though it still seemed close, he couldn't reach it. He stretched his arms out farther, but the Cup began to move toward Ben.

"I can't," Ben choked again. *"Oh God, I . . . I didn't know . . ."*

"Ben, take it," Joby said with sudden urgency, afraid that if Ben failed to share in this experience, it would separate them forever. "Don't be scared. It's wonderful!"

"I never believed!" Ben groaned, still shying from the Cup. *"I never—"*

"It doesn't matter!" Joby urged. "Just take it!"

"He's right," Jake said quietly, standing calmly at Ben's shoulder. "The Cup has made this choice, not you. Have courage. Trust."

Rocking on his knees like a frightened child, Ben reached up at last as if to grasp a red-hot brand, and seized the Cup in both his hands, but before he could bring it to his lips his eyes flew wide, and he seemed to freeze. Joby watched in anxious fascination, wondering if that were how he, himself, had looked when he had touched it. He waited, silently willing his friend to raise the Cup and drink, but Ben remained mesmerized by something only he could see, then cried out as if in grief, and, to Joby's great distress, began to sob without restraint.

Joby wanted to go and shake him, make him drink, but his knees had taken root and his voice had been removed. He could only kneel helplessly, and watch Ben suffer.

Finally, as if it took great strength, Ben turned his head to look at Joby.

"Oh . . . *My Lord,*" he groaned. "What have we done . . . again?"

Still unable to rise or speak, Joby longed to help his friend, his brother, his . . . Some fleeting insight that went through him like a bolt, then vanished. He pursued the feeling, certain that he ought to understand, but not a trace remained. When he looked again, Ben was no longer sobbing, but kneeling over the Cup, eyes closed, seeming as utterly at peace as he had seemed distraught before.

"With all my heart," Ben whispered gravely, eyes still closed. Then, with a radiant smile, he said again, "With all my heart . . . I will."

At last, he raised the Cup, and took a hearty swallow.

And it was gone.

The light, the music, the Cup itself—all vanished in an instant.

Joby found that he could move again, but before he could so much as speak, Ben opened his eyes and turned to stare at Joby with such unfathomable joy and sadness and affection that Joby could only stare back in wonder, unsure if this were even still the friend he'd always known.

27

(Hellfire)

"I just feel like there must have been some reason," Joby pressed as they were finishing the light supper Father Crombie had prepared after returning, or, in Crombie's case, being returned, from the momentous gathering at Burl Creek. "I had it in my hands and didn't drink? It makes no sense. I thought I had."

"You mustn't keep trying to assign meaning to that fact, Joby," Father Crombie assured him. "It came all that way to find you of its own accord! Such a thing is unprecedented in all my years here. You held it in your hands. It spoke to you. Can you not see what *that alone* suggests about your worthiness?"

Ben listened with deeply mixed emotions. Crombie was right, of course, but, for once, Ben understood and shared Job's disappointment. It had quickly become clear that Joby had been shown none of what the Cup had shown to Ben about who the two of them and Laura really were—or had been once, at least. Would Joby have known also, if he'd put the chalice to his lips and drunk as Ben had? There was no way to know, but though Ben now felt sadly isolated from his friend and more than friend of several lifetimes, he was reluctant to tell Joby something of such gravity when the Grail had chosen not to.

"What you must understand, Joby," Father Crombie continued, "is that the Grail is not just a sacred object, bestowed as some kind of reward or badge of honor. It is imbued with life itself, mind, will, and even temperament. If anything, it seems to function as a teacher, or a catalyst, existing to provide extraordinary intervention at extraordinary moments, and seeming to understand what's needed far better than even those who have the need. If nothing else, you can be sure it came to give you some great gift tonight, not just to deprive you of a drink." The old priest smiled.

"I know," Joby said contritely, "and I don't mean to sound ungrateful. There's nothing in my life this hasn't changed, and I've been thinking about what I'm supposed to do now. I mean, there must be something, or why did this happen?"

"Love deeply," Father Crombie replied. "Live fully and well. If you have some destiny beyond that, you'll likely find it soonest by pursuing those two basic goals."

"I'm sure you're right," Joby said, "but I've also been thinking about what we came to ask you about when we were kids." Ben was pleased to notice that the self-scorn that had once accompanied the topic was completely absent now. "I mean, if it's all real; God, the devil, the Grail even, then, do you think that dream I had was more than just . . . Was I really supposed to fight the devil somehow?"

"We are all fighting the devil somehow." Crombie smiled. "Even those who seem mean or sinful are often struggling desperately against Lucifer's influence in their lives. I have no reason to assume that you are an exception."

Joby ducked his head self-consciously. "I guess Swami had a . . . premonition or something that I was going to be . . . well, needed somehow, to help protect Taubolt. What you said, about how Taubolt's borders broke down when I showed up; I was thinking maybe that wasn't something I caused, but something I was sent to . . . to fix, you know?"

"I will trust you with the truth, my friend." Crombie smiled. "I am always very skeptical of assumptions about what God intends, even for myself, much less for others. I would suggest, therefore, that until you see some very clear task before you, and know with great conviction that it is truly and undeniably yours, you should be content with the two endeavors I just mentioned. Loving deeply and living well will prove challenging enough, I think, if those tasks are taken seriously."

Ben could not help smiling at how well the old man knew Joby, and how wisely he employed that knowledge. Joby had always been eager to rush off to battle before nailing down the fort at home. . . . Or had that been Arthur?

"I've a little something in the kitchen for dessert, I think," said Father Crombie, rising slowly from his chair.

"I can get it," Joby said, rising as Ben did the same. "Just tell me where to look."

"No, no. Sit down, both of you," Crombie said with gruff amusement. "If I wanted to be fussed over in my own home, I'd have left the priesthood years ago and gotten married." His grin widened as he turned to totter toward the kitchen. "I've been carried everywhere I went tonight. Make's me feel quite useless."

In fact, it seemed to Ben that Crombie was walking more easily than usual tonight, wondering if the Grail's visit had benefited more than just himself and Joby.

When the priest had gone, Joby looked uncertainly at Ben, and said, "So . . . you seem to have come to better terms with all this."

Ben didn't have to ask what Joby meant."Guess I put on quite a show, huh?"

Joby shrugged. "You did kind of surprise me. I mean, I've never seen you so . . ."

"Panicked?" Ben suggested ruefully.

"Yeah." Joby grinned. "That would be the word, I guess."

Ben nodded pensively. "Tonight was . . . I've always wished the world were a little stranger, Joby—more magical, ever since we were kids. But . . . until tonight, I never really thought it could be. I've made it through some tight spots in my life by sticking to the facts. For a while, once, I worked with this outfit guiding backpack trips for guys with more money than sense sometimes. I was good at putting imagination aside when things got hairy, and sticking to what was *real*. I s'pose that's why I've been so impatient with you sometimes, Joby. I always thought if you'd just learn to deal with the real world, instead of all this . . . subjective stuff, things would be easier for everyone. Then, tonight, those facts I've always been so sure of just burned down and blew away." He looked Joby squarely in the eye, "I owe you some pretty big apologies, Joby. I've got no more idea what's real now than you do. Maybe I never did."

Joby shook his head. "That real world of yours has been just what I needed at the worst times in my life, Ben. You owe me nothing."

"Thanks," Ben said, "for understanding."

"You're still not gonna tell me what you saw, huh?" Joby asked.

"Persistent, aren't you," Ben said, suddenly unable to look Joby in the eyes. He knew he couldn't dodge the question forever, but still had no idea what to say. "I learned some things about who I really am," he tried. "And . . . that's all I'm ready to say yet. Okay?"

Joby searched his face as if trying to guess the rest. "Is there some reason why you think I shouldn't know?" Joby pressed. "Something you think might hurt me?"

Ben suppressed an urge to roll his eyes. Two days ago, he'd have been scornful of such a typical "Joby" take on things, but Ben couldn't kid himself about how he'd have felt if Joby had been the one to drink from that cup, and he had not. "I did learn something about you, actually," Ben said.

"I thought so," Joby said grimly, clearly braced to hear the worst.

"I learned that you're the best of us," Ben said. "Though I don't expect you to believe me. That what you been so afraid to hear all night?" He grinned.

When Joby looked doubtful, Ben just laughed and shook his head. "You are such a piece of work, bro. I don't know who did it to you, but they sure did it good." The laughter left him suddenly as he heard his own remark. There was one part of what he'd learned that night that did need discussing with Joby, and the sooner the better. They still had time, thank God, to avert what had happened to all three of them before, and Ben had no intention of letting that chance get away from him.

Leaning forward earnestly, Ben said, "Joby, I've been doing a lot of thinking about this thing with Laura. We need to talk again as soon as possible. I've decided—"

Before he could go further, Father Crombie reappeared carrying a plate mounded with shortbread cookies. "Gladys gave me these," the old man smiled. "They are food for younger stomachs than my own, however."

"You'll have *one,* at least, I hope." Ben grinned. "We can't just eat them all while you sit there watching."

"I will likely eat them all if someone doesn't stop me." Crombie grinned back. "That's why I am bringing them to you."

Ben saw Joby looking at him with understandable curiosity, and felt bad to leave him dangling, but the subject had been broached now. They'd get back to it soon enough.

"Actually," Father Crombie said, setting the cookies down between them as he lowered himself back into his chair and resumed the conversation they'd been having, "it was a bit unsettling to see the Cup arrive that way this evening; an uncomfortable reminder of what an independent treasure we've all grown so dependent on here. It's been behaving very strangely now for several months, and made quite a spectacle of itself yesterday in front of that storefront preacher, Mr. Cotter. We've had to put someone on guard around the clock in the chapel now. Alfred Cognolio is in there as we speak, making sure no one enters who should not. I spoke to him after returning tonight, of course—just before you boys arrived—and he claims to have seen or heard nothing at all during the Cup's excursion. Had no idea it had left. So much for security.

"It has been decided that the Cup must now be moved to some location much farther from town." Crombie said somberly. "We are considering our choices, but whichever is chosen, it will mean the end of my role as primary guardian. I am too frail to go far from the church anymore."

"I'm so sorry," Joby said.

"I agree with the Council's decision, of course," Crombie nodded, "and feel more privileged than I can say to have spent so many years in its presence. Still, I will miss—"

His voice was suddenly drowned out by Taubolt's emergency siren.

With all the tourist traffic in Taubolt these days, the siren's deafening wail was far less uncommon than it once had been, and at first they just fell silent. But when the siren continued instead of going off as usual after just a cycle or two, Crombie turned toward the rectory doors and murmured, "My goodness. What can be happening?"

"Let's go out and see," Joby said, rising from his chair.

"Got a pretty good view of town up here," Ben agreed.

After helping Father Crombie to the door, they went out into the darkened yard and were shocked to see black smoke illuminated by the ruddy glow of flames billowing up just beyond the rector's garden fence.

"My God! It's the church!" Joby gasped.

"Alfred!" Crombie barked. "He must be hurt, or he'd have come to warn us!"

"I'll go check!" Ben called, running for the gate.

"Wait!" Crombie shouted. "If the Cup is still inside, I must get it!"

"If it's there, *I'll* get it!" Ben said, eager to be off. "Where is it kept?"

"No! You cannot breach the wards!" Crombie protested. "I must do it! Quickly, I need your help, boys!" He held his arms out for support as he hurried toward them with surprising speed, but still far too slowly.

Ben's first thought was that Crombie was nuts, but he also realized that there was no place remotely closer than the rectory for this Alfred guy to have gone for help, or just to sound the alarm, and the fire had clearly been burning for a while, so he might still be inside, in who knew what condition, and the Cup there with him, just as Crombie feared.

Joby was already helping Crombie toward the gate, but if they had to do this, it had to be done faster. Ben ran back and simply hoisted the small man up over one shoulder. "Joby, get the hose!" he called returning to the gate. "Try to train it on the fire."

Joby ran back to twist the faucet on and yank the coiled garden hose toward them.

"Wait," Ben said as Joby reached them. "Soak us down with that."

Seeing the fire now, Joby looked appalled. "You can't go in there!" he said.

"We must!" Crombie protested. "The Cup! We cannot lose the Cup!"

"Hurry up, Joby," Ben said. "Get us wet. We'll be in and out in minutes."

Already lost in planning as Joby complied, Ben hardly felt the water's chill. "Where are you keeping it?" Ben asked Crombie, who endured both his undignified perch and the soaking without complaint.

"In the sacristy, since the incident with Cotter. Just beside the altar."

Good, Ben thought, *not far inside the back door.* This might be easier than he'd feared. "Okay, that should do," he said to Joby. "Bring the hose, and be ready to hit us again when we come out." He was already loping toward the back steps of the church, Crombie still across his shoulder. "If we're not out in a minute or two," he called back as they neared the door, "break the sacristy window, and stick the hose in there."

Happily, Crombie was so shrunken with age that he weighed almost nothing. Ben was up the steps with ease, and yanking at the door, which wouldn't open.

"It's locked," Crombie said. "The key is back at the rectory. You'll have to—"

Before he could finish, Ben set him down, waited while Crombie steadied himself, then drew back and launched a powerful kick at the door, which broke up like so much kindling, shuddering inward on its hinges. The building sucked a loud breath of air in around them through the doorway, then exhaled a blast of furnace heat that made Ben spin away to shield himself and Father Crombie.

"I'm not sure we can do this," he said to Crombie.

"You stay here," Crombie said, already shuffling toward the door. "I'm the one who must go in. I know the wards."

"No way, Father," Ben grunted, hoisting him again. "You ready?"

Crombie merely nodded his assent.

"Take the biggest breath you can," Ben said, and did the same before charging through the door.

The heat was terrible, but not unsurvivable yet, Ben judged, as he turned, intending to dash across the altar into the sacristy. But there was a man lying facedown in front of the altar, unconscious, if not dead.

"Alfred!" Crombie croaked, and began to cough.

Ben set him on the floor, and shouted, "Don't get up. The air'll be better there." Then he ran to crouch by Alfred, rolling him over to find a knife protruding from his stomach. His wilderness first-aid training rushing back, Ben checked for pulses, and lowered his ear to Alfred's open mouth, but it was clearly too late for this one.

There was no time to wonder where who had killed him, or why. Ben ran back to Crombie, coughing now as well, and fearful that their clothes might ignite at any moment. The blaze had clearly started back toward the main doors, but it was racing forward now, probably on the draft they'd created by opening the back door. The altar hangings had begun to smolder

"Hurry!" Crombie moaned over the fire's roar.

There was just time, Ben hoped, to get into the sacristy. Once there, he could smash the window and get them out through that.

"Take another breath!" Ben shouted. Crombie did so, but began to cough, and had to try again. Then, with Crombie bundled like a child in his arms, Ben sprinted for the sacristy door, kicked it in without setting Crombie down, and raced inside. Thankfully, the sacristy was still much cooler than the church had been.

He laid Crombie quickly on the floor, and turned to slam shut what remained of the now knobless door behind them, dragging a chair against it to help block out the heat for at least a few more minutes. Crombie was already crawling to his feet, chanting the words that would breach the wards, as Ben grabbed a tall metal candle stand and rushed to smash out the sacristy window, intent on letting in some air and preparing their exit.

Seconds later, as he scraped the frame clean of glass shards with the candle stand, a stream of water came through the broken widow, spattering his steaming shirt. *Good old Joby,* Ben thought with fierce affection. "We're okay, Joby!" he shouted. "Keep the water coming!" He turned to Crombie and called, "Come here a second!" wanting to wet him down again as well, but the priest just shook his head, continuing to chant.

"There!" Crombie called, stepping forward to open the ornate metal box at which his chant had been directed. But when the doors parted, he only stood and gaped.

Ben rushed to his side, and saw the box was empty.

"We're too late!" Crombie gasped. "It's gone!"

Ben had never heard him sound so desolate.

❋

"Jake! Gabriel, we need you!" Swami shouted, running down the street in tears. It had come—the bad thing he had always feared—without any warning! *"Merlin! Help!"*

The two archangels, dark and light, appeared simultaneously ahead of him, already deep in urgent conversation.

"Try to find the Cup," Swami heard Jake say as he ran toward them. "Until we know where it's gone, I've nowhere to send these people."

"Jake!" Swami began as he reached them, but Jake held up a hand to silence him, and Gabriel swept Swami into a comforting embrace as he and Jake continued talking.

"The Cup may not reveal itself to me," Gabriel said, "especially if I am—"

"No more of that!" Jake cut him off. "I understand your concerns, but we must try, or all is truly lost. Take Swami. It isn't safe to have him here now. Not with what he knows. His gift should be of help to you. The Cup will reveal itself to him if anyone, but he will need a guard."

"No one will guard him more fiercely than I," said Gabriel, "but we both know it will be no quick or easy task. Can you preserve this place until my return?"

"With Merlin's help, perhaps," Jake said. "What choice have we but to try?" A faint smile brushed his lips. "Lucifer's dogs will find a small surprise awaiting them. The enchanter is already preparing it. Our Master bade me let them enter, He did not say *how* I must allow it. Go now. There is no more time. They come."

※

When Ben's face left the window, Joby tugged the hose closer, trying to get more water to them, but instead, the flow abruptly dribbled to nothing. Joby looked back to find the hose kinked in the rectory gate. He tried whipping it straight from where he stood, but couldn't, and rushed back to straighten it by hand. He had just bent down to do so when the church behind him groaned ominously. As Joby turned to look, a roar like jet engines swept through the chapel, and all the windows blew out at once in gouts of flame. Joby whirled away as burning debris rained down upon the churchyard. When he turned back, flames belched from the sacristy window as well.

"Ben!" he screamed, running toward the church with the hose, but the heat made him to pull up short. *"BEN!"* he screamed again. Still clutching the now working hose, he forced himself a few feet nearer, just as Ben came hurtling from the engulfed window with Father Crombie in his arms, both men wreathed in flames

As Ben hit the ground, he rolled himself and his passenger around in frantic, writhing arcs, trying to quench their cloaks of fire. Joby ran farther forward, suddenly heedless of the heat, training his hose as best he could on the moving target until Ben suddenly lay still far enough from the building for Joby to close the distance.

Joby rushed to stand over them with the gushing hose, uttering a wordless shout of terror as he saw how badly burned they were. Father Crombie lay facedown, his clothes half-gone, his once pale skin angry red and charred to black in places. Ben lay beside him faceup, eyes open, breathing raggedly. His once bronze hair was sooty black and altogether absent from one side of his head. That half of his face was a swollen ruin of blistered meat. Of his shirt, only one sleeve and the shoulders remained. The torso this revealed was a charred and oozing wreck. His jeans were scorched but still intact. His tennis shoes looked melted to his feet.

"Oh God, *help!*" Joby shouted, still dousing them with his pathetic stream of water. *"Ben!"* he sobbed. *"God help me! What do I do?"*

"Get help," Ben rasped, beginning to writhe again. "Hurry," he groaned.

Joby dropped the hose and ran toward town, wondering why no one had gotten there yet. Couldn't they see the church was burning? Only then did he see the smoke and flames that billowed up from several more locations around the tiny village.

⚹

"This is what I've been warning them about!" Agnes shouted into the phone, crouched in her bedroom closet as all hell broke loose outside. "But would anybody listen? Now look! There are buildings burning all over Taubolt! It would be almost satisfying if half of them weren't mine! Yes! You heard the sirens! Can't you see the smoke? Well, look outside for heaven's sake! Those kids are going to burn this place to the ground, Karl!" She looked annoyed as Karl buzzed nonsense at her from his end of the line. "Of course it's kids, Karl! What adult could move around so fast? They're probably riding on those damn skateboards!"

⚹

As Basquel soared toward Taubolt's outskirts, the sight of steam and smoke rising in pale columns over several ruined buildings lifted his spirits even higher, and he picked up speed, eager to wreak still more havoc on the Creator's offensive little preserve.

News of the Cup's unexpected departure had sent an almost immobilizing wave of shock through Hell, then a helter-skelter scramble to mobilize. Sitting through Lucifer's dreary session of instructions about who to look for first, and how to strike at whom, and whom not to strike at, et cetera, et cetera, had been the most infuriating bore. Talk about hurry up and wait! Who'd ever thought that they were going to get in at all? The least he could have done was let them at it.

Kallaystra and her little team, of course, had been allowed to leave right away. Privileges of the elite and all. Yes, her little flood of operatives had apparently done their job, but the way she'd crowed and preened about it had been positively revolting.

As Basquel glided toward the nearest buildings, he was overtaken by a sudden wave of vertigo and a terrible sense of weight, as if he were falling, which he realized with a shock, he was! Instinctively, he braced against the impact as he plowed into the ground, utterly dumbfounded to find himself suddenly . . . *corporeal!*

"What on earth?" he blurted out, doubly stunned to hear his own quite audible voice! He had made no decision to materialize! How could this have happened? Worse still, he found that he could not dissolve back into his ethereal form. The weight of his obese bulk alone seemed crushing—the physicality left him near to retching. He stumbled to his—*all Hell's gates!*—his *feet,* and staggered desperately away from the village, knowing that he mustn't be caught like this by anyone. Incarnate, he was utterly vulnerable to . . . well, to all sorts of unthinkable outcomes!

"Basquel!"

The sound of Kallaystra's voice made Basquel flinch. He feared to be caught incarnate even by her—perhaps especially by her. They'd never been that fond of each other. What if she took advantage of his helpless condition?

"Basquel, you fool," Kallaystra said when he ignored her summons, "come this way. We are ordered to retreat!"

"Where are you?" Basquel called, humiliated by his inability to see her disembodied form with his own disgracefully material eyes. "What has happened to me?"

"You've been forced to materialize," Kallaystra replied, cruel amusement all too evident in her voice.

"How?" he wailed, still struggling away from Taubolt. "By whom?"

"By Michael," Kallaystra growled, "and his host of Morningstar's Children."

"They *are* here then?" Basquel blurted out, anger leaping up through the fear and confusion in his breast.

"They are here," Kallaystra's voice intoned from somewhere very near now. "And, as you see, some of them are still powerful. A few steps more, and you will be clear of their spells, however. Follow my voice."

Even as her last words were spoken, he felt the dead weight of his unwanted flesh begin to lessen, and then, to his immense relief, he was free, dissolving ecstatically back into mere thought, will, and vapor once again.

He could see her clearly now, not ten feet in front of him, still looking smugly satisfied at his recent discomfort. This so annoyed him that he might have blasted her with more than mere enmity if not for the presence of so many others all around them.

"Commanded to retreat by whom?" he demanded instead. "I've no desire to go anywhere until these half-breed vermin have been exterminated. I thought we'd gotten the last of them centuries ago."

"So we had assumed." Kallaystra frowned. "But they've been here all along, it seems, hiding in the Cup's shadow, as always. Their ability to force us into flesh changes everything. Lucifer commands our return to Hell to regroup and amend our plans."

"Very well," Basquel sighed, as if merely humoring her with compliance, though she was right. This latest development would require some whole new approach.

❊

As Molly examined the happily marginal fire damage to her store, her disciples began gathering to support her and report on the evening's other disasters. Two shops on Main Street had also been firebombed, though, like Molly's place, they'd been saved from more serious damage by the swift work of Taubolt's volunteer firemen. With poorly disguised satisfaction, Alicia had arrived to inform them that Sam Cotter's so-called mission had been set ablaze as well, shortly after the two shop fires had started, and had burned halfway to the ground. Of Cotter himself there was no sign, and rumors were already circulating that blamed him for having set all five blazes himself.

"What kind of idiot would burn his own place down?" Margery wondered aloud.

"They think he may have done it to throw suspicion off himself," Alicia answered smugly. "They say he bought a lot of paint thinner at the hardware store earlier tonight."

"Then he'll be charged with murder," Sharine said. "What an awful thing about St. Luke's. You should see the mess up there. It's a total loss." She shook her head. "They're saying that man who runs the junk shop was stabbed inside before the fire. And that poor old priest! Everybody says he was the kindest man in town."

"Do they think the other one will live?" Lolly asked sadly.

"No one's saying," Sharine answered, "but I saw them put him in the helicopter." She blanched visibly at the memory. "He looked dreadful."

Just then Carolena arrived in a breathless rush. "Molly! There are people falling from the sky!" she exclaimed in hushed excitement, as if afraid of being overheard. "Naked people! I saw one! With my own eyes! Not more than fifteen feet in front of me!"

"You saw what?" Molly asked. "Calm down, dear, and make some sense."

"The fairies!" Carolena gasped, still at half a whisper. *"I've seen one too!* It happened just after the fires started. He looked *very* disoriented. His back was turned. I don't think he saw me!"

For a moment, everyone stared at her as if she'd belched up a toad.

"I'm serious!" she protested. "Why would I make up such a ridiculous story?"

The ladies looked from Carolena to each other, as if waiting for someone to decide how they should react.

"I knew it!" Alicia said at last. "First those children, now this! I knew it was real!"

"The new age of enlightenment has dawned," Molly said, looking back gravely at her damaged store. "For every gift there is a price. The goddess has exacted her price this evening, and these are but the birth pains as Taubolt brings its gift into the world."

✴

Joby rode beside Ben's stretcher, hardly able to endure the sight of his friend's ruined face, yet unable to look away. Crombie had been declared dead at the scene by the nurse accompanying the paramedic on the helicopter from Santa Rosa; his body would be transported by ambulance, along with Alfred's, to the morgue in Heeberville.

One of Taubolt's two fire trucks had come racing uphill toward the burning church before Joby had run half a block for help. Moments later Jake had appeared, looking desolate, and bent over Crombie's body with tears in his eyes. Then he'd gone to Ben, touched him briefly, and whispered something Joby hadn't been able to make out above the clamor of the fire and those fighting it. Ben's moaning had fallen off then, but Jake had turned to look at Joby as if he were among the burned as well, and said, "There's no more I can do for him. The helicopter's on its way. Stay with him, Joby." Joby had nodded, wondering where else Jake imagined he might go.

When the building was clearly beyond saving, two of the volunteer firemen had come to sit with Joby, sadly explaining that they'd been fighting other fires before anyone had noticed smoke at the top of the hill as well.

"We'll find the bastard who did this," one of the men had said at last.

"Okay," Joby had murmured without looking up from Ben's unconscious form.

Now Ben lay before him under heavy doses of morphine for the pain and sedatives to keep him from twisting off the stretcher. With such burns, they hadn't wanted to strap him down. The paramedic and the nurse hung back politely, quietly monitoring Ben's condition, occasionally checking his IV drip, but not otherwise intruding on Joby's helpless vigil.

Besides the burns, they'd told him, there were head injuries from the explosion and severe respiratory damage. It was amazing, they'd said, that Ben had managed to remain conscious at all, much less get himself and Crombie out the window as he had. "He must be in pretty awesome shape," the paramedic had said encouragingly to Joby shortly after their take off. "He was," Joby had replied, then quickly amended, "is," recalling Ben's radiant face earlier that night, after drinking from the Cup. Joby was glad now that Ben had been the one to drink. Perhaps it would help him live.

"Arthur," Ben moaned without opening his eyes. *"Arthur!"* His voice was a saw blade drawn through chalk.

Joby didn't know what to make of the call at first. Then remembering that Arthur was Hawk's real name, he leaned closer to be heard above the muffled throb of rotors, and asked, "You mean Hawk, Ben? Hawk will see you at the hospital."

"Arthur!" Ben rasped again. Then his eyes opened, and a kind of clarity seemed to resolve behind the ruin of his face. "Joby?" he croaked.

"Hey, Ben," Joby said, managing to smile, longing to take Ben's hand but not daring to touch the burns. "Were you asking for Hawk?"

"You look . . . like shit," Ben wheezed, an attempted smile cracking the seeping wreckage of his mouth.

Joby shoved a fresh upwelling of grief and revulsion aside and said, "Been a rough night, but we're almost there, Ben. You're doing great."

"Crombie?" Ben asked.

"He's okay now," Joby dissembled.

Ben nodded slightly, exhaling like a chorus of whispered violins. For a moment after that he just stared into space, then croaked, "You made my life . . . all the magic in my life, Joby." Ben closed his eyes again "I love you both. . . . I always have."

Frightened by what he heard, Joby leaned closer still, and said, "Laura's going to meet us there, Ben. They called her. She's driving to the hospital."

"She's yours," Ben wheezed. "She always was." He opened his eyes again and stared hard at Joby. "Why won't you ever let her love you?"

Joby struggled just to hold himself together, until Ben looked away, trying to smile again. "I held it, Arthur," Ben exhaled with a look of joy that seemed utterly impossible on that face. "It let me drink. After all this time . . . all I've done. I never thought—" Suddenly, he gasped in pain, the sound like milkshake slurping through a straw. Ben's eyes flew wide as he struggled to draw in another breath that sounded worse. He began to writhe again, and gasped, *"I can't . . ."*

The nurse and paramedic rushed forward, pushing Joby back.

"Intubation," the nurse ordered with quiet urgency.

At that moment, Ben's heart monitor began to shriek, a loud, steady tone, and Joby heard the paramedic mutter, "Shit."

"Ben?" Joby said, his chest constricting in fear and grief.

The nurse was rushing to ready a syringe while the paramedic jammed a tube down Ben's throat. Ben began to thrash, and the nurse lunged forward to restrain him.

"Ben! Don't!" Joby yelled.

"Please stay back," the nurse insisted over her shoulder. Finished with the tube, the paramedic took over Ben's restraint as the nurse thrust her syringe into Ben's IV tube, and injected its contents. While the monitor's alarm continued unabated, the paramedic let go of Ben to prepare a set of the defibrillator disks Joby had seen on countless TV shows. Only then did Joby understand that Ben's heart had stopped.

"Ben!" Joby sobbed. *"Oh God! Don't! Don't!"*

No one heeded him as the disks were pressed to Ben's chest. "Clear," said the paramedic. There was a thump, but Ben continued to lie motionless, and the monitor's monotonous alarm resumed.

"Try again," said the nurse.

"Oh no," Joby wept. *"Oh, Ben, please, God, please don't let me lose him now."*

28

(Tug-of-War)

Laura's sobs grew softer and finally ceased again. They'd cried themselves into a state of muffled exhaustion that now left them side by side in silence for long stretches.

By the time the helicopter had landed on the hospital roof, Joby's grief had already started hardening around his heart. Watching them unload the mangled, lifeless shell of his best and oldest friend, it had seemed possible that he would never feel anything again, until Laura had arrived. Then all illusions of emptiness had been swept aside as they'd collapsed onto a bench in the hallway, crying themselves hoarse in each other's arms before going in search of some more private place.

Now they sat alone in the hospital chapel, numbly suspended between all they'd lost and whatever would come after it. For Joby, that space was full of drifting fragments. What needed to be done when someone died? Who had to be notified? . . . Where was Ben now? . . . Had he been a coward to let Ben and Crombie go in alone? . . . Ben had sent him for the hose—given him his task outside the church. . . . No one had thought they'd die. . . . Where was Ben now? . . . *Why won't you ever let her love you?*

"Laura, we need . . . I need to . . ." He turned to face her, reaching down to take her hands in his.

Her face was blotched and puffy, her eyes bee-stung, her lips and chin still moist with tears and snot. And she was more beautiful to him than she had ever been before, because her grief was so much like his own, because he didn't have to tell her anything about the friend he'd lost, because at the darkest moment of a life that had known so much darkness, he was not alone, as he had been so many times before. She was right there beside him, there to touch and hold, and, for the first time he could remember, he wasn't wondering whether he should let her or whether he could be there for her too.

"I love you, Laura," he said as everything he'd ever felt or tried to feel welled up, desperate to get out before the moment passed. "I love you so much it hurts. And heals me all at once. I'm so sorry that I haven't been there like I should. I know I haven't. But I'm going to now." He began to cry again, but he didn't care. "I'm going to be there for you every second we're together. And every second we're apart, I'll be waiting to be back with you again. I've always loved you. I wanted to marry you way back in high school. I told Ben that the morning . . . I told him I was going to ask you. And then I let you go, and everything's been broken ever since. Everything." He was crying so hard now that he could barely talk, and she was crying too, but the words kept rushing out of him and he wasn't sure they'd stop now if he wished them to. "And when I found you again in Taubolt, I didn't know how to put so many broken things back together. I didn't want to give you broken things. I was afraid you'd see what I'd become while you were gone, and I felt . . . I felt like I should be so many other things for you I'd never been at all—things that had just never even been there anywhere inside me. I never should have let you go. I swear, I've never—"

Laura freed her hands, and pressed her fingers to his lips to stem the flow at last. "There are broken things inside me too," she wept. "Everybody has them, Joby. Ben had them. Arthur has them too, and most of his are my fault. It breaks my heart to know that, but broken hearts are all any of us has to give. All I've ever wanted was you, Joby. All of you. The bright parts and the broken ones, whatever's inside you. I don't care, as long as it's just really you! Ben told me months ago that I should say this to you." Her face began to twist around an effort not to cry. "But I was too afraid. I was afraid you'd leave again." She looked down, too wracked with sobs to speak, and Joby pulled her into his arms. "You're not the only one who hides," Laura sobbed. "But don't hide from me anymore. I see all kinds of good things in you, Joby. Beautiful things. They've always been there, but even if all you can see is darkness, then I'd rather have you love me with your darkness than keep hiding from me. I love you too. I always—"

Joby bent to kiss her mouth, wrapping her more tightly in his arms. She kissed him back, pressing hard against him. He pressed back, wanting her to feel the wound of love inside, the luminescent pain that surged through him healing every other pain he'd ever known. Minutes passed before they finally pulled apart.

"Oh, Joby," Laura wept, throwing herself back into his arms. "That's the first time that you've ever *kissed* me!"

"I'll never hurt you again, Laura," Joby said. "I know I have, but I never will again. I promise that with all my heart."

"I'll hold you to that promise," she murmured into his sodden collar. "'Until the day I die."

❧

The Triangle were not the only ones getting fidgety in Hell's conference room as everyone awaited Lucifer's new instructions. Even Kallaystra was wondering why he should keep them all here twiddling their thumbs at such a moment. Lucifer, however, just kept perusing Joby's dossier which was stuffed with facsimiles of every piece of correspondence between Joby and his parents, or anyone else, for the past three years; transcripts of every phone call, lists of gleaned names, opinions, and anecdotes about himself or others inside the once inaccessible refuge.

"You seem upset, Tique," Lucifer observed without looking from the document he was scanning. "Something on your mind?"

Tique's fingers ceased to drum upon the conference table, but he made no reply.

"I should think you'd feel quite good about the fact that your life may be worth a plug nickel after all, now that the ball is back in play," said Lucifer, looking up at him at last. "Why the long face then?"

"Bright One," Tique said nervously. "The boy is *outside* of Taubolt. Right now."

Good move, thought Kallaystra. *Start dictating to Lucifer. What a numbskull!*

"An astute observation," Lucifer drawled. "Your point?"

"Shouldn't we . . . be doing something?" Tique shrugged uncomfortably.

"Like what?" Lucifer asked, as if genuinely curious.

"Well . . . that would be for you to say, of course," Tique mumbled, looking everywhere except at Lucifer, "but, I just thought that, maybe—"

"Speak up," said Lucifer. "I want everyone to hear this bright idea that you're spiraling so concisely toward."

"Sir," Tique said desperately. "In Taubolt, we'll have to work confined to flesh! We'll be next to powerless! If we struck now, we could do anything we liked!"

"Another stunning insight," said Lucifer. "And again, doing what, precisely?"

"You know," Tique grimaced. "Just . . . get him somehow."

"You mean kill him?" Lucifer asked lightly. "And just scrap the wager altogether? I'd just kill you then, to begin with. What good would that do anyone? Or did you mean cripple him perhaps, just to limit his capacity to do anything that matters later on, good or evil? No? What *did* you have in mind? I'm all ears."

"Not *him,*" Tique said. "I know we're not supposed to do that. But what about the woman? I mean he loves her, and she's right out in the open. There must be some—"

"So," Lucifer cut him off, "after three decades of *wasted* time, we're back to willy-nilly potshots, is that it, Tique?"

Just shut up, Tique! Kallaystra thought, braced for his imminent demise. Her team was small enough already. She couldn't spare even such an idiot with all there'd be to do once Lucifer declared an end to *nap time.* Was even Lucifer unable to think of some way to deal with Taubolt's unexpected defense? Was that what all this delaying was about?

"If I may kibitz, Tique," said Lucifer with unsettling politeness, "as gratifying as it may be to cause Joby grief, our experience to date suggests that grief alone is not enough. What we need is anger. Without anger, he won't learn to hate. And hate is what we're after in the end. Lots of it. And rather quickly . . . thanks to you and your friends."

"If we killed her, that would make him angry," Tique muttered, seeming more oblivious than ever of the precipice before him.

"But angry at whom?" Lucifer asked, as if this were some mere classroom debate.

"Her killer, I suppose. The universe? Does it matter? He'll be angry, won't he?"

"Apparently you weren't listening," Lucifer said crossly. "I said the point of Joby's anger must be hate. Who's he going to *blame,* Tique, if we kill Laura now, so far away from Taubolt? Some drunk driver whom he'll never see again? The *universe?* How's he going to *act* on hate like that? Whose he going to *punish* for it?" Lucifer no longer played at being calm. "I don't need some act of *abstract* evil, Tique, directed at the *universe!* We don't have *time* for that anymore! I need specific, concrete evil directed tangibly and intentionally at some very *real* target! I want *him* to hit the things that *he loves most,* and those are all in Taubolt, Tique, in case you haven't been paying attention! To make that happen, the people he *blames* can't be out here! They've got to be there in Taubolt, all around him every day, stirring the anger and building the hatred, month after month, until his loving little heart is swamped and capsizes in it! *Is that clear?* Drum your fingers on that table one more time, and you'll be lucky if they're all that I remove."

Tique nodded, once, in silence finally.

Lucifer went back to studying the contents of Joby's dossier again. A moment later, his calm seeming restored, he said, without looking up, "However inconvenient they've made it for us, we are going to have to work inside Taubolt, within the limitations of corporeal incarnation. That means making every smallest resource left us, every move and moment, *count.* Thus, unlike many in this room, I'm not going into the field until I've *prepared,* and I know precisely what I'm doing there."

A wave of palpable astonishment swept the room. Kallaystra barely managed not to gape. Had he just said *"I"*? Had he meant it figuratively, or ...? It had been centuries since he'd condescended to fight beside any of them in the field at least for more than minutes at a time.

As if unaware of the sensation he'd just caused, Lucifer looked up and said, "Joby and his lady will undoubtedly be leaving Taubolt again soon for Ben's funeral. Kallaystra, I will spare *you alone* to follow them and work your special magic. The trip should provide an excellent opportunity to remind Joby of just who and what he was before Taubolt caused him such forgetfulness. Please do not dilute Joby's focus with any greater gestures though. From now on, I don't want him to associate a single disappointment in his life with any place but Taubolt.

"While Kallaystra is gone," he continued, "the rest of us will be here preparing for Joby's return to Taubolt with meticulous attention to detail, for once. I am currently compiling a thorough list of who to target there, and how."

Lucifer leaned forward, bracing both arms on the table, and swept the assembly with his disapproving gaze. "I want to make this very clear. I am not *angry* that, given thirty years in which to work, we are virtually starting up again from scratch four years before our deadline.

"I AM ENRAGED!" he screamed, the very walls waffling with the sound. Kallaystra sat in shocked and fearful silence as did all the others. "I once generously assumed that there were some in Hell to whom I could still delegate with confidence, but you are *all* worthless incompetents! So, yes, I'm going *with* you this time to make sure that everyone does precisely *what* I need them to, precisely *as* I need it done! Anyone who falters will be terminated instantly and replaced with someone who can do the job." He leaned even farther forward. "If that means killing every one of you and finishing this campaign alone, don't imagine I will hesitate. The outcome of this wager is far too important to me to pussyfoot around with anymore."

He turned to look directly at Kallaystra. "You may go now, dear. Good hunting."

❧

A single officer! Agnes was incensed. Half the town burnt down, three murders, a maiming, an attempted rape, and countless acts of malicious vandalism in just two months, and Mansfield had sent just *one man*? This was not an answer, it was a slap!

The minute Karl had called to tell her Donaldson had been shown into the building Agnes had so generously donated, not rented mind you, *donated,* for use as Taubolt's new police station, she had donned a suitably no-nonsense outfit, and come down to see what kind of superhero they'd been sent. Because that's what this officer had better be if he were going to deal with Taubolt's escalating crime wave all alone.

She stood in the open doorway, knocking on the jamb and gazing at the jumble of boxes and half-assembled furniture already cluttering the otherwise deserted space.

"Be there in a minute!" called a harried voice from the first floor's other room.

As it seemed he could not be bothered to come greet her, Agnes entered uninvited. She owned the building after all.

A moment later, a lanky, crew-cut young man came through the office's rear door, still buttoning the short-sleeved shirt of his kaki uniform. "Can I help you?" he said, glancing from his busy fingers to smile at her.

For a moment Agnes simply stared. He looked like an ROTC recruit fresh out of college! Or even high school! Not only had the county sheriff sent them just one man, that man wasn't even seasoned!

"My name is Agnes Hamilton," she said.

"Troy Donaldson, ma'am. Very pleased to meet you. Sheriff Mansfield and Mr. Foster both told me to expect you. I appreciate your loaning us this building."

"Us?" she said hopefully. "Have they sent more than one of you after all?"

"Oh. No ma'am." He smiled. "I just meant the county."

"Ah," she said, disappointed. "Well, then, Officer Donaldson, if Mansfield mentioned me, then he'll no doubt have explained that I'm the reason you are here."

"Ma'am?" the young man said uncertainly.

"I've been requesting police protection here for years," she said. "I wrote the letter that resulted in your appointment."

"Well," Donaldson said hesitantly, "I appreciate your vote of confidence, ma'am, but I'd been given the impression there's a fairly broad base of interest in local law enforcement here."

"Well, of course," said Hamilton. "I would hardly have made any such request without knowing the community supported me. Where were you stationed before coming here?" she asked, braced to learn that this was the befuddled youth's first posting.

"Up in Colby, ma'am," he said.

"In command of what?" she pressed.

"Oh no, ma'am." He smiled. "I was just a patrolman."

As she'd feared. An untried rookie. "Well, I hope you brought your ticket book, young man," she said, "because you'll find no shortage of people in need of your citations here." The look on Donaldson's face was further confirmation that he was easily confused. "While I'm sure you've heard about our recent string of ghastly crimes, the most pressing problem day to day here is our unfettered herd of juvenile delinquents."

"I saw that kind of thing in Colby too," Donaldson admitted. "Rural kids with too much time and not enough to do. They can run kind of wild sometimes."

"They congregate in front of public places every day here," Hamilton said, relieved to see that Donaldson understood at least that much, "taking great delight in intimidating customers and performing countless acts of vandalism with no fear of punishment. As the owner of numerous retail facilities here, and a leading member of Taubolt's Chamber of Commerce, I've come to request that you make bridling these noxious youngsters one of your first priorities. Particularly those with skateboards. As you will quickly see, they career through crowds with no regard for public safety and do all manner of irreparable damage, both to Taubolt's businesses and its buildings. I assume there are laws of some kind that can be applied to stop to this?"

"Some," Donaldson nodded. "Regarding public nuisance and reckless endangerment. Loitering and vandalism, of course. Mostly misdemeanors, but that should be sufficient to curb the problem."

"Excellent!" Hamilton said, smiling for the first time. "Well, I just wanted to say hi, and welcome you to Taubolt, Officer Donaldson." She peered over his shoulder at the disorder behind him. "Is your ticket book in one of these boxes?"

"I expect it's somewhere here," said Donaldson, smiling cautiously.

"Then I'll leave you to unpack," Agnes said breezily, turning for the door.

❧

"Well?" said Lucifer. "Have you found them all?"

"Nearly everyone on the list," Basquel said, relieved to be far enough outside of town again to disincarnate for a while. Lucifer had come with them all right, but he'd set up his own heavily warded base camp in an isolated clearing far enough from Taubolt to avoid being trapped in flesh, as everybody else was. Privileges of power, Basquel sighed silently. "Joby and Laura aren't here of course. They're at the funeral."

"Obviously!" Lucifer snapped.

"But I've seen Laura's child," Basquel blurted quickly. "Hamilton and Foster have practically married, which should be useful. Ferristaff is tangling with our environmentalist, as hoped, and in considerable conflict with the local populace over logging rights to some tract of land or other. Cotter's gone, of course. *But we knew that,*" he said hurriedly as Lucifer's frown returned. "There's a lawman just arrived in town that does *not* seem to be on our list. I thought you'd want to know. From what I've seen so far, at least half the town's residents are new, and when you add the tourists, the original population would seem outnumbered by at least three to one. All in all, the situation seems rife with potential."

"Kallaystra's done a decent job, it seems," Lucifer mused. "Better late than never, I suppose."

Resentful of Kallaystra's smug superiority, even in absentia, Basquel added, "There are a couple hitches though."

"Such as?" Lucifer said, instantly more alert.

"Well, I did encounter several wards during my travels around town. Obviously the work of our vile brethren's bastard race. Unfortunately, being corporeal, I was unable to penetrate them."

"So there are places we still can't see," said Lucifer. "I want such places watched, of course, 'round the clock, as soon as you find them, daily reports on who goes in or out. This damned incarnation spell is not angelic work. There's someone very, very strong in there. If we can find out who, and take them out, perhaps we can be free of all this constraining flesh."

As if you *weren't already,* thought Basquel sourly. "Which reminds me," he said aloud. "I've found Molly Redstone too, and you'll be glad to hear that she's convened a very useful group of local gossips who meet weekly to compare their notes on *'fairy hunting.'* They're quite passionate about it from what I've gleaned."

"You're already infiltrating that group, I take it?" Lucifer said.

"They're all women," Basquel said glumly. "I incarnate as a man. The spell doesn't ask me for a preference," he added dryly.

"Then we'll send Trephila in," Lucifer said irritably. "In the meantime, I want Laura's brat observed closely for a week or two. He's become important enough to Joby to do some real damage, I should think, but I want as much data as possible before deciding how best to twist his arm." Lucifer looked morosely away, and said, "It's a damn shame about Ben. Losing Lancelot deprives us of so many useful strategies. This," he said, looking bleakly at Basquel again, "is what comes of blind potshots."

⊠

They were gathered in their sea cave hideout, warded extra heavily, as all once-simple activities were now. Demons. *Real* demons. Hawk had seen two bodies fall from the air himself that awful night, and he had attended the emergency conclave above Mayfield's gallery with everyone else of the blood, but he still had trouble believing it. He knew he'd have found it all very entertaining in a story or a film, but there was nothing cool about it now. Everyone was frightened all the time. No one was supposed to use their gifts at all except in dire emergencies, or to set protective wards. Basically, Taubolt's whole battle plan seemed just a long list of different ways to hide. So that's what they were doing once again today: hiding until someone came up with a better plan.

For Hawk, there was one more frustration. When their elders finally did formulate some more decisive plan, everyone would have their parts to play, except himself. He couldn't change to any other form. He could cast no power outside himself beyond the mildest moods or lures and a few weak wards. He couldn't heal people, as even Joby could, apparently, though Joby hadn't seemed to want to believe it for some reason. He had no prescience. What good was he at all in times like these? His thin blood had always chafed him, but now it felt unbearable.

When he'd voiced these frustrations to Rose, she'd just assured him that his growing abilities as a bard would do far more good out in the wider world someday than any of the "silly little tricks" she and her friends could do. But somehow, Hawk could not see himself standing heroically on Main Street, felling demons with brilliant oratory. Basically, his situation sucked.

"But Ferristaff doesn't own the land!" Sophie was complaining. "How can he file a harvest plan?"

"Jake says he's just tryin' to lure the real owners out of hidin'," Cal said. "Figures they'll come out and sue 'im or somethin' now. Then he'd put the pressure on 'em to sell."

"Sounds like something you'd do, Cal," said Jupiter.

"Wanna get punched?" Cal grinned.

"Wanna catch me?" Jupiter parried, flapping his arms like wings.

"But there *aren't* any owners!" Autumn protested.

"Which is what's got the Council worried," Sky said. "If someone doesn't show up with proof of ownership, Ferristaff might be allowed to buy the land himself."

"No one can *buy* the *Garden Coast!*" shrilled Sophie.

"We got demons on our butt," growled Nacho. "No way we should be diddlin' around with richards like Ferristaff."

"This must be the bad thing Swami always said was coming," Autumn sighed.

"Anybody hear where Swami's gone to yet?" asked Ander.

"Jake just says the same thing as always." Cal shrugged. "He got sent off on some 'secret mission' for the Council."

"Lucky bastard," said Nacho. "At least he gets to *do* something."

"Amen!" said Cal. "Me an' Cob are gonna pound 'im for not takin' us along."

"We shouldn't just be sitting here," mumbled Cob, who'd been uncharacteristically quiet ever since the night of the attack. "I'm sick of hiding."

"What else are we gonna do?" said Cal. "You know somethin' 'bout fightin' demons that the Council don't?"

"Even if we can't fight demons," Hawk said, frowning at his tennis shoes, "we should at least be getting rid of idiots like Ferristaff and Foster. Like Nacho said, we shouldn't have to suffer ticks like that with all this going on. Seems to me we could've gotten rid of that trash ages ago, and I think we should have."

The ensuing silence made Hawk look up to find everybody looking back.

"Not a half-bad idea, Hawk," said Cal.

"Yeah." Nacho grinned. "Got any ideas how?"

"Me?" Hawk said ruefully. "I suppose I could come up with a decent story about it. But that's pretty much all I'd be good for, as everybody knows."

"Well, that's *one* story that would do my heart some good," Tholomey said, grinning. "Make a nice change from all the other ones I'm hearing now."

"Yeah!" said Ander. "Tell us how the land was cleansed forever of Ferristaff and Hamilton, oh great bard!"

"And Greensong." Autumn smiled.

"And don't forget Foster," said Nacho.

Surprised, to find himself suddenly the center of attention, Hawk took a moment to prepare himself, as Solomon had taught him, his mind quickly sketching out the form his tale would take. "Very well," he said, imitating

Solomon's voice and manner, to the amusement of all, "a tale then." And he launched into a set of stories, each more wildly inventive than the last, about how a band of clever children managed to drive out the four greatest villains in the land in just a single night. By the time his story ended there was rapt silence in the cave, and delighted smiles on every face.

"We gotta *do it!*" Cob shouted, the light of mischief in his eyes again.

"Why not?" crowed Nacho.

"Because we're not supposed to use our gifts at all right now!" said Sophie, sounding scandalized. "You all know what the Council said. We're supposed to stay out of sight, not put on a circus for the demons!"

"We could put up wards!" said Jupiter. "Just like we're doing everywhere else! And have people on the watch until we're through."

"And when one of Hamilton or someone goes running through town telling everyone what happened, and the demons figure out who we are?" Sophie insisted.

"Weren't you listening?" Nacho scoffed. "We won' look anything like *us!* How would anybody know who'd done it? I think it's a great idea! You're a genius, Hawk!"

Hawk felt suddenly alight with pride. Solomon had always told him that bards were not just entertainers, but counselors to the mighty and leaders of men. Now, Hawk began to realize what he meant. He fiercely wished that Rose were here to see this, not off on the Garden Coast collecting seeds against the worst scenario with Ferristaff.

"It sounds very cool," said Ander, "but I'm not sure its really such a good idea. The Council's been real clear about laying low. At least we ought to tell them what we want to do, and get permission first."

"Wuss!" Cob scoffed. "They'd just say no! They don't think we can do anything."

"Yes they do," Autumn protested. "They just care about our safety too."

"Autumn's right," Hawk said, recalling a conversation he'd had once with Solomon about the captive-hawk poem. "They respect us. But Solomon told me once that no one ever gets *permission* to grow up. If someone *gives* you your freedom, it's still theirs, not yours—like some kind of loan. See what I mean? To grow up, we have to take our freedom *without* permission. It's the only way it can be done."

"Wow!" said Nacho. "That's some pretty heavy dunkin' dude."

"So, what?" said Sophie. "You're saying we should all just defy our parents now, in the middle of a demon invasion?"

"I'm not trying to tell any of you what to do," Hawk said, a little scared himself of what he was proposing. "Like I said, that's got to be your choice, but I'll be graduating in the spring, and even now my mom cares way too much about my safety to ever give me *permission* to get in harm's way. She'll never really believe I can handle it until she finds out I already have." Hawk felt rather proud of all this sudden insight. "She may not know it consciously, but I think she's secretly waiting for the day I finally *steal* my freedom."

"Oh man!" Cob crowed. "Hawk, you are the *uber-bard!*"

Knowing she was overruled, Sophie threw up her hands as almost everyone there jumped on Hawk's bandwagon. Within minutes they had sorted themselves into four groups, one for each of the first four people they meant to drive out of town. Then all the groups fell into animated discussion about how to achieve their various missions.

Not five minutes later Sky gave a deafening whistle that silenced everyone, and said, "This cave is too small and too noisy. I can't hear myself think in here. We should break up, and each team go find someplace to plan where they can hear each other talk."

"Foster group to my house!" Nacho grinned.

"Ferristaff team can go to my place," Hawk said. "My mom's gone all week."

There was an awkward hesitation while everyone, especially Hawk, avoided acknowledging the reason for her absence. Then Sky already heading for the cave mouth, said, "Hamilton group to the sacred circle."

"Team Greensong can stay here then." Autumn said, smiling.

With that, Hawk led his team, which happened to be the largest, out of the cave, filled with pride. Rose had been right after all. His barding skills did have their uses.

❀

As two birds, a raven and a blue jay, flew away from the circle of trees that four boys had entered half an hour earlier, Cassey lowered her binoculars in exaltation. She'd just *known* that continuing to spy on that ring of cypress would pay off eventually! Her binoculars had given her a very good look at the children as they'd entered this time, and to her delight, she'd recognized one of them. A boy named Jupiter. She'd met him at the market, where he worked, and been quite taken by his name. So astrological!

She turned around and half-sprinted back to town, knowing Molly would want to hear about this right away. Cassey felt certain she would call a special meeting tonight, now that they actually had a fairy's name!

❀

He was out inspecting a work site in the woods. Fallen trees lay tumbled on the ground for as far as he could see into the darkness, an impressive harvest, but he wasn't pleased. Why had none of these been hauled away yet? Was he the only one who knew what work meant anymore? Where were all his men? As if in answer, he heard laughter from the edges of the clear-cut. Gleeful children's laughter. Suddenly, the uncut woods surrounding the site seemed too dark . . . too wild. He turned to run back toward his truck, but his legs would hardly move. He pushed them forward as if through sand while the laughter grew louder behind him. He strained to make his legs obey him, and—

Ferristaff gasped awake.

The dream dissolved, but quiet laughter hung on the air just long enough to leave him certain there was someone in the house. He sat up and peered into the darkness.

"Who's there?" he called gruffly, but only silence answered him. Perhaps the dream had lingered longer than he thought. He glanced at the luminous clock face beside his bed: 3:30 A.M. Outside, tree trunks groaned, wind rushed sighing through the foliage, branches tapped and scrapped against a wall downstairs. Sounded like a storm was brewing. Ferristaff lay back and stared up at the ceiling. It had only been a dream.

But as he closed his eyes, it came again; a childish giggle from downstairs. He bolted up in bed, and pulled the top drawer of his nightstand open. The gun he kept there was gone. He began to fear. Hamilton's teenage vandals must be real after all. Well, children he could handle, gun or no. However fierce their masks might be, he knew that deep down children were scared of nearly everything. One just had to face them down. He got carefully out of bed and crept to the open doorway of his room where he could peer down the stairwell into the entryway and some of the dining room. All was dark.

"You'd better get out!" he called in an angry, no nonsense voice. "Now!" He expected to hear scurrying escape, or frightened silence, but was surprised with more laughter. There were more than one of them, then, and too dumb, or stoned more likely, to know trouble when they heard it. "You think I'm funny?" he demanded. "When you took my pistol, you missed the shotgun in my closet. That makes me a lot more dangerous than you are. Now get out of here, or no one will blame me for what happens to intruders in my home!" It was a bluff of course. He'd left his shotgun in the basement after cleaning it, but how could they know he hadn't two of them?

There was more hushed laughter, and a brief green glow of some sort through the living room door opposite the dining room. He knew where they were now, and that room had no exit but the one he was looking at. They'd hide when they heard him coming down, but he wouldn't go into the living room after them. Through the dining room, he could reach the basement and his shotgun. After that, there'd be no more bluffing. He'd faced much tougher customers in his time than a couple of rural delinquents with a pistol between them, assuming they even knew how to shoot it.

"I gave you a choice," he growled menacingly, "and you chose wrong. Now you're going to pay the price." He started loudly down the stairs, figuring the more noise he made, the more startled they would be. Before he'd gotten halfway down, however, the green glow kindled in the living room again, and grew until it lit the entire stairwell. Unable to imagine what might cast such a glow, Ferristaff had come to a complete halt, when something large flew through the doorway, glowing like a giant firefly! Before he had time to gasp, it wheeled to fly directly at him, talons outstretched, beak gaping wide, a piercing shriek preceding it, a huge, burning owl rushed to rake his face! Ferristaff turned to run, but went sprawling on the steps instead, banging his shins painfully as he lunged at the railing for support. When he looked up there was no owl, but a child standing at the top of the stairs—dressed in glowing bark and leaves—a child with wings, and coal black eyes devoid of pupils!

Ferristaff remained crouched, utterly dumb, staring wide-eyed at the apparition, which was not entirely opaque, he realized. "W-what—" he croaked, but there was another peal of laughter from below him, and he turned to find at least five other creatures like the one above, gazing up at him with glee.

"Is it a toad?" chortled one of them.

"It's not pretty like a toad," said a second. "It's just an ugly lump."

"A stump then?" laughed another.

"It cannot be a stump," smiled a fourth, pointing at Ferristaff's disheveled thatch of iron hair. "It still has leaves."

"It must be a *tree* then!" exclaimed the second child. "An ugly stunted tree! Trees don't belong in stairwells though. What are we to do with it?"

"Cut it down! Cut it down!" shouted all the childlike ghosts at once, swirling into the air like great glowing, windblown leaves, slapping lightly at Ferristaff's face and back and hands and hair as they flew past him up the stairs to join their leader.

Ferristaff yowled in wordless fright as they gusted by. *"Who—what—who are you?"* he babbled hysterically when they had passed.

"We are spirits of the wood," said the creature who had been a owl, no longer grinning. No one smiled anymore. "The ghosts of all the trees you've murdered."

Ferristaff gaped in blank incomprehension, then he murmured, "I'm still dreaming. . . . You're a dream."

"Then *wake up!*" the spirit child screamed. *"WAKE UP!"* And they all flew around him once again, pinching, tugging, swatting, laughing cruelly. "Can't you *wake up?*" cried the leader of them. "Don't you know how to *wake up* from a *nightmare?*"

"Stop! Please stop!" cried Ferristaff. "What do you want from me?"

Immediately there was silence, and Ferristaff uncovered his head to find the "children" settled all around him on the steps again, fixing him with melancholy stares.

"Stop killing us," said their leader very quietly.

"Go away from here," said a second creature.

"Take your saws and trucks and cranes away," said a third.

"And all your men," said a fourth.

Ferristaff looked from face to impossible face and thought, *This isn't happening.* "You," he said, rising to his feet in sudden fury, "you aren't real! I don't believe in . . . in fairies!" shoving one of them aside he ran down the stairs toward his front door. Sometimes in dreams, he thought, getting out meant waking up. But as he reached the polished redwood door, its grain began to twist, the wood to bulge and groan, and all at once a giant wooden mouth, yawned wide before him, screaming at a deafening volume, as if its owner were being flayed. Ferristaff crumpled to the floor in terror, covering his ears, and wailing like an infant. *"Stop!"* he screamed at last. "I'll do anything you want! Just let me go!"

The giant wooden mouth melted into the form of a small wooden boy, who walked out of the door itself to become another glowing spirit like the others. "We will let you go," it said, "if you're gone before tomorrow."

The other spirit children were drifting in the air above him now, settling to the floor around him like huge snowflakes. The leader of them stepped forward and bent down until his face was only inches from Ferristaff's own. "We *want* you to go," the creature said, its eyes suddenly slitted with malice, its mouth stretched impossibly wide, full of terrible needle teeth. It thrust this terrifying visage farther forward until their noses almost touched. "And don't come back," it growled. "For *we* are far more *dangerous* than you." His teeth grew longer before Ferristaff's eyes. His mouth stretched even wider.

"How . . . how can I be out that quickly?" Ferristaff stammered, numb with terror. "I have all these things to pack, my business to—"

"Let someone else do that!" the toothy creature shouted, and Ferristaff felt his bladder go, a wet warmth spreading from his crotch.

"I'll get out," Ferristaff sobbed. "I'll make it up to you. I'll be gone by morning, and I'll have one of my people—"

"Just *go,*" hissed the apparition.

"And so you do not think us just a dream," said the fairy boy who'd stepped out of the door, "we leave you with a gift." He spread his arms, and, from nowhere Ferristaff could see, a flood of stones and bones and broken shells poured from between them to pile up on the floor. Ferristaff stared down at the jumble for a moment, then looked up again to find himself alone. Only their "gift" remained, and he knew with terrible certainty that it would still be there in the morning, though he, himself, would not.

29

(Cold Servings)

The morning after their crusade, Hawk rose at dawn, drove into town, and stealthily returned to their sea cave lair to find several of his fellow crusaders already waiting. The news was good and getting better as he arrived. Ferristaff was definitely gone. Tholomey reported that his front door had been left wide open, their cryptic calling card still piled on the floor inside.

Looking like the cat who'd swallowed the canary shop, Nacho told them all that Foster's lime-green Mercedes had last been seen at 2:00 A.M. racing south from town as if the hounds of hell were on its tail, "which," Nacho said happily, spreading his arms in a sitting curtain call, "they were!" When the cheers subsided, Nacho went on to speculate that, at the speed Foster was driving, he'd now have at least a couple of the tickets that he'd been so excited about giving out to everybody else.

Half an hour later, smiling sweetly, Autumn crouched through the cavern's entrance and informed them that Greensong had experienced a much more "animated" encounter with several of the trees she'd always claimed to care so much about. "We told her that we didn't like having spikes driven in our sides," Autumn said primly. "Then we played a game of hide-and-seek with her. She hid, we seeked. She won. I don't think we'll ever find her now, though it wasn't very fair of her to use a car." Everyone giggled.

All their protective wards had held, and there'd been no sign at all of demons. As further anecdotes were shared, and bragging contests escalated, Hawk sat quietly, basking in the rosy glow of all they had achieved.

His mom had called the night before to say that she and Joby would be coming home today. She hadn't sounded happy, which was unsurprising given what they'd gone there to do. His mother's grief caused Hawk pain, of course, but he hadn't known Ben well enough to take his death as personally as she and Joby did, and besides, now he'd have some news to really cheer them up when they got back. Visions of their pride and amazement danced through his imagination; he saw grateful congratulations from the Council and tickertape parades down Main Street. He imagined Solomon giving him a regal nod as their awards were being bestowed, and saying, *You are a true bard now, young Hawk.* If only Rose had been here, Hawk's happiness would have been utterly complete.

It was half an hour more before they began to wonder where the Hamilton team was. Cob, Cal, Sky, and Jupiter were not known as early risers, and the group was still debating whether someone should go roust their lazy butts from bed when Blue arrived and told them he'd just seen Hamilton in town.

"She was in the coffee bar on Shea Street, asking if anyone knew where Foster went," Blue said, anxiously. "She didn't seem upset at all, except she wanted Foster and couldn't find him. I was hoping Sky and those guys would be here."

"Something went wrong then." Nacho frowned. "I'm going to find Cob."

"I'll go back and look for Jup," said Blue.

Just as they turned to go, however, Ander crawled into the cave, and stood up looking pale and shaken. For a moment he just stared at them seeming to shiver, though it wasn't all that cold. Then, as the cave fell silent, Hawk realized that Ander was crying.

"What's wrong?" Hawk asked with dawning dread.

"Sky," Ander croaked. "And Jupiter," he said, crying harder now. "They're dead."

"What?" Nacho yelled.

"God!" Sophie shrieked. *"Goddamn it!"* she yelled again. *"I told them! I told all of you!"* She burst into tears, as did Autumn. Everyone else sat gaping, their faces drained of color.

Hawk could not move at first, couldn't even breath. It was his fault. He'd talked everybody into this. Steal your freedom, he had told them, and now two of them were dead. Three, Hawk amended numbly. His life was over too. "How?" he heard himself ask, as if someone else had spoken.

"They're calling it an accidental fall," Ander said, "from climbing on the cliffs out by the Circle."

"That's bullshit!" Nacho shouted.

Everybody knew that both of them could fly. They hadn't fallen from any cliffs. If anything, they'd fallen from the air as they'd been murdered.

"It was goddamn demons!" Sophie bawled. *"I told them not to do this!"*

"Has anyone seen Cal or Cob?" Tholomey asked fearfully.

"Jake says they're up in the Garden," Ander said, "where they'll be safe."

Not looking at Hawk, he added, "Jake says the demons know them now. They can't come back to town."

There was nothing Hawk could say, or even think, except that this was all his fault, and everyone would know it, and there would never be a way to take any of it back. Sky and Jupiter were dead! And he was finished here. He was finished everywhere. Imagining Rose's face when she learned what he had done, he just wanted to escape, but how could he escape himself? Hawk's mind began to rifle through some catalog of ways to kill himself, trying to determine which one would be fastest and least painful, until he imagined Rose's face again, when she learned he'd killed himself, and realized, with even greater despair, that he could never do that to her, or to his mother, or to anyone he knew on top of what he'd done already. There was no way out of it. He was going to have to live with this. Forever! And all the "great bard" could think to say was, "I'm so sorry. I'm so sorry," which, he realized, he'd already started saying through tears he'd been oblivious of until now too.

They were all looking at him, some with anger, some with pity, some with what seemed fear, but he had no more power to shut his mouth or stop the words than if he'd been a dummy on some ventriloquist's knee. "I'm sorry! I'm so sorry!" he kept sobbing, knowing he'd be saying those words until the day that he died too.

❁

"You *dare* to lecture *me* on *interference?*" Merlin raged. "*You,* who let two boys die, when one flick of your angelic little finger could have saved their lives? Your *lack* of interference was *unconscionable!*"

"It was obedient," Michael said sternly. "Painfully obedient, yes, but we both known this entire invasion is about Joby. And that attack was clearly aimed at him."

"Lucifer has *told* you that?" Merlin spat. "Might not his ancient hatred of our race be sufficient explanation in itself?"

"And the first two attacked just happen to be particular favorites of Joby's?" the angel asked levelly. "That stretches credibility, don't you think?"

"Half the children in this town are particular favorites of Joby's!" Merlin snapped. "If you were really so astute, you'd have noticed that. As long as such questions are remotely open to debate, I have no intention of letting any of them die like you did."

"Arthur killed a great many children once, hoping one of them was Mordred," Michael said implacably, "while *you* stood back and let him, as I recall."

"Don't throw that in my face just to excuse yourself now!" Merlin shouted, stung to fury "At least I don't keep blindly repeating my mistakes in the name of some abstract concept of obedience. I think and grow! I have a conscience!"

"Which is precisely why I mention it," the angel sighed. "To make you think and grow. We both know why you didn't stop Arth—"

"I should have!" Merlin cut him off, astonished at the angel's cruelty. "I should have thrown Arthur in a tower cell and kept him there until he understood what he was going to do! To himself as well as all those innocents."

"Then why didn't you?" Michael asked quietly.

Merlin said nothing. He did not want to remember it, and he didn't want to say the answer. This angel was trying to twist everything.

"Because you knew his life was no one's but his own," the angel said softly, "the only truly sovereign possession any person has. You understood, as few men ever do, what it would have done to him if you took that choice away, for whatever reason. Now Joby's going to face such terrible choices. Would you prevent him from deciding?"

"Then why try taking choice away from *me,* angel?" Merlin rasped.

"I have not. Nor will I," Michael said, "as you know very well. Have I thrown *you* in any tower cell? Or threatened to prevent you from choosing next time as you chose the last? Have I moved behind your back to alter choices you might make before they even reach you?" he asked pointedly. "I seek only to persuade you to greater wisdom, just as you tried to persuade Arthur once."

"And *failed,*" Merlin said bitterly. "Just as you do now. Had I your angelic powers, Michael, I'd have saved all four of those boys, not just two. And I will do everything within my power to save the next four and the next four after that. I have no cold and callous angel's heart, I fear. If I'm damned for that, so be it."

"And if all of us are damned for it as well?" the angle asked. "Will *that* matter to your supple human heart?"

"Our loving Lord will now damn us all just to punish my misdeeds?" Merlin scoffed. "I have never seen you overreach so, Michael."

"You know what's at stake then, in this wager, I assume," the angel said.

"My grandson's life and many others," Merlin growled, deeply discomfited at having to admit that he did not. "Have you some better information?"

"Not for one who would just use it to further interfere in what he doesn't understand as well as he may think," Michael replied sadly. "But you would be wise to worry about why I dare not disobey the command we all were given, even to save lives that my cold, angelic heart dearly loved many years before you knew them."

The worry this did cause Merlin just increased his irritation. "Yet you've no qualms about my incarnation spell, or helping to conceal the Garden from this invasion either," Merlin countered. "Might those not be construed as interference too?"

"The last time I heard my Master's voice," said Michael, "was days before all this began. He seemed to suggest that morning that I'd have leeway, when the crisis came, to help defend Taubolt *in general*. Thus I have and will. It is a very troubling line to walk, but when it comes to intervening in specific acts so clearly aimed at Joby's heart, my hands are tied, Merlin, as yours should be. *We* are *commanded* not to interfere unasked. How can you continue to 'misunderstand' that?"

Weary of their pointless sparing, Merlin said, "Your own remarks simply make the nature of that command seem even more ambiguous. I made my choice many years ago, and any damage it might cause must surely have been done by now. I still see no reason to abandon my grandson in the middle of this stream."

He turned to leave and said, "I'm going now to interfere some more, I fear. I've heard rumors that this Redtsone woman and her knitting circle have been looking for us. I think it's time someone obliged her with the kind of *real* magic she'll not soon forget. If my own investigations are correct, it was she and her women, not Joby, who led that hell spawn to those boys the other night. If so," he said, looking pointedly at Michael, "the attack upon them had no more relationship to Joby's trial than anything else happening in this town now. Think on *that*, my *obedient* friend."

❊

As the joint memorial service for Jupiter and Sky convened at the community high school in Taubolt, Joby lay on Laura's couch, too exhausted to rise, and too plagued with thought to sleep. As profoundly as he grieved the loss of his two young friends, Joby and Laura had decided to stay here, with Hawk, who had adamantly refused even to discuss attending it himself. Joby wasn't sure how many funerals he could take in one month anyway. His reservoir of tears was badly overdrawn.

Beyond Ben's funeral itself, the journey back to Joby's childhood home had been a nightmare—literally. He'd been subjected to demoralizing dreams every single night. In some, Laura had pulled away from him in the middle of their lovemaking to sullenly admit he'd only won her because Ben was dead. In others, Ben's ravaged body had turned up in the trunk of Joby's car, as police arrived, accusing him of murdering his friend to steal his wife. Fortunately, Joby and Laura had slept together at his parents' house, so each time he had woken in a rigid sweat, all he'd had to do was turn and see her lying there, kiss her shoulder and feel her press against him in the dark, to know that she was *not* there by default. If not for Laura's presence all that week, in fact, Joby didn't know how he'd have survived the trip.

He'd been stung to see how rundown his old neighborhood had grown. The grassy hillsides of his childhood were brown and threadbare now, gouged with ruts and bald expanses of hard, colorless dirt. The neighborhood had seemed a sterile maze of faded stucco houses landscaped in anal geometries of close-cropped grass and olive-drab shrubbery, the streets awash in litter.

In his parents' house, the same paintings had still hung above the same furniture, the same books and knickknacks cluttering the shelves, the same framed photos on the mantel, all as if he'd entered some ghastly museum. At the sight of his high school graduation picture, Joby had felt as if that boy might still be living there, not just on the mantel but in the very air. Eighteen years and nothing had changed, unless the gloom had grown a little deeper, though that had likely been just the weather.

Then he and Laura had come home to Taubolt.

Joby had read somewhere about a form of medieval execution where a plank was set atop the condemned, and stones piled on, one by one, until the person underneath was crushed. Lying now on Laura's couch, Joby could not help but empathize.

They'd returned to Laura's home to find a note in unfamiliar handwriting, saying Hawk had gone to Rose's house, and they should come at once. There, as Clara had horrified Laura in one room with news of two more deaths and the dimensions of Hawk's own disaster, Tom had shocked Joby in another with assertions of demonic invasion and a mind-numbing list of precautions that must now be taken by anyone of the blood, including Hawk and Joby. Almost worse, Joby had been advised to keep all of this from Laura for a host of reasons, topped by the likelihood that she was not remotely prepared to believe any of it, especially amidst so much other trauma.

As Joby lay wondering if there could be anything to the idea of karma and, if so, whether he'd been Adolf Hitler or Genghis Kahn in some other lifetime, he heard Laura coming down the stairs from Hawk's room. He sat up to look at her.

"He won't even speak to me," she said quietly, looking drawn and pale. Her reservoir of tears seemed empty too. Theirs was a dry and weary grief by now. "You want to try?" she asked. "Maybe it's because I'm his mother."

Joby got up off the couch, and stopped to kiss her on his way toward the stairs. "It's *in spite* of that," he told her softly, "not *because*." Then he went up to see what he could do. From the moment Joby had understood Hawk's place in all of this, he'd hardly ceased to think about what he might have tried to tell his younger self if he'd been able to after Lindwald died. Would it have made much difference? Probably not, but the time had come to try.

Laura had left Hawk's door open. Hawk was lying on his bed, staring at the ceiling as he'd done for most of every day since they had brought him home from the Connollys' house.

When Joby's knock got no response, he walked in anyway, sat down on Hawk's desk chair several feet away, and let the silence stretch.

"Hey," Joby said at last.

He might have been a ghost, for all Hawk seemed to notice.

"Sometimes," Joby said, remembering the day he'd found Hawk crying on the headlands, three long years ago, "it helps to talk when things are bad."

Hawk's eyes grew red as his face struggled to remain dispassionate. "I know what you're trying to do," he murmured. "You can't help me. No one can."

Was this what Ben had gone through on the lawn in front of school that day? Joby wondered. At least Joby hadn't had to tackle Hawk and pin him down yet.

"What you and all the others tried to do was brave and well intended," Joby said. "You were trying to help Taubolt defend itself. Everybody knows that."

"Not Sophie," Hawk said stonily. "She told us this would happen. I talked everyone into ignoring her. Everybody knows that too." He went back to staring at the ceiling, the smoldering anger that had briefly lit his eyes evaporating once again.

After they had sat in silence for another lengthy spell, Joby took a breath and said, "I've got a story for you, Hawk, and when I'm done, you'll have to tell me if *I'm* guilty."

Without waiting for permission, he began, for the first time in eighteen years, to speak of Jamie Lindwald's last night on earth, leaving nothing out except for having slept with Hawk's mother after prom.

"So did I murder Jamie?" Joby asked when it was done. "Should I be punished?"

Through the entire tale, Hawk's eyes had never moved from whatever they'd been staring at above his bed for half the week.

"If you're going to condemn yourself," Joby pressed, "you'll have to shoot me too. Can't have it one way for you and another for me. That's not how justice works."

"All you did was drink some beers," Hawk said at last, his eyes still on the ceiling. "Your mistake was *nothing* like mine."

"Glad to hear you admitting it was a mistake," said Joby. "*Everybody* makes those. You think *all of us* should suffer what you're putting yourself through then?"

"They'd told us it was dangerous!" Hawk snapped, finally glancing at him. "I defied the Council! *I* knew better!"

"They'd told us drinking was dangerous too," Joby shot back. "That we were too young. I also defied the edicts of authority. It was *against the law* for me to drink, but *I* knew better *too*—just like Jamie and half the other kids at school did. Stop thinking your mistake was unique, Hawk. The only difference I can see is that you had far, far better reasons than mine."

"Pride," Hawk said, eyes back on the ceiling. "That was my only reason."

"And what's wrong with being proud?" Joby demanded more fiercely than he'd meant to. "Every kid who's ever grown up has known better than his elders somewhere along the way, and nothing ever comes of it for ninety-nine percent of them. You got unlucky. Being unlucky isn't any more a sin than being lucky is a virtue!

"While I was driving back here from Ben's funeral, I looked down to fiddle with the radio, Hawk. Your mom nudged me, and I looked up to find my car way over the centerline. I yanked it back where it belonged, took a deep breath, and forgot all about it. Was it my fault there was no one in the other lane? Does my good luck make me better than you? *Your mom* was in the car, Hawk. I could have killed her. If you're so sure of this unbending justice you're inflicting on yourself, don't be a hypocrite! Get up and punish me for what I could just as well have done to you this week!"

As Joby's voice had risen in frustration, Hawk's eyes had brimmed with tears and begun to spill at last.

"I just want to take it back!" Hawk cried, rigid as a board. "Every minute. That's all I think or feel, but I never can! I never will be able to!"

Joby rushed to pull Hawk off the bed and wrap him in his arms, which Hawk lunged into as a drowning man might hurl himself into a life raft.

"You're just a fallible, good-hearted, deserving human being, Hawk, like all the rest of us," Joby said, crying too now, "with as much right to grieve, and be understood and cared for, and *healed,* as me or anybody down at that memorial service."

As they clung to one another, weeping, Joby realized that for all the pain and anger they'd been dragged into so suddenly, all he felt now was hope, and love, and most of all, gratitude, that whatever he had suffered in his life might somehow have equipped him for this moment.

"I still wish you'd been my father," Hawk half-whispered.

"Will stepfather do?" Joby replied as quietly.

Hawk leaned back to stare at him. "Have you asked her?" he said, hopeful.

"Not yet," said Joby. "Not in the middle of all this, but I'm going to, as soon as we all get a little breather. We both know what she'll say, I think."

For the first time that week, Hawk began to smile, then pulled suddenly away, looking toward his bedroom door. Joby turned to find Laura there, wiping tears from her eyes too. Unsure how long she'd been there, Joby smiled reassuringly and waved her in.

"There's someone here to see you, Hawk," she said quietly, stepping back into the hallway instead.

From out of sight beside her, Nacho and Tholomey shuffled through the door looking timidly at Hawk, who wiped his eyes and stared back at them like a man resigned to execution, maybe even longing for it.

"Hawk," said Nacho, clearly struggling with emotions of his own, "we've come to say—me and Tholomey—we *all* decided that day in the cave. It wasn't just your fault."

"It was a good service," Tholomey murmured. "You were missed though."

Losing his brief composure, Hawk sat on his bed and began to cry again. The two boys came to sit beside him, one on either side, each with an arm across his shoulders as he wept. When Rose peered around the doorjamb and came in to join them, Hawk cried even harder, while Joby went to Laura, who clearly needed holding too.

☒

On the first clear afternoon they'd seen in weeks, quite a parliament of skaters had convened outside the community high school, laughing, jeering, or, when one of them pulled off some particularly impressive maneuver, tapping the tails of their boards on the pavement in approval. The school grounds' wide cement walkways and paved courtyard, low concrete walls, ledges, stairs, and metal handrails provided the kind of terrain skaters loved, and Bridget never chased them off the way so many of the ognibs back in town did these days. Sometimes she even came outside to sit with them and watch as they perfected their ollies, nose-grinds, tail-slides, or, if they were veterans like Nacho, more advanced "flippity tricks."

Having warmed up with a quick series of back-truck tricks, Nacho finished his ride with a seemingly effortless front-side flip, then comboed a radial 360 with a 180 end-over between his legs, while spinning his body 180 degrees to land back on the board in reversed stance before it touched the ground.

The trick won a loud round of catcalls and board banging as Nacho slid gracefully to a halt. He turned to take a little bow, but instead stopped to stare at a boy watching them from underneath the trees that edged their impromptu arena. He seemed seventeen at most, wearing baggy denim pants, ratty tennis shoes, and a long-sleeved, black cotton shirt. He had startling blue eyes and shoulder length sandy blond hair streaked with gold around the bangs and sideburns. His chiseled features were all that saved him from looking pretty as a girl, Nacho thought.

The boy, leaning on a skateboard of his own and returning Nacho's scrutiny, was no one Nacho had ever seen, though that meant very little these days, when more than half the people in town on any given day were no one Nacho had ever seen either. Still, given Taubolt's state of occupation, it never hurt to be suspicious.

"That was tight," the strange boy said quietly. "Can I skate with you guys?"

"It's a free country." Nacho shrugged.

By now, a number of the others had noticed the newcomer, and watched as he lifted his board and started forward with shy determination.

"What's your name?" Nacho asked as he approached.

"GB," the boy muttered self-consciously

"GB?" said one of the younger boys, smirking. "That like the *heebee geebees?*"

Seeing how this embarrassed the new boy, Nacho frowned at the brat who'd teased him and growled, "Give it a rest," before asking GB, "Where you from?"

"Seattle," GB answered, still clearly unsure of his standing here.

"That's a ways," Nacho replied. "Your family here on vacation or something?"

GB looked away uncomfortably. "Wouldn't know."

"What's that supposed to mean?" asked a kid named Barnard. His family was of the blood, but they'd been drawn to Taubolt only weeks before the Cup had vanished, and he was always trying to show he belonged by being suspicious of other newcomers.

"I'm on my own," GB said, still looking no one in the eye. "Just me."

Nacho took a second look, noting that his unkempt condition seemed a tad more authentic than current fashion dictated. "You run away?" he asked.

"No," GB said. "I'm just on my own." He looked Nacho in the eye at last, and said, "I'm lookin' for a job, and a cheap place to rent, if you know one. Just a room."

He was a runaway all right, but Nacho figured that was no one's business but his own, so he stuck his hand out and said, "I'll keep an ear out. Welcome to Taubolt."

GB responded with an expertly hip handshake, knocking his fist against Nacho's as they disengaged. Then he threw his board down and jumped on to ride fakie down the cement walk into a half-cab flip before popping his board up and carrying it to one of the benches without so much as glancing toward the others for reaction.

"Not bad," said Nacho, jumping onto his own board to follow GB's route into a clean 360 shove-it with a 180 foot rotation.

"Sweet," said GB appreciatively.

"HORSE!" said the kid who'd made fun of GB's name.

"Yeah," said another neophyte named Jessie. "You and him, Nacho!"

"He just got here," Nacho objected. "Give 'im a break, you guys."

"It's okay," GB said behind him, then added hesitantly. "If you want to."

"You played horse?" Nacho asked.

GB nodded modestly. "I mean, you'll win, but it'd be fun."

"Nacho's gonna grind him flat," someone whispered theatrically.

It was a tough call. If Nacho refused, it would be like snubbing the guy, but if he said yes, and beat him, these bloodthirsty little board babies might laugh the boy back into the trees. Before Nacho had decided what to do, GB jumped on his board, got some speed up on the walkway, and ollied off the stairs into the courtyard, executing a flawless 360 flip, his feet grabbing the board again before landing, as if they were welded to it.

That resolved the issue. This guy was good enough to look out for himself. In fact, Nacho wondered if he was being sharked by Mr. Modest, here. If so, Mr. Modest was in for a surprise. Grinning, he stepped on his board and matched GB's jump without much effort. Then, coming back up the stairs, Nacho kicked out into the street and ollied up into a long crooked grind along the curb, came off fakie, then popped into a half-cab flip. Boards banged on the pavement behind him, but GB duplicated the trick with apparent ease. GB's next gambit was a front-side half-cab heel flip. There were grunts of surprise and admiration from the others. No doubt about it, Nacho thought, he'd been sharked. This guy was way too good. Nacho got up some speed, and headed into the trick, but as his body came around, the board brushed his foot before completing its rotation, and he barely made the landing. In the courtyard behind them, there was a sudden quiet. This wasn't funny anymore. Third turn, and neither of them even had an "H" yet. Nacho decided it was time to cut things short.

"You're damn good," Nacho said to GB, "so let's ditch the kiddie stuff."

He started kicking fast back down the walkway toward the stairs, did a quick front-side flip, then ollied up huge into a backside grind down the handrail to the courtyard, but his weight was too far back. As he began to fall, the *other* skills that were his birthright leapt up instinctively, stalling his board just enough to make the landing possible. He hadn't meant to cheat. His use of power had been a reflex. But half the kids here were of the blood, and their silence made it clear that they all knew what he had done. Flushed with embarrassment, he turned to GB, searching for some excuse to save his honor with the others by conceding the game without exposing his real reasons to GB and all the other ognib townies here.

Still struggling after some solution, Nacho saw GB looking at him strangely, half a smile playing on his lips before he pushed off down the walk, did the front-side flip and ollied up onto the railing, just as Nacho had. But at the end of GB's grind, he popped into a truly impossible kick flip and nailed the landing in the courtyard below.

The silence now was absolute. Every boy there was astonished, but Nacho knew that any who were of the blood had sensed GB's use of power. GB picked up his board, turned to face Nacho with a look of tense defiance. "Fair is fair," he said quietly.

Nacho's mouth dropped open, a flood of questions scrambling up his throat, none of which could be asked until he got this kid into some less public setting.

Before he could think how, Barnard hissed, "Hey, watch it! Donaldson!"

Everyone turned to see the town's new scourge of skaters park his patrol car across the street, climb out, and swagger toward them.

"It's getting pretty close to dinnertime," the young officer said. "Shouldn't you boys be headed home?"

Everyone looked sullenly away or at the ground.

"Bridget says that we can skate here," Nacho answered levelly.

"If you mean, *Mrs. O'Reilly,*" Donaldson countered, "she may be head teacher here, but this is not her property, so her permission's kind of beside the point."

"Who called you then?" asked Barnard, who'd already been ticketed in town for being a "public nuisance," which is what they called skating these days.

"That's none of your concern." Donaldson frowned. "You're disturbing lots of neighbors in the area, and they're worried that one of you is going to break a leg here any moment. The school board's not too eager to get sued. I'm afraid you'll have to leave."

"Where are we *supposed* to skate then?" Nacho asked, uncowed.

"Your name Nacho?" Donaldson asked with obvious irritation.

Nacho fell silent, alarmed that Donaldson knew his name. He'd been careful to keep a low profile since the officer's arrival.

"Yeah, I thought so," Donaldson said. "Karl Foster told me all about you."

"Foster didn't *know* all about me," Nacho replied.

"There's people here in town who are mighty curious about his mysterious departure a couple weeks ago," Donaldson said menacingly. "You know anything about why he might have left?"

"Got no idea," Nacho said. "Just glad he's gone."

"Well, *I* know you've been out of school for several years now, boy," said Donaldson, "and according to the law, no one's got a right to be on school grounds who isn't faculty or student body." He surveyed the group. "Looks like that may apply to several of you. Now, I'm not here to debate with you boys. You can all leave right now, or I'll start writing tickets for the usual violations. It's your call."

Beyond a tatter of grumbling, all resistance vanished. Everyone began to leave, but as Nacho turned to go, Donaldson said, "Not you. I'll have that board, please."

Nacho turned back to gape at him. "*Why?* I'm *leavin'!*"

"Not fast enough," Donaldson replied, holding out his hand. "Maybe you'll think twice before you question my authority again."

"Wait a minute," Nacho protested, "I—"

"Boy, you can hand me that board, or I can arrest you right now, and show you the *real* meaning of trouble," Donaldson growled. "What's it gonna be?"

It was Nacho's best board. He'd made it all by hand, every inch with loving care. No way he was going to hand it over to this latest tool of Hamilton's. He turned and bolted toward the headlands beyond the school, tossing back a little flow of air, just enough to wrap Donaldson's feet and make him trip. Hearing the man scuff the ground and cuss behind him, Nacho smiled, and poured on a bit more speed than was strictly natural. As he reached the fields, he realized that GB was running right beside him.

"You're of the blood?" Nacho panted warily as they ran. Strangers were not to be trusted these days; strangers with power least of all.

"I heard there were others," GB replied his voice unsteady with something more than just exertion. "Somewhere down here." Nacho glanced over at him, realizing with a jolt that the boy was trying not to cry. "I've been lookin' for a long, long time," GB said.

"How'd you know what you were lookin' for?" Nacho asked, far from reassured.

"My parents told me," GB answered. "Just before the demons killed them."

"What?" Nacho exclaimed, breaking stride to stare at GB.

"He's coming!" GB said, looking back at Donaldson, who was gaining ground behind them. "Come on," he said desperately, urging Nacho to follow as he picked up speed again. "I can't get arrested. They'll throw me out of town, and I've worked too hard to find you guys! Where we gonna hide out here?"

"Can you blink out?" Nacho asked as they sprinted toward the Sacred Circle downhill from the burned out chapel.

"You mean disappear?" GB said. "He'll see us! Don't you care about that here?"

"Course we do," said Nacho. "Do it when we reach those trees. He's far enough behind. When he gets in there he'll just think we took off out the other side."

As they ran inside the ring of cypress trees, they did as Nacho had suggested, remaining still and silent as Donaldson barged in himself a moment later, stopping to glance first one direction, then the other before walking to the circle's center, where he stood breathing hard and looking cross, turning a full 360 degrees in clear confusion.

To Nacho's surprise, he didn't even check if they'd run out the other side, only shook his head and left to trot back across the field toward his patrol car by the school.

"Okay, so tell me that again about your parents?" Nacho said, turning toward GB as they both reappeared.

"They're dead," GB shrugged sadly. "There was a couple of us living up there in Seattle. Not just my family." He shrugged again. "One of us got careless, I guess. I still don't know which one. But the demons found us all." He fell silent, his eyes gone empty with some dreadful memory he clearly wasn't going to describe. "One night," he said bleakly. "That's all it took."

Nacho nodded grimly, thinking of Jupiter and Sky, and of Alfred and Crombie on the night all their lives had changed.

"My father woke me up and said we had to run. Practically threw me out the window. *Find the others.* That was all he said." GB's eyes began to redden as Nacho watched him try to jam his feelings back. "I thought he meant the other families in our group. When he shoved me out the back, I thought he and my mom would be coming right behind me. But I went to all the other houses, and the demons had already been there. One was burning. The other one was full of . . ." He fell silent again. "I hung around for weeks. Went to all the places I could think of where my parents might have tried to meet me, but they never came. No one did."

He looked up at Nacho, his expression haunted. "I hooked up with other kids livin' on the streets up there then. My gifts made it easy for me to steal things, and deal with people, so I was popular. I was careful no one ever figured out how I was doing things, but one day someone started to suspect, so I left before they started talkin' and the demons found me too. I just wandered south for months. Then I started hearin' rumors about some town in California. I heard some guy sayin' in a bus station how he'd been vacationing there when they'd had a bunch of fires, and he'd seen naked people falling from the air. Everybody laughed at him, but I remembered what my father said the night he made me leave. Find the others." GB's satisfaction seemed almost fierce as he stared at Nacho. "How many of us are there here?"

"Lots," said Nacho, amazed at GB's courage. "But I've got some bad news for you too. You've kind of jumped out of the frying pan into the fire here. Taubolt's new name is Demons 'R' Us. They invaded just about a month ago. We've got a couple ancients here who are strong enough to force the fucks to incarnate here in town, but you've picked a bad time to visit, I'm afraid."

"What's an ancient?" GB asked, seeming only excited.

Nacho shook his head, supposing that next to hiding all alone out in the world, eating out of garbage cans, Taubolt must still look like paradise to him. "There's a lot you prob'ly oughtta know," he said. "And if you check out with our certain people, I'll be glad to fill you in. No offense, but we gotta be careful now. I'm sure you understand."

"Sure," said GB. "No one gets that better than me."

"Where're you headed now?" Nacho asked.

"Nowhere," GB said.

Knowing this was probably the literal truth, Nacho felt another stab of sympathy, and said, "Let's go get your grillin' taken care of then. After that I'm goin' home to fix some dinner. You can come over if you want."

"You sure?" GB asked, but the look of gratitude on his face spoke volumes.

"Come on," Nacho said, managing a grin. "It'll be a lot more fun to bitch about that asshole Donaldson with company. Guess we better blink again, though." Donning robes of twisted air, they started out to cross the fields, seeming nothing more to anyone who might be watching than a slow breeze through the long grass.

"So," Nacho asked, "what does 'GB' stand for anyway?"

"Nothin'," GB muttered.

"Come on, what?" Nacho pressed.

"It's stupid."

"I'm not gonna laugh."

GB looked away and mumbled something too quickly and quietly to make out.

"What?" Nacho said, too intrigued to let it go now.

"I said, 'Golden Boy.'" GB sighed, looking mortified.

"Your name's *Golden Boy*?" Nacho blurted despite himself. "Your *real* name?"

"My parents were . . . kind of strange sometimes." GB gave him a look full of earnest appeal. "I'd appreciate it if you'd keep that to yourself. I . . . I go by GB, and—"

"Hey," Nacho interrupted, "your secret's safe with me. Geez. Golden Boy. That sure sucks."

"You're telling me," GB said as they headed toward the street.

30

(Golden Boy)

Dear Sheriff Mansfield,

While I remain grateful to you for sending us Officer Donaldson, I am writing once again to plead for further action. As our county sheriff, I know you share my escalating alarm at the continuing increase in serious crime that threatens this entire rural county's economy by eroding Taubolt's viability as a premier resort destination.

Since summer alone, Taubolt has endured five murders, numerous arson fires, several extremely suspicious disappearances, uncountable acts of vandalism and petty theft, and now, the torching of three more cars belonging to trusting visitors. I might also add that there is increasing anecdotal evidence of escalating drug use among Taubolt's teenagers. While Officer Donaldson performs his tasks with exemplary diligence, no one man can hope to address such an overwhelming challenge alone.

Locally, one hears increasing curiosity expressed as to why this crime spree has been greeted with such apparent indifference by our county's top officials. I am sure that assignment of more appropriate resources to this urgent crisis would go far to rouse the kind of respect and gratitude a man looking forward to reelection would value. Come next year's election campaign, I will happily throw the full weight of my resources behind any man who can demonstrate a credible willingness and ability to restore the peace and security that this charming town took for granted not so long ago.

Appreciatively,
Agnes Hamilton

❈

Franklin stood behind the counter of his hardware store, absently cleaning a case of glass lamp chimneys with an old rag, while watching Taubolt's new policeman stand across the street in the blowing drizzle, writing up some kid who'd dared to skateboard past a few of Shea Street's shops in daylight—not that there were any customers to scare off in such weather. It had blown sheets of rain for three days straight now.

Seemed an awful waste of law enforcement to spend so much time writing kids tickets and taking their toys away, though, in sad truth, this was probably the only so-called crime in Taubolt even twenty Donaldsons stood any chance of tackling. Wasn't much use calling in police to deal with demon mischief.

He shook his head, wondering how much longer he could stick around here watching Taubolt go to seed. Their once pleasant village was nothing now but a brawl of kiddie crime fighting, yuppie refugees, "infrastructure issues," rising violence, dying children, and incarnate demons virtually undetectable (until they vandalized your business or firebombed your car), among the horde of clueless tourists still expecting to pampering. They didn't know Taubolt was an active war zone. Franklin would have gone already except that everything he'd ever had or cared about was here, and there was nowhere it made any sense to go. Not until the Cup was found. If it ever was.

"Hey, Franklin. How are you doing?" Tom Connolly waved half-heartedly as he entered the store, accompanied by gusts of damp air and the sounds of power saws and pounding hammers from farther up the street. Molly Redstone's abandoned shop was being repaired and renovated as the new police substation. Redstone had left suddenly the month before, claiming the devas had directed her to some new "mission" in Colorado.

"What ya need, Tom?" Franklin replied, setting down his glassware.

"A few of those big yellow notepads," Tom said, coming to the counter, "and some manila envelopes." He looked out at the street with a sour smile. "I see he's at it again. Ever vigilant."

Franklin nodded. "Neither rain nor snow nor dark of night can close that man's ticket book. I feel safer every day."

"Hamilton doesn't seem to," Tom said, heading back to the stationery aisle for his things. "You read her latest letter in *The Lighthouse?*"

"I did," Franklin replied, going back to wiping down his chimneys. "Sounds like she expected 'em to station the whole platoon out here, don't it?"

"Sounds like," Tom agreed. "Seems to me she ought to be happy, though. He hasn't wasted any time zeroing in on the worst threats to local safety, has he?"

"No, sir," Franklin said dryly. "Don't know how we ever got by without 'im."

Suddenly, across the street, Donaldson ran to lean in through the open window of his car, then jumped in and sped off with lights blazing, as the kid he'd been accosting watched in open-mouthed surprise.

"Looks like something big's gone down," said Connolly, drawn back to watch with Franklin.

"Hamilton's probl'y caught some of those damn delinquents lookin' at dirty pictures." Franklin smiled humorlessly.

Suddenly, the door flew open, banging loudly on the stop as Blue leaned through it in a breathless panic. "They're cutting down the Sacred Circle!" he shouted.

"WHAT?!!" both men exclaimed in unison.

"They're chainsawing the trees!" Blue wailed. "Nacho's tryin' to stop 'em! And that new kid, GB! Everybody's runnin' down there telling 'em to stop, but—"

"We're comin'!" Franklin cut him off. Already running for the door one step behind Connolly, he was stunned that even demons would try such a thing in broad daylight.

❈

Bridget O'Reilly was last to arrive, delayed by "issues" at school, she claimed. But it was to Joby Peterson that she apologized for being late, Donaldson noticed, though this was Donaldson's conference room, and, officially, his meeting. In reality, of course, this whole powwow had been Peterson's doing, as was the guest list, kindly forwarded to Donaldson ahead of time with brief explanations of local position and importance beside each name, just to help him understand how deep a pile he'd stepped in, no doubt. Why was it always the littlest things that bit you? A touch of routine security clearing on virtually undeveloped public land. Who'd've thunk?

"If we're all here then," Donaldson said, "I'd like to start by thanking you for making time to come down here and help us all understand each other better."

"I'm not goin' to mince words with you, young man," said Franklin Holt—*owner of the hardware and grocery stores*—old *Taubolt businesses,* Donaldson recalled from Peterson's helpful little list. "I'm hopin' *you're* gonna understand *us* better. *That's* what this meetin's about. You were brought to Taubolt a month or two ago by people who've only been here for a couple years. My family has lived in Taubolt for five generations, Mr. Donaldson—*five generations*—and those trees you started cuttin' down last week were old back when my great, great, great, grandfather got here. Can you understand how ill-mannered it was to chop into five generations of this community's life without so much as consultin' anyone who *belongs* here?"

Two minutes in, and Donaldson already felt like a ten-year-old bent across his daddy's knee with his pants yanked down. Personally, he'd have preferred just to apologize and get this all behind him, but, in a town this small, one careless apology could cost him all appearance of authority—especially with Taubolt's cocky kids. He'd be finished here then. "Believe me, Mr. Holt," Donaldson said, trying to look charmingly disarmed instead of just red-faced, "no one regrets that misunderstanding more than I do. Though it pains me to say so now, that ring of trees looked like nothing but a tangled clump of wild old cypress to me then. Had that been private land, I would, of course, have consulted with the owner first. Unfortunately, those trees *are* on undesignated county property, so the county's who I went to."

"But, who told you that law enforcement was about landscaping to begin with?" asked Alice Mayfield. "I understand you were intending to mow and limb the entire headlands. We *like* it 'wild,' as you put it, Mr. Donaldson, as do the tourists on which this town's economy depends. Taubolt's *wild* beauty is part of what they come to see."

"Ma'am," Donaldson said patiently, "I appreciate that point, but my job here is to create a safe and secure environment for this town's residents and those same tourists. Apprehension of wrongdoers becomes extremely difficult, especially working without backup here, when they can just run a block in any direction and hide in the long grass and dense thickets currently surrounding this site. I thought it wiser to deprive Taubolt's criminals of that advantage. In addition, I'm sorry to say, such ready concealment also serves to induce your kids to all kinds of illegal behavior."

"Such as?" scowled Alex Carlson, Nacho's father.

"Much as you may not want to hear it," Donaldson said, "those thickets provide perfect hideouts for kids who want to sit around smokin' dope." He shrugged. "Prune the limbs to five or six feet above the ground, cut some of that grass, their concealment's gone, and lots of people might consider the landscape beautified."

"Ain't you been payin' attention?" Franklin growled. "We don't want our landscape *beautified*! Like Alice said, it's plenty beautiful already—for better or worse."

So much for risking reasonable suggestions. Donaldson thought wearily.

"First of all, Officer Donaldson," said Bridget O'Reilly, "the idea that anybody's smoking dope in that ring of trees is ridiculous. I would certainly know if anything like that were happening a hundred yards behind my school."

Donaldson suppressed a smirk at such naiveté.

"And second," O'Reilly said, "I'm disturbed by the implication, both here and in your conduct elsewhere, that our kids are the 'criminals' you were sent here to suppress. I'm told you've been harassing skateboarders on my school grounds, where I've welcomed them to skate, and even said things to undermine my authority at school."

"Pardon me, ma'am," Donaldson said, agitated, if unsurprised, that such dirt bags had been lying about him, "but, while I did ask one very rowdy group of boys there to disburse, I don't recall saying anything at all about you."

"You didn't tell them that my permission was beside the point?" she pressed.

The littlest damn things, he thought, recalling his remark with cross chagrin. "They've taken that statement completely out of context," Donaldson said. "In fact, I encouraged them to show you *more* respect by insisting they call you Mrs. O'Reilly instead of Bridget, as if you were just another of their buddies."

"Students here are encouraged to address all their teachers by first names, Mr. Donaldson," she replied coolly, "just as we address them. We practice *mutual* respect here. I've been teaching since before you were old enough to drive, and I've never encountered a single shred of evidence to suggest that being thought of as a friend by my students made me less respected, or less effective."

No wonder these kids are so completely out of control, thought Donaldson. "Well, I'll have to take your word for that, Mrs. O'Reilly," he said aloud. Then, in a flash of diplomatic inspiration, he grinned and added, "Though one look at you suggests you're assertion about our relative ages is pure exaggeration."

"Whatever you may think, Mr. Donaldson," she replied sternly, "flattery gets my students nowhere either."

Mayday, mayday. Am surrounded and outnumbered, thought Donaldson. *Urgently requesting backup.*

"It seems to me we're ganging up on you a little, Officer Donaldson," said Peterson, as if reading his mind, "and I assure you, that's not what we came here to do." He directed a solicitous glance at his compatriots before continuing. "I have no doubt that you're doing a very difficult job as conscientiously as possible, and we just want the same things you do, I think. A safe, secure community where people get along the way we did all the time here just a few short years ago."

The puppet master speaks, Donaldson thought. Having let the "bad cops" do their work, Peterson was weighing in now as the peacemaker. He was good, Donaldson had to admit. Better than Hamilton, who employed her troops with all the subtlety of a fire-crazed cow, but did Peterson really think this game was going to fool a trained officer?

"I think we're all on the same page about the headlands now," Peterson went blithely on. "The more important issue, for me, is this business with Nacho and GB."

"Out of my hands," Donaldson quickly insisted, seeing where this was going now. "Those boys instigated a full-on brawl, Mr. Peterson."

"Trying to prevent irreparable harm to a local landmark," Nacho's father interjected, "which, I think we all agree now, was being damaged in error to start with."

"Your boy and his friend broke the nose of a county employee, Mr. Carlson, and destroyed county property, namely two valuable chainsaws. I had no choice but to arrest them. It's a court matter now. You'll have to take it up there."

"Perhaps you're right," Peterson said. "But what confuses us is your decision to recommend lengthy jail time, and to have them hold GB without bail before his trial. This seems neither proportionate, nor constructive."

"Assault is a very serious crime, Mr. Peterson," said Donaldson, irritated to be told his business by a schoolteacher—especially one from such an undisciplined school.

"*Whose* assault?" snapped Franklin. "Good Lord, you are quick to forget your own errors, aren't you! Why can't you be so forgiving with others?" When Peterson shot the man a pleading look, Franklin drew a deep breath, and said more quietly, "This is a damn good boy we're talkin' about. A bit puckish, yes, but I've known Nacho all his life, and if he's got any business in jail, I'll eat three copies of your whole report on this matter."

Donaldson smiled despite himself. The man clearly had no idea how much paper was actually involved. "As for having the other boy held," he continued, overlooking Franklin's tempting bet, "he's an obvious flight risk, and frankly, I'm unclear why we're discussing him at all. A drifter here for less than two weeks? What's he to any of you?"

"Nacho introduced GB to several of us," said Tom Connolly, who'd been silent until now. "He's seems to be a good kid who's just had a very rough time. His folks are dead. He didn't come here to make trouble. He was looking for a job and an apartment to rent as soon as he had an income."

"I've had the chance to get to know him too," said Peterson. "*He* came to *me,* hoping to get back into school. The juvenile justice code is full of talk about 'the best interests of the child,' and rehabilitation, I believe. Does throwing GB into jail just as he's seeking education and a job in a community that wants him seem like the best way to pursue that? However misguided their actions may have been, they *were* seeking to protect their community, not stealing a car or robbing a liquor store."

Geez! thought Donaldson. That kid had sure worked them good! These gullible bleeding hearts wouldn't last ten seconds in the real world.

"All we wish to suggest," Peterson pleaded, "is that, while little seems likely to be accomplished by throwing two wool-headed kids into prison for six months, where they'll likely learn to be real criminals, a great deal might be accomplished to improve this community's relationship with you, and their cooperation with the law you represent, if we could find some more constructive punishment that you felt as comfortable recommending to the court."

"You ever think of becoming a lawyer, Mr. Peterson?" Donaldson smiled, careful to make it sound like a compliment.

"I find teaching adventurous enough." Peterson smiled back.

"Well, I appreciate what you're saying," said Donaldson, "but I've already told you, this is a court matter now, and it's the judge you should be saying all this to. I'd like to help you, but at this point I'm nearly as far out of the loop as anyone else."

Unfortunately, once Peterson bit into something, it seemed he held on like a dead python, and somehow, half an hour later, Donaldson had agreed to change his recommendation of jail time to probation and eighty hours of community service for each of the boys, repairing damage done by skateboards around town, public apologies, and a bit of free expert computer service to the school tacked on for Nacho. *Just terrific,* Donaldson thought, smiling daggers at Peterson's departing back. There went the one thing he'd done since coming to Taubolt that had truly satisfied Hamilton.

✸

As he sat correcting papers, a knock brought Joby's eyes up to find GB standing shyly in the entrance to his classroom.

"GB!" Joby said, getting up to greet him. "Welcome back."

"Thank you, Mr. Peterson." GB smiled uncertainly.

"It's Joby." Joby grinned. "Mr. Peterson's my father, remember?"

"Yeah, okay," GB smiled as they shook hands. "it just still weird, callin' teachers by their first names," He ducked his head. "You know."

"Yeah, I know," said Joby. "It all seemed weird to me when I first got here too. In fact," he said, nostalgically, "it was about this same time of year. You're going to like Christmas here, GB."

"I wanted to come thank you," GB said quietly, "for helping me so much. The Carlsons told me everything you did while we were driving back. And getting me that job. You don't know what it means. I thought for sure they'd just kick me out of town."

"You belong here," said Joby. "We weren't about to let that happen. Have you been over to see Muriel yet at the Heron's Bowl?"

"Yeah," GB smiled. "She'll be fun to work for."

"Just watch out for her sense of humor," Joby said. "Her son's a friend of mine, and believe me, a tendency for sadistic pranks runs in their family."

"I didn't meet him," said GB.

"No," Joby said, feeling the smile leave his face. "He and some friends ran into demons in November. Two of them were killed." The waves of grief were always smaller now, but still managed to surprise him. "Cob was sent away for his own protection."

"Sent where?" GB asked. "Where is there for us besides here?"

Joby hesitated. The Garden Coast's existence was under tighter raps than ever. With Ferristaff no longer around to draw attention to it, everyone just hoped the demons would have no reason to probe so far north. Still, GB had been vetted by several members of the council. The address in Seattle GB had given them checked out: gutted by fire two years earlier, a couple dead, their son still missing. Joby saw no reason not to answer GB's question. He was one of them now.

"He's in a place called the Garden Coast, well north of here," said Joby. "GB, what I'm telling you is one of our most closely guarded secrets. It's vital that no demon ever have reason to suspect it's there. You mustn't speak of it to anyone unless they bring it up. Okay?"

"Sure," GB said. "You get good at keeping secrets on the street. Does Nacho know about it?"

"We all do," Joby said. "Everyone who's of the blood, I mean. That's why I'm telling you. In fact, quite a few of us are up there now working to hide it more thoroughly, and preparing for the worst if it's found. You may end up helping them yourself, once you've settled in here."

"Have you been there?" GB asked.

"Just once," said Joby. "It was quite beautiful, but I'd be of no use up there now."

"Why not?" GB said, giving Joby another shy smile. "You seem pretty helpful."

"What they're doing takes all kinds of power I don't have," Joby said wistfully.

"That's not what I heard," said GB. "If you're of the blood, you've got powers."

"Well, yes, I have been told that," Joby sighed. "But if so, mine are hidden way too well to find. Since all the trouble started I've tried, a couple times, to do things, or even just to sense this power everybody says I have. But nothing happens. I've talked to Solomon about it, and—"

"He's one of the ancients, right?" asked GB, his eyes suddenly alight.

"Yes," Joby said. "I forgot you hadn't met him yet. He and Jake are both stretched pretty thin, as you can imagine."

"So, Solomon said you don't have powers?" GB said skeptically.

"Not exactly," Joby said. "Just that it's much harder for someone who wasn't raised to use them early. He says it's like being French. Either you're born and raised that way, or you're toast."

"Yeah, but . . . maybe I shouldn't be questioning an ancient," GB said hesitantly, "but I'm not sure that's right."

"Well, the proof is in the pudding." Joby shrugged. "Like I said, I've tried."

"You didn't try with me," GB said. "I think . . . I could help you do it."

Having resigned himself once to being a magical retard, Joby wasn't eager to jump through still more pointless hoops. "That's very kind of you, GB," he said, "but—"

"You gotta let me try, at least," said GB. "You've done all this stuff for me. I really wanna do this for you. Okay?"

"Well, what did you have in mind?" Joby said, seeing no way around it without completely rebuffing GB's generosity. Might as well fail one more time and have it done.

"Okay," GB said, heading for a table at the back of Joby's room. "Let's sit here."

"We're going to do it now?" Joby asked. "Here?"

"Good as anyplace." GB shrugged. "We'll be able to see if anyone comes in."

"What exactly are we going to do?" Joby asked, sitting down beside him.

"First, we have to find it," GB said. "Sounds like you lost it pretty early. But it's gotta still be in there, and once you remember what it felt like, the rest'll be like swimming." He smiled. "Once you've done it, you can do it."

"Uh-huh," Joby said, certain that GB was in for a disappointment. "And if there's no magic in there to remember?"

"It's there," GB said firmly. "Nacho says you use it all the time without knowing, so we prob'ly don't even have to look that far back" He turned to Joby, seeming suddenly uncomfortable again. "But, here's the deal. You gotta promise not to tell anyone how we did this, okay?" His expression became grave. "I mean *seriously* promise."

"Why?" Joby said uncomfortably. "What are you going to do?"

GB said nothing for a moment, then, "If I tell you, will you promise not to even tell the Council what I said?"

"That depends on what it is, GB. To be honest, it's sounding like whatever you've got in mind is nothing we should be doing anyway."

"It's nothing bad," GB insisted earnestly. "It's just that . . . when people find out what I can do, they get all tweaked sometimes. So . . . so I just don't let them know I can."

"Are you going to tell me what it is?" Joby pressed.

GB sighed, seeming braced for trouble. "I can sort of get in people's heads and . . . look around for things."

"*You read minds?*" Joby said. Then, less comfortably, "Are you doing it now?"

"No!" GB said hotly. "That's what I'm talkin' about! The minute people find out, they get all paranoid. But it doesn't just happen. I have to work at it, and I *never* do it without permission. Anyone who uses the power at all would feel me in there in a second anyway, but people still treat me like some kind of peepin' Tom," he frowned. "So now I've told you. You can trust me or not. It's your call." His sullen expression made his expectation clear. "If you tell, I'll just go find some other town to live in."

Joby wondered uncomfortably whether other people around Taubolt had been reading his mind. "You can't be the only one who has this gift," he said.

"Most of us can send things *into* other people's minds," GB said, "but being able to pull things *out*; that's rare." He shrugged unhappily. "Lucky me."

"Is it . . . unpleasant?" Joby asked.

"It doesn't hurt, if that's what you mean," said GB. "Might feel a little strange, is all." He looked hopefully at Joby. "You're gonna let me?"

"I might," Joby said, still trying to decide.

"And you won't tell anyone?" GB asked.

"No," Joby said. "I won't betray your trust. But I'm counting on you not to betray mine either by doing anything I'll be sorry for later."

"I won't," GB enthused. "Honest! Okay. First, lay your hands out flat on the table, and I'll put mine on top of yours." When they'd done so, GB said, "Now close your eyes and get relaxed. Think about fallin' asleep or something . . . On a warm day. . . . Let your body just slow down, your breathing, your blood . . . everything gettin' slower."

They were silent as Joby let himself relax, noting that GB's hands were very warm, and getting warmer.

"Okay," GB said. "I'm gonna start lookin'. It feels different for different people. It could feel like gettin' dizzy, or like your ears are ringin', or even like you're forgettin' things. But I won't do anything to hurt you, and I'll get out the minute you ask, okay?"

Joby nodded, tensing up a bit despite himself.

"Okay," GB said, "now, when I find what we're lookin' for, you'll sort of see it—like a daydream. Latch on to that and concentrate until the dream gets stronger. Ready?"

Joby took a deep breath and nodded again, then felt it, right away, like a waterfall of inaudible voices in his mind. "Wow," he whispered.

"Shhhh," GB said. "Pay attention, watch."

For a long while nothing changed. Joby just felt GB's feather-light presence sifting through his mind like a barber's fingers running through his hair. It was kind of relaxing, really. "Nothing's happening," he said at last.

"You always use such tiny brushes of power," GB replied. "I can't find anything big enough to make you see it."

"It feels kind of neat though." Joby smiled. "God, this is weird."

"Keep quiet," GB urged, then uttered a soft exclamation and said, "There!" Joby felt a sudden plunging sensation, as if he'd lost his balance. His hands clamped down involuntarily on the tabletop beneath GB's. "Relax," GB said calmly. "Can you see it? Man! How could *anybody* miss a thing like *that?*"

As GB spoke, Joby had already begun to slip into a dream of astonishing vividness, both frightening and fascinating—not just images but sound and touch—all his senses. Soon GB's voice was all that proved he was still in his classroom.

"Where is this?" GB asked.

"It's the lake!" Joby said, recognizing his surroundings in amazement. "I remember this! This was our swimming hole."

As Joby spoke, the experience ceased to feel like mere memory at all. The rising sun crested trees across the lake to spill across the rock ledge where he sat naked and dripping in the early sun, covered in undulating reflections of sunlight, and feeling suddenly as wild, as still and beautiful as everything around him. Lost in light and warmth, he gazed out across the dazzling water, and became aware of movement all around him in the silence.

Tiny flies danced on the lake's surface. Bees and dragonflies darted all along the shore. Ants searched rocks and pebbles for morsels to carry to their queen. Thistle seeds and iridescent strands of gossamer drifted through the air, back lit with rainbow fire by the rising sun, until it seemed the entire world was one slow, swirling, dance of glinting, golden illumination. It was the strangest feeling, yet familiar in some nameless way as well. A small wasp landed on Joby's arm, carrying the rainbow in its wings, but he felt no fear of being stung, only the tickling touch of kin. A bottle fly, also covered in rainbows, landed on his knee; one more intimate connection with the moving, luminous scheme of life that stretched away across the lake into the forest beyond, and on out of sight. With a surreal surge of wholeness and well being, Joby wondered how he'd stumbled into this sudden fairyland, and what might happen if he tried reaching farther into—

"Whaaaaaaawhoooo!"

The shout and several pounding steps behind him were all the warning he received before Jupiter's body came hurtling past him to land like a depth charge in the lake, drenching Joby and his perch with spray, and shattering the spell.

"Jupiter!" Joby shouted, filled with delight to see the boy alive.

"Were you *blind?*" came GB's voice.

The dream dissolved in shards of light and sound as Joby's eyes flew open, swimming in unshed tears.

"How could you feel all that and not notice?" GB laughed, seeming oblivious to Joby's sudden pang of grief at having had and lost his young friend yet again.

"Feel what?" Joby asked, pulling himself forcefully back into the present.

"That was *it,* man!" GB said incredulously. "What'd you think, your average tourist sees the whole world edged in fire? You could've flown across that lake and taken half the water with you filled with that much power!" GB shook his head and laughed again. "No gifts, huh?"

Joby was astonished. "You mean that feeling was—"

"The power we all tap into," GB nodded, "I anchored that memory in your conscious mind before I pulled out, so it should come back pretty easy when you want it. Now all you have to do is learn to find that feeling in yourself again, then aim it with your will, and things will start to *happen,* dude."

"Like what?" Joby said, still filled with disbelief.

"Let's find out." GB grinned. Reaching into his coat pocket, he pulled out a book of paper matches, tore one loose, and laid it on the table between them. "Here's what you do," he said. "Try to fill up with the memory of that morning—your whole body, not just your head. Then focus that feeling on what you want the match to do until it does."

"That's all?" Joby said. "But I still don't know what I'm doing."

"There's nothin' to know," GB insisted patiently. "Once you've learned to tap in, you don't have to know how it works any more than you know how you're makin' your lungs fill up or your legs move. You just want 'em to, and they do. Tell 'em not to and they don't. For us, the power's built in like that too."

Doubting it could really be so easy, Joby concentrated on the match and reached for the strange ecstasy GB had helped him recall a moment earlier, amazed at how effortlessly the seductive feeling returned now. At first, he imagined the match sprouting wings and fluttering off like a butterfly, but that seemed too hard to hope for on a first try, so he decided just to make it light, since that's what matches did anyway.

Staring at the match, the memory of "power" grow even fiercer within him, becoming a kind of pressure in his face as the image of the match aflame grew more vivid in his mind. With a smile, Joby started to believe it might actually happen, and—

The match went up all at once—not just its tip, but the entire length of it! Joby lurched back in surprise, then lunged forward to beat it out with his cupped palm. He'd been so sure nothing would happen that he'd never worried about scorching the tabletop.

"Kind of a boring choice," GB grinned, "but not bad for a beginner."

Joby gaped at him in stunned disbelief.

"Hey, that wasn't me," GB said with mild amusement. "You're in, man."

"What do I do now?" Joby asked, still in a daze.

"Whatever you want," GB shrugged happily. "Practice, I guess. I can help you if you want, but we'll have to do it someplace private, so people don't start askin' questions. In fact," GB said, looking troubled again, "maybe you better wait a while before you show people, or they'll think it was awful sudden and I'll get discovered."

"All right," Joby said, still too overwhelmed to think straight. "We can meet in my room at the inn or somewhere in the woods." He shook his head in wonder. He'd done magic! Real magic! Snap! Just like that, his whole world had changed again.

❊

Agnes stood inside one of Taubolt's newest boutiques, discreetly concealed behind reflections in the store's large plateglass window, and watched Joby Peterson being fawned over by a crowd of hooligans up the street. Since getting Nacho Carlson and that vagrant boy off the hook, he'd become the darling of delinquents everywhere.

Community service, Agnes thought with contempt. What impression was *that* likely to make on anyone? No one on her side of the issue had even been informed of the underhanded coup where that decision had been made. She'd clearly placed far too much trust in Donaldson—not a mistake she'd make again.

Turning away in disgust, she walked out of the store in a huff just as Peterson's band of thieves produced a burst of braying laughter at some doubtless filthy joke. The sound brought back her first encounter with him in the Heron's Bowl all those years before. The proof of his poor character had been plain even then. What was such a perverse young man doing teaching school? She'd be looking into *that* immediately.

❊

It all seemed very curious, Merlin thought as he stood outside his grandson's room waiting for Joby to answer his knock. Joby had sent him a general delivery letter, of all things, saying he had something urgent to discuss. Admittedly, it was a lengthy hike to Merlin's house up on Avalon Ridge, and, yes, he had been gone a lot, what with all the work involved in defending Taubolt, and it was true that "Solomon" did not have a phone. Still, a letter by post? Joby was lucky it had come to Merlin's attention at all. Why had he not just left a message with anyone on the Council? And why was he not answering now? Mrs. Lindsay had seemed quite sure about seeing Joby come in. Merlin knocked again, suppressing a distasteful hybrid of irritation and concern.

"Come in," Joby called, sounding muffled and unwell somehow.

"Joby?" Merlin called back. "It's Solomon. I can come back if you're sleeping?"

Receiving no answer at all, Merlin's concern increased. Finding the door unlocked, he opened it and peered inside. No one was there. Early evening light poured through the half-open window onto Joby's unmade bed. A chilly breeze ruffled class assignments stacked neatly on Joby's desk. That was all. Yet Merlin had heard someone call to him quite clearly. Seeing Joby's partly opened closet door, Merlin went with growing discomfort to see if Joby were inside it for some reason. When he pulled the door open, however, what he found left him gaping in disbelief.

Leaning into Joby's modest wardrobe was a woman Merlin hadn't seen in centuries, dressed precisely as he'd seen her last, just before she had betrayed him.

"Nimue!" he exclaimed, aghast.

"You remember! After all this time," she grinned coquettishly, "I'm flattered."

Behind him, the merest breath of air and a soft click as Joby's room door closed. Merlin whirled, still dazed with disbelief, to find an adolescent boy of astonishing beauty smiling slyly from across the room. His fair hair was shot with miser's gold, his chiseled features rife with malice, his blue eyes, icy. Merlin knew him instantly for Hell's master made no effort to shield himself from Merlin's probing mind. *"Lucifer!"* Merlin gasped.

"Very good." The fair boy smiled. "Not one of your celebrated Council members has managed to see through my disguise at all. But then, I didn't want them to. If you don't mind, however, I prefer GB at present." The boy moved gracefully to place himself between Merlin and the door, as if that mattered now. "Kallaystra, dear. Come say hello to the man who's caused us all this trouble," GB said, waving vaguely at his body.

"We've met. Several times," she said, stepping out of Joby's closet to stand behind Merlin and run her hands seductively across his shoulders and down one arm. "I wore this," she gestured like a Vegas showgirl—not just at her medieval attire, but at her face and form as well—"in honor of the last one."

Merlin barely managed not to groan. One good forgery of Joby's signature was all it had taken to breach his defenses. How could he have been so stupid? More to the point, in how many dreadful ways would he and who knew how many others pay for it now?

"It's amazing that I didn't guess your identity earlier," said Lucifer. "Able to hide from celestial eyes and fend off the wrath of demons. Who else but that troublesome half-breed, Merlin? Or should I say Solomon? No, wait, it's Mary too, isn't it? So nice to have you sorted out at last, though I confess I'd no idea you were still around."

"I've lived quietly," Merlin said, struggling to maintain his composure. Against Lucifer himself, he'd have stood no chance at combat and little of escape. Against both of them, without more preparation, he stood no chance at all.

The too-pretty boy sidled closer, his every gesture filled with subtle threat. "So what is *your* interest in this matter, Merlin? I'd think a man of your distinction would have bigger fish to fry than the fate of one obscure young man in a tiny town like Taubolt."

"You have the power to destroy me," Merlin said, ignoring the question. "But I will make you pay for it. I *can* make you pay."

"Destroy you?" said the boy. "I've no such intention, old man. Not *yet*. I want you alive to watch as I destroy your *grandson*. That's who we're talking about, isn't it? The grandfather from Taubolt who hasn't any past. The dead old man who gave Joby his beloved book of fairy tales. What a lot of roles you have performed in this affair. It's practically a one-man play, only, you're not the *one man* it's supposed to be about." The boy finally let his mocking smile slip. "You've been no end of trouble, if you want to know the truth, and last time I checked, you were still serving Heaven. Does that place you squarely next to Gabriel on the reservations list for my little summer camp? I think it does," he growled. "And for what? I am bound to win at this point. Even a bleeding heart like the Creator's can justify only so much illegal interference before being forced to default. You can't imagine how much I appreciate your help with that. I'm sure the whole *world* will want to thank you—if there's time."

"The Creator would never have entered into any wager you were bound to win," Merlin said defiantly.

"The Creator's miscalculations are piling up enormously, if you haven't noticed," Lucifer countered. "I mean, if you're going to trot Arthur out again, why on earth would you send Mordred too? It's that kind of cockiness that's lost Him this whole contest."

"Arthur?" Merlin asked, confused. "Mordred? What are you talking about?"

After gazing at him in bemusement, Lucifer burst into delighted laughter, joined by Kallaystra. "You really don't know, do you! Destiny's own device, utterly unwitting! Oh, that's rich!"

"What are you two cackling about?" Merlin asked, annoyed to be caught so transparently off guard. "What's Arthur got to do with this?"

"Spirited away to sleep until the world has need of him again," Kallaystra murmured in his ear. "Isn't that how the story goes?"

Lucifer suffered another bout of giggling, then said, "That you should be the one to bring him back into the world this way is rich enough, but not even to know, now *that* is entertaining. Really," he chortled, "every time I find myself convinced He hasn't any sense of humor, He surprises me with something like this!"

It took another moment for Merlin to decipher their ravings. Then it was all he could do to keep his legs beneath him. His grandson . . . was . . . Merlin nearly moaned aloud to think that his first concession to love since Nimue should have plunged that poor boy's soul a *second* time into such ordeal. "You lie," he insisted palely. "And Mordred was an incest. Joby has no sisters. Not even any cousins."

"A bastard son is a bastard son," the boy said sardonically. "The niceties are unimportant, surely. Either way, your great grandson is going to deliver you grandson to me *again*." He gave Merlin a chiding smile. "Or were you even unaware that Hawk was Joby's child? My goodness, what a lot of things you've overlooked."

"You can't possibly know all this," said Merlin. "You're speculating."

"You'd be amazed at what I know," the boy said icily. "Our dear, trusting Joby has let me riffle freely through his mind. I know more about him now than he does himself *and* about everyone he's met here, everything he's done, everywhere he's been. That little shard of Eden you've all been hiding up north will make a *splendid* bonfire."

"You'll have to get through Michael first," said Merlin. "He will be nowhere near as easy to deceive as I was."

"But, my dear Merlin, I thought we had been over this," said the boy. "Michael is required, just as your were, to refrain from interfering. While I concede that he's a fiercer foe, he's also got a reputation for obedience that, I must say, puts yours to shame."

"The Garden has nothing to do with Joby!" Merlin spat. "Michael's not a fool!" *As I am,* Merlin thought bleakly.

"But it *will* have *everything* to do with Joby when he goes up to help them save it." Lucifer smirked. "Did I forget to mention that I'm teaching Joby magic now? In fact, I'm supposed to meet him for a lesson right here in several minutes. I'll be right beside him when he finds your body. How poignant. He's quite skillful actually. When *I'm* doing all his tricks, at least. What a good thing *someone's* kept him ignorant of what it's really like to use such power, or I doubt he'd have fallen for my useful substitutions."

Merlin could no longer help closing his eyes and looking down in shame. Michael had been right all along. His meddling had brought them all to this. Given Kallaystra's choice of costume, he thought he knew what they intended. They were going to make him fail Arthur again, and in exactly the same way. They would think it deliciously cruel to repeat every detail as perfectly as possible.

"No need to look so sad," Lucifer assured him. "I'll be here to take on Joby's care and feeding while you're gone. Just because I'm administering his wounds doesn't mean I'd let him suffer them alone. I am compassionate that way. In fact, I'm such a softy that, though I'm now intimately aware of nearly every child of dawn in this village, I'm not going to destroy any of them. They're Joby's people after all. Why not let him do it?"

"Joby comes," Kallaystra said at Merlin's shoulder. "He's just outside the inn."

"Alas, it's showtime," sighed the wickedly lovely boy. "And, while I did promise you could watch, I cannot have you meddling anymore."

In the instant left him, Merlin mashed his own tongue between his teeth hard enough to draw blood, and spat on the floor at fallen angel's feet. Praying that Lucifer would simply take it for a final gesture of contempt, he snarled, "I defy you to the—"

"Last." Lucifer finished as Merlin's body went rigid and collapsed. "You've made that stupidly clear several times now." Lucifer and Kallaystra came to gaze down at Merlin's frozen but quite conscious form. "Not to worry," drawled the boy. "I'll make certain they notice you're not dead. I suspect they'll take you to that lovely hospital in Santa Rosa where poor Lance breathed his last—again. They've lots of specialists in stroke and coma there. Your body will receive the best of care, and, of course, I wouldn't dream of leaving your poor, imprisoned mind without a ringside seat here on the home front." Merlin felt his conscious self yanked rudely from his body. "Crystal caves are so passé," the boy grimaced in distaste. "Let's try something more in vogue."

Seconds later, Merlin found himself standing in a vast, deserted shopping mall. Irritating muzak wafted toward him from somewhere high above, and every plateglass window for as far as he could see held bank upon bank of television screens. It seemed that all the stores sold only televisions here, none of which showed anything but Taubolt. It was all far bleaker than the crystal cave had ever been.

But Lucifer had goofed again; for Merlin could still feel the tiny thread that tugged between his spirit here and that tiny spot of blood he'd left on Joby's floor. It would take quite a while to follow that gossamer trail back to consciousness through all the labyrinthine knots that separated Merlin from the bit of himself that Lucifer's spell had missed, but there was nothing to distract him from the task, and he set his mind to it immediately, hoping Joby wouldn't pick this moment to wash his floors.

31

(Making Mordred)

"Six months?" Kallaystra shrieked. "It would be impossible in twice the time!"

"Nonetheless, those are his instructions." Basquel shrugged, his satisfaction so poorly concealed that Kallaystra longed to make cinders of him then and there. "He holds *you* responsible, I fear, for having overlooked the boy's true paternity for so *many* years."

"Malcephalon was still in charge then!" Kallaystra protested.

"Ah, but he's not here to blame now, is he." Basquel smiled.

"Joby and the girl were estranged!" Kallaystra insisted angrily. "She was three thousand miles away, and out of his life forever, we assumed. What reason was there to waste resources watching her and that pathetic alcoholic when Joby was the import—"

"What *reason?*" Basquel interrupted, sounding scandalized. "This was Guinevere, Kallaystra! The love of Joby's life! Of both his lives!"

"Lucifer didn't say that to us *then!*" she snapped, forgetting to contain herself.

"Surely you are not blaming our master," Basquel said, hopeful.

"Of course not," she said through gritted teeth. "I mean only that we *did* and *do exactly* as we're told to."

"Ah. Well, that's wise," Basquel said. "And I'd find some way to do exactly as you're told this time too. You know how touchy he's been since deciding to don flesh like all the rest of us," Basquel pretended to commiserate. "The fact that now, with Merlin gone, his role as GB leaves him the only one still forced to bear that indignity has not helped his patience either."

Daring to say no more in front of Lucifer's latest tool, Kallaystra simply glared at Basquel, wondering if he were really so stupid that he could stand there grinning at her and not see what happened to their master's *favorites* as soon as something made him angry. Having ridden her into the ground, he now clearly meant to tack his own poor planning to her back and drive her off into the wilderness like a sacrificial goat. It would serve Basquel right to get her canned, and end up tied to this post in her place.

"Even if I succeed," Kallaystra fumed, "does he think no one will notice such a drastic transformation and grow suspicious of the little changeling in their midst?"

"I don't think he cares about suspicion now. Even Joby knows we're here. All our master cares is that the boy is rendered pliable in time. Those around him will likely chalk it up to the effect of grief and trauma anyway. Just watch him like a hawk, as they say, and do that voodoo that you do so well." Basquel grinned in smug amusement.

"If I whisper in his ear night and day without ceasing, I will be lucky to achieve half of what our master asks," she growled. Lucifer was clearly setting her up to fail despite all she'd done to get them here. That he had sent a buffoon like Basquel to deliver these instructions was ample proof of his displeasure. But could he really be so stupid as to discard the sharpest tool left in his shed just to satisfy this latest fit of pique?

"Such strategic matters require *direct* communication," Kallaystra said, turning her back on Basquel to go take her life into her hands. "I must speak with him myself."

"Good luck," Basquel said cheerfully. "I shall miss you when you're gone."

Yes, you will, you rotund turd, she thought. *Be careful what you wish for.*

✳

Donaldson hung up the telephone in a state of delirious shock. After reading Mansfield's letter, he had called immediately to make sure it wasn't some kind of hoax. Mansfield had hardly been effusive, rudely warning Donaldson that if he screwed up this time it would be the end of him entirely. But it was true! Donaldson was being promoted to deputy sheriff, and four officers transferred to Taubolt under his command! His substation was even being enlarged to contain a jail! It made Donaldson's head spin!

If anything, he'd been expecting to be replaced at any moment since pissing Hamilton off with his concessions to Joby Peterson in December. That had been a big mistake. As intimidating as Peterson's old-school crew had seemed, it had not taken Donaldson long to figure out who was actually going to call up Mansfield and make trouble. Hamilton had been on his butt like a boil ever since.

Far worse, the town's periodic arsons, muggings, and vandalisms hadn't fallen off at all, yet he'd apprehended not a single likely suspect yet. Whoever was behind these crimes was unbelievably slick. Never any witness descriptions of the perp. Never a shred of physical evidence—except the crime itself. It was beginning to seem downright unnatural. Had detectives sent out from the county seat not been as stumped as Donaldson himself, he was sure his ass would have been grass months earlier. Nonetheless, it seemed that somehow he had not just survived, but thrived!

He got up to do a little two-step around his chair, still clutching Mansfield's letter, which, of course, had made the price tag for this miraculous boon quite clear. Donaldson was expected to restore *complete* tranquility to Taubolt's crime-ridden streets and do it quickly—or there'd be hell to pay. But Donaldson was hardly worried. With four officers in a town this size, who'd get away with anything? The law was going to have some teeth around here now, baby!

His private celebration was still just warming up when he heard someone enter the substation's outer office. He went out to be of service feeling so good that he even managed not to lose his smile when he saw that it was Agnes Hamilton.

"What can I do for you this fine day, Ms. Hamilton?" he asked.

"You seem very chipper," she said dryly.

"Yessiree!" Donaldson grinned. "Spring is in the air! I can feel it!"

"Then I surmise you've heard from Sheriff Mansfield," Hamilton said crisply.

The smile slipped from Donaldson's face. How could she possibly . . . Then it all dropped into place. Hamilton's campaign for more police presence was hardly any secret.

"That's right," said Hamilton with obvious satisfaction. "You've me to thank for your sudden windfall, *Sheriff* Donaldson. When Mansfield called to let me know you'd received his letter, I just had to come by and congratulate you personally, and say how much I look forward to working *more closely* with you in the future."

※

"Well, hi Rose!" Laura smiled. "Welcome back. How was your trip?"

"It was fine. We saw some neat campuses," she lied, unable to tell Hawk's mother anything about the Garden Coast, "but I still plan on going to Brown."

"Arthur will be glad to hear that," Laura said. "But he's not here now, I'm afraid."

"I know," Rose said. "I just left him in town. I've come to see you, actually."

"How nice." Laura smiled. "I'd love to hear more about your college tour."

"And I'd love to tell you sometime," Rose said, more sincerely than Laura knew, "but I've come to talk with you about . . . about Hawk."

"Oh?" Laura said, her smile fading. "Please, come in." As they headed for the living room, Laura asked, "Are you two having trouble?"

"I'm not sure," Rose said, taking a chair beside the windows. "But I think Hawk is. I'm pretty worried about him."

"I see," said Laura as she sat down on the couch. "I am too, Rose. I might as well just say that. He's been terribly depressed since what happened in November. It meant so much to him when you and the others came over after the memorial service. He was a great deal better for a week or two, but then . . ." She sighed and shook her head. "He just started slipping even deeper than before. Nothing I or Joby try seems to help at all. Then, after Solomon's stroke last week . . ." She groaned, covering her eyes. "It just never seems to stop these days! It hit Joby pretty hard, but Arthur! It's been like watching Arthur smothered right before my eyes. I don't know what to do."

"That's what I was afraid of," said Rose, having hoped she'd just caught Hawk at a bad moment in town that morning. "That's how he was with me too. I came back full of things to tell him, and he acted like it all just caused him pain. I ran into Nacho later, and he said Hawk's not even speaking to him anymore. He was pretty irritated, actually, and he's not the only one. It's as if Hawk's *trying* to shove his friends away."

"I'm so sad to hear that," Laura said wearily. "I'd hoped . . . Maybe I should take him to a therapist or something. But I haven't been able to find one any closer than Santa Rosa, and I just didn't want to make him feel . . ."

"Sick," Rose finished sympathetically. "I think he is, though," she said quietly. "And I think something pretty drastic needs to happen, or I'm not sure what he might do to himself once he's managed to shove all of us far enough out of his life."

"He won't be shoving me or Joby anywhere," Laura said fiercely. "Or you either, I imagine," she added more gently.

"Failing to get rid of us doesn't mean he won't just remove himself," said Rose, remembering all too clearly how effortlessly he'd closed her out that morning.

"Have you got any good ideas then?" asked Laura. "I'm running pretty low."

"That's why I came to see you," Rose said. "I can only think of one, and it's *really* drastic. I didn't even want to suggest it to him until I'd talked with you."

✠

Hawk sat inside the dripping cavern where his life had gone awry, feeling like an outcrop of the cold stone surrounding him. No one but himself ever came here anymore. Without Solomon's incarnation spell, demons might be lurking on the very wind. For those of the blood, gatherings of any kind were no longer safe.

Outside the cavern mouth, surf boomed more loudly on the rocks. The tide was coming in. He'd have to leave soon if he wanted to stay dry, but he couldn't seem to move—a thought that summed up his entire existence better than any he'd come up with yet. He almost wrote it down, but even that much willful movement proved beyond him.

Solomon had always said that words had power to make sense of chaos, bring healing, defeat injustice. If so, Hawk was not half the bard he'd once imagined. The notepad on his lap was covered in line after line of writing, each one crossed out more angrily than the last. He'd stopped bothering to erase things hours ago. He'd stopped writing altogether some time later. The voices in his mind these days no longer murmured stories full of wonder and heroic daring, or even weighty consolation. Now they only whispered that his mentor would be dying soon, off in Santa Rosa, as everybody died in Taubolt now—except for Hawk, who deserved no such release.

The voices whispered now that those who'd said such reassuring things to him after Jupiter and Sky had died were merely being "nice" and, having discharged that obligation, only wished to leave both Hawk and what he'd done behind them. Hawk had several times caught Joby and GB coming out of Joby's inn, or wandering from the woods together. He had no idea what they might be doing, but it was clear that in GB Joby had found some new, and doubtless more enjoyable, "project" to occupy his time. One with more potential than Hawk could hope to offer anymore. Even Rose spent days or weeks away from him up on the Garden Coast now. Why sit here in some cave, after all, when *she* could be so *useful* elsewhere? Hawk's inner voices said that even Rose found him easier to take now at a distance. And that was for the best. Hawk felt like a filthy hand that left dark, repellent smudges on any clean surface it touched. It was less painful to be alone than to be caught in anyone's attention being *this*.

Such a short while back, he'd thought nothing could be worse than all the grief and shame and anger he'd been feeling. Now Hawk felt nothing anymore at all, which was proving even more unbearable. All around him people grieved, and cried, and comforted each other, while he, able to let nothing in or out, felt only the hopeless void. In Hawk's mind there was a janitor now, that came each day to sweep away the bodies without a hint of feeling. Something had strangled his heart, and with nothing left alive inside him, it seemed cruel that he must go on living anyway.

His attention was pried from this cesspool by the sound of someone's sloshing approach outside. When Rose's face peered through the cavern's entrance, Hawk remained utterly still, more from inertia than any particular will to hide. But when her eyes had adjusted to the darkness, she found him and came inside.

"What are you doing here?" she asked quietly. "The tide is more than halfway in, and everyone's worried sick about you."

He'd grown so still that it was hard to talk but he tried as he would not have done for anyone but Rose. "Now you can tell them I'm all right."

"Are you?" she asked softly.

What was he supposed to say?

She glanced at the pad in his lap, and asked, "Are you writing?"

"No."

Seeing the hurt in her face, Hawk was surprised to discover that he could, in fact, still feel something. The things coming from his mouth only shamed him more.

"Hawk," Rose said uncertainly. "You're obviously not okay."

You're not the way we want you anymore.

"I'm worried about you," she said when Hawk did not reply. "Everyone is."

You're a burden to everyone now.

"Hawk, please talk to me."

A surly, boorish burden . . . You're offending her.

"What would you like me to say?" Hawk murmured.

"Hawk," she sighed, coming to sit down beside him, "people can get lost in grief. It can bang them up so hard they can't find an exit, and you've been through too much."

You're not as strong as all the others . . . You can't handle this like they can.

Rose reached out and took his hands in hers. *Your hands are clammy and covered in grit . . . She's repulsed but she won't tell you so . . .* "You've got to do something to break out of this."

They can't put up with your behavior anymore.

"Your mother and I were talking," *Even your mother is talking behind your back . . . You're breaking her heart . . . filling her life with grief . . . ,* "and we both think maybe this place is the problem. I mean, Taubolt's under attack, and you know as well as I do that things are probably just going to get worse for quite a while." *They're all dealing with lots of bigger problems than your own . . . If you were just grown-up enough to see that . . .* "You haven't even had a chance to get your head above water before the next wave hits, and if you stay here, it's just likely to go on that way. We both think maybe you should leave for a while." *You should leave.* "I'll miss you terribly, but if you can put some distance between yourself and all this, maybe it would help you heal. I don't think Taubolt's going to be very good for that now," she said, giving his hands a squeeze.

You should leave.

"You could stay with your grandparents for a month or two."

You should leave.

"Even Joby thinks it might be a good idea."

There it was. *Even Joby wants you out of the way while they dealt with Taubolt's real problems.* Hawk wondered whether Joby had consulted GB about it too.

"Hawk, please say something. You're scaring me with all this silence."

You're scaring her . . . You should leave.

In the darkness behind his eyes, Hawk watched his fingers leaving gouges in the muddy rim as he lost his grip at last, and plummeted into the bottomless abyss he'd been staring into all this time. . . . He'd lost her.

"You're right," he said tonelessly. "I'll go."

He found that he could move now, if not much faster than honey over ice. He got up without a word and headed for the cave mouth, unable even to look back.

✸

"The moment is upon us," Lucifer said briskly as the triangle appeared. "I've just pried Joby's eyes open. He's headed up to see her now. Tique, you stay with him until he gets there. He was quite upset, of course, and left me like the proverbial bat out of hell in that jalopy of his. I don't want him driving into a ditch or something on the way. Timing will be crucial here."

Tique nodded sharply before vanishing.

"Trephila," Lucifer continued, "go use whatever time remains to get Laura as agitated as possible. Help her spill some milk or break some dishes. Use whatever's close at hand, and no need to be subtle. Since she's still ignorant of our existence, she's not likely to suspect anything unless you incarnate in her face."

Trephila vanished with a smile.

"Eurodia, you will stay with me in case our machinery should require any adjustment in motion. Kallaystra will have whipped the boy's wounded feelings into heat by now, but he mustn't arrive until it's all over but the crying. If this goes right, it should produce quite a blast." He actually smiled. "In the end, it's always about *timing.*"

☒

Joby took another corner much too fast, and almost lost control. What was left of his rational mind kept telling him to slow down, but the rest of him was no longer listening. He needed to hear Laura tell him that it wasn't true—more, perhaps, than he needed to live through this if it was. That embattled little corner of rational mind kept insisting that it couldn't be true—that she'd never have done this to him—or to Hawk, But after GB's innocent misapprehension, Joby had done the math again and again in his mind, and the answer just kept coming up the same. He could not believe he'd failed to see it for so long, except that Hawk already had a father! Everyone had talked about him, on and on: the abusive, alcoholic, *abandoning bastard*. It made Joby want to bash his own forehead on the steering wheel.

He arrived at last, crunched to a halt on the gravel drive beside her house, and bounded up the stairs. But as he raised his hand to knock, fear stayed his arm. What if it were true? How could he face it? He still hadn't knocked when Laura opened the door, doubtless having heard him on the stairs.

"Joby!" she said. "What's . . . Is something wrong? You look— What's happened?"

Seeing no way to ease into it, he asked, "Was Sandy Hawk's real father?"

Laura's mouth fell slightly open as panic changed her face. "How did you . . ."

"Oh God," he groaned, turning to sit down on her stairs before his legs gave way. *"Oh my God!"* he moaned again, dropping his face into his hands, weak with helpless grief. "How could you do this?" he whispered inconsolably. "To any of us?"

When she didn't answer, he turned back to find her clinging to the door frame, pale and shaking with emotion. "What was I supposed to do?" she pleaded roughly. "Joby, you were headed off to Berkeley with high honors, that whole bright future ahead of you. Was I supposed to crush all that because one night I'd gotten it into my head to seduce you? I loved you more than that!"

Her eyes had filled with tears, but Joby just felt numb with disbelief. "You *loved* me?" he demanded. "So you never let me know I had a *son*? What about all those things you told me at the hospital? How you just wanted all of me—the broken parts and all the rest? What a load of crap! You asked *me* to come out of hiding, and I did! How long did *you* plan to go on hiding this *little detail* from *me*? Forever? What about Hawk? Did you love *him* too much to let him know he had a father?"

"That isn't fair!" she wept, her grief becoming anger in an instant. "I married Sandy so he'd *have* a father! You have no idea what I've sacrificed to spare you from—"

"*Sacrificed?*" Joby cut her off, leaping up as the horror of it all unfolded in him. "*It wasn't your sacrifice to make! You took away my chance to be a father—my chance to watch my son grow up—my chance to be there when he needed me.* Do you know what I've thought every time Sandy's name was mentioned? I thought, how could that *abandoning bastard* leave this beautiful boy? But that abandoning bastard was *me! You made me an abandoning father!*"

"*How dare you!*" Laura snapped. "As if you'd left me any choice! You were a *mess,* Joby Peterson—already half out of your mind with imaginary guilt about Lindwald! What was I supposed to say? Oh, and by the way, I'm pregnant with your child too? What would you have done with *that,* Joby, on top of all the rest?"

"*I'd have married you! Ask Ben! He knows!*" Joby cried, forgetting Ben was gone. "*I told him the morning Jamie died! I was on my way to propose to you!*"

Laura slid down the sill to sit crying in the doorway. "You were in no shape . . . no shape to be a father, Joby," she sobbed into her hands. "Ben told me what you were like when he saw you in Berkeley. Couldn't even leave your damn bed, but you'd have been an *awesome* father, if only *I* had *let* you?"

"If I'd had something in the world to think about besides myself—"

"You—were—in—*no shape*—to be a *father,*" she said more fiercely, wiping at her eyes and standing up again. "Ben saw that as clearly as I did. Give us all at least a little credit before you play the blameless victim."

"*Ben knew too?*" Joby gasped, and all at once remembered, as if he'd just been there, hiding around that corner in the music room at high school, listening to his two most trusted friends discussing what they *mustn't* tell him. "Was I the only one who *didn't* get to know that Hawk was mine?"

"*Arthur!*" Laura shrilled. "His name is *Arthur!*" She began to cry again in earnest. "It was as close to naming him for you as I could come without making Sandy jealous. Can't you see anything? I never stopped loving you, Joby. I'd have given anything to have you there raising our son instead of Sandy, but how could you have—"

"And I condemned that man," Joby groaned, turning from Laura. "Of course he drank! Of course he mistreated you and ran away! There he was, knowing all the while that you were still in love with the man who'd left him holding all my baggage."

Laura made a strangled noise, then screamed, "*Get out! Get out of here, you selfish, monstrous ass!"* She whirled around and slammed the door, leaving Joby on the porch alone. From inside the house, he heard her scream again—no words, just pain, followed by a torrent of heart-wrenching sobs.

⌗

When Joby didn't answer, Hawk pounded on his door again. Joby's car was here, so he figured Joby must be too. He'd already been angry by the time he'd gotten home from his encounter with Rose. Then he'd found his mother, a sodden wreck, on the couch. It seemed there *were* still some things Hawk cared about. His mother's pain was one of them.

Hawk pounded for a third time, and was drawing breath to yell Joby's name, when the door finally lurched open. Joby looked not much better than his mother had, though that bothered Hawk not nearly as much.

"I was sleeping," Joby apologized, looking mournfully at Hawk.

"Pleasant dreams, I hope," Hawk said coldly. "What did you do to my mother?"

Joby only stared at him in dull surprise.

"You know. The woman you just demolished?" Hawk growled. "When I asked her what was wrong, she said to ask you, so I'm asking. What the hell did you do?"

"She didn't tell you?" Joby said stupidly.

"She hasn't been like this since the day my fucking father left," Hawk snapped. "Answer my question, or I'm going to write you off as fast as I did him, and you can fuck yourself 'til Hell freezes over before I talk to you again—not that you'd care, I guess, now that you've got *GB* to kiss your ass."

"Come in," Joby said wearily, walking back into his room. "It's not a conversation to have standing in the doorway."

Hawk followed Joby in, and said, "Okay, I'm inside. Now you'd better tell me fast what happened to my mom, or I'll go right back out—for good."

"Hawk," Joby sighed, folding wearily into a chair beside his stove, "your mother's kept a secret from both of us until today. When I found out, we had a pretty nasty argument, and . . ." Joby looked so bleak that Hawk didn't need him to confirm what he had guessed at first sight of his mother's condition.

"You've broken your engagement," Hawk shrugged.

"You don't seem too upset," Joby murmured sadly.

"Things don't upset me like they used to," Hawk replied, though, privately, he felt the blow as yet another evidence of the universe's enmity toward himself. "So what's the awful secret?" Hawk asked, careful not to sound as if he cared too much.

Joby stared at him in dismay. "I know you're angry Hawk, and I can understand that but I didn't want to hurt your mother. I care about her deeply."

"Huh," Hawk grunted, sitting on Joby's bed. "Just yesterday, you *loved* her."

Joby looked as though he might be going to cry, and Hawk was ambushed by a sudden stab of remorse. Not for the first time, he wondered what was wrong with him, when he'd become so cruel, so eager to wound. But then he thought about his mother's grief-swollen face, and shoved his sympathy for Joby aside. "It's now or never," Hawk said, starting to rise. "I'm leaving Taubolt tonight, like you all want me to. If you won't tell me why my mother's in this shape, I'll wait until she wants to say. Your choice."

"Tonight?" Joby said, sounding startled. "Why so sudden?"

Hawk just turned and started toward the door, tired of being stalled and jerked around by everyone. He had problems of his own to manage.

"I'm your father, Hawk," Joby said behind him.

Hawk turned back to stare, his mind still somewhere headed toward the door.

"Not Sandy. Me," said Joby. "I never knew until today." He hung his head. "I'm sorry. If there's some gentler way to tell you that, I don't know what it is."

Hawk's mind finally finished the turn his body had already made. "You can't be my father," he whispered. "How could you be my father?"

"Your mother and I were in love," Joby said without looking up. "We were together just one time, a few months before we graduated from high school." He looked up at last, his eyes like some Hawk had seen in photographs of concentration camp inmates. "I didn't know she was pregnant. She never told me."

Hawk came back and dropped onto the bed again, feeling like a sleepwalker. "So what was Sandy?"

"He was the man your mother married so that you would have a father." Joby's face was one big grimace of contrition now, which, Hawk would later surmise, might have been what put the idea in his head that all of this was Joby's fault. Whatever its genesis, the idea stuck and bloomed like napalm in Hawk's soul.

"So we spent thirteen years getting yanked around by that fucking, drunken prick, because you had a nice one-nighter with my mother and walked away without asking how it all turned out?" Such a surge of anger welled within him that Hawk had to gouge his hands into the bedspread to keep himself from getting up and giving Joby what he'd so often dreamed of giving GB.

"No," Joby protested urgently. "The next night, someone died. A friend. I felt responsible; everything went to pieces then. Your mother . . . I thought she didn't want to see me anymore. I thought she'd gone to Ben. It never crossed my mind that—"

"It never crossed your mind!" Hawk cut him off, enraged. "Well, it sure crossed mine, *Dad!* Every time my father . . . no, that *strange man* you *left* me with, every time he took a whack at me. Every time he raged around the house on some stinking bender. It *crossed my mind* that this was my father! What I got! What I *came from!* My friends had fathers who played ball with them, *Dad!* Their fathers took them camping and came to school on parent night smelling of aftershave, not barley hops. Their dads were *proud* of them. But I got Sandy, and you know what? I figured that there had to be a reason—that someone must have chosen him for me instead of all those other dads because maybe, somehow, he was all that I *deserved!*" The fury was spilling out of Hawk now like some huge volcanic tapeworm. It felt like throwing up a bad meal. He had no desire to stop; for all that he was clearly tearing Joby to pieces. "Do you have any idea how much time I've spent working all that out?" Hawk demanded. "And now it turns out, oops! That was all for nothing! He never *was* my father to begin with. My *real* father was the good, the kind, the universally admired, Joby Peterson, who'd have been the best damn father in the whole wide world if only it had *crossed his mind to inquire about my existence!*"

Surging to his feet, Hawk said, "Well, It sure has been a treat to finally meet you, *Dad,* but I've got to go now," he turned and stalked toward the door. "Before I beat the fucking crap out of you!"

"Hawk," Joby pleaded in what rags of voice his tears allowed him, "please wait."

Hawk turned back once more at the door. "You stay away from my mom," he rasped. "She's been hurt enough. You stay away from me too. You did without us all these years. No point in complicating your life now!"

Ignoring Joby's further pleas, Hawk stormed from the house and slammed himself into his car. Then he drove, far too fast and with no thought of destination, until he slid into a ditch somewhere well north of town. Without pausing to reflect on his condition or that of his car, he shoved his way out from behind the wheel, and began to walk up the hill, then hopped the fence and headed for the woods, always up, along the path of maximum exertion, trying to burn off all the fury that still pounded through him like the flumes of some huge booster rocket. But his supply of anger seemed inexhaustible, and he stopped at last atop a bald grass hill with no "up" left to travel, threw back his head to face the sky, and screamed and screamed and kept on screaming, a solid stream of mindless rage. And somewhere in that timeless span, he found himself aloft, soaring high above the wooded hills, screeching out the angry hunting songs a wounded hawk carries in its heart. Unlocked by rage, he'd finally found the power, after all those years, to change. He was an equal now—as fully of the blood as any of his peers, and he could think of no good reason to come down to earth again.

✷

"Follow him," Lucifer told Kallaystra as they watched Hawk soar away from Taubolt. "Seeing to his reeducation should be much easier out there. You've done sufficiently so far," he said, turning to pierce her with his eyes, "but remember that I hold you *personally* responsible for *completing* his transformation swiftly. I need that boy ready, and I need it *yesterday*! Fail to keep pace for an instant, and I'll take him from you and give Basquel his chance. You can regain Your strength cleaning toilets in Hell."

"Bright One," Kallaystra said sullenly, "Basquel is—"

"I know," Lucifer cut her off impatiently. "He's not as clever as yourself, but neither is he moody and defiant. He does what he is told without a lot of *attitude.* We're already much too far behind schedule. My plans *hinge* on that boy, and I'm *tired* of having to *improvise* at the last minute because my support staff couldn't cut it."

Without further *attitude,* Kallaystra spread herself upon the wind to follow Hawk.

When she'd gone, Lucifer turned to face the Triangle standing behind him. "Now *that,*" he said more brightly, "was how proper orchestration ought to look. I trust you all took notes."

32

(Spring Break)

Dear Hawk,

    How's your new job going? I'm hoping I'll get to hear about it in person. It's been such a hard winter for all of us that I decided drastic measures were called for, and convinced everyone that we should celebrate spring with a huge party on the beach to cheer up this whole town. Bonfires and barbecue—just like Halloween, but with better weather. Organizing it has been a much bigger job than I expected, but Jake's agreed to take care of security, and Kellerman's band is going to play. I've been putting flyers up all around town, and people are really getting excited. It's going to be wonderful, and I'm hoping you will come. Will you come home for my party, Hawk?

    I've appreciated your letters more than I can say. I'm sorry things got so strange between us before you left, but I hope you know I love you, Hawk, more than ever. That's only gotten clearer in your absence. It would mean so much to me to see you—face to face. Come home for the party, Hawk. Please? I'll make you glad you did.

    Whatever you decide is fine. Just let me know whenever you do.

        Love,

            Love,

                Love,

                    Rose

Rose set down her pen, and read the letter through, wondering if she'd said enough, or too much, or said it right. It was so hard to know. Hawk seemed even more changed in his letters than he had before he left, though she supposed that was to be expected. His entire life was different now. How could he not have changed? Still, the preoccupied and formal tone of his correspondence did little to reassure her. She didn't want to loose him, but even more, she just didn't want him to be lost and it felt so much as if he were, or might be soon. A career in finance? The Hawk she'd known had never cared for things like that. What about his writing? His stories? Where had all that gone?

She read the letter one more time, hesitating at the end. Joby had practically begged her to speak to Hawk on his behalf. She felt awkward about getting in the middle of all that but supposed she ought to try. Hoping that she wasn't shooting herself in the foot, she put her pen back to the paper.

> *P.S. I know you might not want to hear this, but Joby sends his love too. He's heartbroken about the way he mishandled everything, Hawk. If you ever felt like writing him a letter, even just to tell him how angry you are, I know it would mean the world to him. If I've made you mad by saying this, just erase it, and please, please come to my party anyway.*

> *P.P.S. I kissed the paper here.*

❧

There were few corporeal forms the Triangle found more entertaining than those of children. As they crept through the darkness toward Hamilton's house, they couldn't keep from giggling and shoving at each other like the real thing.

"You're such a slut, Eurodia!" Tique teased through whispered laughter. "I can't believe your mother lets you wear such clothes."

"At least *my* face isn't covered in peach fuzz," Eurodia parried with adolescent hauteur. "You look like a fruit stand."

"Shut up, both of you," Trephila grunted, a wicked grin spreading on her adolescent face. "You'll be overheard, and someone will *see* us."

Her two companions burst out in renewed laughter.

As they reached Hamilton's gate, Tique produced a brown paper bag from each of the large pockets on his low-slung cargo pants, and handed them out with stealthy glee before producing two more for himself. A blue flickering in Hamilton's living room window told them Agnes was there watching TV—the news no doubt the nightly news was confirmation of all her darkest opinions about the nasty world.

"I don't think she's gonna like this," Tique said with exaggerated trepidation. "Are we sure it's such a good idea?"

Eurodia said, hefting her bag thoughtfully. "We have been rather naughty lately."

Trephila launched her sack at Hamilton's front door, where it splattered open, spewing its rank, excremental contents in a broad arc across the neatly painted porch.

"Hey, you Nazi bitch!" Tique shouted as his arms swung back. *"Go back where you belong!"* His sacks of doggy dung burst violently on impact, one against the wall, the other in a spray of glass as it crashed through her window to rain across her living room.

"Yeah! Get outta here, you old witch!" shrilled Eurodia, launching her bag just in time to spatter Agnes herself, as she yanked the door open in a rage.

For good measure, Tique pointed at the remnants of Trephila's sack, still hanging by a paste of crap from the door frame, and it burst into flame, causing Hamilton's furious expression to grow wide-eyed with alarm.

"You've been warned!" Tique yodeled as they ran down the darkened road toward Shea Street, squealing with malicious delight. *"Get out of our town!"* He launched a spinning kick at the neighbor's mailbox as they ran past, breaking its post off just above the ground. Spring always made him frisky.

❈

Tom Connolly wondered how to slip the word "manners" into his next few answers as Ryan Garret, a young magazine reporter, concluded the second cell phone call he'd taken since their interview had started.

"Look," Garret told his phone, "this is going nowhere." He gave Tom another apologetic smile and rolled his eyes. "Just have Larry call me, okay? . . . Yeah, well I didn't set it up this way either. It's his problem; let him fix it or have him call me himself. . . . Okay. Sorry. . . . Bye." He flipped his tiny phone shut at last, dropped it back into the pocket of his trendy black coat, then, amazingly, checked his reflection in the glass cabinet doors beside Tom's desk, straightening his hair where the phone had disturbed its perfect shape and grain before turning to smile at Tom again. "Lots of crazy stuff happening at the office today. I appreciate your patience, Mr. Connolly."

"No problem," Tom said politely. "You were asking about Taubolt's recent 'crime wave,' I believe."

"Wait," Garret said, "don't talk yet." He reached down to turn his miniature recorder back on. "Okay. As I was saying, Mr. Connolly, a lot of people here seem to feel that Taubolt's become such a hotbed of unrest because of all the tourist traffic it attracts now, but others think the problem's source is local. What's your opinion?"

"My opinion is that until someone is arrested for any of these crimes, there's no way of knowing who's responsible," Tom said, he could hardly tell *CalTrends* magazine that most of Taubolt's trouble stemmed from demonic invasion.

"Is that an indictment of Taubolt's new police force, Mr. Connolly?"

"That was not my intention," Tom said, "though I *am* of the opinion that a force of five officers is a little ridiculous for a town of something under a thousand people."

"Yes, but as a number of others I interviewed point out, if one counts the tourists here on any given weekend, Taubolt's population is more than triple that now."

"Well, I guess I'd see their point better if all these new officers were investigating or arresting tourists," Tom said. "But I've seen nothing to indicate they are. So far the only population that seems to be getting much attention is Taubolt's kids."

"It's interesting you should say that," Garret replied with new enthusiasm. "You're not the first person I've talked with who seems to think that Taubolt's kids are the real source of all these problems."

"I said no such thing," Tom replied impatiently. "Taubolt's youth are definitely *not* the source of Taubolt's problems, though some of this town's newcomers seem to get a lot of mileage out of saying so. Kids make very safe scapegoats, Mr. Garret. Offending them has relatively few social or political consequences for adults frightened of tangling with their equals when there's a problem. Please keep that in mind when you're listening to those who vilify our children."

Garret's grin had grown steadily wider as Tom had spoken. "That's really good," he said. "I can quote that?"

"Be my guest," Tom growled.

"Great!" the young man enthused, slipping a thin turquoise note pad and matching pen from his breast pocket to jot down a few brief notes. "This article's going to be way better than they thought. It might even get the cover!"

Tom wasn't sure who Garret was congratulating, but he was beginning to regret agreeing to be interviewed.

"As you're obviously aware," Garret said, "lots of people here applaud Sheriff Donaldson's call to close the high school campus during lunchtimes and his efforts to keep kids from congregating in front of shops and other public places, citing some compelling examples of teen inflicted intimidation and property damage. Since you clearly disapprove of Donaldson's current approach, what alternative would you suggest?"

"What I suggest, Mr. Garret," Tom replied with careful courtesy, "is that the more our youth are shamed and punished by those they have no real power to confront, the more they will act like people always act when helpless and ashamed; defensive, resentful, angry, and eventually defiant. Children tend to see themselves as others see them, and if members of this community are sufficiently determined to prove our kids are all really dangerous criminals . . . Well, where there is a will, there is probably a way."

"Mr. Connolly," Garret said, seeming barely able to contain his elation, "you are, without a doubt, the most articulate person I have interviewed today. This sort of divergent opinion is exactly what I needed to drive this article home. I—" His cell phone burst into song again. "That'll be Larry," Garret sighed. He reached out and shook Tom's hand with his right, while pulling his communicator from its pocket with his left. "I think I've got all I need. Thank you so much for your time," he said, putting the phone to his ear, and getting up to go. "Hello," he said, as he left the office. "Yeah, hi Larry. I knew it would be you. Listen, I've got something really hot going here, so I may not be back this evening. . . . Yeah, I already told Johan that. . . . Uh-huh . . ."

Tom sat listening to the man's receding monologue until it was finally eclipsed by the thud of his downstairs door. There'd still been no word at all from those sent in search of the Cup, but Tom prayed word would come soon. He and everyone else who'd once called Taubolt home clearly needed someplace to start over.

֎

"*Hawk!*" Rose screamed joyfully, lunging through the door to wrap him in her arms. "*You came!*"

"Rule one," he said, tentatively returning her embrace. "Never miss a party."

"Oh, I'm so glad to see you!" she said, stepping back to take him in. He wore a long gray overcoat, slacks, and dress shoes, which she thought awfully heavy for the season, though it did make him look sophisticated and more handsome than ever. It seemed he'd even gotten taller, though she doubted that was possible in just five months. "Come in! My folks'll be so glad to see you." As she grabbed his hand to drag him through the door, she saw the small red sports car at the curb.

"You like it?" Hawk asked coolly when he saw her looking. "Rule two. Image counts." He punched her shoulder lightly, as if she were his little sister. "I'll take you for a ride in it. You won't believe the way it corners."

Rose was spared having to respond by her mother's arrival. "Hawk? I thought I heard your voice!" She came out and hugged him almost as fiercely as Rose had. "Tom's up in his office." She smiled. "I'll go up and tell him that you're—" She stopped, staring at the red Miata. "Is that yours?" Hawk nodded, and she gasped, "How beautiful! Did you win the lottery or something?"

"No," Hawk sighed wistfully, "I'm making payments, but someday I'll write even better cars off as a business expense." He offered Rose another self-congratulatory smile.

"Well, do come in, Hawk," said Rose's mother, glancing one more time at Hawk's new car. "I hope you're staying for dinner. I've just started fixing it, and we've got chicken coming out our ears."

"Sounds painful," Hawk laughed, grabbing Rose by the hand. "Come on," he said, as if inviting her to dinner too.

❧

"Are you sure?" Joby asked, handing Franklin the contents of his wallet without even checking to see how much it was.

"Had to take a second look," Franklin nodded. "Got a shiny red sports car now, and clothes like a TV star, but it was Hawk all right. I figured you knew he was comin'."

"No," Joby said, suddenly ashamed to look Franklin in the eyes. "Hawk doesn't . . . we're not on close terms these days." His son had been back in town for at least two days, if Franklin was correct. That Hawk had not let Joby know he was coming was painful enough, if not surprising, but that no one else had told him either hurt even more. "Did you talk to him?" Joby asked.

"I waved, and he waved back, but we didn't talk."

"Well, thanks, Franklin," Joby said, taking his bag of nails and turning to leave.

"Got some change here," Franklin said. "'Less this is a tip," he added wryly.

"Oh," Joby replied quietly, taking the twenty-plus dollars and change from Franklin's outstretched hand. "Thanks. I'm easily distracted lately."

❧

"Big money, Rose," Hawk said in grim, paternal tones. "That's what ruined Taubolt. And the only way to fight big money is with *bigger* money. I'm going to make more money than God and use it to smash people like Ferristaff and Hamilton."

Somehow Rose had imagined that if Hawk would just come home, she'd find a way to fix whatever had taken him from her. Now she saw that only his absence had made such thoughts possible.

"You make it sound so easy." She smiled as best she could.

"Nothing mysterious about money," Hawk said. "It's all just math and attitude. You learn the right equations, make the right acquaintances, the rest will follow. I've already got my foot in several very useful doors back east." He turned to give her one of his new soulless smiles—the one's that never touched his eyes. "I'm a very charming fellow, Rose. And thanks to Solomon, I know how to talk without sounding like a hick. That's all you really need, besides a magic trick or two, and the willingness to say 'money' without blushing."

It hardly even seemed like his voice, Rose thought bleakly.

"Too bad the old guy's never gonna see me do it." Hawk shrugged. "He was always big on justice."

"You mean Solomon?" Rose said, appalled at the callousness of Hawk's remark. He'd loved that man once! "Maybe he will. While he's alive there's still room for hope."

"Hope," Hawk said tonelessly. "That's one idea I may never be able to afford." He turned to her with something in his eyes at last; sadness, which was better than the vacancy. "Maybe I should hire you to hope for me. Want the job, Rose?"

On the verge of telling him off, she saw the longing in his eyes and realized that he was asking her in earnest, the only way he could allow himself to do so. It was the only time he'd asked her help in any way since coming home, and her intended retort dissolved unspoken. "If that's what you need, Hawk," she said quietly, "I'll try."

❊

The day had dawned bright and breezy; perfect weather for an outdoor party. Taubolt needed something joyful now, Rose had argued, something to bring the whole community together and remind them what it felt like to celebrate life as friends. As Ian Kellerman and his band set up their platform, and coolers full of food and drink began to trickle down the stairway to the beach, Michael watched from the bluff tops in his guise as Jake. He was not alone in questioning the wisdom of so conspicuous an event. But the fact that everyone, even tourists, were invited might make it less suspicious to the ever-present enemy, and, in her determination to organize this fete, Rose had pointed out that, precisely because the threat *was* "ever present," there would be no better time. In the end, Michael had been unable to dissuade her or

fault her motives, so it was going forward, with all the mundane and mysti-
cal protections they could muster.

Since Merlin's so-called stroke, the fine line Michael had been trying to
walk between protecting Taubolt and staying out of Joby's trial had become
almost too fine to find at all. Only recently had the angel admitted to himself
how much he had depended on the old man's willingness to rush in where
obedience forced Michael to refrain. Merlin's courage, however ill fated, no
longer merely troubled Michael; it shamed him.

❈

There were at least two hundred people on the beach, laughing around the
barbeques, flying kites, throwing Frisbees, chasing dogs, wading in the small
spring surf with children by the hand, and dancing on the sun-warmed sand
to the raucous music produced by Kellerman's Celts. It was everything Rose
had hoped for, and more. She'd been moving around the beach for hours,
saying hello to friends and strangers, and meeting friends of theirs, receiving
kudos, and enjoying the celebration when she saw her parents standing hand
in hand beside a cooler full of beers and sodas, smiling and laughing like
young lovers. She hadn't seen them look so happy and relaxed for . . . well,
maybe years. She smiled and went to join them.

"Hey there, honey!" her father enthused as she arrived. "Finally got a moment for your old man, huh?"

"You don't look so neglected." Rose grinned, glancing at her mom.

"We're having a wonderful time, Rose!" her mother said. "And we're both
so proud of you. What a marvelous thing you've put together, dear."

"Thank you," Rose replied, leaning in to hug her mother, "for all your
help and for supporting the idea." She smiled at her father. "I know you
weren't so sure about it."

"Rose," he said, joyfully embracing her in turn, "the older you get, the
more I learn from you. I've decided that when I grow up, I want to be just
like you."

Rose had hardly ever felt so happy. "I love you both so much," she said. "I
can't tell you how grateful I am—for everything you've always been and
done for me."

"You tell us all the time," her mother said, "just by being you."

"Okay," Rose laughed, feeling tears gather in her eyes. "Let's not get all
sticky right here on the beach."

"There you go," her father said, winking at her mother. "We've embarrassed
her now. It'll be three *more* hours before she comes to talk with us again."

"No it won't!" Rose protested playfully, then looked around them at the crowd, and teased, "But there must be *someone* here I haven't talked to yet."

That's when she saw Hawk coming down the beach path, and her smile faded. He'd come for thirty minutes that morning, then disappeared for hours. She had begun to wonder if he meant to come back at all. Following her gaze, her parents saw him too and seemed to understand. They smiled their farewells as she hugged them each again before rushing up to keep Hawk from going off a second time.

⚹

Hawk saw her coming well before he reached the beach, and almost turned to flee again. No doubt she'd think he didn't understand how much this shindig meant to her, or just didn't care, or even wanted to avoid her. But none of those was why he'd fled the first time. A beach full of people from his maudlin past, half of whom he'd probably offended before going east, had been uncomfortable enough. Then he'd seen Joby walk from underneath the bridge and hurried back up into town as fast as dignity allowed, wanting nothing less than to come face to face with his—that man.

Now, as Rose approached him, Hawk nudged his sunglasses higher up his nose and hoped he didn't smell too much of beer. He tried to think of how he would explain his absence, but she didn't ask where he had been. She just smiled and waved as if he'd done nothing wrong at all, which, in its way, made him just as uncomfortable.

"What's up?" Hawk asked, determined to match her nonchalance. If she wouldn't admit she was upset, he wasn't going to do it for her. He didn't play such games.

"It's going great, I think!" Rose smiled, turning back to survey the carnival-like crowd below them. She grabbed his hand and led him back down toward the beach. "Tholomey and Blue have got the most delicious chicken going at their barbecue," she said. "Remember that marinade their mother makes? Have you had lunch yet?"

Hawk shook his head, wondering if she really wasn't mad.

"Nice sunglasses," she said.

"Thanks," he answered. "Got 'em at this place in Boston. They weren't cheap, but you can't drive straight into the sunset for five days wearing junk, unless you want to go blind, I guess." He was babbling. *Be cool,* he told himself. *Just shut up, and be cool.*

"I wish you didn't have to go so soon," she said, gazing at the beach. "You'll miss all this amazing weather. Can't you stay an extra day or two?"

"It's gonna take at least four days to drive back, Rose," he said. "I've got a lot of stuff to do at work, and this is unpaid leave."

"I know," Rose sighed. "I'm just not ready to start missing you again."

"I'll come back and get you," Hawk assured her. "Soon as I've made something of myself." Rose was silent in a way that made him feel he'd said something wrong. "I don't want us out there just scraping by while all our dreams die on the vine," he said, compelled somehow to explain. "You deserve to live in style. I want to——"

She turned around and put her fingers to his lips, then leaned in to kiss him. He kissed her back, feeling sick inside. Everything was empty all the time now. . . . Even this.

"So," he said as soon as she had let him go, desperate for anything to fill the empty moment with. "We've still hardly talked about *your* work these days. How's it going up there on the Coast?"

She looked at him sadly for a moment, then turned away as if to scan the beach again, though Hawk wasn't fooled. She'd felt it—the emptiness inside him. Why had he even come back here?

"It's going pretty well," she said, still looking at the beach. "We've prepared almost all the seeds we'd need, and quite a few of the rarest animals are penned or caged and ready to take out quickly if it ever comes to that." She sighed, and said, "I wish they'd find the Cup. Then at least we might know where to take them all."

As he listened, Hawk felt torn between one mind that thought her task made all of his ambitions look like paste and paper, and another that struggled not to sneer at the pointlessness of scurrying around in preparation to go hide again in some new forgotten corner of the world. Would these people never tire of living tiny little lives in fear? This was why he'd left—what he had to get away from.

"Do you think I should?" Rose asked.

Hawk just blinked and stared, realizing he'd become lost in his own thoughts as she'd continued to talk. "I'm sorry. I missed that last bit," he said, his face burning.

She just shrugged. "It doesn't matter. I was only chattering." She reached into her pocket and pulled out a tiny book four inches high and less than half an inch thick. "I wanted to give you this," she said, "before you leave. I've had it since I was a little girl, but I want you to have it now, to remind you of home, and of me."

"Rose, if this is something you care about, I shouldn't——"

She shushed him, and put the book into his hand, curling his fingers around it with her own. "Bring it back to me when you've read it if you want to," she said quietly. "The bent page marks my favorite one." She leaned up to kiss him again, just a brush across his lips, then turned and waved good-bye as she ran down to rejoin the party.

Feeling more sick at heart than ever, Hawk looked down and read the small book's cover. *Flower Fairies of the Winter,* by Cicely Mary Barker. The gift was quintessential Rose, but what was *he* to do with it? He sighed and opened it to find the poem she had marked. There was a picture of a butterfly-winged fairy that looked very much like Rose, wearing a child's gingham dress and perched on a dark branch festooned in small white blossoms. A poem on the facing page was titled, "Blackthorn."

> *The wind is cold, the Spring*
> *seems long a-waking;*
> *The woods are brown and bare;*
> *yet this is March; soon April*
> *will be making*
> *all things most sweet and fair.*
> *See, even now, in hedge*
> *and thicket tangled,*
> *one brave and cheering sight;*
> *the leafless branches*
> *of the Blackthorn, spangled*
> *with starry blossoms white!*

Very pretty, Hawk thought wearily, but a child's poem wasn't going to do the job Rose had in mind. The sheer naiveté of such a gesture might have made him laugh if there'd been any laughter still within him. He shut the book, and jammed it in his pocket, then ambled toward the beach below to get some chicken and, he hoped, a few more beers. Surely no one in a riot like this would ask to see ID. Later, when he'd got his courage up again, he supposed he should go thank her for the gift, but he dreaded having to seem genuinely enthusiastic about fairy poems.

☒

By six o'clock, the time seemed ripe for setting match to powder.

"Hey, GB!" shouted Tique, grinning impishly at Lucifer from within his adolescent guise. "Has Euro gotten back yet? We're almost out of beer!"

"Keep you're voice down, will ya?" Lucifer grinned back. "Ya wanna get us all *arrested?*" Virtually all of Hell's operatives in Taubolt were on the beach by now, disguised as very naughty teenagers. "Light 'em if ya got 'em," Lucifer said in a voice pitched for Tique's ears only. Then he started up the trail toward town. It was time for Agnes Hamilton, or a damn good facsimile, to phone in her noise complaint. Then it was off to haunt the good sheriff's binoculars. Gazing up to estimate the rate of failing daylight, Lucifer smiled to himself and thought again, *It's all about the timing.*

❧

Donaldson didn't delegate calls from Hamilton. He'd come out himself to have a look, and he'd heard the blare of music and the roar of people long before he'd reached the cliff tops. Now he stood gazing down at a far larger crowd than he'd expected. Hamilton had been right. This was way over the line, especially without a permit.

He'd brought a pair of binoculars along, and raised them for a better look. People of all ages gathered around coolers and ice-filled buckets full of cans and bottles. The beach was largely shadowed by the cliffs at this hour, so it was difficult to tell how much of what the chests contained was alcoholic, but he wagered by the party's raucous mood that it was mostly booze. The more he looked, the more he realized how many of the crowd were kids, half of whom held cans and bottles too; flashes of aluminum, green and brown glass. Could have been soda, but he'd have bet his shirt it wasn't. He lowered his binoculars and swept his eyes across the beach again. The dancing crowd was large and getting pretty crazy. Numerous bonfires had been lit as evening approached. No permits for those either. He was amazed no one had called him sooner. He raised his binoculars one more time to sweep the beach's margins, knowing that's where the worst offenders would be hanging out, and sure enough, behind a thicket near the bridge, he saw a group half-hidden in the tall grass, passing around something that sure looked like a bong. Their faces didn't seem familiar, but by now, the light was too poor to tell for sure.

He trotted back across the field to his patrol car, and radioed for backup. Nearly four months after his promotion and the arrival of his team, Donaldson had yet to achieve anything beyond the prosecution of another handful of teenaged pranks and minor violations. Finally, something major was going down right before his eyes, and he'd arrived in time to do more than scratch his head the morning after. He'd have bet his badge that if they managed to bust enough of those booze-guzzling, bong-huffing kids down there tonight, Taubolt's more mysterious crimes would fall off just as mysteriously, at least until Joby Peterson managed to get them all out and onto the streets again.

❋

Kellerman's Celts had been playing tunes back to back for almost thirty minutes, so when they stopped, everyone just assumed they were taking a well-deserved break until Ian started unplugging amps while his band members packed up their instruments.

"Hey! What are you guys doing?" Blue asked. "You're not packin' up!"

"Afraid we have to," Ian said.

"It's not even dark yet," whined Blue's brother, Tholomey. "What's the hurry?"

As more people gathered to express their disappointment and surprise, Ian grabbed one of the remaining mics, and addressed the crowd. "Folks, we've had a great day playing for you all. Thanks for enjoying us so well. Unfortunately, Sheriff Donaldson has sent word down there's been a noise complaint from up in town. We're being asked to stop. So," he smiled and shrugged, "all good things must end."

There were boos and louder protests from all around the platform.

"Well, let's go up and talk to him," Blue suggested to his brother and several others around him.

The idea was immediately encouraged by everyone close enough to hear, but Ian leaned down to put a hand on Blue's shoulder, and shook his head. "Already been tried," he said. "He's been up there half an hour, I'm told, with several other officers. Yours'd be the third group to approach him. Just leave it be. The party can go on without us."

❋

Rose watched with mild disappointment as people left the beach in larger numbers. It was not the ending she'd have chosen, but it had been a tremendous day, and more than served its purpose. By sunset, a lot of older folks and tourists had already left. The young, always last to abandon a party, were soon left gathered in loose rings around each of the three bonfires, sipping drinks and milking the afterglow for all it was worth. Rose stood in one of these with Ander, Blue, and Nacho, when Joby came to join them.

"It was a really wonderful party, Rose," he said. "I haven't had this much fun in ages. It felt really good. Thanks."

Rose smiled. "You're welcome, Joby. Thanks for coming."

"So, how's Hawk doing?" Joby said a little too casually. "I noticed you were talking to him earlier."

Rose reached out to squeeze his hand, then pulled him off toward the water. "I'm sorry he hasn't come to see you, Joby," she said when they had left the firelight. "I tried to tell him he should, but—"

"Hey, hey, hey," Joby said softly, tugging her to a stop. "That's not your problem and not what I meant. I . . . just wondered how he's doing and figured you would know."

"To be honest, I have no idea," Rose sighed. "He's changed so much, and . . . not any for the better, I think. All he talks about is how much money he's going to make and how . . ." She shook her head and looked Joby sadly in the eye. "He talks as if I were just some kind of trophy he intends to win or maybe *buy* someday, as if he doesn't know I'm already his. It breaks my heart, Joby. Maybe you were lucky not to see him."

"I've hurt him pretty badly, haven't I?" Joby said, looking down.

"I don't think it's you," Rose insisted. "Not just you anyway. He's been like this for a while now. I don't know why, and I don't think he does either."

"You're probably right," said Joby, not sounding too convinced.

Someone sent a bottle rocket into the air from the grassy dunes behind them. It went up with a shrill whistle, quickly followed by another, just as Blue came running up to say, "Hey you guys, someone came down to say the sheriff's telling everybody to get off the beach. You think we ought to go?"

"Why?" asked Joby. "It's illegal to stand around a fire on the beach now?"

Before Blue could answer, three more bottle rockets shrilled into the air.

"Fools," Joby griped. "That *is* illegal. Do they think antagonizing him will help?"

❈

"Look at that!" Donaldson spat, watching the second wave of rockets go up. "Flagrant little bastards."

"Probl'y all high as kites," said one of his patrolmen. All four officers were here now, full riot gear waiting back in their cars in case things got really out of hand.

Donaldson shook his head in disbelief. He'd sent none of his men down to the beach itself yet, knowing that most of his intended targets would run the minute a uniformed officer showed up. He didn't want a single one of them to get away before all the exits had been covered.

"I didn't know this town had that many kids," said his second patrolman.

"A lot of 'em prob'ly aren't from here," said the first officer. "Gang types, most likely, come in for the party. Saw it all the time when I was down in L.A. Word of some big rave like this gets out, they come from all around."

"How many would you say we got down there?" asked Donaldson. His head was spinning. Only the crowds around the fires were clearly visible, but there was lots of vague movement in the darkness back from the beach and under the bridge. If they were all inebriated, this could get very, very ugly in a hurry.

"Could be a hundred," said the officer who'd been in L.A. "Maybe one fifty."

Just then Donaldson's fourth officer rejoined them, having been sent to radio the backup they'd called in from Heeberville an hour before. "They say ten minutes," the patrolman reported. "Maybe less."

"Good," said Donaldson. "Those kids have responded to my evacuation order with fireworks. This thing could come apart at any minute. When the backup gets here I want us all ready to move, so get geared up now." He turned to the officer who'd just been in contact with the force from Heeberville. "You told them where to deploy? Down there, at the bridge flats, and up there on the west end of the headlands?"

"Yes, sir."

"You think they understood?"

"Most of 'em seem to know Taubolt, sir."

Donaldson turned back to look at the beach again. "I've got you now," he muttered under his breath. "Every last fucking one of you."

⊗

"So, think we should leave?" Blue asked again.

"I'll go up and try to talk with him," Joby said.

"I'll come with you," Blue offered.

Just then a third phalanx of bottle rockets burst above the dunes behind them.

Joby rolled his eyes, and turned to Rose. "Maybe someone could go tell those yahoos to cut it out?"

She smiled and nodded, heading off into the darkness as he and Blue left for the trail up off the beach.

They'd barely reached the stairs when they heard sirens in the distance.

"What's that about?" said Blue.

"I don't know," Joby said. "They're coming from the south. What's down there?"

"Avalon Ridge." Blue shrugged.

By then, the sirens had grown much louder. "There's a bunch of them," said Joby.

"That can't be . . . for us, can't it?" Blue asked.

"Don't be crazy," Joby said. "Maybe there's a fire."

Suddenly, a line of flashing lights appeared; three patrol cars racing across the bridge. On the bluffs above himself and Blue, Joby heard more sirens. In stunned disbelief he watched two of the vehicles skid to a halt beside the river on the far side of the bridge, their lights still flashing, while more flashing lights appeared atop the cliffs west of the beach. From around the fires below them, there was utter silence as everyone stared in speechless confusion.

"Holy shit," Blue said.

"This cannot be us," Joby said quietly. "This cannot have *anything* to do with us. Something else must have gone down by the river."

"Like what?" Blue said, his voice edged with budding panic.

"This is crazy," Joby said. "Come on." He began to climb the stairs again, two at a time, heedless of his footing in the dim light from the beach fires.

As they reached the cliff tops, Joby could not believe his eyes. A column of officers in full riot gear was coming down the path, silhouettes against the twilight.

"Oh crap," Blue whispered.

As the officers approached, Joby said with careful calm, "Can I ask what's happening here, please?"

"You'd better go," said a voice he recognized as Donaldson's.

"What's anybody done to merit all this?" Joby asked, trying not to sound belligerent.

"I said, go, Mr. Peterson," Donaldson repeated. As the column clearly didn't mean to stop, Joby and Blue stood aside in mute dismay.

"What are they *doing*?" Blue murmured.

Joby saw still more officers gathering in the parking area across the field ahead, and set out to get an answer to Blue's question. The first officer they encountered only shrugged and said he wasn't sure what was going on, but recommended, as Donaldson had, that they leave immediately.

"Can they just do this?" Joby asked.

Before the officer could answer, they heard voices shouting from the beach. Then a crowd of kids appeared at the top of the stairs, running like their lives depended on it. Close behind came two riot-gear clad officers, dragging a third person crying out in pain between them. They were followed by a second group of kids, shouting angrily at the officers ahead of them.

As the first wave of teenagers ran past, Joby was finally able to make out who was being dragged by handcuffed arms wrenched up behind his back. "My God!" Joby gasped. "It's Ander!" Then Joby saw that Nacho led the pack of angry youth behind them, copious streams of blood flowing down his upper lip and chin.

⌘

In a state of shock, Rose thinking to flee up river, had run with many others toward the bridge when all the lights and sirens had appeared. But before she'd gotten halfway there, a hand out of the darkness grabbed her arm and wrenched her to a halt.

"Not that way!" hissed Hawk's voice. "They're parked out on the flats!"

"What's happening?" Rose cried as Hawk dragged her up the hillside through the bushes. "Why are they doing this?"

"I don't know," Hawk growled. "But there's no room in my plans for an arrest record. We have to get out of here!"

As they neared the top of the steep hillside, they heard others crashing through the undergrowth nearby.

"Who's that?" Hawk whispered, stopping in his tracks.

"Hawk?" came Tholomey's voice.

"Tholomey," said Hawk. "Who's with you?"

"Jessie and Autumn," answered Tholomey, as his trio ran to join Hawk and Rose. "They're up on the headlands too. I could swim out, but these guys are all stuck. We've gotta get past the cops and into town somehow."

"Why are they doing this?" Rose demanded again.

"'Cause Donaldson hates us," Tholomey said grimly. "I hear he's got Ander. Have you seen my brother?"

"He went up with Joby to talk to Donaldson," Rose replied.

"Oh, that's just awesome," Tholomey groaned. "Right into the fire."

⌘

In shock, Joby had watched the nightmare go from terrible to worse before his eyes. Illuminated by the headlights of several patrol cars, an enraged crowd of boys shouted angry accusations at officers trying to contain the escalating conflict. As Ander had been shoved into the backseat of one of the cars, his bleeding wrists still cuffed, Blue had rushed to join the others shouting for their friend's release, only to be grabbed by one of the officers, thrown against the car in dumbfounded amazement, handcuffed and pushed into the backseat next to Ander. This had only redoubled the outrage of the others, who stood ten or twelve feet off yelling angrily that this was bullshit and against the law. Within minutes, officers had darted forward to yank two more boys into cuffs and shove them inside other cars.

In Joby's mind, the morning of Gypsy's death was being replayed with lurid intensity; the yelling, the uniforms, the scuffling mob, Gypsy's bloodied corpse lying lifeless in his arms. It was all happening again, but Joby couldn't seem to move or even breathe. He was afraid to speak for fear that one more voice raised might push the button that would make it all explode.

Then he saw Nacho shoving toward the front of the crowd of boys again; his shirt now soaked in the blood still cascading from his nose.

"Nacho!" he croaked, trying to be heard, afraid to yell. "Nacho! Come here!" Nacho didn't hear him. Had he forgotten how much Donaldson loathed him? Suddenly, it was Nacho's bloodied body Joby imagined holding in his arms. Joby took several frightened steps closer to the conflict, and stepped up on the bumper of some civilian car parked there from the party, hoping he'd be seen above the crowd.

"Nacho!" Joby snapped more loudly. "Get out of there!" Amazingly, Nacho heard, and turned to look at him. "Come here!" Joby demanded. "Come here, now!" Nacho just kept staring, as Joby gestured frantically toward himself. "Now! Please!" he yelled, until, to his deep relief, the boy backed from the crowd and started toward him.

Joby leapt from the bumper of the car to grab Nacho's hand as soon as he was near, and dragged him farther from the lights and yelling. "Donaldson hates you," Joby said. "You've got to stay away from that."

"No!" Nacho said, pulling out of Joby's grasp. "Don't you see what they're doing?" Nacho turned to look back at the altercation, and Joby saw that he was crying.

"I see it," Joby replied with urgency. "I've seen it before, Nacho. People could get hurt here. They could get killed! This has to be addressed, but not here! Not like this!"

"You can't just let them get away with this!" Nacho wept, suddenly nothing like the tough hoodlum he was so often accused of being. "Look what they did to Ander," he groaned again. "What they're doing to all of us!"

"I won't let them get away with anything, Nacho," Joby said. "I promise you, I'll see that this is dealt with. But you have to trust me and stay out of it tonight." Tonight, he thought, but not tomorrow, vowing in his heart that someone was going to answer for this outrage. They might get away with stuff like this in the cities, but it wasn't going to happen *here*. He'd had enough of watching Taubolt die.

Around the embattled police cars, the crowd of boys had begun to back away and quiet down. Everyone could see that they were beaten. The conflict disintegrated as quickly as it had ignited, and officers were already starting to mop up the details.

"What happened to your nose?" Joby asked Nacho.

"Donaldson pepper sprayed me," Nacho said. "Right in the face. A couple others got it too, but it was mostly me."

"Why?" Joby asked. "And what did they arrest Ander for?"

"They came marchin' onto the beach like that, and told everyone to go," Nacho grumbled. "Ander asked them why he had to leave, and Donaldson just jumped out and started slappin' handcuffs on him."

Joby could not believe it had been that simple. "So, why'd he spray *you*?"

"I don't know," shrugged Nacho. "I was at least twelve feet behind him. Everybody was. But he was yankin' Ander up the stairs by those handcuffs, and it was breakin' Ander's arms! Then his wrists began to bleed, and everybody started shouting for Donaldson to ease up. That's all I was doin', tellin' Donaldson not to hurt him."

"Here's some ice for your nose," said a voice behind them.

They turned to find an officer holding a cooler full of ice cubes from the beach.

"They're getting some towels from the inn over there," the officer said politely. "It'll probably help if you wet one down and hold your nose shut, leaning forward. Are you having any trouble breathing, son?" the officer asked, with what seemed genuine concern. "Any dizziness or nausea?"

Nacho shook his head, leaning to bleed into the bucket until the towels arrived.

"Okay," the officer said. "I'll check back later to see how you're doing."

Nacho refused even to look up, but Joby thanked the officer, feeling as if they'd all just dodged a bullet.

Five minutes later another officer arrived with the towels. Nacho thanked the man this time, though sullenly, and was wrapping ice inside of one when a third officer called, "Hey, Ted, get over here! We've got another call!" The officer excused himself, and left just as Joby heard his name called, and turned to see Tholomey running toward them.

"Joby, have you seen my brother?" Tholomey called raggedly.

"Yes," Joby sighed. "I'm sorry, Tholomey, but he was arrested. Don't worry though. I'm going to—" Joby stopped short, realizing that Tholomey was crying very hard. "What's wrong?" he asked. "Your brother's all right. He just—"

"You have to come," the boy managed to say before breaking down completely.

"What is it?" Joby asked.

"We were running from the cops," Tholomey squeezed out between sobs. "Hawk and Rose and me. We ran across a street, and—" Tholomey started crying too hard to talk "Rose got run into by a car!" the boy keened. "I think she's dead!"

"Fuck!" Nacho gasped behind him, jumping to his feet. *"Fuuuck!"* he yelled.

"Where?" Joby rasped, his chest seeming to collapse.

Tholomey began to run back the way he'd come, waving for them to follow.

"Where's Hawk?" Joby asked, catching up to run beside the boy.

"He went crazy after she got hit," Tholomey said, his voice a gurgling shudder. "He just laid on top of her and cried at first. Then he ran away, and he was screaming, Joby. It was . . ." Tholomey ran on, crying too hard again to tell him any more.

By now, Joby's face was wet with tears as well. This much grief was *not allowed,* he kept thinking to himself. . . . It shouldn't be *allowed!*

33

(Blackthorn)

For three days Michael followed helplessly as Basquel drove Hawk raging through the woods to bat at trees, scream his larynx raw, sit staring into space, sob himself to sleep, wake sobbing still, and rise to rage again. Before Hawk had even run from Rose's body, the disembodied demon had been riding him, both feeding and being fed by the boy's consuming anguish. Well aware that Michael followed them, the demon frequently looked back to laugh, reveling in the angel's impotence. They both knew that Hawk was being shaped to serve as Hell's H-bomb against Joby, and that helping him in any way would constitute unlawful intervention of the most flagrant kind.

On Hawk's fourth morning in the woods, ragged and disheveled, but seeming more lucid in some frightening way, Michael saw him discover something in his pocket and pull out the little book of fairy poems Rose had given him. At first Hawk only stared at it, dumbfounded. Then he opened it, turning numbly to the page that she had bent.

As the glimmer of tears gathered in his eyes, the boy began to tremble and weep. "'Even now, in hedge and thicket,'" Hawk mumbled hoarsely through his tears, "'. . . starry blossoms . . . white.'" The last word was less than whispered as Hawk peered up around the clearing in bewildered desperation.

"Where?" Hawk croaked. Michael saw Basquel prod the boy cruelly, and Hawk's face jerked toward the sky, *"Where are all the fucking flowers, Rose?!"*

His screams became incoherent as he hurled the book with all his might against a nearby tree, then rushed to scoop it off the ground, and throw it at the trunk again. *"There's no flowers!"* he shouted at the tattered book. *"I hate you! I hate you!"* Falling on the book, he grabbed it in both fists and tried to tear it in half. He was too weak though, after so many days unfed, and, in another moment, pressed it to his chest instead, as if to push it through himself, and wept and wept with such remorse that Michael could not bear it any longer.

No longer did Michael merely *fear* himself a coward, as he had since Jupiter and Sky had died; he *knew*, and in that instant saw the path that had been there right before him from the start. *With the candidate*, his Lord had said. *The folks here are still under your care. The wager don't change that.*

Remorse to rival Hawk's leapt up in Michael's breast. He had not just been afraid of disobedience. He'd been afraid of guessing wrong, of bearing responsibility for losing Heaven's wager through some misstep of his own. He'd been afraid of facing what his brother faced, and Merlin too: damnation. Still afraid of all those things, but no longer able to cling to such excuses, Michael cast aside the safety of unseen sympathy for Hawk, and stepped into the clearing in a form the boy would see and know.

"Hawk," he said firmly. "It's time to stop this. Rose's death was not your fault."

Hawk looked up gaping. "Jake?" he gasped.

"What are you doing?!" The demon howled in a voice only Michael's ears detected. *"You cannot interfere!"*

Concentrating all his anger, Michael thrust a hand toward the Basquel's head. With a shriek, the demon became flesh against his will, bowling Hawk down flat beneath his now considerable physical weight.

"You fool!" the toad-faced demon roared as Hawk struggled in terror to get out from under whatever beast had jumped him. *"You've damned yourself for certain now!"*

"Get off!" Hawk gasped, scuttling away from Basquel in horror. *"Who are you?"*

"That is what has caused your torment for so many months," Michael said grimly, still staring at Basquel. "It and others like it. It's a demon, Hawk."

"What?" Hawk squeaked. *"Where'd it come from? What's it want with me?"*

"Now you've fouled the wager!" Basquel snarled. "This will not be overlooked! You've betrayed your Master's cause to us!"

"I haven't said a thing about the wager," Michael said quietly, "but you just did."

Basquel looked appalled, then, with narrowed eyes, said, "It doesn't matter, now. The wager's already lost, and you're to blame. Explain that to your Master."

"Is that so," Michael replied. "I am commanded not to aid the *candidate* unasked. This boy is no more him than any of the others you've all made yourselves so free with."

Crouched now at the clearing's edge, Hawk stared back and forth between them in stunned incomprehension.

"You've *cheated!*" Basquel screamed. "That means *we win,* and you'll be *punished! Master! Master, come and see what they are doing!*"

"I'm already here," said Lucifer, stepping from beneath the trees, not guised as GB, but as himself, tall and dark to Michael's tall and fair. "Did you really think I'd let you go unwatched all this time with such an important charge?" he asked Basquel.

Michael moved to stand between Hell's ruler and Hawk, saying, "You'll have to deal with me to have him back."

"Have him back?" Lucifer said dismissively. "There's hardly any point now. Not after all this. First Lancelot. Now Mordred. It seems I shall have to improvise *again.* No, Michael, I've only come for . . . *closure.*" He turned to Basquel with ominous calm. "Whose idea was it to stay and chat in front of the boy once you'd been exposed?"

"What?" the creature said, its fear instantly apparent. "I didn't—I never—"

"You did," Lucifer said quietly. "It seems I should have listened to Kallaystra. She may be slow and lazy, but she didn't waste the boy completely, as you have done."

"No!" Basquel quailed, rising to his feet. "I've served no one but—"

"Yourself," Lucifer sighed, throwing both arms up to bath the quaking demon in a brilliant light that flared and vanished leaving only Basquel's final scream behind.

Lucifer looked back at Michael then, smiling unpleasantly. "I know my terms with your Employer do not require you to obey Him. An oversight, I must confess, but who'd have thought so many of Heaven's brightest surviving stars hid such potential for subversion?" Lucifer's grin evaporated. "I still intend to win this wager, and then . . . you know the price for failure in *your* Master's domain, as well as Basquel knew the price in mine. I look forward to seeing what a few millennia of confinement to this forsaken rock pile does to all that fierce self-confidence of yours, Michael."

Before Michael could respond, Lucifer had vanished without so much as a glance at Hawk, who stared openmouthed at where he'd been, then turned to stare at Michael.

"Jake?" Hawk said. "Who was that? . . . Why'd he call you Michael?"

Michael pursed his lips, calculating the damage, and what might be done about it.

"What did they mean about your . . . master?" Hawk insisted.

"You and I must talk now," Michael said quietly. "A very long talk, about a lot of things, but first, let's find you something to eat. You'll need a clearer head for this."

He reached down to help the boy up, but whatever strength Hawk had possessed before seemed drained now. He could barely stand, so Michael bent down and picked him up as if he were a child.

"Jake?" Hawk asked quietly, as Michael carried him from the clearing. "Was it them . . . that killed her?"

"No," Michael said. "Her death was just an accident. A terrible accident. . . . Or I'd have been there."

After a moment, Hawk murmured sadly, "I never thanked her for the book."

"You will," the angel said. "Now rest until I find some food. There will be time for questions then." He looked down to find He looked Hawk already fast asleep against his chest.

❧

Rose had lived quietly at the very heart of all that Taubolt was, and her memorial service overflowed the high school's huge central room through every door. Joby had been at school all day, helping to prepare, and so secured a seat inside where he waited now, reflecting on the week since Rose's death.

Her young friends and former classmates had gathered within hours of the accident and stayed together all that week, traveling from home to home like a large nomadic family. Cooking and sharing meals together, sleeping side by side on floors and couches, they'd gone from grief to laughter back to grief again and again as they remembered Rose and coped with the fresh and devastating wound of her sudden, awful absence. Invited along, Joby had spent much of that week traveling with them, astonished at the strength and honesty and wisdom of these children who had known so little grief before Taubolt had begun to change for reasons no one could explain.

As the town had reeled in shock, Donaldson had been quick to deny any fault in the accident, and express his sympathy with a gesture of "goodwill," releasing all the boys arrested that night without bail to await their court hearings in Santa Rosa later that month. For now, the issue smoldered unaddressed, until the community's more urgent grief was dealt with. But Joby had not forgotten his vow to Nacho that night. When Rose was laid to rest, he would make certain Donaldson paid . . . for everything.

Laid over all of this was Joby's fear for Hawk. Though his new car remained parked where he had left it at the Connolly's house, Hawk had not been seen since running off that night. Joby had spent hours that night driving through the darkened town, then searching the highway and surrounding roads without success. By now, he woke and slept suppressing dread of being the next to grieve a child deceased.

As Rose's parents were ushered through the hushing crowd toward a row of chairs around the center of the room, Ander began to play his guitar and then to sing lyrics that Joby quickly recognized from one of Rose's many poems.

> *"The bark is rough,*
> *against my determined hands,*
> *but still it*
> *does not hurt me.*
> *I have climbed all this way,*
> *with branches cracking in my face,*
> *just to hear the gentle song*
> *of the wind.*
> *I will wait now for a while.*
> *And suddenly the song begins,*
> *rippling and laughing.*
> *The trees will dance*
> *to the happy melody, carrying me with them*
> *as they sway to the*
> *music of the wind."*

Ander played an interlude evoking gusts of wind through leaves, as Joby recalled the first time he had heard her whispering to Bellindi in that thicket on the headlands. She had seemed so strange, if fair, running from him, laughing, with flowers falling from her hair. . . . Could she truly be gone? . . . Did such wounds ever fully heal?

Ander's voice rose again, breaking Joby's reverie.

> *"My life is like the wind that blows through*
> *my hair on a cloudy day.*
> *My life is like the fish that swim*

in the deepest depths of the ocean.
My life is like five thousand years of light
that will never go out.
My life is like the hills,
rolling away forever."

Ander played gently for another bar or two, the notes rolling softly into silence.

As there was currently a dearth of religious ministers in Taubolt, Bridget O'Reilly stood to conduct the ceremony that Rose's parents and friends had prepared. Her opening statements of welcome were brief and unassuming, as were the things she said of Rose before turning to Rose's parents and inviting them to speak.

Tom and Clara stood and turned to face the crowd. Clara smiled; Tom tried with less success. Their eyes were red and rough, their faces pale and puffed with grief. They'd been in near seclusion all that week, attended by just a few of their oldest, closest friends. Joby braced himself for a painful display of grief.

"Rose was conceived on the shores of a lake high in the Sierras," Tom began. A pale smile crossed his face at last. "I can't tell you exactly which one. . . . We saw a lot of lakes that trip."

There was an instant of surprise before the whole room rang with laughter mixed with tears and admiration, for Tom and Clara laughed as well. *What amazing people,* Joby thought. No wonder Rose had been so remarkable.

"We have often wondered," Tom continued when the laughter ended, "if that's why Rose was like she was; because she had been conceived so much closer to Heaven than other people, or in such a wild, lovely place." Clara nodded, and leaned her head on her husband's shoulder, as he continued, "All we knew for sure, was that from the very beginning she was way out in front of us in so many ways."

He smiled at Clara, who said, "I see it especially in her poems. You heard some of them in that beautiful song Ander just played." She turned to smile at Ander, then unfolded a sheet of paper she'd been holding, while Joby continued to marvel at their self-possession. "She wrote this one when she was only eight."

"Above the ponds,
the marshes glazed with ice,

there is a cavern.
It is eternal,
everlasting.
Those who live there
are beautiful.
They never die."

"Eight years old," Clara said again, wiping quickly at her eyes, "and she was already seeing further than I think most of us do at many times her age." Beside her Tom nodded, his sad half smile stolidly fixed. "Tom and I are grateful to have had her for as long as we did. We wouldn't give away a day of it. And we're grateful for all this community has done for her, and for us, through the years. We are very grateful that we were able to be with our daughter just before she died. She came by and told us how much she loved us, and we got to tell her the same."

"We've both noticed how many people she went out of her way to talk with that day," Tom agreed, his voice grown rougher, "how much . . . business she took care of, just before she died, almost as if she threw that whole party to say good-bye to all of us. It may be just our imagination, but we're grateful for that too."

As Tom took a moment to steady himself, Joby wondered how many others shared the wave of fury he felt remembering how her party had ended.

Tom looked at Clara, who nodded, then he turned back to face the gathering and said, "That's really all we have to say."

"We love you all," said Clara. "And we're really very grateful."

When the Connollys had sat down again, Bridget stood to speak again, but stopped abruptly, interrupted by some kind of disturbance at the back of the room. Joby turned with all the others, and saw people near the doorway making way for Jake, behind whom, looking pale and abashed, came Hawk.

Joby leapt to his feet, pushing down the row of chairs to get to his son who, to Joby's overwhelming gratitude, began to press his way through the crowd to meet him. They came together sobbing unreservedly, as people murmured all around them.

"Thank God you're safe!" Joby groaned into his son's shoulder as they hugged. "I was so frightened!"

"I'm sorry," Hawk replied, holding him as tightly. "I'm sorry for everything—the way I've treated everybody."

"I'm just glad you're here. Where have you been?"

"I'll tell you later," Hawk said, pulling reluctantly away. "This is Rose's time."

Joby looked past his son to see Jake still standing at a distance. "Thank you," he rasped, still raw with emotion. "For bringing me my son."

Jake only nodded and stepped back into the standing crowd, as Hawk turned to look at Rose's parents. They were standing now as well, and Joby realized how this must be for them, watching his son returned, while no such hope remained for them.

"I'm sorry to disturb you all like this," Hawk said to them with obvious contrition. "But when there's time, may I say something to everyone?"

"Of course!" Clara said, smiling through fresh tear and coming to embrace him. "Hawk, we're all so glad to see you!"

"Thank you." Hawk wept, returning her embrace as Tom came to wrap his arms around them both. "I loved her. I loved her so much, and I'm so sorry she's gone."

"I know," Clara murmured. "She loved you too, and so do we, Hawk. I'm very grateful that she knew what love was like before she died."

Hawk nodded and pulled away, drawing a long shuddering breath, then went to stand at the center of the room and face the gathered crowd.

"If you don't know me," he said quietly, "my name is Hawk . . . Peterson." He looked at Joby who bowed his head to hide another sudden flood of tears. "Rose was the first girl I ever loved, and because she loved me back, I've never tried to love another." He pursed his lips and struggled for composure. "In the years I knew her, she gave me too many gifts to list, but she gave me one the day she died that I think I'm meant to share with all of you."

Hawk reached into his pocket, and drew out a badly damaged little book, its covers smudged with dirt, its pages torn and wrinkled. He opened it and began to read a poem about a Blackthorn bush blooming at the end of winter. When he'd finished, he looked up and said, "This was Rose's book. She told me that this poem was her favorite. For . . . a long time, after she died, I couldn't see the flowers it talks about, just the thorny branches. But now I've seen them, and I want . . . I want to say . . ."

He looked down at the book again, and Joby saw his hands were shaking. Shoving the book back into his pocket, Hawk looked up again. "A lot of you know I've been . . . treating people badly for a while. I've probably offended some of you deeply, especially Joby, and the Connollys." He hung his head again. "I treated Rose worst of all, right up to the end." He looked up, and said, "I've been . . . sick inside. With anger. Very sick. After Sky and Jupiter died, I couldn't feel grief, or happiness, or hope, or love for anyone, not even Rose. I just felt dead, like I was watching everyone through thick glass . . . not a part of anything. I didn't know why. I just shoved everyone away. By the time I last saw Rose, there was nothing but a hole where my heart was supposed to be, and . . . and that was how I treated her . . . heartlessly.

"But Rose just kept saying that she loved me, and . . . and she gave me this book," His tears began at last, but he didn't stop. "Rose gave me back my heart," he wept. "She broke it open when she died. . . . And all the things I couldn't feel before came rushing out, and it was worse than I can tell you, and I *wished* that I could die, but I didn't, and then Jake found me in the woods, and showed me . . ." Hawk looked down and pointed at his chest. "They're here . . . the flowers . . . growing in the heart that Rose gave back to me." Hawk looked up, struggling to rein in his grief. "I know I'm not the only one. She did so many things for so many people. Those things live on, and I know that someday, you'll be able to look out and see all those small white flowers Rose planted, growing for as far as anyone can see in all directions from the spot where she lived."

Streaming tears, Joby stood, gazing straight at Hawk, and said, "He's right. Because of Rose, I have my son again."

Across the room, Nacho stood as well. "Rose helped drag me away from that dog that tried to kill me. Because of her, I'm still alive."

Bellindi was the next to stand. "Rose taught me to love the forest. Because of her, I know what I want to do with my life."

Behind them, old Mr. Templer wobbled to his feet, leaning heavily on his cane. "When she was younger," he quavered, "Rose kept dragging me over to help Amanda Farley with her garden." He turned to gaze down at the white-haired woman smiling up at him from the chair next to his own. "You all know what came of that." There were tatters of laughter from around the room. "Because of Rose, I have a wife."

The laughter only grew as one by one by one others stood to tell of some small thing Rose had done to change their lives, while Joby watched in wonder as more and more of the flowers Hawk had promised burst into bloom before their eyes.

⊗

Merlin reached up to touch the window between himself and what he'd seen. "You are a *true* bard now, my boy," he said. "My *great* grandson. I'm so proud of you."

Merlin stepped back to look around the empty mall. "Having trouble keeping all your balls in the air, Beelzebub?" he called happily into the air above him. "Hawk is playing a very different tune than the one you called for, is he not?" Merlin did a little jig into the center of the plaza—his first merry moment in so very long—then sighed and sat back down to focus once again on the endless task of winning his freedom.

34

(*Throwing Down the Gauntlet*)

Hawk had dinner going on the stove when Joby trudged into the small rental cottage they now shared, collapsed into a chair, and stared up at the ceiling for a while before scrubbing at his bloodshot eyes. Hawk turned back to his cooking with a frown. Two months of crusading for "justice" had taken a heavy toll on his father.

The very morning after Rose's memorial, Donaldson had issued a warrant for Nacho's arrest, apparently eager to justify his use of pepper spray by claiming Nacho had attacked him as Ander was being cuffed. Joby had gone off like a bomb, visiting every community leader he knew to point out that lots of boys had been arrested that night for nothing more than shouting at a distance, while Nacho had sat bleeding into a bucket for half an hour surrounded by cops who hadn't even mentioned his even more serious supposed offense, much less arrested him for it. By the following day, Donaldson's warrant had been quietly rescinded. By week's end there'd been a huge town meeting at which Donaldson and his faction had faced hundreds of unhappy residents. Donaldson might still have stopped it there just by conceding there'd been errors made and dropping charges against Ander and the others, but he hadn't, so the fire had spread.

"Smells good," said Joby, opening his eyes to smile wearily at Hawk.

"Ready in about five minutes," Hawk replied, stirring what was in the frying pan one more time before going to set the table.

"I can do that," Joby said, starting to rise.

"No, just rest," Hawk insisted. "I'm already on it."

Joby leaned back again with a grateful sigh.

The county sheriff had called Joby personally to tell him what a divisive, conniving, dangerous, possibly criminal element he was for stirring up all this trouble against his sterling men. But Joby had been harder to intimidate than Mansfield had expected. An internal investigator had been sent out to grill everyone involved, then investigators from the state capital. Even the regional senator's office had made inquiries, until Joby's life had become just one long parade of official inquisitions and media interviews, not to mention all the politicking required to keep pressure up and people reassured while the ponderous wheels of inquiry and deliberation had rolled on.

By now, Donaldson's story had sprung more leaks than a rubber raft full of porcupines. There'd been *hundreds* of kids on the beach, he claimed, though nowhere near that many could be accounted for now. Coulson's men had seen *forty* bongs around those fires, and beers in every minor's hand, though not one of these illicit items had been seized that night. Nor had Donaldson shown any proven cause yet regarding those he'd pepper sprayed. It had been a riot, Donaldson kept insisting; but no one else who'd been there had seen it that way, except his fellow officers, of course, and Hamilton, who hadn't been there. Ander had been known for years around the village as a quiet, well-liked boy, a good student and hard-working employee. Donaldson could hardly have picked a worse "criminal" to haul away in cuffs. As week had followed tumultuous week, Hawk had begun to feel almost sorry for the embattled man, who, by now, seemed desperate for peace, but still refused to drop his charges against Ander and the others.

"You want juice or milk?" Hawk asked, going to dish the stir-fry into their plates.

"Juice," said Joby, climbing to his feet. "Thanks for cooking, son."

"Just felt like something edible tonight." Hawk grinned as Joby joined him at the table. "You only get to cook when I'm not hungry, remember?"

"You're just jealous of my skill with Tupperware," Joby parried as he sat down.

Unsurprisingly, Joby had been pulled over twice this month for "fix-it" tickets, but he hadn't wasted any of his precious energy protesting such petty aggravations. He'd just told Hawk it was a fair price to pay for the greater satisfaction of discovering that people of goodwill could still make a difference against corrupt power. The proverbial fat lady hadn't sung yet, but things were looking more promising for Taubolt's kids and less for Donaldson all the time, and Joby was clearly more proud of his community than ever.

Nonetheless, the lengthy campaign had not been good for Hawk's father. Not only was he tired all the time now, he seemed angry too. His whole life revolved around conflict now. On several occasions when Joby had been in the shower, or outside chopping wood, Hawk had heard him muttering and yelling as if Donaldson or Hamilton had been right there accusing him of something.

"Know what day tomorrow is?" Hawk asked as they began to eat?

"Nope," said Joby, scooping food into his mouth. "What day?"

"Saturday," said Hawk.

"Oh," said Joby, looking at him quizzically. "And you're saying this be-cause . . . ?"

"I think we should go hiking tomorrow," Hawk said, "like we used to."

"God, that sounds great," Joby said. "Can't though. Got a meeting with the county mediator in the morning, and the Youth Park Committee in the afternoon. Only day they could do it," he said around another mouthful of stir-fry.

"Cancel it," Hawk said gruffly. "The *youth* can get their park a week later."

Joby looked up, seeming startled.

"Sorry," Hawk apologized. "It's just . . . This is all so out of hand, Joby."

Joby shrugged. "Not much I can do about it. Life goes on, Hawk."

"You've got a life?" Hawk said.

"What's that supposed to mean?"

"Joby, all I've seen you do for months is 'fight for justice.' Maybe if you just got on with your life, and let this thing with Donaldson go, he might too."

"You want me to give up three feet shy of the finish line? With charges still pending against all those kids, and let Donaldson off scot-free? You know me better than that, Hawk." With a wounded look, Joby added, "I'd hoped you'd be proud of me."

"Of course I'm proud of you," Hawk protested. "That doesn't mean I have to like watching you fall on your knife. You're too wrapped up in all the crap that's gone down around here, and I just think it would be good if you just took a little breather. The whole town backs you on this, Joby, and you've brought them all this way. Can't you just let *them* do some of the cleanup?"

"What kind of man would that make me?" Joby said almost scornfully.

"A living one," Hawk muttered. Joby could take this whole integrity thing to such ridiculous lengths sometimes. "It's not like God appointed you to save the world."

"All right," Joby said, leaning back and crossing his arms. "What, exactly, am I *supposed* to be doing while everyone else in Taubolt is finishing what I started?"

"You should get out of here completely," Hawk said. "Take a vacation."

"I live in one of America's premier resort towns!" Joby laughed. "Sunny beaches, magnificent forests, hiking, biking, kayaking on scenic rivers, quaint shops and world-class restaurants overlooking the blue Pacific! Haven't you read the Chamber's new brochure? Where else would I want to go?"

Hawk stared at his food, deciding it was time to say it. "To see mom." He looked up to find the laughter gone from Joby's face.

His father dropped his gaze, and asked quietly, "Has she told you she wants that?"

"No," Hawk said. "But I know she'd like it if you did."

"No dice," Joby said without looking up.

"Dad," Hawk said, an appellation he still found strange and rarely used, but which seemed very to the point just now, "you still love her, don't you?"

"Yes, I do," Joby said. "But I've got no business bothering her unless she wants to see me, and if she did, I'm sure she'd tell me so."

"Maybe not," Hawk pressed. "I understand how you felt when you found out about everything, but she really thought she was saving you, and it hurt her when you didn't even try to see that. Maybe she's just waiting for you to take the first—"

Joby raised a hand to stop him. "If you're trying to make me feel bad, son, you're months too late. I do. I have ... since hours after I destroyed everything."

"I'm not trying to make you feel bad," Hawk growled. "I'm just saying that maybe *you've* got to be the one to fix what happened. Maybe she just needs—"

"Some things can't be fixed," Joby said, looking up at last. His expression made Hawk want to wince. "Once you break them, you just have to make room for what's left." He got up and took his half-finished meal to the kitchenette, turned the water on, and stared into the sink. "I hurt her back in high school, much, much worse than I ever knew, and when she was brave enough to give me a second chance, I promised I would never hurt her again." He laid his dishes under the water, and turned to look at Hawk with steely resignation. "But I did, Hawk. What should I go say to her now? I promise ... *again*? ... Third time's the charm?" He shook his head. "I'm sorry, Hawk. You have no idea how sorry. ... She deserved better, and so did you. But if she wanted to give me more chances, she wouldn't have moved so far away from Taubolt."

✳

"I still can't believe this works!" Joby said in hushed wonder as he set a ring of dandelion seeds spinning clockwise, then counterclockwise in the air above their heads.

"You learn faster than anyone I ever heard of," GB said quietly.

"Well, that would be largely to my teacher's credit," Joby said, letting the ring of seeds disintegrate on the breeze as he turned to grin wanly at GB. His face was pallid with fatigue, his eyes red-rimmed for want of sleep. The sight filled Lucifer with satisfaction as Joby's grin grew careworn, and vanished altogether. "I wish Solomon could see this," Joby said sadly. "He'd be so surprised."

Buck up, Joby, Lucifer thought dryly. *He's missing not a moment of it.* "But you're not showin' this to anybody yet, right?" GB said aloud.

"No, GB," Joby sighed, bending to sit on a tangled hump of tree roots. "I'm not going to blow your cover."

"Just a few more months, and it won't seem so sudden," GB said apologetically. "It's just, if these demons can get to an ancient like Solomon, what chance would I have? If they even suspect I could get into their minds, I'd be dead in two seconds."

"You're really that sure it wasn't just a stroke?" Joby asked glumly.

"I told you; guys as powerful as Solomon don't just have strokes. It was them all right, though I still wonder what he was doin' up there at all when you were gone."

"You're too suspicious, GB," Joby said. "I've known him for years. Besides, he wouldn't have talked to Gladys first if he was trying to sneak into my room."

"Unless he just wanted to be sure you were out," GB insisted. "You said they all used to hide from you, right? Are you so sure they're not still hiding?"

"Hiding what?" said Joby. "GB, I hate to say it, but you're sounding awfully paranoid these days."

"I know," GB scowled, "but can you blame me? Don't you see what's goin' on around here? This isn't just some little band of asshole demons who stopped to look around on their way through. They're *staying* 'til they take Taubolt down *completely.* Every last brick! Why? Why now? What are we really caught in the middle of here, Joby? Has anybody told you? You bet I'm paranoid. You should be too." GB shook his head in frustration. "I finally reach a place I could stay with people like me, I and get here just in time to see it all destroyed. You have any idea what that's like?"

"Yes," Joby said sadly. "I do." His eyes were seeing something elsewhere. Lucifer suppressed a smile, imagining all the many elsewheres it might be. "That's about *all* I ever knew 'til I came here." Joby's red-rimmed eyes focused again. "We've still got Jake, GB, and a lot of gifted people on the Council. They'll think of some way to—"

"Hide?" GB finished for him. "'Til the demons just go away? That's all I see anybody doin'. Who's gonna go away is *us*, Joby. One by one, just like Rose did, and those other guys, Sky and Jupiter, and from what I've heard, a bunch more before them. People are dyin' at an awful rate here, if you haven't noticed. Pretty soon there won't be any of us left to cry about it."

"Gotta have a little faith, GB," Joby said, looking at him with obvious concern.

"You a preacher now?" GB retorted. "Well, here's a Bible quote for ya. '*Ask* and it shall be given. *Seek* and you shall find. *Knock*, and the door will open.' Faith's fine, but someone's gotta *act*, Joby. Someone's gotta find the balls to stop them anyway it takes."

"Which would be how?" Joby asked quietly. "Do you know?"

There's the question we've been waiting for, Lucifer gloated silently. But, as always, timing was everything. Reel the line too fast and it might snap. "Not yet," GB sullenly admitted. "But I'm workin' on it. I'll let you know." He scuffed at the ground, and said, "Sorry if I'm bein' a prick. I just get pretty bummed sometimes."

"Hey," Joby said reassuringly, "I don't need you to be cheerful all the time. We all get bummed these days. I sure do. You're completely welcome to talk with me about it." He looked wearily away. "To be honest, I'm glad you're there to talk with too sometimes." He shook his head. "Hawk's been through so much, I hate to burden him more with my troubles, especially when so many of his were my fault. Laura's gone," he said bleakly. "Everybody else in town is so busy trying to defend what's left." He looked up to smile grimly at GB. "Seems like you're about the only person I've got left that's been through enough shit to really understand and isn't too busy or fragile to confide in. So, by all means, complain away, as long as I can do the same sometimes. Deal?"

"Deal," said GB, reaching out to shake Joby's hand. "Thanks, man, for understanding. I envy Hawk. He's real lucky to have you."

"Not as lucky as I am to have him," said Joby. He glanced up at the sky above their isolated woodland "classroom," then clapped GB on the shoulder and said, "I'd better go. Hawk'll be wondering where I've gone by now."

"Next week then?" GB asked.

Joby nodded. "Thanks again, GB. For all of this. You hang in there."

Oh, I will, thought Lucifer. *Count on it.*

✴

"So I took a quick walk with one of my students," Joby said, seeming genuinely puzzled. "I don't see why that upsets you so much."

"You have time to go hiking with GB?" Hawk shrugged, sounding whiny even to himself. "I thought you had a *Youth Park* meeting."

"I did. It ended a little early. I was already there at the school and so was GB. He wanted to talk about what had happened at the meeting, so we went walking in the woods for, what, forty minutes? An hour maybe? What was I supposed to tell him, Hawk? No, I can't talk with you? My son wanted to go hiking today, and I couldn't, so you can't have me either? Not even for a half an hour?"

"It's half an hour now?" Hawk growled. "Not forty minutes or an hour?"

Joby rolled his eyes. "Look," he said. "I'm here now. It's light for hours yet. You want to go out for a walk? I'll give you *two* hours. Will that help?"

Hawk was too embarrassed, and too angry, to say anything at all. Since returning to his senses after Rose had died, he'd worked hard to repair his damaged friendships around town. Hawk hadn't known GB that well before what he now thought of as "his illness," but the boy was one of Joby's favorite students, and Hawk had felt bad about being so jealous of him earlier, assuming his feelings had been nothing but another symptom of his dark condition. Lately though, he wasn't so sure. GB had received Hawk's repentant overtures more magnanimously than many, but there'd also been something smarmy about his "understanding attitude." Today hadn't been the first time Hawk had caught GB and Joby coming companionably out of Taubolt's fields or woods together. He didn't know what they were always out there doing, but there still seemed something wrong about it.

"What's you're problem with GB?" Joby asked when Hawk went back to sorting laundry without answering his question.

"Sorry, Joby, but I just don't trust him."

"Why not?"

"Look, Joby, you keep talking like you get it, but I don't think you do. Since last August, Taubolt has been under assault by *demons*. I met one, remember? I know you grew up in a dusty suburb where there wasn't any 'fairy magic,' but wake up and smell the coffee! They disguise themselves as people, Joby—strangers! GB came here out of nowhere right in the middle of all this. What does anybody really know about him?"

"You're saying *GB's* a demon now?" Joby half-laughed.

"Do you know he's not?" Hawk insisted.

"You're serious!" Joby said, appalled. "Hawk, Nacho took him straight to members of the Council the day he got here. GB's story checked out fully. He's had a very rough life, and in spite of that, he's been nothing but help in trying to defend this community almost since the day he arrived. Why should I distrust him? Why should you?"

It was true. GB had been checked out by several members of the Council. But then, the Council hadn't recognized the demon riding Hawk's back either, had they?

"That school down there is full of kids who've come to Taubolt in the last few years," Joby pressed. "Am I supposed to suspect them all?"

"No," Hawk sulked. "But most of them aren't . . . like GB."

"You keep saying that, but you never tell me what's wrong with him. Do his eyes flash red or something?"

"He's got such a way with the power, for one thing," Hawk said, sounding pathetic, even to himself, "and such a way with you, for another."

He watched Joby consider him with . . . was that amusement? "You know," his father said at last, "I hate to say this, but you sound a little jealous."

"Forget about it," Hawk said crossly. To his relief, the phone rang.

"Hello," Joby said, after grabbing the receiver. "Bridget! Hi. I just got back" Joby's expression darkened. "That bitch," he sighed. "Wait a minute. Slow down. It's a pain in the ass, but if I have to get a credential now, I'll go get one." There was a longer pause during which Joby's expression went from pained to thunderous. *"What!"* he exclaimed. "Can they just do that? Who do they think is going to replace me?" Joby's expression went from angry, to angry and scared. "Well . . . what can I do?" he asked quietly. "Isn't there anything?" Another pause, and then, "Yeah. Thanks. I'll meet you down there in ten minutes."

He hung up the phone, and just stood looking down at it, his back to Hawk.

"What happened?" Hawk asked anxiously.

"That goddamn *fucking bitch!"* Joby yelled, slamming his hand down on the tabletop. When he turned around, Hawk took an involuntary step away. Veins stood out on Joby's neck and forehead, his face had been transformed by anger. He looked almost like a demon himself. "She's trying to get me fired now!"

❊

"After all the years of work I've done for this district," Joby said, his head hung in furious despair, "everything I've gone through just this summer to protect the very kids they're supposed to be concerned for! I can't believe they're doing this to me! Hamilton, I couldn't care less about," he said in disgust. "Who expects anything else from her, but the school board! And without even talking with me? If Bridget hadn't called me, I'd probably already be fired by now! Were they just going to wait until I showed up at school in September? Announce it in front of my first class?"

Joby finally looked up at GB, realizing that he'd been ranting for at least ten minutes while the boy had simply listened patiently, managing, somehow, to convey genuine concern and sympathy in total silence. The gift of a true fellow sufferer, Joby thought, considering all the far more terrible things GB had been through.

"Taubolt's kids are your whole life," GB said when it was clear that Joby had run dry of words. "You'd die for us. Everybody in this town knows that. You were practically the first person Nacho talked about the night I got here. If the school board's too dumb to see that, they're about to get an education. People in this town will *really* riot when they find out. You've been saving them all summer. Now they'll save you." He came to put an understanding hand on Joby's shoulder. "You'll see. This is never gonna happen, Joby."

Joby had come to meet GB at the appointed time, in their usual spot, because he hadn't been able to contact him in time to cancel, but their magic lesson hadn't really gotten off the ground today.

"Thanks for listening to me spew, GB," said Joby, "but I shouldn't be wasting your time here. Let's learn me some magic."

"Are you sure?" GB said. "We don't have to, if—"

"No, this is what we came to do," said Joby. "Hamilton's preempting enough of my life. I'm not giving this to her too."

"Okay," GB shrugged. "What do you want to try this time?"

Joby thought for a moment, then smiled sardonically as a very therapeutic idea struck him. "Teach me how to blow things up."

"What?" said GB, uncertainly. "What things?"

"I don't care," Joby said. "Anything you want. Rocks, stumps, bugs. Anything big enough to make a decent boom. I'll pretend it's Hamilton."

"Cool." GB grinned. "Okay. Here's what you do."

⚹

As spring gave way to summer beyond the confines of his season-neutral retail environment, Merlin had been deluged with increasingly grim live-action broadcasts in living cosmicolor of Lucifer's revolting predations upon Joby, and all of Taubolt's many boiling conflicts, one of which was coming to a head this evening at the local school board meeting. The question of Joby's future at the high school, which had escalated into a battle royale between Taubolt's old ways and its new, was to be resolved at last.

As he continued mapping out the convoluted path to freedom, Merlin had been turning occasionally to watch the proceedings. The meeting was already in its second hour. Joby's rapport with Taubolt's teens had been praised or denigrated, according to each speaker's sympathies. His lack of certification had been set against his excellent performance in the classroom. Occasionally, the view on Merlin's TV screens zoomed in on Joby, seated in the front row, never speaking unless directly addressed, watching with unreadable expressions as his fitness was debated.

Bridget O'Reilly had just explained again why Joby had been hired without a credential and asked why he couldn't just go get one now. The board had replied that, given Joby's failure to admit his uncredentialed state immediately, his character had become the central issue. Still, it seemed more and more that Joby would prevail.

Then Agnes Hamilton came forward with "new evidence" of Joby's unsuitability.

"When I think of all the things I could have turned you into," Merlin grumbled as she appeared on screen.

"I know many of you are fond of Mr. Peterson," she said, "but this board is not elected to conduct popularity contests. Its mandate is to ensure that those to whom we entrust our children—"

"*Our* children!" someone shouted. "You haven't even got any."

Roger Tanning, the board's president, banged his gavel, glaring at the audience. "Please continue," he said to Agnes when quiet had been restored

"To ensure," she began again, "that *your* children are entrusted to safe and trustworthy persons who teach constructive values. Caring as passionately as I do about both quality of education and the safety of our youth—" There were more rude noises from the audience, quickly gaveled down. "I have assembled a body of evidence that clearly shows that Mr. Peterson is neither teaching constructive values, nor a safe adult with whom to leave your children."

She went on to present a noxious parade of "sworn written testimony," some of it from tourists, demonstrating nothing except that Joby was more sympathetic to Taubolt's kids than to Hamilton's agenda. One accusation, that Joby had referred to Hamilton as "the goblin lady" during a lunchtime discussion with other teachers, merely won Agnes her first big laugh that evening. Even Tanning was starting to look impatient with her.

"As amusing as many of you seem to think this is," she said impatiently, "it presents a very disturbing pattern. Has no one ever wondered why there's hardly a teenager in Taubolt who won't do whatever Mr. Peterson asks at the drop of a hat? Does that seem natural? What other adult do they treat this way? Of course, it's less mysterious when one sees how often he undercuts legitimate adult authority. Of course your children adore him. He tells them what they want to hear, whatever the effect on their behavior afterward. He not only regards his students as personal friends, but treats them like peers, socializing more often, it seems, with people half his age than with adults. Do you really want your children learning from a man who seems to have such difficulty understanding where to place himself on the scale of maturity?"

The audience before her was clearly growing uncomfortable, but not, Merlin thought, with Joby. "Do go on, dear lady," he muttered at the TV screen. "You've nearly enough rope to do the job now. By all means, hang yourself."

"And who are these *'personal friends'* Joby gathers from your cradles?" Hamilton continued. "*Boys*—nearly all of them. Young, pretty boys. Not a girl in the bunch."

Clearly incensed, Joby finally stood, and said, "If I may, Mr. Tanning?"

"I would like to finish," said Hamilton. "He is welcome to respond in his turn."

"If it's brief, Mr. Peterson," Tanning said, ignoring Hamilton.

"I can't see how it would look better," Joby said, "if my younger friends were all girls. I lean toward friendships with male students precisely because there *is* less risk of misunderstanding regarding my intentions there. I would also like to say that I deeply resent Ms. Hamilton's implication here."

"Methinks he doth protest too much," Hamilton said frostily. "I am curious why a man of your polished social skills, respectable income, and, frankly, decent looks, Mr. Peterson, is still single and apparently uninterested in more mature company."

At this, there was an uproar that took quite a bit of gavel banging to subdue.

"Ms. Hamilton," Tanning scowled when he had finally been heeded by the crowd, "I begin to find your remarks *very* inappropriate. Unless you have some substantial proof of the things you are implying, I—"

"I do," she interrupted, unable to conceal the smirk of triumph on her face. "I would like to ask one of Mr. Peterson's students to come forward: a boy known as GB."

Merlin groaned, but morbid fascination kept him watching as GB came forward glancing desolately at Joby in such convincing imitation of remorse that Merlin had to shudder at whatever must be coming.

"Now GB," Agnes attempted a sympathetic smile with rather gruesome results, "just answer my questions as simply and honestly as you did for Sheriff Donaldson."

Joby jumped up again, demanding, "What's the sheriff doing questioning my students? This is no police matter!"

"Mr. Peterson," Tanning barked. "You will be given ample time to address all of this, but I ask you, please, to let us hear what this boy has to say."

Hamilton's smile grew more genuine, if less sympathetic. "GB," she said, "you are a very good-looking boy. I'm sure you know that. Has Mr. Peterson ever spoken to you about your appearance?"

GB nodded, looking at the floor.

"What did he say?" Hamilton asked.

GB mumbled something unintelligible and Agnes asked him to speak up.

"He said I was attractive," GB said, looking humiliated.

Merlin's view swiveled to show the incredulity spreading over Joby's face.

"I see," said Hamilton, adopting a far graver expression and tone.

"It wasn't like that!" GB protested, looking again in apparent agony at Joby. "I was just worried about how I'd make a living when I grew up! That's all."

"Of course," said Hamilton. "And what did Mr. Peterson suggest?"

"He said I had nothing to worry about, 'cause I could be a model."

"A model," Hamilton repeated. "Well, I'm sure he's right. You are, as he said, a very *attractive* boy. Is that the only job he suggested?"

"Well . . . yeah," GB said.

"Nothing else?" Hamilton pressed. "As an English teacher, I'd expect him to suggest at least a couple other things. What about being a writer, or a teacher like himself? A professional athlete even. Didn't he suggest any other options?"

GB shook his head, looking at his feet again.

"And where did this conversation take place, GB; in Mr. Peterson's classroom?"

GB shook his head again, the embarrassed blush returning to his face.

"Where then?" Hamilton insisted.

"The woods." GB frowned.

" 'The woods,' " Hamilton repeated. "Was there anyone else there?"

"No," GB said. "Just us."

"And what were the two of you doing there, out in the woods, alone, when he called you attractive?"

GB looked up at Joby in obvious distress.

"GB?" Hamilton purred. "You're not in any trouble as long as you tell the truth."

Merlin began to curse Lucifer in every language he had ever learned.

"I can't," GB said, looking close to tears. "You wouldn't believe me anyway."

"A tutorial," Joby said, raising his voice to be heard over the growing murmur of the crowd. "GB has some trouble reading. It embarrasses him, for God's sake."

"Is that true?" Hamilton asked GB.

GB nodded, looking properly ashamed.

"Why did you think we wouldn't believe that?" Hamilton asked GB sadly, then turned a far less gentle gaze on Joby. "And why out in the woods, Mr. Peterson? Wouldn't tutoring be better served by a classroom full of books with lots of educational materials at hand?"

"Not for students who are inhibited by institutional settings," Joby replied coldly.

"Is that what you strive for with your students, Mr. Peterson?" she mused. "A lack of *inhibition*?"

"Ms. Hamilton," Tanning interrupted to his credit, "regardless of the truth in this matter, I must ask you to avoid—"

"I apologize," she cut him off. "I just find all this tremendously upsetting. Mr. Peterson, I've another question to ask you. I fear there is no gentle way to ask it, and before you answer, I will tell you that we already know the truth, and have witnesses to back it up, so I'd advise honesty this time. Have you, on any of your *field trips* with students, ever been naked in their presence, or seen them naked in yours?"

Joby just looked stunned at first, then enraged. "We were swimming!" he snapped. "For God's sake, Agnes!"

"Naked. Together," Hamilton said, undeterred. "With children who were your students . . . all *attractive* boys."

As the room erupted into chaos, Merlin could bear no more. He turned away from all the screens and went to work with renewed fervor at finding his way back from this exile Lucifer had imposed. There was nothing he could do from here to help his grandson, and his grandson very badly needed help.

35

(*"Justice"*)

"Can you feel it?" Lucifer exulted theatrically before his assembled demons in the darkened glade. *"Destiny's vast hinges . . . turning!* Soon Joby's rage will crest and fall on Taubolt like a tidal wave, and the gates of Heaven fall at last before our glory!"

Incarnate again after her "janitorial" stint in Hell, Kallaystra checked her nails in the starlight. Was that a chip?

Lucifer did like making speeches lately, but didn't seem to grasp that giving predawn pep talks like some Jazzercise instructor wasn't likely to engender big excitement when he'd *killed* a quarter of the class in just three months. Since losing Hawk to his own petulant stupidity, Hell's mighty leader had been terminating "poor performers" at a rate startling even by his standards—though not Kallaystra herself, interestingly, or any of the Triangle either, despite his *official* position still holding them responsible for every error he had made these past few years.

Whatever he might *say* now, Lucifer clearly knew he *needed* the few *intelligent* operatives left him. The question in Kallaystra's mind these days was how much they needed him. After giving Basquel his just desserts, Lucifer had called her back out of banishment without a single word of apology. She meant to make it through the rest of this alive, of course, but after that it would be a very chilly day in Hell before Lucifer ever saw her face again, much less secured her help.

Most things did seem back on course, though, she had to concede. Taubolt's clueless "ognibs" lived in constant fear of "crime" now, while the minds of their persecuted children roiled with *Rambo*-esque fantasies of revenge upon the hostile adult world embodied in Sheriff Donaldson. Meanwhile, Taubolt's angry merchants had regrouped with fresh determination since Joby's fall from grace, to demand an all out crackdown on "gang activity" in their little town. Even many of the half-breed bastards who dared call themselves "of the blood" were now preparing for defense at any cost. The tinder was so high and dry here that just one match would be sufficient to blow everything to Hell, and, if Lucifer was right this time, Joby was about to strike it.

Their only remaining frustration was Michael's surprising decision to join Heaven's new epidemic of disobedient archangels. He was always there now, thwarting any scheme not directly aimed at Joby. This, in Kallaystra's opinion, was by far the most intriguing development of all. Though it was never said, of course, everyone knew that Michael was the one angel Lucifer truly feared. Once consigned to Hell, as he would surely be now, might Michael not overthrow their current despot and provide some fresh leadership at last? Kallaystra had been thinking about how best to position herself against that possibility ever since she'd learned of Michael's sudden interference.

Realizing that Lucifer's motivational blather had finally ended, Kallaystra's attention returned to the day's instructions he was issuing.

"During your rambles about town," he said, "I want all of you to gather bits of physical evidence on as many of the youngsters Joby cares for as you can: personal effects, strands of hair, clothing fibers, anything that might seem telling at a crime scene. I'll see to gathering Hawk's, myself, of course, when I visit Joby later this morning.

"Kallaystra, dear," he said, turning to face her. "I need you to gather information, please. I want a list of every child in Taubolt whom Joby *doesn't* know."

"But he knows them all!" blurted Tique, mouth on, brain off, as usual.

"Not the youngest ones," smiled Lucifer, seeming unperturbed, then back to Kallaystra. "Concentrate on those newest to Taubolt and not *of the blood,* so Joby won't be recognizing family names. Children less than eight years old should do the trick. He's all about the teens these days." Looking up at the assembly, he said jauntily, "Let's be about our work then. So many lies to tell, so little time to tell them, eh?"

※

Joby stalked through Taubolt's tourist-cluttered streets like an angry shadow, avoiding any eyes that seemed familiar. Muriel's outrage at the school board had been transparent as she'd made it clear that Joby would be welcome as a waiter at the Heron's Bowl. But just making the request had been humiliating for him. Hamilton's obscene maneuver hadn't just cost him his job. Years of accumulated trust and community standing, not to mention self-esteem, had all been plundered in the instant it had taken that selfish whore to whisper "pervert" to his superiors.

Joby's hard-fought campaign against Donaldson, and all the other assholes who'd made youth itself a crime here, had collapsed almost overnight once Joby's own veracity had become suspect. His former compatriots had fallen to quarreling about which of their various pet agendas should take precedence over others now, and within a couple weeks the whole fatigued community had simply thrown up its hands and left the stage to Hamilton and her pet sheriff. Months of effort, once seen by Joby as the culmination of all he'd become here and his crowning gift to the community that had changed his life, were all ashes now, yards short of fulfillment.

Joby was done fighting for "justice." There was no justice in the world anymore; not even here in Taubolt. The Taubolt he had loved was gone. And maybe it deserved to be, given its complacence against despoilers like Hamilton. He'd spent all summer trying to defend Taubolt's children, but none of his so-called friends had done more for him than commiserate when Hamilton had made her move.

As Joby stormed down Shea Street toward his rusty car, he couldn't help recalling the last time he had been this angry—on the streets of Berkeley. Rage haunted both his waking and his sleep now, just as it had after Gypsy's murder. All the distance he had come since then—all the hurdles he'd surmounted, inside himself as well as out—just to end up right back where he'd started! Without Ben. Without Laura. Without hope, or wish to have hope anymore. *This* was what it all had earned him.

Lunging into his car, Joby slammed it into gear and sent startled pedestrians scattering from the street as he pulled out. What did all these tourists think the sidewalks were for? This wasn't Main Street, Disneyland. People really drove here! He sped home daring Donaldson's goons to pull him over now. Joby'd have some magic tricks to show them. What worked on rocks and bugs would doubtless work on cops as well. The image made it possible to smile for the first time in weeks.

As Joby yanked the car into his driveway, he saw GB sitting on the firewood box outside his door. The last time he'd seen the boy, GB had been fleeing the school board meeting in tears. For the first time since that night, Joby found himself grudgingly concerned for someone else. They watched each other as he climbed out of the car.

"I'm sorry," GB said desolately.

"Don't be," Joby growled, walking to unlock the door. "You were just used, the way she uses everybody." As he walked inside, he said, "She had her little ace all ready, anyway. You were just the appetizer." GB still hovered uncertainly outside. "If you're comin' in, come in," Joby said gruffly as he threw himself down to lie on the couch.

"Hawk's not here?" GB asked, stepping timidly in after him.

"He's gone to help out on the Garden Coast," Joby replied. "Said there was some kind of emergency, though he probably just can't stand any more of my company."

GB sat unhappily in Hawk's favorite chair, picking nervously at the upholstery.

"If it's any comfort," Joby told him, "the board's 'Dear John' letter just said I was being let go because I seemed stressed and unhappy in my work." He snorted mirthlessly. "Knew damn well I'd slap them with a wrongful termination suit faster than you could say, 'here's your ass,' if they'd written down the truth."

"Donaldson's gonna start patrolling the shops on Main Streets with dogs now," GB said miserably. "He's tellin' that to every kid he busts."

"Good," said Joby. "This town chose Hamilton's Gestapo. They should have it."

"Nobody chose that, Joby," GB said. "They just—"

"Yes, they did," Joby cut him off. "They could have stopped this if they'd really tried. They could have stopped all of it years ago. They just didn't care that much. I've been forcing help on people who never asked me for it. That was my biggest mistake."

For a while GB just looked at him despondently. Then he said, "Demon attacks are goin' up. Jake's managed to fend 'em off so far, but everybody's talkin' about goin' to the Garden Coast for protection if the Cup's not found soon." He hesitated. "Maybe you should go there right now, Joby."

"Why?" said Joby. "I've got no cause to run away. What else can they do to me?"

"Lots," GB said. "If the demons didn't have it out for you, she'd never have come after you this way."

"Who? Hamilton?" Joby scoffed. "What's she got to do with demons? She just took me down because I like the kids she hates."

"I don't think so," said GB. "Someone had to clue these demons in that we were here. Everybody says what a peaceful place this was. When did that begin to change?"

"The year *I* got here, if you want to know the truth," Joby said darkly.

"Just you?" GB asked. "What about Hamilton?"

Joby thought about it. "Yeah, I guess she came then too. So?"

GB nodded gravely. "And who were Sky and Jupiter after when they got killed?"

."Hamilton."

"And who brought Donaldson to Taubolt?"

"Hamilton," Joby breathed, sitting up as chills ran down his arms.

"She's workin' for them, Joby," GB said quietly. "She has been all along."

"But, there's no way to *know* that," Joby said. "You're just guessing."

"No, I'm not," GB said. "She's one of them. So is Donaldson."

"What, actual demons?" Joby said, incredulous despite his contempt for them.

"No. Hosts," GB said. "Demons aren't anything but air and bad intentions without a physical host. They need the host to make what they want real."

"How do you know this?" Joby said, wondering if GB were inventing all of it for some reason. "Every person of the blood I know has been talking about demons since October, and I never heard a thing about *hosts.*"

"I didn't know any of this either until three weeks ago," GB said bleakly. "When Donaldson questioned me."

"What! He told you?" Joby said, sure now that GB was lying. But why?

"No," GB said even more forlornly. "I saw it in his mind."

"What?" gasped Joby. "You did . . . what you did to me? To him? But you said—"

"I had no choice!" GB blurted. "He did it to *me*! I was so scared! He just pried me open, Joby. I couldn't keep him out, and I was sure he'd know I could see him back and kill me for it! I saw all kinds of things while he was in there, and if he knows . . ."

As GB began to cry, Joby leapt up to shut the cottage door, suddenly fearful of who, or what, might be lurking outside, listening. Then he turned to look back at GB in dawning horror. What the boy was describing was mental rape!

"When they let me go that day . . . I just thought they'd wait to kill me 'til I'd said what they wanted at that meeting," GB wept. "I've been hiding ever since then, expectin' 'em to find me, and . . . finish it. I'm sorry, Joby. I'm so sorry . . ."

"Hey," Joby said, coming to place a careful hand on GB's shoulder, unsure whether it would help or hurt to touch him while he was reliving this. "You did what you could to protect yourself. That's what I'd have wanted you to do. But that was weeks ago. If they were coming after you, wouldn't they have tried by now? Maybe you're okay."

"I don't know," GB said, swiping at his eyes, and dragging himself together. "He *was* pretty busy lookin' for what he wanted, and . . . and it got kind of physical," he added uncomfortably. "So maybe he was too busy to notice me in there lookin' back. Maybe—"

"Physical how?" Joby cut him off, his fury growing with each ugly revelation.

"It takes contact to get into another person's mind that way," GB said grimly. "Keepin' someone's arm cranked back works just as well as puttin' hands together."

"He tortured you?!" Joby yelled. *"Physically?"*

"They wanted you bad, Joby," GB said. "That's why I've been sayin', you gotta go up to that Garden Coast right now."

"No fucking way!" Joby exclaimed. "I'm not running off and letting them—"

"No!" GB shouted him down. "Joby, there's nothing you can do! They'll just deny it, and they've made everyone suspicious of you now. Besides, if I did get lucky, and they don't know what I saw, they sure will when you go howlin' back to town with it. You'll just get me killed for sure! Who you gonna go to, anyway? The cops? The school board? Why not just go to Hamilton?"

"This is fucked," said Joby, rubbing at his eyes as he began to pace.

"The point is, I know them now," GB said fiercely. "A lot of 'em anyway. Donaldson's head was full of their names. You asked me once if I knew what to do about it. Remember? That day we did the dandelion trick? Well, now I do. Now that we know who and where they really are, we can take Taubolt back and make it just the way it used to be. Without their hosts, the demons will be nothin' but a stink on the wind. Jake and the Council will be able to deal with 'em in an afternoon then. But we're not just talkin' about Donaldson and Hamilton. There's at least twenty or thirty more hosts hidden here in town. We've got to get them all at once, and we gotta do it totally *alone,* Joby. We go to anybody else with this, and nine to one, I'm roadkill before sunset. I *need* to know you understand that."

"I understand it," Joby said wearily. "I just got too angry to think straight for a minute, but I'm thinking now. So what's this plan of yours?"

❧

"Good work," Lucifer said, setting down the list that Kallaystra had brought him.

Was that a compliment? she thought dryly. He really *must* be hard pressed.

"Now I need you to find me five adolescent boys. No one *of the blood,* you understand, or known to Joby in the slightest. They must all be 'ognibs' as the vermin call them, and as new to Taubolt as you can find. I'm looking for vivid and violent imaginations, more than usual credulity, and serious delusions of grandeur."

"As you said" she smiled sweetly, "adolescent boys," thinking that any of Taubolt's numerous computer-gaming freaks would fit the bill quite nicely.

"Your task," he went on, "will be to convince them there is real magic hidden in Taubolt, and you need their help to save it. You have three weeks, though I'd prefer it sooner. Joby's still refusing me, but he's very brittle and could break at any moment. When he does, I don't want to give him any more time to think than necessary. Think you can handle the pace this time?" he asked severely.

"Of course," she said frostily. "Coming *out* of hiding is always simpler, especially when half of what I'm telling them is true. Once I've shown the magic to them, what's left for such ready minds to question? How should I describe the help I'm asking for?"

"Tell them that Taubolt's *fairies,* of which you are one, of course, are threatened by an invasion of demons." Lucifer smiled at last. "Explain that there's a spell that will defeat the demons, but it requires five mortal channels."

"I'll have them in three *days,*" Kallaystra smirked. "They'll have had wet dreams that don't excite them half as much as this will."

"Explain the dire need for secrecy, of course," Lucifer added with mock gravity, "and make it clear that great courage will be required, but that they will not be harmed." His smile returned. "What they don't know won't . . . Well, yes it will," he shrugged happily, "but that's all part of the fun, isn't it?"

Kallaystra was quite familiar with the spell he meant. "May I ask who these boys will be used to kill?" she asked.

Lucifer glanced toward the list of children she'd just given him, and said, "Why, all the nasty demon hosts in Taubolt, of course. Didn't I just explain that?"

✖

Midnight found Joby staring up into the darkness once again, sorting through the hopeless web of anxieties his life had become. He'd found GB's plan appalling. How had the boy even *imagined* him capable of *killing* people—demon hosts or not? He wanted very badly to discuss all this with someone other than GB—Jake, the Council, especially his son—but GB was right about at least one thing. Joby had learned long ago that, in a tiny town like Taubolt, secrets known to more than two weren't likely to stay secrets long—especially such explosive ones. With GB's very life at stake, it wasn't

Joby's right to divulge any of what he'd been told. That right was GB's alone.

Sleep had become such an infrequent visitor these past few weeks that Joby had trouble thinking even by broad daylight anymore. He closed his eyes again, trying to translate the fatigue that never left him now into the rest that never came, but the sudden crunch of running steps outside on his gravel drive had him halfway out of bed even before the pounding on his door began.

"Joby!" GB pled outside. "Joby, let me in!" *Pound, pound, pound.* "Wake up!"

Tying his robe, Joby hurried toward the door, flipping lights on as he went.

"What's happened?" Joby asked as GB tumbled from the darkness.

"They're gonna go after the Garden!" GB said, still breathing hard, as if he'd run here clear from town. "I don't know when exactly, but it's gonna be soon. Joby, you've got to decide! We gotta stop them now, or—"

"Wait a minute," Joby cut in. "Just . . . Here. Sit down," he said, closing the door and waving GB toward the couch. "How did you find out *this* now?" Joby asked wearily. "It's after midnight, GB. Couldn't you have waited until—"

"No!" GB exclaimed. "There's no time left, Joby. Don't you get it? They've got us rounded up like cattle here! Everybody thinks we can run up and hide out in the Garden if things get bad, but the demons have found out about it! I don't know how, but I saw! It's in all their heads!"

"Wait a minute," Joby said sharply, his sleep-deprived mind coming suddenly awake. "In whose heads? Don't tell me you've been—"

"I had to!" GB said defiantly. "You may be fine with sitting here and doing nothing, but it's a damn good thing I wasn't."

"Are you *crazy?*" Joby gasped. "What happened to all that fear of being killed? How many people's minds have you been gallivanting through *now,* for godsake?"

"I did it while they were sleeping," GB said sullenly. "I realized that most of them would never feel me there if they weren't awake, and just mistake me for a dream if they did. I wasn't caught, was I?" He frowned almost belligerently.

"I don't know!" Joby said angrily. "*Were you?* Do *you* know?"

"It doesn't matter!" GB protested. "If we don't do somethin' real soon, my dead ass'll just be one more on the pile here. They're gonna burn it, Joby! The Garden Coast!"

"What?" Joby gaped. "How do you—"

"Would you quit askin' that?" GB snapped. "How many times do I have to say it? I've been in their heads every night this week! I have the names of every demon host in town now. See?" He yanked a wad of paper from his back pocket, unfolding it as he held it out for Joby to look at.

Hamilton's and Donaldson's names were at the top, of course. Below these, at least thirty more were written in GB's neat printing. Other than a couple particularly obnoxious shop owners and two members of the school board, which Joby found as gratifying as it was unsurprising, there was not another name he recognized.

"I've never heard of most of these people," Joby said.

"Well, duh!" GB exclaimed. "Whadaya think, they're gonna stand out in front of Franklin's Hardware and wave at us? These are the people *no one* knows," he growled, folding up the list again and shoving it back into his pocket. "They're gonna set the woods on fire all around that Garden place, and burn it to the ground, along with anybody who's up there 'helping,' *like Hawk*," he finished pointedly.

"Oh, God," Joby breathed, not having thought of that yet. "When?" he asked, trying to remember when Hawk had said he'd be returning.

"I couldn't tell," said GB. "It seemed soon, but for obvious reasons, I've been gettin' in and out too quickly to look around for details. So are we gonna stop 'em, Joby, or just sit around and do nothin' like everyone you were complainin' about last week?"

All at once, Swami's urgent plea returned to Joby's mind. *Something bad . . . I don't know what yet. But . . . will you help us save this?* He'd seen all this coming, Joby realized with a shiver down the length of his whole body. They had told him Swami was a seer, but Joby had never . . .

"There won't be anywhere left for us to go," GB pleaded. "We'll be stranded here in Taubolt while they pick us off like hunters at a duck club."

"I can't kill people," Joby murmured in a daze. "I'm sorry," he said, as much to Swami as GB, "but I just can't do this."

"Bullshit!" GB shouted in frustration. "You're doing it right now! You're killing me and Hawk and every other person of the blood you know, Joby! You're killing *us* instead of a tiny handful of vicious haters. They're not even really people anymore. They're just food for what's inside them, hollow shells, burned out years ago by what their greedy, spiteful minds so eagerly invited once. I've been in their heads, remember? It's like pit toilets in there, Joby. Deep down, whatever's left of them is prob'ly beggin' for release. You'd be doin' 'em a favor, but no! You'd rather murder all your friends instead. Is that it?"

"Why don't *you* just do it then?" Joby snapped. "You've been doing magic all your life. If this decision is so simple, can't you just—"

"Weren't you listening when I told you last time?" GB cut in impatiently. "It's a *very big spell*! It's gonna take *both* of us and *five channels*!"

"Which will come from where?" Joby asked, hoping this necessity might buy him at least a bit more time to think.

"I've already found 'em," GB said. "There are some very brave and generous kids in this town, as you already know. And some of them are just as eager to get rid of Donaldson as we are."

"Those people on your list," Joby pleaded. "I don't even know them. How can I kill people I don't even know?"

"It's prob'ly better that way," GB said quietly. "You won't suffer as much later. Joby," he said, sounding almost tender suddenly. "I know this is a terrible decision. I hate them even more for forcing you to make it. I shouldn't have yelled that way, but you do know Hawk, don't you. Will it hurt less to let him die? You knew Rose. Imagine her death times hundreds. You have the power to stop that. All of it. How're you gonna feel, later, knowing that you didn't?" He stood up to come stand face to face with Joby and look sadly into his eyes. "A lot of people are about to die here, Joby," he said softly. "The demons haven't left you any choice about that. You only get to choose who." When Joby failed to find his voice, GB said, "Who's gonna die, Joby?"

"I need time to think about this," Joby said palely as the choice tore through him.

"How much time?" GB said, still quietly, but with clear frustration.

"I don't know," Joby murmured. "A day?"

"You told me once about your friend, Ben," GB said sympathetically. "That fire was their doing too, you know. If you'd had the power to save him then, would you have sat around asking yourself all these moral questions first?"

The question hit Joby like a rock fall. *If he'd had the power then*...It had never even crossed his mind, until now. He'd healed Sky years before, just by wanting him healed, if Tom Connolly had been right. Joby felt dismay spread across his face as he stared into GB's questioning eyes. Why hadn't he healed Ben? Surely Joby had wanted that as badly as he'd ever wanted Sky's recovery...Or hadn't he?...Deep down...had he hesitated...not sure, perhaps, whether to want a rival gone?

"Oh God," Joby whispered, tears welling in his eyes. *"Oh God."* Was he a murderer already? Somewhere deeper in his heart than wherever all these self-ennobling moral qualms were coming from? *Why hadn't his desire been enough to heal Ben?*

"Take your day, then," GB said, breaking their gaze and heading for the door. "I just hope Hawk hasn't burned to death up there by the time you make up your mind."

Joby hardly heard him go. He was still seeing Ben's fire-ravaged face, the moment he had died . . . *She's yours.*

"Not anymore, Ben," Joby whispered, tears streaking down his face. "I failed her too. I've failed everyone I ever loved."

✳

Hawk got back from his shift up on the Garden Coast just after eight, and stopped at Franklin's grocery to get some breakfast fixings. He'd felt pretty guilty about leaving his father at such a time, but he'd seen nothing he could do to help diminish what had happened, and two weeks of Joby's alternation between bleakness and rage had left Hawk desperate for enough distance to get some perspective and regroup. Cooking something really special for their breakfast now seemed like a good way to apologize.

As he left his car to cross the still deserted street, Hawk was surprised to see one of Taubolt's skater types up this early, loitering ahead of him outside the still unopened bakery. He was even more surprised when the boy beckoned him furtively into an alcove between the two buildings.

"You're Joby's kid, aren't you?" said the boy as Hawk drew near.

"Yes," Hawk answered. "Do I know you?"

"Uh-uh," said the boy. "But we all know who you are." He looked around anxiously, then half-whispered, "The fairy lady told us what happened to you."

"What?" Hawk said.

"The demon who was in you," the boy whispered even more quietly.

"Who are you?" Hawk demanded.

"I'm Abe," the boy said, glancing nervously around again, then, even more quietly, "We're gonna make 'em pay—for you, and everybody they been hurtin'."

"Pay?" Hawk said. "Make who pay? What are you talking about?"

Abe suddenly looked frightened. "I just thought . . . We're on your side. We're helping Joby! Please, don't tell 'em I said anything." He began to back away. "I could get in trouble. I just thought you'd like to know." As Hawk gaped, Abe turned and ran away.

"Hey! Wait!" Hawk called after him. "What's this about my father?" But the boy had already disappeared around a corner without ever slowing down.

For a moment, Hawk considered chasing him, but turned and headed back to his car instead. *We're helping Joby?* What was up with that?

Ten minutes later, Hawk came through the door to find his father already up and looking as pale with eyes as red-rimmed as a B-movie vampire.

"Hawk!" Joby gasped, leaping up to embrace him as if he'd come back from the dead. "Thank God! I was so worried."

"Why?" Hawk said, alarmed and confused. "What's happened now?"

"Nothing," Joby said, leaning away, and seeming suddenly unable to look Hawk in the eye. "You're not going back there are you?"

"To the Garden? No," Hawk said, wondering fearfully if Joby might have had a breakdown of some kind. "Why?"

"I just . . . need you here," said Joby, while avoiding Hawk's gaze.

"You look terrible," Hawk said. "What's going on?"

"Nothing," said his father. "I've just . . . I've been having trouble sleeping."

Yeah, right, Hawk thought. And Atlantis had a leaky basement. Hawk's own still too-clear memories of demon possession left him fearful something more than insomnia might be at work here. There were a lot of things about the morning Jake had saved him that Hawk still didn't get. Jake had explained enough to help Hawk understand what had happened to himself, but the ancient had been unapologetic about refusing to discuss the rest. When he'd asked Hawk just to trust him and to keep the little that he had learned to himself, Hawk had seen no reason to deny him anything, in light of all he'd done. But despite the ancient's discretion, Hawk had left that awful morning well aware that something more than he'd been told was going on in Taubolt, and that somehow, for God knew what reasons, he, himself, had gotten tangled up in it. If the demons plaguing Taubolt had come after him, why not his father?

"Joby, what's really going on? I have to know."

"I just told you," his father said crossly. "I'm not sleeping. Is that so hard to fathom given everything they've put me through?"

"*Who's* put you through?" Hawk asked, thinking of the boy in town.

"Who do you *think?*" his father snapped. "Are you the only one in Taubolt who hasn't heard I lost my job?"

Hawk found a chair to sit in, feeling cold and numb. This was definitely not his father talking, unless Joby really had gone crackers in the week that he'd been gone. He knew he ought to smile and nod and go straight to Jake about it now, but Hawk's need to know what was happening, to confront and fix it, was too urgent to suppress.

"I was just stopped by a kid in town who wanted me to know that he's helping my father make the demons pay for everything," Hawk said grimly.

"I have no idea what he meant," Joby said, but Hawk had seen him flinch.

"What is it that you're too afraid to tell even *me?*" Hawk asked fearfully.

"I don't like being called a liar by my own son!" Joby snapped.

"I don't like being lied to by my father," Hawk said levelly, terrified and angry all at once at what might be clinging to Joby's back right now. "If you won't tell me what that kid was talking about," Hawk said, already rising to head for the door, "I'm going straight to Jake and asking him if he knows."

"Stay out of it!" Joby exclaimed. "GB's life could be at stake!"

"GB?" Hawk said, whirling back even more angrily. "What's he got to do with—"

"I *asked* you to stay out of it," Joby said, trying belatedly to curb his temper.

"Just tell me what you're tangled up in!" Hawk demanded, no longer curbing his.

Joby raised his head at last and gazed hard at Hawk. "I appreciate your concern, but I don't want you involved."

Hawk found it suddenly harder to breath, terrified of all Joby's answer implied. "You're my father," he said fiercely. "That makes me *involved.*"

"That's right," Joby said with sudden, steely calm. "And you're my son. I won't put you in harm's way."

"But it's supposed to be okay with me if *you* get hurt?" Hawk parried. "Dad, you've been trusting the wrong people."

"Who else should I have trusted?" Joby demanded.

"The Council, for one, Dad. Have you even tried to—"

"The *Council?*" Joby cut him off. "What have they ever done about anything?"

"What have they done?" Hawk said in disbelief. "They've worked day and night to defend this town! Ever since the night Jupiter and Sky died, they've done more than anyone else to protect the kids you care so much about—including me! Jake saved my friggin' life, Dad! How can you ask what they've done?"

"Like they protected Rose?" Joby pressed, clearly unswayed. "Have you forgotten her already?"

The question was so offensive that it might have sent Hawk from the house had he not schooled himself to remember that the person he was listening to was almost certainly not entirely his father, if it was his father at all. "Rose's death was an accident," he said painfully. "The Council had no—"

"An *accident*," Joby cut in derisively. "If that's what they told you, they lied! Demons killed her, son. Just like all the others."

"How do you know that?" Hawk protested. "Who told you that Rose was—" But he didn't need to finish the question. *"GB,"* he said through gritted teeth. "Why are you so ready to trust *him* instead of me, Dad? I'm your son, remember? Who's GB?"

"He's the one who's been *right* again and again," said Joby sadly. "About my aptitude for magic, about the Council's lies ... and about the kind of coward I've been."

"Okay," Hawk said, fighting tears, "so let GB tell you what to do, but can't you trust me enough to tell me what that is? Just tell me what you're going to do."

"I'm going to give them *justice!*" said Joby. "That's all I'll say about it. I'm sorry, but I won't ... I *can't* just let us all keep dying, one by one."

"What kind of *justice* is GB peddling?" Hawk asked hopelessly. "I'd give up *lots* of *justice* to have you back the way you were ... when we went hiking all the time. When we laughed, and ran, and fed the deer. When everybody didn't hate and fear and kill—for *justice*. ... Can you remember? We had peace here once, and love and joy. We had *beauty,* Dad. *That's* the only kind of justice I want now."

"Things can never be the way they were," Joby said, looking despondently at Hawk. "Time doesn't work that way. It just moves forward."

Forward, Hawk thought dismally, *toward some looming disaster that could not be stopped.* What was he to do? Unable to think of any other way past Joby's defenses, Hawk played the last desperate card he possessed.

"I love you, Dad," Hawk said quietly. "I've loved you since way before I knew you were my father. But I know, in every cell of my body, that you're about to make a terrible mistake. I don't know what it is, but I can feel it coming to destroy you, and ..." His eyes were swimming, and his throat had grown almost too tight to speak, but he had to get this out. "And I can't stay to watch that happen, 'cause watching will destroy me too. I'm sorry, but you've got to chose now: me, or this thing you're set on doing, whatever it is." He couldn't keep his tears in check. "I'll go now and give you time to think about it, but I'm coming back at ten tonight to get my stuff. Then I'm getting out of Taubolt. You can come with *me,* or you can stay and do . . . *your thing.* But if you let me go, I will not . . ." He turned and walked to the door, too torn up to stay another minute. "You've got to choose. That's all. No second chances," he said roughly, and walked out, terrified by what he'd done, and praying, *Please choose me, Dad. Please choose me.*

⚹

Joby stumbled, half-blind with grief, down a wooded trail toward the ocean, needing to move, perhaps just for the illusion of escape, and wishing that a sudden aneurism would make all his choices for him. He'd thought the night before that there'd been no one left to fail, but he'd overlooked one after all. Now Hawk could not abide him either. Joby was nothing but a loathsome pitfall to everyone who tried to love him. He'd have to get a sign to wear: UNCLEAN! UNCLEAN! DON'T GET TOO NEAR!

After GB's departure, Joby had managed only one brief lapse of consciousness just long enough to afford him a nightmare like the ones he'd suffered after Ben's death. It seemed so obvious now what his guilty mind had been shouting at him for so many weeks back then. How had he failed to see it? And if he'd killed his best friend just to steal Laura, why pretend he couldn't do what needed doing for much better reasons now? This really was war after all. Soldiers had to kill people all the time, and that didn't make them murderers. Swami, wherever he was now, had begged Joby to help them on this day. Joby was out of excuses.

By now GB's list of unknown names had acquired the faces of every grasping, vicious entrepreneur and self-serving yuppie loafer who had overrun and fouled his once-beloved Taubolt. They were to blame for this! They'd forced this hateful choice upon him the minute they'd started shoveling all their filth into his home! If someone had to die now because of it, why shouldn't it be them?

Greed, Joby thought, should be a virus; the kind that killed whoever caught it swiftly. Then maybe people wouldn't rush to embrace it so, and soon there'd be no more greedy people. The same for lies, and theft, and every other kind of hurtful satisfaction!

When Joby reached the cliff tops, he headed south along a deer trail in the, knee-deep grass until he came upon a weathered stack of stone half-overgrown in ancient Cypress trees. There he slumped against a rough gray trunk and stared out at the water. The sun had just begun to set behind a narrow band of fog far out to sea, throwing pastel rays of color up into the sky. The scene nagged at him somehow, as if he were remembering what he saw instead of merely viewing it. His mind was clearly going, but who could be surprised at that? Where was that aneurism? What was taking it so long?

"What is it that I haven't done?" he cried. "All my life I've tried, and tried. . . . But everything I touch . . . just turns to ash. . . . Why?"

He began to weep, and hated himself for that as well, and willed the tears to stop.

"Just show me what to do!" he whispered at the sky, watching in vain for any kind of sign. *"I've tried,"* he groaned, weeping once again. "But the world just withdraws, and withdraws. . . . Please! . . . just once . . . just answer me! I need to know . . . what I should *do!*" He looked up in anguish at the clouds, turned salmon in the darkening air. "Please," he whispered one more time. "What have I not given?"

There was no answer but the wind, soughing through the brittle grass and cypress boughs around him. Only wind.

"It's costing me my *son!*" Joby shouted at the air. *"I've sacrificed my son! Isn't that enough? Don't you care at all?"* Receiving only silence still, he left the trees, breathing hard, slicked with sweat, and filled with fury. "Well, *I* will care then! *I* will act!" he raged. "*I* will give them all the *justice* that you've *never* given *me!*"

Joby stalked away then, not back up toward his house, but north, toward town to find GB and tell him he had made his choice. The boy had been right all along. Empty faith was impotent. Only action changed things.

36
(The Final Measure)

Merlin didn't bother watching anything the TV screens portrayed now. There wasn't time. The storm was breaking, and he had to be there when it did.

He was so close, *so close.* And even as he thought this, the last knot slipped away, and he simply *was*! The mall whirled around him and dissolved, as those few, by now barely perceptible, particles of blood drew his spirit back to Joby's empty former room at Gladys Lindsay's inn. Merlin gazed about him in stunned elation, returned at last to space and time, if not yet to his body, which was, of course, no longer here. Having come this far, however, that last step would not be hard. Urgently, he called out to find his flesh, and followed its reply to Santa Rosa.

※

Lucifer sat beside their little fire in exaltation, watching Joby practice the spell by which he'd kill half of Taubolt's children in the morning, including their five teenage channels, who would be consumed as well by the darkness they'd be there to amplify. GB had even managed to convince Joby that their ritual must be performed up on the Garden Coast, at last giving Lucifer access to that offensive refuge too.

It had all come off so perfectly! Like clockwork, in a single year! Whatever had his troop of morons done with all that other time? Lucifer could only shake his head, suspecting they just hadn't any sense of timing. Timing, after all, had been the key.

He should just have faced the unpleasant task of coming here to do the job himself far sooner. There was so much blah, blah, blah in Hell about how domineering, unsupportive and untrusting he was, but look what delegation had gotten him! If not for his misguided urge to nurture all their botched attempts, who knew what Joby might have been by now? Dictator of all America, quite possibly, doing evil of historic significance, instead of just some paltry wickedness like murdering numbers of anonymous children—*again*. Alas, that would have to satisfy at this late date, though there were still enough years left for Joby to do at least a few worse things afterward. That's how it always worked, of course. Get a man to do something so unendurably shameful that he'd do any number of even worse things to hide what he'd become, until he'd gladly burn the entire world just to hide his dirty laundry—from no one but himself, of course, by then.

It was such a simple concept, really. Why did so many of his own employees seem to have such trouble grasping it?

❋

Getting back into his body had been as simple as falling into bed. Getting out of the hospital with it, much less back to Taubolt, would be by far the greater challenge. Merlin found his flesh attached to a labyrinth of life support almost as tangled as the knots by which Lucifer had held him in oblivion. His poor body had become so atrophied that magic was required just to move it now. Still, there was cause for thanks. It seemed nurses came seldom to the bedside of a man who'd been a vegetable for months, so he suffered no interruptions while executing the demanding and often unpleasant tricks required to free himself without setting off alarms. The surprising lack of demonic guards was an unexpected blessing too. Apparently, Lucifer had been that sure of Merlin's helplessness.

Since no one near him was alert to the use of magic, Merlin was able to wander from his room in search of an exit using nothing more elaborate than a few simple cantrips for disguise and misdirection. He stopped once along the way to steal a wallet and some keys, with silent apologies, from the pocket of a busy doctor—along with that man's knowledge of where his car was parked. Merlin frowned on theft, but with so much strength required just to animate his wasted body, Taubolt was much too far away to leap to by any of the usual magic means. The good doctor would see his car again at any rate, and Merlin would be sure the tank was full. In fact, the man would hereafter find his mileage quite improved.

❋

As dawn spread over Taubolt's summer fields, Joby lay awake in bed, having failed to sleep at all for the third night in a row. The moment was at hand, but he felt too paper-thin to rise, though they were doubtless waiting at the school already—GB and his little band of "channels,"—to be taken to the Garden Coast. Joby groaned, and rolled his face into the mattress.

He no longer cared what happened to himself. There seemed no self left for anything to happen to. He'd lost the last thing he had ever cared about when he'd become so angrily absorbed in planning with GB that he'd *forgotten* Hawk's ten o'clock deadline. He had intended to be there, to talk some sense into his son, make him see that nothing was ever that black-and-white, but, God help him, he'd *forgotten,* until coming home well after midnight to find all of Hawk's things gone. Falling directly into bed, he'd thought of little else all night but what Hawk must have made of his failure even to appear. *No second chances.* Those words seemed etched into his soul now.

"*What have I done?*" he groaned.

Forcing himself from bed at last, he stumbled miserably toward the bathroom. It was all a sacrifice. That was the only way to see it now. When he'd done, what he was going to do, he'd probably not even have a soul left, but Taubolt would be saved. That was all that justified his very existence now: what countless others would gain when Taubolt had been cleansed of Hamilton and Donaldson and all their hellish associates.

Then he reached the bathroom, and found the battered little book that Hawk had taped onto the mirror. The only thing his son had left: Rose's book of flower fairies! Seeing it pinned to the reflection of his own ghastly, pale face, every detail of Rose's memorial service returned with razor sharpness—most clearly of all, the moment he had rushed to hug the son he'd feared dead.

Joby staggered back to sit roughly on the toilet, trembling with dismay as an unendurable parade passed before his inner eyes, of all the things he'd loved, but starved or thrown away to feed, instead, the things he'd feared or hated. The last balloon to pass was the memory of his tantrum in the fields the night before. *I've sacrificed my son!* he'd screamed. And it was true. That was precisely what he'd done!

For *what*?

To save someone *else's* children? To save the *Garden Coast*; a patch of old trees and exotic flowers? *In exchange for his son?* What made the Garden Coast that much better refuge than a hundred others they might run to? Had Joby even asked? No! Suddenly it all seemed so preposterous! The entire scheme. The secrecy. The tragic, heroic posses! These were the stuff of adolescence! Fantasies that no one but a boy should be able to take seriously, yet Joby had let himself be led by just such an adolescent, when he, the adult, should have done the leading! How had he allowed it? How could he have *thrown away his son* for *this*? Had Hamilton been right when she'd accused him of not knowing how to act his age?

At the disgust even this brief thought of Hamilton brought him, the remaining scales fell from Joby's eyes, and he saw the awful truth. As stupid as these other reasons were, he'd let himself be led for an even more pathetic one: He'd *wanted* to believe the boy. He'd been so angry, so eager to blame and punish someone, so sure he knew who deserved that punishment, and . . . so sure that *he* was *right*. He'd thrown away the *son he loved* just to purge his little town of those he loathed, as if the world wouldn't merely send another wave of loathsome creeps to Taubolt from its bottomless supply. GB had been wrong. It wasn't just about who died. It was about who did the killing too, or Taubolt would be saved for nothing but a whole new generation of monstrous prosecutors—like Joby had become, or was about to. Hawk had tried to tell him that just yesterday, and it brought Joby grief to know now that he'd have heard his son if only he had listened with his heart instead of with his *righteous* anger.

If demons were about to burn the Garden Coast, both that news and GB should be taken straight to Jake, who was neither demon spy nor gossip, and had proven more than able to shield many other children from attack. Had there been any doubt before, Joby knew now that the biggest ass in human history was himself.

Leaping up, he headed for his room to dress in desperation. There had to be a way to fix this. First, he'd have to go stop this madness and get GB under Jake's protection. However much the boy might hate him for it now, he'd be grateful later. And if not? Ah well. Joby had broken everything else he valued, why not this friendship too? Then Joby would find his son, wherever he had gone, and tell Hawk he'd been right. It couldn't really be too late to choose! Were such bonds broken so quickly? God, he hoped not.

As he yanked his shoes on, Joby decided to call Laura if their son refused to listen. He had hurt her, yes, but she'd never been a petty or vindictive person. Surely she would help him. As he rushed outside to jump into his car, Joby dared to hope. He'd missed Hawk's deadline, but he hadn't done the things Hawk had been trying to prevent. Wasn't that the choice his son had given him; come with me, or do your thing? The clock might have run out, but Joby prayed the choice was still in motion.

☸

As she looked around at Merlin's living room, Kallaystra couldn't help but be impressed. More than half the house was made literally of magic. The old man had clearly lost none of his prowess since she'd been sent to lure him into confinement the *last time* Arthur's endeavors had collapsed. She ran her fingers down a door frame of remarkably believable wood, marveling at how much power must be woven into this structure, amazed, despite her-self, that any mortal man could be so *potent*. What a shame to waste that vir-ile body on a coma. He'd even been strong enough to leave his house protected by a self-sustaining spell that had forced her to incarnate not three steps into his yard. She'd just had time to will herself into Nimue's form one more time for old times' sake, as it took hold.

Tique had intercepted a phone call that morning, to Joby's cottage from the hospital, nervously reporting that Mr. Rand was missing. Incredulous that Merlin had escaped, Lucifer had sent Kallaystra and the Triangle to watch the several locations he thought Merlin most likely to return to, though Kallaystra could not imagine how even such a powerful enchanter would pose much threat wearing a body as far gone as his must be now.

The thought was hardly done before a door slammed shut somewhere in the back end of the house. Kallaystra whirled in alarm. Footsteps echoed down the hallway. Then Merlin stepped into the room and pulled up short, looking as surprised as she was.

"Nimue!" Merlin exclaimed angrily.

"Merlin!" Kallaystra gasped.

He was terribly pale and thin, but she wasn't reassured. Any man who'd got-ten out of Lucifer's captivity and moved that frail body all the way from Santa Rosa, not to mention having made this house from virtually nothing, might be an opponent to concern her even in such weakened condition. "You do seem remarkably improved, but not as well as you pretend, I think," she said.

Merlin leaned against the wall behind him for support, as if hoping she would not notice his discomfort. "I warn you, demoness, weak as you may think me, I've surprises still tucked up my sleeve, and I will not go back a *third time* to that—"

"Perish the thought!" Kallaystra cut him off with an upraised hand. "As it happens, I was just lamenting your wasteful coma." She looked down shyly. "I've always regretted what happened, you know. In all these centuries, I've never found another lover who came within light-years of moving me like you did," she said breathlessly. Glancing around as if to make certain no one listened, she said. "Lucifer is quite distracted at the moment. I'm sure he has no idea that you're here. I could help you get to someplace he would never look." She gave Merlin her most seductive smile. "Then, later, when it's safe, maybe we could make another try at—"

"If you wish to stop me, do so," Merlin said impatiently. "I've not come all this way to trifle with *you*. My grandson needs me."

"Your grandson," Kallaystra sighed. "I could hardly believe it when they told me. Who *was* the lucky woman?"

"I have things to attend to," Merlin said coldly. "Let's get this combat over with."

"Combat?" Kallaystra laughed. "In your condition? What bravado!" she said duskily. "I can think of far more enjoyable alternatives to combat if you're feeling that frisky." That was when she noticed he no longer looked so pale. In fact, his color was improving even as she watched. "What are you—" Then she realized, and knew it was too late to stop him. As if to confirm her theory, a rumbling crash came from the kitchen. "So that's why you came here first," she smiled.

"I think you'll find my *condition* much improved now," Merlin said, still leaning on the wall, but not in weakness. Above them came another crash, then a horrendous cacophony from the far side of the house. Kallaystra suspected that the room they stood in might be the only one still "remodeled." "I'd stored a lot of power in this little battery," said Merlin, stepping forward to confront her, "for emergencies."

"What makes you think I wish to stop you?" Kallaystra mused.

"Why should I think you don't?" Merlin countered.

The time for flirtation was over. He clearly wasn't going to fall for that again. "To be honest, I'm rather miffed with my employer at present." She smiled. "I've served him *very* well, and he's served me like a cheap whore." A look she chose to ignore crossed Merlin's face. "Doubtless he'd expect me to cover his majestic ass again now, but I ask you, has he ever covered mine?" She didn't have to fake the irritation she wanted him to see. "The festivities will probably be underway before you can get back to town, but I think I'd like to let you try," she smiled coquettishly, "for old time's sake, as long as you promise never to tell Lucifer that you were here. It would serve him right to have his *special day* blemished. *He'll* never know I helped you, of course. But I will, and you will, and," she smiled again, "that's enough for me."

"Why should I make deals with you?" Merlin growled with overt disgust.

"Because even if you're able to get past me at the moment, I can surely slow you down," she said severely. "Right now, I'd say speed is of the essence if you want to bother him at all, so promise what I ask, and I'll facilitate. Otherwise, I'll have to fight you. I wouldn't survive any other choice when he found out."

"Fine," Merlin said. "I promise never to tell Lucifer we met."

"Oh no," Kallaystra said. "Swear by something binding, or we have no deal."

"I swear by my immortal soul then," Merlin replied tiredly.

"Really!" Kallaystra jeered. "Do you think me stupid? Your soul's as good as signed and sealed to us already, after all the ways you've disobeyed your Lord's commands. Try something convincing this time, or I may change my mind."

"I swear on my *grandson's* immortal soul," Merlin said less comfortably. "If I ever speak a word of this to Lucifer, Hell may have him. Will that do?"

"Of course not!" Kallaystra snapped. "His soul will by ours by sunset too! Really, what do you take me for? You have one last chance, old man, or I will find out just how powerful you really are, while Joby perishes without you!"

Merlin sagged, and said, "I promise then, on the soul of my *great* grandson, whom you know I love as well, that I will never speak a word of this to Lucifer."

"Hawk's soul." Kallaystra smiled. "Yes, that will do. He is likely beyond our reach now, and I think that you would not betray him. . . . Very well. Be gone, and may Lucifer enjoy the loyalty he's so richly from me earned."

Merlin leaned against the wall once more, and said, "You realize of course, you've left me free to tell *everybody* else."

Before she could react, he was gone, and her scream of rage was buried in a mighty roar of falling beams and masonry as the remaining house collapsed around her corporeal body: drained as Merlin vanished of all the power that had held it up.

☒

GB leapt up eagerly as Joby came around the corner of the school building. "Man, I thought you'd chickened out!" He grinned in obvious relief.

"I have," Joby said, seeing no point in mincing words. "GB, I've had a chance to think things through more clearly than before, and this is not a good idea."

"What?" GB demanded in dismay. *"You're selling us out?"*

"No," Joby said. "I'm trying *not* to sell you out for the first time in months. We'd all have regretted this terribly as soon as it was done. I've been thinking, and I know how I can approach the Council without letting on that you—"

"I don't believe this!" GB cut him off, looking furious and hurt. "You might as well hang us all up on butcher's hooks outside Donaldson's station house right now!" Behind him their five teenage channels watched in confusion. "Did I do something to make you hate me all of a sudden, or have you just been lying to me all along?"

"GB, calm down. I don't hate you. I just—"

"*Calm down?*" GB shrieked. "*My ass is dead!* But that's not your problem, is it. Just go on home, dude. Better yet, take a fuckin' vacation. Maybe when you come back, we'll *all* be dead, and you'll be completely off the hook." GB wiped tears angrily from his reddened face as confusion turned to alarm on the faces of his five young friends.

"Vacation's not a bad idea," came a voice that Joby recognized with shock. "It's the first good one you've had, in fact."

Everyone spun to gape at Solomon.

"*You!*" GB gasped, looking strangely furious. "*How did you—*"

"You'll find your pretty sentinel buried in her work, I fear." Solomon smiled.

"Solomon?" Joby said, feeling numb. "You're . . . How did— When . . ."

"*You meddling maggot!*" GB shouted at Solomon. "You'll regret this day for as long as—" Seeming suddenly to remember those around him, GB's mouth clamped shut.

Meddling maggot? Joby looked from Solomon to GB, feeling extremely light-headed and thinking that he should have had some breakfast. On top of three sleepless nights, Joby had eaten nothing since the previous morning. "GB?" he said, but he couldn't seem to formulate his question.

"I think it's time Joby knew what '*GB*' really stands for, don't you?" Solomon asked. Before GB could answer, Solomon turned to Joby and said, "It's 'Goddamned Bastard,' if I'm not mistaken." Then he threw a hand up toward GB who shrieked in surprise and began to change before everyone's eyes.

Where the flaxen-haired youth had stood, a far taller man with huge wings of black leather, horns protruding from his coal-dark locks, and a long spade-tipped tail now gaped in horror at his own reflection in the school building's plate glass windows.

"*How dare you?*" screamed the apparition. "*I have never looked like that!*" A spastic wave of its hand banished the wings, horns, and tail, but the rest of its appearance remained unchanged. "*We are betrayed!*" it shouted at the empty air above it.

At this, the openmouthed paralysis in which everyone had been suspended shattered. GB's gang of teenagers ran off in all directions screaming in terror. Joby felt, suddenly, too drained to stand. Struggling to remain conscious, he half-sat, half-fell onto the pavement, finally understanding that GB must have been—must be. . . . "Oh, Hawk!" he moaned. "You were right about it all, and I've betrayed you."

"*Moron!*" the demon yelled at Solomon. "Did you think to win *for* him?"

"Joby had made his decision before I even got here," Solomon replied. "He'd already refused your offer. You heard as well as I did."

The senseless words they fired at one another began to swim and swirl through Joby's vision like schools of small black fish. "Win what?" he said palely. But neither man paid him any heed.

"I still had three years left!" snapped the demon, regaining some of his composure. "All you've done is guarantee your own damnation, and won the chance to watch me destroy the last of everything your grandson loves—beginning with *you!*" The demon jerked an arm into the air, and arcs of crackling light flared from his fingers, but Solomon was already wrapped inside a luminescent shell of green, and shot back from within it, streams of violet fire.

Stunned beyond endurance, Joby lost his grip on consciousness.

❊

He settled gently to the grass, like a fallen leaf, and looked around the lawn behind his parents' house, wondering where he'd put his book. He thought about it very hard, then stood up and walked, and walked, beyond his backyard fence, beyond the fields he played in until he found himself before a ring of cypress trees that seemed familiar, though he didn't know from where. There was pretty music coming from them, and a pretty, dark-haired girl waving to him from high up in the branches. He was quite impressed that she had climbed so high.

"The bark is rough," the girl laughed, "but it won't hurt your hands. Come up and listen to the song with me!"

Happily, Joby began to climb. Boys were climbers. That's what his father said. Finally he sat down beside her, laughing in delight at the way everything around him swayed to the music in the wind. Such pretty, pretty music, Joby thought and turned to ask the girl if there were words, but found her holding out a shiny cup he hadn't seen her holding before. Suddenly it seemed that all the music came from inside that.

As the Cup shown brighter and brighter Joby wanted very badly to take a drink from it—more than he'd ever wanted anything before, or, no, maybe once before.

"Can I have some?" he asked the girl, afraid she might say no.

She smiled and nodded. "Yes, but first I have a secret, and you have to tell."

Joby leaned in closer while she whispered in his ear, "Tell Hawk I know, and I am waiting, but for now, he has to live, and love, and do everything he can." She leaned away and smiled again, and Joby didn't know what any of it meant, but didn't think he would forget.

"Can I have some now?" he asked.

She handed him the Cup at last and said, "Feed your heart, Joby."

He pulled it to his lips and drank the way the ocean drinks a river at low tide.

Then a man's voice called his name, and Joby looked up to find the girl gone, the wind a gale, and himself no longer young but grown, trying to grab the thrashing branch with one hand while clinging to the cup with his other.

"Feed your heart," the man's voice sighed again, and though Joby couldn't tell where it was coming from, he knew whose voice it was.

"Why did I forget?" he asked, struggling not to fall as the wind increased. "Why do I keep forgetting?" Afraid not just of falling, but of spilling what was in the Cup, he looked down to find a face beneath the liquid's surface, crowned in bloody thorns!

Lurching back in terror, Joby dropped the Cup and fell seamlessly into running, running from that thorn-crowned face, through empty darkness filled with candles that went out as he approached. Amidst the roar of rushing wind, yet another voice behind him in the darkness started calling out his name. Joby just ran faster. "Joby!" called the voice again, as something grabbed him from behind and yanked him off the ground—

❈

"Joby! Can you hear me?" Jake stared at him and shook his shoulders once again. "Get out of here," he said urgently. "His demons are destroying the village."

Joby found himself held upright, but putting weight upon his feet, he saw that he was fine. In fact, he'd never felt so fit and full of life.

"Go!" Jake ordered again, shoving him away and spinning to block a blast of light from the demon who had called himself GB. Joby found he knew now who that demon was. Beyond the battle raging between Solomon, Lucifer, and Jake, the school was burning, and, as Joby watched, several other buildings through the town went up in gouts of flame. He heard shouting in the distance, saw people running through the streets, and knew that he'd been running too, all his life. Now the running had to stop.

"No," Joby said to Jake, even as the woodsman used his magic to shield them again from Lucifer's attack. "I have to stay."

Jake turned back to face him in distress. "Leave!" he said. "This is beyond you! There's nothing you can do now, except—"

"There's nothing anyone *but* me can do," Joby insisted. "This was my fight all along." He looked Jake squarely in the eye and added, "I was . . . sent to do this."

Jake uttered a low groan, and turned back to where Lucifer was now engaging Solomon. "Stop!" he yelled. "Merlin, stop! Lucifer, the boy has claimed his right!"

There was a sudden stillness amidst the roar of flames and distant panic, as both Solomon—had Jake called him Merlin?—and Lucifer turned to stare at Joby.

"His right to *what?*" Lucifer sneered.

"To face you on his own," Jake replied in weary resignation.

There was an even deeper silence. Then Lucifer began to laugh.

"NO!" Solomon exclaimed. "Joby, you've no idea what that means!"

"I never seem to," Joby said feeling terrified and pale. "But I had a dream once, as a boy, where King Arthur asked me to fight the devil for him, and I said I would. It was such a *real* dream that . . . it took me years to forget it." He looked again in grief at the destruction all around them. "And it's taken all of this to make me willing to remember again." He looked back to Solomon, or Merlin, or whoever the old enchanter really was. "I still want it just to be a dream, but . . . I can't go on pretending, can I."

The old man stared sadly at him, then said, "No," and bowed his head.

"He called you Merlin," Joby said, awe and sadness too mixed to pry apart. "Was it really you then, who told me to be perfect?" Joby asked. "That night in Camelot?"

"No," Lucifer sneered before the old man had a chance to speak, "that was I."

Joby felt something large collapse inside himself after all that trying to live up to Lucifer's fraudulent advice had cost him—and so many others. "I'm . . . glad," said Joby, smiling wanly at Merlin. "I've always liked you."

At this the old man just looked more desolate than ever.

"So, let me understand this," Lucifer said cheerfully, "little Joby has decided to resolve all this by challenging *me* to direct combat?"

No one replied, least of all Joby, who supposed he was simply going to die now. And yet, why would Arthur . . . or whoever that had been . . . have sent him off to do a thing he had no power to do? There had to be some way to win.

"Have I misunderstood?" Lucifer asked when no one answered.

Joby took a breath and shook his head.

Lucifer's mirthless grin fell away. He stretched an arm out, not toward Joby, but back toward the burning town, which had grown ominously silent while they'd talked. There came a groaning rumble, and several buildings simply vanished into a giant hole as a sound like the gasp of some great whale filled the air and tons of water jetted out of cave mouths all around the headlands. For a moment all of Joby's attention was required just to stand as a rolling ground swell passed beneath them. Then other buildings swayed and fell throughout the town, and Joby's courage vanished, but his fear that if he hadn't run so long and hard, all of this might have been avoided, did not.

When the earth had finally ceased to move, Lucifer lowered his arm, and said, "I'll let you take the first swing then, boy, just to make it sporting."

Joby clung in terror to the conviction that there had to be a way. If it was really the devil standing there before him, then he figured it must have been God who'd come to him as Arthur that night. Who else could it have been? And God, Joby was sure, could not have sent him out to face this just to die. So, Joby thought through all the little magic that he knew, and found just one possibility with any potential. Ironically, Lucifer had been the very one to teach it to him. Concentrating on the trick he'd used to blow up rocks and bugs, Joby gathered up the power in himself that "GB" had helped him find, letting it build until he doubted he could hold much more. Then he aimed with all his will at Lucifer's arrogant brain, and stepped out utterly on faith.

For a moment, nothing happened. Then the devil looked astonished, and reached up to clutch his head and howl . . . with laughter.

Joby's focus failed, and he felt his legs go weak with fear.

When Lucifer had finally gasped his last guffaw, and wiped his eyes, and turned to look at Joby, there was not a hint of humor in his face. Only rage burned in those frigid blue eyes, a terrible, unquenchable fever. Joby only hoped that whatever Lucifer was going to do would not last long or hurt more than he could bear.

"I'm impressed," Lucifer growled derisively, "if you had any idea how hard I've always had to work to give your paltry little efforts at magic any strength at all, you'd understand just how amazed I was to feel anything just now. Given your decent from that conniving snake charmer over there, you've got some little power in you, but it's held in check behind so many walls of fear and disbelief that, without my aid, you'd never have been able to lift ashes in a tempest, you worthless insult to my pride."

He stretched an arm toward Joby, as Merlin grasped his head in grief.

"You," Lucifer hissed like water dropped onto a griddle, "have always mattered less than the empty speck of dust shed by a single diatom that dies in darkness on the ocean floor. Tell your beloved *Arthur* that I said so, when you see him next."

The fire was too sudden and too painful to allow Joby any voice, or thought, or movement. Wrapped in steel threads of magma, he endured the endless moment of his death because there was no other choice.

Then, at last, the pain was gone, and, for an instant, he stood, ten years old again, out on Taubolt's beach, the laughing wind riffling through his hair, sunlight sparkling on the water all around him, as the day grew impossibly brilliant, unimaginably clean. Then the glittering scene surrounded him, and entered him, and somehow became him. He heard his own voice giggle, and felt himself dissolved in joy.

Beautiful! he thought. *So beautiful!*

And he was gone.

37

(Heart's Desire)

As Swami tossed and moaned, Gabriel stood watch, uncertainly. Swami's dreams were one of their most potent tools in searching for the Grail, but it always worried him to let the young man suffer. As Gabe leaned down to wake him, the lad's whole body snapped taught and bolted upright with a wordless scream. Gabriel reached out to hold him, but the boy would not be calmed.

"It's come!" Swami cried. "Gabriel! We have to help them!"

"Peace little brother," Gabe said. "It was just a dream."

"No!" Swami said, pulling from his embrace and getting up as if he meant to leave that minute. "No! I saw it!" He began to weep. "They're destroying Taubolt! Gabe, we have to do something!"

"What did you see?" Gabriel asked with apprehension. "Did . . . was Joby . . ."

"Gabriel."

"My Lord?" Gabe asked, joy and fear at war within him to hear his Master's voice again after so many years in exile.

"Come to Me," said the whisper in his mind.

A shiver of dread pass through him. The time for judgment had arrived.

"Little brother, I am summoned by my Master," he said tenderly to Swami. "I must leave you here . . . a while. But take courage. If anyone can help Taubolt now, it is He. Wait here and be at peace, my friend. He will care for you. Be at peace."

He kissed Swami's forehead one last time, with all the reassurance he could offer, and saw the boy unclench. Then he stepped out of the world Swami knew, into another he had been too long gone from and might never see again when this was done.

※

His legs moved of their own volition, step by measured step, along the shadowed path, though he had no legs to move. His progress was calm and stately, though the speed at which he traveled seemed astonishingly fast. He knew the word, astonished, what it meant, but not the way it felt. The light ahead of him was beautiful and always near, though he never seemed to close the distance, nor ever seemed to mind. He knew who he was, and where he'd come from, though not why he was here, or where he was going. But he did not care to know. There was a sense of many others moving all around him, though he was totally alone.

Until *another* joined him.

He saw no one, but felt him there, moving at exactly the same speed beside him, a comfortable, familiar presence that he didn't think to question.

"Jake," he said, just to say the name, though he hadn't any voice. Not really.

"It's Michael, Joby," said the voice without a sound.

"Ah," said Joby, not surprised.

"I have come . . . to bring you," said the person who was nowhere at his side.

"I'm glad," said Joby, though he'd felt no need of a companion until then.

They walked in silence after that, having never made a sound, until, briefly, they were joined by someone else who hovered, never there, beside them in what seemed—another word that Joby knew, but couldn't feel— surprise.

"Gabriel?" said Michael, never speaking. "Have we failed?"

"I do not know. He calls," said the other as silently, then fluttered from their presence, leaving only Joby and the one named Michael continuing alone together toward a light almost close enough to touch, and far enough away to never reach at all.

Then a figure stood before them, here where Joby had never reached anything. Though half in darkness, the figure was familiar in a very different way than all else around them seemed familiar. It was someone he had known. There was a name, and for the first time since he'd come here, he remembered what it was to "want," and suddenly a lot of things returned to him, of which the figure's name was one.

"Ben?" And "joy" was something Joby could remember too. "Ben, is that you?"

"As you wish, Your Majesty," said the other's voice, smiling, "I've been Ben as well."

"Ben!" Joby exclaimed, and found he could have arms now that he wanted them to embrace his friend, who reached to hold him too. "Ben, what are you doing here?" he laughed. "It's so good to see you! You look so . . . *young!*"

"As do you, Your Majesty," Ben said, grinning in the pale light.

"Why do you keep calling me that?" asked Joby.

"You must know, Sire," Ben replied. "I'm sure you do."

"I . . . don't though," Joby said.

"With all respect, Your Majesty, I think you must," said Ben, "or you would not have known me, for I look not at all as I remember looking when I was Ben; no more than you seem much like Joby here. Think hard, and it will come to you. Who were we back in Camelot, my lord? The first time we were men."

"The first time?" Joby said, remembering "confusion" now as well. "Ben, it's me," he said. "I'm Jo—" He stopped, and felt the strangest thing. A flash of red. A ruby glinting in the sun. Set into the pommel of a sword. . . . A sword of silver. A crown of gold . . . a yellow dragon on a field of red . . . a bridge. A quarterstaff. A mighty splash, and himself floundering in running water as Ben stood on the bridge above him laughing at— "Good heavens," Joby murmured, reacquainted, now, with astonishment as well. "Lance! . . . It's you?"

"Arthur," smiled Lance, going down upon one knee. "My Lord and King and brother of my heart. Well met, and God be praised that it should be this soon."

"Lance, get up. Get up," said Joby, reaching down to drag the man back into his arms. "Oh Lance, I can remember now! And . . ." He stood back, "dismay" now added to the other feelings he'd retrieved. "Have we done it all again? Camelot in ruins . . . And Guinevere! I've failed her twice! Oh Lance, I cannot bear it! Am I dead now? Yes, I am, and it's too late to reach her! Too late . . . again!"

"Your Majesty, perhaps it's not," Lance said. "I am sent with tidings that you are not to come among us yet." He looked down sadly. "Sire, you must go back."

"Again?" Joby whispered, wondering if the heavy breath he drew was as real here as pain and disappointment seemed. "I'd hoped all that was finally done," he said quietly. "Am I to pay for failing twice? Is that why I am yet allowed no rest?"

"Sire," said Lancelot, tenderly, "He explains Himself least of all to me." He placed a hand affectionately on Joby's shoulder. "But think. You'll have the chance you craved to find her, and to make amends. I'll not be there to muddle things this time."

"Yes. How selfish of me not to see that," Joby said. "By God, I will! At least, I'll try." He smiled, then barked a quiet laugh. "It seems I cannot even manage dying without several tries. Well," he sighed and turned to leave, then stopped, looked back at Lancelot, and asked with some regret, "is it . . . very wonderful?"

"My Lord," said Lancelot, seeming caught between unbridled joy and sympathy, "if I possessed an angel's tongue, I could not describe it. I know it must be disappointing to be twice turned out, but they do say third time is the charm." He raised a hand in parting. "For now, my lord, good-bye, but we await you with great joy. It will be soon enough, I think. Now go. And, Arthur, . . . kiss her, more than once, for me."

"I will. . . . Good-bye once more then, Lance . . . for now. . . . Good-bye."

✻

Merlin sat amidst the smoking rubble that had been, so recently, the fairest town he'd ever known, and held the lifeless body of his grandson in his arms, and keened as he had never wept for centuries before. As Joby died, Merlin had flown at Lucifer in a mindless rage, prepared to blow a hole in the very fabric of the world if that might destroy the fiend. Then the Creator's summons had rolled over them like thunder, and both angels had vanished in an instant, along with all Hell's demons.

"Oh, Joby! Joby!" Merlin cried, rocking in his pain. "I never should have loved at all, to see it come to this!" He threw his face up at the sky, and sobbed, "Oh, God, forgive me! Please! Forgive me! I should not have disobeyed!"

"Did the devil . . . say . . . I was your grandson?"

For an instant, Merlin didn't understand where the pale voice had come from. Then he looked down in shock to find his grandson's eyes no longer vacant.

"He said he was going to destroy everything your grandson loved," Joby barely more than whispered. "Was he talking about me?"

"Joby?" Merlin gasped. "My God!" he threw his face once more toward Heaven and shouted, *"Oh my God! Oh, thank you! Joby! How are you alive?"*

"I . . . am, aren't I," said Joby, sounding perplexed. "I thought I burned."

"Ah, Joby," Merlin wept, dragging him into his arms "It was not that kind of fire. I'm so sorry that you suffered it, and so glad you're . . . *back*! Oh God! *You're back*!"

With some effort Joby pulled free, and sat up to look around at all the ruin. "There's nothing left at all," he sighed. "I'd hoped all this was just a dream."

"My boy, of course there's something left. There's you, by God!"

"I talked with Lancelot," Joby said. "I remember who I was." He turned to look at Merlin. "I remember you now too, but is it true? Am I your grandson now?"

Merlin nodded, momentarily unable to harness any voice at all.

"So *you* gave me that book about . . . ," Joby smiled, then laughed, "myself?"

"I had no idea," Merlin said, "that you were—*had* been . . . I just meant for you to *know* him, not to *be* him. . . . And you're not, you know. Not anymore. You're you now!"

Joby's gaze turned inward. Then he nodded. "Yes. That was there," he looked bleakly around once more, "not here. But have I failed again?"

"I cannot see what more He could have asked of you. If anyone has failed, it was myself, and . . . and others perhaps. I fear . . ." Merlin sighed, his joy dimmed for the first time since Joby's miraculous return. "I fear that we have terribly betrayed you, Joby. Lucifer may win in spite of all you've done."

"You?" Joby asked. "How? You helped me more than anyone."

"Yes, and in so doing, we've all disobeyed Him, myself and several angels. Perhaps that's why we lost this way. I . . . I should have trusted Him."

"Disobeyed?" Joby said in clear distress. "He didn't want you helping me?"

"His will was never mine to question," Merlin sighed. "Yet I took it upon myself to change the course before you. . . . Not just once, I fear, but many times."

"But . . . didn't He want me to win?" Joby asked in clear dismay.

"I cannot believe He didn't," Merlin said. "But He commanded all of us—everyone who served Him—not to help you unless you asked us to, and you were such a stubborn lad. So quick to blame yourself, to grieve or fight, and try, but never, never would you ask for help! In truth, it was a trial to us all."

"But, how could I have asked you?" Joby protested. "I had no idea any of you were there! Or that I was even in this trial! . . . At least, not consciously," he said uncomfortably. "Not since I was a child, anyway."

"I don't know," said Merlin. "But hereafter, Joby, since it seems you're granted a hereafter after all, I hope you'll try asking help of anyone you can, instead of going through everything so stubbornly alone."

"I'm sorry," Joby said. "From now on, I will but, Grampa, if you wanted me to ask for help, how come you made us think that you were dead?"

"Ah, my boy," Merlin answered, weary with regret. "In my *infinite wisdom,* I imagined I would be of more use to you that way." He shook his head. "By my arts, I saw some trouble coming to my daughter and her child, though not what it would be, and disastrously supposed that I'd be better able to act on your behalf unencumbered by the need to pretend I was just a normal man." He looked at Joby sadly. "Do you know the thing I wanted most for your mother, and for you?"

Joby shook his head.

"A normal life," said Merlin. "That was all."

Joby hugged him then, wringing tears from Merlin's aged eyes again.

"That book was my favorite possession, you know," said Joby.

"I know," Merlin said, seeing no need to tell him it had been made to be.

Suddenly, they were not alone. Joby gaped as Michael stood before them in full angelic glory, as if "Jake" were made of diamond now, with hair of fluid gold and massive wings shot through with rainbow, soft and white as pure sea foam.

"We are commanded to attend Him," said the angel in a gentle voice filled with music, and with sadness Merlin could discern, though Joby likely wouldn't.

"Who?" said Joby, very much in awe. Then, "You mean . . . *Him?*"

Michael nodded, stretched out his hand, and opened up a gateway in the air, through which, instead of burning wreckage, they beheld a glade of soft green grass bedecked with flowers, and ringed in giant trees. "Come," said Michael. "He waits."

Merlin yearned to ask the angel if he knew what judgment was awaiting them, but didn't waste the time, doubting Joby understood a fraction of the moment conveyed in that simple phrase, *He waits.*

❈

Gabriel stood, one last time, he feared, at the right hand of his Lord, while Lucifer glared angrily from the left side of the clearing, commanded to await Michael's return in silence. Between them, the Creator waited on a mossy tree bowl, guised just as he had been in Joby's dream nearly thirty years before.

When Michael reappeared before them with Joby and Merlin, Lucifer gaped at Joby, looking apoplectic, though the Creator's command still held him shut.

"My Lord," said Michael, dropping to one knee and bowing his radiant head.

Behind him Merlin did the same, and Joby too, after staring in amazement at the very "Arthur" he obviously remembered having known and loved in childhood.

"Should friendship be hobbled by such formality, Sir Joby?" the Creator smiled. "Rise, and add the pleasure of your countenance to that of your courtesy."

Joby looked up slowly, and stared some more.

"You *are* allowed to speak," the Creator chided.

"What . . . should I call You, Sir?" Joby murmured.

"Certainly not that." The Creator grimaced. "What would you like to call Me?"

"You . . . aren't Arthur," Joby said.

"No, I am not," the Creator said quietly. "You know that now. As I recall, you always hoped that Arthur would return." He shrugged happily. "Now you have."

"I liked it better, though, when You were Arthur," said Joby still bewildered. "Would it be all right if I just call You Lord?"

"If you find that comfortable." The Creator smiled.

"Lord it is then," Joby said uncertainly. "Do You always look like this?"

"Only for you," the Creator said, beckoning Joby to his side. "Come sit beside Me, Joby. Let us talk the way we used to. I've badly missed our conversations."

Joby came somewhat fearfully and sat down beside the Creator. "We're on the Garden Coast, aren't we," he said, his eyes darting at all the unlikely things and persons around him. "But this is where we came to talk that day too . . . or night, I guess, isn't it?"

"That's right," said the Creator. "And have you guessed yet what this place really is?" When Joby shook his head, the Creator said, "One of a few very precious remnants scattered through this world of a much larger garden you have probably heard called Eden, preserved for Me down through the eons by a few of My favorite people."

"I'm . . . not sure of this," said Joby looking uncomfortably at Lucifer, "but I think he may want to burn it down."

Lucifer made a strangling sound as if he might be going to rupture.

"Ah yes," the Creator sighed, "there is so much we should discuss, but first, I fear, we must endure one last spate of lies. Lucifer, you may speak now."

"I won!" the devil shouted, as if uncorked. "I claim victory by default!"

"On what grounds this time?" the Creator asked wearily.

"Well, look at *You*!" Lucifer gasped. "Even *You* are interfering now! There are years left before this wager's over! *You've* violated the most fundamental term of our—"

"The wager ended hours ago," the Creator cut in firmly. "Lucifer, you *killed* the *candidate.* Our terms made *that* part very clear," he turned to Gabe, "did they not?"

"That Lucifer not deprive the candidate of life itself or the power to choose unless and until the boy's unequivocal failure has been confirmed before valid witness," Gabriel said. "That was the term agreed to."

"And was Joby deprived of life itself by My opponent?" the Creator asked.

"Obviously not!" Lucifer blurted before Gabe could answer. "There he is in front of You, quite alive!"

"*Was* he dead?" the Creator asked Gabe, patiently.

"He was," Gabe said. "I saw him on the path, myself."

"There you are," the Creator shrugged, turning back to Lucifer. "He was dead, but now he's not. . . . You seem to have a lot of trouble with that concept."

Lucifer began to tremble like a broken steam engine. "Surely," he protested, "You're not going to pretend this contest was anything like fair!"

"On that, I must agree," the Creator nodded. "It was hardly fair to anyone but you, who could do anything you liked, while all the rest of us were required to sit bound and gagged, just watching."

"Are You *pretending* anybody actually *did* as so *required*?" Lucifer shrilled.

"I did," said the Creator. "And your wager was with Me. We've been over all this before. If you've nothing new to say, I'd like to move along to more pleasant matters."

"Oh no," Lucifer growled. "No indeed. There are still some very *unpleasant* things to tend to, and if You think I'm going to walk quietly away with even one of them undone, You're not half as omniscient as You claim."

"Believe Me, Lucifer," the Creator sighed, "you're the last one I'd expect to leave an unpleasant thing undone. What is it that you think is left?"

Lucifer blinked, and stared. "You may think to get away with claiming victory where none was had," he said in righteous indignation, "but at the very least, I have some damages to collect before I go. Their souls belong to me now! All three of them, by indelible rights far older than any wager we have ever made! You know how long You'll last if You violate those rules. You'll have no authority at all! You'll be as impotent—"

"As you," the Creator finished for him coldly. "I'm aware of that."

"Well?" Lucifer demanded, breathing hard and smiling most unpleasantly. "You speak of truth and fairness, of rules and technicalities meticulously observed. Now it's time, *My Lord,* to demonstrate Your vaunted *impartiality* and *justice* or give up any pretense of the moral authority that is Your only claim to rule. I want them *damned,* just as *I* was damned, for disobeying Your will."

"Did they?" the Creator asked levelly, his wide gray eyes fixed unapologetically on Lucifer's incredulous face.

Lucifer looked around at all the other gaping faces in the clearing as if expecting them to share his outrage. "Don't be absurd! Everyone here is well aware of the countless times Your two pet angels and this hoary old enchanter have violated Your command against uninvited intervention! *That one,*" he spat whirling to point at Merlin, "has been at it since masquerading as a hag clear back in Berkeley!"

Gabe saw Joby give his grandfather a startled look.

"Ah, then as you, yourself, admit," the Creator said, "it was only my *command* they violated. Not my *will.*" He shrugged. "I will concede that, had they disappointed me by doing otherwise, I doubt you *could* have lost this wager, Lucifer."

Gabriel turned to stare in confusion at his Master, as did everyone else in the clearing—even his unflappable brother, Michael.

"What kind of . . . *insanity* . . . is *that?*" Lucifer choked.

"When you first proposed this wager at that café in New England," the Creator said with frightening severity, "you suggested—no, *insisted* very firmly—that my creation was inherently corrupt. 'The rot in this insufferable contrivance of Yours has gone clear to the core.' I think those were your *exact* words. I disagreed, as you'll recall, and when you proposed your wager, saw My chance to settle what seemed to Me a very important question. Was the core of My creation inherently corrupt?

"While you set out to prove that, if I let you bring all Hell down on the shoulders of one barely suspecting boy, for half a lifetime, without any interference, he'd do something very naughty, I chose to wager something more *imaginative. I* was betting that, *at the core,* My creation was so *soundly* imbued with the laws of love and faith, compassion and *real* justice, that even if I, Myself, should command it to ignore those laws, it *would still not do so.*"

The Creator smiled at everyone around the clearing with unbearable affection and . . . was that gratitude? "At your urging, Lucifer," the Creator said quietly, "for the first and only time in all of time, I uttered a command that did *not* express My *will.* And not one person in this clearing violated My *will* to keep that command." The Creator turned first to Michael, then to Gabriel, and said, "Not even you, my angels, who have so seldom been required to think for yourselves in all these many eons."

"But, Lord," Gabriel stammered, "if You wanted us to think for ourselves, why didn't You just ask us to?"

The Creator looked at him, a bit nonplussed. "Ah well," he sighed. "As I recall, Rome was not built in a day." He smiled at Gabriel with great fondness and sympathy, and said, "You are often much too anxious, my beloved friend, but I am very grateful to you for having been so quick to put love before blind law. Never give yourself to despair again, Gabe. I do not abandon anyone who has not very clearly wished Me to."

Seeming unable to summon words sufficient to the occasion, Lucifer released a gurgling shriek, and began to jump up and down like an angry child, stamping flat the grass beneath his feet. "But, it's not *fair!*" he raged. "You can't let them all go when You threw all of us in Hell for—"

"I know you're very disappointed," the Creator said, as one might try too soothe a child, "but don't you see it—still? These others only disobeyed My command because they *love* all that I love." A deep sadness crossed the Creator's face. "You, on the other hand, have always *hated* what I love, even on those rare occasions when you do obey My commands, and you know very well I didn't make the Hell you live in."

When Lucifer opened his mouth to object, the Creator waved a finger. "Don't waste the breath. The others I cast to earth with you made of their confinement this very paradise that surrounds us now. You could easily have done the same, and still may do so, if you *will*. Even now, I make you the offer I made them. You could all return to Heaven once again."

"If you are referring, Sir," Lucifer sneered through clenched teeth, "to that offensive invitation to surrender my divinity for the paltry honor of *mingling* with the *hoi polloi* at your *little club,* my answer remains the same. I will never suffer *death,*" he proclaimed defiantly, "nor validate the kind of imperfection You indulge. I'll persist until I have succeeded in prying open those *loving eyes* of Yours to the truth about how flawed, and, yes, *inherently corrupt,* this anthill of yours is! Then, *You* will owe *me* an apology!"

"Very well," the Creator sighed. "But, since you're so concerned with *perfect observances,* I *will* hold you to every last detail of what we wagered, including your offer to abort those '*messy, messy,*' conflicts you were planning."

"Have I any power to refuse?" Lucifer replied stiffly.

The Creator shook his head. "You'd better go then. I'm afraid you have a pretty *messy* house awaiting *you.* By way of friendly warning, there are some among your minions who feel you acted rather precipitously when you killed

Joby several years ahead of schedule. They seem to think your *timing* was a little off."

Lucifer turned in smoldering rage to face the others in the clearing. "You were all in this together from the start, and I will make certain no one is left in Heaven or Hell who doesn't see very clearly what you have done!"

"That's very generous of you," the Creator said. "Now, if you'll leave without further histrionics, I *won't* tell your *loyal* servants back in Hell what you'd have done with *them,* had they succeeded in helping to secure your victory."

Lucifer paled, and vanished in an instant.

"My Lord," said Michael deferentially, still on one knee when Lucifer had gone, "We are . . . none of us, to be . . . punished then?"

"What for?" said the Creator. "Failing to sacrifice all that I love most, even to spare yourselves damnation? What kind of employer would punish such behavior?" He shook his head. "Punishment has rarely much to do with justice anyway."

Gabriel sat heavily on the mossy bowl behind him, so weak with inexpressible relief that, were angels capable of unconsciousness, he might well have fainted.

"None of you can know how long I've waited for this day!" the Creator chuckled. "Michael, stand, and look at Me." When Michael did so, he said, "The love I know you've always born Me, dear old friend, is at last truly *perfected.* Can you not see that?"

Michael gazed at him a moment, then turned back to look at Merlin, who was grinning like a simpleton. Then both of them were laughing, though Michael's laughter soon faltered, and he turned back to face his Master. "There were children that I should have saved," he said, with obvious remorse.

"Yes, there were," the Creator replied gravely. "You did not know that at the time, and you do know now that they are well provided for and happy where they are."

To Gabe's surprise, his Master turned to Joby then, and said severely, "Stop that now. The time for such lies is past." When Joby looked up startled, the Creator said more gently, "Of course I hear you. I have never, for a second, ceased listening to your heart. Not in all these years. Ben had suffered much graver injuries than a pair of broken legs, Joby. If not for your desire that he should live, he would have died much earlier that night. His life had

run its proper course. The Cup had shown him this, though he didn't understand until that moment all of what he'd seen. He already knew then who all
of you had been before and knew he mustn't stay to put Guinevere through
all of that again. The choice was his that night, despite you, Joby, as it should
have been." As he reached out to embrace Joby, the young man buried his
face in the Creator's robes and cried as freely as a child. "You've been trained
to think in such disastrous ways," the Creator said in quiet sadness. "And yet
you never ceased to try, through so much disappointment, so many twisted
outcomes. Everything My fallen angel ever taught you about yourself is lies,
My beloved champion. You did very, very well."

"But I saved nothing," Joby wept. "Ben, and Laura, Hawk and Gypsy, all of
Taubolt. Everything I ever loved is lost. I did nothing but survive!"

"Sometimes," the Creator said, "just surviving takes far greater strength
and courage than winning glorious victories does. Sometimes just surviving
is the greatest victory anyone can ask. Now, though, it is time to heal the
wounds you've suffered in My service. Stay here with Me a while in this
Garden, and feed your heart, Sir Joby."

⚔

Joby idly arranged the objects on his desk again, though they'd been
straightened countless times already. It had been a maddeningly quiet day at
the counseling center.

Gazing out his office window, Joby started picking out people on the
street and trying to imagine what their lives were like. So many of them, he
supposed, must have wives or husbands to whom they said, "hello," each
morning, and "good night," each evening; children who jumped into their
arms when they got home. Maybe that one had played basketball or soccer
back in high school, confident and content with himself as he'd gone off to
college. Had he enjoyed a normal sex life, found a normal job, fallen normally in love and had a normal family—and taken his marvelously normal
life all for granted? Objectively, Joby knew that all these people's lives were
composed as much of loneliness and frustration as of brighter things; and a
great deal more boredom than he himself had been subjected to for quite
some time. Still, he couldn't lose the feeling that being normal must be more
wonderful than anyone who'd been so ever suspected. At very least they all
belonged in so many ways that Joby never would.

Turning from the window, Joby had to concede that his life had not been
dull or meaningless. How many people could claim to have helped save the
world, or had their lives explained to them, face to face, by God? He was

sure that most would gladly throw their *normal* lives right out the window to have anything at all explained to them by God. But they didn't really know what that would mean, did they, any more than he would ever really know what being normal meant to them.

He gazed into the middle distance and shook his head. . . . He really had talked with God. . . . Face to face. . . . That would never cease to astonish him. And he had been a king in ancient England too . . . and still remembered most of it. He had put the Grail to his lips—at least once, maybe twice. He often longed to drink from it again, but once or twice would have to do, he suspected. He had befriended fairies, and seen a patch of Eden, and palled around with angels, and, oh yes, been Merlin's grandson. *The* Merlin! He'd even been dead, and gotten to come back—a couple times—knowing now that there was nothing all that frightening about dying, if you'd lived even a little well.

He drew a heavy sigh.

Ironically, all that was just the problem. Having done so much before the age of forty, what was left to occupy all of his remaining years—especially as it seemed his heritage was causing him to age so much more slowly than most. He'd once have thought that talking face to face with God would leave every mystery and problem solved, but it had only left him with a whole new set of even broader mysteries and a lot of insight that explained, but somehow didn't change, so many things. The Creator had implied that Joby had unfinished business still ahead of him, but had refused to say what any of it was. Joby was still waiting for some clue.

He caught himself straightening his desk again, and almost slapped the guilty hand.

When the subject of reward had been broached, Joby had first asked if all the children killed in Taubolt might be brought back to life, but the Creator had explained that they'd each accomplished what they'd lived to do, and were already deeply tied to marvelous new lives, which they would likely leave as reluctantly as they had left their last ones. When Joby had asked about being allowed to live his own life over as it should have been without the wager, the Creator had conceded even that was possible, if Joby truly wished it. But then He'd pointed out that doing so would mean undoing all that Joby had accomplished, putting all those lives, not to mention all that angelic evolution, back at risk until someone else had succeeded or failed as the wager's candidate in his place. Joby had not, for an instant, entertained any thought of putting all creation back at risk just to get his own little pig-in-the-poke back.

And the thought of *choosing* to put someone else through what had been done to him was . . . just not thinkable.

There was only one other thing that Joby truly wanted now: another chance with Laura and his son. He wanted them back desperately, but had quickly realized how awful it would feel to think they might be with him only because the Creator had somehow compelled it. The Creator had sadly concurred that Joby would have to win them back himself or, if that failed, accept that loss with all his others.

So far, however, Joby hadn't even found them. He was immensely grateful now that Hawk had left him just before the end, still shuddering to imagine his son caught up in what had happened, but when Joby had tried calling Laura, the number Hawk had given him was disconnected with no forwarding number. So, he simply waited now, praying that one of them would find *him,* though unsure of how they'd go about that either.

After Taubolt's destruction, Joby had said good-bye to his grandfather, whom the Creator had kept behind for some mysterious other business, and returned to Berkeley. There he'd found Sarina raising her and Gypsy's son and running this nonprofit counseling center. Joby hadn't even known that she was pregnant when he'd fled town after Gypsy's death and had feared at first that she might despise him for having left without so much as good-bye, but she'd just been delighted to see him again, and offered him work screening her new clients. He'd told her very little of what had really happened to him in the intervening years, sure that if he'd done so she'd just have offered him *services* rather than employment.

His desk well straightened now, Joby went out to the waiting room to find a magazine, smiling to discover more headlines about the sudden cessation of hostilities between India and Pakistan, and the wave of reconciliation spreading across Africa. No, for all he'd lost, he'd have changed nothing, knowing what he did now.

Which was not to say that he'd avoided the "Why me?" syndrome altogether.

In the Garden, the Creator had shown Joby not only how deeply he had been deceived, but how his parents' lives had been manipulated too, leaving Joby filled both with grief and gratitude for all they had endured on his behalf. He visited them often now, as close to them as he had been before the bad old days had started. But when he watched them loving one another in their countless little ways, Joby found it hard to imagine ever finding such a love himself. Not anymore.

"'Scuse me, man. You the guy I'm s'posed to see for counselin'?"

Joby looked up to see a tall black man standing in the center's entrance. His tattered clothing did nothing to diminish his athletic build and chiseled features. His large brown eyes seemed more fitting for a doe than for a man. This guy could leave the streets to do modeling work tomorrow, Joby thought, not that he'd ever be caught suggesting such a line of work to anyone again.

"I'm the guy you see *before* the counselor," Joby said. "Come into my office."

When the man had seated himself, staring around with wide-eyed fascination at the office's rather dull furnishings, Joby handed him the first of several forms. "Just basic information," Joby said, "to give us an idea of what you're skills and background are, the issues you want to work on with us, that sort of thing. You want any help filling this out, just ask." A lot of their clients had trouble reading or writing.

"Huh," the man grunted, examining the form with the same childlike interest he had devoted to the rest of Joby's things. Not very bright, Joby suspected. The good-looking ones never seemed to be, he thought, wondering why that was. A moment later, however, the man began writing in a lovely hand faster than Joby could credit.

When the man had handed back the questionnaire, Joby looked down to get his name, and said, "So . . . Rafe, is it?"

"Short for 'Raphael,'" the man explained.

"Great," said Joby. "Do you have a last name Raphael? You've left that blank."

"Just Raphael," the man said, sounding concerned. "That all right?"

"Sure," Joby shrugged. He looked farther down the form, and froze. In the "Past and Present Employment" section, there was only one word written: "Angel." He felt his skin prickle, and looked back up at the man's perfect features and doe-like eyes, wondering how he could possibly have been so blind. He was about to ask the angel what it was doing here, when he paused again, suddenly unsure. This *was* Berkeley. Half the people living here thought they were angels, or demons, or Jesus Christ, and this *was* a counseling center after all. If, by some weird chance, this guy *was* just one more paranoid schizophrenic, Joby didn't want to say things virtually designed to inflame his psychosis.

"Well, Mr. Raphael," he said. "It says here you were, or are, I guess, an angel?"

"Yes," said Raphael soberly.

"Right," said Joby. "That's a great profession. Mind if I ask what an angel would need counseling about?"

"I'm jus' here to work on the whole independent livin' thing," the man said. He looked back toward the door. "Tha's what the sign says, right? 'Independent Livin' Skills'? Tha's the new thing out here now, but I gotta confess, it's been a very—" He turned back to Joby, looking appalled, and said, "Sorry, man. I didn't mean to say that."

"What?" asked Joby.

"'I gotta confess,'" the man said uncomfortably. "Did that offend you?"

"Of course not," Joby said, less certain than before whether this was an angel or just a very good-looking lunatic. "Why would that offend me?"

"I don't know!" Raphael exclaimed. "Tha's just what I'm talking about. He wants us makin' all these decisions for ourselves now, but I can't even tell what's gonna offend folks anymore. This new 'everybody start thinkin' for yourself' thing is a real . . . What's that thing they all say down here? A real bitch?"

"They do say that," Joby grimaced, "but I might not use that one, if I were you."

"There you go!" the angel said, throwing up its hands.

"So let me get this straight," said Joby nonplussed. "Angels actually need human counselors to work through independent living skills now?"

Seeming suddenly unable to contain himself, Raphael threw back his head and laughed, looked at Joby again, then bent double, laughing twice as hard. "Not too bright, huh?" Raphael grinned when he'd finished laughing. "Is that what I just heard? The *heroic* ones aren't either, it seems. Why is that, I wonder?"

Immediately recognizing his own earlier thoughts, Joby's face began to burn.

"That's right." Raphael grinned. "You may have saved the world a little, but don't get cocky, Rocky. You ain't the judge of me." He laughed again at Joby's reaction. "That's a good one, isn't it? 'Don't get cocky, Rocky.' Yeah, I got all kinds a good ones since I started hangin' out 'round here, man."

"I thought it was considered rude to read minds without permission," Joby said.

"That was before we started thinking for ourselves." Raphael smiled.

"So, you can't have come all the way from Heaven just to yank my chain," Joby said, trying to suppress his irritation. "Don't tell me He needs another crash test dummy."

"Ooooh. We still a little angry, are we?" Raphael said, his brows raised.

"As you say, I may have saved the world a little," Joby drawled, "but now I find myself a little cut adrift, except for visits from the occasional comic angel."

"I see you've started working on that self-pity thing again too," the angel mused.

"Sorry," Joby sighed. "You're right. Old habits die hard, don't they? To be honest," he said wistfully, "I was kind of hoping you'd come because He did need something. I think I'd even handle being a crash test dummy better than this boredom."

"I've come to deliver a letter," Raphael said more soberly, removing a pale green envelope from the pocket of his coat, and laying it on Joby's desk.

Joby picked it up, wondering what kind of letter required delivery by angel mail. The outside was completely blank. After a glance at Raphael to see if this was going to be another joke, Joby opened the flap and removed the single sheet of stationery inside, unfolded it, and caught his breath. He'd have recognized her handwriting in the dark.

> *Dear Joby,*
>
> *Hawk and I are together here, and miss you very, very much. Your grandfather has explained everything to us—the things you went through all your life, and what was really happening in Taubolt, and, dear God, what happened after Hawk left. It's been a lot to absorb, but I can hardly deny any of it when I'm surrounded every day now by things that seem like miracles. Am I the only one who can't pull apples from the air, or change into an animal? Hawk tells me even you can do some of these things. Is that true?*
>
> *What I'm trying to say is that I wish I had known any of this, and been there when you needed me. We both do. Your grandfather says you'll understand. I know he's right.*
>
> *Joby, both Hawk and I love you very much, and wish that you were here, if you wish to be. I hope you wish to be. While we're alive, there's nothing that can't be patched up, is there? I don't know what else to say. Your grandfather tells me this will reach you, though he hasn't told me how. He says I mustn't tell you where we are now, which I guess I understand, and I'm not sure we have an address at the moment anyway. But he says that you will find us.*

Come find us, Joby.
I love you,
Laura

P.S. Dad, this is Hawk. I know what you chose, and I will never doubt
you again. I love you too. Come home.

P.P.S. I finally know how Measure's tale ends. . . . Tell you when you get
here ☺

"So," said Raphael, resuming his comedian routine, "y'all gonna sit here fertilizin' your self-pity, or go grab the good things you still got?"

"Where are they, Raphael?" Joby said, wiping tears from his face, clear at last about the nature of his unfinished business, and overwhelmed with gratitude. "Why can't she just tell me where they've gone?"

"Not really safe to tell you." Raphael looked around them pointedly. "The air's got ears, as you should know."

"I thought no demon could get near me now," said Joby.

"There are lots of ways to hear things without 'getting near,'" Raphael scoffed. "Even your kind can do that. And it's not *your* safety we talking about now anyway. That's why they have no address."

"Then how am I supposed to find them?" Joby protested.

"Follow your heart," Raphael said. "You'll get there."

"Oh for crying out loud," Joby complained, "What, am I in the *Wizard of Oz* now? What's that supposed to mean?"

"Just what it says," Raphael told him soberly. "Follow your heart, Joby. *It's* got the compass. It always did. And don't forget to give Hawk Rose's message."

Joby stared at him. "So, what, I just get in my car and start driving?"

"Sounds good, and if you gonna do it, I wouldn' wait aroun' here askin' questions all day neither, beeyatch" Raphael japed.

"Are you serious?" Joby asked. "Just get in my car? Right now? . . . And just drive . . . anywhere?"

"Hey," the angel shrugged, "least you ain't got to hitchhike this time." He stood up to go. "This has been very helpful, Mr. Peterson." He smiled, went to the door, then turned and said, "I'd be goin' pretty soon, like right away then, huh? And remember what they always say: third time's the charm!" He winked and shut the door behind him.

For a minute, Joby simply stared. Then he got up and rushed to follow

Raphael, unable to believe that those were really all the instructions he was going to get. But when he yanked the door back open, he found no trace of anyone.

Running to Sarina's office, he stuck his head in through her open door, and said, "Sarina, I'm sorry, but I have to go."

"Okay," she smiled, "it's slow here anyway. I'll cover it. See you tomorrow."

"No," Joby said. "I mean, I have to leave completely. Maybe for a while. I . . . just didn't want to go without saying good-bye this time."

She looked at him, confused. "What? . . . Why? How long are you going for?"

"I'm not sure," Joby said, beginning to realize how many things he was walking out on. "There's not much stuff in my apartment yet, but if I'm not back in time to pay the rent, you can have it all, okay? Use it here, or just give it all away. I'm sorry to ask this, Sarina, but I don't think I even have time to go home."

"Joby what's going on?" she said, clearly alarmed.

"I heard from Laura," Joby said.

"That's great!" she exclaimed. "But why—"

"I'm not really sure," he said, embarrassed. "It's complicated, but I . . . I think I've got to go right now. I'm sorry. Is it okay?"

"Okay," she said, looking concerned again. "Will I ever see you again?"

"I . . . don't know." Joby shrugged. He darted in to kiss her on the cheek. "You're a peach, Sarina, and you're doing a real fine thing here. It's been great to see you. Thanks for everything. Good luck! Good-bye!"

"Good-bye!" she said as he ran for the exit. "Good luck!"

A moment later, he pulled into traffic still wondering where he was supposed to go. He filled his tank at the first gas station he saw, and bought a toothbrush and some other things at the mini-mart there, then got back on the road, and headed west because the light seemed nicer that way.

He chose the Richmond–San Rafael Bridge because of its name. That took him to Highway 101, where he headed north until he realized he was driving to Taubolt. Even though it wasn't there anymore, he couldn't think of any other place to go. Taubolt was the only place this highway had ever gone that mattered.

Now what? he thought an hour later, as he approached the point where he would have to leave the highway or keep on going. It was getting on toward sunset. There was a hitchhiker standing at the off-ramp, who would be hitch-

ing in the dark before much longer. There'd been a soft spot in Joby's heart
for hitchers ever since the night he'd fled to Taubolt, so he pulled over as the
young man ran to meet him.

The guy pulled Joby's car door open, and they both just stared.

"Joby!" said the boy.

"Swami?" said Joby in amazement. "What on God's green earth? You're
back! Has anybody told you?"

"Yeah," Swami answered glumly. "I've already been there, and I knew anyway. I just came back to make sure no one's left behind. What a trip running
into you, though!"

"Tell me about it!" said Joby. "Geez, it's great to see you!" Then, recalling
what Swami had been sent away to look for, Joby asked, "Did you find it?"

"Not yet," he said. "But we will."

"Well, get in," Joby told him. "I'll take you wherever you're headed now. I
have no idea where I'm going anyway."

"Great!" said Swami, jumping in beside him. "Let's go."

"Where to?" said Joby.

Swami gave him an odd look. "Not really safe to give directions out here."

Joby's mouth went dry. "You *know* . . . where I'm supposed to be going?"

"Don't know where you *were* going, but I know where you should go
now." Swami grinned. "They'll all be glad to see you."

"Are Hawk and Laura there?" Joby asked.

"Of course," said Swami. "Almost everyone. And you're a hero, you know."

"Why?" asked Joby. "I destroyed their town."

"More like moved it." Swami shrugged. "And you saved the Garden Coast,
just like I always knew you would."

"How the heck do you figure that?" Joby asked.

"Haven't you heard?" Swami said. "That whole stretch of coast has been
declared *severely* unstable. Nobody's gonna be allowed to rebuild a thing
there now for years. Maybe never!" He grinned at Joby. "I knew somehow
you were gonna save it, Joby. I just didn't guess you'd do it this way."

"Lucifer won't care whether he's allowed to rebuild," Joby said. "How
does that protect the Garden from him?"

"Demons we can deal with," Swami said. "With the Creator's help, that's
covered now for good. It's the *people* we had to worry about. Protecting the
Garden on a coast crawling with tourists would've been next to impossible.
But almost no one will be going anywhere near there for ages now. Taubolt's

gone. Everybody thinks the place is dangerous. Who's gonna want to vacation there?"

"So where are you all going to live now that Taubolt's gone?"

"I just told you," Swami smiled, "it isn't really. Sooner or later, every flower dies and goes to seed, Joby. That doesn't mean there's no more flowers. Taubolt's just blooming somewhere else now. It wasn't just a place, you know. And even though we haven't found the Cup yet, I found something almost as good—even better in a way. Oh, and by the way," Swami grinned, "in gratitude for your heroism, the Bobs have canceled all your debts."

"What debts?"

"Here's a tip," Swami smiled enigmatically, "never tell imps you'll 'owe them.' Not even as a joke."

"Well, I'll be d—" Joby suddenly reconsidered his choice of words.

"Hawk's gonna be pretty glad to see you," said Swami. "He's started writing his *masterpiece,* but he's gonna need a lot of help from you."

"I don't think so," Joby said. "My son's twice the storyteller I'll ever hope to be. His grandfather saw to that."

"Don't you even want to know the title?" Swami asked.

"Sure. What is it?"

"The Book of Joby." Swami grinned.

"Tell me you're joking," Joby groaned.

"Nope," Swami chuckled, "We can't wait to read it, but Hawk doesn't know a lot of the story yet, so your help *is* gonna be kind of crucial."

"I was told my suffering was over," Joby sighed, though, of course, he was very pleased. "Well, let's not just sit here on this shoulder gabbing. Which way do I go?"

"Just drive." Swami grinned. "You're already headed in the right direction."

(Have a Little Faith)

It was late September, and the Creator had invited Gabe to come catch the end of the baseball season at a sports bar in Tucson, Arizona. They sat at a small table on the upper deck, just two more cowboys throwing down a beer or three before the game.

At the moment, all the bar's TV screens were still tuned to the last few moments of a weekly magazine show devoted, this week, to the sensational earthquake that had recently demolished California's premier resort town of Taubolt. Gabe and his boss had watched spectacular footage of the devastation narrated by a stream of experts explaining the event's geological origins, many unpleasant consequences, and, of course, the rather bizarre stories told by more than a few survivors. Gabe had listened with interest as several still traumatized tourists and ex-residents described monsters throwing fireballs at buildings, and pushing down walls without ever touching them. At present, a nationally renowned psychiatrist was explaining the concept of mass hysteria.

"During a particularly traumatic event of this kind," the doctor said excitedly, "entire crowds of people can, by unconscious consensus and amplified power of suggestion, all project the same meaning onto what they're undergoing. They literally *share* a hallucination."

"Fascinatin'," the Creator murmured. "It'd only work on Californians though."

"This phenomenon has been amply documented on numerous occasions," the psychiatrist continued, "during natural disasters like this one, and also during large, emotionally-charged religious gatherings, such as mass sightings of the Virgin Mary in Europe, for instance, though some of those may be traceable to the poisoning of communal grain supplies by molds such as ergot."

"Don't think she'd like the sound of that," mused Gabriel.

"No way," the Creator agreed. "Mary keeps a *spotless* kitchen."

"Think she's watchin' somewhere?" Gabe asked.

"For that guy's sake, I hope not," the Creator said, tipping back his hat. "You know how she gets when she's chafed."

While they'd been talking, the program had moved on to an interview with one last quake survivor. She was an elderly woman with long disheveled hair piled in a disorderly bun. It had been dyed, but not recently enough to hide the white roots showing at every part. Her makeup seemed hastily applied, and her whole demeanor mildly hysterical, as if she were a very old Ophelia. The screen caption read, "Agnes Hamilton: prominent former resident of Taubolt."

"Well, of course I plan to fight the ruling!" she snapped. "Never allowed to rebuild anything again? That's ridiculous! Everything I had was invested in that town! Don't they understand that? If things are a little bit unstable, reinforce them, but they can't just shut me out that way. I was a very wealthy woman! That town was my life!"

The camera zoomed in on her distraught expression just as she wiped a fleck of spittle from the corner of her mouth, smearing her lipstick.

"Poor woman," the Creator sighed.

As the credits ended and they rolled a beer commercial, Gabe turned to the Creator and said. "I've been wonderin' about somethin'. May I ask?"

"Whadda *you* think?" the Creator smiled, still gazing at the commercial.

"Right," Gabe said, embarrassed. "Okay, well, I'm happy as anyone, of course, about how everything came out, but . . ." He really wasn't sure he should be asking this.

"Spit it out, compadre," the Creator growled.

"Well, what if You had lost? You *could* have lost, couldn't You?"

"I can do anything." The Creator grinned.

"Then, what would You have done?" Gabe said.

The Creator shrugged and took another pull at his beer. "I'd have ponied up, I guess, just like I promised. I'm no cheater. You know that."

"You'd have just wiped everything out?" Gabe said. "Even me?"

"Yup," the Creator said grimly. "Sorry, pardner, but a promise is a promise."

"And made everything over according to *his instructions?*"

"Well, now, that's the problem, ain't it?" the Creator said. "Seems like old Lucy kinda overlooked the fact he's a part of creation too. He does that a lot. You noticed?"

Gabe was too dumbstruck to answer.

"Soon as I'd wiped every last thing out," the Creator continued, scratching the back of his head, "I'd have asked for his instructions, of course, but if he wasn't there to give 'em . . . well, a plain old post 'n' hole man like Me oughtn't presume to guess what a brilliant mind like his would've wanted. I s'pose I'd just have had to make it all up again without him." He grinned. "You think?"

Gabe was shocked, not just at the plan's simplicity, but also at its callousness. "With all due respect, My Lord, what about all the good and loyal beings . . . well, like myself?" he said, daring to express a little of the umbrage he was feeling. "It wouldn't have bothered You to wipe us all out just to get my brother off Your back?"

The Creator tipped his hat so far back it nearly fell off, looked surprised, and said, "Well, I'd have brought you all right back, of course. 'Cept for old Lucy maybe. Who said I wouldn't? There's no rule says I can't bring You back, is there? *I* sure never wrote one." He gazed at the ceiling and murmured, "Why does everybody seem to have such trouble gettin' that?" He looked back at Gabe, and said, "Have a little faith, for cryin' out loud."

Gabe felt a total fool. "I should have known, My Lord. I apologize for—"

Before he could finish, the Creator had his hat off and was slapping Gabe on the head with it. "Now cut that out!" his Master growled. "Just when you finally start showin' a little spirit? What you wanna start apologizin' for?" He donned his hat again, grinning at Gabe's amazed expression. "I'm gettin' us another beer," he said. "Oh look. The game is . . . Awww hell," he groaned, gazing toward the door. "Look who's here."

Gabe turned to see Lucifer all duded up like an oil baron on some TV show.

"What's he want now?" Gabe asked unhappily. He looked at the Creator and said, "You don't think . . ."

"Hell, no," the Creator frowned. "He'd never try again this soon. It's prob'ly just the weather brought him down here. Hot as hell out there today."

"Yeah, but why *this* bar?" said Gabe. "He has to know we're here."

"Good thinkin', Gabe," the Creator frowned. "Could be right. Let's skedaddle."

"Where to?" Gabe asked as they stood up to go.

"How 'bout Seattle? Lucy hates the weather there. We could get some coffee, and still catch the game."

"Yes," Gabe said, still hesitant to question his Lord's suggestions, "but if it is us he's looking for, and not just the weather, will that be far enough?"

"Damn," the Creator grinned. "Got yourself another point, Gabe." He dropped way too much money on the table, and tugged his hat down real low to hide his face. "Remember that little discothèque in Prague?" He smiled. "That might be far enough. Let's just go. The team I'm rootin' for is gonna lose this game anyway."